THE SHIVADH ROMANCES: VOLUME I

Fête For A King
Infinite Jes
The Lady And The Tiger

by Sam Starbuck

The text of this book is set in Garamond.

This volume contains the tenth, eleventh, and twelfth books published by
Extribulum Independent Press
extribulum.wordpress.com
Printer's Row, Chicago, IL

Nameless – 2009
Other People Can Smell You – 2009, Retired 2022
Charitable Getting – 2010
Dr. King's Lucky Book – 2011
Trace – 2011
By The Days – 2011
The Dead Isle – 2012
Six Harvests in Lea, Texas – 2020
The Found Fortune Deck – 2022
Fête for a King – 2022
Infinite Jes –2022
The Lady And The Tiger – 2022
The Shivadh Romances: Omnibus Volume I – 2022

ISBN 979-8-9859604-6-4

Infinite Jes and *The Lady And The Tiger* contain some material which may be triggering or upsetting, although generally brief. For a full list of content warnings and spoilers, please turn to the last page of this volume.

2022 was a real wild year, guys.

FÊTE FOR A KING

This book is the result of an anonymous ask I received in my Tumblr inbox. It is dedicated to that anonymous reader, and more broadly to all the anonymous readers who have come into any of my inboxes to spread joy and inspiration.

PROLOGUE

EDDIE RAMBLER TOOK a bite of the sandwich he'd just been excitedly gesturing with, closed his eyes, groaned, and staggered backwards in pretend shock.

His theatrics didn't bother the octogenarian who had made the sandwich for him in his food truck. Very little had bothered the man, except for when he'd been asked by the episode's director to take off his Red Sox cap because they couldn't have sports logos or unsponsored brand names on the show. There had been a tussle over that which had only been settled when Eddie suggested he turn it around backwards, which had at last led to peace.

Now, watching Eddie pretend to be bowled over by how good his sandwich was, the vendor just grinned and said, "Ya ain't got sammiches like that in California, yeah?"

"Sure ain't," Eddie agreed, pretending to wipe sweat off his forehead. "Hey man, thanks. You know you're the oldest food truck chef I've ever interviewed? What's your secret to a long life?"

"Rye bread," the guy cackled, and Eddie laughed too.

"Thanks for keeping it new even at eighty," Eddie said, clapping him (very gently) on the shoulder. He turned to the camera, gave it a winning smile, and delivered a line he still, somehow, wasn't tired of after five years on air: "And that's... Truly Tasty."

He held the pose until the director gave him a thumbs up, listened for "Wrap on *Truly Tasty*, episode 72!" to reassure him

1

that filming was genuinely over, and then turned back to the sandwich guy again.

"Seriously, this is a great sandwich," he said. "I'll make sure they send you a link when the show goes live."

"You don't issue it on VHS?" the man asked. Eddie paused, horrified, and then relaxed when the man cackled again. "Just pullin' your leg. See you around, huh?"

Eddie nodded and made his way into the crowd of techs, mics, cameras, and all the rest of the small traveling circus required to film an episode of food television, at least the way Eat Network liked to do it. The network was a little old fashioned, but if Eddie wanted to feel cutting-edge he could post to Photogram anytime and keep wooing that under-25 crowd, most of whom (if comments were any indication) were literally learning to cook from Eddie Rambler: celebrity chef, host of *Truly Tasty*, and eater-about-town.

Most of the people running produce stalls at Haymarket, Boston's enormous open-air farmer's market, paid him zero attention other than to look annoyed by all the filming equipment. On the fringes, a few shoppers cast strange looks his way, and a handful of fans were waiting for autographs. Two were even wearing the signature loud floral-patterned shirts he sold on his website, with the linked-T logo on the breast pocket. He stopped only briefly to let hair-and-makeup clean the foundation off his face before he wandered over to the fans.

"Thanks for coming out today, guys," he said, shaking hands and accepting photos, cookbooks, and the odd kitchen implement to sign. "We always appreciate the support."

"Are we gonna be in the show?" one of the younger ones asked. His dad elbowed him gently.

"Tell you what, I'll talk to editing, do my best," Eddie said. "Might not be much of a shot but we'll try, okay?"

"Wicked cool!"

"Sure thing." Eddie gave the kid a fist-bump and winked at

his dad. "I'd love to stay but I got a plane to catch. You all keep it new and I'll see you on television, huh?"

He ducked into the tiny trailer that combined equipment storage, lunchroom, and wardrobe into one compact space, grabbing his duffle bag from where he'd stashed it on top of the fridge.

"Is that seriously all you're taking?" one of the PAs asked him, holding out his plane ticket.

"Travel light, kiddo," he said, shouldering the bag. "I've got a phone charger and a credit card, which is more than I had when I started in this business. You need anything else from me? I gotta be at the airport soon but I could shoot some B-roll if we make it quick."

"We'll make do," she replied.

"Great. Hey, pass a note to editing, try and get a few shots with the fans in the loud shirts in the background into this one."

"Got it," she said, noting it down in her phone. It was difficult to get used to people taking him seriously, even when he was being serious. Probably some combination of the floppy bleach-blond hair, chunky sunglasses, and floral shirts; people tended to mistake him for a blue-eyed California himbo without much going on upstairs. Still, that look had gotten him this far, and very few people who met him made the mistake more than once.

"Thanks. And let everyone know I blew town? They've got like eight weeks without my dumb ass looking over their shoulders."

"Quite a vacation," she agreed, grinning. "Where are you going again?"

Eddie hesitated, for once at a loss.

"I'll get back to you on that," he said.

EIGHT WEEKS UNTIL
THE CORONATION OF HIS MAJESTY
KING GREGORY III

THE PALACE OF Askazer-Shivadlakia was enormous in terms of places one might call home, but as castles went it was actually quite small. Gregory's father referred to it as *tasteful*, and most of Gregory's school friends who'd visited said it looked like a setting for a fairy tale, although their tone said the fairy tale was probably a modest one. To Gregory it was simply home, and at the moment he was gazing up at it from the harbor town below, longing to be back there.

Still, occasionally one had to put on the formal dress uniform of the royal family – no medals or sashes, but expensive sober black touched here and there with gold braid – and do a goodwill lap. Especially with the coronation looming. He wanted to make sure that his people understood he was doing his best not to inconvenience them, and that this would all be over in a few months. For them, anyway. For him, it was just beginning.

A local artisan was demonstrating a pattern in the tapestry he was making, which normally Gregory would find interesting, but his mind had begun to drift to everything left to accomplish before the coronation. He glanced up at the palace again, wistfully. Alanna was in the palace, with her reassuring lists and spreadsheets.

The bunting was already out in the town of Fons-Askaz, along with the royal insignia banners and the window decorations featuring Gregory's face. Askazer-Shivadlakia did love its pageantry.

And at least, he thought, as he thanked the artisan and climbed into the car that would take him home, it was one less thing for him to worry about. He relaxed into the seat of the car and took the ride back to the palace to relax and calm his mind.

Alanna was waiting for him at the door, bless her, with a soft sweater for him to change into. Gregory gratefully passed the stiff uniform jacket to his valet and struggled into the sweater as she launched into the report she knew he'd want.

"Flowers are set," she said, gently tugging the collar of the sweater down over his head. He nodded his thanks and pulled it straight. "Just got word this morning."

"Very glad to hear it. Does make me feel as though I'm getting married, however," he replied. "If you tell me I need to pick out a font for the invitations..."

She laughed. "No, I've done that already. And we've made a date for the cleaners to do a deep scrub and airing of all the guest rooms."

"Any word from the tailor? I'd love to have him here sooner rather than later, get the robe fitting out of the way," he said, leading the way down the hall towards his office.

"Working on it. I guess there was some kind of issue getting them out of storage."

"The robes or the tailor?"

"Probably both. He did the fitting for your father's robes too, so he might be immortal."

"Mm. A vampire around the place would certainly add flair," Gregory said, grinning. "And how are the arrangements coming along for father's funeral?"

Alanna actually opened her mouth to answer that, then checked herself and smiled at him.

"Very funny, Your Highness," she said.

"I have to keep you on your toes, Al," he replied.

"His Majesty the king, your father," she drawled, "would like to have dinner with you this evening. He said it was about details for his retirement, but I think he has ulterior motives."

Gregory didn't have a chance to agree with her before he heard his name called, a *basso profundo* shout – "GREGORY!"

He turned towards the source of the roar and saw his father, King Michaelis, at the other end of the hallway, attended by his own crowd of aides and assistants.

"Sometimes it's like he's with me even now," Gregory said to Alanna, who nodded, poker-faced.

"DINNER!" Michaelis called. "TONIGHT!"

"Of course, Father," Gregory called back. Michaelis nodded and stalked onwards, intent on whatever royal business he still had to handle with two months to go until his retirement.

"Oh! And I have great news," Alanna said, checking items off a list on her tablet as they continued. "The chef you asked for? He arrived late last night. He's settling in now, with plenty of time to get the menu set and the catering up and running."

"Ah, the coronation banquet, right," Gregory said, recalling faintly some conversation they'd had about this. "Who'd you get?"

"Eddie Rambler," Alanna said, perplexed. "Like you asked for."

Gregory came to a stop, turning to fully face her. "Eddie... Rambler?"

"The TV chef," Alanna replied. "He hosts *Truly Tasty?*"

"He hosts what," Gregory said flatly.

"I thought you asked..." Alanna began, then hesitated. Gregory had known Alanna since childhood, and the look on her face was very familiar; it was usually a look they gave each other when they'd gotten into some mischief too big to simply scamper their way out of.

"You said...you said you wanted the 'Keep it new' guy, right?" Alanna asked hesitantly.

"I said I wanted someone who would keep things new,"

Gregory replied, relatively certain that was what he'd said, though his memory of the discussion was cloudy. He'd been distracted by something, probably some request of his father's. "I wanted to show the guests that we're truly a twenty-first century modern monarchy."

"Well…he's definitely modern," Alanna pointed out.

"We hired the host of a TV food show to cater my coronation banquet?" Gregory asked.

Before Alanna could reply, her tablet bleeped; she looked down, equal parts distracted and, he could tell, searching for a distraction.

"He just posted a new Photogram video!" she said brightly, holding the tablet up for him to see, then blinked when she saw Gregory's face. She tried to tuck the tablet away, but he tapped the play button before she could.

Eddie Rambler, six feet of loud blond celebrity chef, had posted a video filmed in the palace kitchen. Gregory's personal palace kitchen, the one that served the royal family directly, not even the larger kitchen that served palace staff and guests.

Gregory tapped the tablet again and raised the volume just in time to hear Rambler say "The Democratic Monarchy of Askazer-Shivad…nokia," followed by an encouraging noise from Simon, the royal family's personal chef. Alanna jerked the tablet away from him and closed the window.

"I was looking for modern like a nice gastropub," Gregory said. "Not like a dive bar." He kept his tone gentle, because he suspected this was as much his fault as hers.

"I am so, so sorry," she said.

"No, it's fine," he replied. "We can explain there was a mistake."

"I thought you'd want a famous chef to do the banquet – "

"These things happen," he told her. "It's a minor speed bump. If that. More like a small pothole."

"Do you want me to tell him today?" she asked. "He just got

here."

"No, I should do it," he decided.

"Oh, no, that's not – "

"I'm responsible for the country, and the palace," Gregory told her. "When mistakes are made, regardless of how, I have to fix them gracefully. Anyway, it was just a miscommunication. And I don't punish my staff for honest mistakes."

"Are you sure?" she asked.

"Well, maybe a little," he said, giving her a smile. "Come on, I'm going to make you watch."

She winced, but followed him bravely as he made his way to the palace kitchen.

Eddie set the phone in its little tripod on one of the palace kitchen's stainless-steel prep counters, pressed the record button, and backed up until he was perfectly framed in the phone's selfie-mode reflected footage.

"Well, I told you all I had a surprise for you," he said with a wink. "Guess what? I'm in Europe! I've been hired by the crown prince of…" He faltered, then, sighing. "Ah, man…."

He darted forward to rotate the camera on its tripod; Simon LeFevre, a gray-haired man in pristine chef's whites, had been warned this might happen. He gave the camera a narrow, skeptical look.

"Say it again for me, Chef?" Eddie pleaded.

Simon nodded and poured centuries of French gravitas into his voice as he said, "The Democratic Monarchy of Askazer-Shivadlakia."

Eddie gave him a quick "ok" gesture before turning the camera back on himself.

"I'm gonna get it," he announced. "Here we go. The Democratic Monarchy of Askazer-Shivad…"

Despair rolled briefly through him, even though he knew this would be great content.

"…nokia," he finished, then pressed a hand over his face.

"You're getting closer!" Simon said encouragingly. Like a natural-born star, he leaned in so the phone mic would pick up his voice even though it wasn't recording his face.

"Thanks, Chef," Eddie nodded, letting his hand fall. He put on a fresh smile. "Anyway. I've been invited here by the royal family to cater a coronation banquet. I'll be coming to you live and in living color, only on my Photogram, for the next two months!" he pointed down, to an imaginary logo bug he could add in post. "So if you want all the news, remember to subscribe!"

Simon looked at him like Eddie's ancestors were ashamed of him, but Eddie made *sacrifices* for his followers.

"It's crazy here," he continued. "I'm staying in a genuine palace and everything! I promise lots of content, some tours if I can sneak past the palace guard, plenty of quick cooking lessons, and hopefully a few selfies with the royals. Okay, that's all for now – peace out and you know I mean it when I say: keep it new!"

He shot the camera the peace sign, then hurried forward to end the recording. Simon went back to the stove, shaking his head, but Eddie knew he'd charmed the reserved Frenchman. He picked up his phone and made a few hasty adjustments to the video before slamming that post button with a paragraph's worth of hashtags.

"I really wanted to get that right," he said as he worked. "Help me out? Askazer…"

"Shivadlakia," Simon repeated.

"Shivadlakia," Eddie managed.

"It takes time to learn to let it roll off the tongue," Simon said. "The important thing is to try."

"Well, trying's all I have," Eddie said, settling himself on a stool near the prep table. "You sure you don't mind me in your kitchen?"

"No, I have seen your show," Simon said. "I know you are a

true chef in a carnival barker costume."

Eddie clutched his chest, but Simon was unperturbed by his suffering. A timer went off on Eddie's phone, and he hurried to one of the four nearby ovens, pulling out the cast-iron pot he'd had in there.

"Here we go," he said, removing the lid and inhaling the fragrant steam. Simon peered into it, interested. "Looks great. You want a sample? Hey, when do you think I'll get to meet the prince?"

Simon looked past him, towards the doorway of the kitchen.

"Very soon," he murmured, and Eddie turned.

Crown Prince Gregory ben Michaelis, soon to be King Gregory III of This Place He Was Definitely Going To Memorize The Name Of Soon, stood in the doorway. Eddie had done at least a little research, but even if he hadn't, Gregory's face was everywhere. There were even posters in the train station announcing his coronation and welcoming tourists and diplomats who were going to be attending. Still, it took a few seconds for it to sink in. This was a royal prince, after all, and he was also insanely hot.

The posters and photographs didn't do justice to the deep olive of his skin or the short-cropped dark curly hair above equally dark eyes; in the pictures he was wearing a high-collared, gold-edged dress jacket, but the real prince was wearing a burgundy sweater with a simple diamond pattern across his shoulders, as well as a somewhat imposing expression. Behind him, a slight young woman with long brown hair, a sweet face, and a tablet clutched in one hand looked extremely alarmed.

"Prince Gregory," Eddie heard Simon say. "May I introduce Chef Edward Rambler. Chef, this is His Highness, Crown Prince Gregory."

"Whoa," Eddie said, and then screamed, briefly, internally. He'd done enough panicking on enough national broadcasts to keep from doing it externally, at least.

"Beg pardon?" the prince asked, blinking.

Eddie decided to lean into his initial reaction. "Whoa! Wow, here you are! Your Highness! It's such a pleasure. Do I bow, or do I shake hands?"

"Either is acceptable," Simon told him, clearly teasing, at the same time the prince said, "Ah yes, Mr. Rambler. I – "

"Oh, call me Eddie," Eddie said, deciding on the handshake and reaching out. Prince Gregory took his hand automatically; he had a firm handshake even when surprised. Nice hands, too. Warm. Eddie ignored that and leaned around the prince, because he'd just realized who the alarmed woman was.

"Alanna, right?" he asked, shooting her finger-guns because the prince was in the way of a second handshake.

She nodded, and Eddie turned back to the prince. "This lady is great! She hired me and really got me set up. I'm super excited to be here to help out with the coronation. It's a new one for me."

"Ah, yes, about that," the prince said, and Eddie knew an opening for a pitch when he saw one. He held up a hand.

"Don't say another word yet," he warned. "I know you probably have a vision for your coronation banquet, but I want to rock your world for a second before we dish." The prince started to say something, but Eddie was already heading for the pot he'd just taken from the oven, and he'd sold enough hard ideas to enough rich show-business types to know that the key was continually talking until they broke down.

"So a banquet is a big deal, but you hired me, right?" he asked, rummaging in a drawer for a tasting spoon. Simon handed him one. "Thanks, Chef. So I know you want to keep it new, and I figure maybe a little relaxed. It's a formal occasion but we can set a real easygoing tone with the food, make sure it's comfortable as well as high-brow. The hard part's over by the time you get to the feast, right? So I have a ton of ideas but just consider this first: hot sandwich bar."

He scooped up a mini-meatball, made sure it had plenty of

sauce on it, and turned to the prince, who said, "I really need to – "

"Taste this, I know!" Eddie replied. "It smells amazing, but trust me, there's truth in this advertising."

"You see – " the prince tried again, but Eddie held the spoon in front of his face.

"Here, taste," he commanded. It was, actually, a little gratifying that even a prince couldn't disobey the command to try some of Eddie's food. He took the spoon from Eddie's hand and sampled the mini-meatball with genuine consideration. Simon was already offering another one to Alanna on a toast point.

"Tarragon mini-meatballs in red pepper marinara," Eddie announced. "You get a big pan of these and you stuff 'em in an olive oil roll with some fresh basil or rosemary..."

The prince had finished chewing; Alanna was watching him, her mouth still full, and it only then dawned on Eddie that there might be a subtext to the conversation that he wasn't privy to.

"You made this, just now?" the prince asked, swallowing.

"Well, I improvised with what Simon had lying around," Eddie admitted. "If you don't like the flavor profile we could go with a traditional marinara, maybe a little more garlic in the *meats'a'ball...*"

He put a fake-Italian accent on the last word, trying to anchor them firmly in the lighthearted world he'd been pitching, but all Prince Gregory said was, "This is your concept for the banquet?"

"Well, one idea, sure," Eddie ventured. "Easy to prepare, easy to serve, keeps the line moving. Not just these, obviously. You get five or six different hot dishes – meatballs, some spicy chicken, sausage, sweet potato curry or fried butternut squash for a vegetarian option – and you got some guys dishing the hots into the breads. Add a condiment bar, you're good to go. Passed apps beforehand, plenty 'a side dishes. Simon says he'll do the cake, which is great, because I am many things but I am not a pastry chef."

He watched the prince carefully, but the man had a pretty good poker face. Now was perhaps the time to let things simmer, to let him consider; Eddie glanced at Alanna, who had been both kind and fun to talk to when setting all this up, but she was still eyeballing her boss.

"Well," Prince Gregory said finally, "It's a little informal for what I had in mind, but I'll consider it as an option."

"Red sauce," Eddie replied. "Nobody resists the red sauce. Up top!"

He held up his hand for a high-five, but he had definitely misjudged something about the situation. The prince just stared at him. Eddie shot a pleading look at Alanna, and after a split second she leaned around the prince and finished the high-five. Well, he at least had one ally on the royal side.

"Simon," the prince said, turning to the other chef. "Include these with dinner tonight, if you would. Father will want to try them. Service as Mr. Rambler – "

"Eddie," Eddie said. "Or Dude," he added jokingly.

It backfired immediately. "Service as Mr….Dude recommends," the prince finished. "I'd like to see a range of your 'hot sandwich' options, but I'll want some menus for a multi-course sit-down dinner as well, and perhaps a few other concepts as they come to you. Speak to Alanna tomorrow morning about a meeting, when you're ready, to go over your ideas."

"You got it," Eddie answered, hiding most of his glee and all of his amusement. The prince, without another word, turned and left the kitchen, Alanna trailing behind him with a little wave goodbye.

Eddie glanced at Simon and saw Simon was already looking sidelong at him. Eddie broke first; Simon didn't exactly crack up laughing, but once Eddie started to laugh he deigned to give him a good-natured chuckle.

"Mr. Dude," Eddie hooted. "Oh man. What a stuffed shirt."

"He's a good man at heart," Simon replied, shaking his head.

"I've known him from a child. He'll govern well."

"Hope so for your sake," Eddie said. "Anyway, doesn't matter. He liked the meatballs and I can work with the rest. I just gotta un-stuffify him a little."

"I wish you luck in your quest," Simon told him, and went back to prepping for dinner.

Gregory didn't stop walking until he was in his office, down the hall from the kitchen. It was the place he was most at home, at least nowadays. In the middle of the room, with its bookshelves and worktable, wide bay windows and prized antique telescope, he felt like he could, in fact, rule wisely. At the moment he felt mostly taken aback; he turned to face Alanna, not sure what to say.

"So," Alanna said finally, after a few seconds of silence. "Good job firing him back there."

"I didn't know he could actually cook," Gregory said, because it was all he could think about. The little spoonful of food, a simple meatball in piping hot sauce, had shocked him into silence. Simon was a good chef and had taught Gregory to appreciate good food, and apparently Rambler knew a thing or two about good food too.

He also hadn't thought the man would be quite so good-looking in person. On the television, on the rare occasions Gregory had seen it in passing, he always looked sort of...

Well, trashy. Might as well admit to his own snobbery. In person, moving, speaking excitedly, he was a very good looking man. Tall, with dark gold hair bleached white at the tips and deep blue eyes, he had a compellingly mobile face. And that ridiculous flowery shirt didn't hide the fact that the man was built like a...like a Viking, or a tree. A Viking tree, perhaps. Solid enough to climb.

"I didn't know he could cook like that," Alanna admitted.

"It was really good!" Gregory exploded.

"I know!" Alanna replied, equally surprised and excited.

"Is all his food that good?"

"I hope so!"

"He just made that up out of whatever was lying around…" Gregory circled his desk, dropping into his chair. "Alanna, not firing him would uncomplicate both our lives."

"Mine more so than yours, but yes," she said.

"And he can cook."

"He can *cook*," she agreed. Gregory understood the distinction. He could still taste the faint bite of sweet pepper in the sauce.

"Okay. So we have a chef. That's good! We'll just find a way to tame his…natural exuberance in front of my father. And maybe me," he added ruefully. Alanna carefully wasn't smiling. Gregory pointed at her. "In the meantime, you're on high-five duty. In fact, that's now a permanent part of your job. I'm appointing you to high-five anyone who wants me to high-five them."

That did break out one of her better smiles, the one that dimpled her cheeks. He saw it less now, as her boss, than he had when they were children and she was his friend. She still was his friend, it was just… boundaries were being renegotiated in light of his coronation.

"You're lucky you're pretty," she said. "I have a few things to deal with. Do you want me to set you an alarm for dinner with His Majesty?"

"No, I've got it covered," he said, and she turned to go. "Don't wear yourself out," he added, genuinely concerned.

"I'm fine. Save me a meats'a'ball!" she called as she left.

The palace had a formal dining room of course, for state dinners and feasts and the various diplomatic parties Michaelis had thrown and Gregory would be expected to. It was a big, echoing room with unfortunate baroque decor that Gregory would like to streamline, but the historians would clutch their pearls. The family dining room, where the royal family ate most of their meals, was smaller and more modern, not subject to the same attempt at awe as most of the palace. Gregory arrived just as the hot dishes were being set on the table, and saw a rustic bowl of Eddie Rambler's meatballs placed at his father's elbow, along with a plate of crusty bread.

"Quiet day?" he asked Michaelis, helping himself to a cup of stew while his father dished up some of the meatballs.

"For the most part. Every day I do a little less," his father replied. "Bread?"

"Please, and I'll take those when you're done, too," Gregory replied. Michaelis passed over the bread, then took the stew in exchange for the meatballs. "Well, that's the point of the handover, so that the chaos is out of the way before the coronation."

"Having gone through my own, I can tell you, you're very optimistic about how well these things work," Michaelis replied.

"You know me, Crown Prince Optimism," Gregory said. "I'm sure there'll be wrinkles, but it's not like you're leaving for an eight-month cruise like Grandfather did when you were crowned."

"Never forgave him for that."

"You seemed to recover," Gregory pointed out, amused. "Something in particular you wanted to discuss?"

"I can't enjoy dinner with my only son and heir?"

Gregory grinned at him. "You can, but you sounded like you had something on your mind earlier."

"Well, sort of. I received some comments about your impending reign today."

Gregory sat up straighter, perturbed. If his father's aides were questioning his competency, or worse, some of the Parliament members –

"Don't look so distraught, it's nothing to do with your qualifications," Michaelis said soothingly. "Anyway, I'd fight that battle for you if they questioned them. I've taught you all I know about statecraft and diplomacy. And I think some of those fancy schools I sent you to taught you something about economics."

"I didn't mail-order the MBA," Gregory agreed.

"I hope not. If you did, I overpaid. No, I think you're ready to be king and most people agree with me. And I'm very proud of that," Michaelis added, giving him a meaningful look.

Gregory narrowed his eyes. "And thank you."

Michaelis set down his spoon. "But I think once the coronation is over, it's time to seriously consider finding a partner."

Ah. Back to that, then.

He supposed it was good of Dad to face the issue head-on, at least. A lot of royals would either ignore an inconveniently gay son or try to evangelize him back to heterosexuality. Michaelis had always been good about not doing that, and once he'd gotten past the initial surprise, he'd been supportive. Still, it didn't stop him from insisting on a semi-annual discussion of Gregory's lack of a husband.

"Dad," he began warily, and Michaelis winced, cutting him off.

"I know, I know you don't want to rush things, but this is important. You need someone who can make sure your plans go forward if you get sick – or, Heaven forbid, you die."

"This is great dinner conversation."

"Would you prefer it be breakfast conversation?" Michaelis asked, which was an annoyingly good point. "You need someone to be able to step in at a moment's notice, someone who carries the authority of the king without needing all the paperwork to back them up. It's not just that, either. The people should see that you have a…a backup plan. It's for the stability of the kingdom as much as anything else."

"I just don't think the backup plan has to be a spouse," Gregory said.

"Yes, I heard you the last time someone brought this up. You can think all you want, Gregory, but that won't turn the tide of public opinion. You need a visible, present, and appropriate helpmeet and workmate."

"I have Alanna."

"And if you married Alanna, cousins or not, there would be great celebration in the country," Michaelis said. "But as it stands now she won't be your assistant forever. And she deserves someone who could give her more than a sham marriage. You aren't going to marry Alanna."

"No," Gregory admitted.

"Good," Michaelis said, surprising him. He blinked across the dinner table at his father.

"Good?"

"See, here's the part I don't think you ever hear when this comes up," Michaelis said, leaning forward a little. "You need a companion too, son. It's hard going this alone. You need someone you can vent to at the end of the day – someone who looks after you and lets you look after them. You need a refuge from the throne. Like your mother was for me."

"Doubly unfair to Alanna, then. She wouldn't get much in return and she wouldn't even get paid for it anymore," Gregory said, trying to lighten the moment. His mother Miranda's death was still a tender topic years later, but if his father was going to pitch it this way, he had to ask. "Who's been there for you since Mom died?"

"Never mind that. We're talking about you, not me," Michaelis said shortly, which was precisely the kind of non-answer he always gave when Gregory brought her up. "Look, we are very traditional in some ways but you know nobody here would care if you had a king consort instead of a queen, and there are options for heirs. You just have to have *someone*."

"King consort," Gregory snorted.

"Fine, give him whatever title you like."

"Duke of Buckingham."

"Eh what?" Michaelis asked, looking puzzled.

"Sorry. Dumb joke," Gregory said. "James the First of England had a boyfriend. He made him Duke of Buckingham."

"Well, then make him a duke, it doesn't matter," Michaelis said, waving it away with typical Shivadh arrogance, as if the monarchy of England was a minor concern next to the throne of Askazer-Shivadlakia. "The point is, whoever or whatever he is, he'll need to be brought up to speed on royal etiquette, start learning to step in for you if he has to. He'll have to have all kinds of PR briefings."

"You're not really selling me on this," Gregory pointed out. His father, halfway through a bite of meatball, didn't reply. "There's not a lot of spare time. You know better than anyone that running the country takes a lot of work."

"And you know better than anyone that one has to make time for one's family," Michaelis said, and then delivered the killing blow. "If you don't, I'll do it for you."

Gregory set his silverware down. "No."

"I could hold a ball," Michaelis threatened.

"Dad, no – "

"Every eligible bachelor in the country," Michaelis said with relish. "I'll import a few. A foreign spouse is always good for diplomatic relations. Maybe one or two millionaires from America."

"You can't," Gregory protested, even though he knew his father was joking.

Probably. Mostly.

"There will be waltzing," Michaelis said darkly.

"You wouldn't dare."

"Then you've got to do it yourself," Michaelis retorted.

Gregory sighed. "At least think about it, all right? Get Alanna to help, she knows all your exes, and she probably has better taste than you do."

"Now that's just mean."

"It's you, or Alanna, or the Ball," Michaelis said, spooning one of the meatballs onto a crust of bread and popping it in his mouth as if that decided things.

"Fine," Gregory replied, more than ready to change the subject. "I'll talk to her. What do you think of those meatballs, by the way?"

Michaelis swallowed thoughtfully. "Pretty good. I was just thinking I should ask Simon to put them on the regular rotation. A bit different from his usual."

"The new chef made them, the one Alanna hired to do the coronation banquet," Gregory said.

"Well, he seems talented. Although I don't know about meatballs in red sauce for a coronation."

"I've asked him for some other ideas. I think he has plenty."

"I look forward to hearing more," Michaelis said. "All right, let's lay business to rest. I've been thinking of overseeing some upgrades to the fishing lodge…"

In the groves of the palace grounds the next morning, the dew was drying and the sun was barely peeking over the mountains. Birds were bathing or hunting breakfast, the sky overhead was a deep cloudless blue, and the light was at the perfect angle for filming.

"Good morning to everyone who's keeping it new on Photogram!" Eddie said. "It's a beautiful day. I've had a good breakfast – thank you Simon – and I'm escaping the palace early today."

He started to walk, keeping the selfie stick as stable as he could, trying to capture as much of the natural beauty behind him as possible. "I think the first thing a good chef in a strange new country should do is get out and socialize. Meet the people, learn about what they're eating, start tracing that path from farm to table, you know? So here I go!"

He twisted to show them the road down to the village, walking backwards briefly, the quaint glow of lit houses visible behind him.

"I'm going to learn everything there is to know about…" he paused dramatically and then squinted down at his hand, "Askazer-Shivadlakia."

He held up his hand to the camera, grinning, showing the words written on it. "Nailed it. Anyway, I'm going to be way too busy eating everything and meeting everyone to take video myself, but keep your eyes peeled for photos! I'm sure it'll be Truly Tasty."

He finished with a wave at the camera, ended the recording, and uploaded it without even any editing. Practically rustic, and very satisfying. With a clean heart and a hunger to learn, he picked up his pace heading into town.

Gregory ben Michaelis hadn't become crown prince of a small country by sleeping in, any more than Eddie Rambler had become a television star that way. Some of his staff didn't love morning meetings, so he made concessions and never started one before 8:30. Still, by the time the daily briefing rolled around, he was more than ready with marching orders for the day, taking in reports and handing out assignments.

He was just finishing up when the beeping began.

"Lastly," he said, "I know it feels like this is some kind of strange summer break before school starts again, but there are things we just can't start work on until after the coronation."

Alanna's phone beeped, but she ignored it, so he did as well. "This is why it's so important that after the coronation, we be ready to hit the ground running," he continued. "Do what you can now and keep the first month of the new reign – "

Her phone beeped again. Gregory shot her a questioning look, but she shook her head, not looking at it, mouthing, "Sorry."

"Keep the first month of the new reign free," he said. "I mean entirely free. No concert tickets, no hot dates."

The staff laughed, which almost covered the sound of a third beep. Alanna looked down at her phone, finally silencing it, then frowned.

"I promise I'll make it up to you once we're on stable ground," Gregory finished. "Okay. Most of you, your suffering is over for the day. Those with morning meetings with me, get yourself some food, give the kitchen your lunch orders, and come back to settle in."

They filed out, chatting amongst themselves, and Gregory caught Alanna by the elbow before she could leave.

"Even for you that was a lot of texts," he said, smiling to show he wasn't annoyed. "New boyfriend being clingy, or should I worry for the state of my country?"

She gaped at him. "Uh…it's the country, actually."

A brief shot of adrenaline ran through him; his father had handled various crises over the years, and this might be his first.

"What's wrong?" he asked. "Why didn't you interrupt the meeting if it was serious? Has something – "

"No, sorry, it's not…" She rested her hand over his, reassuring. "There's no emergency, exactly. They were status updates from the palace communications office, I just need to find out what's going on. Traffic to the national website is spiking."

"The national website? Like – are we being *hacked*?" he asked in disbelief.

"Not the government intranet. The tourism site," she said, and then did a double take. "Did you just ask if we're being hacked?"

"We might be! Why is the tourist website getting traffic, are we in the news?"

"I'm not sure…" Alanna brushed past him to the small television mounted in one of the bookshelves. "I asked them to find out how people are finding us, what they're searching to get there…"

Her phone beeped again as she was turning on the television, and she blinked at it. "Oh. Ah."

"Oh, ah?" Gregory echoed.

"Well, the good news is, I don't think anything bad has happened," Alanna said.

"What's the bad news?"

She gestured with her phone at the television.

"…nation of Askazer-Shivadlakia is trending this morning after a series of Photogram posts from celebrity chef and influencer Eddie Rambler," a news anchor said, as an image of Rambler appeared next to her.

"Eddie Rambler crashed our website," Alanna said, her voice rising in suppressed amusement.

"Rambler has been hired by Crown Prince Gregory ben Michaelis to cater his coronation banquet," the anchor continued, and then she smiled, and Gregory had a great foreboding. "What everyone seems to want to know this morning, though, is whether Prince Gregory is looking for a queen."

Gregory's official royal portrait, which they had admittedly posted as part of the press packet on the tourism website, replaced Rambler's. Alanna giggled softly as Gregory hit mute.

"He posted a video to Photogram this morning and he's been putting up photos ever since," she said.

"Find him and calm him the hell down," Gregory said.

"I have to say," Alanna continued, ignoring him and scrolling Photogram on her phone, "he's doing a great job of showing off the country. Great PR, if you ask me."

"I don't need good PR, Alanna! I need to get through my first few months as king without the entire world staring at us."

That was a good point he hadn't even thought he was making until he made it, and it snapped Alanna out of her amusement.

"I'll put someone on it," she agreed. "Look, this is why you hired a social media manager for the palace. It'll be fine. Katie's probably feeling very smug."

"Katie in Communications?" Gregory asked, sidetracked.

"She's been telling us to bolster our site infrastructure since the coronation was announced and she got louder about it once she heard a famous chef was coming to cater for us."

"Ah, the joys of I-told-you-so," Gregory nodded. "Look, don't – don't yell at Rambler or anything," he added, because Rambler probably hadn't done it intentionally. Photogram had a way of just…getting out of hand. At least he assumed; he didn't have one personally, but it seemed like Alanna was always telling him about some drama the other noble cousins were getting into on the app. "Don't make him take down the videos, just tell him to tone it down."

"Of course," Alanna said. "Let me handle it, you have meetings all morning."

"I very much do," Gregory sighed. "Okay. Budgets."

"Top left drawer, and in the Finance folder on the shared drive."

"Right. I'll take it from here, you deal with the website situation."

"Always a pleasure, Your Highness," she said.

Once she was gone, he turned the television off entirely, muttering *looking for a queen* dismissively under his breath. That was the last joke he needed anyone to make right now, including himself, but it was a little bit funny, he supposed. He wondered if he should get a Photogram of his own, just for spin control, or to see what Rambler had actually said about the country. Or about him.

Then his staff started trickling back in, at least the ones he needed to meet with, and the idea was shuffled to the back of his mind to make way for more important affairs of state.

Eddie was in a bakery in town, elbows-deep in bread dough and loving life, when the Palace caught up with him. He didn't even know they'd been chasing, but he supposed he should have expected it.

"Mr. Rambler?" came a voice, and Eddie began extracting himself from the dough, while the baker who had been graciously teaching him how to make Askazer twist-bread looked on in amusement. "Eddie?"

"The invitation to call me Dude extended to you, light of the palace," Eddie replied, finally getting free and turning around to face her. The baker's teenaged daughter, who was filming him with her phone, hastily ended the video when she saw who it was. "Did I miss an appointment?"

"You crashed the internet," Alanna said, a hint of a smile twitching around her lips.

"I hate it when I do that," Eddie said to Baker Junior, who giggled at him. "Hey, shoot me that video, would you? Have you got a Photogram?" At her nod, he added, "Then you edit and post it, tag me, and I'll link to yours. We'll get you to influencer in no time. Okay," he continued, rubbing his hands together to clean them of dough and turning back to Alanna. "What'd I do again, now?"

"You namedropped the country on your social media," Alanna continued. "It brought down our tourism website."

"Oh, snap. I didn't even think about that. Is it causing a lot of problems?" Eddie asked, frowning. "Are people like trolling the prince or something?"

"No, but it's giving Communications a headache," she said.

"The palace would just like you to tone down the media blitz a little."

"Oh sure, I can pull back on posting to a couple of times a day, at least when it comes to PR stuff. I was just having a great time, there's so much good food here. If I'd known Aska..."

He looked imploringly at her.

"No, you have to learn to say it," she said, hands on hips.

"She's onto me," Eddie said to the baker. "Aska...zer... Shivad... lakios."

"So, so close," she replied, finally grinning.

"If I'd known *your country* had food this good I would have been here years ago. I'm about to be the guy who discovered Askazer twist-bread and brought it to the masses."

"The masses here have had it for about five hundred years," Alanna replied.

"Touché."

"Look, I'm really sorry," she continued, subtly leading him out of the bakery's kitchen. "Truth is, the prince doesn't need more eyeballs on him right now."

"I mean, he's throwing a coronation."

"That's why," she said. "It's not that I want you to stop talking, because we could use the tourism. We just weren't ready for...you."

"I'm not trying to condescend here, but I just obliterated your tourism website, so I need to ask: do you actually have a Communications office?" he said. There was a dark car decorated with the seal of the government parked nearby; it was clearly where she was headed, but he hadn't quite finished his tour yet.

"We do – "

"Oh, sweet, then no problem. I'll just coordinate with them. I do it all the time when I do state tours. I'll have my guy back in the US send me the standard packet, we can make up a strategy," he said brightly. "I love a strategy."

"You do," she repeated, clearly disbelieving, as someone got out of the car and held the door for them.

"I do, I live for that stuff. Okay, like, this is fine," he said, waving to the car, "But I need five minutes. It's for salami. Can I have five minutes for salami?"

He could see Alanna weighing whether this would actually be five minutes or closer to fifty; he squeezed his thumb and forefinger together, pleadingly.

"It's going to look really bad if I have Security pull you out of a salumeria," she told him.

"Yes!" he pumped his fist and raced for the storefront he'd seen earlier, with cured meats in the window. He burst inside and hustled up to the bemused clerk behind the counter.

"I have this much money and I want one of everything," he said, holding up a bill he'd changed from American money earlier.

"Not enough," the man shook his head, but he was already pulling various paper-wrapped sausages together. "I'll give you the tourist package plus fish salami."

"Fish salami," Eddie breathed, eyes widening. "That sounds terrible."

The man grinned. "It is. Punishment for being pushy."

"I'll come back and behave better, I promise," Eddie said, passing the cash across and getting a bundle of anonymous tubes in return. "Which one's the fish?"

"That's for you to discover," the man told him.

Back outside, Alanna was looking at her phone. As he skidded to a stop in front of her, she held it up, showing a timer at the 4:30 mark.

"See, thirty seconds to spare," he said as he climbed into the car, stuffing salami into an already very full messenger bag. Alanna, sliding in after him, offered her purse. He put what he hoped wasn't the fish salami into it. "There's more where that came from."

"You'd be surprised how many men tell me that," she informed him gravely.

"I like you more every hour, Alanna."

"Probably for the best, because I'm here mainly to spoil everyone's fun," she told him. "Driver, to the palace, please."

"I thought that was Prince Gregory's job, spoiling the fun."

"Unkind." She swatted him gently on the arm. "His Highness has a lot on his mind right now."

"And it's your job to smooth the way, eh?" he asked.

"I do what I can. I'm very good at it and I enjoy it, so it's not usually as annoying as I pretend," she said with a grin.

"I think you and I are gonna get along just fine," Eddie replied. "You set me up with your people and I'll text my PR folks, and in the meantime we'll pretend to be a power couple off to take over Monaco, how's that sound?"

"We did once try to invade Monaco, around the 16th century or so," Alanna said.

"Imagine what might have been," Eddie told her solemnly.

Askazer-Shivadlakia was not a large country, or politically important, or particularly wealthy. Traditionally, ruling it was tedious, but rarely a struggle; a good job for a man who liked math and thought diplomacy was exciting. Gregory did sometimes wonder if earlier kings got as stressed out by olive crop yields as he did, and if they'd felt as much like they were drowning when they came up on the coronation.

From where he sat, on the bench under the big bay window of his office on the palace's ground floor, he could see a couple of the old kings – two were in portraits in his office, and one (so it was rumored) was buried in the ornamental garden just past the road leading up to the palace entrance. The sun was setting over the grounds, turning the garden golden and the road into a deep black streak among the grassy hills. He'd meant to move away from his desk for a few minutes to enjoy his dinner, but he'd only picked at the meal, and now he was lost in contemplation of the sunset.

There was a smart double-rap on the door frame, Alanna's efficient knock. From the doorway, she said, "Penny for your thoughts."

He sighed, not looking around. "Shivadh currency is pretty strong right now. You could get a lot more and better thoughts for a penny in France."

"I like the personal touch. Hand-crafted by a traditionalist," she replied. He turned to shoot her the best smile he could manage. "I mean it, Greg. Anything I can help with?"

"No, not yet," he said, turning back to the landscape. "Just ticking off a few things on the to-do list. Stuff I've been avoiding for a week."

"Like what?"

He shrugged. "You ever stop and look at something you're doing and think maybe you bit off more than you can chew?"

"Yeah, the first six months I worked for you," Alanna replied, coming to sit on the other end of the bench, more or less forcing the conversation. It was something he appreciated about her; she knew when to push.

"I wasn't that bad," Gregory protested. "Besides, you knew what you were getting into."

"Even for you it was a lot," she told him.

"It wasn't."

"You were named crown prince and your first diplomatic act afterward was to adopt a puffin while you were on vacation in Iceland."

"I rescued the puffin," he retorted, still annoyed that she was bringing up the puffin a year later. "And I gave it back. You don't give things back if you adopt them."

Alanna smiled. She also knew that needling him about the puffin might take him out of himself a little. He rolled his eyes at her.

"So, what puffin is worrying you this time?" she asked. "Even if I can't help as your staff, I can help as your friend."

"It's probably more a staff problem," he said. "Dad's brought up some deficiencies in my palace management."

Alanna's brow furrowed as she frowned. "Like what?"

"I think I need to put a meeting on my calendar," he said. "Make it two – no, three months from now. When we're well clear of the dust of the coronation."

"Okay," she agreed, opening the case on her tablet. "Who's attending?"

"You, me, head of Communications for a start," he said. "Head of our tourism office, too. And add my father but make his invite optional."

"Sure," she replied, fingers dancing over the screen. "What do I call it?"

"Initial planning meeting, royal wedding," he said.

"Getting married?" Alanna asked, laughing. When she saw his expression, the laughter stopped abruptly. "I mean, really? Do...do I know him?"

"Not yet. Well, probably not," Gregory replied. "I need you to help me find him. It's a planning meeting to manage finding me a spouse. Come prepared to brainstorm."

"If you want me to set you up – "

"No, I don't want to rope romance into this," he said. "I want to find someone appropriate. I need a king consort, not a boyfriend. Diplomatic, preferably royalty from somewhere nearby or with sufficient wealth that he knows what he's getting into. Potentially open-minded on the subject of adopting children and having extramarital affairs."

Alanna, quietly, closed her tablet case again.

"Greg," she said.

"I told you this was a staff thing, not a friend thing."

"You cannot meeting-minutes yourself a husband," she said.

"I'm sure it's been done. Probably by kings before me," he

pointed out.

"Love isn't a function of government!"

"I'm not looking for love, Al. I'm too busy for that. But Dad's not wrong that I need a partner, and the sooner the better. If we find someone with a reasonably even temper and decent ego we can make it work. Actually, a narcissist might be just the thing," he said thoughtfully.

"Might as well just marry me," she said.

"That's what Dad said. I would, but it'd hardly be fair to you. Anyway, I'm already out; people would know it was a sham if I did that. And you deserve a paycheck for what you put up with."

"But your husband doesn't?"

"It's not like being king consort doesn't have perks. And if I like the look of him and he doesn't mind me, we could make something work. I know it's a tall order but there can't be that big a shortage of sensible, good-looking gay men in Europe."

"There's a shortage of that in this room," Alanna drawled.

"Ouch!"

"I just mean you're not being sensible. But you are being…royal," Alanna sighed. "I don't suppose Jerry – "

"Jerry's my cousin," Gregory said.

"So am I!"

"Yeah, but you're disqualified for other reasons. Anyway, Jerry's also straight. And a buffoon."

"People like a buffoon. Fine, not Jerry," Alanna said. "I'll start a list, but I'm doing this under protest."

"If you think about it, a husband-search is probably the most royal thing I've done," Gregory said, as she opened the tablet again.

"Royal pain in my ass," Alanna retorted. "Invite sent, but we will be circling back on this."

"You and my father both. Your country thanks you for your service."

"Hm." She stood up, tucking the tablet under one arm. "Try

to get to bed before midnight, huh? The spreadsheets will wait a day."

"That's a lie, but I'll do my best."

He let her kiss him on the forehead, then turned back to the window as she left.

SEVEN WEEKS UNTIL
THE CORONATION OF HIS MAJESTY
KING GREGORY III

AFTER DRAGGING THE entire internet to their doorstep, where Askazer-Shivadlakia became a meme for about 29 hours, Eddie Rambler laid low. At least that was what Gregory assumed he was doing. He didn't see him much around the palace, and while Rambler didn't stop posting completely, he did seem to be working well with palace communications about when and where to share his glamorous life in a small European kingdom. Gregory asked Alanna for a daily update on the Photogram situation, but after two days of that Alanna took his phone away and maliciously installed Photogram on it so that he had to check it himself. He considered using his new account to become an influencer, just to annoy her, but that would have been funnier when they were kids.

He was just finishing up for the day, about to check Photogram as a break from paperwork, when he looked up from his desk and caught sight of the chef through his window.

At first he didn't realize who it was; the sun was down and the figure on the road wasn't much more than a vaguely two-legged shape against the last red of sunset, with a weird bulge on one side and a single, strange antenna. He moved to the window, open to let in the summer air, and confirmed to himself that it was Rambler. The bulge was a bag slung over one shoulder, and the antenna resolved itself into an archery bow.

Before he could withdraw, satisfied, Rambler saw him and

lifted his bow in greeting, cutting across the grass to the window instead of following the road.

"Evening, Your Highness," Rambler said, coming to rest his arms on the ledge of the window, just below chest-height. "Working late?"

"Good evening, Mr. Rambler," Gregory said, feeling strangely formal and awkward, standing above him. Rambler didn't seem bothered by it.

"I told you, Eddie's fine," Rambler said.

"Eddie," Gregory agreed, casting around for some way to resolve the height disparity. He ended up seating himself on the bench, which at least put them closer, though it still felt odd. "What are you doing out at this hour?" he continued.

"Oh!" Eddie said excitedly. "Fishing! The lake fish come up to feed at dusk."

Gregory cocked his head at him. "You were bowfishing?"

"I've been learning." Eddie jostled the bow slung over one shoulder. "Found out that the National Conservation guys, your park rangers? They teach classes in it at the lake east of the palace."

"We're very proud of our heritage," Gregory managed.

"You should be. I haven't had this much fun in years. You get your bow and you stand in a little boat like a stand-up paddleboard, and you push out onto the lake – and when the fish come up to feed, whap!" Eddie smacked the window ledge for emphasis.

"Yes, I…grew up here, we went bowfishing when I was a boy," Gregory said.

"I'll be honest, I didn't think it'd work," Eddie said. "But check it out!"

He flicked the bag off his shoulder and lifted it up. It turned out to be a wicker basket, containing several fish. They were average size, plump from the bounty of springtime in the lake. They looked healthy, which pleased Gregory as a monarch, and there were a respectable number of them with only small wounds, which impressed him as a sportsman.

"That'll show me to be skeptical," Eddie said, shouldering the basket again. "Anyhow, I'm gonna clean these while they're fresh and pack them in ice for Simon. Maybe do a late-night fish fry. Hey, have you eaten?" he asked, brow furrowing. "Getting late, Your Highness."

"A few hours ago," Gregory said. "I was just – "

"Great!" Eddie interrupted, and started *climbing through the window.*

It was just far enough off the ground to be difficult, but even as Gregory went to help him through, he hauled himself up and swung his entire body over the ledge, in a move more reminiscent of a parkour video than a cooking demonstration. Gregory blinked at him as he slid lightly over the sill and into the office.

"Hope security doesn't come after me for that," Eddie said, dusting himself down.

"We don't have guards on the windows," Gregory replied.

"Probably to your credit, means nobody wants to kill you that badly," Eddie said, heading for the door that led out into the hallway. "Come have some fish with me."

"I…if you insist," Gregory managed, following as Eddie made a beeline for the kitchen.

Once there, Gregory made his way to a stool at the prep table as Eddie settled his fishing bow in the corner and bustled around, digging out knives and bowls. He put a pot on the stove and poured oil into it, heating the oil while he gutted the fish deftly.

"You look like you've done this a lot," Gregory observed after a while, for lack of anything else to say.

"Oh, yeah," Eddie said, sleeves rolled up, muscles in his forearms flexing as he worked. "I used to sling fish at a fry shack. I could probably do this in my sleep."

"Sounds like a difficult job."

Eddie gave him a curious look as he laid the fish out in a neat row on a prep tray and began filleting two of the biggest. "Not usually what people say when I tell them that. Fry cooks don't get the kind of respect TV stars do."

"Well, there's hot oil involved, which as a royal I'm very familiar with," Gregory said, and Eddie's jaw dropped.

"Was that a joke about boiling oil?" he asked, delighted. "Where'd you pull that out of?"

"When you're attending boarding school and they know your father's a king, you get all kinds of good material," Gregory told him. "My friends used to call coming over to my room for evening study *storming the castle*."

"Wild. Did you get Vlad the Impaler jokes?"

"Mm, no, I think we're too Mediterranean for that," Gregory said. "One of my teachers called me Prince Charming for a year, though."

"That's equally wild but way less cool," Eddie said.

"How so?" Gregory asked.

"Not cool for teachers to do it, that's punching down. Kids don't need that kinda stress."

"It wasn't terrible. It was good-natured, and if I couldn't hold up to that, I'd never hold up under all this," Gregory said thoughtfully. He'd never thought much of the ribbing he'd gotten over being a prince; it was just people who didn't fully understand the situation and were probably trying to process the strangeness of his existence. But it was a little nice to see someone having sympathy for the mortified fourteen-year-old Prince Charming.

"Uneasy lies the head, eh?" Eddie asked kindly, whisking something in one of the bowls. Gregory looked at him in surprise, startled as much by the literary reference as by a sudden return to reality from his thoughts.

"It kinda spoils my schtick, but I *can* read," Eddie added, grinning over his shoulder. "And Shakespeare was low entertainment for rude mechanicals, so I guess it's on brand."

"It's from one of the histories, though, isn't it?" Gregory asked, hoping it wasn't from *Macbeth*.

"*Henry the Fourth, Part Two: The Empire Strikes Back,*" Eddie agreed.

"No, part two would be *Attack of the Clones,*" Gregory said thoughtfully.

Eddie let out a startled laugh, almost dropping the fish he'd been about to put in the batter. He set the fillets down and turned to Gregory.

"That is the nerdiest thing I've ever heard royalty say," he declared, pointing at Gregory. "You just had that right there at the front of your brain."

"In my defense, Alanna really loves the prequels," Gregory said, which set Eddie off again. He laughed his way through battering the fillets and laying them carefully into the oil, then set the old wind-up timer Simon kept by the stove.

"Do you like Shakespeare?" Gregory asked, curious now.

"Usually I joke that I've just spent a lot of time in parks," Eddie said. Gregory frowned. "Because Shakespeare's always happening in a park somewhere?"

"It takes an unusual level of dedication to see *Henry IV part 2,*" Gregory said. "It's not really park fare."

"Man, this is *really* going to spoil my schtick," Eddie said, washing his hands and gathering up a mesh straining spoon, big enough to scoop out the fish with. "There's a reason I went into TV, my friend. I majored in theatre." He put a dramatic flair on the last word, bowing regally. "Of the thirty-nine-ish plays of Shakespeare, I've seen thirty-six."

"Which ones are you missing?"

"Well, I've never seen *The Winter's Tale,* that's just bad timing on my part. I've never been sober for all of *Titus Andronicus,* so I don't know if that counts. And I've never seen *Twelfth Night.*"

"*Twelfth Night?* Really? Isn't that one *required* to happen in parks?" Gregory asked. He could recall seeing at least three versions of it. Even his cousin Jerry liked *Twelfth Night.* He called it a banger.

"I've been saving it for a special occasion," Eddie said. "I mean, I've read it, I know what it's about. But like, I saw *Hamlet* three times in two years for school, more if you count all the movie versions I had to watch. Do you know how boring *Hamlet* gets?"

"Some would say it begins boring," Gregory said.

"Well, I didn't want to ever be the kind of douchebag who thinks, *Man, Twelfth Night again?* I want it to have the preciousness of rarity," Eddie finished, flipping the fish deftly in the oil. "I'm going to wait until I hear about a really great production of it and also it's my birthday or something, and then I'll just go all out with it."

"That's an oddly charming idea," Gregory said.

"Thanks, I'm full of 'em," Eddie replied with a grin. "Does Askazer-Shivadlakia have a state theatre or anything like that?"

"That was good, you didn't even have to look at your hand that time," Gregory pointed out, amusement in his tone taking the sting out of the words.

"Thanks, I've been practicing," Eddie replied.

"We have a small national theatre, but it's mainly for cultural preservation. Most of the arts in the country are independent. We subsidize a lot through grants, but there are constraints on how far the government can dictate how the money is used."

"Guess I asked the right guy," Eddie said. "Well, I can't advise you to fund any of the histories and most of the tragedies end badly for the kings, but the comedies have some decent princes."

"I'll bear that in mind."

"I suppose it's a lot, running a country," Eddie mused, poking the frying fish. "I mean, you must know that kind of information for everything that happens around here."

"Some of it I outsource," Gregory said, as Eddie scooped the fish onto a sheet of brown paper he'd found. "And if I didn't want the job I wouldn't have taken it."

"Aren't you kind of obliged, though?" Eddie asked, salting the fillets and tearing the paper into pieces to wrap them in. "Malt vinegar?"

"Probably, somewhere," Gregory replied, gesturing at the pantry.

"Helpful." Eddie rummaged in a rack of bottles nearby. "Aha!"

"Askazer-Shivadlakia is a democratic monarchy," Gregory continued. "Power doesn't automatically pass within families. The king has to be confirmed by a popular vote. The kind of personality who wants to be king tends to run in families, so it's convenient that I'm the king's child and wanted the job, but if I hadn't we'd just have held a general election."

"Wait, so you're *elected?*" Eddie asked, disbelieving. "That's *beyond* wild."

"It's not really different from electing a president, although the scale is smaller, of course," Gregory said. He'd developed a little patter for this explanation years ago, around the time he had seriously started considering election to kingship when his father retired. Eddie gathered up the fish in bundles and brought the bundles over to him as he explained. "We had a traditional monarchy, but one of our recent kings – Gregory II, actually, I'm named for him – saw what was happening in Russia just before the Revolution. He decided some pre-emptive democracy might be in order. A small country like ours needs stability and wants one person in office long-term, so generally rule is a life term once elected. But if the people don't like the king, it's possible to call a vote of no-confidence and a new election." He accepted the brown-paper bundle of fried fish Eddie offered, pulling a piece off to taste it. "That's very good. You can tell how fresh the fish was."

"Thanks. Hey, hang on," Eddie said, pulling out his phone. "Say cheese."

Gregory huddled behind his fish a little, trying to show it off as the real star.

"Can't hurt that you're photogenic," Eddie said, setting the phone aside and biting into his own fish dinner. "Has a king ever actually been voted out?"

"Gregory II's son was voted out," Gregory said. "He lost to my grandfather."

"He lost to…so you're named for a guy you're not related to?" Eddie asked.

Gregory swallowed a mouthful of the succulent, crisp-crusted fish before replying. "Our sense of tradition is strong. He's a spiritual ancestor, anyway. Reminder to be a good king."

"Tell us, Crown Prince Gregory, what makes a good king?" Eddie asked, holding out his fish like a microphone. Gregory smiled.

"A strong head for detail," he said. "Empathy, diplomacy, statesmanship. And since I'm elected I do have to be at least a little popular. Have to mind my manners. No boiling oil. Except for fish."

"No boiling oil is a pretty low bar to clear," Eddie replied.

"It does take more effort than that," Gregory admitted, as Eddie set the rest of his fish aside and picked up his phone again. "I'm not…really a natural at the likability part."

Eddie frowned down at his phone. "Well, they voted for you, so you can't be too bad at it."

"Hadn't thought of it that way," Gregory said, pondering this. He'd thought of it more like…a force of nature. He was of age and wanted the job, and he was the king's son, so it was easier for the voters to simply let it happen. The idea of people voting for him because he was well-liked, rather than convenient, was a novel thought.

"Is it okay if I upload this?" Eddie asked, flashing the phone at him to show the photo he'd taken. It wasn't half-bad, even if less of it was of the fish and more was of him than he'd hoped. His hair looked fine, and he was giving what Alanna called the

Smolder with his eyes. "Comms said I could upload any photos taken personally, as long as everyone gave verbal consent. The fish think I should," Eddie added, pointing to the now nearly-empty cone of paper with a smile.

"I suppose," Gregory said. "You'd know better than I would, it's your Photogram."

"Prince Gregory…strong…Photogram game," Eddie said aloud as he typed, then looked up. "Any opinion on the fish?"

"I should probably make some kind of comment about fried fish being a sometimes food," Gregory said thoughtfully.

"It's fish! It's good for you. Omega-3s and all that."

Gregory grinned at him. "Hashtag truly-tasty?"

"Ah, you've been reading my posts!" Eddie shook a finger. "A good catchphrase is worth its weight in gold, especially as a hashtag, but it's all just showmanship. I'm postin' this without any scolding about fried food."

"Fair enough," Gregory replied. "I really should get back to work."

"Well, I'm a fry cook who majored in theatre so I'm not qualified to manage affairs of state," Eddie said. "But I think you should know, fish fried by me is the highlight of any day. It can only go downhill from here. So if you want to get some sleep – and buddy you look good but you do look tired – I think you should throw in the towel."

"You'll be my excuse, eh?" Gregory asked.

"There's photographic evidence of it on the internet," Eddie said solemnly.

He was tired, and the food was warming; he felt like his shoulders had dropped a few inches just from the last half hour.

"All right," he agreed. "Next time, though, I won't be bribed by fish."

"I'm sure I can come up with something," Eddie said. "Sleep well, Your Highness!" he added, calling after Gregory as he left the kitchen.

He made it to his bedroom, left most of his clothes on the floor, and fell into bed, asleep almost as soon as his head hit the pillow.

SIX WEEKS UNTIL
THE CORONATION OF HIS MAJESTY
KING GREGORY III

"GOOD MORNING, READERS and friends and everyone who is keeping it new!" Eddie said into the phone camera. It was being carefully held by Simon, who had foolishly allowed himself to be roped into it.

Eddie felt good, and he knew he showed it. He'd been plotting this for days, but he'd been a little surprised when Alanna agreed to his plan. He suspected she'd said yes so readily in part because she could see the tired, drawn look on the prince's face as easily as he could.

"I'm blown away by the hospitality of Askazer-Shivadlakia – take that, haters, I finally learned to say it – and I'm going to showcase some of that for you today," he continued. "People love their food here and they love to show it off!"

He held up a slice of the fish salami, which was…well, it was certainly new, he told himself.

"But I've worked my way through all of the cured meats, so I think fans of the show know what that means…" he blew air through his lips in a staccato drumroll as he flung the salami aside. "It's time for cheese!"

Simon very patiently kept the phone still while Eddie waved his arms in the air, miming like he was at a football game, cheering wildly.

"But cheese is too good to eat alone," he continued. "I love to share a plate. And when you're planning a shindig like the coronation banquet, you have to know what the belle of the ball wants. So stay tuned to Photogram today! As soon as I'm done filming this, I'm going to go find Crown Prince Gregory and convince him to come with me!"

Simon, otherwise unflappable, looked up from the camera screen and said, "What?" in a voice full of shock, outrage, and delight.

Eddie, knowing it didn't get funnier than that, reached out and took the phone, ending the recording.

"Are you really going to interrupt the prince's day for cheese?" Simon demanded, as Eddie threw a million hashtags on the video and posted it immediately.

"Well, I'm gonna try," Eddie said, pocketing the phone. "Wanna come see me work?"

"I should have made popcorn," Simon replied, following him down the hallway. They could hear the prince's voice in his morning briefing; Alanna, standing just outside the doorway at the back of the crowd, gave a little wave when they approached.

"...discuss this again after the coronation," the prince was saying. "In the meantime, if my father tells you something different, it is still his kingdom. If you're concerned about conflicting orders, speak to Alanna, she'll make the final determination. Alanna?"

"Here, Your Highness," Alanna called.

"Keep me in the loop on any miscommunication."

"Never happier," she replied, to scattered laughter.

"All right, everyone's dismissed," Gregory said, and people began to file out, a few nodding at Eddie or Simon as they left. Alanna stepped into the office, and Eddie put his head in the doorway.

"Ah, Eddie! And Simon. Did you need something?" Gregory asked. "It's only that I have two minutes before a two hour meeting."

"I'm going to say something you're not going to like, and that is this: Ditch it," Eddie said.

Gregory laughed. "I wish, but it's vital. If you can't cover it before the meeting, maybe email me a summary? Or talk to Alanna, she's good at condensing."

"Nah," Eddie said.

"…nah?" Gregory asked, raising his eyebrows.

"Ditch the meeting, come to town with me. I need your opinion on cheese."

"It's a major export but a luxury brand, so we can't depend on it for revenue," Gregory said promptly. "If the economy tanks we all eat very nice cheese nobody else will buy, but the crown will need to subsidize the producers."

"You could be eating very nice cheese in ten minutes without an economic recession," Eddie said.

"Affairs of state – " Gregory began, but there was a soft beep from his phone. He looked down at it, frowning, then up at Alanna.

"Did you just cancel my meeting with the Agricultural Cabinet?" he asked Alanna.

"I had one of those in college," Eddie said to Simon, who nodded sagely. "Great for growing tomatoes."

"No, the meeting's still happening, I just removed you from it," Alanna said. There were two more beeps. "And the follow-up briefing, and the accounting re-evaluation meeting after that."

"I created that meeting," Gregory said.

"No, you requested it, I created it, which means I can kick you out whenever I want."

Gregory rubbed his eyes. "Al, I can't get off on the wrong foot with my entire Agricultural Cabinet."

"I know," she said. "I'm bringing in the duke. He's not doing anything, and they all like him."

"Jerry's never doing anything, and he exists to be liked," Gregory said. "He's not going to understand one word in three they say to him."

"But I will, and I can condense it for you," Alanna said. "Greg. This is your last few weeks before you're king. Go have some fun." He opened his mouth, but she barreled onward. "All the crops and their statistics will still be here after the coronation, and so will all the meetings. You need a day."

He looked back and forth from Alanna to Eddie, and Eddie could tell when he realized this had been planned.

"All right," he said, standing and spreading his hands in defeat. "Let's go. Show me this amazing cheese."

"Triumph!" Eddie crowed. Gregory followed him out of the office, Alanna locking up behind them. Simon headed for the kitchen, and Eddie held the door to one of the side entrances of the palace, which would set them on a footpath down to the main street of town.

Once they were out of sight of the palace, Eddie dug in his bag and pulled out a hat, passing it over. It was bright blue and said TRULY TASTY in tie-dye patterned embroidery on the front. The prince accepted it, perplexed, and once his hands were full Eddie placed a pair of blue cat's-eye sunglasses on his face.

"What is this?" Gregory asked, pulling the glasses off to inspect them.

"I got you a disguise," Eddie said. "Glad I didn't have to talk you out of wearing the uniform with all the braid and stuff, actually. Can't have you mobbed while we're in town."

"Eddie, I'm the prince of a country with a smaller population than Manhattan," Gregory answered, but he did put the hat on. "People are going to know it's me." His phone beeped again and he frowned at it. "Did you post about this on Photogram?"

"Well, a lesson I happen to have learned in Manhattan is that if you look like you don't want to be recognized, most people will mind their own damn business," Eddie answered. "Of course people are going to know it's you, you're highly recognizable and built like a Greek god. This is a hint you want them to pretend they don't."

Gregory clearly didn't have a response for this, but he also clearly tried very hard. "Do you know, in theory the kings of Askazer-Shivadlakia are descended from Apollo?" he managed.

"Explains some things," Eddie said. "But you're not a hereditary king."

"Again, it's the spirit that counts," Gregory said, putting the sunglasses back on. Between the hat worn brim-forward like a nerd, the slightly askew glasses, and his upright royal posture, he gave the impression he was actively *trying* to seem awkward. "How do I look?"

"I haven't known you very long," Eddie answered, holding up his phone in selfie mode to show him his reflection, "but I feel confident in saying you've never looked less royal."

Gregory let out a startled bark of laughter at his own appearance. He reached out and tapped the photo button, preserving the image. "Do not post that to Photogram."

"No, that one's for the scrapbook," Eddie agreed, pocketing his phone again. "I'm not kidding about the cheese, though. Let me tell you my impressions so far and you can spout every fact you ever memorized about domestic cheese production."

The walk into town was educational. Eddie thought he'd learned a lot from talking to cheese mongers, but most of them were craftsmen who made small-batch cheese, or retailers who bought wholesale from the one large manufacturer, further inland, where most of the dairy farming was done. Neither group had the overhead view of things that the prince did, and they didn't want to. Eddie did; he liked to know how things worked, and he'd done very well for himself by making content that traced things back to their origins. He'd packaged it up in beach-bum slang and easily digestible sound bites, but it was all there.

Gregory knew the cost of everything his country produced, where it came from and where it went, but he also looked at all of it in terms of the passage of time. If the global economy suffered, what would happen to his people? If there was a sudden uncontrollable demand for some product his country produced, where could the supply chain be supported? Could local delicacies be made elsewhere and simply stamped with the royal seal? How long could that last before the assurance of quality that came with the king's seal was watered down?

"….which is why I think tax subsidy endowment accounts are so vital," Gregory said, as they arrived on the doorstep of the first cheese shop on Eddie's agenda. "It's a hard sell to people who don't understand endowment finance, though."

"I can imagine," Eddie replied. "And this was all super cool, but now I want you to try a thought experiment."

Gregory nodded, attention focusing.

"I want you to consciously attempt to forget that tax subsidy endowment accounts exist and think about how much you like good food," Eddie said. Gregory's brow knitted. "We're not here to judge the quality of king's-imprint domestic product. We're here to pick out some cheese you really like for a party you're super excited about."

"I think super excited would be an extremely generous term for my feelings on the coronation," Gregory replied.

"Thought experiment," Eddie reminded him. Gregory nodded and seemed to genuinely be making the attempt. Eddie pushed the cheese monger's door open. "All right. Come with me."

Alanna reflected, an hour into the Agricultural Cabinet meeting, that the downside of being the right hand of the prince, soon to be king, was that you had many of the same boring experiences he did without any of the luxury.

Not that Gregory lived extravagantly; King Michaelis and his son both had relatively simple tastes and preferred sport and statecraft to partying or lavish spending. The queen had been more fond of the finer things in life, but even she hadn't been particularly fancy by royal standards. And Alanna had a title, or would when her grandmother passed, and she didn't even want that one.

But the point was that Alanna was in this meeting so Gregory wouldn't have to be, and nobody was calling *her* Your Highness.

On the other hand, she'd volunteered for this when Eddie suggested his plan to her, thinking Gregory could use both the time away from his desk and a little PR boost with the populace. Eddie Rambler had a golden touch; where he went, people followed, emotionally if not literally. He'd raised the profile of Askazer-Shivadlakia significantly. Even among their own people, being seen out with him could only be good for Gregory.

Her phone vibrated silently every so often and she kept an eye on Photogram, but as promised Eddie was being restrained. The photos he was posting were good quality, he always named the shop in the photograph, and so far nobody locally following the Photogram seemed to have caught up with them.

Jerry – more properly Gerald, 12th Duke of Shivadlakia – fidgeted in the chair next to her and tapped her phone with the cap of his pen.

"How's it going?" he mouthed.

"Seems fine," she whispered back. Jerry nodded and ostensibly turned back to the meeting. He was asking, if not especially well-informed questions, then at least not the most obvious ones. Jerry's family were old landed nobility from before Askaz and Shivadlakia had combined into a single country, and they had apparently bred for charisma. They had been kings, on occasion, but more often regents, and sometimes what Jerry referred to as evil advisors. Not that Alanna didn't have a few of those in her own history, she supposed.

Gregory's family on his father's side were relative newcomers, immigrants from only a handful of generations back, which was perhaps why they treated rule like a civic duty, while Jerry treated it like a quaint chore. Jerry could have stood for king if he'd wanted, but he preferred to make himself amiable and be otherwise useless. In that sense he was a good tool to have around the place. He could be deployed effectively against annoying bureaucrats, overly friendly grifters, squabbling government ministers, and once, memorably, a handsy ambassador bothering palace staff.

A shift in the air pressure of the room told her she'd missed something; people were stretching, speaking to one another, or rising to leave the room.

"Five minute break," Jerry said to her, cracking his neck. "Want me to see if I can stretch it to fifteen? You look like you could use a nap."

"No, my mind just wandered," she replied. "Did I miss anything vital?"

"I'll tell you later. It's all locked away up here," he added, tapping his temple.

"I'm sure there's empty space enough."

"You're a monster, Al," he informed her.

"Pain builds character," she replied ruthlessly. "Anyway, it's for Greg."

"Sure, you say that. I think you just want the chef to give you your own cooking show," Jerry said with a grin. "I know it's not just getting Gregory out of his office for a couple of hours. What's going on?"

Alanna shrugged. "I felt like he needed a reality check."

"Why?"

She sat back, staring up at the ceiling, relaxing while she could. "He wants me to find him a husband."

"Oh saints," Jerry cackled. "He has met you, right?"

"It's not that! I'd be extremely good at finding someone a husband. I have great taste in men and I'm highly efficient," she protested.

"Physician heal thyself, then."

"I don't want a husband, Jerry, I don't have time for one. The point is, the king's on him to get married for the good of the country, he's feeling a little raw about it, and he's busy. So he made me set up this husband-hunt meeting for after the coronation."

"Huh." Jerry slouched down next to her, contemplating this. "That's kind of sad."

"It's extremely sad and it's very out of touch in that dumb way he gets," Alanna sighed.

"He can be deeply stupid about other humans," Jerry agreed.

"So I thought if he got out and talked to someone who didn't work in politics for a few hours he'd maybe relax a little," Alanna said. She held up her phone, which was flipped to Eddie's latest post. It was, for the most part, just an anonymous pair of hands holding a large flat wheel of cheese. If she didn't know what Gregory had been wearing that morning or if she didn't recognize the insignia of the royal family of Askazer-Shivadlakia on his ring, she wouldn't know it was his hands holding the wheel. "He seems to be having fun."

"Well, then our suffering is not in vain," Jerry said. "Look out, better sit up straight, someone's coming to talk to us about figs."

It was afternoon by the time Eddie and Gregory said goodbye to the last of the cheese mongers and turned back towards the palace. Neither of them had bothered with lunch, but Gregory felt warm and expansive, pleased with what he'd seen and full of good food he'd sampled all morning. Eddie, who was carrying a messenger bag that was significantly heavier than it had been when they set out, whistled as they walked.

"You know, I think that was potentially more educational than the Agricultural Cabinet briefing would have been," Gregory said, enjoying the breeze off the beach below Fons-Askaz as they climbed the gentle incline back to the palace.

"See, I knew you'd have fun," Eddie replied.

"It's important. I want to be able to confidently speak about every aspect of our farm-to-table pipelines, and that naturally includes cheese," Gregory said, already organizing a campaign in his head – something to do with a line of exports, perhaps.

"And also you had fun," Eddie said. Gregory shot him a tolerant look.

"Yes, I also had fun," he agreed, removing the hat but keeping the sunglasses on.

"And we found some great food. Not sure what I'm doing with some of it yet, but nothing goes to waste in Simon's kitchen," Eddie said cheerfully.

"If nothing else, fondue's very popular here," Gregory said. "Might have a family dinner, invite in some of the cousins."

"That reminds me, I was curious," Eddie said. "Who's the duke that Alanna got to stand in for you today?"

"Ah, Jerry. His family's been in state politics forever. He and Alanna and I were thick as thieves as children. At school he was always a year ahead of me and making my teachers grateful I was so well-behaved. He gets into some small scrape about once a year to keep us humble, but he's very good at making other people feel important."

"He's not like…out for your job though, right?" Eddie asked. "I'm not in *Hamlet*, is what I'm asking."

"Well, we do live in a park. But no," Gregory assured him. "He's a good man on your side in a pinch. Sort of a big brother. Cousin on my father's side."

"It's good when family gets along," Eddie mused. "Especially when it's a family business, which I guess this government sort of is. My family does okay but I can't imagine the yelling we'd do if we had to rule a whole country."

"Are you all chefs?" Gregory asked, wondering what kind of

family brought up a man like Eddie.

Eddie burst out laughing. "Oh, no. Most of my family work in Dad's auto shop. Those that work at all, anyway."

"Auto shop!" Gregory blinked at him.

"Sure. My dad specializes in trucks and does van art on the side. His sister works on beach buggies that my mom rents out from her surf shop."

"You have a pedigree I was wholly unaware of," Gregory observed, staggered by this information.

"Yeah, they put it in the puff pieces whenever someone needs a bio of me but it doesn't come up a lot," Eddie said. "They're all pretty free spirits. They don't like a lot of attention, so I try to keep them out of the spotlight."

"And you didn't care for that life?" Gregory asked.

"Well, I had a great childhood. All that stuff's awesome when you're ten and someone else is driving. I like surfing, and I'm okay with an engine. But I got older, wanted something different." Eddie shrugged. "I had bigger dreams than opening a taco stand next to the surf shop."

"I suppose we're opposites, in a way," Gregory said.

"How so?"

"I bought into the family tradition. You climbed out. Nothing wrong with that, just...different."

"I don't think it's opposite, exactly," Eddie replied, frowning – more like he was puzzling it out than like he disagreed. "You wanted to be king, didn't you? Nobody pressured you?"

"No," Gregory said. "Father has always said it's a job you have to choose, and my mother agreed. I could have gone into business or law, or – I suppose I could have opened a taco stand, though I don't think they'd have been delighted by that."

"So we both saw what we wanted, and we both looked at the consequences of reaching for it and accepted them," Eddie said. Gregory considered this as the palace came into view at the end of the road.

"That's...true," he allowed. "I have strong feelings about this place. I saw how hard my parents worked to protect it. It's a noble calling, at least I think so. And I like it, too."

"I gotta say I never thought of 'television chef' as a noble calling," Eddie said, as they drew closer to the palace. "But it's kinda how I treated it anyway. I knew kids who wanted to be famous but I didn't want fame, exactly. I just wanted to talk to a lot of people about something I really loved. Fame's mostly one of those consequences."

"Huh," Gregory said.

"What?"

"You're right, I don't think we are opposites." He took the sunglasses off, leaning against the lintel of the doorway into the palace. "And I had better go deal with the consequences of the Agricultural Cabinet."

"I'm glad you could come out today," Eddie said. Gregory held out the sunglasses and hat, but Eddie waved a hand.

"The merch is free. Hold onto it for the next time you need to ditch," he said.

Gregory felt unaccountably touched by this; not only the gesture of finding him a ridiculous, useless disguise, but offhandedly giving it as a gift, and implying there might be another need for it in the future.

"That's kind, thank you," he said.

"Pay you twenty bucks to wear the hat instead of the crown at coronation," Eddie added, and Gregory laughed.

"I'm afraid I can't oblige that one. I hear the host of this show is a real beach bum."

"Yeah, well, wish me luck, this beach bum has a bunch of menus to present to his uptight new boss on Monday," Eddie replied. Even the ribbing for being a little uptight felt kind, like he knew Gregory didn't get much friendly teasing anymore.

"I'm sure I'll have some commentary on your Photogram posts to review by then," Gregory said. With a wave he ducked inside, leaving Eddie enjoying the sun on the palace steps.

Thirty seconds later, as Gregory was entering his office, his phone beeped. Eddie was posting to his Photogram, a selfie in the garden. It was captioned "Can't believe I just forgot to get a selfie with Crown Prince Gregory in a *Truly Tasty* hat. Letting you down, guys, it won't happen again."

Gregory tapped the image to Like it, making little hearts dance around the text, and then headed to the conference room to find Alanna.

FIVE WEEKS UNTIL
THE CORONATION OF HIS MAJESTY
KING GREGORY III

EDDIE WAS REALLY getting to like the palace of Askazer-Shivadlakia. It wasn't just that he had a cool room with a great view of the grounds, or that it was full of art and interesting people. It was that it felt like a home in a way a lot of places didn't. He'd cooked for celebrities in their mansions, he'd cooked in museums and on sound stages and even in a couple of what, in America, passed for castles. But most big institutional buildings, even if he liked them, just felt a little soulless. They were event spaces, not homes.

The palace here was different – it was a working building, the decor incidental to the real business of governing. The kitchens were beautiful (Simon's doing, he felt sure) and the hallways were draped in tapestries and lined in slightly worn rugs that softened the feel of stone underneath. And all of that was for a purpose, not for show.

He'd spent most of the morning in the kitchen with Simon, putting the finishing touches on his lunch presentation to the prince, going over checklists and the printed menu copies to make sure nothing was missing. Now the cold food was packed in a cooler and the hot food in a basket lined with tea towels, and he hummed cheerfully to himself as he gathered them up, making his way towards the prince's office.

"Eddie!" a voice called, and he turned in time to see the

prince himself emerging from a conference room.

"Your Highness," he called back, waiting for Gregory to catch up with him. He had a tablet under one arm and was dressed the least formally Eddie had ever seen him, in a t-shirt and worn dark trousers. "Casual Monday?"

"Wh – oh," the prince looked down at his clothes. "I was getting fitted for the formal robes this morning, and they're dusty – they warned me to wear old clothes." As if to demonstrate, he sneezed, and a light flurry of powder floated off him. Eddie, without thinking, shifted the basket to the same arm holding the cooler, and brushed Gregory's shoulders clear of the remainder. "Thank you," Gregory said, dusting the rest of himself down. Eddie patted him on the shoulder, enjoying the muscle underneath briefly, and then rebalanced himself, cooler in one hand, basket in the other.

"I hear there's a good drycleaner in town," Eddie said, as they turned to Gregory's office. "I don't know if they do royal robes."

"Apparently the dust is part of the tradition," Gregory replied. "Is that samples in your basket?" he asked hopefully. "I haven't had lunch yet."

"It is, and it's both still hot," Eddie held up the basket, "and still cold," he continued, holding up the cooler, "so we should hustle."

"I've had some thoughts about those cheeses," Gregory said, and Eddie cheered a little internally.

"Me too!" he said, as Gregory led the way into his office. "I'm looking forward to – "

Eddie broke off, because Gregory had stopped a few paces inside the door. There was a man sitting in one of the office's guest chairs, book in one hand; even if his face wasn't on half the currency in the country, Eddie would have noticed his resemblance to Gregory. This was Michaelis, the current king. He'd just gotten accustomed to thinking of the prince as Gregory, and the renewed awe for the grandeur of Askazer-Shivadlakia's royalty filled him.

"Father," Gregory said, sounding both surprised and annoyed.

"Good morning," King Michaelis said, putting away the book he'd been reading. "Mr. Rambler, I presume. Pleasure to meet you."

"Your Majesty," Eddie said, remembering his manners. "The pleasure's mine."

"What are you doing here?" Gregory asked.

"Well, I know Alanna marked me as optional on the meeting invite, but for all your jokes it's not like I actually have died," Michaelis said. "This is almost as much my party as it is yours, in a way, and your mother used to like having me do the gala catering sampling with her. I thought I'd offer my opinion."

"Sure you didn't just want more of those meatballs?" Gregory asked. Eddie chuckled, which drew both their attention, a fearsome thing in itself. "Eddie, are there enough samples?"

"Sure, the more the merrier," he said, sidling past Gregory to begin unpacking the food onto the desk. Gregory sat down in the other guest chair. Eddie decided to stand, just in case sitting in the presence of the king was a political thing.

"I heard about your trip into town for cheese-sampling," Michaelis continued, speaking to Gregory as Eddie unpacked. "I thought I'd see if it was productive." He turned to Eddie. "Obviously the reception is extremely important, but the palace trusts you to produce a good meal without too much guidance. I want to make sure Gregory's time isn't taken up with incidentals. It's easy to be distracted from affairs of state. Such as the Agricultural Cabinet," he drawled at his son.

"Great for growing tomatoes," Eddie tried again, but the joke still fell flat. He wondered if he could get away with making it a weed joke instead. Not in front of the king, that was for sure.

"It's fine, once or twice," Michaelis said. "Everyone thinks it was charming of you to go yourself, and Gerald handled the cabinet competently. I just want to make sure it was worth it."

"So, I have four menus," Eddie said, because there wasn't any great place for that conversation to go, and Gregory seemed tense. "We can mix and match the foods a little depending on what you like." He handed the four printed menus to the king, who set them on the desk to share with his son. "On one end of the scale we have my personal favorite, the hot sandwich bar with passed apps, which we've already discussed a little. On the other end is a multi-course royal meal *a la russe*, with personal service by the waitstaff. Let me introduce you to some herbed clay pot chicken on peasant bread rolls."

He'd crafted his menus with local food in mind, but Alanna had made him well aware that the prince also wanted modernity. He hadn't counted – and clearly neither had Gregory – on the king joining them, and Eddie had no idea what the man's tastes were, other than what he'd gleaned from Simon's standard dishes. But all the food was good, which went a long way towards satisfying even the most exacting of parents, and Eddie had thought to bring a bottle of wine from the country's highlands ("Well…highland, there's just the one mountain," the wine merchant had explained) which smoothed the way a little more.

Going through the menus and the various hot and cold dishes that accompanied them, Eddie decided the tension between father and son probably wasn't normal. He prided himself on being a pretty good judge of character, and Michaelis didn't seem like a bad dad, or Gregory a disappointment. This was something else, which meant that until it came to a head he, at least, could probably safely ignore it. Maybe they would do the same.

So he kept serving and talking, two things he was good at, and ignored the vague elephant in the room. Still, he breathed a little sigh of relief when they finally reached the end of the presentation.

"I think if nothing else we've established something pretty

vital," Gregory said, having finished off the last of the dessert nibbles.

"What's that?" his father asked, waving away Eddie's offer of a top-off on his wine.

"It's going to be great food regardless," Gregory said. "This was delicious, Eddie, thank you."

"It was good," Michaelis agreed. Both he and Gregory saw the 'but' coming, Eddie thought. "But the quality of the food is expected. It's only one aspect."

Gregory looked annoyed, but Eddie cut off a potential fight. "I'd love to hear your thoughts on that," he said sincerely, not moving to tidy away the plates or containers of food.

"The coronation is a ritual as much as an event. Everything about it should be a unified whole – dare I say a *magical* event, without getting too flowery about it," Michaelis said. "We call ourselves kings at this point, at least in part, because we have a cultural love of pageantry. We want things to look their best and impress those around us."

"I want that as well," Eddie replied. "Do you see anything in what I've shown you here that you think fits in best?"

"Well, I can't say I'm thrilled with the idea of a hot sandwich bar," Michaelis said.

"Yeah, the prince wasn't either," Eddie agreed. He shot Gregory a grin, a hint to stay calm, because he was looking more annoyed by the second.

"Smacks of a Las Vegas buffet," Michaelis continued.

"There's a time and a place for that style of service," Eddie replied. "Maybe this isn't it."

"I like it," Gregory said, a little sharpness creeping into his voice. "The family feeling of it. Maybe not the format, but…"

"This is an affair of state," Michaelis said.

"Yeah, but Dad, I can't stand the formal dinner thing. *You* don't even like it."

"No, but I had to learn to live with it to keep others happy.

You might too. Not to say it has to happen at your coronation," Michaelis said, making a calming gesture with one hand. "But the coronation will set a tone."

"Exactly! I want us to seem approachable as well as impressive. A six-course meal is nobody's idea of a good time even with food this good. Too much sitting down."

Michaelis, to his credit, seemed to consider this. "And nobody likes a compromise."

"No," Gregory agreed. Both men looked at Eddie, who nodded as if he was considering this deeply. A good eighty percent of being a television host was looking like you were actively listening.

"I'm not out of ideas yet," he said, although he *absolutely was*. To cover, he started cleaning up the desk.

"These recipes – the flavors are great," Gregory said. "Don't throw the food out just because the look isn't right yet."

"But I do urge you to find a balance between informality and elegance," Michaelis said. His phone beeped. "And I'm afraid that's my afternoon appointment with the royal librarian."

"Need a book recommendation?" Eddie joked.

"Apparently I'm expected to dictate my memoirs," Michaelis said sourly. "Gregory, I'll see you at breakfast tomorrow."

He leaned over and kissed his son on the forehead, a seeming conciliatory gesture, and left. Eddie slowed his cleaning, waiting for Gregory to speak first.

"I am so, so sorry my father ambushed you," Gregory said finally.

"Sounds like he ambushed both of us, but it comes with the job," Eddie replied.

"Oh, for me too, I guess."

"Are you okay?" Eddie asked carefully.

"What?" Gregory replied.

"Well, obviously it's tough. He looks like he's feeling iffy about you playing hooky with me for cheese."

"He'll be fine. He's just worried about the coronation, like me. It's coming out in weird ways. You're not seeing him at his best."

"I'm not sure I made a great first impression," Eddie said.

"I'm guessing you have a lot of experience defying first impressions," Gregory replied, and Eddie laughed.

"Sure, that's true, I'm really more of a second-look kind of guy."

"Anyway, it's not his decision. Ultimately, it's mine, and whether or not he likes you, I do. So he'll have to put up with it."

Eddie smiled, genuinely touched. In show business it was rare for someone to stand so firmly behind anyone else. "Thanks. That means a lot – "

He had closed the basket on the pile of dishes, and was just picking up the cooler when Gregory held up a hand.

"By the time we get to the reception, I'll be king," Gregory said.

"Yeah?" Eddie replied, confused.

"It hits you in waves," he said. He let his hand drop to rest on Eddie's arm. "You realize what'll be different, and…that morning I'll be crown prince, and that evening I'll be king. The mistakes will be mine to make, so I guess…don't worry about my father. I'm on your side."

"I think I'm supposed to be on your side," Eddie reminded him. Gregory looked down at his hand and pulled it back slowly.

"Well, that's probably a question for the philosophers," he said. "Anyway. Just do some thinking, maybe build another few menus – will you have time?"

"All I got is time, baby," Eddie grinned. "Sure. I'll knock his socks off next time."

"And if my dad doesn't like my coronation banquet, the world won't end."

"Yeah, but it'll be uncool, and I'm here to prevent that."

"I'm reliably told I'm uncool anyway," Gregory said. "Do

you need help getting that back to the kitchen?"

"Nope, it's fine." Eddie gave him the peace sign as he left. "I'll keep it new for you, boss!"

"That's Prince Boss to you!" Gregory called. Eddie chuckled, but by the time he made his way back to the kitchen he was more thoughtful.

Whatever Gregory said, this was clearly both a big deal and a significant problem. At this point more than Eddie's professional pride was on the line; besides, he'd given up on professional pride when he did that special where he had to do a kick line with a bunch of sports mascots. He wanted Gregory to enjoy his coronation, and impress his guests and his dad.

"How was it?" Simon asked, looking up from his dinner preparations when Eddie walked in.

"So-so," Eddie said thoughtfully. "Little soon to tell."

"What went wrong?" Simon inquired.

"Nothing wrong, exactly. King came to the tasting," Eddie said, unpacking the cooler and shoving leftovers into the big fridge. "He wasn't big on what I had to show."

"Not the food, surely. He knows good food, and yours is good," Simon replied.

"Thanks – no, the sandwich bar idea. He said it smacked of a Vegas buffet."

"I've had very good meals at buffets in Las Vegas," Simon replied.

"When the hell were you in Las Vegas, Chef?"

"I wasn't sprouted in Askazer-Shivadlakia, you know. If you want to learn about gourmet food, there are many places to study. When I was young I was offered Las Vegas or Paris, and I don't like Paris," Simon told him.

Eddie turned to stare at him. "You're French," he said.

"What has that to do with anything? You come from California, do you love Los Angeles?"

He had a point, and Eddie made a face to acknowledge it.

Simon smiled.

"You had three other menus," Simon continued. "None of them appealed?"

"Well, the prince doesn't want a formal meal. They've got real conflicting opinions on what they do want. I'm supposed to come up with something that's modern, traditional, innovative, and on-brand, all at once."

"This is a terrible burden for a man who earns his living on the internet," Simon said, mock-solemn.

"You make fun, but this is serious! I want to make a good impression." Eddie looked around. "You got any dishes I could wash?"

"Sink is full, if you want to, but the staff will do it later," Simon told him.

"I'll do it. Good for thinking, dishwashing."

"If you say so. I don't like dish soap, either," Simon said, turning back to the prep table. "I leave you to your thoughts."

Gregory didn't always eat dinner in the family dining room, and lately he hadn't been there much, preferring to take a plate up to his room or eat in his office. For dinner, Alanna had brought him a plate as a check-in, and he thought Simon had probably heard about the tasting to judge from the composition of the plate.

Simon had been their chef since he was a child and knew all his favorite comfort foods: Askazer twist-bread, roasted vegetables with fresh herbs from the kitchen garden, and a slice of spiced meat pie. Not too much of any one food, but altogether it had been very satisfying.

He decided it would be a nice break to stretch his legs and bring the plate back himself; gathering up the remains of the meal, he locked his computer and stepped out into the hallway. Previous kings looked down on him from paintings as he passed, but they were old friends, and anyway he knew most of their scandals and secrets. A perk of being raised a prince was a healthy disrespect for royalty, he supposed.

It was amazing how productive work and a good meal had raised his spirits. Everything seemed a little brighter this evening, and perhaps he didn't even need to put in a few more hours tonight. Nobody would die if he waited until tomorrow to complete his current work, and the idea of a good book before bed felt indulgent, inviting. Even the kitchen looked friendly, with a warm wash of yellow light spilling out into the hallway and the sound of voices inside.

He stopped to listen, wondering what they were talking about. It was like lying in the dark listening to your parents talk in the other room, as he'd often done at their fishing lodge when he was a child.

" – His Majesty is retiring for a reason," Simon was saying, his voice drifting out over the sound of spoons against pans. Gregory wondered what they were cooking – dinner had already been served, but he knew Simon preferred to eat later, after the family meal was served. "He knows it's time for someone younger to take the reins, someone with more modern ideas, and Prince Gregory is ready."

"At least it seems like he's happy it's his son," Eddie answered. There was a soft noise, a sort of *fwoom*, and the brief smell of alcohol burning. "Nicely done."

"Thank you. My point is, perhaps the king doesn't handle this so well."

"That's what the prince said, yeah."

"So he takes it out on the food, maybe. Your food, I mean."

"Well, the food never did anything," Eddie replied. Gregory leaned against the wall, just outside the doorway. From here he could see Simon at the stove, tossing vegetables in a stir-fry. "Food's just there to be delicious," Eddie continued. "Kinda like me. Hey! I'm gonna put that on a t-shirt. *Food is here to be delicious, just like me.*"

"That's very funny," Simon intoned. "All this is temporary, anyway. It will all settle down. These things feel more important in the moment than they truly are."

"Yeah, probably."

"And Prince Gregory will be a fine king. Very popular already," Simon said. Gregory smiled to himself, pleased at the praise.

"I don't know anything about kinging, so I can't speak to that," Eddie said. "But he's a nice guy. Funny, when he forgets to be a prince. If he weren't a prince…"

"He'd likely still be in politics," Simon said.

"Well, maybe, but I meant, if he weren't a prince, about to be a king, I'd definitely consider asking him out."

Gregory blinked, shocked.

"Would you now," Simon asked, sounding amused.

"Sure, why not? Good looking man, pretty personable. If I met him in a bar I'd like him. He's probably got some princess from another kingdom lined up, though. Or maybe a Hollywood movie starlet," Eddie said. "Looks like that and royalty too? The ladies must be three-deep."

"One would think," Simon said drily.

"Anyway, I need to do some thinking," Eddie continued, leaving Gregory back in the earlier conversation, still in shock. "Maybe do some research. Like, royal traditions. We could base the meal in that."

"It would be interesting. I can tell you where to look."

"That'd be great," Eddie said.

"The palace library has several books of past chefs' recipes, there may be something in there on special events as well – "

Gregory, realizing he probably shouldn't get caught lurking in the doorway, turned to retreat; the movement shifted the plate in his fingers, and before he could recover he'd fumbled it right in the doorway, sending it crashing to the ground.

He startled as badly as both Simon and Eddie did; they looked over, immediately concerned, and Gregory gaped at them for a second, wordless.

"Prince Gregory!" Simon announced, at the same time Eddie said, "Oh, snap!"

"I...the plate," Gregory managed. "I was just bringing it back, it slipped – "

"Are you okay?" Eddie asked, as Simon pivoted smartly towards the little closet where the mop and broom were kept.

"Yes, I'm fine..." Gregory looked down at the fragments of china. "But the plate. It slipped."

"The palace has no shortage of plates, Your Highness," Simon declared, returning with the broom, gently nudging him with the handle to back up so Simon could sweep up the fragments.

"Come on in, take a load off. Have a snack," Eddie offered, taking his elbow to guide him into the kitchen.

"Oh, no, I should go," Gregory said distractedly. Eddie let go of his elbow, but his hand hovered nearby. "Simon, I'm so sorry – "

"No matter," Simon said easily.

"Thank you for sweeping it up," Gregory told him earnestly. Simon nodded, clearly bewildered by his behavior. "I'll get out of your way."

"That's not necessary – " Eddie began, but he was already out the door. He faintly heard Simon call, "Sleep well!" before he took the stairs up to his apartments two at a time.

When the prince was gone, Eddie took the dustpan from Simon and crouched, holding it while Simon swept the broken plate into it.

"What was that all about?" he asked, picking the silverware out of the debris.

"I've no idea. I suppose dropping the plate startled him," Simon replied.

"He doesn't seem the kind to get jumpy over a little broken crockery."

"No, he never has been," Simon agreed. "He well knows we have plenty of plates. It's not even the good china," he added with a sniff.

"Maybe the king isn't the only one who isn't handling the coronation well," Eddie mused. He lifted the dustpan and carried it to the big garbage bin in the corner.

"Mm, perhaps. Alanna mentioned he's been moody," Simon remarked. "I will have to take matters into my own hands."

"Lord, what does that even mean?" Eddie asked, fascinated.

"More regular meals and higher protein," Simon decided. "Also more oil and butter. I will make a cake. Sugar, good for energy. Good pastries, lots of chicken and beef, and desserts." Simon rubbed his hands together, pleased.

Eddie put the dustpan away and came to rest both hands on Simon's shoulders. "You are a chef after my own heart, LeFevre."

"Hey, all you friends and fans out there!"

Eddie's voice was a little tinny through the phone speakers. His usual bright, cheerful tone was tempered, but Gregory wasn't paying a lot of attention to that; he was mostly absorbed in his own thoughts. It was early, and he was still in bed, but his phone had told him Eddie posted a new video that morning, so he'd rolled over and opened it, curious.

"I hope everyone's still keeping it new," Eddie continued in the video. He did a full rotation with the phone, catching the sunlight on the front facade of the palace as well as the mist rising over the gardens. "Isn't it beautiful country? Reminds me of the California foothills. Whenever I feel like I'm in need of inspiration these days, I come out here and look around. Get it? Look around," he said, and spun the opposite direction to give another 360-degree view. It was endearingly ridiculous, which Gregory was beginning to suspect was Eddie's whole point. He was ridiculous, but it was an earnest ridiculous, and there wasn't a hint of self-deprecation in it. That was just how Eddie Rambler was and he didn't care who knew it or disliked it.

It served him right for listening at doorways, Gregory thought, not for the first time since he'd dropped the plate the night before. He'd fled to his rooms after the kitchen incident, and hadn't slept especially well, mortified at his own behavior and confused by his reaction to Eddie's remarks. It wasn't like he'd never heard anyone say he was handsome, or even that he was nice. But it was more often tabloids or random strangers saying it, not people he knew.

Definitely not people in that inbetween state Eddie occupied, somewhere between stranger and friend. Eddie knew him just well enough to like him, which was very flattering, but he hadn't read Gregory's press (condescending when he was younger, sometimes brutal after he came out, but you couldn't let that affect you). Eddie didn't know him personally well enough to know he was gay.

It was nice to be liked for himself, though. Some men liked the dream of being with a prince more than they liked the idea of actually going on a date with him. And some liked the novelty of 'a prince' more than the reality of 'Gregory'.

He didn't think of himself as someone people were attracted to, he supposed. He wasn't inexperienced, but he knew himself to be a little shy in social situations where he didn't have the diplomatic script to fall back on. The idea of an attractive, successful, interesting person like Eddie, who clearly could have his pick of partners, suggesting a date with Gregory – essentially a quiet bureaucrat – was just…weird.

Nice, though, Gregory thought, as the video of Eddie rolled on.

"You can see one of the closest farms, just over there, and I'm told all the dairy grazing is up that way. These are the winter pastures, closer in to the sea, so the cows are all up in summer pasture right now while it's still warm. And down here," Eddie turned again, pointing to the coast. "You can see the fishing boats coming in, and the ice trucks bringing fresh meat in along the coast road. And that mountain! I'm told they joke they just have a single highland, but what a view!"

Eddie whistled low, pointing to the high mountain rising behind the palace. Gregory grinned. The only joke as tired as "we've just got the one highland" was "you're not a local until you make the One Highland joke". Eddie was doing what he did on all his TV shows – arrive somewhere, make himself at home, and show off the local culture. Nice to see his country getting the Eddie Rambler treatment.

Perhaps he should ask Simon to gently let Eddie in on his secret. Could be a fun time.

"Slight setbacks recently, but I'm not worried," Eddie said in the video. "I know you all can't wait to see the shindig I throw for the new king, and I promise to document every moment I can of it, but right now we're still in the planning stages. Anyone who tells you the life of a professional chef is all chocolate tastings and kitchen tours is selling you a line. Still, if you love what you do, the hell with everything else, right? I'll get through it."

He looked contemplatively up at the mountain.

Gregory, suddenly frustrated, closed the app and let the phone fall into the blankets. There wasn't the slightest point in considering a fling with Eddie, let alone actually allowing one. He was an employee, technically, and neither of them had the time for personal pursuits at the moment. Gregory himself was trying to convince Alanna that a political arranged marriage was a good idea. And Eddie was…well, Eddie. If he was out, Gregory didn't think it was very far, and Gregory'd had enough of closets.

Eddie was a goofball who made dumb jokes, and he certainly wasn't appropriate for a king consort, which was the whole point of dating anyone at this point. An American television chef wasn't going to leave it all behind to co-rule Askazer-Shivadlakia, even if he did like the food.

Pointless. Eddie was simply a kind man who was nice to look at, and an amiable employee who would be gone in less than two months. Best leave him to menu-making and get back to the business of ruling.

Three days later all of that went to hell.

He wasn't sleeping well, or rather, he wasn't sleeping often. When he did sleep it was deep and thorough, but he'd wake restless, or have too much nervous energy to manage more than a few hours. He had actually gotten out ahead of most of his work the previous day, however, so that morning instead of going early to the office he put on a pair of old running shoes, some jogging shorts, and a long-sleeved shirt, and went out to do a lap of the grounds.

There was a pretty good trail that circled most of the palace gardens, with scenic views and packed dirt, excellent for running. The whole loop was a decent level run, long enough to test his endurance, and nobody was likely to be around at five in the morning –

Except Eddie Rambler, who almost sent him sprawling.

Gregory was finally getting out of his own head, zoned out and enjoying the run, when there was a movement ahead on his left and someone called, "Prince Gregory!"

He startled, nearly tripped, and skidded off the path to a stop, wide-eyed. The shape moving ahead resolved itself into Eddie

Rambler, a blond-tipped shadow next to one of the ornamental cherry-blossom trees.

"Eddie," Gregory panted, leaning over to rest his hands on his knees. "You startled me."

"Sorry! I thought you saw me," Eddie said, holding up his hands in a show of innocence. A canvas bag hung off one wrist. "Didn't mean to interrupt your workout."

"It's fine, I need to catch my breath anyway," Gregory said, straightening.

"Nice morning for a run."

"Yes, I thought so. Do you run?"

Eddie laughed. "Only from the cops. I just kind of assumed it was a nice day for it."

"Most runners don't really differentiate, to be honest," Gregory said. "If the world hasn't ended, it's a nice morning for a run. Walk you back to the palace?"

"Sure, I'd be happy for the company," Eddie agreed, falling into step with him.

"I always seem to catch you sneaking back with treasure," Gregory said. "What is it this time, spear-hunting boars?"

"No, I – wait, you have wild boar?" Eddie asked, distracted.

"Is that good or bad?" Gregory asked.

"Could I seriously go spear-hunt wild boar in a royal forest? I think if I do they legally have to write a folk song about me, right?"

"Oh, ah. Maybe. You could, is what I mean, but I don't recommend it," Gregory said. "They're large and very angry. But yes, in theory."

"Have you?"

"Hunted boar? No. I feel that we've fallen into some kind of rabbit hole," Gregory added, wiping his face with his shirt. He glanced at Eddie, who seemed flustered. "So you weren't out hunting."

"I was down at the harbor, looking over the catch. I thought about suggesting a clambake for the coronation, but boy did I get told."

"Ah, yes," Gregory agreed. "Shellfish at a party is bad luck. Old superstition. Something to do with drowning. Or more likely, one too many parties where they got bad oysters. Also, definitively not kosher."

"Shame. Anyway, I didn't want to come back empty-handed, so I stopped at the butcher and got chicken wings. I figured I'd make my infamous Trash Tower."

"Should I ask?" Gregory inquired.

"Play your cards right and you can have some," Eddie replied. "Come up to the kitchen, I'll show you how it's made."

"I really shouldn't," Gregory said. "I have to change, and I have a full day ahead – "

"Won't take long, wings cook fast."

"It's just…" Gregory trailed off, unable to come up with a good excuse. He didn't especially want to come up with an excuse, was the problem.

"Look, I know your dad probably thinks I shouldn't take up your time," Eddie began.

"It's not that – "

"It's okay, I get it," Eddie said, still sounding very reasonable about it. "Tell you what, I'll bring you a slice when it's done, instead. It's definitely not appropriate for your coronation but that's not really why I'm making it."

Gregory paused, considering this, realizing he was simply being a coward. He had the time, his father's feelings on the chef weren't really all that negative and certainly weren't going to impact his own feelings, and he liked Eddie's company.

"No, I have time for anything called the Trash Tower," he said. Eddie looked surprised. "Will it horrify Simon?" he asked, starting to walk again.

"Oh, it horrifies everyone," Eddie assured him.

"What goes into it?"

"It's really something you witness more than a recipe you can explain," Eddie replied.

Simon was in the kitchen when they arrived, but he was doing something complicated with dough; he gave them a nod when Eddie greeted them and placed an apple in Gregory's hand as he passed, but otherwise ignored them. Gregory settled himself at one of the prep tables while Eddie set his cargo down.

"I invented it when I was about twenty," Eddie said, going to the fridge and taking out a bowl of mashed potatoes from some previous meal, as well as some cooked vegetables. "It's mostly about the presentation, but it's also about feeding a bunch of hungry college students with whatever they bring you to cook. It's flexible, but there's a sort of platonic ideal, and it has thankfully been many, many years since I didn't have enough money to buy exactly what food I wanted."

"This is a dish with a platonic ideal," Gregory repeated, skeptical.

"Most dishes have a platonic ideal, but only the Trash Tower is brave enough to admit it," Eddie said. "Want to help?"

"Dare I?"

"Grate cheese," Eddie told him sternly, placing a block of cheese from the fridge and a grater in front of him.

"All of it?"

"Most of it. I'll let you know when to stop." Eddie went back to the bag he'd brought in with him, unloading not just chicken wings but also turkey sausages and an enormous bag of potato chips.

"Didn't figure they kept these in the palace," Eddie said, when he saw Gregory looking at the bag. "Keep grating," he added, opening the bag to let the air out and promptly crumpling it up to crush the chips.

"Yes, Chef," Gregory replied. Simon laughed from his pastries as Eddie began laying out chicken wings on a roasting pan.

"Anyway, the basic premise of my relationship to cooking is that there is a simple, satisfying way to make almost any food," Eddie continued. "Simon, the oven?"

"Still hot from the pastries," Simon replied.

"Awesome." Eddie set the oven temperature a little higher and returned to the wings, sprinkling them with seasoning. "Every time I make a recipe, especially if I'm developing it for a cookbook or an episode, I ask myself which parts are necessary, which parts people might not know. And I try to do something fun with it, so that people who do cook for fun won't see just another recipe for, I don't know, pot roast or lasagna."

"Keeping it new," Gregory said.

"That's it exactly." Eddie put the chicken in the oven and set a frying pan on the stove, swirling oil into it.

"It's a very…youth-culture friendly slogan," Gregory said. "Good marketing, I guess."

"Turned out to be."

"Didn't you come up with it for the TV show?" Gregory asked, surprised.

"Ah! No, the show came later. I didn't come up with it, anyway."

"Who did?"

"Technically a Chinese emperor," Eddie said, like that was the most normal thing in the world. "Ch'eng T'ang, in the 18th century. But I sound like a real new-age asshole when I put it that way. I got it from Ezra Pound."

That clarified absolutely nothing and opened several fascinating new avenues into the inner workings of Eddie's mind, but Gregory honestly wasn't sure where to start.

He finally settled on asking, "Did *he* get it from the Chinese emperor?"

"Yeah, more or less. There's a story about Ch'eng T'ang having a bathtub with an inscription on it about how necessary it was to renew yourself daily. It's meant to be a lesson in good government," Eddie continued, digging in the pots and pans and coming up with a bundt mold. "Pound read about it in a book on Confucian moral philosophy."

"Where'd you come across it?"

"Modernist theatre. Modernism is all about renewal, and they all say Pound said it first, and as we've established, he got it from Ch'eng T'ang. Now, on the one hand, Modernism could be super playful, which is kind of where I plant my own flag. On the other hand, you start edging into Futurism, at which point renovation, making it new, gets a lot more about like...clearing away rubbish, erasing the past. It all goes very Mussolini after that. Not here for it."

"A good lesson to take away," Gregory agreed.

"I think so. Still, the philosophy is pretty sound. I took it as a sort of personal slogan. I really like the idea of always being in renewal. You keep what's already there, you just change it up a little. Always have a solid ideal to adapt from. Then you know where to fall back to, if you have to."

"A very Shivadh sentiment," Simon remarked. Eddie began stir-frying the vegetables, and for a while the crackle of oil and sizzle of some sauce he was concocting drowned him out.

Gregory, his duty done to the cheese, watched as Eddie began assembling...whatever it was. The chicken roasted while the vegetables fried, and then the frying pan was set aside while Eddie mixed more garlic into the potatoes. Then the still-hot chicken wings were pulled from the oven and stripped, Eddie making soft *hah* noises over his singed fingers the whole time, and the meat tossed with the vegetables.

It came together with remarkable speed after that. Eddie laid a few remaining whole wings in the bottom of the bundt pan, then stirred up the potatoes and pressed a layer on top of the chicken. He alternated layers of potato, vegetables with chicken, cheese, slices of sausage, and crushed potato chips, until the cake pan was full and all the other pots and pans were empty. Then he carefully covered the pan with a platter, flipped it, and tapped out a perfectly molded mountain of food, topped with golden wings, oozing with melting cheese.

"Behold, the Trash Tower," Eddie said. "Ready for the finishing touch?"

"I'm intrigued and aghast," Gregory told him. Eddie picked up a bottle of hot sauce and striped it sparingly in one direction, then patterned mayonnaise across it, sprinkling the last of the potato chips over all of it.

"Bravo, that looks terrible," Simon observed.

"Take my picture with it, every time I make this people lose their minds," Eddie ordered, handing Gregory his phone with the camera open. Gregory lined up the shot of Eddie holding the Trash Tower, snapped a few for good measure, and then passed it back as Eddie set the platter down.

"My kingdom has never witnessed anything like it," Gregory said.

"Few have. Well, made by me, anyway. I published the recipe a few years ago and it's pretty popular for tailgating, apparently."

"Do you excavate it from the top down, or from the outside inward?" Gregory asked.

"Slice it," Eddie replied. He took a knife from the rack and cut two slightly wobbly slices, tipping them out into bowls, topping each with one of the whole chicken wings. "Simon, you in?"

"No, I have eaten, and I need to take the pastries in to the breakfast room. Shall I tell your father you've eaten also?" Simon asked Gregory.

"Thanks," Gregory said with a nod. Eddie offered him a fork and he dug it into the food in the bowl, trying to get a little of everything in one bite, instinctively understanding that was the best way to attempt this. Eddie watched him sample it, awaiting a reaction.

"Well, that's different," Gregory said thoughtfully, still

chewing. "I like the crunch from the chips."

"I do a vegetarian version with mushrooms, too, and there's one with rice," Eddie said, starting on his own. "Some of my better work," he pronounced, after couple of mouthfuls. He leaned against the prep table, next to Gregory, and took out his phone, opening the photo app to study the pictures of him that Gregory had taken. "Oh hey, that's good work," he said, even as he cropped and color-adjusted the image.

"Easy subject," Gregory replied, between bites. It somehow tasted better the more you ate.

"I do my best," Eddie answered, amused, dropping the image into a Photogram post. He set his bowl down to concentrate on typing out a caption. "Trash Tower by Eddie Rambler, photograph by Crown Prince Gregory," he said as he typed. "Anything you want to add?" he asked, looking up.

Gregory had leaned over his shoulder to watch him work, and their faces were very close; Gregory saw Eddie's eyes dart down to his mouth, and his lips part.

"I suppose just that it's surprisingly good," Gregory heard himself say, the diplomat-politician part of his brain on autopilot while the rest of him vanished in a brief whirl of fantasy. Eddie seemed frozen, surprised perhaps. Gregory dipped his head, and Eddie's eyes closed –

And then Gregory's phone beeped, loudly.

He jerked back, setting the bowl down and digging in his pocket. He was suddenly aware he was sweaty and disheveled from his run, halfway through breakfast, and Eddie was probably just startled by how close he'd been.

"It's Alanna," he said. "She wants to know if she can move my nine-thirty to eight-thirty..."

He twisted to consult the kitchen clock; eight-ten.

"I need to shower, I need to get dressed," he said, pocketing his phone and picking up the bowl. "All right if I take this...?"

"It's your bowl," Eddie said with a grin. "Go, get ready for the day. Glad you liked it."

"Thank you, Eddie, really. And keep me posted on that brainstorming for the menus," Gregory said, and hurried out of the kitchen just as Simon was returning.

He tried to put it from his mind for most of the day, but meetings and palace business were hardly compelling enough to keep him from replaying the moment. Especially since the bowl, from which he'd eaten every scrap of the Trash Tower, sat on his desk until lunch, when palace staff replaced it with a plate of spaghetti that very clearly had Eddie's meatballs in it (they were popular in the staff kitchen too, or so he was informed). And in the afternoon his phone notified him that Eddie had posted to Photogram. Reluctantly, he set it aside for later.

Eating dinner with his father did put a damper on his thoughts, but then Eddie Rambler, curse him, was waiting in his office when he got back to it afterwards.

The chef was sitting at the window, feet propped up against the bookshelf to one side, playing a noisy game on his phone; when Gregory walked in he grinned at him and turned off the game, but he didn't get up.

"Do you know, I got Simon to try some of the Trash Tower? I told him it was better as leftovers, which is kind of a lie, but it got him to eat it," he announced, by way of greeting.

"What was the verdict?" Gregory asked, unable to resist that infectious smile.

"He told me that the only reason my ancestors weren't ashamed of me for putting mayonnaise in it was that he wouldn't consider what I'd used real mayonnaise," Eddie said. "It's potentially the most devastating burn I've ever gotten from a fellow chef, but he polished off the whole slice, so who really won?"

"Who indeed," Gregory replied, settling into his chair and spinning it to face Eddie in the window seat. He found he didn't want to ask why he was there, enjoying the friendly camaraderie of it too much.

"I put the whole conversation on Photogram, you should check it. What a hoot," Eddie declared. "I had a question for you, though."

"Fire away, you've caught the future king in an indulgent moment," Gregory told him.

"Well, I went to the royal library to do some reading this afternoon and I thought, I really don't know much about how the country sees you. Like, what public perception of the nobility is here. I think your dad was right, I do need to factor that in more, even if thinking about it doesn't mean I *use* it," Eddie said. "And so eventually I got on the internet and looked you up."

"Brave man," Gregory murmured. Eddie let his feet fall and leaned forward.

"I have to admit that one, I did not know you were gay, which normally wouldn't be relevant for a client except that you're the first out gay king of Askazer-Shivadlakia," Eddie said, tone growing serious. "And two, my immediate thought was that if I had known that, I would have come at this from a different angle, because that's a big fuckin' deal, man."

"Well, it is, and it isn't," Gregory said, mouth a little dry.

"And that was my third point," Eddie agreed. "I then thought that maybe I *shouldn't* treat it any differently, because obviously you aren't. Like no requests for, I don't know, rainbow cakes or anything."

Gregory made a face.

"Do not tell me rainbow cakes are tired or tacky, I love a rainbow cake," Eddie said, pointing at him warningly.

"No, but they're not appropriate for a coronation," Gregory said.

"Maybe. We can debate that some other time. And you

know, I'm sure you don't want it to be about that, you don't want to be The Gay King, you just want to be a king," Eddie said. Gregory nodded. "Which, I feel you, because like…I did that same math when I started my media career."

Gregory stared at him, perplexed.

"I'm bi," Eddie said. "I'm also super private about my personal life, not just that part of it, but the whole thing, so it wasn't a huge deal to me not to talk about it. But it's important in the sense of, I don't know, principles? So we had to have like…meetings about it with the network. They weren't thrilled, which is about par for the course. And I thought, okay, this doesn't have to be what I'm about right now."

"You were all right with that?" Gregory asked.

"Weren't you?"

"I came out in college," Gregory said with a shrug. "As soon as I'd sorted myself out and figured out how to…how to be me in public. But Askazer-Shivadlakia is very different from America. We don't have some of the same hangups."

"Obviously, or you wouldn't have been elected. My point is, yeah, I was okay with keeping it quiet until I could get myself established, and that's…kinda recent. So I'm not out. But I'm not like, *ashamed* of myself. That's the math I'm talking about."

He got up from the window seat, and Gregory saw what was coming with just enough clarity to know he could pull away from this if he wanted. He just…didn't want to.

So he didn't get up, not when Eddie did or when Eddie crossed to his desk, or when Eddie leaned over him, hands on the chair's armrest, face close to his once more.

"I didn't imagine you checking me out this morning," Eddie said. Gregory, slowly, shook his head. "And you haven't got anyone?"

"No."

"Mm," Eddie said thoughtfully. His eyes darted from Gregory's eyes to his lips again, then sideways, then back to his face.

"But it's unwise," Gregory said. "I can't offer much, and you're an employee – "

Eddie laughed. "I'm a contracted caterer. You're not king of my country, and I'm not particularly in the market for anything permanent."

"But I am. I need a king consort."

"Right this second?" Eddie asked. Gregory shook his head again. Eddie pulled back just a little, crouching in front of his chair, not quite so intimidating. "Then I'd like to offer you, Your Highness, a little fun while you wait for your own Prince Charming."

Gregory leaned forward and down, catching Eddie's mouth in a kiss; Eddie's hands went to his neck, thumbs on either side of his jaw.

It lasted about two seconds before Gregory overbalanced and Eddie, not in a stable position to begin with, tumbled backwards.

They ended up on the floor of his office, Eddie propped on his elbows, Gregory sprawled over him. Eddie laughed as Gregory rolled and got to his feet, reaching down to help him up. He abused the help by pulling Gregory in close and kissing him properly this time, both of them on a level. Eddie wrapped one arm around Gregory's waist.

"Lock your door and let's make out," Eddie suggested.

"I have to work here," Gregory said.

"You practically live here."

"Yes but I don't live *here*," Gregory replied impatiently. "I have an apartment with comfortable chairs and a bed and a lot more privacy."

Eddie's mouth drew up in an amused smile. "A bed, huh?"

"I'm an extremely ambitious man," Gregory told him.

"Servants won't find it weird you taking me to your apartment?" Eddie asked, but followed him when he started for the door.

"They're called staff, and they go home at night."

"Ironic," Eddie remarked, as Gregory led him into the hallway and down towards the back stairs behind the grand staircase. Gregory thought he saw someone in one of the side-hallways, but nobody emerged, so he started up the curving staircase, Eddie behind him.

"How so, ironic?" he asked, turning left at the landing and following the hallway with its row of windows that would lead them to his apartment.

"The staff get to leave, the king never does," Eddie said.

"Well, a king serves his people," Gregory replied, hoping he hadn't left his rooms messy. He couldn't think of anything particularly embarrassing that might be visible, but normally only his valet Jonas ever saw it, and Jonas was a quiet, nonjudgemental man in his sixties.

Eddie, if he even noticed such things as mess or interior decor, clearly didn't care. He followed Gregory into the sitting room, then grabbed him by one hand and beelined for the large curving sofa in front of the windows, tumbling down onto it and pulling Gregory into his lap.

From here, Gregory could look out at the sunset over the palace grounds, with the town below almost visible; he could look down at Eddie's upturned face, delighted and intent.

Or he could close his eyes and lean forward into a hell of a kiss, so he did that.

Just outside the grand staircase of the palace of Askazer-Shivadlakia, Jerry (Gerald-12th-Duke-of-Shivadlakia, he'd learned in a sing-song when he was little) intercepted disaster and, as usual, dealt with it.

Well, perhaps "as usual" was pushing it, but Jerry had a nose for drama and a knack for getting into it, so when he'd seen King Michaelis coming from one direction towards Greg's office, and Greg coming from his office with another man in tow, he gauged distances carefully and then moved to intercept.

"Uncle Mike!" he said brightly, as the king approached. "Just the man I was looking for."

"Right now, Gerald?" Michaelis asked, sounding tired. "I'm looking for Gregory."

"Already gone to bed," Jerry replied, which wasn't technically a lie. "Saw him off myself."

Michaelis got the slightly suspicious look he often got around Jerry, but Jerry supposed he deserved it. The whole family had expected him to be the responsible one, to babysit Gregory and Alanna despite only being a year older, and the whole family had been endearingly disappointed. Jerry regretted very few things in life, at least so far, and being a fellow troublemaker with those two wasn't one of them.

"I suppose it can wait until morning," Michaelis grumbled.

"Well, what's it about? Maybe I can help," Jerry said.

Michaelis looked genuinely surprised. "Help....with what?"

"Whatever you needed Gregory for. This time of night it's either a real emergency or something that should wait for morning," Jerry pointed out.

"I'm afraid it's royal business," Michaelis said, but Jerry could tell he'd successfully distracted the king from his mission. Gregory owed him one.

"In that case, it can definitely wait until morning," Jerry said with a grin. "Anyway, with all the coronation plans going off, I'm feeling extremely neglected."

Michaelis rolled his eyes, but a faint smile crossed his lips. "All right. What is it you need, Gerald?"

"I actually had a question for you. It's about farming."

That drew the king up short. "Farming? You?"

"It came up during the meeting with the Agricultural Cabinet the other day," Jerry said. "I'm becoming very interested in olives."

"Are you feeling all right?" Michaelis asked.

"I can have interests in the welfare of the country, you know," Jerry said defensively.

Michaelis, to his credit, looked apologetic. "You can, of course, and I'm sure both Gregory and I would be thrilled if you took an interest. What is it you'd like to know that you couldn't get from the Cabinet?"

"Oh, long term stuff, mostly. You know – the royal vision," Jerry said. "We don't have to talk about it now but I'd like to get on your calendar."

"Won't be my vision much longer, but Gregory and I have had some discussions…" Michaelis looked thoughtful. "I'll have a meeting arranged. You, me, and Gregory."

"Oh, ah – that'd be fine, but maybe after the coronation?" Jerry suggested.

"Why?" Michaelis asked.

Jerry rubbed his jaw. It wasn't really his business and both Gregory and his father could be stubborn about being told when they were being stupid, but after all, that was why Jerry cultivated a specific air of daffiness. People would accept a lot more advice from an idiot than an equal, for some reason.

"There's a lot on his plate," he said finally. "The coronation, taking over royal duties, briefings…maybe the unnecessary stuff can wait a little while."

"Do you think he's not up to it?" Michaelis asked. Jerry blinked.

"Uncle…nobody's up to that much," he said gently.

Michaelis seemed to consider this, which was kind of impressive.

"Is he struggling?" he asked. Jerry frowned.

"Why ask me? I barely see him these days."

"Yes, but he'd tell you things he wouldn't tell me."

That was true enough. Gregory had confided in him at school, inasmuch as he did anyone. Not for a while though, now. Jerry wondered if he confided in anyone anymore. Al might know.

"I think anyone would," he finally said, diplomatically. "I'm sure if he starts to really drown he'll speak up, but Gregory's idea of drowning and our idea..." he made a weighing motion. He hadn't meant to get quite this deep just to keep Michaelis from walking in on his son with a secret lover, but, well, carpe diem.

"It's a good point," Michaelis said, eyes going distant. "Very good point. Well. Thank you, Jerry. Speak to Alanna about setting up that meeting whenever you think is best. But I'm going to hold you to that interest in olives," he added, shaking a finger at him.

"Absolutely," Jerry promised. "Goodnight, uncle."

"Goodnight, Gerald," Michaelis said, and went back the way he'd come, towards his own apartments in a different wing of the palace. Jerry, deciding this was enough hard work for the week, slumped onto the grand staircase, resting his head against the post of the banister.

"Deftly done," said a new voice, and Alanna stepped out from the shadows. Jerry, startled, clutched his chest.

"You could have helped," he said, scowling as she sat next to him.

"And ruin the moment? You did fine. Though I should warn you, if you keep behaving competently, they'll keep giving you work."

"I could take an interest in things," Jerry protested. "I might be turning over a new leaf, for all you know."

"Well, you did Gregory a favor, anyway, so I suppose I should thank you. What was all that about?" Alanna asked.

Jerry shrugged. "When did you come in?"

"Just as you buttonholed His Majesty."

"Ah. Well, you didn't hear it from me," Jerry said, tapping the side of his nose. "I was preventing trouble. Himself was coming down the hall looking for Greg just as Greg was taking an *amore* up to his rooms."

Alanna blinked at him. "An *amore?*"

"Boyfriend? Or at least, a date. I didn't get a good look but it was definitely an assignation."

"He isn't even dating anyone right now," Alanna said. "That was the whole point of the arranged marriage discussion."

"Well, he's clearly doing some arranging," Jerry replied. Alanna still looked unsettled. "He's a big boy, Al, I'm sure he's fine."

"It's not that I'm worried about," she said. "All this stress…he's not himself."

"I don't know. I don't see him as much as you, but seems like the best stress relief possible just followed him up the stairs."

"Creep," she said affectionately. "Thanks for covering, though."

"All part of the royal service. I am interested, you know."

"In Greg's *amore?*"

"No, sorry, back a few changes of subject," Jerry said. "In the olives. When I was talking with Uncle Mike. The agricultural meeting got me thinking. I didn't know crop planning was such a precise science."

"Precision hasn't usually been one of your strong suits," Alanna pointed out.

"No, but I love all that kind of planning stuff. Timetables. Like those word puzzles they used to give us in school."

Alanna twisted a little, resting her chin on his shoulder. "Well, well. Everyone's growing up at last."

"Slander," Jerry said.

"Maybe, but I'm giving you a new job," Alanna said.

"I didn't have an old one."

"Fine, I'm giving you a first job," she said. "His Majesty listens to you because he knows you have no political agenda, which is a belief you can only weaponize for a short time. From now until the coronation, your job is to run interference on the king. Get him to leave Greg alone as much as possible outside of meetings. And if this *amore* hangs around, keep him out of the king's way."

Jerry looked down at her, eyes wide. "Keeping the prince away from the king?" he asked. Then, delighted, "Am I the evil vizier?"

"If you do a good job I will have Gregory officially appoint you vizier when he's king," she said.

"We haven't had a vizier in a hundred years," Jerry said, pretending to be star-struck. "What would I even do?"

"Nothing," Alanna said, "but with great drama."

"Sold," Jerry replied, and kissed her temple. "Go to bed. I'm headed there and Gregory's clearly already gone."

"Fair enough. If you find out who the *amore* is, let me know," she said, standing and dusting the seat of her trousers. Jerry gave her a thumbs up, then leaned back on the stairs to watch her go.

Eddie left the royal chambers (as he called them, narrating the adventure silently to himself) around midnight, well-satisfied with the world. He didn't expect to run into anyone, but he wasn't truly at ease until he'd made it back down to ground level and through the main hallway to the guest wing.

Eddie came from a family of people for whom the world held endless possibility, and he was rarely surprised when his unorthodox life brought him to new adventures. Still, this was high on the "didn't predict that" scale. After a couple of seasons of success on television he hadn't really blinked at being hired to cater a coronation, but there was still a certain spice in going halfway around the world to make out with the soon-to-be king of a delightful little coastal city-state.

In private, away from his office and staff, Gregory was different. He'd seen a little of it in their walk to town, and their morning meeting in the garden, and – really almost anytime he was in Simon's kitchen or in Eddie's company without others around. The tension in his body dissipated, and his face became startlingly expressive. As he unlocked the door to his own suite, Eddie beamed to himself over Gregory's dark eyelashes and half-open mouth from a few minutes before.

It couldn't be easy to be one of the few visibly gay royals on the continent (in the world? Eddie didn't pay much attention to royalty, usually) but Gregory had apparently been very intentional about it, and he went about enjoying himself the same way, without the least hint of shame. If, perhaps, a little exaggerated dignity.

Well, at least they'd gotten past him calling Eddie "Mr. Dude."

Very well past.

Eddie settled cross-legged on the foot of his bed, checking his appearance in the selfie-camera view on his phone before hitting record.

"Evening, friends and fans," he said, keeping his voice low. "I'm pretty sure it's like lunchtime where most of you are, but I'm keeping quiet because it's late here. Just thought I'd say a happy goodnight to everyone – every day here brings new challenges but also new delights. And at the end of the day I'm always ready to sleep. Even if it's just so I can get up tomorrow and try again."

He gave them his goofiest smile, wondering if Gregory watched these videos. "So I'll say goodnight to you locals here in Askazer-Shivadlakia, and I hope everyone in America's having a wonderful afternoon, and...well, good morning to Japan, I guess."

He put up the peace sign, tilting his head towards it. "Everybody eat at least one really good meal today, okay? Night, you all."

FOUR WEEKS UNTIL
THE CORONATION OF HIS MAJESTY
KING GREGORY III

GREGORY WOKE, THE morning after his evening with Eddie, feeling energized and cheerful. It didn't immediately occur to him why, until he spotted his shirt, lying across the sofa where Eddie had tossed it last night. Gregory had tried to catch it, to set it aside in a more orderly kind of way, and Eddie had laughed and distracted him.

"Not everything's gotta be filed," Eddie had said, and the sentiment had struck a chord he hadn't really examined at the time. Now, looking back, the reminder that sometimes you had to simply let a mess be a mess had felt very freeing. The whole world didn't have to be in order before he could be crowned.

Pleased at the idea, he took a little longer in the shower than usual, and Jonas had come and gone with his clothes, whisking away the messy shirt and leaving clean ones. Gregory dressed, deciding on a bright blue shirt from the two the valet had left, and met Alanna in the hall on the way to breakfast.

"Good morning," he said, wondering if Eddie might be pestering Simon in the kitchen. "Sleep well?"

"I did, thank you," she replied, flipping her hair over her shoulder. "You look nice."

"Thank you. Begin as you mean to go on, I guess," he told her. "Not to trumpet the perks of being king, but it's easier when you have staff who pick out your clothes. What's my first meeting this morning?"

"The usual briefing, but otherwise you're open until about two. Because of the – "

"Budget meeting that I need to do the numbers on," he agreed, peeking into the kitchen. Just Simon, frying eggs.

"Good morning, Your Highness," Simon said.

"Morning," Gregory replied. He held up three fingers to indicate how many eggs he wanted and Simon nodded. As they headed to the dining room, Gregory caught Alanna smiling at him in a way that made him suspicious, but he couldn't put his finger on why.

Michaelis was at breakfast, eating toast and reading something on a tablet; to Gregory's surprise, Jerry was also up and working his way through an omelet. Alanna took a scone from the dish and settled in, spreading it with jam.

"Good morning, Gregory," Michaelis said, looking up briefly from his tablet. "You look well rested. Bed early last night?"

"And some good sleep," Gregory agreed. Jerry made a soft noise, but when Gregory looked over all he saw was an innocent smile.

"Just as well. Have you got a few minutes this morning?" Michaelis asked. A look crossed Jerry's face that Michaelis seemed to register. "I'll try to keep it brief," he added.

"Sure, after the staff meeting. Al – "

"Adding it to your calendar," she agreed, tapping on her phone.

"You should go to bed early more often. You're in high spirits today," Michaelis said, somewhere between approval and a grumble. The others bit their lips. Gregory wasn't sure what was going on, but it looked like Al and Jerry might be conspiring. Given one was his assistant and both were family, it'd probably be to his benefit to stay ignorant.

"I'll bear that in mind," he said, as Simon came in with the eggs and more toast. "I didn't see Eddie in there with you this morning, Simon."

"Ah, no," Simon agreed. "I think he's spending much of the day with the Conservation officers. He seems very determined on the subject of wild boar."

"Hear there's good eating on those. Acorns all winter and berries all summer, makes them tender," Michaelis remarked. "The nonkosher butcher pays top dollar. Devil to hunt, though."

"Alanna," Gregory said, considering things, "Could you block off the hour before the budget meeting today? Just mark it busy on the calendar."

"Sure. Anyone to add to the meeting?"

"No, I want to have time to clear my head beforehand. If anyone has issues today, they'll know to come to me before one."

"Shall I hold lunch, Your Highness?" Simon asked.

"No, I'll be going out," Gregory said. Simon's eyebrows rose. "Actually, can you pack a lunch? On the large side. I'll take it with me."

"Of course," Simon replied, as Alanna set the meeting in the calendar. "It will be ready in the kitchen at one."

Not everything had to be filed, and Eddie had been clear he was here for a good time. Gregory could make a little mess in at least one corner of his life, for now.

The palace of Askazer-Shivadlakia was technically public property. The grounds, including the lake, fishing lodge, trails, and a portion of the forest, were administered and cared for by the conservation corps, which Gregory's grandfather had founded. Because of this, there was a visitor's center not far from the palace, and that had to be where Eddie had taken his bowfishing lessons. It was probably where he was trying to convince some poor conservation officer to let him hunt a wild boar.

Gregory hummed to himself as he made his way down the

trail to the visitor's center, the small basket of food swinging from one hand. Not only was he getting a well-needed breath of fresh air before an all-afternoon meeting, but he'd have a good lunch by the lake with Eddie.

Besides, Eddie probably hadn't packed a lunch, and it was a nice gesture. Although…

He stopped outside the low fence of the visitor's center. Eddie had been very casual about this – they both had – and bringing him a picnic lunch after they'd spent the previous evening on the couch together…

"Your Highness!" Eddie's voice rang out from the left, and Gregory turned to see him, two conservation officers, and (unsettlingly) a man with a guitar, all loitering on the rocks at the edge of the lake's beach. "Come over, we're all down here."

"So I see," Gregory replied, steeling himself for an awkward moment. "Have you found a folk song about the wild boar yet?"

"How'd you know?" Eddie asked, laughing.

"I saw the guitar," Gregory said. The man with the guitar smiled at him respectfully.

"What brings you out here?" Eddie asked.

"Oh, I ah…" Gregory held up the basket. "I wanted a break from work, and imagined you hadn't brought a lunch with you."

Eddie beamed at him. "From Simon?"

"Well, I definitely didn't make it," Gregory said, passing the basket over. The conservation officers gave him a nod as they left, and the man with the guitar high-fived Eddie and walked off down the beach. Eddie began unpacking the basket onto a flat rock, gesturing for Gregory to take the slightly more sloped rock next to it.

"Join me, Simon packed more food than even I can eat," he said, laying out bread and cheese, a little jar of mustard and a pot of olive oil, some dried figs. "Productive morning, I hope?"

"Yes, very. Not as interesting as yours, I imagine," Gregory said.

"Well, I definitely learned a lot," Eddie agreed.

He looked up in time to catch Gregory watching him, and Gregory smiled. Eddie matched it, and then they were both laughing quietly.

"This was very sweet of you," Eddie said.

"Not a little over the top?" Gregory asked.

"No, why would it be? Got you out of that stuffy office, and tells me you wanted to see me."

"I wouldn't want to be obvious."

"Why not? I would," Eddie replied. "I like being obvious. Means nobody ever doubts where you stand. Why wouldn't you want to spend time with me? I'm delightful. I definitely didn't expect I'd get to see you today, or at least not so soon, and that's great."

Gregory considered this. There was a charm to being obvious, he supposed, especially if you were as charismatic as Eddie. It was refreshing, to say the least.

"Well, then I'm glad I came down," he replied.

"Me too. Now, let's eat," Eddie pronounced, and Gregory nodded and bent to his food. "You listen attentively while I tell you the legends of your people I have just now learned from a park ranger."

Later that evening he was glad he'd taken a break; the budget meeting, infuriatingly but also expectedly, ran long. Staff brought in dinner during the course of it, and by the time he'd finally handshaked-and-armclapped the last of the attendees out the door, it was late.

He considered going in search of Eddie, even stopping by his suite, but decided against it. Eddie was a perceptive man; he'd have seen that Gregory was in a meeting and found some other entertainment.

When he reached the door of his apartments, there was a neon pink sticky-note on the handle that read "DO NOT DISTURB" in Eddie's sprawling hand.

Gregory grinned, plucked it off the knob, and tucked it in a pocket as he stepped inside.

The light was on in his bedroom, and he could see one of Eddie's loud-print shirts against the bedspread. When he leaned in the doorway, he could see the rest of Eddie as well – still in his clothes, loud shirt included, but sprawled on top of the bed, asleep, one hand on his chest and the other above his head.

He had a post-it note stuck to his forehead that said, "Disturb".

Gregory plucked it up and laughed; Eddie startled awake, and then tilted his head against the pillow.

"Hey, thank you for disturbing," Eddie said, smiling warmly.

"One does one's best. You didn't need to wait up," Gregory said.

"Good, because I clearly didn't. What time is it?"

"Only about ten."

"Power nap, then," Eddie said, sitting up and crossing his legs. "I thought you might want a friendly ear after the late meeting. Or a friendly hand," he added, waggling his eyebrows. Gregory sat on the edge of the bed next to him and then flopped back, stretching. Eddie rested a palm on his stomach.

"Listen, I will not be hurt if you are tired and want me to fuck off," Eddie said. "Just so we're clear."

"Not at all, I'm glad you're here. But I'm not sure I'm the most inspired person right now, given I've still got the words 'fiscal year' imprinted on my eyelids," Gregory replied. "Just so your expectations are correct."

"No expectations here," Eddie said. "If you want me to stay – "

"I do."

"Well, good," Eddie answered. He leaned over, filling

Gregory's vision, and kissed him. "Want a truly wild suggestion?" he asked, against Gregory's mouth.

"I'm learning the folly of saying yes to you," Gregory said.

"How about you go to bed and I will also go to bed, but in this bed, and we can continue the conversation when we wake up?"

Gregory could feel the moment his muscles relaxed, the drop from King Ascendant to Crown Prince all the way down to just Gregory.

"That sounds amazing," he said.

"I know!" Eddie sat back and reached out, pulling him upright. "Go get changed."

Roughly eight minutes later, in a worn old shirt and cotton shorts, Gregory shuffled under the covers and felt Eddie climb in behind him, wrapping around his body like a large, sleepy bear. He closed his eyes and let himself go blissfully slack.

"I've never said this to anyone before," Eddie said, as Gregory drifted off, "But I'm going to enjoy the hell out of sleeping next to you."

The next morning, when he woke up and Eddie was indeed still in the bed – sprawled out over Gregory's chest, gently snoring into his collarbone – Gregory managed to find his fast-dying phone in the bedclothes and text Jonas not to come in until summoned. Eddie mumbled sleepily into his chest.

"Time 'sit?" he asked.

"Early yet. Just letting my valet know not to interrupt us," Gregory replied, patting Eddie's pale hair, sticking out wildly from his head. "Sleep a little longer if you'd care to."

"No, I'm up," Eddie decided, pushing away just enough so that he could roll over onto his side. Gregory plugged the phone into its charger and then turned to face him, curious. "Sleep well?"

"I did, yes."

"Good. Al worries you don't sleep enough."

"Ah, Al to you too now, is it?" Gregory asked, amused.

"She's great. And she cares a lot about you."

"I know. I care for her, too. It's not often the noble families have children who get along. Lots of attempted murders between cousins in past generations."

"Huh." Eddie rolled onto his back, looking up at the ceiling. "Must be weird, having roots that deep. Like, how far back can you go in the family tree?"

"Not terribly far on my father's side – two, three generations past him, when they arrived in the country. My mother was old nobility, I can probably get back fifteen generations on her side. But yes…there's a strong foundation of history to stand on. Thank goodness, all things considered. You sound like you're close to your family. Surely you understand what that's like."

"A little." Eddie shrugged. "It's really just my parents, though. My mom's parents are big hippies, they've been in a couple of cults, and we're not actually sure where they are at any given moment. They've got a VW Bus and a will to wander."

"My goodness."

"Good people but not like…dependable. And Dad's parents don't like him so they don't see us much."

"Whyever not?" Gregory asked.

"They're real Stepford types. They don't acknowledge I exist."

"Because you're a TV chef?"

"Among other things. The shame and horror," Eddie said, grinning. "Dad and I don't like them either so it's no big deal. They think I'm trashy, that's all. Lots of people do."

Gregory thought reservedly of his objections when Alanna had hired Eddie. *I wanted gastropub, not dive bar.* Eddie laughed, and Gregory realized it must have shown on his face.

"Yeah, that's about the size of it," Eddie said, though

Gregory hadn't even spoken. "Look, I do a show about working-class food and the working-class people who make it. Restaurants that I put on the show get huge bumps in business. If I like the food, I invest as a silent partner. I've got a portfolio of dive bars and greasy spoons from Bangor to Baja. Hell, after the coronation I'm going to drop a few grand in Askazer-Shivadlakia, too. Luxury cheese exports and handicrafts. My folks raised me to believe in what I do. Other people don't have to."

"A very healthy way to live, I suppose."

"It has its pain in the ass moments, but I do love it. There's real freedom in not giving a damn. Sooner or later I'm going to get tired of television, being on the road all the time, and I like knowing my whole identity isn't tied up in it. I can walk away if I ever want to."

"No firm ideas for the future?"

Eddie shrugged against the sheets. "How do you make fate laugh?"

"Announce your plans," Gregory said. "We've heard that one in Askazer-Shivadlakia."

"Which reminds me, realistically, this week we need to set the theme and menu for the banquet."

Gregory groaned, covering his face with his hands. Eddie rolled, propping himself up, and kissed the backs of Gregory's hands.

"Don't worry. I'll pull something off, I always do. You have a good kitchen staff, they'll help, and I'm going to try to source all the food locally, so we won't need to worry about shipping delays."

"If we can't come up with something that Dad likes, I think we should just go with the formal meal," Gregory said.

"You're the boss. It's not interesting, but it is safe. I'll have Alanna set a final tasting for the end of the week, we'll make sure your dad's in a good mood, and I'll do my best to knock his socks off. In the meantime," Eddie added, pulling one of Gregory's hands away from his face, "I should shower and sneak out before anyone's up. Wanna come shower with me?"

That was the week guests began trickling in for the coronation. Not many at first, since there was a full month until coronation, but distant family began returning for a nice long holiday on the coast, and a handful of reporters started to set up shop and look around for local color. Gregory began to be interrupted with requests for interviews, local television spots, and occasionally a royal favor for a family friend.

He was running late for a call-in to a podcast recording, and was literally running from the conference room to his office, when he burst into the main hall and almost bowled over a crowd of elderly women. He skidded to a stop, startled, and as one they turned to look at him with interested eyes.

"Your Highness!" Eddie called, from the middle of the knot of women, at least a head taller than any of them. "Everybody curtsey!"

Gregory stared, mortified, as two dozen women, all visibly over the age of sixty, dropped into dainty curtseys they'd clearly learned in school as children. Without even meaning to, he fell into tradition as well, stiffly bowing at the waist, deep enough to demonstrate his respect for their age. A few laughed.

"All right, nonnas, come on, this way," Eddie continued, leading the women towards the big staff-canteen kitchen. "Show a little of that Shivadh hustle!"

He wanted to stop and find out what was going on, because it certainly looked interesting, but his phone beeped insistently. He put it from his mind as he ducked into his office, where Alanna had already set up a mic for recording. It wasn't until that evening, eating dinner in the family dining room, that he remembered what he'd seen.

"Did you happen to see the gaggle of grannies in the castle today?" he asked Alanna over a bowl of pasta – an old highland recipe with thick noodles and seared, thin-sliced beef.

"Oh yeah! Eddie had them in to give him a demo. You're eating the result," she said, pointing her fork at his bowl. He looked down, surprised. "He wanted lessons in hand-pulled noodles and what we do with them around here. He rounded up every woman in town who still makes her own and threw a party."

"A noodle-pulling party?"

"Can't argue with results," she said. "He's got kids coming in tomorrow to help him learn how to make cookies. Don't worry, I got releases signed by the parents and there are plenty of chaperones."

"Doubt that's going to help with the coronation feast."

Alanna looked complacent about it. "You never know. Anyway," she added, studying her phone, "You can take some of that to-go if you want, you don't have anything booked for this evening."

He frowned. "Why would I want to take some to go?"

"I don't know. If you wanted some later, or to share with someone," she said airily.

Gregory stared at her, setting his fork down. "Who would I be meeting that you didn't know about?"

Alanna gave him a look. Gregory felt his eyes widen.

"I don't know who he is and I don't need to – " she began, but he cut her off with a gesture.

"It's not serious," he said. "I mean – it's not a relationship, not really. It's just some fun. I had thought we were being discreet."

"Like I said. Don't know who he is," Alanna said. "Frankly, I think it's good for you."

"Is this what you and Jerry were giggling about at breakfast the other day?" he demanded.

"Yes," she said unrepentantly.

"Does Dad know?"

"If he does, it's not from me or Jerry. But no, I don't think so."

"Well, small mercy."

"Why?" she asked. "I'm sure he'd be thrilled. Isn't this what he – ah," she said, as Gregory pointed at her.

"A little too thrilled. And he's not a candidate, anyhow," Greg said.

"That's a cruel thing to say about a date." Alanna looked appalled.

"He's not interested in long-term, is what I mean. And even if he were he wouldn't..." Gregory searched for the word. "I don't know that he'd enjoy the royal life."

"Well, as long as you're having fun," she said.

Gregory considered this. "You know, I think I am."

"Good." She gathered up her phone, standing. "I'll see you tomorrow morning – yell if you need anything."

"Alanna," he called, as she reached the doorway. She turned. "You know if there was someone serious I'd tell you. I value your opinion tremendously."

She grinned. "You'd better. Until tomorrow, Your Highness."

Eddie, still dotted here and there with flour and hugely pleased with himself over the noodle lesson, was helping scrub down the big kitchen that fed most of the palace staff when someone walked in and said, "You!" loudly at him.

"Indeed, it is I," he replied, bowing low and flicking a tea towel off his shoulder in a salute. When he straightened, a man with a faint resemblance to the royal family was staring at him. "I'm afraid I haven't read my Who's Who, but you're probably one of the noble cousins, huh?" Eddie asked, grinning.

The man dodged someone going past with a pile of dirty plates and hustled into the kitchen, squinting at him.

"You're Eddie Rambler," he said, surprised.

"Most of the time," Eddie agreed, offering one slightly damp, soapy hand, then wiping it with a towel before re-offering it.

"Oh! Sorry, I'm Jerry," the man said, taking his hand. "Gerald, Duke of Shivadlakia."

"You're the bad example!" Eddie said, delighted.

Jerry laughed. "Is that how Greg described me?"

"It's how everyone describes you," Eddie said. "They also always add they think I'll like you, which is either a statement about me or a testament to your likability."

"Probably both," Jerry said. "Sorry, about three separate facts are coming together in my head and I'm still sorting them out. You're here to cater the coronation."

"Yep," Eddie agreed, going back to wiping down the steel prep counter.

"It's only the last time I saw you I didn't realize you were, well, you," Jerry said. "I'd have introduced myself before now if I'd known. Offered to show you around, sort of thing."

"Wouldn't say no now," Eddie replied, wondering where Jerry had seen him earlier. "Well, actually, I would, but only for tonight. If you're into giving tours I'll take a ticket for tomorrow."

"Honestly, I wouldn't know where to begin. And I'm sure you've been kept very busy," Jerry remarked. "How's preparations coming?"

"It's a work in progress," Eddie replied. "Hey, I've been asking everyone today, what's your favorite food?"

"Cocktails," Jerry replied.

"Huh. Actually, that might be helpful," Eddie said thoughtfully. "I'm considering a kind of country house murder mystery vibe, given everyone's going to be in tuxes and gowns anyway."

"I'm being fitted for my gown tomorrow," Jerry said.

"I'm sure you'll wear the hell out of it."

Jerry laughed. "I see why Greg likes you. And a little bit why Al says Uncle Michaelis is…"

"Of no strong opinion?" Eddie asked drily. "Yeah. He might go for the cocktails thing, though, as long as I don't actually present it as *country house murder mystery*."

"Murder vibes not appropriate for a coronation?" Jerry suggested.

"I think it's fine, but you can see the problem he might have. Anyway, he wants a formal dinner. If I can pull him in with swanky custom cocktails, he might be more open to innovation in the food." Eddie gave the table a final swipe, then turned back to Jerry. "Thank you, Your Grace."

"My, you've been reading the comportment books! Jerry's fine. I don't stand on ceremony." Jerry clapped him on the shoulder. "Keep up the good work."

"Keepin' it new," Eddie said, and Jerry laughed as he walked off.

"Psst – hey!"

Gregory, leaning back in his chair with his boots up on his desk and phone in hand, looked up from a muted Photogram video. The video showing Eddie making cookies with children – including what looked like some of the younger noble cousins – and when he looked away it was to find a real-life Eddie leaning in the window of his office, arms resting on the sill.

"I was just catching up on your extremely busy day," Gregory said, pointing at his phone. Eddie grinned.

"So you know that I have cookies to share," Eddie replied.

"I have a feeling we'll be eating cookies until my diamond jubilee."

"Do you get one of those if you're elected? I guess nobody's going to say you can't have one. Anyway I have a bag of cookies," Eddie said, holding up a bag in one hand, "and also a bag of wine," he added, indicating a slim backpack on his back.

"Sounds like you're on your way to a grand adventure," Gregory remarked.

"Come along. I'm going to hide out in the gardens and watch the stars come out."

Technically, he shouldn't; he had to finish this speech soon to get it to the communications people tomorrow to be doctored up and returned to him so he could give it at the opening of the royal vault so they could get the crown jewels out.

So that he could be crowned with them, which still felt surreal.

On the other hand, he could blow the speech off, at least for a little while; it was bound to be relaxing, and he'd had a full day.

Eddie cheered when Gregory dropped his boots to the floor and got up, coming to kneel at the window bench and look down at him.

"What kind of wine?" he asked.

"Why, are you picky?" Eddie retorted.

"I want to know my coronation banquet chef is pairing wine with cookies properly."

"Not intentionally, I just stole what I saw. It's a Riesling, that's a dessert wine! It'll be fine."

Gregory nodded and slid around, dangling his legs out the window; Eddie stepped back and he dropped down, grateful for Eddie's steadying hands.

"Here," Eddie said, offering him a bar of shortbread. "For the journey."

"How many cookies have you already eaten today?" Gregory asked, nibbling on it while they walked.

"Not that many. I learned how to eat for an audience years ago," Eddie said, clearly leading the way to some goal he had on the palace grounds. "The rule is that you never take more than one bite for the camera. You watch any food television host. They take one bite of everything. The rest is a camera cut that leaves the meal to your imagination. It's part of why food shows make people hungry."

"That's a good trick."

"Small bites and big reactions," Eddie said. "Key to what I do."

"It's not far off how one gets a law passed around here, either," Gregory replied. "It's good shortbread."

"Potato starch," Eddie said.

"Oh yes?"

"Probably doesn't help with law making, but it's great in shortbread." Eddie ducked through a gap in a high hedge and led him into a little clearing that looked down on the harbor. From this angle the town was almost across the water from them, lights slowly going on in shops and houses. They'd barely penetrate the darkness once the sun was fully down.

The backpack Eddie brought had two bottles of wine wrapped in a blanket; he set the bottles aside and shook out the blanket, spreading it on the ground before opening the first bottle with a corkscrew on a pocket-knife. Gregory settled himself on the blanket and leaned against his shoulder, watching him pour.

"We have a bouquet of cookies for you this evening, some of which may even make it into the coronation menu," Eddie said, handing him a glass of wine. He opened the other bag and revealed a covered bowl stocked with various sweets. "The only ones not included are the tricolors, because those take like two days to make."

"I've had tricolors. Very fond of them, actually."

"Duly noted," Eddie replied. "I'm tempted to veer away from anything with nuts for the official event, but there are these, which are walnutty things, and these almond whatses, and some of the chocolate chip cookies have pecans in them."

"Yes, the very famously traditional Shivadh chocolate chip

cookies," Gregory drawled.

"Chocolate chip cookies have been around since the 1930s. Almost a hundred years. I actually had a look in some of the previous chefs' personal cookbooks in the library, you know when chocolate chip cookies made it here?"

"I couldn't begin to guess."

"Me either. The notes don't say. But chocolate chips made it here in 1946. There's records of chefs using them instead of full bars of chocolate because you could get the chips but not the bars. Some kind of rationing issue. Anyway," Eddie said, "your granddad ate chocolate chip cookies in this palace, that's good enough tradition for me."

"Then me too, I suppose," Gregory said, taking one.

"Wanna eat it like a food host?" Eddie asked. Gregory gestured for him to continue. Eddie held up a cookie, broke off a chunk about the size of a coin, and popped it into his mouth. He rolled his eyes, groaned in appreciation, and waved the hand not holding his wine glass dramatically. "Now you."

"I'm not going to groan like that," Gregory warned, but he did break off a chunk like he'd seen Eddie do, and when he ate it he couldn't help but nod in appreciation.

"All that dignity's going to catch up with you one day," Eddie said.

"Probably already has. Too late to do anything about it now," Gregory said. He began picking at the other cookies, trying a little of each, while Eddie explained what each was and told stories about the kids who'd brought the recipes. By the time he'd sampled everything, the first bottle of wine was empty, and they were both lying back on the blanket, staring upwards, Eddie giving a sort of impromptu lesson in the history of the cookie.

"I thought you studied theatre in school," he said, as Eddie paused in his discussion of the uses of date honey in early recipes for baklava. "And somewhere in there you must have learned to cook. When did you have time for history as well?"

"I had a lot of backstage time during rehearsal and access to a good library," Eddie answered. "I like history. Might go back and get a degree in it someday."

"You don't think it would be strange? Going back to school as Eddie Rambler?"

"Sure. Strange as attending college as Prince Gregory ben Michaelis to begin with," Eddie answered.

"I suppose that's a point." Gregory rolled over, propping himself on his elbows. Eddie gazed up at him serenely. "You could put out a line of dormitory cookware."

"Don't think it hasn't crossed my mind. Always thinking, me," Eddie said. "That reminds me, I've got a question for you. I've been asking everyone lately, just to see what they say."

"Of course."

"When you were a kid, what was your favorite food?"

"Hm." Gregory thought about it, plucking at the grass just at the edge of the blanket. "You'd think it would be something unique – something only served in Askazer-Shivadlakia."

"Like what?"

"Oh, I don't know. Kuzhui, perhaps."

"Kuz what now?"

Gregory smiled at him. "Kuzhui. It's a kind of casserole made with flaked fish."

"That certainly sounds unique."

"But when I went off to boarding school, eating in the dining hall every day…" Gregory shrugged. "It was good food, but it was meant to feed a lot of growing children very quickly. And school wasn't nearby, so the food was different, too. I did miss Simon's cooking."

"What did he make that was so good?"

"Not the fish casserole," Gregory said. Eddie chuckled. "No, what I really wanted that first holiday home from school was potato salad."

"Potato salad!"

"Sure. It was a very specific cold potato salad my mother used to pack in a thermos, for when we went to the fishing lodge. That first day, we'd get there just before sunset. My father would bowfish, and my mother and I sat in the boat and ate potato salad on crackers, and read books. At least until I was fourteen or so, and Dad started teaching me to bowfish too."

"That sounds nice, actually," Eddie said. "Simon's recipe?"

"My mother taught him to make it. She learned from her family chef. We still have it once in a while, but usually only at the fishing lodge. We don't go boating as often anymore. What about you?" he asked, aware he was rambling back into nostalgia.

"Oh, I don't go boating much either," Eddie said. Gregory nudged him with an elbow. "Well, I do make a decent potato salad."

"But what was your favorite food?"

Eddie tucked his arms behind his head, closing his eyes. "It's a little gross."

"Fish casserole," Gregory reminded him.

"Well, also the food isn't material, it was part of something bigger. Kind of like how yours is, actually. On weekends or whenever we could weasel out of school, my folks would throw us in the car and take us on day trips or overnights to, I don't know, wherever – national parks, tourist traps, different beaches with cool waves for surfing. Plenty to see in California if you drive pretty much any direction from the coast. We'd get up super early, pack the car with games to keep us busy and coolers full of lunch, and hit the road. Eventually we'd stop off somewhere and eat lunch at a picnic table or on the beach or whatever. It was the travel that made it special."

"What was in the lunches?"

"Chips, for sure. Celery sticks, peanut butter. Cheese and crackers – real cheap cheese, bless my parents. Bananas. Soda and juice. And we all made our own sandwiches so we'd have what we liked, then we'd wrap them in waxed paper and put them in the very top of the cooler, so they'd stay cold but they wouldn't get soggy."

"Very rustic," Gregory remarked.

"That's a charming word for it. Anyway, a sandwich eaten out of a waxed paper wrapper, that was my best meal."

"Any kind of sandwich?"

Eddie opened his eyes, amused. "I had a specialty. Peanut butter, banana, and bacon bits, with hot sauce."

Gregory knew he couldn't keep the look off his face, so didn't try. Eddie pointed at him, snickering.

"That's what my siblings looked like. Kept them from trying to steal my sandwich, though."

"It'd keep me from trying, certainly."

"Don't knock it. Although probably all the fresh air and getting to skip school contributed to the flavor." Eddie sat up, stretching a little. "There's a lot here that reminds me of home. It's that balmy warm weather in the evenings, especially. Really beautiful nights you have in this burg."

"We put them on specially for visitors."

"As long as it doesn't rain, your coronation's probably going to have gorgeous weather."

"I hope so. I won't see much of it. Trapped inside most of the day making oaths and wearing extremely heavy hats and robes."

"Huh," Eddie said, in a way that made Gregory look up at him. "That is a shame. You and your dad are both pretty outdoorsy, right?"

"I suppose so. A little less now that he's older, but yes."

"And everyone loves a picnic," Eddie said thoughtfully. Gregory sat up too, watching him.

"What are you thinking?" he asked.

"Well, picture this," Eddie said. "Coronation's over. Everyone's leaving the, what, the throne room?"

"Yes."

"Stuffy in there?"

"Extremely."

"Late afternoon. We're all ready for a drink and something to eat. Everyone's in a good mood because their very handsome and charismatic new king has been crowned."

"Thank you," Gregory said.

"Welcome. As they leave the throne room, they're guided outside into the palace gardens – "

"Charming, but we can't make diplomats sit on blankets," Gregory said, catching his drift.

"No, I wasn't going to. I was thinking cafe tables, like they have at the bistros in town. Draped in checked tablecloth, in the kingdom's colors. Lawn chairs with cushions. Not formal, but very well presented. And on every table there's a picnic basket."

"Like a gift," Gregory said, enthralled by the idea.

"The baskets have a bottle of wine, little jars of mustard, jam, honey – people love stuff in little jars," Eddie said. "Snack foods. Cookies to eat with the big cake Simon can bring out at the end of the meal."

"But what's the meal itself?"

"In the basket, finger sandwiches in waxed paper – maybe beeswax wrap, that's more environmentally sound. Fresh whole fruit. But that's just the foundation. Here's the spectacle," Eddie said, turning fully to him. "Just as everyone sits down, waiters come out of the palace with thermoses. Two for each table. Hot soup in one, cold potato salad in the other. Your mother's recipe. To honor her. What kind of soup does your dad like?"

"There's a mushroom soup – "

"Perfect. Hot soup, cold potato salad, sandwiches, snacks, fruit, wine. Easy to prep – time intensive but not difficult to make. Easy to get everything I need, too."

"I like it," Gregory said. "I like the idea of – being king at that banquet."

"Will your dad go for it?"

"Maybe. Probably. If we make the presentation formal enough."

Eddie grinned. "We, huh? Well, let me come up with a sales pitch for him."

"How?"

"Not sure yet, but I'll figure it out. This time the presentation will be more for him than for you anyway. I can think about that later. I'll give it to him this weekend, that'll give me a few days to pretty everything up."

Gregory saw real pleasure and interest in Eddie's eyes, which were lit up with the idea. He leaned in and kissed him, feeling oddly as though he could capture a little of that euphoria.

Eddie made a soft noise and grabbed the front of his shirt, deepening the kiss. Gregory figured this one was on Eddie to write down and file away and work on, so he let himself be distracted for a while.

Eddie held up his phone, camera aimed outward for once, and called, "Simon! Simon, turn around."

Simon, standing over a pan at the stove, announced, "*Je refuse!*"

"Aw, come on Simon!"

"I will not be held hostage to a telephone," Simon continued, sounding as even-toned as ever.

"You're the hottest new food media star, though," Eddie pleaded, circling to one side. "Give them all a look at your beautiful face!"

He caught just the edge of Simon's eyeroll, which was enough encouragement for him.

"I am not a performing internet monkey," Simon said, but he did give the camera a dry look.

"Hah, looking good. So tell us what you're doing," Eddie

said, aiming the camera down into the pot.

"I am checking the doneness on the potatoes," Simon told him. "For potato salad."

"And why potato salad?"

"Because you have a harebrained scheme," Simon announced.

Eddie turned himself and also the phone, so that he could capture Simon in a shot with him. "It's true. All my schemes are like this," he told the camera. "But you like me anyway, huh?"

"You're charming, so I forgive you," Simon said, shaking a finger at him.

"I'll take it. What goes into the potato salad?"

"Palace secret. But I can tell you that you must include cider vinegar and garlic. And of course it helps if your personal paid chef made it for you."

Eddie laughed. "Personal paid *celebrity* chef. My followers made you a fan club. They've got t-shirts and everything."

"Silliness," Simon said. Then, almost as an afterthought, "But I would like one of the t-shirts, please."

Eddie stopped the recording before he started laughing, but only just.

"That's awesome," he said. "Thanks. I'm going to tag a staged video of me making potato salad onto the end of that, and it'll go out this afternoon."

"Pleased to oblige. I do want one of the shirts. My nephew's birthday is coming."

"That is a kickass uncle gift. Are you sure you're going to be able to handle the volume of potato salad we're going to need for the event?"

"I won't be doing most of it. Everyone else can peel and slice and such. I'm just there to make sure the herbs all go in, in the proper amounts," Simon reminded him, carrying the pan to the sink and straining the potatoes. "I always liked this recipe. The queen knew exactly what her people's tastes were."

"Wish I could have met her."

"Me too. I'm curious what you'd make of each other. Probably similar to your and His Highness's first meeting. Maybe less awkward," Simon allowed. "A very gracious woman, Her Majesty. Gone too soon – a very sad illness. Ah, well, but soon we'll have a new king and perhaps a king consort."

"Thanks for the subtle hint, but I figured it out," Eddie said. Simon shot him a sidelong grin. "Hard to believe he's in the market for a husband. He seems pretty married to the job."

"He's asked Alanna to help him find a suitable man," Simon said. Something in his tone caught Eddie's ear.

"Suitable?"

"An arranged marriage. Very traditional but *rather* outmoded." Simon carried the potatoes to a mixing bowl and began shaking them in gently.

"He's looking for a, what, a mail-order prince?" Eddie asked.

"In her words, he wants the whole thing done with," Simon replied. "I'm not worried. She will talk him out of it. Or at least into letting her manage his relationships for him."

"We'd all be in better shape if Alanna managed our lives, probably," Eddie agreed, thoughtful. "Arranged marriage. Not a very good deal for the prince, I feel like."

"How so?" Simon asked.

"Well, we know why he's looking, and *we* know he's a decent guy," Eddie said. "But what kind of person puts themselves up for an arranged marriage with a king they've never met? You get maybe one or two royals who feel like he does, but you're going to have to pick them out of all the con men and attention hounds."

"Royalty is good at sorting the wheat from the chaff. This is fortunate for us," Simon replied.

"Let's hope so. Anyway, not your problem or mine, right?" Eddie asked, though he felt oddly pensive about the idea. Gregory deserved more than a political ally. In private he was kind and fun and intensely vulnerable. It would be too easy for someone to take advantage of that.

On the other hand, most of the really awful ones would probably be scared off by the public nature of it – too much work for some, with the king being a functional part of the political system. What would that job even be like?

"When the queen was alive, what kind of job was it?" he asked. "What did she do, on a daily basis?"

"Ah, Queen Miranda. She did a great many things," Simon told him. "She traveled. Ambassador of culture. She was in several advertisements for national tourism. If the king couldn't attend a social function, she represented him. Eventually she brought the prince to such things to train him."

"She was old blood, though, that's what the prince said. That kind of thing probably has to be picked up when you're a kid."

"They have a saying, actually," Simon said. "The lord's father is the stableman's son."

"Uh…" Eddie frowned, trying to parse this out.

"It means that the best partner for a noble is a commoner," Simon translated. "Destined lovers in Askazer legends are often of different classes. Yes, Gregory's mother was the daughter of an old house, but that house had many maids and butlers marry into it. It's the name that comes down, not the bloodline exactly."

"Like how Prince Gregory is named for a king he isn't related to," Eddie said.

"Exactly. He'll look among the nobility, here and outside the country, but it's also very likely his eventual consort will come from the town, or get off a tourist bus, or have family who sell fish harborside."

"A place after my own heart," Eddie said.

"Mine also. I could never leave here, once I arrived, even if I did have to learn English," Simon said.

"I was going to ask, but it seemed rude. It's a weird country to be speaking English, this deep in mainland Europe," Eddie remarked.

"Bah. Some English colonial nonsense three centuries ago." Simon waved a hand. "I think they kept on after kicking out the English purely to annoy the French."

"Seems to be working," Eddie pointed out.

Simon gaped at him for a second and then laughed. "True! Now," he added, "come with me. You can help me make *real* mayonnaise."

"I have made real mayonnaise before!" Eddie protested, but he followed Simon to the big walk-in fridge for eggs.

THREE WEEKS UNTIL
THE CORONATION OF HIS MAJESTY
KING GREGORY III

IT WASN'T THAT it bothered Eddie, exactly, but the idea of a man like Gregory settling for an arranged marriage – probably to a virtual stranger – gnawed at him. It felt out of character. Not for Crown Prince Gregory or King Gregory III, that was very much in his wheelhouse, but for Gregory the man?

It felt like a building block of the wrong color – it fit the shape, but the design wasn't right. Not that it was Eddie's business, considering they'd already agreed this would be a fun way to pass the time and not a commitment. He'd be gone in less than a full month. Still – Gregory didn't need that and neither did Askazer-Shivadlakia.

The night before Eddie was supposed to present the new picnic idea to Michaelis, Gregory actually came and found him, which he didn't normally; usually Eddie searched him out instead. This time, Gregory turned up in the kitchen after dinner, eating an orange for dessert and watching Simon tidy away the dinner pans while Eddie prepared the picnic basket for the following day. Eddie took the hint and put a little hustle on, then agreed to "a quick meeting in my office" with the prince.

Now, lying in Gregory's bedroom, breathless and relaxed, he let his curiosity get the better of him.

"I feel like I gotta ask you something," he said, "but it's definitely none of my business and probably annoying."

"I'm positive I've heard you ask that kind of question before on your show," Gregory said.

"Have you been watching my show?" Eddie asked, delighted.

"It's streaming," Gregory answered, defensive. "And Alanna said there was one about fried pork belly I had to watch because just seeing it raises your cholesterol."

"Oh yeah. That episode was a lot. But actually most of the questions get cleared beforehand. I'm not a journalist, I'm just a hungry dude. And I don't know them. Not as well as I know you, anyway," he said. He watched Gregory consider this.

"You might as well ask. If I don't want to answer it, I simply won't."

"Is it true you're going to get Alanna to find you a husband?"

Gregory let out a bark of laughter, a shock reaction. "Did she tell you that?"

"Simon said you're considering an arranged marriage."

"That's more accurate. Sure, I have a meeting about it set for after the coronation."

"Why?" Eddie asked. "I mean, if you were just a dude that might be different, but you're the king. Royalty mates for life, usually. It's a big mess if they don't."

"So?"

"So you want to spend your life hitched to a stranger?"

"Don't we all, in some way or another?" Gregory asked. "We're very, very lucky if we get to choose our bosses. Friends start out as strangers. There are politicians in my cabinet I would prefer I didn't have to work with, but until they die or I do, here we are."

"But this is a life mate. Someone you're going to sleep next to."

"It's much more important that I'm going to work next to them," Gregory said, eyes dark but not sad, exactly. Perhaps a little resigned. "I'd love to marry for love but time is fleeting and it's a little impractical."

"Well, I'm not here to throw stones. I'm just curious," Eddie said. Gregory gave him a smile.

"Some would say I'm young to commit my whole life to governing the country," he said. "It's a much more complicated, difficult thing than a marriage. And – and if someone did love me, my duty is to the country. It'd be hard on him."

"Your parents did okay."

"Let you in on a secret," Gregory said, inching closer. Eddie leaned in. "They were absolutely in a threesome with the country."

It was Eddie's turn to laugh in shock. "Gregory!"

"It's true. A love like that, where we both loved each other *and* the work, I'd jump for in a minute, but the odds aren't on my side. So, I'll find someone agreeable, who likes the country and puts up with me, and we'll figure the rest out as we go."

"Well, it's your life," Eddie said. "I have a suggestion, though."

"I'm all ears."

"You are..." Eddie narrowed his eyes, pausing for effect, "...*amazingly* good at sex. I'm going to suggest that you make sure whoever you end up with, they appreciate this about you. You can't waste your talents on an unappreciative audience."

"Well, that's very flattering. I'll do my best," Gregory said, rolling over to kiss him. "In the meantime I'm happy to share."

The following evening, King Michaelis and Crown Prince Gregory took a stroll through the palace, starting in the rarely-used throne room and following the path that, presumably, attending visitors would take to the garden.

"What've you got planned?" Michaelis asked, but Gregory just grinned at him.

Outside, on the flat stretch of grass and flowerbeds of the west garden, bordered by hedges, a single elegant table was standing, covered with a tablecloth in the checked blue-and-orange of the flag. Behind it, slightly to one side, stood two waiters, each holding a thermos, and Eddie, holding a printed-out menu. On the table was a picnic basket. As they arrived, Eddie pulled out one of the chairs.

"Your Majesty, Your Highness," he said. "I have a new concept for the coronation banquet to show you."

Michaelis gave him and then the chair a measured look, but he stepped up to the table and allowed himself to be seated. Gregory sat himself, eyes on his father, hoping a more immersive experience would help.

"Prince Gregory said something to me that inspired me," Eddie continued. "He liked the idea, so we thought we'd give you the practical demonstration."

"On the lawn?" Michaelis asked. Eddie nodded. "Well, I'm interested."

The king reached for the picnic basket, tipping it towards himself to unpack it. The wine came out first; with long habit Michaelis handed it to Gregory, who took a corkscrew from Eddie to open it while his father unpacked the rest. There were small packages wrapped in white paper, little jars of mustard and slightly larger ones of pickles, a pot of soft cheese, a bowl of fresh fruit.

"Allow me to present to you an elegant, full service, traditional coronation picnic," Eddie said, as the waiters came forward. They laid a pair of bowls in front of each man, one pouring soup while the other gently spooned potato salad. Michaelis unwrapped one of the paper packages, studying the finger sandwich with interest until he saw the potato salad.

"I told Eddie about how we used to have it when we went fishing," Gregory said quietly.

Michaelis nodded, picking up a fork, taking a small bite. Gregory stifled amusement at the idea of his father knowing the one-bite rule.

"I want you to picture this whole field full of tables – six to eight seats per. Each table has a basket with sandwiches, fruit, assorted other foods and wine," Eddie said. "Music, dancing…everyone's happy to be celebrating the coronation. Your favorite soup – "

"And the queen's favorite picnic food," Michaelis finished. For a half a second, Gregory wondered if the whole idea touched a nerve, if the reminder of his mother was a little too painful. But then Michaelis tilted his head to look up at the chef, and his face was thoughtful, not pained. Slowly, his eyes crinkled, a smile crossing his face. "Well, she would have loved this idea."

"I'm glad to hear it," Eddie said sincerely.

"Croquet," Michaelis added, and Eddie's smile turned puzzled.

"Come again?"

"Ask Alanna where the croquet sets are," Michaelis said. "We have a number of them. And I believe some kites, as well. For the children. We can purchase some if there aren't any."

"I will…absolutely do that," Eddie said. He glanced at Gregory, who tried to telegraph calm. If his father was making contributions, then he'd made up his mind to approve.

"It's been ages since we had a garden party," Michaelis said.

"A picnic, dad," Gregory replied.

"It's a garden party," Michaelis declared, and Gregory made a choice not to die on that hill. "Have Alanna find some appropriate live music. Hire extra waitstaff if needed. Very well done, Mr. Rambler."

"Thank you, Your Majesty," Eddie said.

"You can go up to the kitchen," Michaelis said to Eddie, and then to the waiters hovering nearby, "You as well. We'll bring in the plates when we're done."

Eddie, clearly reassured, retreated with the staff. Gregory took a bite of the potato salad, as good as it ever was.

"I really liked this idea," he said, as his father tried the soup.

"Yes, so do I. It's very suitable," Michaelis said. "And also pleasant," he added tolerantly, when Gregory opened his mouth. "I know that's important to you. Clearly so does this chef."

"He's a thoughtful man, once you get to know him," Gregory said.

"Well, I did always try to teach you to dig deep. It's a wise king who looks for the truth, let alone finds it."

"That's a really high bar to set right now," Gregory said. "I was hoping for the first few years we'd just be happy if I don't get voted out. A quest for an objective truth is more of a fifteen-years-into-a-golden-age kind of a thing."

"I waited at least ten before I did mine," Michaelis agreed.

"And what objective truth did you find, Dad?" Gregory asked. Michaelis looked up and around, thoughtful.

"I couldn't say," he said. "But you were born about ten years into the reign, if that helps."

Eddie was waiting for them when they came inside. He wasn't obvious about it; the kitchen was empty as they put their plates in the sink and the basket on the counter, but Gregory saw him lurking near the back entrance and told his father to go on ahead, that he'd see him for breakfast tomorrow. As soon as Michaelis was gone, Eddie emerged, fists clenched in triumph.

"He loved it, right? He totally did. You have to actually give me the high five this time," he said, and held up his hand. Gregory gave him as good an imitation of his father as he could muster, looking him up and down, then raised one hand to tap his palm lightly against Eddie's.

"I knew it," Eddie crowed, breaking into an ugly, enthusiastic dance move. "Man this is going to be a slam dunk, easiest dinner I ever catered. We're gonna be under budget, I'm gonna look like a boss, and you are going to have a really great banquet," he said, dancing around Gregory. "They're gonna think you are the coolest. Am I in charge of buying the kites or is that an Alanna job?"

"She'll assign it to staff," Gregory said. "I'm pretty sure they'll have to buy new croquet sets anyway. We used to use them to tap the fig trees to get the ripe ones down before harvest. We definitely destroyed at least two sets."

"Aw, tiny Gregory with a big wooden mallet, beating on a fig tree. I wish there was footage," Eddie said.

"Thankfully, there isn't. That was very well done, Eddie," Gregory said. "He's fully in. There was some feedback on the sandwiches and he'll undoubtedly have notes about the wine pairings but I will pay you extra to be tolerant."

"No need. I'm happy to hear his thoughts. The royal sommelier had some strong opinions on the wine too," Eddie said, calming himself down. "Okay. So. Tomorrow, I'm going to have to shift into high-gear asskicking mode. Do you want to celebrate tonight, or should I come find you in a couple of days after I've gone on a blitz of food-buying and menu preparation?"

"Come by tonight," Gregory said, tilting his head in the direction of his rooms. "Give me an hour or so? I have to wrap up a few things."

"Sure. I'll spend the time coming up with a secret knock," Eddie said.

"I'm on pins and needles," Gregory told him. He leaned in briefly, stealing a kiss, and then left the kitchen with a spring in his step, while Eddie redoubled his triumphant dancing.

The knock, when it came, was quiet, but also extravagant and complicated, really more of a drum solo; it was still going on when Gregory opened the door.

Eddie, both fists upraised and knuckles at the ready, beamed at him and let his arms fall, then bent to pick up a carton next to his feet.

"This is, technically, business," he said, brushing past Gregory into the room. "You are being crowned king, which is a big deal, Sweet Prince, and that calls for champagne."

"Isn't 'sweet prince' from *Hamlet*?" Gregory asked.

"It is," Eddie agreed, pulling tiny piccolo-bottles of champagne out of the carton.

"And isn't it what his friend calls him when he's dying?"

"Goodnight, sweet prince, and flights of angels sing thee to thy rest," Eddie agreed. "It's also what you're supposed to quote to lift the curse if you've said 'Macbeth' inside a theater. It's a turn of phrase, gorgeous. The point is, I have some champagne for you to sample, both so that we can celebrate and so that you can choose what you'd like served for your toasts."

Out came a series of tasting glasses, as well as a bowl of coffee beans and a sleeve of saltine crackers.

"Sip lightly, swallow, give me your notes, then sniff the coffee, eat a piece of cracker, and rinse your mouth with water," Eddie said, as he began opening bottles. "You can spit if you want, but I didn't bring a bucket."

"You've done this before," Gregory said.

"Yes, but not often. Believe it or not, there's not a lot of call for wine tasting in burger joints," Eddie said, offering him the first glass.

The tasting was fun; with a little of the pressure off he could enjoy the flavors and the zing of the bubbles. All but one of the wines were true champagne, and the last one was a California sparkling wine that Eddie explained came from a vineyard where he had an investment.

"Just for fun," he said, and Gregory leaned into him, warm and tipsy from the drink.

"You are fun," he agreed. Eddie laughed.

"I do my best," he said. "Enjoy this. I won't be around as much for a while."

"I am." Gregory inched closer, until Eddie put an arm around his shoulders. "I'll miss you when you leave."

"You won't have time. I've seen your schedule. And anyway, I'll be back," Eddie said. "Now that I know what a hot spot this place is, I'll have to film an episode here. Maybe do a whole season in Europe. What passes for diner food in these parts?"

"Couldn't say. I'm sure you'll sniff it out, though."

Eddie laughed into his hair. "I am good at that. You'll let me do at least one segment in the palace though, right? My loyal fans will know if you don't. They recognize the kitchen now."

"As long as you promise not to poach Simon," Gregory said.

"Simon wouldn't leave even if you fired him."

"Nice to have loyal staff."

"Loyal hell, he just knows he's never gonna get his hands on appliances that nice anywhere else."

Gregory laughed hard enough to snort, and then laughed at that. Eddie was warm under him, and for at least a little while the kingdom could look after itself.

"C'mon, let's get you to bed," Eddie said, half-lifting him and dragging them both to the bedroom. "You can miss me all you want tomorrow."

TWO WEEKS UNTIL
THE CORONATION OF HIS MAJESTY
KING GREGORY III

AFTER THE MENU was approved, the time flew by. Gregory saw Eddie less than he'd like; he was distracted with interviews and photo sessions, logistics meetings for the coronation, and multiplying meetings as his father handed off duties one by one. Still, he tried to sidetrack whatever walk-and-talk he was on so that they passed the kitchen. If Eddie saw him wave, he'd grin and wave back. If he didn't, it was generally because he was so deep into something that he didn't notice, so at least he was keeping busy as well.

"I don't think there were nearly this many pressmen at my coronation," Michaelis said one afternoon, coming into the office as a cameraman and his partner left. "I'm not sure if I should be jealous."

"I wouldn't. There's just more…I don't know, news, now," Gregory said, waving a hand. "And when Eddie put us on Photogram, it got a lot of people interested. I think there's ten or twenty real, proper influencers who are going to feature us. The cafes in town are keeping track of how many foreigners call them cute and authentic."

"Influencers," Michaelis said, rolling his eyes. "They didn't have that when I was crowned, either."

"I've been thinking of becoming one. It doesn't seem overly difficult, especially if you've got a palace," Gregory said with a grin. Michaelis nodded, amused. "You could host a podcast. Talk about statecraft, diplomacy. Pressuring your son into running the country."

"I pressured you!" Michaelis pretended outrage. "When you were *five* you told me you wanted to be king."

"And what a mistake that proved to be," Gregory drawled. "Did you need something?"

"Not in particular, just to see how you were holding up."

Gregory tapped the end of his pen on his blotter. "Doing all right, actually. There's less waiting around now, and things seem to be going smoothly. Busy, but tolerable."

"I'm glad to hear it. The rest of the palace is going wild. Can't walk through a door but someone runs past with bunting or place settings or some damn thing."

"Ah yes. Alanna's been scarce, I thought that might be why."

"That chef has everyone on the jump." Michaelis studied him. "He's very enthusiastic about the garden party."

"He's just pleased you liked it. So am I."

His father seemed about to say something else, then changed his mind. "Well, it's one small moment in what I think will be a very long reign. They trot out that old footage of me being crowned once a year, but nobody remembers all the details anymore, and thank goodness. Try not to blaspheme or fall on your face and you'll be fine."

"What even counts as blasphemy anymore?" Gregory wondered aloud, as Michaelis rose to leave.

"You'd know better than I would," Michaelis told him. "Come to breakfast tomorrow, I want to see you eat a full meal."

"Promise, Dad," Gregory said, and Michaelis lifted his hand in acknowledgment as he left. Gregory heard Alanna call a greeting to the king, and then she was ducking into the office, tablet at the ready.

"Well, it appears I have open office hours," Gregory said as she sat down. "Keeping busy, I hear."

"Yes, but no disasters yet. Probably means there's going to be one right beforehand, but it'll be useful on my resume eventually," she said.

"You're not pulled too tight?" Gregory asked. Her smile softened.

"No, I'm fine. It's reminding me how much I love planning parties and how very happy I am I don't do it for a living," she said.

"Dad said Eddie has the staff 'on the jump'," Gregory said.

"I think they're all breathing a sigh of relief he'll be gone for a couple of days," she said, and Gregory frowned.

"Gone?"

"He might not have told you – there's an issue with the, ah, mushroom supply," she said, checking her notes. "He's going to drive down the coast, try and buy up any he can find in bulk. It'll take a few days to get to Messina and back."

"No, I hadn't heard. I hope it's a productive trip."

"I think he wanted to get out of the palace, give everyone a breather, maybe take some time for himself, too," she confided. "It must be hard, coming all the way out here for two months."

"Well, he travels a lot, I suppose he's used to it," Gregory said, wondering why Eddie hadn't told him. True, they hadn't seen each other much, but he would have wanted to know – he could have arranged for a car, and staff to help if he wanted it –

Which was of course when Eddie knocked on the open door.

"Your Highness," he said, and then with a nod, "Hey Al!"

"Eddie," she replied. "I was just telling Gregory about your trip down the coast."

"Oh yeah! Man, I wish you could come, but it's a little more than a jaunt to Fons-Askaz," Eddie said. "Don't worry, though, I'll be back in plenty of time. I was coming to let you know about it. Should have known Alanna would get here first."

"Will you be all right driving?" Gregory asked.

"Oh, sure. Simon's lending me his car. I've heard tall tales about Italian driving but I grew up in California, I should be fine."

"Sounds like quite the trip," Gregory said with a grin that was only half-forced. "Come find me when you return, I'd like to see these mushrooms you're on a mission to find."

"Will do, boss," Eddie said, and trotted off, probably back to the kitchen. It took Gregory a second to register the look on Alanna's face.

"No," he said, pointing at her.

"Oh yes," Alanna said.

"Alanna, do not – "

"The dive bar chef is the *amore!*" she cried.

"The what?" he asked, startled.

"Jerry and I called your mystery boyfriend the *amore* and it's the guy who *you said* was more dive bar than gastropub!"

"He's not my boyfriend and I'm not having this conversation with you," he told her. "Besides, I didn't know him then."

"You're dating the chef! It's just like Gregory II's father did, you remember we had to learn about it in history…"

"It's nothing like that," Gregory said, trying for dignity and probably failing. "It's not a romance. I've told you that much! It's just…convenient."

"I hope it's more than convenient," Alanna said. "I mean I hope it's fun. He seems like he'd be fun."

Gregory sighed. "Yes. He is fun. And being honest, last week I think it kept me sane."

"I know! I just didn't know it was him," Alanna said.

"You can't tell anyone, Al. It's nobody's business."

It was her turn for dignity. "You insult us both by suggesting I'd tattle. I wouldn't do that to you or him."

"I don't even want you talking to Eddie about it, I don't want to make it any weirder than it already is."

Alanna got up and rested against the desk, leaning over him. "One, you could not make it weirder if you tried, because you're super weird. Two, Eddie's a nice guy, so I hope you've talked with him about the temporary nature of this."

"I have, I promise."

"Good. Three," she added, standing and heading for the door, "I want you to think about this moment in a couple of months when you propose, in all seriousness, an arranged marriage."

Gregory sighed. "Message received, Al."

"Just so it is."

When she was gone, Gregory leaned back in his chair and stared at the ceiling. He didn't want it to be weird; in fact, he wanted it to be as normal as it could be. If he weren't king, or if Eddie weren't famous and living on another continent most of the time…well, one couldn't invite someone to immigrate on five weeks of acquaintance, and Gregory *was* king, or nearly. He and Eddie were on different paths. That happened, and you simply had to enjoy the paths before they diverged. With any luck, he'd meet a couple of prospective king consorts he'd like just as well as Eddie, but who could actually stay in Askazer-Shivadlakia.

"Holy crow, friends and fans," Eddie said, sitting in a taverna that had agreeably allowed him to film there in return for some publicity. "Did you all ever think I'd be coming to you from Messina, Italy?"

He pointed up and around him in all directions. "I didn't even know Messina was a real place until like…probably college," he said. "And that's not my fault! Half of Shakespeare's plays are set in real places and the other half are in like, whatever, fairyland, and you never know which is which. In case you're wondering, *Much Ado About Nothing* is set in Messina, which is real, and it is also where this video is set."

He grinned at the camera. "I'm here on a mission to get some mushrooms, but if I had a little more time or budget this would absolutely be an episode of *Truly Tasty*. So I'm going to give you a little mini-episode and cut here to a cooking tutorial in the kitchen right....now," he said, and hit stop on the video. The cooking tutorial, by the taverna's hip young owner, was already in the can, and he joined up the two videos and tossed them on Photogram.

One of the best things about Photogram was that if you posted, people knew where you were. His parents never worried about him if he had posted there within the last twelve hours, and it was easy to let people know you'd reached your destination safely. He wondered if Gregory had a notification set up, or just saw them whenever he happened to think of it.

Nuts; he was here to buy mushrooms and see the city, not worry about the king-to-be. It was one reason among many other and probably saner reasons that he'd decided on the trip. He was into the crown prince, in a way he recognized was more than just surface attraction, but Eddie himself had been the one to suggest it could just be a good time. Couldn't go back on that now. It wasn't fair to Greg, and it wouldn't exactly be easy on Eddie either.

No, he'd take a few days to get out of the palace, and when he came back he'd be in a shallower state of mind. He could hang out with the crown prince, who among other things badly needed a little pressure release, and who in any case was a lot of fun to be around. They'd finish up the affair, say fond and already-nostalgic goodbyes, and in a hundred years Eddie could tell his grandkids he'd shacked up with a prince, and nobody would believe him.

His phone rang, a number that wasn't in his contacts, and he picked up with a cheerful, "Yello!"

"Eddie," Gregory's voice was both amused and dry.

"Uh oh, what'd I do now," Eddie said.

"I saw the video. You're supposed to be here for Askazer-Shivadlakia, not canoodling around with Messina."

"She means nothing to me," Eddie said dramatically. "It was the heat of the moment."

"Hm, it was the smell of the pasta, I have a feeling," Gregory answered.

"The things they do with fettucini," Eddie replied, lowering his voice and leaning into the phone. "I should have come to Italy when I was like twelve."

"Pretty sure you were still in school at twelve."

"Not if I could help it. Anyway, it's just the one video. I'll be back tomorrow. Day after tomorrow in the morning, at the latest."

"Did you find your mushrooms?"

"And then some. Almost positive none of them will kill you."

"It would be highly operatic to be poisoned at my own coronation, but yes, I'd like to avoid that fate," Gregory said.

Eddie grinned. "Only the best for the king. Hey, can I call you later tonight?"

"What, you aren't going drinking with that chef from your video?"

It struck Eddie that the prince was jealous, which was hilarious. "Yeah, but you know you'll be my first call when I'm maudlin drunk."

There was a pause, and then Gregory cleared his throat. "Look, this is a favor you absolutely don't have to do."

"What is it?"

"Don't go out tonight. Get yourself a cup of gelato and have an early night instead," Gregory said. "Or don't, it's a stupid request – "

"I'm not especially stoked to get drunk with chefs. Having been a chef, I know what we're like," Eddie said. "Gelato and an early night, no problem."

"That's all right?"

"It's fine, Greg," Eddie said. "Good excuse, actually. See you tomorrow, huh?"

"Tomorrow," Gregory echoed, and hung up. Eddie put his phone on the table and sat back, considering.

Well. Gregory ben Michaelis, crown prince of Askazer-

Shivadlakia, missed him and didn't want him going out with someone else. Flattering, and touching too; Eddie liked Gregory and enjoyed the idea that Gregory liked him as much. Trouble, of course, it was trouble in a couple of ways, but it was also nice to be missed.

The truth was that being a celebrity was fun, but it wasn't why he'd gone into show business. He liked teaching people about the world, and experiencing it as he did so. He was already tired of being on the road so much; he'd done enough *Truly Tasty* to get a sense of American cuisine, and what newcomers were bringing to it. If he wanted to settle down, maybe start a real cooking show in a kitchen of his own, he could. He'd always figured it'd be in America – Hollywood or New York, or even somewhere like Austin or Chicago. But…here he was, in Italy. Askazer-Shivadlakia was within spitting distance of Italy and France, two great countries for food. It had a climate like his home in California, and a leader that really seemed to care about agriculture and food and the links between them.

I could stay there, he thought. *It'd be dumb, but I've been dumber.*

On the other hand, no need to overstay his welcome. It was probably less cool a place if you were a resident who had to pay taxes and take out your own trash and stuff. He'd maybe get back to the palace faster than he'd intended, but then he'd cook this meal, celebrate the coronation, and head back to America to consider his next move.

Alanna came in as Gregory was hanging up with Eddie, and she grinned annoyingly at him.

"We are too old and our friendship is too valuable to me to fire you out of spite, but I haven't ruled out having you framed for sedition," he said.

"Greg, I love you, but you couldn't frame a poster without

my help," she replied.

"I'm about to be king of a whole entire country."

"Try doing that without your to-do list," she said, and he gestured defeat. "Was that Eddie?"

"As though you didn't know," he replied.

"He has a very audible phone voice," she admitted. "Sounded like he missed you."

"Did it?" he asked, a little wistful.

"Sounds like you miss him, for sure," she said.

"He'll be back tomorrow, so he says."

"Faster than expected. So why are you sulking in your sulk fortress?" she asked.

"I'm not sulking. I'm just…considering everything," he replied. "The coronation's getting closer, lots of stuff is happening. Things are moving very fast."

"This sounds silly to say," she said, "but you're only king of one very small country."

"And not even that yet. No, I know. It's a big job, but not President of the United States big."

"At least you're a useful king," she said. "Are you getting cold feet about it? Or is this something else?"

He folded his arms on the desk, resting his chin on them, slumped over. "Remember when you told me to think about how I'm sort-of dating Eddie when I think about that arranged-marriage meeting?"

She nodded, the amused expression fading from her face.

"It's months away. I don't know why I'm thinking of it. But…"

"Difficult to consider the idea when you've got someone you like close to hand?" she asked.

"I do like him. But it isn't that way and it can't be."

"You keep saying that," Alanna replied, raising an eyebrow. "But you don't ever really say why. I get not wanting to just blurt out that he isn't marriage material again – "

"He isn't marriage material *for me*. I like him. I think he's nice and funny. He's less intense in person than he is on his show."

"I have to say I watched the show and I still didn't expect him to be so…real," she agreed.

"That's the problem, though!" Gregory said, sitting back again, looking up at the ceiling. "He's *so* real. He's a person, not a political prop, and even if I wanted him to be that, he never could. He never *would*. He has no other way of being, he's not a diplomat or a royal. He has no manners, he has no training for something like this. He grew up on a beach in California. He's a TV star. He's a *tacky* TV star. It's something he's proud of."

"Why shouldn't he be?"

"Well, exactly," Gregory said. "But I have to be honest about how that would probably go. I can't consider people who wouldn't be suited to the throne."

Alanna was quiet for long enough that he looked at her curiously. She was thoughtful, clearly considering something.

"With all due respect," she said finally, "And I'm saying this both as your friend and as your employee, I think you're wrong about Eddie. In a couple of ways."

"How so?"

"I think he'd make a great royal. People love him. He makes that easy. He might work hard at making it easy, but he does it, and he seems to enjoy it. People genuinely like him, because he's genuinely likeable. Not just Americans, either. Your subjects love him."

"You can't be serious," he said. "You've told me what he's dragged us into. All the influencers and such."

"They know that's not his fault, and they like that he loves the country enough to want to share it. Honestly…you and your father have to make the laws, you have to make unpopular decisions sometimes, and they get that, but they don't have to like you," Alanna pointed out. "They already voted for you. Eddie's like the fun parent. He's spent a lot of time here, talking to people.

Learning about the food. He hasn't imported a single thing for the banquet except these mushrooms and even then it's only because we didn't have enough. The food's all local, and so is the decoration. The picnic baskets are from a basket weaver in town. I didn't even know we had a basket weaver."

"How'd he find them, then?" Gregory asked, distracted.

"I have no idea. No clue where he got all his new ideas about dairy farming, either, but the milk board is interested. And he knows more than you think," she added, before Gregory could follow that tangent down a rabbit hole. "Ever notice he always addresses you and your father properly? He always gets your titles right."

Gregory thought back. He hadn't noticed, probably because he was used to it. But it was telling that Alanna had.

"Remember when he had the kids in to do the cookies?" she asked. He nodded. "After they made the cookies, he took them on a palace tour. He had a lot of stuff written on his hand, but he was very enthusiastic about it."

"Did you go on this tour?" Gregory asked.

"Well, I'd eaten the cookies, I couldn't skip the tour," Alanna said reasonably. "The point is, whether or not you want to marry a guy you've only known five weeks, he has the skills a royal spouse needs. I'm not saying you should and definitely I doubt he would, but I don't think you should write off the idea wholesale."

"I don't know if people would find him as whimsical on a throne as they do in a kitchen," Gregory said.

"Do you think they'd do better with some stranger you don't even know that well?" she asked.

"If the stranger is the better partner, they should. I have to put the country first," Gregory pointed out.

"Then you definitely shouldn't be dating a guy who brought a bunch of tourists here," Alanna replied, voice tart.

"Alanna."

"Your grandfather was a commoner when he became king. I

know his wife's parents weren't thrilled with him being their son-in-law *or* the king, but he won the vote and he's a famous, beloved legend now. Putting the country first means listening to what it actually needs, not what you think it should need."

Gregory studied the ceiling. "Well, it's a nice idea."

"You know I've got your back whatever you decide. Eddie Rambler isn't your last chance for a relationship unless you make him your last chance, and I don't think he'd love it if you did. But if you're doing a husband-search you could do a lot worse."

"I do listen to you, you know," he said. "I'll think about it."

"That's all I can ask," she said. "I'll see you for breakfast, huh?"

"I'll be there."

"Goodnight, Your Highness."

When she was gone, he stretched, rose, and closed the window, locking the office up after himself.

It *was* a nice idea. But not exactly practical.

Eddie arrived at the palace after dinner the next day. Gregory caught a glimpse of him through a window, unloading box after box of mushrooms from the car, in dirt-smeared shirtsleeves and a wrinkled pair of cargo shorts. He looked so good that Gregory caught his breath, and then felt stupid for thinking a t-shirt and cargo shorts were sexy. But the flex of Eddie's arms carrying the boxes in was nice to look at. And the easy way he moved, at home here already, made all of Gregory's resolutions to continue to treat this lightly very difficult to keep.

"Hey!" Eddie said, as Gregory stepped out of the side door to greet him. "Good timing! Here," he said, and plopped a box into Gregory's hands. He took it out of instinct, then stared down at it.

"How many mushrooms are you feeding us?" he asked.

"They cook down a lot," Eddie said. "Plus, I figured if I'm cleaning you out of mushrooms so completely I've gotta go to Italy for more, I might as well get everything I can. Anything we don't need, I'll dry them and you can give them out to your subjects as a coronation gift. But I really gave them to you just now so I could do this," he added, and leaned over the box, kissing Gregory briefly. It was fast and discreet enough that Gregory almost wished he'd taken a little longer. "You'd have loved the drive and hated me stopping to take selfies every ten minutes on the way down."

"Probably," Gregory agreed, as Eddie took another box from the back of the car, leading the way inside. "I'm glad you enjoyed yourself."

"I'm definitely going to need to do a show in Italy," Eddie said as he set the mushrooms down in a corner with the other boxes. "Maybe a special miniseries of some kind. I could call it Rambling Down Italy."

"Keep It Noodle," Gregory said, and Eddie burst out laughing as he went outside to lock up the car.

"That's good! I'm stealing that," he said. "Glad to be back, though. Italy's been around for a couple thousand years, it can wait, and I have cooking to do here and..."

He leaned in close, holding up a paper-wrapped object from his pocket.

"Let me make you breakfast in bed tomorrow," he said quietly. "I have a truffle."

"Just what every young man loves to hear," Gregory replied, but he kept his voice soft too. "I'd like that."

"Then let me shower and get changed, and I'll drop in," Eddie suggested. Gregory nodded. "Okay. I'm gonna go make sure the mushrooms are stored and let Simon know I'll pay for the interior detailing on his car. Wait for the secret knock."

"It's really more of a drum solo," Gregory said, but Eddie just laughed and ducked back into the kitchen.

Eddie did the drum solo about forty minutes later, but he also let himself in when it was done; Gregory, who'd brought a few reports up to his rooms to read while he waited, set them aside and made space for him on the couch while Eddie put a small bag of food in the refrigerator of the kitchenette.

"Do you ever get to stop working?" Eddie asked, coming to join him on the couch. He sounded less petulant than many would have – more curious, like he was…concerned, almost.

"Eventually," Gregory said. "I mean, most nights."

"But it won't be like this for you when you're king, all these fifteen hour days? I realize this is hypocritical coming from a chef, but at least when I'm filming I get mandated union breaks."

"Oh – yes, this is temporary. There's just a lot to take in, a lot of transition plans to make," he said. "Some staff are leaving when my father does, so this week I've also been looking at resumes and considering revisions to our pension plan. And there's a lot of decisions to make for the coronation even now."

"Mm, which crown to wear?"

"Fortunately that one's out of my hands, but you're not far off. Decor for the throne room, finishing touches on speeches, making the final call on seating arrangements."

"Seems a little beneath you," Eddie observed.

"Well, sometimes two of the people attending have parents who hate each other, and you just have to seat them together and hope for the best because a third person needs a seat at a different table so that nobody gets stabbed over certain votes taken ten years ago they're still mad about. Sometimes you have to shuffle the feuding members of a family so that they can't needle each other about who got Granny's good china. Babysitting petulant petty nobility won't be the majority of my job, but it's probably good practice regardless."

"Maybe a lottery would be easier. Pull a number and let the chips fall. If people fight, they fight. A stabbing would probably liven things up," Eddie said. "Although it's hard to enjoy my cooking when that kind of shenanigan is happening."

"Don't tell me it's the first time you've been in the kitchen when someone's been stabbed," Gregory replied. Eddie laughed and grabbed him, pulling him over to straddle his lap.

"I've lived a sordid life, for sure," he said, hands firmly on Gregory's hips. "But I feel like I'm moving up in the world lately."

"Ah," Gregory bent to kiss him. "Kept man of the crown prince. I see."

"Am I?" Eddie asked, amused. "You did seem very jealous of my Italian friend in Messina."

"Well, I don't get you for very long," Gregory said, and something in Eddie's face made him uncomfortable enough to add, hurriedly, "And I was concerned about the mushroom expenditure."

"I kept all the receipts," Eddie said, whatever feeling he'd been having flitting away. "Anyway, let me prove to you I missed you."

"I'd very much like that," Gregory told him, and bent in for another kiss.

The next morning, Gregory woke to a clank and a swear-word, and rolled over in bed to find Eddie rummaging in the kitchenette. He'd located a frying pan and a mixing bowl, but seemed to be on a quest for something more complicated.

"I don't have a stand mixer," he called, and Eddie straightened from his inspection of a cupboard.

"I'd be horrified by that but Simon has three, so the ratio of stand mixers to residents in the palace is okay," he said. "Do you have a mandoline slicer?"

Gregory grunted, sitting up. "I have no idea."

"Well, I'll make do," Eddie decided, cracking eggs into the bowl. Gregory noticed the precious paper-wrapped truffle sitting nearby.

"You didn't actually have to make me breakfast," he said.

"And give Simon first crack at the truffle?" Eddie threw him a smile over his shoulder. "French toast or scrambled eggs? I brought fixings for both."

"French toast, please," Gregory said, and Eddie nodded. While Eddie cooked, he checked his phone – no urgent emails, no impending disasters – and put on a robe, settling back on the bed when Eddie brought him a plate. The french toast was lacey at the edges, a delicate brown with gold highlights, and atop each piece were paper-thin shreds of truffle.

"You do, fortunately, have sharp knives," Eddie said, settling across from him with his own plate. Gregory took a mouthful, enjoying the earthy bite of the truffle against the gold crunch of the fried bread.

"They don't get much use," he said. "I'm not what you'd call an enthusiastic cook."

"Well, nobody's perfect," Eddie said. Gregory rolled his eyes. "If you were an enthusiastic cook I'd honestly start to be worried. Royalty, politician, bowfisher, and he looks good in a suit. If you could cook, too, you'd be some kind of experimental clone. Do you sing?"

"And play the piano, neither especially well," Gregory said. "Little hypocritical of you to ask, don't you think?"

"What's that mean?" Eddie asked, pretending to be wounded.

"Shakespeare-quoting, truffle-hunting celebrity, a TV star and influencer and he *can* cook?" Gregory recited, in a decent approximation of Eddie's accent. "What else do you do, appraise gemstones and raise racing pigeons?"

"If it helps, several people have tried and failed to teach me to knit," Eddie said.

"Off with his head," Gregory replied soberly. Eddie laughed as he took another bite of his breakfast. "I was thinking, though."

"I'm in trouble now."

"Eddie, really," Gregory protested. Eddie subsided. "I know this coming week leading up to the coronation is going to be busy for both of us. But if something goes wrong, or if you need me to back you on something, come find me."

Eddie nodded, considering this as he swallowed. "Deal, but I have a condition."

"Oh?"

"I want to know you're eating and resting, and I can't do that myself. If necessary I will sic Jerry on you."

Gregory gave him a half-smile.

"So if I don't see you in the family dining room for at least one meal a day, I'm gonna break out the big guns, okay?" Eddie tilted his head. "And that's not part of the job. It's because I like you and I see how hard you work. Can't have the king passing out during the coronation, either, it'd really harsh the reception."

"I'll do my best," Gregory said. "Though I will also say it is possible to bribe me with desserts."

"I'll bear that in mind," Eddie replied, laughing.

ONE WEEK UNTIL
THE CORONATION OF HIS MAJESTY
KING GREGORY III

GREGORY WAS ASLEEP, or rather barely on the verge of awareness. He knew he was warm. The sheets were soft, and he could feel the light weight of the blanket on top of him, insulating him from the world.

And then Eddie Rambler called, "GOOD MORNING!"

Gregory opened his eyes just in time for Eddie to peel back the blankets, uncovering his head and shoulders. The light in the room was dim, but still enough to make him squint.

"Up and at 'em," Eddie said. "It's a busy day for me and probably the last time I'll get to see you for very long until the coronation."

"Why?" Gregory asked, more of a plea to the universe than a request for explanation.

"It's crunch time. This morning I need to drive into town and I think you should come along. Keep me company."

"Town?" Gregory managed.

"We gotta load up on picnic baskets and haul them back here so the kitchen staff can start packing them," Eddie explained, correctly interpreting his question. "Simon's busy boiling every potato ever, and the rest of the staff are helping when they can, but they've still got regular meals to serve."

"Mm." Gregory swung himself mostly out of bed, groping for his robe. Eddie put a mug of coffee in his hand instead.

"Thank you. This wouldn't have anything to do with me missing dinner yesterday, would it?"

"I told you if you didn't have at least one meal a day in the family dining room, I'd be forced to take action," Eddie said.

"I meant to. I did eat."

"I know, or I would have done this last night."

"Not that I'm not glad to see you, but you are a lot first thing in the morning."

"Baby, I'm a lot all day," Eddie said, and Gregory couldn't disagree.

He hadn't seen Eddie much since his triumphant return from mushroom-hunting, but then neither of them had much time to spare at this point. As he dressed one-handed, sipping from the coffee cup in his other hand, Eddie gave him a rundown on what he'd done and what he still had to do – which Gregory suspected was more for Eddie than for himself. What had been prepped, what was left to prep, and what was currently in progress meant much more to Eddie, logistically, than it did to him.

Caffeinated and dressed, he trooped after Eddie towards the garage, but put out a hand to stop him from taking Simon's car again. Instead, Gregory pulled the dust-sheet off a pickup truck at the back.

"We can take my car," he said.

"Your car?" Eddie asked, studying the battered vehicle.

"It has more cargo space," Gregory explained.

"Does it have a floor?"

"Don't be so picky." Gregory hoisted himself into the driver's seat, taking the key off the dashboard, and Eddie clambered up into the other side. The truck engine purred when he turned the ignition, to Eddie's surprise (and a little to Gregory's). He eased it out of the garage and onto the main road leading away from the palace.

"I learned to drive in this car," he said, as they bounced down the road.

"I'm gaining a new respect for you and your secret, reckless disregard for your own life," Eddie replied.

"I think the gardener had it before I did. But it's pretty good for running around the countryside when I don't want the pomp and circumstance of an official motorcade."

"Yeah, the pomp got beat out of this thing years ago," Eddie said. "Not that I'm judging, I have a deep appreciation for useful junk."

"Don't listen to him," Gregory told the dashboard.

"How are you, anyway?" Eddie asked, eyes carefully on the road. "Feeling okay about getting crowned in a few days?"

"Surprisingly, yes," Gregory said. "Possibly I'm just too tired to sustain any kind of anxiety about it, but I think I'm honestly okay. It'll be a big change, of course, but I've done all I can to be ready."

"You're not worried about the actual event?"

"Oh, no, big state occasions don't bother me. I mostly just repeat what they tell me to repeat. As long as I don't mess up the oath of office or drop the sacred orb of rule, I should be fine."

"The sacred orb of rule?" Eddie asked. "Is that like an actual orb, or is it a kind of metaphorical..." he trailed off when he saw Gregory suppressing a smile. "You lying liar."

"There was, once!" Gregory protested. "I think my grandfather got rid of it. He said it was just an encumbrance."

"A real pain in the orb," Eddie replied. "Can't blame him, though. Change can be a good thing."

"I like to think so. I hope my constituents see it that way," Gregory replied. "I'm not going to make a bunch of policy decisions right up front, but I'm setting up a lot of dominoes for incremental change. You're part of that, actually."

"Me?" Eddie asked, delighted.

"Well, you're keeping it new, aren't you?"

"Doing my best," Eddie agreed.

"There you go. I don't want to drag the country into the

modern era; it doesn't need dragging. It's just going to be a waltz in that direction. With lots of breaks for snacks," he added. Eddie laughed.

"I like that. A waltz into the future," he said. "I've been thinking about that a lot myself."

"What, modernizing? Photogram isn't new enough for you anymore?"

"Funnily enough, no. There's always another platform on the horizon," Eddie said, watching the landscape pass. "More, I've been thinking about making changes. I'm in a place where I can write my own ticket, which I don't think really came home to me until I just…up and left the country for eight weeks to come here. I have money, I have social clout, I have a network. If I didn't want to do *Truly Tasty* anymore, I wouldn't have to."

"Don't you?"

"Well, I'd like to see it continue, but there's no shortage of people who could take over. I don't mind it, I'm just looking at a lot more possibilities outside of it than I used to have. And the network isn't the one who calls the shots anymore. I could do a new show, or no show at all. I could come out if I wanted."

Gregory glanced at him. "Considering it?"

"Yeah. Making some plans. Nothing I've told my PR team yet, but they knew this was coming eventually."

"I wish you more luck than I had."

"Why, what happened?" Eddie turned to him, brow knitting.

"Nothing specific, just the usual savagery from the tabloids. Dad wasn't thrilled at first but honestly I think mostly because of the press. He's come around since," Gregory added.

"I'll at least hold off until after the coronation – can't be stealing your thunder," Eddie said. "The point of it all is that if I say I'm bisexual or talk about a history of relationships with men, and the network tanks the show or fires me, I don't need them. I don't need *Truly Tasty*."

"What would you do instead?"

"World's my oyster. Could become a personal chef like Simon, but I think I like attention too much," Eddie said ruefully. "Think I mentioned opening some restaurants. I could rest on my laurels. Sell a line of cookware on Photogram. But I've been thinking I'd like to do something less intense. Maybe a traditional cooking show."

"In a studio?" Gregory asked, amused by the visual. "With one of those tastefully cluttered kitchen sets?"

"Studio, maybe, I don't know. Short videos are trendy at the moment and I could do fifteen, twenty shorts in a day. Spend a week on set and stock my Photogram queue for the year. Not that thrilling, though." Eddie sighed. "It's just there's so much food I still don't know how to cook. I'd like to do something where I learn a new dish each week and teach it to the viewers. Eddie Gets Educated."

"Right after Keeping It Noodle, the Rambler tour of Italy," Gregory laughed. "The internet will love it."

They turned onto the main street of town at that point, and Eddie directed him about halfway down, and around to a loading dock on the back. The shop owner, clearly out early specifically to meet Eddie, looked startled to see his king-elect behind the wheel. He bobbed a little bow, took the signed invoice back from Eddie, and vanished into the shop. Gregory, distracted by loading box after box of baskets into the truck, vaguely registered the man handing a solitary basket to Eddie, but didn't think anything of it until they were back on the road.

"Hey, pull over here," Eddie said, after a few minutes of contemplative silence. He gestured to a scenic overlook that gazed down onto the bay and harbor, brilliantly blue in the early morning. Gregory, obedient, pulled the truck into the turnoff and parked it.

"Last Photogram selfie?" he asked, as Eddie got out of the truck.

"No, come on out! I have a surprise for you."

"For me?" Gregory asked, joining Eddie, who was pulling down the tailgate of the truck and perching himself on it comfortably. He had the single basket he'd taken from the shopkeeper carefully cradled in one arm.

"Yeah, c'mere," Eddie said, patting the gate next to him. Gregory slung himself into the space Eddie indicated as Eddie turned to face him. He accepted the basket, perplexed, and lifted the hinged lid, revealing a jaunty blue-and-orange striped fabric lining, in which sat a small paper carton. He lifted the carton out and opened it, torn between confusion and delight. It turned out to be a small cake, about four inches square, covered in white frosting, adorned with blue and orange birds.

"It's a congratulations cake!" Eddie said, excited. "It's for your coronation. Man, that came out great," he added, admiring it.

"Bit small for the feast," Gregory said, but he knew his voice gave away how touched he was.

"Ah, this is all for you. Well, and a little for me," Eddie admitted, taking two forks out of the basket. "It seemed like…I don't know, all this fuss is more for the country than for you. You're going to have to spend the whole time vowing or praying or glad-handing. So this is a cake of your very own. Nothing better than cake for breakfast."

"Thank you, Eddie," Gregory said, accepting one of the forks and taking a corner off neatly. "Lord, that's good," he added, around the first mouthful. It was a chocolate cake with what tasted like pomegranate filling between its two layers, and some kind of extra-rich frosting.

"Yeah, you all make some pretty decent cakes," Eddie said, taking a lump of frosting from the other side. "I'm glad you like it."

"I do. The coronation will be fun, but…well, I suppose in the way being married is fun," Gregory said. "The day is all about the person, of course, the king – I mean I will be the one the cameras are on all day. But everything will happen around me. I'm a bit at the whim of fate at that point."

"Well, now that I know you don't have a sacred orb of rule, I might have to make one out of a water balloon and really liven up the coronation," Eddie said. Gregory laughed, taking another bite of cake.

"You wouldn't really," he said.

"No. I'm irreverent but I'm not mean. Anyway, I won't have the time. Once you sit down, I stand up and start moving."

"Hm." Gregory considered it – all of it, really. The warmth of the truck's tailgate under them, the chocolate and pomegranate, the bright blue of the water below, the shadow of the palace behind them. It was wonderful; it was *comfortable* in a way little in his life ever was. Very tempting, in some ways.

"Who was the best king?" Eddie asked, helping himself to more cake. "Like, in all of the history of the country, which king was the greatest? Who is Askazer-Shivadlakia's King Arthur?"

"Gilles Roman y Askaz," Gregory said promptly. "He was the king who united Shivadlakia and Askaz and made it stick. Tradition says he's actually an ancestor of Alanna's but we've never bothered to verify it."

"I'm picturing Alanna in armor on a horse and I'm not hating the visual," Eddie said.

"I think he did do some conquering in his youth and he was a famous swordsman, but he united the two nations through diplomacy and charm. He married a Shivadh princess."

"Slay a dragon first?" Eddie asked, grinning.

"Sadly for us, no. There's an epic about him on a wolf hunt, but it's declasse at this point, since we like wolves and maintain a conservation program for them." Gregory offered Eddie the rest of the cake, setting his fork aside. "He already had two mistresses – "

"Oho!" Eddie cackled.

"It was a *long time ago*," Gregory retorted. "Anyway, he was out riding the border of Askaz, and oral history tells us he was trying to think of a way to unite the sea-bordered Shivadlakia with his own inland kingdom, because he knew with unfettered access to a harbor his merchants would be unstoppable. He was considering invading when he saw a beautiful woman bow-hunting a deer. She shot the deer but it leapt, and it fell on his side of the border. She shouted at him not to touch it because it was hers, he shouted back it was on his land and that was poaching, and she got so angry she pulled him off his horse and tried to take a swing."

"Love at first sight," Eddie said.

"For him, it was. He supposedly wrote in a letter to someone or other that he knew instantly that she was his…well, the old language isn't precise when it comes to being translated into English, but roughly, he knew she was his soulmate."

Eddie digested this, along with some cake, pondering it. "What happened to the deer?" he asked finally.

"That's what you want to know?"

"Perfectly good venison going to waste. I hope he let her take it or he's no gentleman."

Gregory grinned. "He did. More or less. While she was butchering it he built a fire and offered to cook some, because it meant she'd hang around a little longer while he figured out who she was and how to get her to come meet him again."

"So he cooked his love a meal?" Eddie beamed. "My kind of story, Greg."

"More than you know. There's an apocryphal version that I've always been fond of, which says it was the princess's brother that shot the deer and got into a fight with him over it, and he married her to stay close to him," Gregory said. "It is historically confirmed that the queen's brother was a close advisor to the royal family for their entire reign."

"Close advisor," Eddie said, eyebrows waggling.

"Well, exactly."

"No shit!"

"They're the reason the country has a...relaxed attitude about that kind of thing. At least, that's my theory. I can thank Gilles Roman y Askaz for my stellar reputation despite my many handsome boyfriends," Gregory said, grinning sidelong at him. "I'm surprised you didn't come across at least one version in all your folk research, but it's not a story we tell often to outsiders. Might have to change that when I'm king, maybe commission a play from the national theatre."

"Well, as long as it's in a park, I'll come watch it," Eddie said.

"That'd be nice. But you're leaving soon – we'll have to schedule it for some future visit."

"I could leave soon," Eddie said, looking out over the harbor. "Or I could stay a little while longer."

Gregory tilted his head. "After the banquet, you mean? I assumed you'd have a lot to do, given all your plans."

"Sure. But I could do them all here." Eddie turned to him. "Especially if the network wanted to cancel me, I'd really have no good reason to go back to the US. I'm several hours away from my biggest demographic here, so I could do pretty much what I wanted without having to give a damn about my numbers. I said I wouldn't cheapen your coronation by making it about me, and I meant that, but a week or two after..." he shrugged. "I think...I know what I said a couple of weeks ago and I *know* it's only been a couple of weeks, but I think there's something here worth staying for. Isn't there?"

Gregory knew what he was asking, and it made him lightheaded, but the little anchor deep inside him, the one that was preparing to be king, held him back.

"The problem," he said slowly, "is that it would be...nice, and convenient, and maybe even as good and functional as you think – but it would be a solution to a problem, and I don't want to make you that."

"What, good and functional?" Eddie asked lightly.

"A solution," Gregory said. "You're a person."

"I like solving problems," Eddie pointed out. "I don't mind it."

"I'm worried that would change," Gregory replied. "My life, Eddie – it's not my own. It belongs to the country. Anyone who serves the country has to feel the same, and you've only just finished telling me about how you can finally do just as you like. I wouldn't ruin that for you, not for anything."

Eddie seemed to be considering this, with none of his usual blithe disregard for reality.

"I suppose I see what you mean," he said at last. "And we've had the conversation about...sacrifice."

"So you understand," Gregory said, relieved, because honestly if Eddie had tried to argue...

"I do. Not sure I completely agree, but I understand," he said. "And...at least this way it's settled. Come on, let's get going," he added, hopping down and heading for the door of the truck. "Busy day ahead."

"You're all right, though," Gregory said, a half-question, as he started the truck up again.

"Sure," Eddie replied, his smile sunny and, as far as Gregory could tell, real. "I'm the one who said this could just be fun. And it has been, so no regrets," he added, and kissed Gregory on the cheek before settling back on his side of the truck.

THE CORONATION DAY OF HIS MAJESTY KING GREGORY III

EDDIE, STANDING IN the kitchen in his most comfortable shoes and his tallest chef's hat, clapped his hands for attention. Simon, three sous chefs, and innumerable prep chefs and waiters all looked up from where they were setting up their stations.

"Greetings, patriotic comrades," he announced, and they laughed lightly. "Welcome to zero day. In less than twelve hours we will be feeding the nobility of Askazer-Shivadlakia – "

He waited for the applause over his flawless pronunciation to die down.

" – as well as diplomats, politicians, industrialists, rich fuckwits, and other powerful people from powerful places," he said. "If you have ever brought your A-game, I need it today. Don't think about the time limit or what's going on in the palace, just think about making the absolute best, most impressive food you can make. Nobody is getting fired for screwing up today, so if you do screw up you need to tell me as soon as possible so I can fix it. Is there anyone who does not know what they're doing?"

He held up his own hand, to a sprinkling of laughter.

"Is there anyone who has a question or a problem?"

Silence.

"In that case, get going," Eddie said, clapping Simon on the back. "Battle stations – let's show 'em what we're made of!"

Coronations didn't come around very often, which Gregory supposed was probably for the best. He hadn't been born yet when his father was crowned. He'd been to one or two in other countries during his childhood, but he'd generally been given a toy to play with quietly while his mother and father paid attention to the ceremony. He'd been through portions of his own crowning in rehearsal but not the whole thing at once, and he didn't realize how dull some parts were.

It opened with a reading of the history of the monarchy, which was mostly boring because Gregory already knew it and also they didn't keep any of the interesting trivia in. To keep his mind occupied, he counted fancy hats in the audience and tried to decide which, if any, would be likely to become a meme; then he tried valiantly to put a name to every face he could see, and awarded himself about a 75% success rate. He identified at least one Photogram influencer who had managed somehow to sneak in, but before he could find a way to notify anyone, the sergeant at arms had noticed and quietly taken her phone away. She looked annoyed until Gregory caught her eye and winked at her, which settled her down and made her blush a little.

He returned his attention to the reading just in time for the master of ceremonies to reach the end of the recitation.

"King Michaelis I, son of King Jason I the Interloper," the man intoned, filling the word *interloper* with amused irony. Most of the population, Dad included, thought it was hugely funny that Granddad, the duly elected king, was called an interloper. That's what you got for interrupting a few centuries of hereditary rule, Dad said. "Today, we crown King Gregory III, son of King Michaelis I and Miranda, Queen of Askazer-Shivadlakia, duly elected by ballot of the will of the people of Askazer-Shivadlakia."

First time bowing; Gregory stood, bowed, swooped his robes a little to situate them more comfortably, and sat back again. There was polite applause.

His father, in a special audience alcove where very few other than Gregory could see him, rolled his eyes. It was going to be a long day.

Still, there were moments when Gregory felt a strange spark, a sense of unreality that this was happening. It was almost supernatural. In rehearsal, stuff like kneeling to accept the ceremonial sword, wrapped in a length of fishing-boat hawser, had seemed silly at best. Now there was the hush of a room of witnesses, and the hairs on his arms stood on end as he took the sword.

He did struggle to stay awake during some of the singing, which was operatic and not really his bag. And then, the crown was finally placed on his head...

Well, he was probably just tired, and overwhelmed from the long day. It was just that when he felt it settle over his hair, a crown his father and grandfather and at least a few of his mother's ancestors had worn, he felt like there was a sudden tether in his chest, tying him to his country, rooting him as part of the land. He understood, if only fleetingly, old legends about the king's spiritual communion with the people.

Then the kneeling pages were rising and the master of ceremonies was coming around from crowning him to shake his hand, and people were taking pictures and beginning to stand to process out from the very humid throne room. Gregory stood, waiting by custom until the last of the witnesses had left. Michaelis, second-to-last out, stopped to give him a brief hug and whisper a reassurance in his ear before leaving.

"And now I'm king," Gregory III murmured to himself, before gently shedding the official robe of office on the throne and walking to the doorway, where Alanna was standing with his uniform jacket.

"Good job," she said, helping him into the jacket and smoothing it across his shoulders.

"I do sit *and* bow like an absolute champion," he replied. She beamed.

"Ready to party till dawn?"

"Is that a coffee?" he asked, blindsided as she produced a

covered cup from a little table nearby.

"Cold brew, sugar, milk," she said, and he gulped it greedily. "Thought you could use a pick-me-up."

"Thank goodness. Do I have three minutes for the restroom?"

She nodded and took the cup back from him as he dashed across the hall. By the time he emerged, Jerry had joined her. He was wearing a magnificent floor-length orange evening gown with blue trim, and orange opera gloves to match.

"Come on, come on, everyone's in the garden," Jerry said, leading him towards the party. "It looks amazing, Greg. Sire," he added impudently.

"So do you. Out to make every tabloid front page tomorrow morning?" Gregory asked, gesturing at the gown.

"Do you like it? Figured it was about time I did something unexpected, and it takes a little heat off you."

"Thank you. It does suit you," Gregory agreed. "By the way, Alanna says I need to make you my vizier. What did you do to get made vizier?"

"Never you mind. Is there a ceremony?"

"Not that I know of, but I'm sure you can invent one. Make yourself up a robe and some kind of medallion of office while you're at it," Gregory answered, and stepped through the doorway into a kind of warm fantasy world.

The garden had been filled with tables covered with checked tablecloths and a basket on each, just as Eddie had described. Overhead, paper lanterns were hung from wooden poles, waiting to be lit when it was dark out. There were croquet wickets set up at the far end, past the small stage for the musicians and a temporary parquet floor that had been installed for dancing. People were finding their seats, poking curiously at the baskets, and making small talk with one another, enjoying the warm afternoon. A traditional Shivadh folk quartet was tuning up on the stage.

The nearest people noticed Gregory emerge and began to clap; the applause rippled outward, and Gregory smiled deprecatingly and gave a wave, the same wave his father often gave at state events. Jerry subtly broke a path for them as Alanna guided him to the king's table, where Michaelis, Jerry, Jerry's mother, Alanna's grandparents, and a handful of diplomats were seating themselves. The diplomats looked aghast at Jerry, but the nobility didn't even bother batting an eye.

"Crown's crooked," Michaelis said, reaching out to Gregory to straighten it. "There. Can't look disreputable for at least another few hours."

"Thanks," Gregory said distractedly, seating himself. Around them, everyone else took their seats too. There was what felt like an indrawn breath, and then from seeming nowhere an army of waitstaff appeared, thermoses in hand, laying bowls before the assembled guests to serve out the hot soup and cold potato salad. People began to eat hungrily, chattering to each other about the weather, the coronation, the food. Gregory felt he should probably make the speech he'd prepared, but the noise level was rising...

Jerry, catching his eye, stood up and began tapping his spoon against his glass, calling for quiet. Voices settled, and even the clink of spoons in bowls stopped.

"Attention everyone! As your new grand vizier to the king, allow me to introduce to you King Gregory III, who has some notes prepared," he said, bowing at Gregory, who stood and nodded back.

"Thank you, Gerald," he said, which drew a face from Jerry. "I promise to be brief. Gathered dignitaries, friends, allies, and I'm sure one or two spies..."

The crowd laughed on cue, thank goodness.

"I would like to thank you all for attending the coronation today," he said. "I am so pleased and proud to represent the third generation of my family to rule by popular acclaim. I hope I will rule as wisely – and as long – as my father," he added, nodding at Michaelis, who acknowledged it with a wave.

"Ruling a kingdom is an incredibly complex task, and my ministers and staff have been very patient with me," he continued. "Tomorrow we begin a long job of work, maintaining the peace and prosperity the country owes to its people. All I can do is keep a hand on the rudder. I trust you all to tell me if we're steering into rough waters."

He took a breath, because it seemed difficult to catch it. "In the meantime, we are grateful for your ongoing support. I would be remiss not to credit our dear Alanna, who was instrumental in planning all of today; my father, King Emeritus Michaelis – " he paused for applause, and his father looked faintly embarrassed but nodded regally, "– and all of the palace staff, who have been very tolerant of the disruption to our normally quiet life. I hope you also enjoy the wonderful picnic meal, cooked by our very popular and very...boisterous friend, Mr. Eddie Rambler, and our palace chef of many years, Simon LeFevre."

He saw movement out of the corner of his eye; Simon giving a little wave, standing next to Eddie at the edge of the picnic ground, both in chef's whites pristine enough they must have changed for the feast.

"As I expect any member of the palace to do, Alanna and my father, our staff and friends, have also often reminded me of my responsibility to serve the country first, to preserve the best of our traditions, and to maintain a sense of awe at the honor I've been given," he said. "Please enjoy the food, the dancing to come, and the company of one another in this spirit: that today we celebrate not only a coronation but a long tradition of excellence in our small but proud nation."

He sat down amid cheers and applause, and a renewed interest in the food; Michaelis leaned over and said, "A good speech. Glad you kept it short."

"Me too," Gregory replied with a grin. "Thank you, father."

"I do wonder, though," Michaelis said, as he started on the mushroom soup.

"Oh? About what?" Gregory asked.

"Well, your mother and I raised you to serve the country and consider the needs of others, given how fortunate we've been," Michaelis said. "Lessons you took to heart, obviously. And all this talk of duty to country is fine and admirable."

"But?" Gregory asked, curious as to where this was going.

"But I wonder if I forgot to tell you that a king should also be happy," Michaelis said.

"I wouldn't have taken the job if I didn't love it. Of course I'm happy," Gregory assured him. "Starving, but happy."

"Good. Eat up now. People will want to come bend your ear soon enough," Michaelis said. "Gerald!"

"Uncle?" Jerry asked.

"Do your best to keep publicity hounds and that woman who snuck in from the internet away from Gregory for a bit, would you?"

Jerry laughed. "That woman from the internet has more followers than the population of the country, but I'll do my best."

"Make sure she gets her phone back, it can't harm anyone at this point," Gregory added. "Find her somewhere to sit, tell her the king apologizes for the inconvenience, and get her to share any flattering photos she may have managed to take."

Jerry laughed. "On it, boss," he said, and took a glass of wine and a sandwich with him as he wandered off.

"Don't let him give her your phone number, you'll never hear the end of it," Michaelis said.

"I doubt he'll remember past *go talk to the pretty woman from the internet*," Gregory replied. He craned his head around to see if Eddie was still there, but he'd disappeared, probably back into the kitchen with Simon. Michaelis followed his gaze.

"The staff will look after themselves," his father said. "And they have outdone themselves on this soup, so let's not make their work meaningless by letting it get cold."

Gregory smiled and bent to his dinner. "Right you are, Dad."

Eddie set up the camera on a tiny portable tripod, perched gently on a sculpted topiary bush with a flat top. He checked the stability and then the angle, adjusting it so that the just-lit lanterns and a small sliver of the party was visible behind him. Finally, he pressed the record button, pulling his hat off.

"I don't mind telling everyone, I am worn out," he said, giving them a wide grin to show it was a good tired. "Everything went off without a hitch, though – or at least with only the normal number of hitches. I know you all come here for the real talk that I don't always have time for on *Truly Tasty*, so this is your semi-annual reminder that screwups in a kitchen are normal, and the mark of a good chef is in how you handle the unexpected. But today we had very few!"

He held up a hand, gesturing to the party going on behind him. "For all my followers in-country, congratulations on your new king! He did great today and I'm sure he'll rule wisely. They're partying until dawn and so should you. For the rest of my followers, it's like mid-morning where most of you are, I think? Maybe don't start drinking until you get off work. I was gonna go grab a cocktail myself, but I think I'm ready for bed. My work here is done, honestly. All except the dishes, anyway, and someone else is being paid to wash those."

He laughed, mopping his forehead with the edge of his hat.

"I was thinking about staying a few extra days but I traveled light coming here, so it's easy enough to pick up and go – you know me, I always have places to go, stuff to do, new food to eat. So tomorrow morning I'll probably be off on a new adventure!"

Behind him, the music struck up, which he took as a cue to wrap – his followers didn't like music or other noise under his videos, generally, unless it was kitchen noises.

"You all got a great place here," he said. "I know my motto's always been about keeping it new, but there's something to be said for age – newness is about reinvention, reimagination, not necessarily never getting to touch any history. You can't change something if you don't understand it, after all. Anyway, I'm gonna miss this place. Might make it back here someday soon though! I'd like to do a show that brings people a real taste of the region. Next time you see me I might be on a train, or in Paris, or maybe back in Messina – but for now this is Eddie Rambler, reminding you to keep it new, and signing off."

He stopped the recording, taking his phone off the tripod and settling onto a decorative bench that was probably older than America, and definitely older than he was, to do a few minor edits. There was the sound of a throat clearing, and he looked up, startled.

"I didn't want to interrupt your recording," King Michaelis – ex-king? Was it really King Emeritus? He should have looked up what you call a former king – stood nearby, hands in the pockets of his sober black uniform.

"Your Retired Majesty," Eddie said. "Give me thirty seconds and I'll check with the internet what I'm supposed to call you."

Michaelis gave him a tired smile. "Technically still Your Majesty, but that will become confusing, I suspect. For direct address, I find 'Your Grace' rarely goes amiss. Vague enough not to break protocol, strange enough it's probably an honor to be called it."

"Well, Your Grace, what can I do for you? Sneaking off for a smoke?" Eddie asked, feeling a little daring.

"I was coming to find you, actually," he said.

"Oh, no – is something wrong – "

"No, nothing to worry about," Michaelis said quickly. "It's a great success, in fact. Many, many drunk people."

Eddie smiled. "How's the king?"

"He's holding up. I wanted to speak to you about him, actually. May I sit?"

"It's your bench, technically," Eddie said, gesturing to the other half of it, turning to face him as the former king settled himself. Michaelis held his hands between his knees, leaning forward, seemingly in thought.

"I'm not sure, when Gregory was born, that we wanted him to be king," he said slowly. "His mother was ambivalent about the nobility, having come from it, and we both knew by then that it could be stressful. Difficult. You've seen, I think, what Gregory's been up to since you arrived."

"Seems like a lot of work, but he likes it," Eddie ventured.

"He does, thank goodness. I think the only reason I trust it's his choice is that he so clearly saw how conflicted we were over the idea. He'll be a good king as long as he keeps his wits about him." Michaelis inhaled, let out the breath, then breathed in to speak again. "I made an error with him, though. I think I made him think that it was all or nothing, that service to the crown meant one couldn't have things for oneself. I thought he'd see that he and his mother were precious to me for reasons having nothing to do with her being the queen or him being my heir. But before the coronation – a few months ago – I told him he needed to find a partner. It's an important role in our government, the…well, traditionally the queen, but that's a loaded word when one's son prefers men."

Eddie couldn't help himself; he snickered. Michaelis glanced at him and nodded.

"Just so," he agreed. "Perhaps I put too much pressure on him. And perhaps the affair you've been having with my son really is just a last fling before he takes on all this responsibility."

That dropped the smile off Eddie's face. "We didn't know you knew."

"I didn't rule a country for decades by being unobservant," Michaelis replied. "I'm not angry. Even if I were, what would I do about it? You're both grown men. I'm just telling you I know, and also that if…if it is more, then you, and I, and Gregory all have a significant problem."

Eddie tilted his head. "Which is?"

"He clearly thinks he needs to marry someone appropriate. Someone of the blood, or at the least someone who can help him rule. Perhaps he thinks that isn't you, and perhaps it isn't, but…"

"Ah," Eddie said. Michaelis gave him a curious look. "That's not it, but you're close."

"Do tell."

"He said I was a solution to a problem," Eddie said. Michaelis nodded. "But he also said I was a person, and he wasn't going to treat me like I wasn't."

"Well." Michaelis considered this. "That is both the smartest and stupidest thing he's said since the puffin incident."

"The…puffin…?"

"I'll let him tell you that one – or better yet, ask Alanna," Michaelis said. "I suppose what I'd like to know is…are you? Or could you be?"

"A solution?" Eddie shrugged. "Who knows? I like him. I like him enough I asked to stay, and I respect him enough that when he said no, I agreed. Do I think it would be weird and cool to be – " he grinned at Michaelis, " – *queen* of a country? Sure. It's soon to know exactly how I feel about your son, but I love this place. I could see a life here. But it's all still new and shiny to me, and he's smart not to ask on those terms."

"But on other terms, you might stay. Just to see," Michaelis said slowly.

"I'd have to wrap up some business in America and I don't know how good your spies are, but I'm about to very publicly come out as bisexual, which could draw attention Greg doesn't want if I do stay. But sure, if I had a reason that wasn't about the king, I wouldn't mind."

Michaelis nodded. "When were you planning to go?"

"Tomorrow, early."

"Ah. There's a little more broken heart there than evident?"

Eddie blinked at him. "Yeah, maybe."

"Well, before you go, speak to Alanna," Michaelis said. "She may have some final business for you."

Eddie nodded, puzzled and confused but also well aware that something momentous was happening. "Thank you. I'll do that."

Michaelis nodded and stood, dusting down his trousers. "Goodnight, Chef."

"Goodnight, Your Grace."

Michaelis snorted, heading back towards the party, and Eddie sat on the bench for a good five minutes, trying to work out what exactly had just happened, before he came to his senses. He looked down at his phone, pushed the post button on Photogram to send the video he'd filmed before the king arrived, and then stood up, stretching, and went to bed.

FIRST DAY OF
THE REIGN OF HIS MAJESTY
KING GREGORY III

G REGORY HAD GIVEN the staff the day off after the coronation, which was the only rational thing to do. Most of them had worked for days leading up to the coronation and some had worked until dawn the night before, serving at the party. Giving the administrative staff the day off meant they could give most of the kitchen staff the day off as well.

He'd told Simon he should take the day, but he doubted Simon had listened, and the smell from the kitchen told him he was right. He popped his head in to find Simon making crepes at the stove.

"Good morning, Sire," Simon said with a small grin.

"I'm going to have to get used to that. Morning," Gregory yawned, already missing Eddie's noisy presence in the kitchen most mornings. Better this way, but...he'd probably feel the absence for a while.

"There are crepes also in the dining room, and fillings to put into them. Leftovers from last night, mostly, but I've cooked the last of the fruit in a sugar syrup, there are mushrooms sauteed with shallots, and the potato salad is always better the second day, you know."

"Surprised there's any left."

"A very popular dish," Simon agreed. "Any requests?"

Privately he wondered if there were any chicken wings

available, but that was just silly nostalgia.

"No, I'll browse the dining room," he said. "Coffee?"

"In the carafe."

"Dad?"

"Awake and scheming. Being king always kept him out of trouble," Simon observed.

"I'll do my best to find him a hobby," Gregory replied. "I'll be in the dining room if anyone comes looking."

Simon acknowledged him with a wave as he left, sleepily ambling his way to the dining room. When he was about ten feet away he heard Alanna's voice, slightly raised, vigorously defending...thick-cut bacon?

" – supposed to have texture," she was saying, her voice strident. "You're supposed to really experience it."

"Flavor is an experience," said another voice, and Gregory stopped, startled. "When you slice it thinly, the fat renders out – "

"Exactly! The fat's supposed to be there!" Alanna argued.

Gregory hurried forward and then stopped again in the doorway, perplexed by the scene in front of him.

Michaelis was sitting at the dining table as usual, quietly eating a crepe stuffed with fruit, a little bowl of oatmeal at his elbow. Alanna was sitting near him, tablet discarded on the table, hands gesturing as she vigorously defended traditional Askazer bacon, which had more in common with pork belly than American breakfast meat. She was turned slightly so that she faced...

Eddie, who was sitting next to her and apparently arguing with her for the benefit of his camera, which was filming the whole thing from the far side of the table.

Eddie's back was to him and blocking Alanna's line of sight to the doorway, but Michaelis had a clear view and noticed Gregory immediately.

"Sire," he drawled.

Alanna's head shot up in surprise; Eddie turned, but not to Gregory. Instead he reached out and ended the camera recording before twisting around.

"Eddie," Gregory said, realizing how obvious he sounded even as he said it.

"Way to interrupt filming, Your Majesty," Eddie replied. "That was great though," he added to Alanna. "We can continue discussing how wrong you are later."

"I'm not wrong!" Alanna insisted.

"She has strong feelings about pork," Eddie told Gregory.

"Better her than me, I guess, I don't eat it," Gregory said. "What are you doing here?"

"Eatin' breakfast," Eddie said. "Starting trouble. The usual."

"He's good at both," Michaelis put in.

"I thought you were leaving," Gregory said.

Eddie chuckled. "Saw my video, huh?"

Gregory held up his phone. "Photogram sends me a little notice when you post."

"Plans changed," Eddie said. "Just waiting for my PR guys back in the states to wake up before I run this up their flagpole, but engagement's been off the charts since I got here and Alanna says once they fixed the tourism website they started getting tons of interest. In the next six months they expect tourism's gonna double – overseas tourism might even triple."

"…and?" Gregory asked, bewildered, finally coming into the room to sit down. Michaelis pushed a bowl of potato salad towards him gently.

"And that means that the communications team needs some help," Alanna said. "We're hiring Eddie."

"I'm going to make a bunch of videos on like…local culture," Eddie said. "You know, where to get the best coffee, how to talk to the locals, the best way to get the train here from Paris, that kind of thing. Where to rent bicycles and where to ride them. Oh! And how the surfing is. Excited to try that."

"I thought you were going to start a cooking show," Gregory replied.

"I could, but I can do that anywhere I've got a clean corner of a kitchen to cook in," Eddie said. "I can cook here as well as anywhere."

"Here, in Askazer-Shivadlakia?"

"Well, I finally learned how to pronounce it," Eddie said, as Simon came in with a fresh plate of crepes. "You'll help, Simon, won't you?"

"I'd like a raise," Simon told Gregory.

"Probably due," Gregory agreed, turning back to Eddie.

"Anyway I need to file a bunch of tax stuff, but there was no reason not to get started immediately, so I asked Alanna for her thoughts and she said Americans do bacon wrong, which is a hill I was surprised to find I would die on," Eddie said.

"Keep eating Askazer bacon and you probably will," Gregory replied, deciding that whatever was going on, it was probably best to just lean in. He spooned some potato salad into a crepe and took a bite. Eddie turned to Alanna and gestured at Gregory as if to say, *See? The king agrees with me.*

"Oh, like I've never told him to his face he's wrong and stupid before," Alanna sniffed. "Sire, I'm going to hire this man but I'd like it recorded that he's wrong about bacon."

"Keep me out of it," Gregory said. "He's your problem now."

"I strongly doubt that," Michaelis murmured, and Gregory and Alanna both looked at him in surprise. Eddie seemed smug. Michaelis, finishing his oatmeal, stood and set his napkin aside, bending to rest a hand on Gregory's shoulder.

"Be happy, sire," he said, turning to leave. "And good luck!" he called from the hallway.

"Does he….?" Gregory pointed after his father, but he was looking at Eddie.

"Apparently we've been 'obvious'," Eddie said, employing

airquotes. Then, possibly just to annoy him, he added, "And he thinks a good 'work life balance' is 'important'."

"So I'm coming to understand," Gregory admitted.

"Look, nothing's set in stone," Eddie said. "But it wouldn't be awful if we decided to consider the possibility. I'm extremely charming and functional once you get to know me."

"Sure, that's what they all say," Gregory replied.

"Your dad seems to have pulled a u-turn on me from where he was a few weeks ago, anyhow," Eddie offered.

"He has very strong opinions."

"Yeah, that definitely doesn't run in the family," Alanna put in, gathering up her tablet. "I'm going to tactfully withdraw and let you two figure this out," she announced. "I'll have your nine o'clock briefing ready, Greg, but I can tell you it's going to be a blank page because anyone who didn't take the day is hungover or still drunk."

"Good, I suspect I'll need some time," Gregory replied, not looking away from Eddie as Alanna left. They were quiet for a few seconds, Eddie patiently waiting for something, Gregory sorting his thoughts.

"You understand," he said slowly, "you will need a royal visa to remain in-country and work for the palace. The normal visas generally take several weeks and if you want to make official content for royal communications, we'll have to fast-track that."

"Well, I know a guy," Eddie pointed out.

"And if you hold a royal exception visa, you represent the royal family," Gregory continued thoughtfully. "That's a heavy responsibility, Eddie. I'd want to personally teach you what you needed to know. And everyone here knows everything about the royal family, so our attentions towards you won't go unremarked."

"I think I'll survive," Eddie said quietly.

"If you, say, wanted to have dinner with me. Or go bowfishing at the lodge. People might talk."

"I'm ready to let 'em if you are," Eddie said.

"Yes. I suppose I am, actually," Gregory replied. Eddie reached out and tugged Gregory's wrist, pulling him out of his seat and into Eddie's lap, which was undignified, but also felt right. The way the coronation had. Like a puzzle piece settling into place, or a tether being tied.

"I have an idea for a coming-out video but it's gonna require multiple filming locations and some special effects," Eddie said, his face serious. "There may be some extremely tacky choreography. I can't promise good taste."

"Why start now?" Gregory asked, and Eddie cracked up laughing. Gregory leaned down to kiss him, fingers threading through Eddie's wild hair, eventually settling in the bright pink collar of his loud flower-print shirt.

EPILOGUE:
THE CORONATION ANNIVERSARY BALL
OF GREGORY III

EDDIE CHECKED HIS tie and waistcoat one final time, turned to his king, and said, "Tasty?"

Gregory, adjusting his collar in the mirror, rolled his eyes and nodded. Eddie shot him a grin.

"I'm in very nice black evening wear," Eddie said, wrapping his arms around Gregory from behind. Gregory took the opportunity to fix Eddie's cufflinks. "The flower pattern on the waistcoat is extremely traditional, the tailor said so."

"After you asked him what the loudest possible print you could get away with was," Gregory pointed out.

"You love it."

"I am, in fact, extremely fond of your loudness," Gregory agreed. "It's a real failure of character on my part, everyone says so."

Eddie kissed his neck and released him, hopping up to sit on the low table in the dressing room. "You ready for tonight?"

"Sure. What's not to enjoy? It's the one year anniversary of the coronation, the party will be mellow, and you'll be there."

"As your boyfriend for the first time."

"Nonsense," Gregory said. "Everyone knows we've been dating. You've been at every state event I could drag you to. This is just a formality, introducing you as a companion to the king. I'd have done it sooner if you asked."

"No reason to. Like you said, everyone knew. Nice to make it official, though," Eddie said, beaming. "And I have to say, I love all the fuss. I have never met anyone who likes drama as much as the whole population of Askazer-Shivadlakia."

"It's not drama, it's pageantry."

"I'm sure they love drama too. Bet you if we staged a fight, the entire country would be up in arms. You could start a civil war."

"The country was united centuries ago. If I tear it apart because I had a fight with my boyfriend, I'll never live it down," Gregory told him. "Now, you remember about the processional?"

Eddie nodded. "It's not like I haven't seen one before. You're called and you process into the ballroom, then your father and the family, then heads of Parliament. The royal dates come after. Fun to be with them instead of waiting for you to arrive this time."

"But you'll be first, so you'll need to listen sharp for your name."

"Mr. Eddie Rambler!" Eddie boomed.

"Well, Edward, but yes," Gregory said. There was a strangely tense pause. "Eddie?"

"When I gave the announcer the little card with my name, I wrote Eddie on it," Eddie said. "Is that okay?"

"It's a formal announcement. They'll use your legal name regardless of what's on the card."

Eddie frowned. "But they'll just assume it's Edward, right?"

"Generally they make a note when they do the background check, but in your case they probably just looked up your pay stub from…" Gregory trailed off, because Eddie's eyes kept getting bigger. "Your legal name *is* Edward Rambler, isn't it?"

"Uh, the Rambler part's right," Eddie said.

"Your name's not Edward?" Gregory asked. "We've been dating for a year. Simon told me your name was Edward. My father's been calling you Edward."

"Look, it's not that I don't like my name," Eddie said. "Or that I have a criminal past or something. Well, I do, but not like that. I just never think about it until it's already awkward."

"Eddie, what on Earth is your name?" Gregory demanded, in his best royal tone.

"In my defense, it's easier than Askazer-Shivadlakia," Eddie said.

"MR. THEOPHILE RAMBLER AND LADY ALANNA DASKAZ!" a voice called, and Eddie did his best to proceed forward with dignity.

Technically, Alanna should have gone into the ballroom with the royal cousins, following Gregory. She was high enough born, and she was very evidently one of the King's favorite people. But tonight she was on the arm of a visiting diplomat who was going in with the heads of Parliament, so she was relegated to the Very Important Dates part of the processional.

"I cannot believe your name is Theophile," she said, as she and Eddie descended the stairs to the ballroom. "How did you get Eddie from Theophile?"

"My parents are hippies with real weird theology," Eddie said around a smile for the cameras. "Everyone called me Ted but one of my brothers couldn't say his Ts, so everyone started calling me Ed. Eddie is just more TV-friendly."

"I would have given you so much endless flak for being named Theophile, but that's actually very sweet so now I can't," Alanna said.

"You are reacting way more maturely than Gregory," Eddie told her, handing her off to her adoring diplomat and making his way to the king's side, in the line to receive their guests.

"I don't even know who you are," Gregory said, eyes still

forward as Eddie joined him.

"That's not what you said last night," Eddie answered. Gregory's lips twitched.

"Where were you last night? Because I was in bed with some guy named Theophile."

"Alanna thinks it's a very nice name," Eddie said.

"When we were both six I watched Alanna eat a ladybug," Gregory replied.

"Insect protein is the food of the future."

"Sweet nothings," Gregory sighed, as the procession ended. There was a blast of fanfare, and a string quartet struck up what Eddie had come to categorize as Royal Family Muzak: light enough that it didn't interrupt conversation, constant enough to be pleasant background noise. Later there would be waltzing, which in this particular royal family always sounded like a threat. Eddie was looking forward to it; this was his first official outing as Gregory's date, where before he'd always attended these things as a guest of the palace.

Usually he took the first dance with Gregory, had a few interesting conversations, and then slipped away while Gregory still had two or three hours of politics ahead of him. It wasn't that he especially minded the politics, but he didn't want to be a distraction, and he liked to take a stroll on the grounds and listen to the party from a distance before heading to bed. Tonight, however, something a little different was on the menu.

"I should demand a traditional Shivadh name," he said to Gregory, as a line formed for people to greet the king.

"So good to see you," Gregory said to a visiting Italian dignitary of some kind, and then to Eddie, "I don't even have a traditional Shivadh name. They tend to be quite complicated."

"Welcome! Man, that jacket looks great on you," Eddie said to the Italian, who beamed at him. "I bet I could rock a Shivadh name. Can't be more obnoxious to say than Theophile."

"Beloved Theophile, I am begging you to focus," Gregory

said, and Eddie shot him a grin before composing himself to be as proper as he knew how to be.

Alanna found Jerry hiding in a corner with a cocktail, which was impressive considering they were only serving wine at the ball. She raised an eyebrow at it; he looked unrepentant and offered her a sip.

"No, I'm still on the clock," she told him, leaning against the wall next to him, watching the reception line as the last of the visitors met the king. "Squiring the diplomat and keeping an eye on Gregory for signs of panic."

"As if Greg ever panics at these things. Don't know how he does it."

"I think he likes it. Normally you do too," she pointed out. "Why are you pretending you're not hiding behind a decorative ficus?"

"Do you remember the girl I dated my last year in boarding school?" he asked.

"I remember the grievous bodily harm she threatened you with."

"She's here with her successful husband and their adorable young child and I'm pretending to be petty about it," he said.

"Pretending," she replied skeptically.

"I thought it would make her feel good, and also it means if she still wants to kill me she can't get close enough," he said.

"Well, it's one way to live," she replied. She watched as Gregory, his duties done, took a few steps back and signaled the string quartet to strike up dancing music.

"Theophile looks thrilled to be doing the most boring job on the planet," Jerry said.

"I can't believe that's his name." Alanna shook her head.

"I can, he looks like a Theophile. I've always thought so,"

Jerry said, mock-serious. Alanna thumped him on the arm.

"Be nice. It's about to be a rollercoaster of an evening," she said.

"What? Why? Did you invite my ex to come say hello?"

"Just wait for it," Alanna told him.

"Still mad at me?" Eddie asked, as he and Gregory took the floor for the first waltz. He was happy to take the formal black gloves off, but after shaking a million hands in the reception line, he was prepared to admit he understood why the royal uniform included them.

"I'm not mad," Gregory told him, sliding an arm around his waist. "This is actually very funny. You'll find out why in about two minutes."

"What happens in two minutes?" Eddie asked. "Do they call my name again for some reason?"

"No," Gregory said, as the music began. "Don't worry about it."

"You're lucky I'm extremely laid back and actually won't," Eddie said.

"I do think I've had good luck," Gregory told him. "I didn't expect you'd tolerate this end of the business so well, Eddie."

"What, the parties? Love a party, you know me."

"I'm only saying, it's difficult to truly know what you're signing on for, dating the king," Gregory said. "I didn't think you really knew what a relationship with me would mean."

"Oh, I absolutely didn't, the last year has been buck wild," Eddie said. "I love both you and this country, but I had no idea what I was getting into."

"You don't regret it, I hope."

"Not for a second," Eddie told him.

"I have to admit, I didn't think you'd be willing to stay in

Askazer-Shivadlakia for months on end, let alone consider a life here."

Eddie gave him a warm grin. "Listen, I love America too, but it can't offer me socialized healthcare, let alone a Mediterranean paradise with the king at my feet."

Gregory nodded, seemingly lost in thought for a moment as they danced, and Eddie sobered.

"This is my home now," he said, more earnestly. "I'm on a permanent visa, I'm running a business here…it's not where I thought this job would take me, but my life is here. Hopefully, with you."

Gregory nodded, and then stopped moving. Eddie, surprised, stopped also. So did the music. Everything was suddenly very, very quiet, and all eyes were on them.

Gregory put his hands in the pockets of his dress trousers, then removed them as fists, offering them to Eddie like a grandparent with a piece of candy, making a kid guess which hand it was in. Behind them, someone gasped.

"Greg, what's going on?" Eddie asked in a low voice. Gregory just nodded at his hands. Eddie, perplexed, tapped his left hand.

Gregory turned his hand over, opening it to show his palm. There was a thin silver ring resting in it.

"This is how we propose in Askazer-Shivadlakia," Gregory said. Eddie stared down at the ring. "You got the ring first try, good job."

"Oh snap," Eddie said. Gregory's face took on a faintly put-upon expression.

"Say yes, dumbass!" someone hissed. It sounded like Jerry.

"See, I can't," Eddie said, and Gregory turned pale. Eddie patted his own pockets madly. He'd put it in one of them –

He came up with the little bag out of his waistcoat pocket and hastily dumped the contents into his hand. He hadn't intended to be so public, so he'd just gone with a gag ring, with a giant plastic "diamond" full of glitter in the top. He offered it to Gregory, who stared at it in shock.

"Good timing, bud, I was going to propose in about an hour," Eddie said, and Gregory burst out laughing.

"You absolutely ludicrous clown of a human being," Gregory said, taking the joke ring out of Eddie's fingers and dropping the slim, elegant silver band into Eddie's palm. "I'm dating a cartoon. It's come to this."

"Technically," Eddie said, staggering from Alanna's hug as he put his ring on, "You're *marrying* a cartoon. I'm as surprised as anyone."

"Did you know?" Gregory asked Alanna, who giggled. "She knew I was proposing to you," he said to Eddie. "You knew," he accused, turning back to her, "and you let him think he was going to propose to me, and – "

"She helped me pick out the ring," Eddie confirmed. "We had to mail-order it. Nobody makes a ring ugly enough around here."

"In front of my entire family and half of Parliament," Gregory said, wiping the tears of laughter from the corners of his eyes.

"I was going to be subtle about it," Eddie protested. "You're the one putting on the dog and pony show! Ah – wait!" he cried, pulling his phone out of his back pocket. "Photogram!"

Gregory started laughing again, but he held out his hand so Eddie could get both hands in the picture. The rest of the party crowded around to congratulate them, or got in line for celebratory champagne.

Eddie spoke aloud as he typed the caption for his Photogram. "*Someone get me the name of a good wedding caterer.* Hashtag *shivadh-life*, hashtag *marriage*. Oh shit," he added suddenly, looking up at Gregory. "Did you throw this whole-ass ball just to propose?"

"Well, it was convenient," Gregory said, twisting the ring

around on his finger. "I know it's relatively soon, Eddie, but – "

"Hey, I had the same speech written, how 'bout that," Eddie told him, gently cutting him off. "When you know, you know."

Gregory kissed him, carefully decorous for the cameras, and then turned to Alanna.

"Guess what you get," he said, and she stopped laughing abruptly.

"What?" she asked warily.

"You get to plan the wedding," he told her.

INFINITE JES

CHAPTER ONE

"UNTIL A FEW months ago, not a lot of people knew about Askazer-Shivadlakia, the little country by the sea," Jes Deimos said, reading off a script but doing a good job of sounding like they weren't. "Maybe geography students with very niche grants, or historians interested in the effect of the Russian Revolution on European monarchy." They paused, to audibly end the paragraph and also give the editor a little space to work with later if he needed it.

"But recently the country became a meme and a hot new Photogram destination – we'll get to that later – and suddenly it was everywhere. Even then, you might assume you've never *met* anyone from Askazer-Shivadlakia. You'd probably be right...unless of course you've been to one of my live shows. Because then you've met me!"

Noah leaned in towards his mic and said, "And me!"

"That's my son, Noah," Jes said.

"Hey everyone!" Noah added. Jes gave him a thumbs-up.

"I was born in Askazer-Shivadlakia, and Noah and I are both Shivadh. This season on *The Echo*, we're moving back to the Old Country, to see what's changed and to learn more about one of the only democratic monarchies in the world," Jes continued. "We've been back for family vacations, but never for very long. There are several reasons for that, all of which we'll be exploring along with the politics, history, culture, and daily life of our parentland. I'll be coming to you with weekly updates – "

" – and I'll be doing my own show for my listeners," Noah

added.

"We're lining up guests as we speak, including one or two celebrities," Jes continued. "Join us in the echo, won't you?"

They held the silence until the recording light went off.

"Solid take," came the voice over the speaker, and Jes gave the tech a nod. "We're on a ten minute break."

"Thank you, ten minutes," Noah acknowledged. The tech grinned at him as he left. "How'd I sound?"

"You always sound perfect," Jes told him. Noah rolled his eyes. "You do! It's those youthful vocal cords. This is why, if I ever catch you smoking, you're both fired and grounded."

"Yeah, yeah," Noah replied, waving a hand. "Do you think they listen to the podcast in Askazer-Shivadlakia? I mean, aside from Nona and Granddad."

"Metrics say there's a small listenership. Probably mostly relatives, even after you take Nona and Granddad out of it. Not unusual for American podcasts," Jes said. "If I did true crime we'd maybe have a bigger audience and I wouldn't have to rob a bank to send you to college."

"Why go to college if you could rob banks?" Noah asked. "Bet people in Askazer-Shivadlakia will listen after you start posting episodes."

"I hope so. If I'm going to move back home, I can at least make a little trouble while I'm at it," Jes said. "Still okay with the move, kiddo? It's not easy to start fresh in the middle of high school."

"Not that hard," Noah mumbled. Jes felt a swell of sympathy for the kid. It was tough to be both smart and shy as a fifteen-year-old who was only famous on the internet.

"Well, it'll be an adventure. But if you get homesick or anything you tell me, okay? Family before business," Jes reminded him. "The podcast is never as important as you are, you know that."

"My podcast is way more important than you are, though,"

Noah told them, grin returning.

"The thanks I get for bearing and raising you," Jes scolded.

"Can I go get a snack from the vending machine?"

"Sure, here," Jes said, and passed him a couple of dollar bills. Noah bounced out of the room, and Jes sorted through the script folder, making sure they hadn't left anything out for today's recording session. The ad for the new season in Askazer-Shivadlakia should have been the last of it.

It might be rougher on Noah than he expected, Jes thought, but the kid was young and resilient. Jes wasn't sure how they themself would cope. It wasn't that they didn't like Askazer-Shivadlakia, but they'd been gone for ten solid years before ever going back, and even now they hadn't been back for more than a week since leaving –

Well, since running away, really.

But the world was changing, and there was a new king on the throne – a gay king, out and proud, and word through the queer and expat grapevines was that Askazer-Shivadlakia was a particularly friendly place to be right now. Lachlan needed them, and politically it wasn't a bad time to be moving back.

"Hope you know what you've gotten yourself into," Jes muttered.

It wasn't easy to travel incognito as a king, even the former king of a very small country.

Michaelis ben Jason, King Emeritus of Askazer-Shivadlakia, had developed a couple of techniques over the years. His son favored driving around in a battered truck and trusting the population to ignore him, which seemed to be working well, but Michaelis had loved spy novels as a child and enjoyed the occasional disguise. For many trips he'd worn a sort of subtle costume meant to imply he was either a tourist or a businessman;

currently he had a goatee, which was doing a lot of the work, combined with a nondescript brown suit and a pair of spectacles.

It helped that his portrait on the currency was a few decades out of date at this point, but he tried not to think about what a great natural disguise crow's feet were.

The train between Paris and Askazer-Shivadlakia was a full-day trip, but that didn't matter to him; it wasn't like he had a busy schedule. He'd made the trip mainly as a favor to Simon, the royal family's personal chef, who needed some supplies most easily acquired there. Simon hated Paris for reasons Michaelis had never inquired about, and didn't like having to spend two days on a train round-trip and an overnight in the city, so Michaelis had volunteered.

It got him out into the world for a while, and he'd enjoyed himself – finished a book and started another on the trip up, shopped in Paris not just for Simon but also for himself, and had a good dinner in a nice outdoor cafe. He had a new book for the trip back, and when he got tired of the book, the train carriage was just busy enough to do some enjoyable people-watching.

They weren't that far from his stop when he noticed one of the other passengers, a dark-haired teenage boy in very American clothing, plastered to one of the windows a few rows up, craning his neck to see where they were going. His traveling companion, who Michaelis couldn't see much of over the edge of the seat, appeared to be asleep.

"If you're looking for the border marker, we passed it about ten minutes ago," he said, and the boy's head turned sharply, startled. Michaelis gave him a reassuring smile. "We're officially in Askazer-Shivadlakia now."

The boy scrambled out into the aisle, coming to Michaelis's row. He had a little bag with him, slung over one shoulder.

"Do you live here?" the boy asked, and if his clothes hadn't identified him as American, his accent would have.

"I do," Michaelis said. "I'm just coming back from Paris."

"We came through there from New York," the boy said. "I'm Noah. I'm moving to Askazer-Shivadlakia."

He pronounced it with the casual cadence of someone who was used to saying the words, not like an American at all, and Michaelis tilted his head, interested. His eye caught the cord emerging from the bag Noah carried, and Noah saw him notice it. He opened it up to reveal a recording device of some kind.

"I'm a broadcast journalist and I make podcasts," the boy said hastily, running the words together like he'd rehearsed them but hadn't had a lot of opportunities to use them. "Can I interview you and record it?"

Michaelis raised both eyebrows. "You're very young to be a journalist."

"I know," Noah said with a grimace. Michaelis smiled.

"Certainly. Take a seat," he said, moving Simon's hamper to the floor. "I'm Mike."

"Thank you for letting me record," Noah said, pressing a button on the device in the bag. "Why are you going to Askazer-Shivadlakia? I mean going home, I guess."

"I was in Paris, picking up some things for a friend. What were you looking for? Was it the border?"

"Oh, no," Noah said. "I saw the border sign. I was looking for the synagogue."

"Ah!" Michaelis nodded. "Should come along soon – you'll know because the train blows a warning whistle when it crosses a main road just before it. You won't see it for long, but the view is superb."

"Have you been in it?"

"Oh yes – often, when I was younger. My father made sure we went every week. Not as much once I was grown and working – High Holy Days, mostly. Should go more often, to be honest, now that I can."

"What do you do?" Noah asked. "For work, I mean."

"I'm recently retired. I used to work in government. Very

boring stuff," Michaelis assured him.

"What do you think of the new king?" the boy asked.

"Hard to know yet," Michaelis said, a little amused. "He's only been king for two months."

"But do you think he's going to do a good job?"

"I certainly hope so. He seems to be, so far." The train's whistle went. "There we go, here, switch with me…" He shuffled aside and let Noah take his window seat. The boy lifted his phone, camera app open, but Michaelis noted with approval that he leaned the phone on the sill of the train's window, so that he could record it but also watch the real thing pass by at the same time.

"There it is," Michaelis said, almost as excited as the kid was. The Grand Synagogue of Askaz was well worth watching for, even at speed from the train. It rose out of the flat landscape like a jeweled treasure box, sunlight glittering through dozens of stained-glass windows, ornate pomegranates crowning the corners, stone songbirds adorning the roof gutters. It was a long time since he'd seen it through a newcomer's eyes.

"Wow," Noah breathed.

"You should go and see it, if you can," Michaelis told him, once it was past and Noah had stopped the video recording. "They do tours, if you don't want to attend a service."

"We're going next Friday," Noah said. "Maybe. Soon, anyway. What else do you think I should do in Askazer-Shivadlakia?"

Michaelis could hear a certain tone in the boy's voice that said this was a Proper Interview Question, but he'd been interviewed by many older, stupider people asking much less interesting questions.

"Well, the palace is architecturally very interesting, and the grounds are at their peak right now, in the spring and summer," he said. "The conservation officers teach bowfishing lessons on the lake, but you'd probably have to get permission from a parent for that. There's a little art museum in town, and I know the king's been thinking of building a science museum. I suppose there's not a lot for a boy your age, though," he added, frowning. "No… amusement parks or malls or whatnot. We do have very good internet, though."

"What do you like to do?" Noah asked.

"Oh, be outdoors, I suppose," Michaelis replied. "Never got to do as much of that as I liked when I was working. Hiking, fishing, swimming."

Just then, the train's conductor came over the loudspeaker – "Fons-Askaz, next stop Fons-Askaz in three minutes!"

"That's my stop," Michaelis said.

"Mine too! I did some reading, it means – "

"Caesar's Fountain, yes," Michaelis said, amused.

"Noah?" a voice called, and Noah looked up only a little guiltily. Whoever he was traveling with was moving around now, gathering up bags from beneath the seats.

"You'd better go get ready," Michaelis added.

"Thanks for the interview. Here," Noah said, and gave Michaelis an actual business card. He hadn't been handed a business card in probably a decade – it was all digital now, or so he'd thought. "If you want to hear the podcast you can listen there. Maybe I'll see you in town!"

"Maybe," Michaelis agreed, tucking the business card in his pocket. "Very nice to meet you, Noah."

The boy shook his hand and dashed back down the aisle; Michaelis heard him call, "I'm here, I was just doing some recording."

He would have gotten up and introduced himself, but just then the conductor announced they were arriving at the station. In the bustle of getting himself and his luggage off, and dodging around other people trying to do likewise, Michaelis lost sight of the boy and his guardian. Then staff were there to collect him up into a car, and he was being whisked back to the palace.

"Simon!" he called when they arrived, leaving the driver to

take his bag, carrying the hamper into the kitchen himself.

"Your Grace!" Simon replied, hurrying up to take the hamper out of his hands. "Thank you. Oh, beautiful," he added, popping the lid up to look inside, examining the cloth-wrapped cheeses, the packets of herbs, and the steel kitchen implements he'd asked for. "Exceptional."

"Happy to be of service," Michaelis replied. Behind Simon, he could see Eddie, Gregory's boyfriend, pulling something out of the oven. "Pizza again, Edward?"

"Hot slices ready in five," Eddie confirmed, sliding the pizza onto a nearby board. "Welcome back, Your Grace. Have fun in Paris?"

"I did, actually, thank you. I'm in time for dinner, then."

"Sure. Greg's not even down yet. Running late because of some kind of argument about tariffs. Not sure what tariffs are, but I'm strongly against them in general, for his sake."

"Import-export fee, essentially," Michaelis replied. "I'm sure he'll be along soon."

"Go on ahead into the dining room. This has to stand first and I need plates," Eddie said. Michaelis gave him a nod and headed for the small dining room nearby, where the king and his close family generally took their meals. The king was, as Eddie had warned, not in evidence, but his cousin and assistant Alanna was, so he probably wouldn't be too late. Jerry – Gerald, 12th Duke of Shivadlakia and technically the king's vizier, an honorific bestowed mainly as a joke – was also there, working on a Sudoku puzzle.

"Welcome back," Alanna said, as Michaelis pulled out a chair. "Shopping go well?"

"Paris was delightful. Usually is," Michaelis agreed. "A nice change of scenery."

"Eiffel Tower still standing?" Jerry asked.

"I didn't inspect it personally, but it seems fine," Michaelis replied. "What new trouble have you got into while I was gone?"

"None at all, I've been very well behaved."

"Mm, you must be feeling ill."

Jerry pretended to be wounded, then got distracted when Eddie arrived with the pizza on a tray in one hand and a stack of plates in the other.

"If you're tired of pizza, Simon said to tell you he also has soup and sandwiches," Eddie announced, "but this is a new crust to keep things interesting."

He presented a slice to Michaelis first, then to Jerry because otherwise he'd have had to fend him off with the serving spatula. Alanna, either more patient or just not as eager for pizza, took hers with more dignity.

"Which iteration is this, Eddie?" she asked, tearing off a piece of crust to sample it.

"Ah, this is Eddie's Perfect Pizza Pie test version 4.2," Eddie said, seating himself and setting out two more slices, one for himself and one for Gregory. "Malt crust, more sugar in the sauce, surprise cheese."

Michaelis, who had been dissecting the slice in front of him with a fork, looked up curiously. "*Surprise* cheese?" he asked.

Eddie gestured at Jerry, who was already halfway through his slice. "It's just Provel. I thought the cheese needed a little more grease. Promise I didn't poison it."

"No point now, I'm reduced to harmlessness already," Michaelis said, breaking off a small chunk with his fork and tasting it. "Decent," he pronounced.

"I don't think you could ever be harmless, Uncle Mike," Jerry said.

"Well, politically," Michaelis said. "I'm getting extremely good with a bow, even off the water. Thinking of going on a boar hunt in the autumn. That's a very elder king thing to do and Edward's keen, aren't you?" he asked Eddie.

"Anytime you want. I'll carry your bags and make sausage after," Eddie agreed.

"Seems a shame to go to all the trouble for something Uncle Mike won't eat," Jerry said.

"I'll eat them," Alanna said, smiling at Eddie.

"I'm in it for the hunt, Gerald," Michaelis replied. "You don't eat pork sausage either, don't talk to me about sausage."

"If I never hear about sausage again, frankly, I'll have lived a full life," a voice announced, as Gregory arrived in the dining room. He bent to kiss Eddie hello, then settled in next to Michaelis with a nod. "Welcome back. Nothing against boar sausage in theory but it's another damn luxury export. We could've been the Geneva Freeport, but no, we chose ethics and cured meats instead of catering to the richest men in the world."

"I warned you," Jerry said. "A moral stance is an invitation to ruin."

"Jerry, what you said was *you can't get in trouble if they can't catch you*," Gregory replied. "Malt crust?" he asked Eddie, who nodded.

"The spirit was there," Jerry said. "Anyway, your dad and Eddie are planning their own deaths."

"Boar hunt," Eddie explained.

Gregory nodded. "Yearning to have a folk song written about you, I remember."

"Because His Grace was just grumbling about harmlessness," Alanna said, and something in her tone made every man in the room look at her.

"Do you take issue with my grumbling?" Michaelis asked, genuinely surprised. Alanna was a sweet girl; not a truly malicious bone in her body, which meant this was about something else.

Alanna and Gregory exchanged a look. Michaelis gestured back and forth between them. "What's this conspiracy? You've already got the throne, there's no point murdering me now."

"Alanna – and Eddie too, to be fair – has mentioned to me that you…talk a lot about how useless you think you've become," Gregory said. "It's become a little worrying, I think."

"It's just small talk," Michaelis said.

"Is it?" Gregory asked. "I know handing off governance wasn't easy."

Michaelis glanced from Alanna to Eddie, and then at Jerry, who gave him a shrug.

"I wasn't in on the conspiracy," Jerry said.

"Nice to know I have one ally, even if it's only because he's clueless," Michaelis said.

"That's fair," Jerry agreed.

"Dad, this isn't a coup, you don't have allies and enemies," Gregory said, rolling his eyes. "Nobody's staging an intervention. Just making sure you're all right."

"I'm fine," Michaelis said. "A little bored, but I'll adjust. That's what retirement is. You have to complain about it before you settle in. Probably why your grandfather disappeared for months after my coronation."

"Well, so long as you know we're here for you," Gregory said.

"The royal family's only allowed two emotions per year," Jerry said to Eddie, who nodded. "I always feel so privileged to see it."

"All right, let's let it go," Gregory said. "Alanna, what am I doing tomorrow, aside from slowly losing my mind at the damn EU?"

Michaelis leaned back, letting the conversation wash past him, full of palace operations he was no longer a part of. Jerry scooted a little closer.

"Offer stands, Uncle Mike," he said. "I could get you a reality show in no time flat. Call it *The Retirement Plan*."

"*Old Idiot Yelling*," Michaelis replied.

"I mean, that probably has great SEO."

"What on earth is an SEO?" Michaelis asked.

"Search Engine Optimization? Means you're easy to find when someone searches you."

"Easier to find than I already was as king of Askazer-

Shivadlakia?" Michaelis asked, raising an eyebrow.

"…you've got me there," Jerry admitted.

"Thank you for the offer, Gerald, but I'm not quite that desperate yet," Michaelis said.

"Your loss," Jerry said. That was the nice thing about Jerry: he might be a troublemaker at times but he was generally low-maintenance, one-on-one.

Michaelis poured himself a glass of the wine that Eddie had paired with the pizza, frowning when the flavors didn't quite mesh. Eddie raised an eyebrow at him and gestured at the wine; Michaelis nodded and Eddie made a note in his phone. Maybe he ought to spend more time with the man; they'd gotten off to a slightly rough start, but Eddie was settling in nicely. And he was good for Gregory, very obviously so.

On the other hand, Eddie then began Photogramming his new pizza, and Michaelis was still very wary of social media. Maybe wait a while longer. Plenty of time to plan that boar hunt.

"Who were you talking to, anyway?" Jes asked, disembarking from the train that evening. They kept an eye out for their parents, but the platform was crowded with people coming and going. Fons-Askaz wasn't as quiet and sleepy as it used to be, they thought.

"Just a guy coming back from a trip, I guess," Noah replied. "He was showing me how to tell when the synagogue is coming."

"Oh, when the whistle blows! Yeah," Jes said. "You were careful?"

"I'm always careful," Noah said, affronted.

"Yes, but you are also a wild child who talks to strangers."

"I am a journalist," Noah informed them. "I was recording."

"And someday I'm sure your recording will be evidence in the kidnapping case," Jes said, ruffling his hair. He batted them away. "You're taller than me now, tell me when you see Nona and Granddad."

A shriek split the air, and Noah's head jerked around; he blurted "Uncle Lachlan!" and took off running. Jes stayed where they were, hobbled by the luggage, as Noah threw himself into the arms of a tall man with wild hair and multiple tattoos – including a few that looked new since the last time they'd seen him.

"JES!" Lachlan yelled. "HE'S TOO BIG!"

"I keep saying," Jes said, as Lachlan dragged Noah back to where they were waiting. They accepted a hug from him and then he turned to hug Noah again, ruffling his hair.

"Look at you, honey," he said to Noah. "So tall and so ready to break hearts! If you want to. If you don't want to, that's valid, and you could break laws instead."

Noah grinned at him. "Not ace so far, but I'll let you know."

"And not in prison for lawbreaking either. Shame. Well, notify me if I need to buy a new flag at any point. Your parents were parking the car last time I saw them," Lachlan told Jes. "I'll take you there. *I'll take you there,*" he sang the last part again, in a soulful voice. "*Ain't nobody cryin'...*"

"Come on, Uncle Lachlan, that's the Staple Singers," Noah said. "Give me a challenge."

"Later, princess. My charm offensive against your Nona continues, and she doesn't like singing in public."

"Lord," Jes sighed.

"Deep breaths. It's only temporary until you find your own place. I've been fixing up the studio, too! All the equipment's in, but I was waiting for Noah to help set it up."

"Thank you," Noah sing-songed.

"Sure thing. How was your trip? Everything go smoothly?"

"Noah made friends," Jes said. "He's getting a jumpstart on the podcast already."

"I got a list of some stuff to see from a guy on the train," Noah said.

"Well, once you're moved in and recovered from the jet lag, we'll get the sound stuff set up and Jes can entertain themself while I take you touring. And Great Auntie Carla has ordered you to come to Friday night dinner," he added, including them both with a look.

"See, we've already got a social calendar and dinner plans," Jes said. "Thanks for coming, Lachlan."

"Of course. Couldn't wait to see you," Lachlan said, planting a kiss on the shaved side of their head. "Chin up, shoulders straight. You only need to be home six hours a night to sleep."

"It's not that bad," Jes said.

"We'll find you somewhere permanent to stay fast," Lachlan assured them.

Jes squeezed his hand, grateful for the support, and waved back when they saw their father waving from the car.

CHAPTER TWO

MICHAELIS HAD BEGUN to loathe his weekly visits to the library, which in itself was upsetting. Ordinarily he loved the library, but now he was visiting to dictate his memoirs to the royal librarian, and it was an exercise in frustration for them both.

Still, he'd scheduled his trip to Paris to interfere with the last one and he'd missed a further two already, so he really did have to attend this one. Even if it was just as difficult as the previous ones had been.

The problem, he supposed, as he left the librarian's office after yet another terrible hour, was that it was difficult to talk about some of the more sensitive political topics, and equally difficult every time he mentioned Miranda. But it wasn't as though he could ignore her in his history – she had been a vital presence on the throne, sometimes better at ruling than he was in those early years. And he didn't want to ignore her. He wanted her memory preserved.

He stopped near the big library doors, gathering his dignity and calming himself. He did what he'd found useful since her death, and pictured himself collecting up all the little pebbles of memory from that day, picturing them cradled in his palms. Mentally, he carried them to a cavern deep in his mind and set them there, near the entrance, smoothing them over until they were indistinguishable from all the others he'd left. Then he walked backwards away from them, until he could open his eyes.

He felt better already – calmer, more ready for whatever might confront him when he left the library.

He emptied his pockets onto the study desk next to him, just to make sure all his notes were in order. Tucked into one of them was a square of stiff cardstock – the business card that Noah from the train had given him.

NOAH DEIMOS
AUDIO ENGINEER - PODCAST HOST
HE/HIM

He took his phone out as he descended from the library to the ground floor, tapping in the website address from the card. There was one of those automatic feeds from Photogram, and he was startled to see footage from the train ride. He waited until he was outside to push play, and when he turned up the volume he could even hear himself say "There it is," excitedly, and Noah's soft "Wow," before the video ended. It reminded him of trips with Gregory and Miranda, sightseeing in between diplomatic stops and trade negotiations.

The website also had a link to a pair of podcasts – *The Echo* and *The Echo Junior*. He added them to the little widget that played the podcasts (Jerry hated it when he spoke about them that way, which was half the reason to do it) and took his headphones out of his pocket.

The walk from the palace to the fishing lodge wasn't long, and once you got used to the scenery it also wasn't that interesting. A good opportunity to see what the kid was about. He tapped open *The Echo Junior*, because Noah's name was attached to that one. The latest episode was called "Teaser Trailer: Season Five" and was only two minutes long, so he skipped it and went to an earlier one titled "Am I The Product?"

It was an interesting discussion, to be sure, about who profited from social media and who provided the content. Even without knowing much about the subject matter he could tell it wasn't a deep dive – it was made by and meant for youth. Still, that was helpful in its own way. Noah and his guests spent a lot of time explaining how social media worked on a basic level, which was quite educational. Michaelis mainly knew of Photogram as a tool the palace used sparingly and something Eddie had used to upend the entire country without even trying. Probably for the best that Eddie now worked for the palace and was taking a more measured approach.

He let the episode play through as he arrived at the fishing lodge and let himself in. It was really too big for one person, but staying full-time at the palace held less appeal for him right now. Besides, one didn't need to fill space just because it was there. He listened to another episode as he changed out of his suit and made a cup of tea.

The third episode had a different host, and when he checked his phone, it said this was *The Echo*, hosted by someone named Jes Deimos, apparently a relative. He paused it – plenty of time to encounter the grown-up version of Noah's podcast later – and instead switched over to some music before bed.

Still, the events of the day bothered him. He knew a historical record of the reign was important – he'd consulted other records himself – but the librarian had Michaelis's official diaries, and the whole point of being king was that if you did it right, nothing especially interesting ever happened. Interesting was the enemy of good rule. Still, the process shouldn't be boring, for him or for the staff, and it was. It was *astonishingly* dull. Michaelis was growing to dislike himself for how uninteresting he was managing to be.

The coolest he'd probably been in years was on the train from Paris, he thought. Showing off the synagogue, advising a newcomer on what to see and do in his home.

He picked up the business card again, studying it, and noticed there was also an address printed on it. Reverb Podcast Network's studio was located in Fons-Askaz, the harbor town below the palace – right on the main street, not even that far away. A podcast studio in Askazer-Shivadlakia seemed like a very modern thing to have, and probably quite interesting.

He sat on the bed, considering this. Obviously the kid was too young to help, but surely someone at the studio was responsible for him, and that person probably knew how to conduct an interview that wouldn't make him seem like a droning old bore. Jerry had suggested a reality show –

Gregory had also suggested a podcast. Months ago, and mostly in jest, but…it had a certain appeal. His speeches had usually gone over well, in no small part because of his voice, and as soon as he'd worked that out he'd made sure to preserve it. Miranda used to say he sounded like a bass drum wrapped in velvet, which had always made him preen a little.

Well, no harm in asking. And it would probably please Gregory, who clearly was fretting (unnecessarily!) about his mental state.

Resolved, he laid out casual clothes for the following day, mapped the location of the Reverb Podcast Network's studio on his phone, and went to bed.

The recording studio, if he had the address right, was in a small block of offices at one end of the high street. He wasn't in a particular hurry and the weather was clear and warm, so he walked into Fons-Askaz at a leisurely pace, with the wide town harbor on his left and the palace up the hill on his right, until he got down far enough that the palace receded into the distance.

The building was old and didn't look well-kept. When he let himself into the main entrance he found a grubby, quiet hallway inside. Third door down was the studio and the handwritten hours card taped to the door said it had been open for an hour, so he turned the handle and peered inside, a little wary.

It opened into a small waiting room with a few seats and two tables, one of which was near a window looking out on the harbor.

That one was occupied –

"Noah!" Michaelis said, startled. He hadn't expected the boy to actually be here. The dark head of hair at the table looked up, and Noah beamed.

"It's Mike, right?" he asked, bouncing to his feet. "What are you doing here? Did you look up my podcast?"

"Yes, in a way," Michaelis said, coming into the waiting room and letting the door close softly behind him. A light over another doorway indicated someone was recording, somewhere. "That's how I found this place. Are you making a podcast today?"

"No, not today," Noah said. "Babysitting some guests for the other podcast."

"Right, *The Echo*," Michaelis nodded. "You do the Junior version – I listened to a few episodes."

"Oh cool! Is that why you're here? I'm definitely going to put you in an episode, but it won't be out for a while," Noah said. "I could do another interview if you thought of more stuff to see."

"I wouldn't mind, but I'm here to speak to whoever owns the studio," Michaelis replied. "I've been thinking of doing a podcast myself."

Noah blinked at him. "About Askazer-Shivadlakia?"

"Maybe indirectly. If I promise I won't steal your thunder, can you introduce me?" he asked.

Noah was opening his mouth to reply when several things happened at once.

The recording light over the door went out and the door itself opened. A handful of people emerged, more or less filling the little space. One of them said, startled, "Your Majesty!"

"Esta?" he asked, surprised to find an MP in a podcast office – although Esta Jerome had been a junior MP during his reign before advancing and was still very young, so perhaps he shouldn't be.

"Noah?" one of the other people said, and Michaelis squinted past Esta, trying to determine if he recognized them.

After a second he realized he couldn't even place their gender, let alone their face.

They were fairly short, with curved hips and a flat chest, what he'd have called a feminine face with a strong jawline. Their bleach-white hair was combed into a pompadour on top of their head, the sides shaved. They looked older, closer to his age, but dressed like one of Gregory's fashionable school friends, in a tailored shirt and a kilt in purple and black.

"Uh, Boss, this is Mike, the guy I interviewed on the train," Noah said.

Esta said, "Mike?" in an intensely amused voice. The man next to her gasped dramatically.

Michaelis tried to stop gaping at everything happening around him and summoned forty years of dignity as a king.

"I was just speaking with Noah about his podcast project," he said.

"Noah," the other person said, going to the boy. There was an unmistakable family resemblance – the same narrow face and snub nose, dark heavy brows and pale eyes, but this one had the Shivadh accent, if a little faded. "Did this man introduce himself properly to you?"

"I'm afraid I was incognito when we met," Michaelis answered. He gave Noah a brief nod of a bow. "Michaelis ben Jason, King Emeritus, at your service, young man."

Noah stared at him. His – mother? Parent? Boss? – nudged him gently. It occurred to him this was probably Jes Deimos, though that was not especially helpful.

"Nice to meet you," Noah said. "Again."

"Esta, thanks for the interview," the person who was probably Jes Deimos continued. "Lachlan, can you walk her out?"

"Can I come back and eavesdrop after?" the man called Lachlan asked. He looked like he was savoring this.

"No," the person said.

"Fine. Bye, Noah, be good," Lachlan said, and then it was

Michaelis, Noah, and this mystery person.

"I go through this a lot," Michaelis said, "but I think you have the advantage of me."

"Jes Deimos," they said. "I'm Noah's parent."

"I gathered. I'm sorry, the boy did nothing wrong – he didn't know who I was when we spoke," Michaelis said.

"Boss, he said he wanted to talk to the owner of the studio," Noah said. "About um. Doing a podcast."

Jes Deimos' face managed to combine "amused" and "deeply unimpressed" in a way that was pure Shivadh.

"Are you the studio's owner?" he asked, still trying to cover his surprise. "I was under the impression Noah had just moved here."

"I'm a partner," they replied. "You want to do a podcast?"

"Yes. Well. I'd like to ask about them. I really know very little, but I listen to some, and they seem…popular," he said.

"Normal mid-life crises usually involve a shiny car, not a recording studio," they said.

"I'm afraid I'm a few years past mid-life and I already have a shiny car," he replied evenly. To his surprise, they laughed.

"Well, all right, we're a public studio and we do offer our services. I assume you have all the funding you need. Have you lined up any marketing or advertisers?" they asked, heading for the door in the other wall. "Step into my office."

"I only came up with the idea yesterday," he said. He held the office door for Noah, looking back; the boy seemed surprised, then followed them in.

Jes's office was a small cubby lined in noise-dampening foam, with a large glass window looking in on a recording studio. He suspected it might double as a second studio at times.

"So, tell me why the former king of Askazer-Shivadlakia wants to do a podcast," they said, sitting down at the desk, gesturing him into another seat.

"Traditionally, if a king retires rather than dying on the

throne, one of his emeritus duties is to dictate his memoirs to the royal librarian," Michaelis said. "It's considered an important historical record. Kings have often consulted the previous memoirs for precedent. Even after the monarchy became democratic and our needs, in terms of advice, were different."

"Ish," Jes said.

"Beg pardon?"

"Democratic-ish. After all, your son is the third generation in your family to be elected."

Michaelis shrugged. "My son and I both won fair elections against strong candidates, which is more than can be said of some American political dynasties. Why, are you bucking for the job?"

Jes laughed again, seemingly startled by the retort.

"That's fair," they agreed. "Your memoirs aren't a full explanation, though."

"No, I suppose not. I've been doing my best, but it's very tedious," he said. "And, as a former king, one does feel useless. I didn't want to keep on in international politics, and Gregory has the country well in hand. I suppose I'm searching for a challenge. A podcast seemed like a chance to learn a new skill, perhaps improve my storytelling. I'm afraid most stories involving my reign are not very interesting, but I don't need to be a sensation."

Jes studied him, which was a little unsettling, but the entire encounter so far had been. He glanced at Noah, who looked excited.

"I'm going to act self-interestedly here," Jes said finally. "Because it's not every day a former monarch walks into my office and wants to hire my services. But I think it would also be genuinely useful to you to see how podcasts are made before you decide you want to make one. They're more work than they seem, and most podcasters don't get past the seventh or eighth episode."

"Good lord," he said.

"So I'd like to invite you onto my podcast," Jes continued.

"*The Echo*?" Michaelis guessed. Noah snickered.

"The same. You can follow me through an entire episode, from idea to finished product, and if you think you're still interested at the end, we can discuss next steps."

"Boss," Noah said. Jes looked at him. "Dibs."

Jes threw their hands up in the air and sat back, groaning, a reaction that surprised him; Noah grinned and pointed at them.

"Fine. Noah did get you first," Jes told Michaelis. "Technically I'm inviting you onto his podcast, *Echo Junior.*"

"Or we could do a collab," Noah said. "We make a podcast about making a podcast. You can be the point of view, like we teach you how to make it," he said to Michaelis. "Then if you want to make your own, you can."

Jes had seemed irritated by Noah's dibs, but now they looked at Noah like...well, the way he'd looked when Gregory was taking his first wobbly steps into politics.

"I think that sounds like a fine plan," he said to Noah. "How do we begin?"

"We have a brainstorming meeting on Tuesday," Jes said. "You can come to that. How do I put something on the calendar of the former king of Askazer-Shivadlakia?"

Michaelis spotted a little pile of business cards on the desk, and picked one up; it said, on the front

JES DEIMOS
BROADCAST JOURNALIST - AUDIO PRODUCER
THEY/THEM

Well, perhaps that explained a few things. He turned it over, took a pen from the cup on the desk, and wrote out his email address, passing it to them.

"This is your personal email," they said, studying it. "Not the palace one that goes to a screener."

"Yes?" he replied, perplexed.

"You don't use a secretary?"

Michaelis shook his head. "There's not much call for my services, as I said. Anyone who wants me for official business goes through the palace. For personal concerns, the email suffices."

"Well, I will have my secretary send you an invite," Jes said, passing the card to Noah, who got out his phone and immediately started tapping away on it.

"Can I ask," Michaelis said, standing to leave, "why Esta Jerome was here?"

"Nervous about an MP speaking to a journalist?" Jes asked, standing also.

"I think you overestimate the level of power I wield or the amount of control I want," Michaelis said. "I like Esta; she's sensible and she's a great supporter of the king's initiatives. She's destined for high office if she keeps on the way she's going."

"I'm sure she'll be glad to know it. She's a friend, and she's in local politics, so I wanted to interview her, that's all."

"I look forward to hearing the interview," he said, as Jes held the door for him. "I'll see myself out. Until Tuesday. Noah, good to see you again."

"Your Majesty," Noah said, and Jes elbowed him. Michaelis smiled and let himself out into the hall. He had just stepped into the sunlight outside when his phone buzzed and an invitation to *Echo/Jr Weekly Brainstorming* appeared on the lock screen. He accepted it and pocketed the phone again.

Well, a radio journalist of indefinite gender and a kid who wasn't afraid to commandeer the former king of his country into a podcast scheme. If nothing else, life was certainly looking more interesting, at least as far as next Tuesday went.

As soon as the former king was gone, Jes slumped against the wall outside their office and slid down it until they plopped on their ass on the floor.

"Wow," Noah said, because Noah was their child and therefore a little bit of an asshole sometimes. "You really had the sass turned up high. Did he kick you when you were a kid or something?"

"Shh, I'm decompressing," Jes replied, and Noah sat down next to them. "Only you."

"Me? How is this my fault?"

"Only you would make friends, randomly, with the king of your native homeland!" Jes said. "I didn't expect a former monarch to walk in today. I would have put more product in my hair."

"Your hair looks fine."

"That's missing the point, but I suppose that's my fault too, probably," Jes groaned. "And now he wants us to teach him how to do a podcast. I'm going to have to show the king how to run a soundboard."

"You taught me."

"Your brain is young and elastic, love," Jes said, pulling Noah into their side.

"He is kinda old."

"Watch it. He's not that much older than me."

"He seems like he learns stuff. You know how some people just never learn stuff. He looks like that's not him," Noah said, considering it. "If he was king for all that time he must've been pretty good at keeping up."

"You'd be surprised what politicians can get away with, especially when they're pretty. But you may be right. I suppose we'll find out," Jes said. Their phone buzzed and they checked it. "Ah. Lachlan wants to know if the coast is clear and he can come back in to scream with us about what just happened. Would you go get him? I need a minute of silence to rethink my life choices."

"Yeah, I got it," Noah said, getting to his feet and heading for the door. A minute later, Lachlan could be heard making a series of high-pitched enthusiastic screams, growing ever closer.

Jes got up and dusted themself off.

"Oh my *shit*, that was the ex-king," Lachlan cackled, throwing himself through the door, down the hall, and into their office. Jes followed more calmly. Noah, wisely, went back to his work in the waiting room. "He is hot in person. That steel gray hair? And legs for days. *And* that voice. Bet he can purr like a cat. What did he want?"

"Podcast advice," Jes said.

"He could read the dictionary and we could sell it. Did you give him your number?"

"I think he took a card," Jes answered, frowning.

"Did you give him my number?"

"Lachlan, I love you, and you are a beautiful person inside and out, but the former king, who was married to the same woman for his entire reign and lost her tragically to illness less than a decade ago, is never going to sleep with you."

"He might be bi. Anyway, the royals demonstrably have no taste in men. His son is dating Eddie Rambler."

"Even if he is bi, he doesn't seem the type for casual sex."

"I'd marry him if it was required, I'm not doing anything more interesting," Lachlan said, putting his feet up on the desk.

"Your husband and infant child might take issue."

"They'd recover. By the way, did you see him check you out?"

"I saw him visibly trying to figure out what pronouns to use. Thankfully the business card was a hint. Hopefully he picked up on it."

"I think he liked your hair. Good thing you wore the kilt today."

"I'm sure he's seen nicer knees. Did you want something?"

"Other than another three days minimum spent drooling over King Michaelis? Not particularly. Let's go have an early lunch with cocktails."

"Lachlan, seriously," Jes said. "Don't tell the world about

this, okay? I don't need that kind of publicity and I'm sure he doesn't. He sounded like it took a lot for him to come here."

Lachlan sobered, folding his hands over his stomach. "Of course, Jes. Promise. Nobody hears it from me."

"And if you behave yourself, you can come sit in when we do the tech stuff, maybe show him how to check his levels."

Lachlan waggled his eyebrows. "I'll be the soul of discretion."

"I'm sure you will. Anyway," Jes continued, pushing his feet off the desk. "Let's go over scheduling. The number of people who want studio space is kind of shocking, to be honest."

Michaelis was at breakfast in the palace on Friday, which surprised Gregory when he walked in. Usually, if he was planning to stay at the palace over the weekend, he didn't show up until dinner time.

"Might just be you and me for breakfast," he said, helping himself to a scone from the basket on the table. "Alanna took Jerry to do some errands, and it's Eddie's slow day so he was still asleep when I left. How's the lodge?"

"Still standing," his father replied with a smile. "I came up to see you, actually."

"Well, you know I always like to see you around the place. Anything in particular we needed to discuss?"

"Nothing official. I was thinking of going to Kabbalat Shabbos tonight at the Grand Synagogue, and wondered if you wanted to come."

"Oh, that sounds nice," Gregory said thoughtfully. "And I should go more often. Kingly thing to do, now that life has settled down. Any particular reason?"

"Not really," his father said, in exactly the tone of voice that would once have made his mother suspicious of ulterior motives.

She would have asked him about it, and Michaelis often did need to be prodded a little about his thoughts. But Gregory had always felt when his father was being devious, adventure was in the wind. He didn't need to know the precise nature of it.

"Well, I'm in, doesn't look like I have anything on my calendar," he said, consulting his phone. "All right if I invite Eddie? He probably won't come, but he likes to be invited to things."

"No objections. Meet at the staircase? I can drive us."

"Sure. Are you in the palace today?"

"No, just came up to see you. Need anything from me?"

"Actually, if you can put your head in at Parliament briefly, Sorensen is still treating me like I'm a stand-in until you get back. Can you be boring about fishing at him for half an hour?"

"Love nothing better," Michaelis said. "There's a man who desperately needs to retire but his district simply won't stop electing him. Irritating him is always a pleasure."

"I'm seeing to the issue. There's a junior MP who could replace him handily, they just need a bit of help strategically. Alanna's hatching something."

"Very good." Michaelis grinned at him. "Now, tell me what you think of this news out of Italy last week…"

It was the best spirits Gregory had seen him in for some time, and after breakfast he enjoyed watching his father take one of his most irritating MPs down a peg. Perhaps the fishing lodge was doing him good, instead of the harm Gregory and his cousins had worried about.

It used to be that a Shivadh king, arriving to any service at the Grand Synagogue, would basically take over the show — received in splendor, seated in honor, and generally distracting from what should have been religious observance. Michaelis had read several historical accounts in the library by rabbis who'd been very angry about it. But that was one of the many changes Gregory II, his son's namesake, had introduced. He'd stopped attending any religious observance entirely, and then when he began again it was subtly, quietly. It was tradition by now, several generations strong, that the kings of Askazer-Shivadlakia basically slunk in the back like tardy schoolchildren.

Michaelis liked it. They arrived about five minutes late, both in the sober black uniform of the royal family, and slipped in through a side door, held open silently for them by an usher. There was a bench in the back specifically for the royal family, and he settled himself next to Gregory on it. The air inside was pleasantly cool, but the light was a deep warm orange, sunset streaming in through the big windows from the west while indigo night was falling in the east. And this had always been his favorite service to attend, between the singing and the murmured prayers. Welcoming Shabbos and a late dinner after, that was a good evening in his mind.

He didn't know if Jes Deimos and their son would be attending, but Noah had said they planned to at some point. He wouldn't admit to something as blasphemous as going to synagogue just to see someone he was curious about, but it was high time he got back here, as Noah's questions about how often he went had proved.

It was good, anyway. He could feel his shoulders dropping, and Gregory seemed to be relaxing too.

He did spot that knot of white hair, very visible in any crowd – Jes Deimos, about halfway up in the congregation, Noah a lanky shadow next to them. Noah looked like he was having more fun than his parent was. A pair of older people next to them, probably Noah's grandparents, seemed happy enough to be there. The man he'd seen at the studio, Lachlan, was behind them, and occasionally squeezed Jes's shoulder.

And of course, someone took Michaelis's picture.

He didn't notice at the time, but it didn't take long for the photo to get out. He wasn't even asleep that night, in his rooms in the palace, when Gregory knocked on his door.

"I don't think this is an emergency," he said, "but it's very funny and also something you should know."

He switched on the television in Michaelis's living room and held his phone up, pairing them. His phone's screen appeared on the TV, showing a picture of him and Gregory, in their matching uniforms and their kippahs with the royal crest, sitting attentively on the royal bench. It had been posted to Photogram, with the caption *Kings greeting the Shabbos Queen. You love to see it.*

"Is that a Shivadh Photogram?" he asked. "Not an influencer or someone, I mean." Gregory nodded. "Hm. Bad form to be taking pictures in shul, but I suppose at least they had good intentions. Decent photo, too."

Gregory tapped a button and a very, very long string of comments unfolded.

"Oh dear," Michaelis said.

"It's mostly positive, at least about us," Gregory said. "Some people agree with you they shouldn't have done it."

The first comment, upvoted the most, was *I didn't think old Mikey'd been back since Queen Miranda passed. Good for him.*

"If I was offended every time someone called me that I'd have quit the job thirty-nine years earlier than I did," Michaelis said, as Gregory scrolled. "Anyway, they aren't wrong. It's been years. My own fault."

Another comment near the top was *Pair of deadass foxes.*

"That's a compliment, isn't it?" Michaelis asked.

"Yes. There are roughly fifteen separate comments calling you a silver fox," Gregory said, amused.

"Again, I've been called worse. What are they calling you?"

"Well, one person said I was a Shivadh snack, which is about the most absurd. The most upvoted compliment was that I'm short, dark, and handsome, which made Eddie laugh. There's not a lot of real ugliness, and half of Askazer-Shivadlakia downvotes it whenever it pops up, so it's essentially invisible the second it appears."

"Mm, and it's not like we didn't get all that before," Michaelis agreed.

That's cool and all but isn't it kind of super disrespectful to Jews? someone had written. *Shouldn't you be invited before you go to services?*

Michaelis opened his mouth but Gregory said, "Wait for it," and opened the comments thread below.

Found the American gentile, the first comment said.

Imagine having to be invited to the synagogue you were married at, the second one added.

Harold, they're Jewish, the third one said. Michaelis cracked up laughing.

"I recognize that joke, Edward taught me that meme!" he said. "You're right, this is funny."

"Now that the country's the center of social media attention, it might go on like this for a while," Gregory said, disconnecting from the television. "I'll get briefings from comms regularly, but I was wondering if you wanted to know when you show up on social media."

"Do you think it's necessary?"

"I don't know yet. It's all new to me, too. Generally it's been kinder to us than the tabloids, but it can get vicious and there's no editor to stop it when it does. Nobody to sue, either."

"Hm." Michaelis crossed his arms, considering. "I don't really need the flattery. I made it a point never to read my own reviews unless they had genuine impact on the governance of the country. That said, I do want to know if something's brewing that you or I will need to manage. Can't have myself turned into a meme every time I go for a walk. What does Edward think?"

"Eddie's an influencer," Gregory said. "He manages his spin himself, and he's much better at it than we'd be."

"Then I think I should ask him to keep an eye on my hashtag, or whatever they're using to identify these things, and if he sees something I should know about, he can tell me."

Gregory was biting his lip. Michaelis raised an eyebrow.

"Eddie said the exact same thing. He's the one who found this one," he said, wiggling his phone. "Says he's happy to do it but wasn't sure you wanted him to."

"As long as it doesn't waste his time," Michaelis replied. "He's technically palace staff now, he shouldn't be made to overwork."

"Oh, believe me, nobody has to make Eddie overwork," Gregory replied. "I didn't realize we were *both* fifteen-hour-day kind of people."

"This brings up a point," Michaelis said, because he'd been turning it over in his mind since seeing Deimos earlier. "Did you know there's a person in Fons-Askaz making a podcast about the country?"

"What?" Gregory asked.

"I don't have much information about it yet. An expat moving back from America. They say they're going to do a series about Shivadh culture, the country…probably your rule. They've already spoken with Esta Jerome."

"Can you send me what you have?" Gregory asked, brow furrowing. "Copy palace comms, perhaps?"

"It didn't seem malicious, for what it's worth," Michaelis said. "Esta wouldn't stab you in the back."

"No, but this is still the kind of thing one has to keep an eye on. I'll speak to Esta about it."

"I wouldn't do that yet," Michaelis said. "Just…I'll send you what I have in the morning, you can look it over then."

"You're sure?" Gregory asked. Michaelis pulled him in by the back of the neck, kissing his forehead, a reassuring gesture since Gregory's childhood.

"Trust me. This doesn't have to get resolved tonight. I'm keeping an eye on it too. Remember, it's Shabbos. At least take the night. Go spend some time with Edward. Get some sleep."

"Fine. It's a good idea," Gregory said with a smile, conceding. "Sleep well, Father."

"You too," Michaelis said, and when Gregory was gone he settled into the couch to read for a while, pleased with the world despite the presence of Photogram in it. It was, actually, a little nice to be in the public eye again, and one did like to hear every once in a while how handsome one was.

CHAPTER THREE

MICHAELIS SPENT THE weekend at the palace, mostly puttering around. He went running in the mornings, worked on the massive project of putting forty years of his papers in order, and played football with the weekend staff, though his knees protested later. On Sunday, he spent the afternoon with Gregory in the kitchen, tasting various dishes Eddie and Simon were concocting. He'd always liked the royal kitchen and Gregory had loved it from childhood, so it wasn't exactly a trial.

Whenever he could, he had his headphones in, and Jes Deimos's voice in his ear.

He knew Gregory was listening as well, and both of them had plenty of reason; if a prominent journalist was going to do an entire series about the country, they ought to know as much as possible. Palace comms wasn't thrilled, but Gregory didn't seem overly worried after he listened to the trailer and a few of the earlier episodes.

And *The Echo* was fun to listen to, purely for entertainment – Michaelis could see why it was popular. Deimos was never aggressive, exactly, but they had a way of pulling a person apart with exacting slowness to get at the meat of what they had to say. He'd have to watch himself a little around them, but that could be fun, too.

They did human-interest pieces and political reporting; an entire season dedicated to the lives of students at a New York performing arts school, and one where they did nothing but interview people the listenership had nominated as thought leaders of the day. They did retrospectives on old news stories that had apparently revolutionized how people saw certain historical events, and they had a running, years-long series on sexuality and gender identity that Michaelis probably could have used when Gregory was coming out, and Gregory definitely could have. They chronicled almost the entirety of their friend Lachlan's marriage, from his third date with his now-husband to the day they adopted their child. They did an episode about what it meant to identify as butch, followed by one about what it meant to come out as nonbinary, to explore genderqueer identities. There seemed to be a lot of discussion and disagreement about the vocabulary, but even that was an education.

He didn't always listen to all of an episode, or every episode in a season, but that was sort of the brilliance of podcasts, he thought; you could just jump around as you pleased, most of the time. He kept a list of other shows they recommended, and his player filled up so fast he had to slim it back down again. Most of the voices were American, but not all, and the more he listened, especially in the evenings when his time was hard to fill, the more intrigued he became. By Monday night, when he was settled back in the lodge with a glass of wine and *The Echo*'s first episode about Askazer-Shivadlakia, he was looking forward to the brainstorming meeting the following day. And he was secretly a little pleased that he was *in* that first episode, taken from Noah's recording.

At Mike's request, Deimos said, voice rich with amusement, *though we have some more information about what he recommends to see and do, we're holding off on sharing it for now. You'll be hearing from him again!*

Tuesday dawned stormy, an unexpected summer rain drumming on the tin roof of the lodge by the time Michaelis woke, so he exercised rare royal privilege and called up to the palace to ask someone to drive down with his car. Normally the trail from the lodge to the palace was a nice morning stroll, but he wanted to look like a genteel retired royal rather than a drowned rat.

And he asked for the Jaguar.

Well, Deimos's remarks about mid-life crises had stung a little, and on the off-chance they caught him pulling up, the sight of the bottle-green Jag he'd been given for his fiftieth birthday would be amusing.

When he arrived at the studio, Jes and Noah actually were outside, but not for any good reason he could see. Noah had his arms full of equipment wrapped in plastic, and Jes was escorting him hurriedly to a van already full of the stuff, a huge umbrella in one hand. He parked the Jaguar behind the van and climbed out, pulling his coat's hood up to keep the rain off his head.

"What's going on?" he called through the downpour.

"Leaks!" Jes yelled back. "Meeting's canceled!"

"How bad a leak?" he asked, baffled by this, and then looked at the office building, which had water pouring out of the front door. "What in the…"

"Kinda bad!" Jes said, as Noah thrust the equipment into the van's open door.

"Let me help," he said, running through the streams filling the front walkway, up to the building's entrance. Inside there was an inch of water in the waiting room of the office. He darted back out into the hall, dodging drips and streams, and lunged for the fuse box he'd seen earlier, pulling it open and flicking all the electricity off.

"What're you doing?" Jes demanded, coming inside. They kept the umbrella up, but Noah ran past them both into the darkened office.

"Turning off the electrics. If the water reaches the outlets and they're live, we'll all die very unhappily," he said, switching on the flashlight on his phone to illuminate the hall. "How can I help?"

"We've got most of the delicate stuff out. It's just furniture and one of the heavier pieces of equipment," they replied. Noah was clattering around in the studio, from the sound of it. "I didn't know this place was made of cardboard when we rented it."

"It does seem to be worryingly disintegrating," Michaelis

said, looking around. "Who else is in the building?"

"As far as I know, nobody. At the time I thought that was great, less noise, but now I'm thinking this is probably why we got it cheap. Dammit," they growled, running fingers through their wet, disordered hair. It dripped onto the baggy sweatshirt they were wearing, creating a constellation of darker dots on the already damp grey fabric over the NYU logo. They sloshed forward, Michaelis following. "Noah?"

"I can't get the board on my own!" Noah yelled.

"Here, let me," Michaelis said, slogging to where Noah was trying to wrestle something flat, wide, and enormous off the table. "If you cover us with the umbrella, we can get this out together," he added to Jes.

"I don't think there's room in the van for it and me," Noah said. "If we can get the board in the front seat you can drive it back, and I'll wait here."

"Not indoors, this is a death trap," Jes said. Michaelis, hefting one end of the board, eyed it speculatively.

"I've got a car," he said.

"You've got a Hot Wheels. It won't fit in the back seat you don't have," Jes said.

"So put it in the van. I'll take Noah and follow you to wherever you're taking it all," he replied.

"Shit, I don't even know. My parents' garage, maybe. They're going to love that," Jes sighed. "But it's dry, at least. Mostly."

"Let's get it out of here," Noah urged.

They managed to haul it out to the van and load it into the front seat, upright, belted in like a passenger, then huddled under the umbrella to confer.

"That's the last of it," Noah said. "Unless you want to – "

He was cut off by an almighty crash; behind them, part of the roof of the building caved in. The family Deimos stared at it.

"You know," Michaelis said, "I think I'm going to have a word with our municipal government about building inspectors picking up the slack a little. We have safety laws in this country."

"That'd be helpful, yes," Jes said. "What a disaster."

"At least you're out, and this looks like very difficult equipment to replace," Michaelis observed. Thunder crashed. "We should get inside. Look," he added, because both of them seemed miserable and he was starting to really feel how wet his socks and shoes were. "There's a cafe down the block that's probably structurally sound. Let's take a break and dry off. I'll buy you a coffee."

They looked more bewildered than anything, and he understood the feeling, so he hustled both of them down the sidewalk and into the cafe, where other equally-wet people were drying out. A few of them looked his way and whispered to each other when they walked in, but Michaelis settled Jes and Noah at a table and then went to the counter, where the barista at least knew him slightly and wasn't entirely bowled over by him walking into her cafe.

"Your Grace," she said. "You look like you've been through it."

"There has been," Michaelis told her, "something of an incident. Could I lean on your patriotic spirit for a couple of dishtowels?"

"I know their regular orders," she said, nodding at Jes and Noah. "Yours plus theirs?"

"Please," he answered, swiping his card as she rang him up.

"No charge for the towels," she said, handing him a stack from under the counter. "I'll call when the drinks are up."

He carried the towels back to the table, using one to dry his face and passing the others to Jes and Noah. Jes seemed glad to be able to put their hair in order, and Noah was mostly dry once he'd patted all the rainwater he could off his legs.

"Well, you aren't seeing us at our most professional," Jes said, through the towel, "but you are, I have to say, seeing us at our most resourceful."

220

"I've found professionalism to be vastly overrated, generally," he replied. "Glad I could help."

"Thank you," Noah said, poking his parent with a finger.

"Yes, we do appreciate it," Jes added, giving Noah a look. "Can we pay you for the coffees?"

"Consider it a down payment on my podcasting lessons. Though I don't think you'll be back in that particular studio anytime soon," he said.

"We've got two weeks' worth of shows in the can," Noah said to Jes, who looked annoyed and disconsolate. "I can do some extra-fast editing once we record and if we can get a new studio set up we won't really miss much time."

"Should you not be in school?" Michaelis asked, realizing it was early May and the schools generally didn't let out until June.

"He's enrolling in the fall. By the time we got set up here, he'd have three weeks left, so we decided not to bother," Jes said. "Didn't seem worth it to send him to school just for exams." They gave him a challenging look. "Going to narc, Your Grace?"

"Beneath the notice of a king," Michaelis answered, amused. "No, it's not my business, and he seems like he's learning something, anyway."

"I could be doing that project on fundraising you wanted me to do," Noah said to Jes. "If you let me take some pictures in the studio I can – "

"You can't go back in there," Michaelis interrupted, appalled. "It's not safe. The whole damn thing looks like it's going to slide into the harbor."

"I'm light," Noah said to him with a grin.

"Allow me to introduce you to the wild child," Jes sighed. "He's right, Noah. We'll shoot some of you looking sad and wet next to the van. Hah! We can call it Noah and the Flood."

Noah made a waifish, pathetic face. Michaelis smiled.

"What do you need the funds for?" he asked. "I would hope it was insured."

"We were renting. Even if the building is insured the money mostly won't come to us, and our business insurance is going to take an eternity to pay out. We've got to rent a new space, which means new deposits and costs. We'll have to get it all set up again, and replace at least two of the mics well before insurance pays, if it ever does. We put up the soundproofing ourselves, so we'll have to either buy more or wait to salvage what's in there. It's...doable, but not great," Jes said. "We're living with my parents right now. We were planning to find a place and move out, but we can use the rent budget if we have to."

The barista called "Deimos!" and Noah got up to go get the drinks. Michaelis rested his chin in his hand, considering. There were arts grants available and he was sure he could divert grant money for this, but it would look like personal use, given he wanted to use the equipment as well. But...the fishing lodge was technically state property, and it had plenty of empty space. Damn thing was built like a bunker – in fact, the basement had been expanded into one –

"That's very imposing," Jes said, and he looked up from his thoughts.

"What?"

"The face. You look like you're bored at the UN," they said, gesturing to his face as Noah set a coffee in front of him.

"I'm sorry, I was just thinking," he said. "I'm staying at the fishing lodge right now, out on the palace grounds. The basement was built out as a bunker during the war. It's already pretty soundproof. You only need my permission to use it, which I'm more than willing to give. And there'd be no charge."

"Ah," Noah said, and they both looked at him. "Can I record this?"

Michaelis grinned at him. "Want a second take?"

"He's already recording on that damn pocket mic, he's just asking for permission now," Jes accused. Noah flushed. "Noah!"

"It's fine, I expected no less from a *broadcast journalist*,"

Michaelis said, gently teasing. "It really is, I don't mind," he repeated to Jes, who didn't look entirely appeased. "I suppose if you're making a podcast about Askazer-Shivadlakia this is probably very good material."

"You're still supposed to ask before you start recording," Jes said. "That's basic ethics."

"Can we get back to the bunker?" Noah asked. "I want to record in a bunker!"

"It seems as though your day has been pretty much wiped clean of meetings," Michaelis pointed out. "At least come and see if it would be useful to you. If not, we can always take the equipment to your parents'."

Jes nodded. "All right, we might as well take a look. One of us is going to have to ride with you in the Hot Wheels, though."

Half an hour saw them running through rain that had only slightly lessened; Noah, leggy and with the energy of youth, outdistanced them both and got into the van. Jes yelled, "Noah!" in a frustrated tone that Michaelis remembered from when Gregory was a teenager: annoyance and resignation rolled together, that their fifteen-year-old had made a unilateral decision they didn't agree with.

"Get in out of the rain before you yell at him," he said, holding the door on the Jaguar for Jes, who looked askance at him but climbed in. He circled around and got behind the wheel, shaking water off his hands and arms.

"He knows he's supposed to ask first, and only drive the van on side roads," Jes said.

"He's fifteen. You let him drive it at all?"

"Well, sixteen is the legal driving age in the US, you know," they replied. "Sometimes when it's just you and your thirteen-year-old kid and you have to get recording equipment somewhere, you have to improvise."

"*Thirteen?*"

"This is why I can't punish him too badly for it, I created

him," Jes said, as their phone beeped. Michaelis could see the single word text from Noah: *Dibs...?*

"It's not far to the lodge, and mostly on a back road," he offered. Well, Gregory had been captain of the shooting team at school when he was fifteen, and giving a child a rifle was arguably a worse idea than putting them behind the wheel of a car.

"*Fine*," Jes said, typing out a message back. "*Next time ask.* And, send," they said. "You'll have to drive ahead, to show him where to – oh, no," they said, as he started the car.

"What?" he asked.

"This is the shiny car, isn't it. You drove your midlife crisis car here just to tweak me?"

He shot them a smile and pulled out of the parking space, gesturing for Noah to follow him.

The disintegrating recording studio was relatively close to the turnoff for the back entrance to the palace grounds; it didn't take them too long to pull onto the bumpy road to the fishing lodge. In deference to the equipment he drove slowly so Noah, apparently a cautious would-be driver, could follow at a sedate pace. Normally he would have pulled around to the front of the lodge, but there was a loading dock down into the bunker, so instead he guided the Jaguar down the ramp and into the covered underground garage.

"Well, this is...definitely...concrete," Jes remarked, getting out. Noah bounced out of the van and looked around eagerly.

"Is this the bunker?" he asked.

"Through here," Michaelis said, leading them deeper into the dimly-lit garage and through the thick entry door. Inside, he took off his drenched shoes and wet socks, and saw the others following suit.

The bunker had been renovated from a simple cellar into a long-term shelter, and the previous royal family had lived there for a period during the war. It had a series of empty bedrooms at the back, a little kitchen off to one side, and a large central room that had served as a war room of sorts, with an extremely yellowed and outdated map of Europe still on one wall. A smaller room off to the side had been a playroom and nursery for the royal children once; beyond that was a network of corridors connecting different parts of the bunker to each other, old walled-off boltholes, supply closets, and the garage. It would have been unpleasant to live in, and some of the rooms were now simply storage, but it was well-lit and well-ventilated, and quiet.

"We could put up like four studios in here!" Noah called from one of the former bedrooms. "The soundproofing's already great! Little bit of foam, run some extension cords...this'll work!"

"As you can see, it's also watertight," Michaelis drawled. Jes cracked a smile as they examined the ancient cookware still on the shelves in the kitchen.

"I can't object to the rent," they said. "And Noah approves, so we can work with it. I never knew this was here. I mean, the fishing lodge, we did field trips as kids, but they didn't show us the bunker."

"Shame. It's very historic – they ought to start showing it on tours. But it's also not very useful, empty like this," Michaelis said.

"You're living here?"

"Upstairs in the lodge proper. It's a little nicer," he said.

"Why not at the palace?"

Michaelis shifted uncomfortably, looking away. "Well, the whole point of retirement was that I could spend more time fishing," he joked, but Jes didn't laugh. "Beats trying to rule a country."

"Well, if that's your yardstick, life's a breeze," they said. "Noah?"

"Yeah!" Noah emerged from the back, looking around interestedly. "This is super punk rock," he declared. "It's awesome, we could definitely fix it up."

"There's parking and space," Jes agreed, looking around. "Are you sure we won't disturb you?"

"Separate entrance, and concrete ceilings. I probably won't even notice you're here," Michaelis said. "During daylight hours you'll have lake access, too. The conservation officers don't love strangers out on the grounds at night, but the view at night's a little lacking anyway."

Noah had his phone out and was already taking selfies.

"Come on, kid, let's get the equipment loaded in," Jes said, casually putting their child in a headlock and dragging him away. Michaelis followed and was promptly tasked with fetching and carrying, since he had no clue how anything should be set up. He brought most of the equipment in, while Noah set it up and Jes settled into a dusty chair to inspect each piece and do any triage for later repair. By the time Noah said they were set, it was past noon.

"Come upstairs," Michaelis said. "Have lunch before you go."

"Coffee and lunch? The generosity of the king knows no bounds," Jes said, following him up the stairs.

"Former king," he corrected with a smile, elbowing the door to the main lodge open.

Jes had to admit, when they'd arrived at the studio that morning to find it falling apart, they hadn't expected to be eating lunch in a warm, dry bungalow with the former king.

Noah, the bottomless pit, was plowing his way through an entire bag of potato chips, which didn't seem to bother Michaelis, who had set out makings for sandwiches and left them to their own devices while he took down plates and cups. The lodge was large, meant for entertaining, and it wasn't difficult to tell how little space Michaelis took up – the kitchen was tidy but lived-in, and there were newspapers folded up next to the nook in the kitchen where he clearly ate his meals. The formal dining room and ballroom that they remembered from childhood field trips were closed off, but the living room that the kitchen opened into had blankets on the sofa, books strewn around, and a jigsaw puzzle on the table in the corner.

"This kitchen is huge," Noah said, settled at the dining table in the corner. "I think our whole apartment in New York'd fit into it."

"Used to be two," Michaelis said. "The old kings were more observant – needed the separate kitchens. My father had it converted to the one big one, put in the bar between the kitchen and the living room, did a few other renovations. He had to have the whole building rewired – before it couldn't even support the one refrigerator, always blew fuses when I was a child. Really should replace that fridge," he added. "The renovation was mostly to make it easier on the caterers when we entertained out here. It's pretty big for one person, but I suppose if I ever wanted to throw a dinner party I'd be glad of it."

"And it's just you? I suppose I assumed you'd have a chef and a couple of maids," Jes said, settling in next to Noah.

"I could, but I didn't see the point. I'm not what you'd call an inspired cook, but I can shift for myself, and Gregory would miss our chef, Simon, if I took him away. Not to mention he'd be incredibly bored just cooking for me," Michaelis replied. "It keeps me busy."

"Do you have to keep it pretty neat?" Noah asked. "If it's historic, I mean."

"Usually nobody's living here long-term, and there aren't any school tours left this term," Michaelis answered. "In any case, I'm a fairly tidy man. Gregory's the messy one. Don't put that in any podcasts," he added, pointing at the recorder sitting out on the table. "Can't have the king mad at me."

Noah made a careful note on his phone, checking the timestamp on the recorder.

"Well, you are all business, aren't you?" Michaelis asked.

"Suppose you've been apprenticing for a while."

"Is that what I'm doing?" Noah asked Jes.

"You can call it that if you want. I kind of like the ring of it," Jes replied. "Noah Deimos, apprentice podcaster."

"Shame you already had the business cards printed," Michaelis said.

"Oh, no, the business cards…" Noah looked at Jes in alarm. "They were in the office."

"Well, then it's a chance to print some new ones," Jes told him. "They have the wrong address on them now anyway. I'm sure we're going to spend the next week thinking of things that were in that office. Probably for the best we hadn't decorated."

"At least this way we won't lose much time," Noah said. "We could be up and recording again this afternoon if we wanted. Can we offer studio space to the people who wanted to rent some?" he asked Michaelis bluntly.

"We'll have to invoice for equipment and time – can't charge for the space itself," Jes said. "Might actually bring our prices down, which could bring in more artists. Don't mind that."

"Well, it sounds like you know what you're doing. Just keep them from wandering. I'll get you a set of keys for the garage entrance," Michaelis replied, more agreeably than Jes might have, if it meant strangers were going to be in their basement all day. "Convenient for me, I must say."

"Ah, his true motives are revealed," Jes said to Noah. "See, you're getting good at this interview thing."

"I'm known to be nefarious," Michaelis said. "I promise I won't be a nuisance, though."

"Why's it so crazy down there, anyhow?" Noah asked. "Walls a foot thick, weird hallways going off to nowhere."

"The fishing lodge dates back a couple of centuries," Michaelis said. "You'd probably have to look in some archive, somewhere, but what I've heard from various sources is that it originally just had that single big room, essentially a cellar. It was used as a shelter during the First World War, but it wasn't really *designed* as one. Then Gregory II – "

"The one who made it a democracy," Noah said.

"It's like the single fact about this place he knows," Jes told Michaelis.

"More than some know," Michaelis replied. "Gregory II had it reinforced after the war, and about fifteen years later when he saw what was going on next door, he decided to expand it into a space they could live in. Hide in. If they had to."

"Hide from what?" Noah said.

Michaelis fixed him with a level gaze. "Who would we have been worried about, in 1935?"

Noah's eyes widened. "Nazis?"

"Italy's on our doorstep. Germany's not that far away," Michaelis said. "Gregory II was an unusually farsighted ruler. He anticipated a lot of 20th century history. Askazer-Shivadlakia basically emptied out in the 1930s – he sent as many people away from Europe as he could. Our own private little diaspora within a diaspora."

"And the royal family hid here?"

"For a time. We – the country, I mean – were incredibly lucky. Not many roads or rails in or out of the country, nothing at the time that would support a tank, and we could booby-trap the lowlands and the harbor. We had some foreign support from the Allies, too, though it's not entirely clear as to how. We made it just slightly too painful for anyone to bother with us. We're of no strategic importance and we were surrounded by enemies. So I think," he said, taking a sip of water, "that more than one army looked at this little country and said, *we'll deal with you later.*"

"But they never did," Noah said.

"No, the Americans came up through Italy first. We gave them a good beach-head. There were some Shivadh soldiers among them, actually, there's a memorial in town. We didn't get out of the war without harm, but…" he shrugged. "We survived.

We're the only Jewish monarchy in Europe. Which Gregory is discovering has its own issues," he added.

"See, this is good material," Noah said. "Boss, there's maybe a history episode in it."

"Perhaps," Jes said. "Maybe Michaelis wants to be the one to tell that, though."

"Don't know. Always a little dicey, bringing it up," Michaelis said. "Some ugly conspiracy theories are attached. I'd want to make sure I had all the facts first."

"How would you see your podcast working, anyway?" Jes asked. "Like one story a week? Formal interviews? Do you want to get the royal librarian involved?"

"Couldn't say. I hardly know what I'm doing, which admittedly is a feeling I haven't had in a while," Michaelis said. "I've been listening to yours, though. And a few others. I don't think I care for those shows where it's just one person talking. That's really nothing more than a book on tape, eh? No disrespect to them, but a conversation – like the shows you do – that's much more interesting and I'll need all the help I can get."

"But you did spend forty years deep in European politics," Jes said. "I know Askazer-Shivadlakia used to host diplomatic talks as a neutral ground. You were king when the Berlin Wall fell."

"I wasn't king of Germany," Michaelis pointed out.

"No, but it must have had ramifications for you. Hang on, this is Noah's job," Jes said. "Let's step back a little. You don't like your storytelling, that's what we should tackle first."

They looked at Noah, who considered it. Michaelis waited patiently, working his way through half a sandwich.

"Can you tell us one of your memoir stories?" Noah said at last. "As if you were dictating to us. Like, show me what's boring you, I guess. Don't tell a boring story, just tell a story," he added, seeing Michaelis's expression. "And then we can help you."

Michaelis sat back for a minute, finishing his bite of food, took a sip of water, and thought about it.

"Well, I left off with some trade negotiations about six months before Gregory was born," he said, and launched into a story that was so unbearably boring that Jes was actually shocked.

Watching such a charismatic man suddenly lose his entire persona was baffling. Two minutes into it they looked to Noah, who seemed equally surprised. Three minutes in, Michaelis stopped of his own accord and spread his hands.

"You see the problem," he said, with a self-deprecating smile.

"At least you're aware of it," Jes said. "That was extremely boring, but I've been bored by professionals who didn't even know they were doing it."

"It's mostly 'cause it's about something boring, I think," Noah said.

"It's important, though," Michaelis replied. "This kind of detail. It's the kind of thing I used to look up in the indices when I was a new king, so that I'd know what to do. Maybe it's better written down," he added. "Not good fodder for a show."

"You do have to pick and choose, with audio media," Jes agreed. "An interview format would probably be more helpful. Or, maybe not an interview exactly, but something structured. We can workshop it. There's plenty of time, anyway, it's not like you have a deadline."

"Why didn't you ask your dad?" Noah asked. Michaelis frowned.

"Ask him what?"

"Why didn't you ask him stuff instead of looking it up? He was still alive, right?"

"It's complicated," Michaelis said. "The simplest way to put it is that I wanted to prove I could rule without him looking over my shoulder. And also the second I was crowned he left the country on an eight-month goodwill cruise."

"Nice work if you can get it," Jes said.

"He wrestled control of the country from an incompetent

tyrant and affirmed democratic rule of law. I feel like he earned it," Michaelis replied.

"This is already way more interesting than the trade negotiations," Noah said to Jes.

"Good, then you're on the right track," they replied.

"My opinion on my father's round the world cruise isn't really relevant, though," Michaelis pointed out.

"I suppose you'll need to decide if you want to be educational or interesting," Jes said. "It's an ongoing tension in this business."

"Wouldn't one ideally want to be both?" Michaelis asked.

"Sure, but you can't be both one hundred percent. And fifty-fifty doesn't always satisfy either."

"Nobody likes a compromise," Michaelis murmured, almost to himself.

"You're a politician," Noah said, like he was reasoning something out. Michaelis nodded. "So it's like writing a speech, isn't it? You have to share information but keep people interested. Did you have to learn to do that? Or was it, like, natural?"

"I had rhetoric and oration at school," Michaelis said. "But you do learn as you go, in my line of work."

"Then you can learn this too!" Noah said brightly. "It'll just take practice."

"I appreciate the encouragement," Michaelis said. Jes caught the faint hint of amusement, but they could tell Noah hadn't, nor was he meant to.

"We've monopolized you for long enough today," they said, gathering up the remains of their lunch to dispose of it. "Noah and I should really see about talking to the landlord."

"I'll get you a key to the bunker – come and go as you like," he replied, ducking out of the room. "Back in just a minute."

"Do not sass him more and ruin this for me," Noah hissed when he was gone.

"I haven't sassed!" Jes replied. "What am I ruining?"

"A super cool concrete bunker in the middle of a literal forest

I didn't know was here!"

"It's the palace grounds. It's a public park."

"Still. This place is great and free and probably has secret passages and hidden rooms," Noah said.

"There is a missing wine cellar," Michaelis replied, coming back into the kitchen, a set of keys in one hand. He passed them to Jes. "Somewhere under the lodge. Supposedly, anyway. Let me know if you find it."

"Thank you, again," Jes said, as Noah got ready to go. "This is really generous."

"Public property," he reminded them. "Your taxes at work."

"Well, I'll make good use of it, then," Jes said. "We'll reschedule the brainstorming meeting and send you an invite. Good day, Your Grace," they added, with a hint of sass just to tease Noah, and left the former king to the rest of his lunch.

CHAPTER FOUR

TIME BEGAN TO pass surprisingly quickly after that. Michaelis often dropped into the bunker in the mornings just to make sure Jes and Noah didn't need anything. They sometimes came up at his invitation to have a meal in the lodge, especially now that he had meetings with them to discuss the podcasts. Eventually Noah took to popping in and out at random, since it was easier to go through the lodge to get to the lake than it was to circle around from the bunker. Michaelis suspected on occasion it was also easier to rummage for snacks in the lodge pantry than go into town for them, but a stray granola bar or sandwich wouldn't break the royal pension.

Michaelis found his days much busier, and felt like he got out into town more; he went back to Friday night service, too. He knew Jes saw him there, but they didn't mention it, so he didn't either. Noah had homework for him on how podcasts worked, and he did some research of his own as well.

Eddie had taken Michaelis's request to hear about anything relevant to him rather liberally, and began sending him memes. Every few days he'd send a link to a Photogram post or video, or simply a photo someone had taken of Michaelis and captioned amusingly; apparently there was somewhere called r/shivadhkings that followed him and Gregory religiously. It was all rather flattering; if any of the comments were cruel, Eddie thoughtfully wasn't sharing those, or was dealing with them through the palace comms team.

Two weeks after the Great Flood, as Jes called it on their

latest episode of *The Echo*, he came downstairs in the morning to a serious discussion, Noah's voice a little panicked, Jes sounding not entirely confident either.

" – won't be the worst thing in the world if we have to stay with Nona and Granddad until autumn," Jes was saying, as he walked in.

"Won't be great either, though," Noah replied. "You hate being there, and I guess I get why now. Even in New York we could always find somewhere."

"It's different here – it's a beach town. As soon as it gets warm, everywhere fills up, and it got warm super early this year. Even if there are places to rent, they're rented by tourists, and it's worse this year. Granddad's had offers on my bedroom that have made me seriously consider sharing with a random tourist."

"Why is it so bad?"

"Tourism's up. Eddie Rambler made it the place to be. Which we will definitely cover in our *Why Are We A Meme* episode," Jes said, and then saw Michaelis in the doorway. "Hey! Come in, we were about to get started reviewing the script for your first episode with Noah."

"Still looking for a place?" Michaelis asked, as he went to the kitchen, where a carafe of coffee was still steaming. "Every apartment in town can't be rented."

"No, but those that aren't are either expensive or about as durable as the studio was," Jes replied.

"I had a meeting with Alanna about that," Michaelis said, stirring sugar into the coffee. "She's going to push it to Parliament – new housing, maybe subsidized housing, and definitely more stringent building codes. A lot of the older buildings are from before my time and were exempt from previous changes in the law. Gregory will make sure things are put in motion. I wish I could say whoever built that mess could be beheaded but I'm afraid we did away with summary execution."

Jes laughed. "It's good of you to even have the king take an interest."

"Well, that's what he's there for." Michaelis sipped his coffee, considering. "In general the palace has been in support of Edward's, ah, enthusiasm about Askazer-Shivadlakia, but we certainly weren't prepared for how it would impact infrastructure. I don't think anyone in the world is truly prepared for Eddie Rambler."

"What's he like?" Noah asked. "He seems cool."

"He's very engaging. Surprisingly, also a good cook. Most of these TV chefs aren't, I have a feeling." Michaelis came to the table, settling in and accepting a tablet with his script on it from Jes.

"I saw a rumor on the internet that Edward isn't his real name," Noah said.

"And do you have an opinion about rumors on the internet?" Michaelis asked mildly. Noah grinned.

"Mostly lies, and only sometimes fun ones," he said. "Why do you suppose he'd do it? Change his name, I mean."

"Well, show business," Jes said. "People sometimes have to change their names for whatever reason. Anyway, I did," they added.

"I suppose I could have changed mine when I became king – some kings of Askazer-Shivadlakia did, way back in the past," Michaelis said thoughtfully. "That would have been too strange for me, though. Gregory thought about it, but only when he was a teenager."

"What did the rumor say Rambler's real name was?" Jes asked.

"Didn't, but they said they bet it had to be rough to change it to Eddie Rambler," Noah said.

"He does have a way of disturbing things," Michaelis said. "Such as, unfortunately, the housing market."

"Should see if we can move in with him," Jes joked to Noah. "It's fine, we'll find a place. If not now, then when the season's over, after the olive harvest."

"You'd be welcome here," Michaelis heard himself say, without even thinking about it first. They both looked at him. "The lodge, I mean."

"Down here?" Jes asked.

"No, that would be unbearably grim. There's space upstairs. You've seen the only working kitchen, but there's an otherwise self-contained suite you could use. Two bedrooms, sitting room, bathroom – I'm in the single bedroom suite at the back, but the two-bed is what we used to use when I was king, and it's serviceable. Or you could each have your own, but those are in the upstairs wing which gets quite warm in the summer."

Noah looked to Jes, who was studying Michaelis with an expression he couldn't quite discern. He hoped, more or less, that they weren't seeing right through his poker face, to how much the silence of the lodge sometimes troubled him.

"We can't live here *and* work here for free," they finally said. Michaelis smiled faintly.

"Technically there's probably some kind of grant you could get to be an artist in residence, so you could be getting paid to live and work here, but I see your point," he said. "Shivadh pride, you know," he added to Noah. "If you like, fix yourself a fair rent and make out a check to the steward of the palace; he'll know what to do with it. I'll get you his name."

Jes looked away, and he could tell his remark about pride had touched a nerve. "I'll think about it."

"Offer stands, no deadline," he replied, and sipped his coffee again. "Now, let's go over this script."

The next morning, Michaelis came out to find Noah in the lodge's kitchen, not the bunker, peering into a cupboard.

"I keep the crown jewels in the fridge," he said, and Noah

laughed. "What are you looking for?"

"Coffee?"

"Ah, here," Michaelis said, taking it down from a different cupboard. "Guess this means you and Jes are moving in?"

"Yep." Noah sounded a little strained about it, so Michaelis let him make the coffee while he took down mugs and got cream from the fridge. "Nona and Granddad weren't pleased. They wanted me and Boss to stay there forever. Big fight, even though Boss only said we were considering the offer. I think the grandparents are going to sulk for a while."

"I'm sorry to hear that. Gregory wasn't pleased when I moved out here, but at least he understood."

"Nona and Granddad aren't pleased by much," Noah continued, watching the coffee drip. "Boss says I'm lucky they love me."

"Ah."

"We used to come here for a week in the summer, or for Passover, but I guess they were on really good behavior then because Boss made it clear that if they weren't, we wouldn't come back. I didn't notice until, like, last year."

"Parents and children…" Michaelis shrugged, a bit at a loss. It was very American, all this sharing, but then Noah was young and had grown up there.

"Sure, but I don't think Nona and Granddad even like *each other*. Wild, right?" Noah asked, turning around. "I wouldn't marry someone I didn't like."

"People get stuck, I suppose. My son considered an arranged marriage for a while. My fault, I pressured him. I forget not everyone marries young like I did."

"How old were you?" Noah asked.

"You should read more Shivadh history," Michaelis said with a smile. "I was nineteen."

"But you liked them, right?"

"Indeed, I loved her very much." Michaelis got up and picked up one of the mugs, pouring from the quarter-full pot, to avoid further discussion. "Well, I'm glad you're both here. And if you want to leave in autumn, a lot of places will open up. If you don't want to live in town, there are cabins in the highlands, too."

"Really just the one highland," Noah said, a fossilized old Shivadh joke, and Michaelis burst out laughing.

"Who taught you that old chestnut?" he asked.

"Eddie Rambler's Photogram."

"Bless. If you want to live in our one highland, I can make some recommendations."

"Who was laughing?" Jes asked, struggling through the front door with an enormous suitcase, the overalls they were wearing streaked with dust. Noah ran to help them. "I heard you from outside."

"Noah was entertaining me," Michaelis called. "Welcome to the lodge."

"Thank you, we'll try to keep being funny," Jes said, as Noah wrestled the bag away and carried it off. Michaelis poured another mug of coffee and passed it over. "Gorgeous. Noah and I will go out today and buy our own food. We wanted to leave early."

"Noah mentioned some strife," Michaelis said.

"Of course he did." Jes sighed. "Spilling our family drama…"

"Every family has some. Gregory used to enjoy dredging up old scandals from royal families past and sharing them over dinner, or doing reports on them for school. Nothing I haven't heard a dozen times before."

"I put your bag in your bedroom," Noah announced, returning. "And I checked the studio calendar, you have the whole afternoon off to unpack while Lachlan and I record with Michaelis."

"All business," Jes said fondly, ruffling his hair. "Let's at least have breakfast first. Actually, we were going to go out — can we buy you breakfast?" they asked Michaelis.

"I wouldn't mind. There's a little place down by the beach

that does a traditional fried breakfast," Michaelis suggested. It was cheap and hot, and he felt like a bit of salt air this morning.

"An entire fried breakfast?" Noah asked.

"I still have the Jaguar here," Michaelis said.

"We'd have to strap Noah to the roof. No, come on, we'll take the van, and you can have a fried breakfast just this once," Jes said to Noah. Michaelis went to get his shoes, already pleased. He couldn't imagine why he hadn't thought of going down to the beach for a nice breakfast before now.

"Hello listeners! I'm Noah," Noah said, settled with ease in front of his mic.

"I'm Michaelis," Michaelis added.

"I'm Lachlan, hi!" Lachlan chimed in.

"And this is *How To Make Some Noise*," Noah finished. "Your weekly podcast about podcasts."

"So, Noah, tell everyone why I'm here," Michaelis said.

"Michaelis is the retired king of Askazer-Shivadlakia, and he's going to be making a show about his life and work," Noah said. "But how much do you know about podcasting?"

"Absolutely nothing," Michaelis confirmed.

"So my job is to get you up to speed on how a podcast gets made, and show everyone else how it's done as well. Next time we'll start at the very beginning, so everyone can follow along, but this time we're going to discuss our setup a little."

"Very first question: if you're the host and I'm your guest, what's Lachlan doing here, buried behind all that technology?" Michaelis asked.

"Aside from looking gorgeous?" Lachlan put in.

"Goes without saying," Michaelis intoned, and Lachlan laughed.

"In most recording studios, the producer who watches the

audio levels and keeps us on track is in a separate room with a glass partition, so they can see us but won't make noise on the microphones," Noah said. "But we're recording in this awesome old bunker, which is mostly concrete, so we can't put any windows in and it's tough to run cords through the walls. Lachlan's going to stay cozy in here with us, and you'll all hear him occasionally."

"Not that I mind," Lachlan said. "More time to admire Michaelis."

"I'll try to remember to comb my hair," Michaelis replied.

They'd scripted this out, at least to an extent; Lachlan, rather sweetly in Michaelis's opinion, had asked if he felt all right about a little silliness over his looks, and he'd said he didn't mind, as long as it was clear it was all in fun. Nobody wanted to be condoning harassment on air, but a joke every now and then didn't hurt anyone.

"In a few episodes we'll come back to the technology in more detail," Noah said, launching into the meat of the show. "Lachlan is producing for us because he's been in radio for about ten years, the last three of those here in Askazer-Shivadlakia…"

It really was odd, Jes thought, how easy they found it to settle into a new routine. A few weeks into living at the lodge, it felt like they'd always been there; they knew where the laundry was and how to nudge the elderly fridge just right when the door wouldn't immediately open. Noah was slowly exploring every nook and cranny except for Michaelis's rooms, and he'd been out in the little boat moored at the lake dock a handful of times, alone but always under some kind of adult beachside supervision.

Often, in the mornings, Jes came into the kitchen to find Michaelis had already made coffee and gone out; aside from his old-fashioned morning athletics, they weren't sure what he did, but he didn't seem annoyed by their presence. Most evenings if they wanted to find him he was in the living room, reading. Sometimes, when Noah got on a kick about experimenting with Shivadh cooking, he'd sit at the kitchen bar and watch, offering frequently useless suggestions until Noah made him text the palace chef for help. Jes had never met Simon, but probably owed him a couple of beers, the way Noah and Michaelis pestered him.

It was such a deep relief, too, not to wake up to their parents sniping at each other every morning – to pour some coffee, linger over the morning news before starting work on the various stories they were chasing, greet Michaelis when he came in from running or a morning swim, and make breakfast for Noah without criticism or commentary from anyone else. They felt...in control again, in a way they sometimes hadn't even in New York. There was something to be said for predictability, which twenty-year-old Jes would have laughed at, but twenty-year-old Jes didn't know who they were or what they wanted or how to get it. These days, they generally had a handle on at least two of the three.

As far as Jes knew, Noah's podcast with Michaelis was going well. They had their hands full with the rest of the network. They were long-distance supervising a few network podcasts still being made in New York, working on their own, and helping with the various clients coming into the bunker to do one-off recordings. A surprising number of locals were interested in recording audiobooks, either their own modest efforts or books for family who needed audio. There were even a few musicians, none especially promising but all very earnest. If Jes wanted to discover the next big star from Askazer-Shivadlakia, they supposed they'd have to wait until Eurovision like everyone else.

It was a busy life, but it was a living, and it had its little pleasures.

One of them was just coming in through the front door now – Michaelis, fresh from a swim in the lake, bare-chested with a towel over his shoulders, swim trunks still damp. Jes leaned on the counter and pretended to be engrossed in their coffee.

"Morning," Michaelis called, padding into the living room.

"Ah, morning," they replied, looking up. "Good swim?"

Hello, pectorals, Jes thought. *Greetings, biceps.*

"Middling. Looks like it's going to storm, so I got out early. I'm sure my obituary will be many things, but I hope it won't read *Former King Dies In Freak Lightning Strike*," he said.

"Good to know; I was thinking of going out today. If it's going to pour, I'll stay in."

"Storm should clear up soon. Good beach weather coming this week, I think. Have a good day in the studio," he added, passing down the hallway towards his suite.

Goodbye, ass. Adieu, calves.

Michaelis was exactly the kind of mistake twenty year old Jes would have made, an older man with a deep voice and a significant amount of power. New York was full of men like him and some of them were even as good-natured as he was, though not many. Jes suspected, however, that while his wife had passed he still thought of himself as married, not widowed, and married men were a mistake they had learned *not* to make.

In any case, he was literally making it possible for them to run their business, and that deserved caution too.

Still, Jes was old and wise enough to enjoy the view without needing to buy the property. If Michaelis didn't mind walking through the lodge in his swim trunks, Jes wasn't going to object.

Eddie emerged from the shower to the usual morning noise – Gregory moving around, dressing and drinking coffee, exchanging a few words with his valet before he got on with the day. Often he had the news on, but more frequently these days it was audio – back episodes of *The Echo*, or short daily podcasts about world events. This morning it was clearly a podcast, but it wasn't about the news, exactly.

"Is that Michaelis?" Eddie asked, over what sounded like Gregory's father talking about microphones.

"It's the first episode of his show with Deimos's kid," Gregory replied. "It's great and also very weird to listen to."

"Is he flirting with that dude?" Eddie asked, eyes going wide as another male voice said something and Michaelis chuckled.

"Their tech guy, Lachlan," Gregory said. "That's what's a little weird."

"I didn't think your dad swung that way."

"As far as I'm aware, he doesn't, but he doesn't tell me everything. And remember, my love, we don't have the same hangups some Americans do. He wouldn't care if someone thought he was dating this fellow, it's no harm to him."

"But it's still weird for you?" Eddie asked.

"Hearing your father flirt with someone on a globally available medium wouldn't be weird for you?"

"Point. Are you okay with it? Because of your mom, I mean."

"I'm a little surprised he is, to be honest. I went to therapy, I've done the work," Gregory said. Eddie wrapped his arms around Gregory's waist, knocking his forehead gently against the back of Gregory's head. "When she died he just…kept working. I mean, it's possible he got some help and didn't say, but I don't think so. It's good to hear him having fun, anyway."

"Maybe he's getting some help now," Eddie said, gesturing at the speaker as Michaelis laughed.

"Maybe so," Gregory said, sounding pleased. "Either way, nice to hear. Haven't heard that in a while. Good for Dad."

CHAPTER FIVE

MICHAELIS AND NOAH seemed to be doing well with *How To Make Some Noise*, so Jes had tried to stay out of it. Noah was supposed to be helping Michaelis figure out his own podcast as well, but Jes didn't want to pressure either one of them. Michaelis didn't seem hurried, and Noah was a kid, not a pro they were paying to get the work done. If he did go into the family business, he'd need to know how to take initiative without a manager prodding him on. Prodding was Jes's job as a parent, not as a producer.

Still, whenever they knew Noah and Michaelis were talking about the show, they kept an ear cocked, and probably for the best. Sometimes you had to learn by failing, after all.

"I understand you're frustrated," they heard Michaelis say as they passed through the lodge one evening after dinner, and they stopped to listen to the two arguing in the kitchen. "I am trying, Noah."

"I know! That's what's so annoying. You are trying but we're not getting anywhere," Noah said.

"Then that's not my fault."

"I didn't say it was!"

"All right, well, what haven't we tried?" Michaelis said. "We've been brainstorming, clearly that hasn't worked. Maybe we should try coming at this from some other angle. How do I make things interesting without being indiscreet? How do I pick out what's interesting in the first place?"

"How can you not know what's interesting?" Noah demanded.

"It's my life, Noah, I lived through all of it, none of it seems all that compelling to me," Michaelis said, which was...actually rather worrying. It was the kind of thing Jes had heard depressed friends say, and they thought he'd moved past that a little.

"Hey," Jes said, leaning in the doorway. Both of them looked up, Noah visibly upset, Michaelis desperate. "This doesn't look like the book club I signed up for."

"Very funny, Boss," Noah muttered.

"Cranky," Jes said, going to him and rubbing the back of his head affectionately. He didn't bat them away, so he couldn't be too mad. "You're getting frustrated and Michaelis is getting tired."

"Well, he's being frustrating," Noah said.

"I'm sure he is, he probably had classes in how to frustrate people," Jes said, dropping Michaelis a wink. He nodded, tilting his head in understanding of what they were doing. "Which is all the more reason to tag out. You guys have been working on this for weeks. Why don't you let a pro handle this one."

"I could be a pro," Noah said rebelliously.

"Someday you will, but this calls for drastic measures only I can do safely," Jes said, rummaging in the fridge for a post-dinner snack. "Go be a kid for a while. You're off the clock."

Noah seemed to relax a little. Perhaps he needed the reminder more often. "Can I stay up and video chat with Mart?"

"Might as well," Jes agreed, pulling a handful of grapes off a bunch and eating them, one by one. Inspiration struck them and they smiled. "Go on, give Mart my love. Michaelis and I are going to play the questions game."

"Fine. But we're not done," Noah added to Michaelis.

"I never dreamed we were," he said, and Noah gave him a sharp nod and went off to the suite. "Who's Mart?" Michaelis asked when he was gone.

"One of my New York friends. She's a drag queen, and she's usually getting ready for work right around the time he goes to bed now, so to get to stay up and talk with her while she puts her makeup on is kind of a treat."

"Good. He deserves it after putting up with me. I forget how young he is."

"So does he," Jes sighed. "And then he loses his temper."

"He's trying to help," Michaelis said, circling to sit at the kitchen bar, on the other side from them. Perfect. "It's not his fault he's got very dry clay to work with."

"Nor his fault that he's fifteen," Jes said, finishing the grapes and washing their hands. "He's better at the technology than you but he hasn't got a lot of experience being a teacher."

"I'm out of practice as a student," Michaelis said.

"I don't really think you need to study," Jes replied. "What you need is something to knock yourself loose."

Michaelis spread his hands. "Your cunning plan?"

"The questions game." Jes went to a cupboard and took down a box they'd uncovered a few days before. "Found these. I assume they were for entertaining at some point. We are going to play a game I learned coming up in my journalism career."

Michaelis watched warily as they unpacked a set of shot glasses, lining them up in the middle of the counter. They each bore the royal crest. He picked one up and touched the crest thoughtfully.

"Now, you can just say no and walk away, and I will still respect you. But I think this will help, so I want you to keep an open mind," Jes said.

"A game, you say," Michaelis said, setting the glass down.

"It's a little like truth or dare. I'm going to try and help you figure out some really interesting stories to tell," Jes said. "Which can be uncomfortable."

Michaelis blinked again. "Hence the shots."

Jes produced, from under the counter, a gray-green bottle. Michaelis leaned back from it as if it had an evil aura.

"Shots of Davzda," Jes announced.

"Absolutely not," Michaelis replied.

"It's fine, it's the legal stuff."

"That doesn't make it better," Michaelis observed.

"It's a little better! The legal stuff hasn't got any psychedelics in it and it's only fifty percent alcohol by volume. Practically speaking, it's just gin," Jes told him.

"It tastes like beach sand," Michaelis said. "Goes down like it too."

"That's the salt content. It's medicinal," Jes continued, pouring out a series of shots. "You can't get this stuff in America, I had to import it while I lived there. Cheers," they added, and did a shot. It burned, tasting like bad decisions and yes, beach sand.

"You are going to die," Michaelis told them.

"Not me. So listen, here's how it works," Jes said, making soft little hacking noises around the words as the alcohol lingered. "I ask you uncomfortable questions. If you can, you answer them. If you don't want to answer, you have to do a shot."

Michaelis frowned. "What's this meant to accomplish?"

"You royals, so direct," they replied, getting water glasses down from the cupboard and filling them. "It's meant to ease you in, so that after a while you're drunk enough to answer the question anyway. And if you won't answer any questions, you pass out fast, don't waste my time, and get a hangover as punishment."

He seemed to study the shots in front of him. The fumes wafting off them were practically visible.

"I'd like to set some boundaries," he said finally.

"I wouldn't have guessed," Jes replied drily.

"Nothing about Gregory," he ticked the first rule off on his index finger, looking at them. They nodded.

"Fair, this isn't about him," they said.

"Nothing about my wife," Michaelis added, touching his middle finger with his thumb. "I'll talk about her if I please but she's not an open topic for an interview."

Jes felt their heart crack a little. "All right," they agreed.

"Thank you." He touched his ring finger with his thumb.

"And I'm allowed to pass without drinking if you ask anything that might threaten the security of the country."

"How would I know you're telling the truth?" they asked.

"I'm an honorable man," he answered. Jes gave him a skeptical look. "What? I did a great job here..." he gestured outward at the country. "I'm trusting you not to take advantage of me if I get alcohol poisoning from this..."

"I reserve the right to renegotiate," Jes said. "And if you can tell me off the record I want the tea."

"The tea," Michaelis snorted. "Fine. But on that note, nothing goes further than us without my permission, tomorrow, in the cold light of day."

"Smart," Jes said. "Agreed. You want a shot to start with?"

"I don't even want a shot to end with. I might get through this entirely sober," Michaelis declared.

"Who is the sexiest world leader you've met?" Jes asked.

Michaelis looked at them, looked at the shots, considered it, and downed one, no chaser. He didn't even wheeze, but his ears turned pink.

"All right, I'll softball you," Jes said, laughing. Michaelis folded his arms on the counter and gestured with one hand.

"Go on, then," he said.

The thing about the questions game was that it was really two games. There was the drinking game, of course – innocent but a little dangerous, maybe even a little sexy. Ultimately it felt fun, whether or not it was helpful in this case.

But the second game, Jes had learned, was a chess game, one the other person hopefully didn't know you were playing.

With Michaelis, the trick was to start out easy, with questions he could answer without feeling self-conscious – then throw in just a few that might make a shot seem attractive. Get him closer to doing at least one more shot, but never make it seem like too much at once. With Davzda involved and with him already on edge about the idea…

Michaelis looked askance at some of the early questions – *How did it feel to be crowned? What's the most boring story you have? Who do you think is the most famous person you've ever met?* – but every now and then Jes would throw in something which sounded innocent and which also made his eyes dart to the shot glasses.

He did his second shot half an hour in, his third ten minutes later, both regarding his opinion on certain world political figures. Jes pulled back then and gave him time to forget he already had the equivalent of about half a bottle of wine in him. They gave him a glass of water, made him drink most of it around more softball questions, and then said, "Okay, this is a little personal, but bear with me."

He gestured for them to continue.

"Why did you move out here to the lodge? And don't say it was for the fishing. You've got two fish in the freezer and haven't gone out on the lake since Noah and I arrived."

"Could have gone in the early morning and cooked them for breakfast," he pointed out. "You wouldn't even know."

"We'd smell the fish."

"Only if I caught any. Maybe they weren't biting," he replied. Then he shrugged and, without being prompted, continued. "Of course it's not for the fishing. If I can't tell a polite lie by now I shouldn't have ever been king."

Jes leaned forward, propping themself on the counter separating them from the former king. "So? Why?"

Michaelis studied the nearest full shot glass, then shook his head. "It was pragmatism. Gregory's very new on the throne, but he's more ready than I was – he's the first king in generations who actually got the right kind of training for the role. My father was naturally good at it and I was a quick study, but Gregory was both born and trained to do this kind of work."

"So?"

"So he ought to be given the chance to do it. People don't like change and they don't want to learn new ways of doing things. Can't have them come round looking for me when they should be talking to him. I go up and knock around in my old office sometimes in case anyone really needs me, and I stay up at the palace on weekends, but…" he shrugged. "Best if I fade into the wings for a while."

"Hm," Jes said, and he tilted his head.

"What, hm?" he asked.

"It makes me think of Jean Valjean," they said.

"How so?"

"Have you read *Les Miserables*?"

"No, the thing's a doorstop," Michaelis replied. "And I just don't care that much about France. But we had several touring versions of it come through, and I believe a few years ago a local school put on a production. That was…certainly an experience."

"So you know the basic plot, right?"

"More or less."

"At the end of the book, he's got his daughter settled in with her husband, and he's making sure she's taken care of," Jes said. "He figures his sordid past might someday come out, so he sets about making sure he can't taint her life with it. He won't even sign their marriage contract, he fakes a wound to get out of it. He moves away, starts making her call him by his name instead of father, that kind of thing. And he makes it…easier for her to lose him. Because he knows he's dying."

Michaelis seemed to consider this, distracted from earlier questions by the idea they'd suggested.

"I have no intentions of dying anytime soon," he said at last. "And I'd rather not distance myself from my only child that way. But there's this thing about being king, and I don't know if I can explain it."

Jes gestured at him to take his time. He nodded, chewing on

his lip.

"Gregory and I both joke about the Shivadh love of drama," he said. "A good kind of drama. The people want a show. You know," he said, and Jes nodded. They did know; the country probably only still had a king because it sounded more fun than having a president. "So, we are Shivadh. I'm not immune and he certainly isn't. There's a feeling you have as king, a connection to the country. Even an elected king, there's something different about it. You aren't only a politician. You think, this country is mine to care for, and if I'm lucky and good at it, it'll be that way for most of my life. I felt it, and I know Gregory does. I want him to get to experience that without me standing in the way, or even casting a shadow. And I'm a little jealous, because it's not mine anymore," he added ruefully.

"That's a staggering loss," Jes said. It was; it made their heart ache to think of it. It reminded them of leaving Askazer-Shivadlakia when they were young. To give it up when you were an angry child was one thing. To give it up after dedicating your life to it...

"Well, I don't love drama *that* much," Michaelis said dismissively, but he wouldn't look them in the eye.

"It is, though," Jes insisted. "You had a life's purpose, and you passed that on when you knew it was the right thing to do, but you still had to lose it. That's hard, and people shouldn't tell you it isn't."

"Nobody's told me that. Least of all Gregory," he said with a laugh. "I just – thought I'd come out here and lose myself for a little while, until that all subsided. All that...feeling."

"Has it?"

Michaelis looked at them, looked away, and then picked up one of the shots, grimacing as he downed it.

"Do you think it will?"

He shook his head and did another one, which was a lot even for a veteran of the game.

"Fair enough," Jes agreed. They picked up the bottle and two of the empty shot glasses. "Come on."

"Where are we going?"

"I'm tired of standing and those stools aren't very comfortable," Jes said, walking out of the kitchen. They could hear the stool's legs grate against the floor as Michaelis followed.

Jes settled on the floor, back against the sofa, and put the shot glasses on the coffee table, filling them both. Michaelis seemed to ponder this, then set down his water glass next to the shots and sank to the floor on the other side of the coffee table, gracefully, legs crossed. After brief consideration, he rested his arms on the table and leaned forward to put his chin on them. It was probably the most he'd slouched in years, Jes thought.

"I can see how you came to prominence as a journalist," he said. Jes gave him a gentle smile.

"I did that because I worked extremely hard and kissed a lot of ass," they said. "Go on then. Take a break, that was rough. Have some more water. Ask me a question."

"Hmf." He watched them with his dark eyes, considering while he took a sip of water. "Why did you leave Askazer-Shivadlakia, all those years ago?"

Jes thought about it, but they weren't quite ready to discuss that outside of a therapy office – and the point wasn't for them to share, not really, but to build trust.

They picked up a shot, gave him a look, and downed it.

"All right," he said. "When you came back, did you really move halfway across the world just to do a podcast?"

"If I wanted to cheat, I could just say no, and not elaborate," Jes pointed out. Michaelis was silent. "Also, that is such a politician question."

"I'm a politician."

"I'm well aware." They shifted a little, settling in. "No. For one thing, a podcast about Askazer-Shivadlakia is never going to be especially lucrative and I unfortunately do not have a large inheritance or a suspiciously dead rich spouse. I have some money, enough to do this, but not enough that I can stop working, or do just as I please."

"Then why?"

"A few reasons," Jes said. "The most significant was that Noah was struggling. He's such a smart kid, but he's awkward and too old for his years, which is probably my fault, and he just…couldn't find his place, in school, with his cohort. I thought, well, the schools here are better, they're smaller, and it's a chance for him to reinvent himself if he wants."

"He doesn't seem at all awkward to me," Michaelis said.

"Well, my friend, you are a grown man and kind of a nerd, of course you're a kindred soul," Jes pointed out. "I'm sure he'd get along well with your very nerdy son Gregory, too."

"Gregory Three," he murmured, and they didn't understand until he continued. "Gregory Two was his namesake. Nice man, so I'm told, but not a very good father. Raised an extremely useless son."

"Yes, I did have year three history," Jes chided gently.

"Sorry. Do go on."

"Go on with what?"

"You said Noah was the most important reason. As a father, I agree. As a king, I still want to know why else you came back. I don't get the impression it was patriotism."

Jes considered doing another shot, but hell, the odds of Michaelis even remembering this in the morning were slim.

"Your son is gay, and still took a very public job that complicated his life more than almost any other would," they said.

"Tell me about it," he replied.

"I respect that a lot. I know that this place is…more permissive – more accepting? I'm not even sure of the word," they admitted. "But it's kinder for someone like me, that was always true. Now there's this precious, fragile growing thing, this community here that people are trying to build, in a place that's good for us. To have a gay king is…a little patch of sunlight for people who need it to flourish. America is *so hard*, Michaelis, you have no idea. Everywhere can be hard but it felt like it was getting harder, in a way I didn't like and didn't want for my son. I didn't feel safe, either. Lachlan isn't even from here, but when he told me I needed to come back, he said I should come *home*. I thought, if Lachlan can feel like this is home, I might feel safe here too."

"Do you?"

"So far, yes," Jes said. "Doesn't hurt that I have a powerful patron."

"I don't like that word," he said. "Patron. I'm not patronizing you. I have no power."

"Of course you do. You've given us a place to work, a place to live. People in this country still look to your example."

"I'm not a powerful patron," he insisted.

Jes fought the urge to make a joke, because it did seem important to him. "Fine. You are…an influential friend. How's that?"

"Better," he agreed. He sat up straight, took one of the shots, and threw it back, without a question, without prompting. Jes refilled it calmly, hiding their surprise.

"Can I ask another?" they asked.

"Of course. That's the point, yes?" His smile was open and warm, unguarded, and it felt a little like a gift.

"Yes," they agreed. "What's the most important political lesson you learned, back when you were studying the other kings? What I mean is, what was most relevant to you, from them?"

"Difficult to say," he said thoughtfully. "I think…maybe the Echardt Scandal. Well, it's called that. I feel like it'd barely be considered sensational compared to what you see on Photogram, at least up to a point. In the memoirs you can read the story in the words of the royals who had to deal with it, and it taught me a lot about…a lot," he finished. "Echardt was a powerful man about three hundred years ago. He held some loans the king at the time had used to...I think he had financed a minor war."

"Oh, only a minor one," Jes said.

"We're a very small country, major ones happen without our input," Michaelis pointed out.

"I'm sorry, continue."

"Well, this Echardt kept a mistress, and also a...mister," Michaelis said. His speech was slower, less exact than usual, his vowels round and soft. "His man wrote to Echardt's wife, fed up with being second fiddle I suppose, and told her anonymously that her husband was being unfaithful. Doesn't seem very bright, if you ask me."

"Why not?"

"More likely to get the boyfriend dumped, eh? And if not that, get Echardt thrown out of his own home, and at that point he's less likely to keep a consort of any kind."

"I suppose that's true," Jes agreed.

"Anyway, wife goes to Echardt and says, is this true, he says no, of course not, and secretly dumps the boyfriend. Who, crucially, goes to the girlfriend."

"This definitely was not in the history books," Jes said.

"Bet it is if you know where to look," Michaelis replied, with a level gaze only slightly marred by the fact that he wasn't entirely focusing. "So the girlfriend goes to the wife in person and says her husband's playing an even wider field than she thought. Echardt doubles down. Absolutely not. Faithful to the end. Well. There's two women fighting with Echardt inside his house and one cheerleading ex-boyfriend standing outside, and the commotion got bad enough someone called whatever passed for law enforcement back then. Whole thing came in front of the king. Out of deference to Echardt, it was in private, more or less."

"To the debts Echardt held, I think you mean."

"Which is also why the king said that the man should sort out his business himself. He knew he didn't want to cross the man holding his loans. He knew that the consorts didn't have the means to cause a real fuss and the wife could be, ah, stifled."

"Gross."

"Undoubtedly. But the wife turns out to know secrets both royal and financial, and it gets fiddly here," Michaelis continued, fingertips dancing around the table. "I'd have to look up what exactly went on. The girlfriend and boyfriend both left town, which was a smart decision. The wife eventually put the screws to Echardt and said, either you sign it all over to me and leave too, or I'll bring you down by force with what I know."

"Do we...do we know her name?" Jes asked. "I have a statue I'd like to put up."

He put a finger to his lips. "Sh. Let me tell it. Echardt tells his wife he's not leaving and if she tries to end him he'll kill her. She pitches a fit – I would too – and it comes back to the king. King's obviously not pleased at all by this."

"Why? Seems like either way, he gets rid of this asshole."

"You'd think," Michaelis said. "But remember, this is all happening more or less in private, which starts to look more and more like a cover-up. People know the king is close with Echardt but not why. King says to Echardt, I told you to fix this yourself. Echardt thinks this time if he hints about the loans the king will support him and, like a fool, the king panics and does. He tells the wife, if she publishes she can be sure she *will* be damned."

"What did she do?"

"She published," Michaelis said with relish. "Made all his papers public and wisely went into hiding. Echardt fled with the clothes on his back. But that's not why it was so important. One of the papers indicated that not only did Echardt hold debts wildly beyond what was publicly known, but some of the loans the king took out didn't make it to the military."

"Where did they go?"

"The boyfriend."

Jes let out a little gasp. "The boyfriend was double-timing him with the king?"

"The boyfriend was blackmailing the king."

"Fuck!"

"I know!" he said. "So here's the kingdom now broke, the king's been caught paying off some banker's boyfriend for lord knows what reason, the banker's fled, the boyfriend's fled. The people are furious. And of course, the wife is essentially ruined. She got her revenge, but the money's obviously not coming back now. She can't stay in hiding from the king forever and she has limited time in which to harness the anger of the citizenry. So she does what any resourceful woman would do."

"Oh do tell," Jes said.

"Off with his head."

"What?" Jes asked, shocked.

"She raises an army, deposes the king, has him beheaded, and takes the throne."

Jes blinked at him, trying to formulate a response. After a while, they said, "So there might already be a statue of her."

Michaelis dissolved into laughter.

"No statue," he said, snorting with glee. "Maybe there should be. There are a couple of very good portraits in the palace. Her name was Queen Alekha. Dozen-or-so times great-grandmother of my wife, Miranda, actually."

"Well, don't mess with your wife's family," Jes said.

"One of the many lessons this has to teach us," Michaelis said. "But there were others. Everything I did as king, in those early years, I thought about the king who wanted to make Echardt sort this out himself. If I thought something was best handled in secret, I did it in public. If I thought it would be a bother to fix a problem that touched on the safety of the country, I made certain I never let it out of my sight. A king isn't there to make pronouncements, he's there to run the damn country."

"His personal dignity and safety be damned?" Jes asked.

"He is no longer a person. He's a king. At least, from eight to six every day. Outside of that, his duty is to those he loves.

Echardt and the king together did everything wrong. I'm not in support of beheadings, obviously, but…"

"Fuck around and find out," Jes said.

"A very succinct lesson I took very much to heart," he finished. "If you like that story, remind me to tell you sometime about my theory that Meyer Lansky saved the country from the Nazis during the war. Or the reason the town is called Fons-Askaz. Noah would call that one *wild*."

Jes stared at him. There was something here, something percolating, and when it bubbled to the surface they grinned.

"What?" Michaelis asked.

"This is it," they said. "This is the podcast."

He looked around. "Isn't," he replied. "You don't even have Noah's little pocket recorder."

"No, I mean conceptually. That's how you make this podcast. Okay, so maybe some of the stories you want to tell you can't, and some of the stories you ought to tell are interminably boring. But you still do have stories to tell. You tell a short version of a story from your life, maybe redacted if you have to, and then you talk about how history got you there. Or you start with a historical story and link it to one of yours. People eat that up," they finished. "You've named at least three of those stories you could tell just in the last fifteen minutes."

Michaelis took a while to mull this over, or possibly he'd lost his train of thought. Finally he looked up at them, glassy-eyed.

"So this is good," he said.

Jes grinned at him. "Oh, you are tanked."

Michaelis nodded gravely, very slowly, swaying a little where he sat. Jes laughed.

"Well, a breakthrough means success, we can finish for the night," they said, downing the last shot on the table. Michaelis tried to stand and made it most of the way up before he staggered. Jes caught his arm and steadied him; he leaned in against them, warm and close. His head bent forward, face tilting over theirs.

"Hi, Jes," he said softly.

"Hey, stranger," they replied, trying to stay light, trying not to think about how easy it would be to kiss him. It would also be taking advantage – and unwise even sober. "Come on. I'll walk you home."

"That's funny, because it's twenty feet in that direction," he informed them.

"Yes, I was aware," Jes agreed, gently moving him forward. They got a shoulder under his arm, wrapping their arm around his waist in order to guide him down the hall to the suite. He leaned against the wall outside the bathroom while they rummaged for painkillers, handing two pills to him with another glass of water and watching as he downed them.

"All of it," they said, and he obediently finished the glass. He stumbled into the bedroom and settled on the edge of the bed, unbuttoning his shirt.

"Can you get undressed all right?" they asked. Michaelis nodded, then nearly fell off the bed. "Well, if you fall over, try to land on a rug."

He gave them a warm grin, then a wave of a hand to show he'd heard and understood the joke. Jes turned to go, but just as they reached the door, he called, "Jes?"

"Mm-hm?" they asked, turning around again.

"This was…a good idea," he said, apparently measuring his words. "A terrible, good idea."

"I'm full of those," they agreed.

"I'm glad you're here, you and Noah," he said. "It's usually very empty. Very quiet."

"I'm glad too," Jes said. "Goodnight, Your Grace."

"Night," he agreed.

CHAPTER SIX

THE NEXT MORNING Jes woke late, but not too hung over. They staggered out into the kitchen to make coffee, not expecting Michaelis to have done it, but Noah was up first and had put it on to brew. They sat down across from him at the little dining table, nodding thanks over the lip of the cup.

"How'd it go?" Noah asked, shoveling cereal into his mouth. "Sorry about yesterday."

"Don't worry about it. Tempers get a little high sometimes. Michaelis is a dad, he understands. He won't hold it against you."

"Well, I'll tell him sorry too later."

"That would be a good thing to do," Jes said encouragingly. "Anyway, he ought to be in good spirits if he's not absolutely miserable with a hangover. We made progress."

"That fast? Way to make me feel great, Boss."

"It's my job to instill crippling self-esteem issues in you, isn't it?" Jes asked innocently.

"It's an unfair advantage that when you interview someone you get to use alcohol."

"Boy is it ever, just wait until you're older," Jes said. "Do you want the elevator pitch for his podcast or not?"

"Sure. Maybe even the five-minute taxi-ride pitch."

Jes smiled and pitched the concept to him the way they would a producer, something Noah hopefully would be one day if he went into broadcasting. He listened attentively, nodding, and took time to consider it when Jes was done.

"I like it, but I think you should do the show with him instead of me," he said finally, finishing his breakfast. "We can keep on doing *Noise* together, but you should do the history one with him. I can't keep up with that much research when I'm in school."

"You think he's up for something this research-intensive himself?"

"I mean, what else is he doing?" Noah gestured around the lodge with his spoon.

"Good point. Would you like to produce for it?"

"I can do it until school starts. Maybe Uncle Lachlan can after that. We should have *Noise* wrapped by then and I can focus on *Echo Junior.* I wonder if Michaelis would introduce me to Eddie Rambler if I asked," Noah said. "You know if he shouted out the podcast it could really spike our numbers."

"Nothing hurt by asking, though I wouldn't get my hopes up. I'm sure Rambler's a busy man," Jes replied. "What are you up to today?"

"Editing for *Echo Junior.* Can you come with me into town later?"

"Sure, I need to get groceries. Run along, entertain yourself."

"I usually do." Noah put his bowl in the sink, gave them a quick hug around the shoulders, and ran off to fulfill his destiny, or whatever it was he did when they weren't paying attention. Jes focused on coffee, eventually on breakfast and the morning news, and by the time they looked up again it was ten in the morning.

Even hung over, Michaelis should probably be up and moving around by now, but Jes hadn't heard anything. They supposed they should bring him some coffee, as compensation for the shots the night before; after considering for a moment they poured out a mug, added a dash of cream to approximate how he liked it, and went down the hall, rapping gently on his suite door.

"Come in!" his deep voice came through the door, and Jes pushed it open.

They expected to see him still in bed, or suffering in the chair by the window. Instead he was sitting on the neatly made bed, legs crossed. He was in a pair of dove-gray pajamas, the same shade as his hair, and he had a book open in his lap, reading spectacles perched on his nose. He looked like a professor having a leisurely Sunday morning.

"Brought you some coffee," they said, holding the mug up. "It's past ten, I thought you might be too hungover to move."

He looked up, eyes wide. "Past ten already?"

Jes nodded at the clock on the wall. Michaelis blinked but accepted the coffee.

"I woke up still drunk," he said, closing the book and setting it aside. "Don't think I've done that since my twenties."

"College?" they guessed.

"Mm, no, first Purim as king."

"Oh lord."

"Thank goodness there's no video. Anyway, I wanted to look up the details of that story I told you, about Queen Alekha? Got distracted by her biography."

"Great story," they said, leaning against the bedside table.

"Yes, but I don't like not remembering the details. So damn much to remember once you get to my age," he said. "I raided the books we have here but I'll need to go up to the library to get the proper citations. Mostly sober by now, I could go soon."

"I'm surprised you remembered telling me the story."

"Well, I don't remember getting to bed, so I probably owe you a thank-you," he said.

"You already did."

"Excellent. Thank you for making me drink water, too. The headache is mild, though it may be stubborn," he added, rubbing his forehead. "Only what I deserve, I imagine."

"Are there many stories like that one about Queen Alekha? That you know of, I mean."

"Oh, more than a few. Probably many I don't know of, as well. I mentioned Meyer Lansky, didn't I? I'll see what I can bring back from the library today on a few of them. You and Noah working?"

"I'm taking Noah into Fons-Askaz this afternoon, but nothing much otherwise. Want some company in the library?"

"Very much, if you'd like. It's a nice walk up to the palace, and Simon will be pleased to be able to make us some lunch."

"I would like that, I think," Jes replied, smiling. Michaelis smiled back. "Feels good, eh?"

"What's that?"

"Having a hook. When you figure out exactly how to get the story told."

"Yes, I suppose it does. How does one do it from here? Like a book report?"

"Try it like Noah said. Write a speech," Jes suggested. "From there we'll work out how to turn it into a dialogue."

He nodded, sliding off the bed. "I'll be going up in about half an hour. Meet you on the porch?"

Jes left him to dress, packing a bag for the walk to the palace. Pocket recorder, just in case; notebook, phone, and charger. They did a quick check of their hair to make sure it was fine, then after a brief consideration in the mirror they added a little highlighter to their cheeks, darkened their eyebrows, and considered lip gloss before deciding against it.

The day was warm and Michaelis seemed inclined to be quiet on the walk along the lake, so they left him to his thoughts. The palace came into view slowly, through the trees and up a slight incline. When they passed into it through a side entrance, the halls were cool and quiet.

"Parliament's in session, but it's across the building, we shouldn't be disturbed," Michaelis said, leading them through the corridors. "I think – "

"Father!" someone called, and the king of Askazer-Shivadlakia emerged from the other direction, looking startled. Michaelis stopped, as startled as the king, and then...

Jes watched Michaelis light up, subtly but unmistakably, at

the sight of his son. His shoulders squared a little, his smile went wide, and his eyes grew more animated.

"Gregory! I thought you'd be in session," he said, clapping Gregory III on the shoulders.

"We're on a short recess. I didn't know you were here today! We should get lunch, later, if you'll be around. Eddie and Simon are experimenting with molasses, which should be exciting," the king said. His eyes darted curiously to Jes.

"Ah, I'm doing some research," Michaelis said. "This is Jes Deimos, I mentioned – "

"The podcaster!" Gregory beamed at them. "Yes, I've been listening. You're doing the show on Askazer-Shivadlakia and helping Dad with the memoirs project."

He bowed in the Shivadh fashion, deep to demonstrate respect, and Jes debated curtsying, then bowed back. To their shock, as they came out of the bow, the king winked.

"Always glad to see an expat coming home," he said. "We need people like you here. Your interview with Esta was food for thought. And I am working…slowly," he added with a grimace, "on the housing issue. Are you here for long? At the palace, I mean. You should come to lunch too."

Michaelis raised his eyebrows, a question on his face; the message was clear enough, that they didn't have to actually *dine with the king* if Jes didn't want to.

On the other hand, Jes hadn't got where they were in life by saying no to things like that.

"I'd love to," Jes said.

"Great. I'm going to go harass people who need harassing. One o'clock? Yes? Be prepared for barbecue sauce," the king said, and ran up the stairs two at a time. Jes watched him go, a little bemused, then turned back to Michaelis.

"I may not have mentioned he's a fan," Michaelis said. "Or, at least, an avid listener."

"Is it going to be strange if I'm there for lunch?" Jes asked.

"I don't see why it would be. Last time I had lunch with him, Edward and my nephew Gerald made him mediate an argument about Hot Pockets."

"Has he ever eaten a Hot Pocket?"

"I'm not entirely clear on what they are, to be honest," Michaelis admitted.

"You didn't arrange this, did you?" Jes asked, as they began to climb the stairs.

"What, an introduction? No. I meddle in his life now and again when it matters, but I try to keep out of it unless he's truly flailing. And I assumed if you needed my help getting someone in the palace to listen to you, you'd ask."

"Thank you. Safe assumption to make."

"Through here," Michaelis said, pushing open the door of the palace library. "Let's see if we can find some primary sources on Queen Alekha."

When Eddie Rambler walked into the royal dining room for lunch that day, he was met with a full table: Gregory, one of his MPs, the King Emeritus, Alanna, and a stranger Eddie didn't recognize, but someone he definitely wanted to meet. He pushed the wheeled cart in front of him into the room and began unloading bowls of barbecue sauce onto the table, followed by a platter of roasted chicken and a sheaf of paper.

"I have six kinds of barbecue sauce and I'm going to need you all to fill out a survey," he announced. "Simon and I are having a difference of opinion regarding traditional Shivadh sauce, and half the internet is going to start setting cars on fire if we don't resolve it soon. It's Esta, isn't it?" he asked the MP.

"Good to see you again, Eddie," Esta said.

"You I have not met, but your hair is spectacular," Eddie added to the stranger, who had ice-white hair piled on top of their head in a fabulous pompadour.

"Dad brought a guest for lunch," Gregory said, accepting a kiss on the cheek and a hefty plate of chicken. "This is Jes Deimos, they're staying at the fishing lodge."

"Oh! And doing the shows we've been listening to. Nice to meet you. I also like your voice," Eddie said cheerfully, setting out the sauces. "Do you eat chicken? I can grab some crudites if not."

"Chicken is fine," Jes said, smiling at him. "Nice to meet you. My son and I both follow your Photogram."

"Cool! Here, help yourselves," Eddie said, putting spoons in the sauces. "Left to right, sweet to savory. I'm not saying where Simon or I fall on the issue, so that you can be impartial."

He settled in as they began passing the food around, sampling carefully and thoughtfully. Alanna was on her tablet, not unusual, but Gregory seemed in good spirits and Esta was pretty fun when she wasn't talking politics. Michaelis was quiet, but he often was. Eddie had recently observed to Gregory that his father was the definition of still waters running deep, and Gregory had laughed and agreed.

"You're recording out at the fishing lodge now, aren't you?" Eddie asked Jes, leaning in to be heard over the conversation going on around them.

"His Grace really scored points with my son on that one," they said, nodding. "He's over the moon to be recording in a historical bunker, and he loves the lake. Of course, it's been helpful from a practical standpoint, too."

"I heard about the storm, but only what you put on the podcast and second-hand information from Greg. I'd have paid a lot to see His Grace running through the rain with a soundboard," Eddie said with a grin. Jes laughed.

"It was more than I expected to see," they agreed. "Worked out well for us in the end. The lodge is beautiful."

"I've done some filming at the lake. Gorgeous country."

"You really do like it here, don't you?" Jes asked. "That's not an act for those tourism bits you do."

Eddie nodded. "Simon – the royal chef, kind of a partner in crime – he told me that after he arrived, he couldn't ever leave. I know the feeling. We're still figuring everything out but I'm liable to be here a while. From the sound of it, you have more complicated feelings about the country, though."

"It's different when you're born here, I suppose," Jes said. "Born here and not a royal, anyway," they added.

"I can imagine. We're keeping exalted company now, though, huh?"

"Or they're slumming it, I haven't decided."

Eddie grinned, delighted. "Oh, I'm going to drop that idea on Gregory at some point. He'll be enraged. Love to enrage him," he added fondly. "Making one of the royal family lose their temper, even if it's just in fun, feels like a real accomplishment."

"Tell you a secret?" Jes asked, and Eddie nodded eagerly. "I got Michaelis to play a drinking game last night."

"Wait, really?"

"He did shots! It was *great*. Do recommend. He's funny when you loosen him up a little."

Michaelis had terrorized Eddie the first time they'd met, but with time and experience he'd come to realize it probably hadn't been intentional. And anyway, Gregory and Alanna were both worried about him lately.

"Probably did him a world of good," Eddie said. "He's been struggling a little, Gregory thinks."

"I got that sense, yes. But we're making great headway on his podcast now."

"Well, if you need a hand from the palace…Michaelis has a lot more pull than I do, but I'm here," Eddie said. "Always happy to help."

"Actually, it's not exactly what you're offering, but I was wondering if you'd consider coming on one of the podcasts," Jes said. "Noah'd give an arm to have you on *Echo Junior.*"

Eddie nodded. "Sure, that'd be a kick. Who should I talk to about scheduling?"

"I'll have Noah get in touch. What's a good way to reach you?"

They were in the middle of exchanging information when Eddie caught Michaelis watching them; he had an expression on his face that was difficult to read, but it was a reminder that this was a man who'd known Eddie was dating Gregory for weeks before saying anything. He had an awareness of the people around him that bordered on uncanny, and a career politician's sense of when to deploy it.

"So, Your Grace," he said, when Michaelis saw him looking. "Are you Jes's boss, or are they yours, now?"

"I think I'm either client, student, or building superintendent, depending on time of day," Michaelis replied.

"Don't forget barista," Jes added. "He rises at dawn, which is extremely unsettling, but it does mean there's usually coffee in the kitchen when I drag myself awake. I was alarmed when he wasn't around this morning but it turns out he just got lost in research."

"Which reminds me, I'd like another hour or so in the library this afternoon," Michaelis said, pushing back from the table. "Jes, if you'd like to head back to the lodge, I'd understand."

"No, I'll come with you," they said. "But then I do have to get home. Noah wanted me to go into Fons-Askaz with him this afternoon."

"Right. If you'll excuse us – Your Majesty," Michaelis added to Gregory with a bow. Jes said their goodbyes and followed him out, and Eddie sat back in his chair, relaxing slightly.

"Well, you made a friend," Esta said. "Gregory asked me along because I know Jes, and he was worried they'd feel a little at odds, but you kept them occupied. Not that I mind either way. Not every day you get to have barbecue chicken with two kings."

"I like Jes. I've been very charmingly roped into appearing

on their kid's podcast," Eddie said. "And then your dad just glared the shit out of me, Greg."

"You'd think you'd be used to it by now," Alanna said.

"He hasn't glared at me in weeks, at least!"

"No, he hasn't," Gregory said, eyes slightly narrowed, still on the doorway.

"Greg," Eddie said, half a question.

"Mm?" Gregory looked at him, then shook his head. "Sorry. Just strange to see Dad cheerful again."

"Gregory," Alanna said, sounding a little appalled.

"You're the one who thought he was depressed! Eddie, I want you to spy for me," Gregory said. "When you're down at the lodge to do the podcast, just…see how he's doing."

"On it," Eddie agreed. "I love it when he gives me jobs," he told Esta.

"It's lost its novelty when he does it to me," she replied.

"All right, subjects," Gregory said. "Off with you all. Leave your questionnaires with Eddie. Eddie, go entertain yourself," he added, leaning over to kiss him. "Tell Simon whatever he thinks is right, I support him."

"Traitor," Eddie replied affectionately.

"Can't be a traitor when you're the king!" Gregory called as he walked out the door.

Michaelis had really only intended to make a few last notes and clean up, but as soon as he and Jes were back at the little study desk, Jes settled in with one of their finds and took their notebook out. He shrugged to himself and sorted the books into stacks — one pile to be left behind with a note not to be moved, one pile to take back with him, and one pile that could safely be given to the librarian to be re-shelved. The early afternoon light streamed in through the windows, warming his back. It dappled Jes, sitting in the chair across from his, turning their white hair subtly gold.

He'd enjoyed lunch, but seeing Eddie charm Jes so effortlessly, the way he seemed to do everyone – even Michaelis, who was fond of him and certainly felt Gregory could do worse – well, it had raised some kind of tension in him that he wasn't comfortable with. It wasn't anger or annoyance, and not jealousy precisely. Perhaps envy. Not of either one of them, though, which was what was perplexing him. It was the sense that he'd found...something interesting, something unique, and now the rest of the world also knew about it, when he'd thought he was the only one.

Ludicrous, of course. Jes wasn't some bauble that had washed up on the beach. In any case, plenty of people knew how interesting they were. They made their living being interesting for people. He supposed it wasn't that different from his own career.

He'd done a little research on them after they'd started working in the bunker, even before they and Noah had moved into the lodge. It only made sense to vet people who were in such close proximity, and if he hadn't done it, sooner or later someone at the palace would have. Probably had, in fact – he'd be willing to bet Gregory had a dossier on them on his desk, whether he'd looked at it or not.

Not that it would contain much to be concerned about. Jes Deimos was Shivadh-born with a US resident visa; they'd left Askazer-Shivadlakia at sixteen (that was a little surprising, but made sense in retrospect) and worked mostly odd, under-the-table jobs until their mid-twenties, when they'd gone to college. After that it was a somewhat distinguished career, first as a journalist and writer, then in audio media. They'd written a book of essays that had middling reviews, and sold a film script of some kind at some point, though it didn't appear to have been produced. They had a following in America that was significant enough they could live on revenue from advertising on the podcast network. He gathered few were so fortunate.

Noah had been born in the US, but children born outside Askazer-Shivadlakia to at least one Shivadh parent were still citizens themselves, so he had all his paperwork in order – national healthcare card, youth ID, even a youth worker's permit so he could draw pay with the podcast network. He'd be enrolling in school in Askazer-Shivadlakia when the term began in October. Jes was the only parent listed on his Shivadh birth certificate. Whoever his other parent was, they didn't appear to be in the picture.

So, that was the family Deimos – comfortable but not wealthy, working hard for what they got. Famous in a very niche and specific way, not unlike himself. Jes was referred to in interviews and by interviewees as a kind person with an intellect like an ice pick, and now Michaelis saw why. He didn't remember all of the previous night but he remembered enough to know that he'd been drinking with someone who was fifteen years younger than him and absolutely on his level when it came to dissecting what it was people felt, thought, and wanted. The politician said it wouldn't do to get on their bad side. The man was intrigued.

Jes was bent over the book, slim shoulders tilted a little where their head was turned to study the page. They looked like someone Degas might have painted, if he'd been around for the 21st century. Perhaps Caillebotte.

He cleared his throat softly, and they looked up.

"If you want to take Noah into town before the shops start threatening to close for the day, we should go," he said. "You can take a few books with you if you like – I plan to."

"Oh, thanks," they said, closing the book and stretching. Michaelis flicked his eyes away. "I think for now mine can stay here. You know at lunch I got Eddie Rambler to consider doing a spot on *Echo Junior*?" they added, as he led the way towards the door. "Don't tell Noah, I want to spring it on him at dinner."

"Good for your podcast, I think," Michaelis said, descending the stairs.

"Great for it, if he's willing to promo it. And he seems like a nice guy."

"I think so. He adores Gregory, so in my opinion he has excellent taste."

Jes laughed. "Picking out china patterns?"

"The palace has plenty of china," Michaelis replied, which made Jes laugh harder. They stepped out into the humid summer air and, to his surprise, Jes put out their hand, palm up.

"What?" he asked, staring at it.

"Give me your books," they said.

"Why on earth?"

"Because I want you to discuss what you learned about the Echardt scandal, and you talk with your hands," they replied.

"I do?" Michaelis said, frowning, but he put the books in their hands.

"When you get excited, mostly. Has nobody ever mentioned it?" Jes asked. "And if you've got something in your hands while you're talking, you get annoyed by it."

"My father did that, too, come to think of it – moved his hands a lot, I mean. Now I'm trying to think if Gregory does it."

"No. Well, not exactly. I don't know him very well, obviously, but he *likes* to have things in his hands when he talks. Waves his fork around and stuff," Jes said. "You're very kinetic, both of you."

"Are you sure?" Michaelis asked, and then noticed with mounting perplexity that even as he asked it, he turned his right hand over, palm up, a questioning gesture. Jes's eyes went from his hand to his face, then back to his hand. "Well. That's unsettling to learn at an advanced age."

"Pfft. You're what, fifty?"

"Sixty-one."

"Get out of town."

"I'm afraid so. But thank you," he said, pleased by their disbelief.

"I've been doing some very incorrect math. Well, you look fifty and might be sixty-one but you keep talking like you're ninety. In America, you'd technically be taking an early retirement, slacker," Jes teased.

"Fair enough," he said, falling back on self-deprecation. "I've been useless since leaving office."

"I don't know what's so bad about being useless, anyway, doesn't seem like such a sin to me," Jes said. Michaelis felt himself stop, shocked by the idea. Jes stopped too, turning to look at him. "What?"

"I...nobody's said that before," he said, confusion washing over him. "Usually it's some kind of platitude. Or a reassurance I'm still necessary. Nobody's just...said I could be useless and that was fine."

"For what it's worth, you're actually being extremely useful to me, but you don't have to be. I love being useless. A week's vacation doing nothing on the sofa? Favorite thing in the world," they said.

"And here I am making more work for you," he pointed out.

"Don't worry, I'll still find time to be a drain on society at some point," they replied, turning and continuing down the path. "Come on, keep up. Noah's going to start texting me soon if I don't get back."

He hurried to catch up, but he couldn't think of a single word to say.

"Echardt," Jes prompted gently.

"Right! Right," Michaelis said, and started talking, putting his thoughts in order as he went. It still wasn't a coherent telling, but he could feel the story taking shape, little turns of phrase here and there that he'd have to remember later. The research had been good, and repeating the story was helping. Jes mostly listened, his books tucked under their arm, a faint smile on their face. It *was* nice not to have books in his hands while he talked.

Noah was out on the dock in front of the lodge when they

returned, feet in the water, playing some game on his phone, apparently without a care in the world. Michaelis looked at the boy and wondered if he'd ever been so young. If he had, it was hard to remember.

"Come on, kid, put some shoes on and get the keys," Jes called, and Noah hopped to his feet. "His Grace has homework and I promised you a trip into town. Unless you want to come," they added, turning to Michaelis.

"No – as you say..." he gestured at the books they were still carrying, and they put them back in his hands. "Have fun."

"Bye, Michaelis!" Noah called, running for the van, pulling his shoes on as he went. "See you for dinner maybe!"

Michaelis waved them off and headed inside, reflecting on how much the Deimos family filled the place, and how quiet they left it when they were absent.

They'd been in the van for all of thirty seconds when Noah said, "You know, I thought carrying someone's books when you like them was, like, something people in the forties did."

"He talks with his hands," Jes replied. Well, it'd worked on Michaelis.

Realistically, they'd missed out on that kind of thing when they were in school – carrying someone's books when you liked them, even if you'd rather die than act on it. Partly because of who they'd been, partly because they'd left school a little too early, grown up a little too fast. It felt good to finally get to do it. A little thrilling that Michaelis had allowed it.

"Sure, don't they all," Noah replied. "Uncle Lachlan's going to lose his mind."

"Uncle Lachlan's not going to hear about it from you, is he?" Jes asked.

"What, like he's going to judge you? He thinks Michaelis is

good looking and fun. They're always bantering on the podcast."

"Michaelis *is* good looking and fun, yes, and it was very nice to carry his books. But you know you don't always have to act on that kind of thing."

"Again, this talk?" Noah asked.

"I want you to internalize that just because someone is good looking doesn't mean they're good for you."

"I'm pretty sure you've said on the podcast, on record, that they can still be a good time, though," Noah pointed out.

"That was a mature podcast and I am shocked, shocked and dismayed, that you have listened to a podcast rated 17+," Jes said.

"I edited that episode."

"Which is why I didn't get more explicit. Listen, Noah, I know that brain of yours is still growing, but do a little mental weight-lifting and tell me how you think flirting with the former king of the country you just moved to would go."

"How about I do a little mental weight-lifting and point out you already are?" Noah asked. "I'm not mad about it. I like Michaelis. He got us the studio and a place to stay."

"And do you want me to endanger that?" Jes asked.

"Oh," Noah said.

"Oh," Jes agreed. "Look. We both like him. It's a little weird for me because I also think of him as the king of my country, but I can see the human under the crown. I think his podcast is going to be pretty cool and I like being his friend. Maybe flirting a little. But a friend is all I'm going to be, for both our sakes."

"What if he likes you back?"

"I think Michaelis still misses his wife," they said. "I don't think he's looking for more from anyone else. And if he is, well, I'll figure that out if he acts on it. No use making plans for something that probably won't happen."

"You're not going to discourage him by carrying his books," Noah said loftily, and Jes shook their head and smiled.

CHAPTER SEVEN

"ARE WE HOT?" Jes asked, pointing at the mic, and Lachlan replied, "Just the hottest."

"Fantastic," Jes said, while Michaelis grinned at Lachlan.

"Ready to go, then?" Michaelis asked.

"Almost. But first, I have a present for you," Jes said, taking a paper bag from under the table.

"What on earth for?" Michaelis asked. "Is this a podcast tradition? I didn't think to get anyone gifts."

"Not exactly. And normally I would never recommend what we're about to do, so don't tell Noah that I'm setting a bad example," Jes told him. "But you know, the only real reason this podcast exists is that you and I were drinking together. And it was over drinks that we figured out how to make it work."

"Yes…" Michaelis said warily.

"So. This is our new tradition to open the show," Jes said, and thunked down two shot glasses from the bag.

"Oh, oh no, Jes – "

"Oh yes!" Jes said, producing a tiny gray-green bottle of liquor. "I promise I'll pour lightly."

"We are not doing *shots* before we even start," Michaelis said, as Jes poured two very shallow shots. "This is Davzda, this is a terrible idea."

"Well, then here's to terrible ideas," Jes said, lifting their shot. Michaelis groaned and picked his up, tapping it against theirs.

"Dozine," he said, a traditional Davzda toast, and drank when they did. "It tastes more dreadful every time."

"Clears the throat for talking, though," Jes said, and coughed as if to prove it. "Three, two, one. I'm Jes Deimos, creator and host of *The Echo* and executive producer of Reverb Podcast Network."

"I'm Michaelis ben Jason, King Emeritus of Askazer-Shivadlakia and recent poisoning victim," Michaelis said.

"This is your guide to Shivadh royal history, and we call it...*All On Mike*," Jes said, their voice deep with amusement.

"Still can't abide that name," Michaelis muttered, but loud enough for the mic to catch it. Jes just laughed.

Lachlan said, "Give me a brief hold for theme music..." and then when he pointed at them, Jes launched into the start of the script.

The first episode of *All On Mike* ("Don't Mess With Alekha") went up a few weeks later on a Thursday, because Thursday was the day for that kind of thing, apparently. Michaelis very carefully did not ask about numbers. Still, Noah spent all day wandering in and out of the lodge, announcing mysterious things like "Engagement is sky high" and "Someone said you sound like Benedict Cumberbatch's cool dad."

They'd left the "cold open" in, where Jes convinced him to do the shot of Davzda, and late in the afternoon Noah came in and said, "Davzda is trending. I bet the king's going to be furious."

"Why would Gregory be furious?" Michaelis asked.

"Everyone's trying to get some after hearing you talk about it. They're sold out in town. There were like, five bottles in all of America and one of them just sold online for six hundred dollars. Bet you tomorrow all the trendy food websites will have Davzda cocktail recipes."

"Well, a lot of people will die, but these are the sacrifices we make," Michaelis said.

"So there's going to be a shortage because all the sellers will export," Noah said. "Demand way up, but supply stays the same. Or if they hike supply, they can't do it super fast. How do they even make it?"

"There's...one distillery," Michaelis said, realizing what Noah meant. The palace would probably have to shell out emergency funds to get the distillery up to capacity.

"Lucky them," Noah said, and went back to monitoring metrics. Michaelis texted Alanna rather than Gregory; she said it was fine, that there was a *strategic Davzda reserve* that Gregory was going to empty out, and that there was a present on the way. He'd just received the text when a delivery driver knocked on the door.

"Your Grace," the woman said, with a bow that was made much more difficult by the enormous food package in her hands. "Compliments of the palace and Mr. Rambler, who said he'd come cook for you but he figured you'd like to celebrate in your own way."

Michaelis took the hamper from her, handing her a tip in return. "Thank you. Does he want a reply?"

"No sir. It's a very nice podcast, Your Grace," she added, seemingly on impulse. "The whole country's talking about it. We're trending again."

He smiled. "Lovely to hear. It's nice to be of service."

"Have a good evening," she said, and dashed back to her delivery van. Michaelis carried the hamper into the kitchen and opened it, texting a photograph to Eddie. The response came from Gregory – *You sounded great. Eddie and I are both very proud.*

It's only a podcast, he texted back.

Love you, was all he got in reply. He set the phone aside and began unpacking just as Jes and Noah emerged from downstairs.

"What's this?" Jes asked, leaning on the kitchen counter.

"Gifts from an admirer," he replied with a smile, setting out packets of meat wrapped in butcher's paper, a basket of new potatoes, and a box with what he suspected was a small cheesecake in it. "Gregory and Edward sent their regards and congratulations on the podcast."

"My admirers always sent flowers when I lived in New York," Jes said.

"Well, Americans, you know. No sense of substance," Michaelis replied, tossing a bag of cookies from the hamper to Noah. "Don't spoil your dinner too badly, I'll cook for you tonight. Oh, dear," he added, removing the last object in the hamper. It was a gray-green bottle of Davzda, but without the label. And he could see the mushrooms floating around in the bottom.

Jes whistled. "Well, now you have your very own illegal Davzda."

"Where the hell did Eddie Rambler dig this up?" Michaelis asked. "This is the real, old-school stuff with the mushrooms in it."

"Like an LSD cocktail," Jes agreed. "Do a shot or two of that and you'll think you've seen the divine."

"Don't even think about it," Michaelis told Noah, who was studying the mushrooms with interest. "I'm going to put this somewhere for very specific emergencies, possibly involving the end of the world."

"But you're cooking dinner?" Noah asked.

"Absolutely, as long as you're free," Michaelis said, glancing at Jes, who nodded. "Good. We'll have a celebration. We'll go boating and I'll catch us a few fish, so we'll have steak and fish on the grill."

He put away the various foodstuffs while Jes and Noah yelled to each other in their suite about what they were wearing and what they should bring. Noah wanted to bring his phone just to take photos with but Jes wanted him to get off the screen for a while; eventually they let him wear them down. Michaelis found a packet of dry rub in the hamper, so he prepared a pair of steaks and left them in the fridge to rest while he packed the potatoes in foil to be stuck into the coals, then fetched his bow and fishing kit from his room. By the time he'd changed into shabby old clothes for fishing and made sure he had what he needed, Noah was already preparing the boat at the dock.

Michaelis loaded bow and kit into the boat and made sure its ballasts were set properly; if you had to stand in a boat on open water and fire an arrow straight down into the lake, you generally wanted to make sure it was the most stable boat possible. He was just finishing up when Jes dropped lightly into the little craft, relaxing into the padded bench at the stern, aviator sunglasses slightly askew on their face. Michaelis felt a stab of affection that he hid by testing the draw on the bow.

"I can show you how, if you like," he said to Noah, who was undoing the mooring rope. "I taught Gregory when he was a little younger than you, but he'd studied archery in school."

"Can I just sit and watch and take videos?" Noah asked. "Promise I won't post them without showing them to you."

"I don't mind. Wouldn't be the first time. There's probably footage around from before you were even born," Michaelis said, kicking them off from the dock. "Right, if you're not going to fish, you row, how's that sound?"

"Where to, pal?" Noah asked, putting on what Michaelis imagined was a New York cabdriver's accent.

"Out that way, just shy of the middle of the lake," Michaelis said, pointing. "Then let the oars drop into the water."

Bowfishing was a Shivadh tradition, but it wasn't all that commonly practiced anymore; Michaelis was just a hobbyist, but he'd always enjoyed it. It used to be Miranda in the bow of the little boat, with Gregory in the stern curled up with a book or telling Michaelis all about the school year, while Michaelis at the oars basked in the presence of his family and waited until dusk for the fish to start to rise.

Now it was Jes in the stern, in a pair of baggy cargo shorts, wearing a t-shirt reading *Askazer-Shivadlakia* in a stylized sports logo font. They were sunning themself carelessly, one earbud in with the sound so low he couldn't even hear it in the silent stillness of the lake. Noah was between the oars, leaning over one side of the boat to study the clear water below. Not replacements; very different from his family, these two, and he couldn't think of them as his in the way he'd thought of his wife and son. But Noah had Gregory's studious curiosity and, like Gregory at fifteen, was all elbows and knees. And Jes…often made him feel the same way Miranda had, like there was a peace at his very core.

He examined the bow, making sure the wood wasn't cracked or brittle anywhere, as he considered this. It didn't occur to him for about ten minutes that the memory of Miranda hadn't hurt, not the way it often did.

"How long do you have to wait?" Noah whispered.

"Any minute now," Michaelis replied, drawing an arrow from the quiver in the bottom of the boat. He got to his feet slowly, adjusting to the gentle rocking of the boat, and took a handful of crumbs from his pocket, sprinkling them on the barely-rippling water. He heard the soft click of Noah's phone recording him.

"The trick of this," he said quietly, nocking the arrow and drawing it back, "is patience, but also endurance. You can't draw the bow when you see the fish – it's got to be before they rise, because otherwise when you do, the boat will rock and scare them off. Can't skip arm day," he added with a smile, repeating something Eddie had observed when he was learning.

"How long can you hold a bow like that?" Noah asked.

Michaelis saw a trout rise, hugely fat from summer feeding, and loosed the arrow before he thought about it. It hit the water with a resounding thwack, and the fish floated up to the surface, speared neatly on the shaft.

"Long enough," he said with a satisfied look, reaching down to shake it into the bucket. The arrow was wet, but didn't seem to have any damage, so he nocked it again.

"I always thought it was pretty medieval," Jes said.

"In a bad way?" Noah asked, still filming Michaelis, who

followed a shadow with the arrow for a while until he realized it was a piece of plant floating past.

"No, it just seemed kind of pointless," Jes said. Michaelis caught their eyes flicking over his arms, bare up to the cuffs of the t-shirt. "Very compelling in person, though."

"Shush," he murmured. "You two talkers are scaring off the fish."

Noah fell obediently silent, and Jes just looked at him over the top of their sunglasses. Michaelis ignored it, focusing on the water, flinching but not firing when a skater-bug skimmed past. After a few minutes he eased the bow down and took another handful of crumbs, scattering them slowly.

The fish burst to the surface, five or six of them flailing up at once as they sometimes did. He quickly nocked the arrow and fired, and then from habit held out his hand. He'd taught Gregory to pass him fresh arrows, but Gregory of course wasn't here – and yet an arrow slapped into his palm anyway. He drew and fired a second time, and a third when Noah passed him another one. Three fish, two neatly speared and one clearly shot but missing its arrow, floated up.

Michaelis crouched and set the bow down, pulling the fish into the bucket.

"That was very helpful," he said to Noah. "How did you know to hand them to me?"

"Just made sense," Noah said, shrugging.

"Well, you've earned your stripes today," Michaelis told him. Noah preened. "Mind rowing us back? I want to clean off the arrows and stretch my shoulders."

"You got it," Noah said, bringing them around with an expertise that said he'd probably been out in the boat, alone, when Jes and Michaelis weren't looking. Well, let the kid have a few secrets. That was part of growing up. He'd done it himself, fifty years ago.

At the dock, he let Noah tie up while he set the gear on the boards; Jes climbed out gracefully, and then instead of moving aside so he could join them, leaned back down and offered him their hand. He cocked an eyebrow at them, then took it and let them hand him out of the boat, not really stabilizing or lifting him, but very charming nonetheless.

"That's usually my job," he said.

"Gender roles are for wimps," they replied. Michaelis laughed. "Come on. Isn't it nice to have someone help you out for once?"

"Seems that's all anyone does these days, but yes," he agreed. "I'll clean the fish."

"My chivalry definitely does not extend to gutting fish," they agreed. Noah was already taking the gear back up to the lodge.

"Noah, bring the steaks on the plate in the fridge, please," Michaelis called, and Noah nodded. He caught Jes smiling at him sideways, and smiled sideways back, well pleased with the world.

It was a pretty good day, Jes had to admit. Michaelis might not want to pay attention to it, but the podcast was a success by first-episode standards and the buzz was pulling in a few listeners to the other shows as well. They'd had a light day of work, they'd gotten to watch Michaelis flex his arms and shoulders for whole minutes together, and there was surf and turf in their future. They stood at the grill and gathered up chunks of charcoal from the nearby bag, building the fire carefully to burn hot and fast at first.

Nearby, Michaelis was at a very elderly outdoor sink, showing Noah how to clean the fish. Out of deference to Noah's cries of "super gross" he was cutting one of them down to filets for the city child, but he left the heads and skin on the others, the better to grill them Shivadh-style. Jes hoped one of those was for them.

They stuck the potatoes right in among the coals as soon as possible – those would take a while to cook. They raked coals to one side to make a slightly cooler area for the meat just as Michaelis brought it over.

"It's all yours," they said, gesturing with the tongs. He accepted the tool with a nod and set to work. Jes retreated to the line of low-slung beach lounge chairs nearby.

"If you want to go swim, Noah, this won't be ready for a while," Michaelis called. Jes didn't even hear a response, just a shriek and the splash of a teenager cannonballing into the lake. "He's taking well to country life."

"He still thinks it's a treat," Jes said. "Normally he only gets this kind of outdoorsiness when we visit here."

"Do you suppose he misses the city?"

"He hasn't said he does. It's a lot quieter here after New York, but you know how kids get jaded when they grow up somewhere," Jes replied.

"And what about you?"

"Who's the interviewer now?" Jes asked, laughing. "Well, yes, there are some things I miss – delivery pizza, for one – but surprisingly not as much as I thought. I mean, New York will still be there if I want to go see it. This place is better for us now."

"I'm glad to hear it," Michaelis said.

"Were you concerned I'd be leaving once the podcast about the country is done?" Jes asked.

"No, that wasn't why I asked," Michaelis replied, leaving the food to cook while he washed his hands at the sink. "I remember enough from the question game to know there's also a good reason you are here in this country. Just wondering what you had to give up to come back."

"Not as much as you'd think. I do like it here. When I left, I just wanted out. What kid doesn't want to kick their hometown off their heels and see the world? I might have kicked a little harder than necessary, but in my defense my parents really needed a kicking. I left because of them. I came back for myself."

"I can't claim to know how you feel, given I literally took my father's job from him and then gave it to my son, but I know it can be difficult."

"Remember when you came to the studio and I got salty with you about being hereditary king in everything but name?"

"Faintly, yes," he said sardonically.

"I know you had a legitimate election, and I think you probably had a great reign, which I missed most of," Jes said. "But I am also still very mad at people who get to have the kind of good relationship with their dad that you had."

"Ah." Michaelis nodded. "If it's any consolation, you've done a great job with Noah. Easy to tell."

"Well, he's a good kid," Jes said.

"Hope he's a hungry one too," Michaelis replied, turning back to check on the food. Jes lay in the sun-dappled shade under the tree cover and let themself drift, enjoying the quiet and the smell of charcoal, and Noah's occasional shouts from the lake.

"All right, this fish is almost overdone and the steak's pink," Michaelis said eventually, nudging their chair with his foot. "Noah! Dinner!"

"Coming!" Noah called, and ran up the dock, ducking under the outdoor shower head near the sink to rinse off. Jes got up to wash their hands and then took the platter of meat from Michaelis, who followed with the potatoes. As they settled in at the table, Jes realized what they were seeing in him – the same brightness he showed whenever Gregory was in the room. It was like the real Michaelis was emerging from a thin, dark shell. If this was what he'd been like as king, no wonder he'd been good at his job. He was always kind and usually fun, but this Michaelis was charming as well.

He wasn't a bad cook, either, they thought, as he put one of the head-on fish on their plate and served the filets, with deep grill marks and crisp brown edges, to Noah. Jes ate eagerly, savoring something that tasted like the best parts of their childhood.

"Michaelis," Noah said, phone set into a little portable tripod and filming him, "how do they make Davzda, anyway? The real stuff that's not legal."

Michaelis set his fork down, clearing his throat. "I suppose it's like absinthe. You start with spirits – if you post this, you should put a disclaimer that this is not a recipe," he said abruptly.

"Promise," Noah said.

"There's a mildly hallucinogenic mushroom that used to grow – and does not anymore, so visitors please don't go pulling up mushrooms on your hikes – in the highlands," Michaelis continued. "The mushrooms would be dried in hot salt. They become very salty, obviously. Then you'd add a couple of those to a bottle and fill it with distilled spirits – which was usually home-made to begin with, so it's always been difficult to gauge the alcohol content. Some people add other spices if they want their drink to taste like, I don't know, regret and cloves instead of just regret. The hallucinogen leeches into the alcohol as the mushrooms rehydrate, so if you shake up the bottle first, you get a little high on top of the alcohol when you drink."

"What if you don't shake the bottle?"

"Then the last person to drink has quite the time."

"Did you ever drink the real stuff?" Noah asked.

"Not intentionally. Once when I was very young and making poor choices in friends."

"But was it fun?" Noah asked, grinning.

Michaelis smiled. "Eat your fish, Noah. You can make your own mistakes when you're older."

Michaelis had learned, somewhat recently if he was honest, that when something was going right, when things were swimming in his direction, he shouldn't question his instincts or feelings. He'd always been analytical, a good quality in a leader, but retirement had meant a readjustment in his thought processes.

He'd been pleased with the gift from the king – still novel and amusing to think of Gregory as the king – and he'd enjoyed boating and fishing, and tending the food. Building the fire was always the part he'd disliked, and Jes had simply gone to do it without even mentioning it, which was gratifying. Dinner was both good and celebratory.

Now, full from dinner and laid out in one of the lounge chairs, with Jes in the one next to his and Noah dutifully clearing the table, he refused to question why he felt so happy or what he could do to hold onto it. Instinct would tell him, and questioning things would only shorten the pleasure of them. Instead he simply folded his hands over his stomach, shoulders twinging pleasantly, and contemplated the lake until his eyelids drooped.

He was more than half-asleep when he felt a soft touch, fingertips ruffling his short hair. The pressure against his scalp felt good and for a second he leaned into it, until he realized he wasn't sure who was doing it, and then he startled awake.

The touch vanished. He sat halfway up, turning; Jes was still in the next chair over, lying on their side facing him, their hand hovering in the air, looking stricken.

"I'm sorry," they said. "I should have asked first, you just had a leaf on your hair, and it's softer than I expected – "

"No, it's fine," he said. "I was almost asleep. I wasn't sure where I was for a moment."

"Ah. Still. I know better," they said, giving him an only slightly brittle smile. He cast around for how to say that he'd liked it, and then felt stupid for a split second.

"It was nice," he said. "Just unexpected. I liked it. I'm not accustomed to, uh. Touch."

He glanced at their hand, still in midair, and then back at their face; they saw the look and hovered their hand closer. He nodded and laid back, eyes open now; they skimmed their fingers through his hair, brushing against the grain, sending tingles down his scalp.

"I was a kid, but I remember there was an absolute scandal

when you cut your hair right after the coronation," they said, after a few moments of absent stroking. He closed his eyes. "My mother said you looked like a shorn lamb."

"The seventies were over," he replied. "Time to be a king."

"Was that why?"

"Honestly? I had to wear the crown a lot, at the start," he said. Their fingers dug into his temple before moving back to the tense muscles just behind his ear. "Hair kept getting caught in it."

"Ever practical," they replied. "It does get a little lonely out here. I can see how an unexpected touch might startle you. Every morning when Lachlan gets here I make him give me a hug just so I don't get out of practice."

"Well, you can do this whenever you like," Michaelis murmured. "Feels fantastic."

"Might take you up on that. Or I might make you cook me fish that good again, as a tax."

"I saw you coveting the heads."

"Noah thinks it's weird. He always has. I don't know, you try to raise them in all the old ways…"

Michaelis chuckled. Jes's fingers dug into the crown of his head, blunt nails creating sharp just-this-side-of-pain pressure before they spread their fingers wider.

"Sleep if you want," they said. "It's only me and Noah here."

He nodded against the touch and closed his eyes, but he stayed awake for a while, the better to enjoy it. He felt a little guilty, but he couldn't bring himself to care; their fingers were warm and soothing, pressing out knots of tension and scrubbing at the base of his skull. When they finally flattened their palm on the crown of his head again, then left it there, he slipped into sleep.

Jes could tell the moment Michaelis slept; the muscles in his jaw went lax, and the last lines of tension around his eyes smoothed out. They left their hand on his head, resting on the short silver hair, watching him sleep.

It wasn't exactly that the idea of the king as a man was foreign to them; Askazer-Shivadlakia was a small place and the Shivadh people weren't overawed by their rulers even before they started voting for them. Living with him certainly humanized him too. But when they were a kid the king was a more distant figure, and every time they were reminded he was human it amused them.

Michaelis had a healthy respect for Davzda until he'd had a few shots of it. He was a tidy man. He liked the outdoors; he was a runner and swimmer, a bowfisher. It was clear he'd spent as much time worrying about his parenting as Jes currently was. He smiled quick and sharp, the way he did many things. He had a startle reflex, and he liked having his scalp rubbed.

They really shouldn't have done it without asking, but he didn't seem like someone who had a particularly high guard against such things. At least he hadn't been angry, just confused.

He wasn't one of Jes's friends back in New York, always hugging and casually touching, sitting hip-to-hip on sofas, dancing close in clubs. He was a widower with an adult son and not much to occupy his time, and nobody much to touch him.

They sat back and picked up their book, reading while Michaelis breathed softly and slowly in the next chair. Noah finished cleaning up and went back down to the dock, this time to sit on it and pitch pebbles into the water.

Well, Michaelis didn't have anyone to touch him and Jes wanted more touch; there was an obvious solution there, and they watched Noah skip stones and strategized about it. Michaelis was obliging when he saw someone with a need, much less stubborn than he would be if he was faced with an offer of help. He could see sense, and he didn't seem particularly averse to touch, just surprised by it.

The sun was just barely down when they got out of the chair and nudged Michaelis awake.

"Noah snitched that there's a cheesecake inside," they said. "Noah, come on, dessert."

Inside the lodge, Jes sliced up the cheesecake and distributed plates. While they ate, Noah showed Michaelis how he was editing the fishing video to make it look more professional.

"Okay, I'm gonna go look at the metrics and do some stuff," Noah announced at last.

"Please, I am begging you to be a normal child and play a video game," Jes said.

"If you insist," Noah said, in such an obvious imitation of Michaelis at his most dignified that even Michaelis laughed.

"I'll be out here for a while. Put yourself to bed when you get tired and remember to brush your teeth," Jes said. "Goodnight, love you," they sing-songed, and Noah chimed in on the last few syllables. Michaelis took their plates to the sink and stretched.

"I should probably turn in," he said.

"Come, sit for a little while," Jes told him, heading into the living room. He followed, then grinned as they grasped his shoulders and maneuvered him to the sofa, settling him on the cushions not quite next to one arm. He looked a little surprised when they dropped down next to him, back to the arm of the sofa, swinging their legs up to prop over his lap, but he didn't object.

"Keep me company," Jes commanded, placing a book from the side-table in his hands.

"What are you doing?" he asked, but he propped the book open on their knees.

"Sitting with you. Reading," they replied. "Objections?"

"Not materially, just curious."

They leaned their head against the back of the sofa. "I told you I miss all the hugs I used to get, and I thought maybe you'd like sitting here too. Seemed like you were a little starved for touch this afternoon."

"I do fine," he replied, looking down at the book.

"I'm sure you do, but fine is only adequate. Anyway it's not about you, egotist. When I was twenty I'd have gone clubbing to celebrate something like this. Might have thrown a huge dinner party when I was thirty-five." They nudged his chest with their knee. "At forty-five, what I want is someone else to cook me dinner and then keep me company while I read."

"Let me tell you, at sixty all you ever want is a nap," he said, settling in. Keeping his right hand on the book, he rubbed his jaw with his left, and then very deliberately rested it on Jes's ankle, propped next to his thigh. His palm was warm on the top of their bare foot, thumb cupped around the curve of their leg.

Jes took out their cellphone and scrolled through the news app, looking for anything interesting or timely for the podcast. For a while there was just the soft noise of his book's pages turning, and the faint, distant rumble of whatever shoot-em-up game Noah was playing.

Eventually, Michaelis's hand twitched; Jes watched as his thumb swept up their ankle and then back down, an absent soothing movement. Still engrossed in his book, he did it again, and then settled into a slow rhythm with it, apparently unaware he was doing it. It felt wonderful – intimate in a weird, Victorian way, the touch of a hand on an ankle, but also innocent. Nothing meant by it, nothing demanded. He was simply comfortable enough to touch them.

He kept it up until at last he yawned, raising his hand to cover his mouth, and set the book aside.

"Bed?" Jes asked.

"Mm." He leaned back to let them lift their legs up, then slid out from under them, stretching as he stood. "Thank you. Sleep well."

"You too," they said, and watched him go, admiring the lines of his shoulders through his shirt. Well, one could dream, and in the meantime perhaps they could help each other.

Perhaps he might want them both to stay here in the fall, and if he did, Jes didn't see how they would be willing to say no.

The next morning, instead of lingering in the doorway as he usually did, Michaelis came into the kitchen while Jes was staring sleepily at the toaster, willing it to toast faster. He nudged them out of the way with a hand on their hip, helped himself to the still-brewing coffee, and then brushed their elbow with one hand to get their attention, passing them the jam.

Jes smiled to themself and, when he got in their way trying to scramble an egg, hip-checked him to make him move over.

Eddie had actually been a little hesitant to do a podcast with a kid, even a kid like Noah. He'd listened to *Echo Junior* enough to know that it was a fine show for teenagers and actually pretty smart, but one never knew how much of that was editing, or even Jes stage-parenting their son. He'd agreed easily when talking to Jes because he had a policy of never saying no to something unless he had to, but he'd had his doubts.

Emailing back and forth with Noah had put his mind at ease. Noah was a young professional, with release forms to sign and a very thorough explanation of what he could expect. Further, the kid was *fun* – he wanted Eddie to tell funny stories and give advice, not just talk about the tourist initiative or his thoughts on food trends. He'd asked, too, what Eddie thought would be a neat thing to do for the podcast.

Remembering Gregory's request to do a little casual spying, Eddie had said, "Why don't you interview me while I'm cooking? I could come cook dinner for the fam at the lodge, and you could record while I cook, then we'll do a roundtable while we eat."

He felt it was working out exceptionally well. He'd arrived with groceries and a couple of recipes in mind to find Noah and Lachlan already set up with recording equipment – a wireless mic for him, stationary mics at the stove and cutting board to record ambient cooking noises, and thick quilts temporarily stapled to the walls to muffle echoes.

Michaelis and Jes were meant to be two of the dinner guests, he knew, but perhaps out of respect for Noah's creative process they didn't show up until the meal was ready. Jes opened and poured the wine while Michaelis, former king, diplomat, and imposing son of a bitch, set the table. Eddie's mind was a little blown by the image.

"How did the interview go?" Michaelis asked, as they settled in to eat.

"Really well, I think," Eddie said, and Noah, mouth already full of goat "Askazer Style," nodded agreement. "I love talking while I cook. My very first cooking show was this dumb little cable access thing I did in college," he added, helping himself to some bread. "It was just me and a camera in a corner of a dorm kitchen, and I used to lock everyone out so I could film. Which turned out to be a huge mistake. I don't know if you know this about me – I'm sure His Grace knows and would agree – but I am a people person."

"I'd venture to say you are the most people person I've met in a long career in politics," Michaelis added drily.

"So the show sucked," Eddie said. "Because I didn't have anyone to talk to. No outlet for my natural charm. One day I forgot to lock the door and a couple of guys walked in and just kinda – stared at me and I stared at them, and then I said well, you're here, you want some tacos?"

"Nobody ever says no to tacos," Noah said.

"You are correct. And that particular video got super popular on campus because it was funny. Because I had an audience, someone for the viewer at home to identify with. It went into my audition reel when I got my big break at Eat Network."

"You learned to play to your strengths," Jes said.

"Yes, but also to recognize what they were. Sometimes we're the only ones who know that what we're good at is worthwhile. Like, you gotta value what you do, or else why do it?" Eddie asked.

"Why wouldn't people value being friendly?" Noah asked.

"Oh, the usual damaged reasons. You're not cool enough, you're too nice, you talk about stuff nobody cares about," Eddie said. "Nuts. That's just people who are afraid to make friends."

"It's a very good strategy," Michaelis said. "Difficult to execute sometimes, but wise to have as an option. Being… unexpectedly transparent. Sincere."

"Yeah. Though sometimes in show business you do just have to pretend to be real cool until they're not looking," Eddie agreed.

He let his mouth run without paying too much attention to it, a skill he'd cultivated over years of interviews. He wanted to stay engaged with the podcast but he was also watching a fascinating silent dynamic play out around the dinner table, and a part of his mind was distracted trying to figure it out.

For a start, this wasn't the dry, slightly cutting Michaelis he was accustomed to, a man who strode through life efficiently and without much pause for other peoples' opinions. He seemed calmer – he might have objected to the word, but Eddie thought perhaps even *softer*. Gregory had been right, there was a change, and it was particularly visible at the dining table of the lodge, in the company of friends.

Or, perhaps, in the company of Jes Deimos. They were seated next to Michaelis, frequently stealing vegetables off his plate, which he had apparently rotated specifically so they could. Michaelis watched Jes when they spoke, and when he spoke to Noah he occasionally glanced at Jes as if he wanted to be sure what he was saying to their kid was okay. It must be an awkward form of quasi-co-parenting, living with a precocious kid like Noah but not being officially any kind of dad.

When Eddie finished the story he'd been telling, Lachlan cleared his throat and turned his laptop to face them. Poor man was eating off his lap while he continued to keep the sound going – Eddie made a note to leave him a special helping of dessert.

"Found the video online," Lachlan said. Eddie's twenty-one-year-old baby face, under a pile of disorderly blue hair, stared out at them blurrily.

"Oh, wow," Eddie laughed. "There I am, making tacos for nobody. About fifteen seconds from now – yeah, hit play – there I go, there's the deer in the headlights," he said, as the onscreen Eddie froze in the middle of assembling a taco. Two figures were standing in front of the right side of the camera, out of focus.

"Oh hey," Eddie on the video said. "You guys look super high. You want some tacos?"

Lachlan was grinning over the edge of the laptop; Noah and Jes were both laughing, and Michaelis's chuckle was a deep rumble underneath. Eddie glanced over in time to see Jes wipe a tear of laughter from the corner of their eye and glance at Michaelis, affection and delight in their look. Perhaps they'd been concerned about him too, as the palace had been. They seemed happy to see him laughing.

"I forgot I told them they looked high," Eddie said, as Lachlan closed the window and went back to work. "Wasn't wrong, though. I know because the tacos weren't nearly as good as they said they were."

The rest of dinner went fine, but he was still chewing over what he'd seen when he arrived back at the palace, making his way up to Gregory's rooms. The king was on the sofa, for once without the requisite pile of spreadsheets or diplomatic reports, reading a graphic novel that one of Eddie's brothers had sent him in their last package. Eddie dropped down next to him and flopped dramatically against his shoulder. Gregory absently rested his chin on Eddie's head.

"Interview go well?" he asked, setting the book aside.

"Yeah, and the goat came out nicely too," Eddie said.

"Well, what's really important here?"

"Making goat edible is important," Eddie informed him. "Anyway, Noah had a good time and I think he got some strong audio, and he and I talked about getting the podcast network some publicity."

"Don't work yourself too hard," Gregory said.

"This is my favorite kind of work, after cooking," Eddie said. "It'll be fine, I'll roll it into some other stuff I'm doing. And your dad and Jes had a good time, I think."

"Oh yes?" Gregory said.

"Yeah. I know you were curious, and it's not like I could go through his underwear drawer or something – "

"I didn't want you to take it that far," Gregory said.

"But he seemed content. You know how you said it was weird to see him so happy? I think what's weird is just…seeing a change in someone. Maybe you got used to him being unhappy."

"That's possible," Gregory admitted. "I told you when you came here that he wasn't at his best."

"I remember. I think he's good now, though," Eddie said. "I think he's enjoying having people to look after. Maybe people who look after him. Hard for him to do that with you right now, you know? Maybe he missed it."

"I suppose," Gregory said. "But he's all right, you think?"

"Yes. I don't think you need to worry about him," Eddie said. He kept his thoughts about the way Jes and Michaelis looked at each other to himself, for now.

CHAPTER EIGHT

ONCE THE FIRST episode of the podcast came out, it felt like something locked into a rhythm – like a clean shot with a bow, or a gear shifting correctly in a car.

Michaelis spent most of his mornings now in the library, happy to be back with a good purpose. He spoke with the librarian about writing the boring parts of his memoirs down and doing the podcast on the interesting ones, and the man gave him a relieved look and permission to go ahead. In the afternoons, he recorded with Noah or Jes, or he worked on scripts – mostly his own, but sometimes looking at Noah's as well, helping with grammar or pointing out what wasn't clear. He broke his own rule about not reading his reviews and read the comments on his episodes, looking for ways to improve, relieved that he was apparently too old to take any of the uglier criticism personally. They all just came off so childish, like toddlers clamoring for attention.

Often, in the evenings, he or Jes would find each other and settle in on the sofa to read, or to exchange dry looks while Noah watched reality television.

"Gregory has an invitation for us," he said one evening, studying his phone while Jes and Noah bickered about what was on television.

"Us?" Jes asked, curious.

"Eddie's been trying out the surfing all along the coast, and he thinks he's found the best spot. He and Gregory are doing a little video thing for the Photogram this week of the two of them surfing. He wants to know if I'd like to come along, and you both as well. He says he struck a deal with Noah about publicity."

"Noah?" Jes prompted.

"Professional dealings, confidential," Noah said with a grin. "Eddie just said after the interview that he thought we should have a higher profile. He said he'd find some opportunities. We're paying him in studio time at some future date."

"Savvy, that one," Michaelis murmured. "Well, I wouldn't mind a trip to the beach, but if Eddie's been there it'll be full of tourists and Photogram models."

Noah looked like he was actually excited about the idea of a beach full of Photogram models, which was when Michaelis remembered that Noah was fifteen, and the vast majority of the Photogram models in Askazer-Shivadlakia at the moment were teenage girls from Italy and France who found boys with American accents extra-interesting.

"Can we, Boss?" Noah asked. "It'd be rude to turn down an invitation from the king, right?"

"Entirely up to you," Michaelis said to Jes. "If you'd like, I can just take Noah."

Jes gave him a sweeping look, and Michaelis wondered if they were considering all the times he'd come in from swimming without a shirt on.

"No, we'll both go, and please thank Gregory for the invite," they decided. "But you, Wild Child, have to promise you will put sunscreen on every single time I tell you, and you, Your Grace," they kicked him gently, "have to keep him in eyeshot. No letting him wander off to canoodle with the Photogrammers."

Spotted in the sun: King Gregory III of Askazer-Shivadlakia takes a break from politics to hit the waves with his boyfriend, influencer and celebrity chef Eddie Rambler. Video via Photogram.

Askazer-Shivadlakia is this summer's hottest

and hardest to pronounce ticket thanks to
Eddie Rambler, who spread the country's fame
among his hip social media following during
the king's recent coronation. While movie
stars and tech moguls sun themselves in
Monaco, the young, the broke, and the
photogenic have made tracks for this tiny
beachfront country, to fill your feed with
sun-kissed smiles, quaint cafes, beautiful
vistas, and friendly local color.

Also at the beach to watch the king wipe out
was his father, His Grace King Emeritus
Michaelis, along with GenX nerd idol Jes
Deimos, who chatted with a steady stream of
Photogram influencers and podcast fans.
Deimos's son Noah, an influencer in his own
right, stuck close to the royal family and
eventually gave up his phone to catch some
sun with a beach read. The Deimos family is
working with the royals to produce a series
of podcasts about life in "The Ask".

"I can hear my father bellowing from this side of the veil,"
Michaelis said at palace breakfast, when he saw the puff piece on
their beach trip. "*They call my country The Ask? They call the country of
the Askazer warrior and the Shivadh noble The ASK?*"

"Grandfather did love a good bellow," Gregory agreed.

"So strange he didn't pass it on," Jerry said, with a grin at
Michaelis.

"There's a time and place for yelling. If you knew it, you'd be
king instead of that one," Michaelis said, pointing at Gregory.

"Want me to put the kibosh on?" Eddie asked around a
mouthful of breakfast. "It's a hashtag on Photogram but I can slap
that shit down and make them thank me for it. If I can learn to
say Askazer-Shivadlakia, these idiots can."

"The tourism office might have input on that," Alanna said.

"I say this as advice, not command, but if you let them brand us as The Ask your ancestors will curse us," Michaelis said, and Jerry cackled with laughter.

"I have to say, Greg, it's a great picture of you," he continued. "Uncle Mike looks fantastic too."

"I didn't see a picture of me," Michaelis said, frowning.

"Down at the bottom, here." Jerry passed him his phone.

It was a fairly flattering photo – Jes was actually the focus, barefoot in the sand in their vintage-style one piece, watching Gregory surf. Michaelis was just behind them and to one side, wearing Gregory's spare rash guard and a pair of plain blue swim trunks, damp hair ruffled up in a cowlick like he'd always had when he was younger.

"Look at you, fashion model," Alanna said, nudging Michaelis gently.

Michaelis nodded absently, studying the picture. He did look nice, and unless someone was looking very closely or projecting very hard, they wouldn't see that his eyes were on Jes, and the smile on his face was more affectionate than was proper. He was the widower king emeritus, after all, and Jes could have their pick of people, outside of a difficult curmudgeon they'd accidentally charmed.

"Could you send me the image, Jerry? I don't know how to do the little picture doodad," he said. He did know how, but complaining and making Jerry do it was a form of entertainment.

"Actually, that's a pretty good quote, Your Grace," Alanna said. "The country of the Askazer warrior and the Shivadh noble. Is that from a book, or did you make that up?"

"It's just something like my father would say," Michaelis replied. "If you quote me don't say warrior, I don't like that to represent Askaz. Say scholar. Or say Askazer poet and Shivadh scholar, that rolls off the tongue better and it's no less true."

"The people of Askazer-Shivadlakia are poet scholar warrior

philosopher kings," Gregory said to Eddie. "We think somewhat highly of ourselves."

"Ain't bragging if it's true," Eddie said. "Learned that from bumper stickers in truck stops all the way across Texas. Anyway, I'm glad Jes and Noah could come to the beach too. Those kids are going places."

"Isn't Jes about fifteen years older than you are?" Michaelis asked.

"I was born an old soul," Eddie replied.

"Save us from Californians," Michaelis said.

"Tell you what, I wouldn't want to be on the wrong side of Jes Deimos," Jerry said. "Have you heard their podcast?"

Everyone looked at him.

"What?" Jerry asked.

"Father is *on* their podcast. Eddie's promoting them. The rest of us have been listening for months. What have you been doing?" Gregory asked.

"Making trouble," Jerry replied unconcernedly.

"For whom?" Michaelis inquired.

"Never you mind, Uncle Mike. The point is, there goes someone who could ravage you emotionally and destroy you professionally but also I want their skincare regimen," Jerry said. "If I were the settling-down type I'd propose."

"I'd dearly love to see that," Michaelis replied.

"Some day you're going to trip and fall for someone headlong, Jerry, and I hope I'm there when it happens," Alanna said sweetly. "Your Grace, I'll pass along your supernatural prognostication about The Ask to comms. Eddie?"

"Yep, let's go confab," Eddie said, rising to follow her out. "What if we didn't call it The Ask, but made that like a slogan. *We're here – Just Ask!*"

"You're not genuinely concerned, are you?" Gregory asked, as Jerry trailed after them to offer his own suggestions.

"I just think it's tacky, and not tacky in a good way, like

Eddie," Michaelis said. "The tourism is good for us but we can't let it be our guiding principle. At least, that's my opinion," he added conscientiously.

"I do value that, you know."

"As well you should," Michaelis said with a smile. "Any other dilemmas I can advise on?"

"Not at present. You've got your hands full, anyway."

"Yes, it's been pleasantly busy lately." Michaelis stood, tugging on his jacket. "I'll be in the library this morning, but probably not around for lunch. Recording early this afternoon and then Noah asked for some help with school preparations. He needs to get enrolled somewhere and apparently he has several options, so he wants my advice."

"The Highlands School is the most well-funded. Probably the best teaching overall," Gregory said.

"Yes, but it's a long trek up there on a daily basis, and Jes tells me Noah's schooling is something of a formality. He's an independent learner, as if that wasn't blindingly obvious. I suspect he needs patient teachers more than prestigious ones."

"Well, I'm sure he'll figure it out. Good luck," Gregory said. "There's always an opening at Institut Alpin, or can be if I write him a letter of recommendation."

"Hurrah for the old school!" Michaelis cried as he left.

"I don't see why school even matters," Noah said, when they sat down at the conference table in the bunker that afternoon to go over his options. Jes had a couple of shiny pamphlets from the local schools, and Noah had his laptop open to the websites. "You dropped out and you did fine."

"I did not do fine, I had to get a GED and then go back to school while working full time and it sucked," Jes said. "Let's try and avoid that for you."

"And you probably should at least know how trigonometry works, even if you forget the details as I clearly have," Michaelis said, studying Noah's previous school's transcripts. "The good news is you're a little ahead of most Shivadh students your age, so you can go into – what would Americans call it? Junior year? And have time to fit in without worrying about catching up."

"Yeah, as if that's ever happened," Noah muttered.

"It could happen now," Jes said gently. "You'll be the cool new kid at school."

"I just think I could learn this stuff faster on my own."

"And possibly you could," Michaelis agreed. "But school isn't just learning or socializing, it's an ongoing experience. It gives you something in common with other people. Which, if you want to stay in Askazer-Shivadlakia, will be important. You're a citizen, but that doesn't mean you know everything about living here yet."

"Learning a lot though," Noah said, rebellion still in his voice.

"All good points, but sometimes, kiddo, you just gotta jump through a few hoops in this life," Jes said wearily.

"Oh. Well. If it's just hoops," Noah replied. Michaelis glanced at Jes, wondering if it could be that easy. "Two years of jumping through hoops is a real pain in the butt, but if that's all it is, I can probably do that. As long as I still get to do the podcast and stuff."

"Thank goodness for small favors," Jes said. "Does this get you any closer to figuring out which one you want to go to?"

"Why do they start so late?" Noah asked. "Doesn't school normally start in September most places?"

"The olive harvest," Michaelis said. "Olive season is August and September, and children were needed at home to help. Not as many people farm olives now, but all the kids still go out to the groves, make a little extra pocket money. Most of the teachers work in the groves over the summers, too."

"Can I go do an olive harvest?" Noah asked Jes.

"Sure, you've got your youth worker's card," Jes said. "Do an episode on it. Or I will."

"Let's focus on getting you enrolled, so you at least have somewhere to go afterward," Michaelis said, trying to redirect both parent and child towards the pamphlets. "The Highlands School is arguably the best, but – "

"No, it's too far," Noah said.

"Well, of the ones close enough for you to attend day school and decent enough you should consider them, that leaves the Western Lowlands School, the Yeshiva, and this strange place down by the harbor in Fons-Askaz where you spend one day a week on a tall ship," Michaelis said, picking up the pamphlet for the Maritime Academy. "I should have paid more attention to our accrediting board when I was king."

"It looks like a military school but it's not," Noah said. "The messageboards say it's actually pretty cool. You can set a lot of your own curriculum once you pass the basics and I can test out of most of them. And it's close."

"Very snappy uniforms," Jes said.

"Don't love uniforms on the whole," Noah replied dubiously. "But they are unisex, so I have to give them that. I could go to school in a kilt."

"I'm fond of them," Jes replied. "You ever wear a kilt, Michaelis?"

"Too much of a breeze for me," Michaelis said. "Does come with a handy place for storing one's wallet and keys, though. I can't recommend the Yeshiva unless you want to be a rabbi, but the best I can say of the Western Lowlands School is that it's...adequate."

"Snob," Jes told him. "He went to boarding school," they said to Noah.

"Really?"

Michaelis nodded absently. "Institut Alpin. It's called the school of kings, but not on my account. Lots of powerful peoples' children are educated there. It's in the Swiss Alps, very cold in the winter. I loved it. Gregory tolerated it well. It's a great education, but not, I think, for you."

"Why not? Other than the obvious, that it's a Swiss boarding school like something out of an 80s movie about an evil stepmother," Noah said.

"It's very structured and traditional. They would try to train you for a life I don't think you want," Michaelis said. "If you want to go into hedge fund management or high civil service – "

"Blegh. No offense."

"None taken. I always told Gregory, you have to want the job," Michaelis said. "I did, he did. You, young broadcast journalist, do not. Are you thinking of journalism school?"

Noah glanced at Jes, who shrugged. "Don't ask me, kid, it's your life. I can advise, but I can't pick it out for you."

"What if I don't know?" Noah asked.

Michaelis considered it. He'd known pretty young, and Gregory had too. If he hadn't known, he definitely wouldn't have gone to Institut Alpin, as much as he'd liked it there.

"If you aren't working directly towards a goal yet," he said slowly, "then there's no point going somewhere that's going to try to push you towards one you might not want. You should...explore, I suppose. Like your parent did – learn what's out there in the world. In a structured way through formal education, and not by running off to another country," he added, when he saw Jes's look.

"Huh." Noah sifted through the pamphlets again. "It'd be cool to learn, like, knot tying and sailing and stuff. And useful, I guess. I could get credit for the podcast."

"Sounds like the Maritime Academy would be a fine choice, then," Michaelis said.

"Anyway, most schools are pretty much the same, aren't they?" Noah continued. "Reading, writing, arithmetic. College prep, school dances."

"I suppose in some respects, but not all. I had to take comportment at boarding school, and they still taught it when Gregory went," Michaelis said.

"Comportment?" Noah asked, grinning.

"Of course. Manners, dancing, table etiquette, how to address nobility. All of that. A good skill set for a king to have."

"What kind of dancing? I mean, I guess not like...Photogram dances," Noah said.

"No," Michaelis laughed. "More like *Strictly Come Dancing*. Ballroom," he clarified. "I've probably spent more time waltzing than you've spent alive."

"Funny to think of you dancing," Jes said.

"Why?" Michaelis asked.

"I don't know, I suppose I think of the king as the guy who sits on the throne and watches others dance."

"Great opportunity for diplomacy, dancing. Everyone should know a little," Michaelis said. "And a waltz is easy, so you can talk and dance at the same time."

"It never looks easy on the dancing shows," Noah said.

"Of course not, they want you caught up in the drama of it all. Here, I'll show you." Michaelis took out his phone, scrolling through his playlist for a waltz and putting it on, the music low. He stood up and offered Noah a hand. "I'll teach you how, it doesn't take long."

"Ginger Rogers did everything Fred Astaire did, backwards and in heels," Jes said.

"Yes, I have seen that t-shirt," Michaelis informed them. Noah narrowed his eyes at Michaelis, but got up and took his hand. "Now. As your parent says, generally the lady has to dance backwards, but in Askazer-Shivadlakia, if she's of higher rank than you, you have to. And what if you have two men dancing, like now? Or if you're dancing with someone like Jes? A gentleman, Noah, always knows both parts, and defers to his partner's preference."

"Doesn't sound like much fun, being a gentleman," Noah said, as Michaelis positioned them on the open floor.

"I've always enjoyed the gallantry aspect of it," Jes said. "Getting to make someone feel special. That transcends gender."

"Or it ought," Michaelis agreed. "All right, so if you lead, we do a simple box step…"

Noah was a quick study, as Michaelis had expected, but he didn't seem particularly enthusiastic about it. Which was fair; unless you were training to be king, he supposed it wasn't a very relevant life skill a lot of the time. After teaching him to lead and at least to know when he was following, he let Noah go back to the table, idly paging through the Maritime Academy pamphlet again.

"Here, kid, let me show you how it's done," Jes said, getting up. Before Michaelis could come up with either an excuse or a good reason they shouldn't, Jes had placed one hand in Michaelis's and the other under his arm, in the leading position.

"Sure you're up for this?" Michaelis managed. "I've done this a lot more often than you have."

"That's cute, but drag and ballroom dancing are like half an inch apart," Jes said. "I've waltzed with men in heels higher than your opinion of yourself right now."

"Burn," Noah commented, sitting back to watch.

"Noah, turn Michaelis's old-dude music off and get my phone," Jes said, giving Michaelis a narrow look. "Track two on the dance beat playlist."

"Oooh," Noah said, queuing up some fancy pop song Michaelis wasn't familiar with.

"Quickstep," Jes told Michaelis, and about half a second later swept him off his feet.

He knew how to dance, that was automatic, and he could do a quickstep while following, but Jes had a bounce to them that he barely kept up with, and they were less cautious about banging into the furniture than he was. It took a few bars to get his feet truly under him, but then it was – well, fun, swinging around the room, letting Jes direct the movement, keeping his focus on their face to keep from getting dizzy. Noah was singing along to the song in the background, and when it went to a typical pop-music bridge, Jes spun around and said, "Okay, now you."

He jumped into the lead role, keeping their orbit a little tighter just in case they'd been straying near furniture, and for the last minute of the song was really only paying attention to Jes, not even to the music or Noah or the room spinning behind them.

When the music ended, they swirled to a stop and Michaelis stepped back and bowed. Jes lifted his hand in theirs and kissed the back of it, grinning. It felt like an electric shock ran through his body.

"Okay, that was a little cool," Noah said, somewhere in the distance.

"Thanks," Jes said, turning away to sit down again.

Michaelis stood there for a moment, startled and confused, lit up with a desire he hadn't even thought he was capable of anymore.

Jes was fun and interesting and had flirted before, but that had just been entertaining, nothing expected to come from it. Now – very abruptly – he *wanted.*

"Getting your breath back?" Jes asked from the table, where they'd settled back in with Noah.

"Ah, yes. And some water, I think. Anything for you?" he asked, going to the sink to compose himself. It wasn't entirely successful, but at least it put some distance between him and that dance.

"No, I'm good," Jes replied. "Thanks, that was fun."

He had to get his breathing, and his pulse, and his damn emotions all under control. This wasn't an accidental affectionate look at the beach, this was bound to be obvious. He took down a glass, slowly, and filled it with water. By the time he'd downed half of it, his body at least was settled back into itself.

He came back to the table, sitting across from Noah, who was chattering at Jes about enrolling and school supplies and uniforms. All very familial. Like Noah was a second son, blithely unworried about the crown.

This was... this was probably unwise. Not just his being here, pretending at parenthood of a child that wasn't his, but this sudden, sharp, bewildering attraction. He couldn't act on it. Jes lived here, they were working together, and – he'd spent his whole life with women, well, with a single specific woman, who he was well aware he was not entirely over and probably never would be. Unfair to Jes. And he had no idea how to go about navigating anything more complicated than he already had with Jes.

But he wanted to. He wanted to learn how to. Also unfair to make Jes show him.

He considered this while Jes and Noah battled their way through the paperwork. If this was just his libido waking up after a few years of grieving, it could go right back to sleep. He wouldn't hurt Jes that way simply because they were present and available and possibly even amenable. He'd enjoyed knowing they thought he was attractive, noticing it and encouraging it, when he knew neither of them wanted it to go anywhere.

Now his mind whispered that there were all kinds of places it could go. Some of them were thrilling. Not all of them were good.

Well, that was what research was for, he supposed. He liked books, but he'd be at sea trying to find books about this. Jes, on the other hand, liked people – going to first-hand sources, finding experts, talking to witnesses.

He leaned forward briefly to pick his phone up off the table, pulling up his text messages.

Word with you tomorrow? he asked Gregory, not expecting a swift reply, but one came back almost immediately.

I have some time in the afternoon. Anything urgent?

No. Personal business, not political. Nothing to worry about.

Lunch? Gregory asked.

Prefer it in private, Michaelis said, hoping Gregory wouldn't push and inquire why.

But nothing's wrong? I could do three, but earlier if you need it, Gregory replied.

Nothing's wrong. Three is fine. See you then, he said, and set his phone down again.

CHAPTER NINE

His FATHER MIGHT have told him not to worry, but when Michaelis arrived at Gregory's office the following afternoon, something was definitely wrong. He was tense in a very specific way – posture intent, shoulders back, face a careful blank. He wasn't upset or angry; he was confused, and Gregory knew his father well enough to know how much he hated being confused.

"Come over to the window," Gregory said, settling on the bench by his big office window. "I get tired of the desk and you're not a job applicant."

"I thought you were finished with hiring the new staff."

"We are, mostly. Though if you want a job I'm pretty sure there are some open," Gregory said, as Michaelis settled next to him. "It didn't sound serious in text, but it looks pretty serious from here. What's going on?"

"I want to ask you something," Michaelis said. "I think you might have more expertise in some areas than I do. I have a bit of a modern dilemma, but I'm not sure how to ask about it, to be honest." He gave Gregory a dry smile. "Difficult for a man to go to his son for advice."

"If it helps, technically you're also my subject," Gregory said, bumping his shoulder against his father's. "How can the king advise?"

"I don't want to pull you into something that isn't your responsibility," Michaelis said, studying his hands. "And if you don't want to answer any of this, you don't have to."

"Now I'm a little worried," Gregory said. "You're not in

some kind of legal trouble, are you?"

"Hah. No. That'd be easier, actually. I know how to pay a bribe."

"Dad!"

"Well, politics was different when I was young." Michaelis slouched backwards, a move Gregory recognized – he did it himself when he was uncertain what to do and annoyed by it. "All right. I know when you came out, lord, a decade ago now, you were older than a lot of people do it these days. You took a while. To be sure of yourself. To know what you wanted to do and how to do it."

"Yeah. You were still the first person I told," Gregory said. "Well. Mom, then you."

"And I'm glad of that. I know I haven't always been perfect about it. I was so pleased you felt you could trust me, and I'm grateful you…tolerated me."

"It wasn't like that," Gregory said quietly. "I could always see you were trying."

"I was," Michaelis agreed. "I was just very worried about how the world would treat you. Never worried about you, yourself."

"I know."

"What I want to know is…how did you know? I know you struggled, you weren't sure…did you just wake up one day knowing, at last?"

Gregory frowned, considering this.

"Well. Around ten or so, you sort of start to get the message that things are going to change, you get told about the birds and bees and that someday you'll find girls interesting for new and exciting reasons," he said at last. "Even in Askazer-Shivadlakia, we're so small, most of the media comes from elsewhere and at least when I was growing up it was very heterosexual. The implication was always that starting to like girls, that's when you start to grow up. It isn't true, but a lot of people think it is."

Michaelis nodded.

313

"So I kept waiting to grow up, to find girls interesting, and I figured maybe I was just…a late bloomer or something, but I realized eventually that wasn't going to happen. And I wasn't sure what I felt about boys was right, either."

"Oh, no, Gregory – "

"Not like that!" Gregory said hastily. "I didn't think I was *wrong* or something. Maybe I didn't like anyone! I just couldn't be sure what I was feeling. So I had to test it out. And eventually I worked out that it was going to be men, for me. After that I still had to work out how to tell people, or even whether to tell people, given I wanted to be king. I had your public relations office do a poll, did you know?"

"You did what?"

"When I was nineteen. I had them do some secret market research about whether Askazer-Shivadlakia would elect a gay king. Good news is, they came back 91% positive on the idea, and here I am, so well done us."

Michaelis chuckled, which was good – at least he wasn't as panicked as before. "Of course you did market research."

"Got to, these days. The point is, by the time I came out, I had some kind of ground to stand on. But no, it wasn't sudden. It took time."

"And a lot of work, it sounds like."

"Well, I did almost fail French Lit. I was distracted by a boy." Gregory grinned sidelong at him. "Why do you ask? Are you at the chapter in your memoirs where your extremely awkward twenty year old son tells you he's gay? I can come on the podcast and talk about it, if you want. I don't mind."

He could see his father considering how to answer, considering whether to lie. He cut that off quickly.

"Is there something you want to tell me?" he asked. "Like…are you seeing someone? You know it'd be okay. Mom would want you to be happy – "

"That's not exactly it," Michaelis said. "There's a person I care for, yes. I would actually be concerned you wouldn't be comfortable with me seeing someone after your mother passed, so that's good to hear. The problem is that I don't know precisely how I feel, and I don't want to get involved if I'm going to hurt them, even inadvertently. With your mother I knew, in a heartbeat, there was a specific day and hour that I knew, and that knowing didn't go away until she died. I was so certain with her and now nothing in my life is certain, anywhere."

He sounded distressed, like this one thing had somehow managed to put his entire life into a tailspin. Gregory turned on instinct and pulled him into a hug, tugging his father's head down to his shoulder. It said a lot that he went without protest, and stayed there for a while. They weren't really either of them big on hugging, but apparently everything was out the window today.

"It's a lot of change," Gregory said at last. "The last few months. I know how you feel. All this is kind of new to me, too."

Michaelis nodded and finally leaned back. "Thank you."

"Well, however I can continue to be awkward," Gregory said with a smile. Michaelis matched it, then looked away. "Seriously. You know what you and Mom had was not the way these things normally work, right?"

"What?"

"Nobody falls in love with their soulmate in their teens and spends the next few decades happily ruling a country with them. You are literally some kind of fairytale prince," Gregory said. "Most of us have to fight to get something like that. You and Mom were effortless, but that's not how this normally goes."

"You have Edward," Michaelis said.

"I do, yes, and I love him, but he is so much work, you have no idea," Gregory said. "And I dated a lot of people before him, and he dated a lot of people before me. We had breakups and hurt people and got hurt, that's how dating is. What you're feeling now is what the rest of us spent our twenties feeling."

"Oh," Michaelis said.

"Yeah. It's okay to worry about hurting someone if you don't know how you feel, but that's just going to happen sometimes, I'm afraid," Gregory said. "The fact you're worried strongly suggests whoever this person is, you do care about them."

"Mm."

"Dad, listen…is it a guy?" Gregory said. "Because the drift of this conversation reminds me of being twenty again. It's fine if it is, I'm actually on much more solid ground with sexuality crises. There are books I can recommend."

"It's Jes," Michaelis said.

"Ah. Oh. Wow," Gregory said. Immediately, he could see it – Jes was attractive, seemed like an interesting person, and they'd been working together, living in the same building if not the same rooms. It actually explained a few things. "I can see how that would be – "

"Complex, yes," Michaelis agreed. "I do think they're interested, I'm not completely blind to this kind of thing, but the last thing I want to do is begin something and then turn coward. I get the sense Jes has probably had a lot of that in their life. I don't want to add to it."

"Does that seem likely?" Gregory asked hesitantly.

"Not likely, but possible. I don't know, Gregory. I don't know if I could be with anyone who wasn't your mother," Michaelis said, clearly frustrated. "Before now I'd have said I was fine being alone."

"Oh, Dad," Gregory said.

"I was," Michaelis insisted. "And then I met Jes and I had something to occupy my time again. And if it's just that I feel useful around them, them and Noah, that's not enough to sustain anything real."

"You don't know if you like Jes or just the person you are around them," Gregory said. Michaelis nodded. "You really can't do anything by halves in your life, can you?"

"I wouldn't get too smart about it, that gene's in you

somewhere too," Michaelis replied.

"Yeah, well, that's Eddie's problem," Gregory replied. "Is this useful at all, what we're doing here?"

"Yes. I think so. It's one more thread to pull on trying to unravel all this," Michaelis said. "I do appreciate it."

"Do you, uh, want the books anyway? There are a couple on genderqueer relationships that might help."

"No. Well. Maybe make sure you know where they are. You know me, I like to muddle through on my own."

"Another thing that will probably eventually become Eddie's problem," Gregory sighed. "What can I do to help?"

"You've done it, as far as you can, I think," his father said. "Just having someone else's perspective is helpful. Do you…like Jes? That matters too, you know."

"From what I've seen of them, yes. But you're a grown man and so am I, I don't have to like the people you date."

"I'd prefer if you did."

"Then yes. I like them," Gregory said. "And I'm pleased you've found something that makes you happy, whether or not you do anything about this potential thing with Jes. Come talk if you need to, you don't have to make an appointment. I'll make time."

"You're the king, you know that's not how this works."

"When I was twelve you canceled Parliament for the day because I was having a nervous breakdown over acne. If you didn't want me to make time for family you shouldn't have led by example," Gregory said with a smile.

"I'm your father, that's different."

"Not really, but that's a discussion we can have some other time. Come talk whenever you need to, I always have time for you. Though maybe not Tuesday nights if you can avoid it."

Michaelis looked at him curiously as they both stood. "What's on Tuesday night that's so vital?"

"Date night with Eddie. It's for your own good, you don't

want to walk in on anything."

"Ah. Duly noted." Michaelis hesitated, then hugged Gregory again. "Thank you."

"Anytime," Gregory said. "Even Tuesday if you have to."

When his father was gone, Alanna knocked on the doorway.

"I just saw Michaelis leaving," she said. "He looked confused, and I only know it was confusion because I almost never see that expression on his face."

"He's going through some things," Gregory said vaguely.

"Aren't we all," Alanna replied. "Is he okay?"

"He will be. He usually is. Ready for afternoon debrief?"

"Of course. Excitingly, the first of the building projects should go through budget approval tomorrow..."

It was not a long walk back to the lodge from the palace, and Michaelis felt that he could use a truly long walk right now. He thought better when he was moving, and the lake felt mockingly serene. How dare it be so scenic when human beings had to deal with turmoil like this?

He almost laughed. He was much too old to be so dramatic, even being Shivadh. Still, instead of taking the trail around the lake back to the lodge, he took the road directly down into Fons-Askaz. At least the act of having to keep out of the way of foot traffic and cars felt suitably chaotic.

He was conscious, in a way he wasn't usually, of the murmurs that surrounded and followed him. Locals knew him and didn't care much, but the tourists were thick on the ground and all of them clearly recognized him, some consulting the cash bills in their hands for comparison. He kept his expression abstracted – not forbidding, just a little distant and, hopefully, unapproachable. He saw one person take a selfie with him in the background, but ignored it.

What was the point of having trained to rule, having ruled for decades, and having graciously handed over rule to his son, if he couldn't get a handle on this? Gregory was right, hurting people was sometimes simply a part of having relationships with them, and that obviously meant this shouldn't happen. Jes didn't deserve that and Noah certainly didn't. Even if he did know how to handle this, the possibility was still there that he'd screw it up. So, he would need to figure out a way around it.

That, at least, was a plan. It let him slow his pace a little, his shoulders relaxing a fraction. Fine; that was a problem to solve instead of an intractable roadblock.

He turned down an alley off the high street, stopping at the little side-door bakery he knew was there. They had a nice new awning with a more prominent sign, probably on account of the increased tourism, and also a few new items in the bakery case. One of them was a pastry that looked like a panda – the sign in front of it read "PAIN-DA CHOCOLAT" – and Michaelis examined it with curiosity.

"You would not believe how many tourists buy them just to take a photo," the baker said with a grin. "You make one cute pain au chocolat or a clever sort of cake, you've made your sales for the week."

"Why a panda, though?" Michaelis asked.

"Who knows, Your Grace? My daughter suggested it. Someone else was already doing birds and rabbits."

"Hm. Well, it's still your pain au chocolat, isn't it? Two of the pandas in a box, and a sausage roll – the lamb, if you have it."

"Want the roll hot?"

"Please."

Bakery box dangling from his fingers and sausage roll in hand, he felt a little better about the world. There was a scenic overlook on the harbor not far away; while the promenade had a number of people on it, the benches were empty. He sat and ate and watched people come and go, letting things simmer until he felt ready to consider them. That was the way his mind worked, he knew that well enough – it took time for the gears to grind all the way around, but he could be patient.

His phone beeped, eventually, and he looked down to a text from Eddie.

Don't jump :D it read, and he opened it to find a screengrab of a Photogram of himself. Someone had taken his picture, sitting on the bench, looking contemplative, and posted it while he was still sitting there.

They'd captioned the photo *Nice to know even the former king has sadness dinner sometimes.*

He considered it, then texted back, *Edward, life has become very recursive.*

Not sure what that means, but let me know if you need a ride home or someone to talk to, Eddie replied.

No, I'm fine. It wasn't a sadness dinner, it was a nice snack.

Eddie sent him a thumbs-up icon. Michaelis sat back and let a smile drift across his face, just in case anyone else was concerned. A few people nodded to him as they passed and he nodded back. Eventually he stretched a little, rising to go to the railing and watch a sailboat tacking into the harbor.

One thing he had learned in his career was the control of strong emotions. Especially when he was new on the throne, he couldn't show if he was upset or angry about something. He'd thought of himself not as two people but as two parts of a person – the king, and Michaelis. Back then, if Michaelis was angry, he slipped into being the king. A little distant, very dignified, full of authority. He'd been twenty-one when he was crowned. What else could he do?

He hadn't had to use that kind of thinking in years. As one got older, all the politics seemed increasingly petty. Important, but not important enough for passion. He'd developed a level head, and he just needed to find the level again.

Well, he'd done it once; he could simply retreat a little into the king again, when things got intense. It would protect both him and Jes, and nobody would come to harm. If they couldn't have that…potential, as Gregory called it, well, one couldn't have everything in this life.

Content with this, he turned from the sailboat, docking safely in harbor, and began the walk back to the lodge.

When he let himself in, Noah and Jes were in the kitchen; Jes looked up from their half-eaten dinner and smiled. Michaelis nodded and held up the bakery box.

"Wait until you see what nonsense I found," he said, and Noah took the box from him while Jes kicked out a chair so he could sit.

"PANDA CROISSANTS," Noah crowed. Jes took the one he handed them and tore into it with delight while Noah looked for the best lighting to photograph his.

And the king Michaelis had decided to be, his very important and careful armor, simply evaporated. All his resolve and his plans, gone in a flash. He couldn't even regret it.

There was a restaurant in town – near the bakery, actually – that had nice views of the water and did extremely good pasta. He was pretty sure he could get a reservation there without too much trouble. He'd wait a few days, make sure the weather would be fine, and ask Jes to have dinner with him, as a date, to see how it would go.

It would have worked, probably.

Instead, it was all Noah's fault.

Michaelis had found the restaurant's phone number, and had meant to speak to the palace scheduler, who could swing him both the best table and an ideal time, but his days were so busy now. He was recording a new episode with Noah most of the morning, and in the afternoon he had retakes to do with Jes, as well as some kind of weird sound check Lachlan was insisting on.

They were nearly done, at least he hoped, and Lachlan was talking about possible vocal rest and not having any dairy for a week, when Jes's phone went berserk.

Michaelis, blinking at the strobe lights and sirens coming from the phone, jerked backwards. Jes grabbed the phone and fumbled to silence it, while Lachlan leapt up from his seat.

"What the hell was that?" Michaelis asked, but Jes just held up a finger and set the phone down, tapping the answer-call button on the screen.

"Noah, is that you?" they asked.

"Emergency ringtone," Lachlan said to Michaelis softly. "Noah uses it if he needs to interrupt recording."

"Hey Boss," Noah said, voice staticky over the speakerphone. "Can you hear me okay?"

"Sure can. What's going on? You're echoing – where are you?"

"Uh, you remember when Michaelis said there was a secret wine cellar?" Noah asked.

"No – did you tell him that?" Jes asked, looking at Michaelis.

"I'm here, Noah. I do remember saying that," Michaelis said. "It was just a rumor, though."

"I think I found it," Noah said. "I kinda fell in. You might have to come get me out."

"Wild Child, I am going to tie you to a chair," Jes said. "Are you okay?"

"Nothing bleeding," Noah said cheerfully.

"That's not an answer," Michaelis said. From the look on Jes's face he wasn't the only one startled by how stern he sounded.

"Might have a twisted ankle. Nothing else hurts," Noah said, more meekly. "It is dark and the spiders are large, so if you could hurry…"

"Where are you, relative to the recording booths?" Jes asked, getting up with the phone and walking out into the bunker.

Michaelis followed, Lachlan on his heels.

"Okay, so the room Michaelis said was the bunker's nursery?" Noah said.

"Yes, I know the one," Michaelis answered, leading them across the big meeting space and through the doorway.

"There's a hallway on the other side," Noah said.

"The one that goes to the north end of the garage?"

"Yeah, that one. You know the weird wood panel in the middle of the wall?"

"Yes, my son," Jes said, voice turning vaguely threatening, and Michaelis could see why – the panel had been pulled down and laid on the floor. "Noah, did you – how did you even get that off the wall?"

"I didn't! It fell off, I heard it fall so I came to investigate," Noah said over the speaker. They could hear his actual voice as well, if only faintly. "There's a secret room behind it! You try to resist a secret room!"

"I'm gonna hang up, we can hear you," Jes said, and put the phone away. "Noah!"

"I think there is actually a lot of wine here!" Noah's voice drifted in.

Jes climbed through the strange, half-plastered hole the wooden panel had been covering. Michaelis eyed it warily.

"This is some nonsense haunted-house bullshit," Lachlan yelled through the gap.

"Thanks, Uncle Lachlan, I want that on a t-shirt," Noah called back.

"Michaelis! Lachlan! Stop being dipshits and come in here!" Jes yelled. Michaelis let Lachlan squeeze through and then followed, scraping up his face when he met an unexpected jut of broken wood in the wall.

"Girl, the demolition of it all," Lachlan said, joining Jes at the edge of a gaping hole in the floor of the weird little room they were in. Unlike the rest of the bunker, it had dirt walls and wood floors.

"It's a miracle he even got a phone signal out to you," Michaelis said, using the light from his phone to study the wooden beams propping up ceiling panels, which were showing distinct signs of rot – warping and flaking, eaten away completely in places, and cracked badly in others.

"The wifi can get in here from the hallway," Noah called up. "I wouldn't go anywhere in the lodge that I couldn't get wifi."

"Nice to know you have one boundary," Michaelis drawled.

"Did you fall through?" Jes asked. "You sound like you're about twenty feet down."

"Only a little," Noah said. "The hole was already here. There used to be stairs at one end. I kinda fell through the last few stairs and then they fell in after me."

"He's very calm about this," Michaelis said to Lachlan.

"He's the only one," Lachlan replied. Jes lit up the flashlight on their phone and aimed it down the hole, catching Noah's dirty but apparently unharmed face.

"I don't think even Lachlan's going to be able to reach you," they said.

"I am not dangling my ass down into that hole unless I have to, either," Lachlan replied.

"Can we call the fire department? Or, um, a mountaineer?" Noah suggested.

"I don't want you in that hole a second longer than necessary. This entire room isn't stable," Michaelis said.

"Well, unless you can levitate me out…"

"Rope," Michaelis said. Jes looked up at him. "There's plenty upstairs. Stay here with him and try not to move around too much. I'll get some rope and a pulley."

"What the fuck do we do with a pulley?" he heard Lachlan ask, but he was already slipping back out into the hallway, running full-tilt for the stairs.

Upstairs he headed for the supply shed next to the lodge. It was a catch-all for anything one might need – spare oars and swimsuits, fishing poles and bows, camping gear, and emergency supplies. No ladders, which was something he was going to address at a future date. He pulled down two coils of rope that looked relatively new, then rummaged for a pulley, which fortunately came already attached to a tripod – he guessed it was for getting small boats in and out of the water. After a second of consideration, he also took a knife from the shelf and a plastic tarp from the pile near the door.

He had to shove it all through the gap before he could get through, Lachlan taking the supplies while Jes kept up a running conversation with Noah.

"He's recording it, because of course he is," Lachlan said.

"Great content, though," Michaelis replied, even as he became aware it was probably not the appropriate thing to say.

"I know, I'm so pissed he thought of it first," Lachlan replied.

"Okay, Noah, I'm going to drop a tarp and a knife down to you," Michaelis said, kneeling at the edge. The only light in the room was Jes's phone light, lying on the floor next to them; he should have thought to take a lantern as well. "While we get this set up, you cut the tarp into strips. I want you to wrap your arms in them from palm to elbow, because that's where you're going to lock the rope, around your arms. The tarp will protect your skin. How are you at a dead hang?"

"What the hell's a dead hang?" Noah asked, sounding alarmed.

"Never mind. Just get to work," Michaelis said, and let the tarp fall. "Knife coming down, watch yourself," he added, and leaned as far into the hole as he could before dropping it. The floorboards creaked ominously.

"If the floor gives way I am going to throw a shit fit that will be so loud it'll get us rescued," Lachlan said.

"Don't brag if you can't back it up," Michaelis advised, examining the tripod. The problem was the size of the hole and relative smallness of the room – no space for the tripod to actually sit. They'd have to just use it as a pole. "Here. We can't sit this on the floor so someone's going to have to hold it here at an angle. Do you think you can keep this steady while I pull Noah up with it?" he asked, handing the pole to Jes so they could test the weight.

"Lachlan, come help," Jes said, fixing their arms around the pole and leaning back. Lachlan got in front of them, resting it across his shoulders.

"I'll hold, you anchor," he said, and Jes moved back to keep the tip of it steady on the floor.

Michaelis unwound one of the coils of rope and began feeding it through the pulley, the same as he'd hitch it to bring a boat out onto a dock.

"Start getting ready to brace now," he said, as he paid out the rope, hanging over the open gap. "Noah, let me know when it touches ground."

"Got it!" Noah said.

"Great. Grab it at shoulder height and wrap your arms in it, so that it locks in place."

"Like the guys who do the silk acrobatics," Noah said.

"Sure," Michaelis agreed. "Let me know when you're ready. I'm going to pull you up but if you can keep your abdomen tense and your knees lifted we'll get you up a little faster. Safer, too."

"I'm ready!"

"This is going to be really ugly for about three minutes," Michaelis said, and began to pull.

Lachlan groaned and then swore, not especially obscenely but still quite imaginatively. Jes grunted and kicked one foot out to brace themself, heel digging into the soft wood. Michaelis pulled hand over hand, as fast as he dared, throwing his weight back on each tug, gradually moving backwards. Noah's arms appeared above the gap and then his face; when his shoes were visible, Lachlan swung the pole sharply to the left.

Noah and Lachlan tumbled onto the wood floor together

and the pole clattered to the ground; Jes skidded in the opposite direction, and Michaelis went backwards with a thump, now that the tension was off the ropes. He gasped for a second, breath knocked out of him, and then pushed himself up on his elbows.

Lachlan was helping Noah to his feet and hustling him towards the door; Jes was scrambling up to offer Michaelis a hand, and he let himself be tugged to a sitting position, then got his first deep breath and pushed himself upright as Jes gathered up their phone.

"Go, this isn't safe," he said. "I'll follow, just get up to the lodge."

They nodded and slipped out, and he cut himself again getting through, but at least nothing collapsed before he managed it. It took him a while to climb the stairs, still winded, but the chaos upstairs was at least under control when he arrived.

Noah was sitting on the kitchen counter, getting checked over by Jes. Lachlan fussed around the boy, helping him get the crumpled tarp off his arms and clucking over the bruising there. Jes, satisfied there were no broken bones, noticed Lachlan's skinned elbows, and got the first aid kit from under the sink. Michaelis, still getting his lung capacity back, leaned in the doorway and watched, gently stretching his arms.

He was just starting to think about quietly disappearing to clean the dust and sweat off himself when Lachlan turned around and blurted "CARRIE!" at him in a panicked voice.

"Oh, shit, Michaelis," Jes said, fumbling the first aid kit. He looked behind him, wondering what was wrong.

"Your face," Lachlan said, as Jes set the kit on the counter and went to him, pulling him into the kitchen. They held up his hand in theirs, staring at it. He realized his knuckles and palms were scraped raw, red rivulets drying in tracks down his wrists on both arms. To his shock, his shirt was covered in still-damp blood.

"It looks worse than it is," he said, confused. "Nothing hurts, they can't be that deep. I don't know where all the rest of the blood is from – "

"Inside you!" Lachlan yelped.

Jes was wetting a towel in the sink, and he saw their hands shaking from the adrenaline crash as they carried it over. They rubbed the cool towel gently against his forehead, bringing it away stained red, and then ran it down one cheek –

His face erupted in sudden, stinging pain, like antiseptic ointment on road rash. He let out a startled bellow.

"Found where the blood came from," Jes said. "Sorry, I'll be gentler."

He braced for a second swipe and managed to hold still, even when Lachlan actually did follow Jes's cleaning with spray antiseptic. The pain in his face, at least, kept his mind off the newly discovered rope burn on his palms that Jes was trying to clean. He heard Noah taking pictures behind them and shot the boy a scolding glare.

"You really tore yourself up," Lachlan said. "If there is any good wine down there, you should call dibs."

"I think it's probably state property," Michaelis said.

"Not if the state never finds out about it. If you don't want it, at least let me loose before you report it. Ah, scalp wound," Lachlan added, working his way around behind Michaelis's ear. "Lie back and think of Askaz, darling."

Lachlan finally got everything disinfected to his high standards, and Jes wrapped the worst of the rope burns in gauze. When they were finished, Noah got off the counter, eyes huge and sad in the way only drama-filled adolescence allowed.

"I'm really sorry," he said. "I didn't want anyone to get hurt."

"We know, Wild Child," Lachlan said quietly.

"You've got to be careful," Jes said, sounding more anxious than angry. They rubbed his back. "We'll talk about it later. You're not in any trouble and I'm sure seeing what happened to Michaelis is punishment enough if you were."

"Sorry, Michaelis," Noah practically whispered, head hanging low.

Michaelis rested a bandaged hand on Noah's arm, wincing, and then pulled him forward. As soon as he was close enough, he wrapped him in a hug, face pressed to his dusty hair.

"Small price to pay to get you out safely," he said, as Noah's arms wrapped around his waist. "Glad you weren't hurt, Tavat."

Jes, he could see, recognized the word, though Lachlan and Noah clearly didn't. He let go and held Noah away from him, giving him a quick once-over.

"Why don't you go wash up? If anything starts to hurt, call Jes at once," he ordered, and gave Noah a gentle push.

"I'm gonna make sure everything in the studio gets saved and shut down properly," Lachlan said, moving towards the bunker stairs. "Nobody fall through anything until I get back, I have an extremely delicate constitution for this kind of thing."

Michaelis took the towel from Jes, refolding it to find a clean patch. He pulled his bloody shirt off and tried to rub his neck clean. Jes turned and sat on the counter, next to him. After a minute or two, they laughed and put their hands on their head.

"That was really, really scary," they said. "My child almost literally fell down a well like in an old Lassie movie."

"He's definitely your kid," Michaelis said, moving to stand in front of them, still trying to get blood and grime off his neck. "But also, I'm pretty sure having an unstable secret wine cellar hidden behind a warped old board in the hallway is a liability."

"Are you saying I should sue?"

"Rather hoping you won't, but you'd have grounds," he said. They leaned forward and rested their forehead on his bare shoulder. He covered the nape of their neck with one hand and leaned his head to the side, speaking quietly, mouth close to their ear. "He's safe, Jes. Kids get into scrapes. Of all the dangerous stuff he could do at his age, this is remarkably wholesome."

"I'm still terrified."

"What kind of parent would you be if you weren't? He's not

even my kin and I was scared, too."

"Bet King Gregory never fell in a wine hole."

"My son once crashed a golf cart into a water hazard and nearly drowned half the royal cousins and himself."

"That doesn't sound like him. Was he drinking?"

"No, he was seven. But he definitely did the driving on purpose, which is more than you can accuse Noah of. Did get me out of ever having to go golfing again, which I hated, so in the end I suppose I should be grateful."

Jes rested their fingertips against his ribs, trembling slowly subsiding. They turned their head further, pressing their nose into the hollow of his throat.

"Jes – " he began, worried.

"Please, don't make me feel weird about this," Jes said. "I just – "

"No, no, shh," he said. "I'm not objecting."

He considered his next words carefully. Jes, apparently not aware they were supposed to wait, lifted their head and kissed him.

He felt like he sort of tumbled into it, letting them run the show, until good sense kicked in and he pulled away gently. He didn't go far; no one had that much self-control.

"Can't get a word in edgewise with you," he said. Jes laughed nervously. They looked a mess. He slid his hand around from where it still cupped the back of their head, so that he could cradle their cheek.

"I want this very badly," he said in a low voice. "I've seen enough to know you probably do too. But there's some reason you always pull back, and I've never pushed it either. That's fine, I didn't expect it to go anywhere. This, now, is a stress reaction, and that's fine too. It just means…I'm not going to hold you to anything you do right now, and I'm not going to do much until I know you're really good with this. Or until we're both more in our right minds. Now is not a good time for this. Later will work just as well."

"I was worried it might endanger the network, us getting entangled. We were working in your home, and then we moved into it…and I was worried about Noah," they said. "If it went badly. He might get caught in the crossfire. I never, ever wanted him to get trapped between two people who hate each other."

"Not like your parents," he guessed. They nodded miserably. "I would never hurt that boy intentionally. Or you."

"Yeah, I'm seeing that," they said.

Michaelis leaned in slowly, giving Jes time to meet him halfway. When they kissed, he could taste chalky plaster dust and his own blood. Jes pushed forward and his mouth opened, scrapes on his cheek singing in pain. It felt spectacular, dangerous and satisfying. He stepped in and slid his free hand around their waist, their arms resting on his shoulders. When he finally retreated, because he could hear footsteps, they looked dazed.

"Lachlan's on the stairs," he said. "We'll talk later? Perhaps tonight?"

Jes nodded and gave him a quick last kiss, then turned in time to see Lachlan emerge from below.

"You both look like you've been through a small war," he said. "Not to be the pragma queen instead of the drama queen but Jes, we are going to need to rebook the last few appointments for studio time today, unless you want me to keep going."

"No, that's not fair to you or them. I can help call and make the changes," they said, glancing at Michaelis.

"I should make some calls about the wine cellar. We're going to need a structural engineer and a historian, which sounds like the start of a joke," Michaelis said. "I'll do it from my rooms."

He showered first and then called Gregory, who was equal parts alarmed and intrigued. They had to have a brief debate about whether Michaelis or Noah needed formal medical care, which required a promise to see a doctor if anything else started to hurt, but eventually Gregory agreed that rest was probably best. He forwarded the call to the palace switchboard, which connected

Michaelis to the head of the historical society. By the time he'd made all the necessary explanations and arrangements with three separate offices of the palace, he was exhausted and crashing fast. He dropped onto the bed to rest for a few minutes, and more or less passed out.

He woke when someone sat on the edge of the bed; Jes, it turned out, looking clean but weary. He sat up, leaning in from behind, and didn't so much kiss their shoulder as tiredly rest his mouth there. They raised a hand to stroke his hair, cautious of the long cut on his scalp.

"How's Noah?" he asked.

"Lachlan's watching a movie with him. I said I'd see how you were doing."

"No worse than I was..." He looked at his watch, "...an hour ago when I was having a very surreal conversation with the royal sommelier. And how are you?"

"Better. I know now's probably not what you meant when you said later, but I have questions."

"It's all right. I've had some rest and you've had a bath, so we could be worse," he said. Jes didn't laugh.

"You said you want this," they said.

He propped his chin on their shoulder. "Indeed."

"I don't get the sense that you're casual about dating."

"You are very correct."

"And I don't do that unless I think someone is going to be around for a while, for me but also for Noah. People who are safe. Stable."

"I'm doing my best," he said.

They turned to give him a quick kiss. "I know. Which puts a lot of my worries to rest. But I also need to know that if we do this, you're going to be cool with my identity – and yours. That you aren't going to bolt because you're too straight for this."

"I was worried about that too. I didn't want to give you a false impression. Asked Gregory for some advice, actually," he said. "It helped, but I couldn't really talk to him about some things. Not a child's job to help his father out like that."

"How do you mean? Incidentally, I'd love to hear Eddie's take on this."

"I considered it, but I didn't feel ready for what I might hear from the sage Eddie Rambler. What I couldn't tell Gregory was that – I loved his mother, but it was for her, the…essence of who she was. If she'd been a man I might still have loved her, I don't know. And Gregory reminded me that what we had was unusual; we spoke this weird personal language for each other."

"So…*are* you straight?" Jes asked, looking perplexed and concerned.

"I'm not often attracted to anyone, to be honest. I think perhaps because there was no room for that while Miranda was alive, and we fell in love when I was eighteen. After she passed, well, grief tends to smother that kind of thing. In my limited experience, all of the people I've felt attraction to have been women until now, but I don't have a problem with the fact that you aren't one. I like you, Jes, and I want you. There are reasons this might not work, but…I was planning to ask you to dinner before all this happened."

He kissed their throat, then leaned forward as they twisted around to kiss him on the mouth.

"Well, maybe you are a little queer, then," they said, amused. He held up his thumb and forefinger, slightly apart, and they nodded. "When were you making moves, anyway? You said you never pushed. When did you even drop hints?"

"Jes," Michaelis said. "Did you think I was walking around shirtless after swimming because I wanted to air dry?"

"Oh. Well. That was very nice," they said. "I said hello to your biceps every morning."

"Glad to hear it." He leaned close, voice soft. "I enjoyed it. I had no expectations, but I saw you noticing. I liked that."

Jes turned to him, impulsively. "Let me take you to dinner

tomorrow instead," they said. "Instead of you taking me, I mean."

"Sounds fine," he said. "But I'm willing to put out now. How much time do you think we have?"

"They're watching *Dune*."

"So we could do dinner and at least half an hour of foreplay and still have plenty of time."

"How much foreplay did you intend?" Jes asked, sounding intrigued.

"Dealer's choice," he replied. They kissed him again, deep but gentle.

"You're right, this is coming from stress," they said. "No need to rush."

He nodded but didn't move away; they both sat there for a while, touching quietly, until he sighed.

"What?" they asked.

"I'm going to have to wear concealer to make the scrapes on my face look less intense," he said. "First time I've ever been the one putting on makeup for a date."

They smiled, patting his cheek. "If you want, I know a lipstick that would look killer on you."

"Pass, but I appreciate the thought. Next time I have to wear some for television, maybe."

"Get some more sleep. One of us will wake you for dinner," they said. "I'm going to go listen to Lachlan rhapsodize about Sting's abs."

"Oh, it's the David Lynch one? We could have a whole relationship before that one finishes. Have fun," Michaelis replied, as Jes stood and headed for the door. They turned and gave him a smile so bright and full of promise that he didn't manage to speak before they'd gone.

He slept a little more, waking eventually when his scrapes started to bother him. He found a clean shirt and walked, slow and stiff, out to the front of the lodge. Jes and Noah were both asleep on the couch, *Dune* still going on mute, and Lachlan was in the kitchen.

"Sit, I'll bring you something," Lachlan said. "It's only canned soup, but it's hot and salty, just like me."

Michaelis nodded gratefully, seating himself and taking the bowl with care.

"How are your scrapes?" Lachlan asked.

"Not too bad. Bet you're bruised to hell from holding up that pulley," Michaelis said.

"Back's going to be purple all over," Lachlan said good naturedly. "But like you told Noah, it's a small price to pay."

Michaelis nodded. Lachlan studied him.

"You said something else, too, when you said that. Something you called Noah," he said. "Tavan?"

"Tavat."

"Is that like a new name he's trying out, or a nickname or something? Unless you're not allowed to tell me."

Michaelis shook his head. "I just said it in the moment. It's in the old Shivadh language. You're not Shivadh by birth."

"No, I'm from Massachusetts. Married in. Jes introduced us, actually. Why?"

"It's a little complicated. We have this…legal tradition, not a law but more of a cultural rule, that some things only princes are allowed to do. But because we are exactly that arrogant, we also say, well, every Shivadh is royalty, everyone is a prince, so anyone can do these forbidden royal things if they dare to. Tavat is what you call a person who is so self-assured that they, as an ordinary person, act like a royal."

"So it's a compliment. Like calling someone brash or daring. Oh! Like the Shivadh version of Wild Child, right?"

Michaelis gave him a measuring look, but Lachlan, as loud as he could be, wasn't indiscreet.

"Yes, coming from anyone else," he admitted. "Coming from me, it's different. Usually you'd translate it to English, especially for a youngster like Noah, as something like…princeling. Little daring prince. But I'm the king. Former king. So when I call someone Tavat, it's layered."

"Almost like saying he's an adopted son," Lachlan said quietly.

"I care about both of them."

Lachlan nodded. "My husband and I adopted. She was only a few days old."

"I listened to the podcast about it. Sounds harrowing."

"It was, but I wouldn't trade it. I would absolutely jump in a wine hole to keep my child from getting a bumped head, let alone anything worse."

"Then she's a very lucky child." Michaelis smiled. "But even if I didn't feel…paternal towards Noah, he is Tavat anyway, you know. A Shivadh princeling if ever I met one. If he manages to survive to adulthood I'll be interested to see where life takes him."

Lachlan sipped his drink. "And Jes?"

Michaelis looked past him to where Jes was sleeping, Noah tucked up against them.

"I didn't know them when they were young, but yes, I'm sure they would have been considered Tavat. Leaving home so young, returning in triumph years later, that's practically mythological. If I were still king, I'd need to coin a word for them. Caez, I think."

"What does Caez mean?"

"Some words for king, like Kaiser and Tsar – and, incidentally, Askaz – descend from the Latin, Caesar. It's a family name, but obviously when we think of Caesar we think of emperors, of men. Caez is just a…part of a word. There's no gender involved. It would be a neutral name for a monarch, or the spouse of one."

"Do you mean you'd call them that, or you'd make them one?" Lachlan asked, arching a brow.

Michaelis arched one back. "Objections either way?"

"Only that you two come from pretty different worlds. But Jes is old enough to look after themself. You looked after a country, I assume you can handle them." Lachlan glanced over his shoulder. "It was hard for them to come back here. You made that easier, so I'm inclined to be grateful. And you're pretty, so it's hard to hold much against you," he added with a grin.

"Been skating on my looks all my life, no reason to stop now," Michaelis said, taking a sip of the broth left in his bowl. "Stay here if you want, but I suspect you'd like to go home and have your husband fuss over those bruises. I can look after Jes and Noah."

Lachlan nodded. "Thanks. I'll see you tomorrow, probably?"

"Sure. Unless Noah's not feeling up to recording."

"Are you sure you will be?"

"It's all surface," Michaelis said, gesturing at his face. Lachlan looked skeptical. "Well, we'll know tomorrow."

Lachlan nodded and gathered his keys and briefcase, leaving quietly enough that neither Deimos woke. Michaelis tidied what he could in the kitchen, then went into the living room and gently settled on the sofa next to Noah, resting an arm over his shoulders, palm on Jes's bicep on Noah's other side. Noah woke and turned to look up at him, curious.

"Go back to sleep, unless you want some dinner," Michaelis said softly. "Lachlan went home, but I'll be here."

Noah nodded and closed his eyes again, head tilting over to rest against Michaelis's shoulder. Michaelis tugged the remote gently out of Jes's hand and flicked the channel over from *Dune* to the news, but he spent more time watching light play over Jes's face than he did watching the muted television.

CHAPTER TEN

A TRIO OF people arrived at the lodge the following morning, and looked horrified when Michaelis answered the door.

"Your Grace," Joann, the historian from the palace, gaped at him. "What happened?"

"Lost a fight with the wine cellar," Michaelis replied with a smile, gesturing them inside. Overnight, bright blue-purple bruises had developed around the scrapes, which themselves were angry and red. "Please, come in."

"Did you actually go exploring in it?" a rough-hewn man asked. "I'm Bennet, by the way, Your Grace. I'm the engineer."

"Pleasure," Michaelis replied. "No, one of my guests fell in, and we had a time getting him out. It's why I wanted you out here today, to make sure nothing further collapses."

Hugo, the palace sommelier, gave him a nod. He'd come to Askazer-Shivadlakia with his brother Simon when they'd been hired for the kitchen, and Michaelis had known him a long time; he was interested to see how he'd react to what might be down there.

"There should be coffee, if you'd like some," he said, leading them down the stairs. "And Noah – the boy who fell in – says he's okay to answer some questions about what he saw."

"Oh, the one you're working with!" Joann said. "I've been listening to your podcast – both of them, actually. A bit fast and loose with some of the history but one can't expect rigorous scholarship for something like that."

"Well, I'm happy to get notes," Michaelis said. "But right

now, the cellar's my concern."

Jes and Noah were in the kitchen downstairs, going over something on a tablet; Noah waved when he saw them, and Jes shot Michaelis a warm smile. He gave them a nod.

"So – coffee, or would you like to speak with Noah here, if he's free, or do you want to see the cellar first?" he asked.

"Boss canceled all my stuff today," Noah said. "I can show them if you want, Michaelis."

"I'd like to see it, and to speak with you, Noah," Joann said. "Hugo's interested in whether you took notes on any of the vintages."

"Yeah, I got some pictures," Noah said. "Okay, come on."

"Do not go in that room again," Jes cautioned. "And don't eyeroll me!" they added, as Noah gave them a tolerant look. He led the trio off, already talking with Joann, and Michaelis accepted a cup of coffee from Jes gratefully.

"He seems to have bounced back," he said.

"Faster than I will," Jes agreed. "Or you. Those scrapes look nasty this morning."

"I was thinking about that," Michaelis said. "I really would like to have a few days to heal up before I'm out in public and subject to Photogram. I don't want to postpone," he added, before Jes could say anything, "just perhaps to do something a little more private. I thought about asking Simon if he'd do a nice meal for the two of us, but I didn't want to presume."

Jes grinned into their coffee. "Good, I like dancing lead in this relationship."

"I thought you might. Hence asking," he said.

"Hm. Let me think about it. I'm sure I can cook something up that will keep your poor scratched-up face out of the limelight," they said. "I did cancel the recording with Noah today, so you're free to fly off if you like."

"No, I'll stay close. Just in case."

"I know how you feel," Jes said. "Very sweet with that

nickname, by the way. Tavat."

"I thought you recognized it. Lachlan asked me to explain it. I think he's clocked us."

"He won't say anything to anyone. Noah hasn't asked about it? Tavat, I mean."

"He probably doesn't remember. I'll talk to him about it eventually. I know there's not much to this whole idea of genetic personality, but he is so Shivadh, Jes. Tavat to his bones."

"I know. I was hoping he'd be a little milder than I was. I guess he hasn't run away from home yet and he doesn't seem to hate me, so progress is steady but slow."

"Well, at least he's somewhere people understand. And if I'm not recording today I'll just keep an eye on the cellar project, maybe run up to the palace to let Gregory know what's going on." He bent to kiss them, the movement surprisingly natural. "Don't work too hard today."

In the hallway, Bennet the engineer was carefully widening the hole in the wall with a crowbar and a mallet, squaring off corners and breaking away the rough ends of wood that had scraped Michaelis as he'd gone in and out. He had a slim lantern with blinding LEDs set up just inside the entry.

"This used to be a door before it was a hole," he said, as Michaelis approached. "I don't know when or how this happened, but you were right to get everyone out of here as fast as possible. The soil's been eating the wood for decades."

"That wood panel's been there since I can remember – at least forty years," Michaelis said.

"Wouldn't surprise me." Bennet poked his head through. "It's a mess in here. I can't let you folks in until I get scaffolding up."

"How long?" Hugo inquired.

"To scaffold the interior? Couple of hours. I'm going to have to build out a walkway to the hole in there, get down, brace the floor from underneath, then put more bracing in up here. I can put in some kind of dumbwaiter thing so you can get the wine out. I'll have to haul out debris anyway. You two oughta take the kid and go talk to him somewhere more comfortable, this won't be ready for anyone until well after lunch."

Michaelis gave Noah a look, silently asking if he wanted company; Noah shook his head and led Hugo and Joann back the way they'd come.

"Guess this is what nailed you," Bennet said, hefting a chunk of wood.

"I didn't even feel it at the time," Michaelis said. "By the time we got Noah out, I looked like an extra from a horror film."

"Honestly? You're lucky you didn't bring the entire floor down when you pulled him up," Bennet said.

"Should we have waited?" he asked.

"No, that'd just increase the risk, and it's probably cold down there. Looks like a natural cavern of some kind from the photos, and those don't warm up in summer. He'd have risked frostbite or hypothermia if he was down too long. He said you rigged a pulley – good thinking."

Michaelis smiled. "Thank you. Not a skill I've often had to put to use."

"So this is the famous lost wine cellar," Bennet said. "Suppose you want lots of documentation. Photos and such."

"As much as you can. I'm more concerned about any kind of collapse affecting the rest of the building. Is the lodge safe to use?"

"Oh yeah. This is outside the footprint of the rest of the building. I'll get upstairs and mark off outside where it is so you don't walk there – that's a sinkhole waiting to happen – but the bunker's sound, and the lodge is anchored to the bunker. Safe as can be."

"It was absolutely terrifying," Michaelis said, unsure why he was confessing this to the man whose main responsibility in the palace was making sure nothing fell down. "I was very worried for Noah. Jes was in here and they'd fall if the floor collapsed...I wasn't sure we could get him out with just the rope, either."

"I can imagine," Bennet said sympathetically. "I've been in one or two collapses – after the fact, of course, to brace them up. I was in that one you got a bug in the king's ear about, the office building by the harbor?"

"Yes. I saw the roof fall in on that one."

"Well, either you're cursed to cause building collapses, or blessed to survive them," the man said.

"I suspect it's not me," Michaelis said. "Noah's got a knack for trouble."

"So it's for the best you're around. Go on, I'll take it from here. I know where the loading dock is. Better call some of my people to help out. You mind us doing the work today?"

"Better today than later."

Bennet tipped an imaginary hat. "Then good morning to you, Your Grace. Next time you see me you'll be standing in a safe wine cellar, hopefully sampling some of the good stuff."

"If there's anything salvageable I'll see you get a bottle," Michaelis said, and went to make sure Hugo wasn't being excessively French at Noah.

"I have a thought," Jes said to him, when he returned to the kitchen.

"I've heard your work, you have many thoughts," he replied.

"About the date," they said. "But it's a little different from what you or I were thinking of."

"Well, I'm open to ideas."

"Lachlan's mother-in-law, Carla, made a standing invitation to us to come for Friday dinner," they said. "Tomorrow's Friday, you could come with us. It'd get us out of the lodge and be sort of like a date. But low-key because there'll be like five other people on the date. Including Lachlan's baby daughter and my teenage son."

Michaelis let a smile spread across his face. "Jes, that sounds delightful."

"Are you sure?" Jes asked. It was obvious they hadn't thought he'd like the idea.

"We didn't meet in a vacuum," he said. "Noah's important to both of us. Lachlan's good opinion is important to me, too, and I've wanted to meet his husband. A family dinner sounds about our speed, don't you think?"

"Well, we can ditch everyone else afterward if we want to. Dinner's usually over by about eight and Carla likes to kick us out by nine."

"Are you coming to dinner, Michaelis?" Noah asked, arriving with Hugo still in tow.

"Yes, I think so," Michaelis said.

"Boss, Great-Aunt Carla said there's an art fair in town on Saturday so I can sleep over if I want and you say it's fine," Noah said.

Michaelis gestured at Jes, trying to indicate *even better.*

"All right, but you have to text me goodnight and send photos from the fair," Jes said.

"I'm going to take Hugo to see what you've got in the kitchen upstairs. He says he wants to make sure you're restocked," Noah said.

"Don't let him touch the Davzda," Jes said sternly. "I'm saving that."

Friday afternoon, Jes emerged from one of the recording booths to find every surface in the bunker's elderly kitchen covered in dusty bottles of wine.

"I see the cellar's getting cleaned out," they said, studying the bottles on the island curiously. "Anything drinkable?"

343

"Almost all!" Hugo said excitedly.

"Hugo's over the moon," Michaelis said. "They're doing inventory now. He's helping select some bottles to set aside here at the lodge. Also, I regret this in advance, but…" he nudged a crate with his foot. "That one's full of Davzda."

"Good, we can sell it and put Noah through college," Jes said.

"Actually, some of this does belong to Noah," Michaelis said.

"How do you figure that?"

"Salvage law. He's entitled to ten percent as a finder's fee. By value, not mass, but still. Either you can sell a lot of wine and subsidize his school tuition, or buy him a very nice car, or you'll have great vintages for every life milestone he celebrates. I recommend this one for a wedding," Michaelis added, indicating a cobweb-covered bottle.

"No, surely for a first child," Hugo said. "The red – "

"Hugo, you and red wines," Michaelis sighed.

"Just because you don't like a strong tannin!"

"We have been having this fight for twenty years," Michaelis said. "I'm not having it again today. Pick me out something nice to take to a dinner, I have to impress someone."

Hugo sniffed, but handed him a bottle. "This one is fine. It wasn't meant to be aged, but aging won't have made it worse."

"And it's a nice rosé. All right." Michaelis presented the bottle to Jes. "Please say you're impressed."

"Couldn't tell you, my knowledge of wine starts with Manischewitz and ends at Three Buck Chuck," they said.

Both men looked mystified.

"Hugo, bear in mind when selecting for Noah that he has an immature palate and so does his parent," Jes sighed. "We'll probably want to sell most of what we get."

"Of course," Hugo bowed. "Your Grace?"

"You know my taste," Michaelis said. "I need to get ready for dinner. I'll see you upstairs," he said, cupping Jes's elbow briefly and heading for the door, wine still in one hand.

Hugo watched him go, then turned to Jes and offered them a bottle.

"Red is much better," he said. Jes took the bottle, nodding.

"I will bear that in mind," they said gravely.

Lachlan and Stephen's baby daughter, Bonnie, was clearly the star attendee at dinner, even though it included both Lachlan's business partner and the former king of the country.

Michaelis understood. Bonnie was Carla's only grandchild, and she was reasonably adorable. Noah, who he would not have thought would be enthusiastic about an infant, immediately took Bonnie from Stephen's arms and held her throughout dinner, feeding her spoonfuls of puree.

"He likes to be an uncle," Jes said to Michaelis after dinner, when they saw him watching Noah with perplexity. "He's had aunties and uncles and zazas his whole life. He finally gets to be older and wiser than someone."

"Ah," Michaelis nodded. "Well, Bonnie doesn't lack for support, that's for sure."

"She's one of the reasons we considered coming back," Jes said. "Lachlan and I met in New York a long time ago. He moved here to be with Stephen, and when he and Stephen adopted Bonnie he said *'something something family*, time to come home'," they said drily.

"I hope you're at least a little glad you did."

"I am," they said, sipping the wine Hugo had sent. They shot him a smile. "Didn't expect it to turn out quite this way, but I can't object. Carla," they added, in a slightly louder voice. "Did I tell you about the second time I met His Grace?"

"This sounds like it's going to be embarrassing," Carla said, folding her hands under her chin. "Sure you don't want to save it for your tell-all book, Jes?"

"Not embarrassing, just funny," Jes said, nudging Michaelis with an elbow. "The first time we met I told him midlife crises usually involve shiny cars, not podcasts. The second time, he pulls up to the studio in a classic green Jaguar."

"Which you called a Hot Wheels toy," he said.

"Honey, it looks like a Hot Wheels toy. Those things don't look real," Lachlan said.

"He rolls up in this Hot Wheels like that's going to impress us," Jes continued.

"I wasn't trying to impress anyone," Michaelis protested. "I just thought it was funny. I told you I already had a shiny car."

"He did look very heroic, soaking wet and trying to help rescue the tech," Lachlan said.

"You weren't even there," Michaelis pointed out.

"Noah sent me so many photos," Lachlan said. "When Jes writes the tell-all book there's going to be one of those old fashioned middle sections that's just photographs of you looking bedraggled."

Michaelis sat back, gesturing at his still-bruised face in resignation. "My lot in life these days."

"Isn't it more interesting, though?" Stephen asked. He was much quieter than Lachlan, but when he did speak he generally had very keen things to say, Michaelis was noticing. "I mean, as king, when was the last time you literally fished someone out of a pit?"

"Used to wish I could cast a few people into them," Michaelis remarked. "Very politically expedient, your average pit."

"Well, the wine's good, anyway," Carla said, drinking the last of hers. "And I'll be the envy of all the old biddies around here tomorrow for hosting the King Emeritus. But I'm afraid now I'm going to kick you all out except Noah, because he's going to stay up with me watching awful old horror movies."

"Don't give yourself nightmares," Jes said, kissing Noah's

forehead as they rose to go. "Remember, text me tomorrow so I know you're still alive, and be home by dinner."

The evening was fine, still warm even well after sunset. Lachlan and Stephen were off to go for a drive down the coast with Bonnie; Michaelis and Jes declined the offer of a ride back and walked instead. The palace, rising up on their left, was ablaze with light.

"Gregory's entertaining the MPs. I think it's his favorite part – not hosting Parliament, but the evening entertainment in the summer," Michaelis said. "He loved those parties as a boy. The last few years of the reign I fell out of the habit. Nice to see it back."

"I suppose Eddie does the catering?"

"Do you know, I haven't asked? Since you arrived, I've been too busy to attend. I'd say we should go, but aside from a few of the juniors it's not the most scintillating conversation," Michaelis said.

"I sort of like that I've been a distraction," Jes said, as they turned off the main road of town and up the footpath, which forked left towards the palace or right towards the lodge. They pushed open the little unlocked gate that said NO ACCESS AFTER SUNSET and held it for him to pass through.

"I certainly haven't minded," he agreed. "It feels nice to have purpose again. And the company doesn't hurt."

Jes smiled. "You know, half my New York friends don't believe I know a royal. Generally the ones who knew me when I was twenty and really punk and more than a little messed up."

"You seem to have come through all right."

"Took some time. Everyone needs time to grow up, though," they said, and he let his fingers drift out to catch their hand, squeezing it. They held on and walked a little closer. "Well. Maybe you didn't."

"Depends on how you look at it. In one light, my destiny was set by the time I was twenty-two," he said. "But when you lock yourself into a path that young, once the path ends..." he shrugged. "I had a great marriage. I had a great reign, too. Wasn't ready for what came after. So I got at sixty what you got out of the way at twenty."

"Are you saying you're a little messed up?" they asked, teasing.

"Who's to say? I suppose it's a warning you may need to be patient with me."

"Michaelis," they said, stopping, and he turned and stopped as well. "If I didn't know that you required patience by now..."

He opened his mouth, a little offended, and before he could retort they broke down in laughter.

"The look on your face!" they hooted. "Oh no, can't tell the king he's sometimes difficult!"

He grinned. "All right, fine. But to be fair, I always fix my mistakes."

"You haven't gone back and fixed that one reference you got wrong in episode two."

"I did not get that reference wrong," he said, pulling them closer, "and I am going to win the fight with my detractors who are slandering my scholarship. I have citations."

"Save your citations for the show notes," they said. They looked past him, towards the lodge, lit only with a single lantern hanging from the eaves over the front door. "Would you like to come back to mine tonight?"

He considered them, a little cautious. "Are you sure?"

"If you want to wait, I don't mind," Jes said. "But if you can't see a reason to, I can't."

He glanced back over his shoulder. "I'm not looking for reasons, no. Although it did occur to me I have no idea if I'm any good in bed."

Jes laughed and leaned against him, forehead resting in the hollow of his throat. "Are you kidding me?"

"I was with one person most of my life. I might be terrible at this," he said, which only made Jes laugh harder. "Mocked, all I get is mocked. I was king!"

Jes propped their chin against his chest. "Quitter."

Michaelis raised his hands to cup their face and kissed them. "Not in this. Come on."

"We could give you a few shots of Davzda if that would help," Jes teased, as they kept walking. "Noah's a liquor magnate now, we can raid his stash."

"You have the worst ideas," he said, but on the porch of the lodge he pulled them in close again, arm around their waist. "Some other night, perhaps. I want to remember tonight."

"Good," they said with a smile, and pushed the door open. "Me too."

EPILOGUE

MICHAELIS CAME OUT of the recording studio, one afternoon in late spring, to find a flotilla of teenagers clustered around the big conference table in what used to be the bunker's war room.

"I understand we've been invaded by sea," he said, faced with a gaggle of youths in navy-blue polo shirts, brick-colored yachting shorts, and boat shoes.

"Hi, Michaelis," Noah called, slightly louder over a desynchronized chorus of children murmuring *Your Grace* shyly. "Study group."

"It will definitely take study if you want to defeat the Spanish Armada," Michaelis agreed. "Have you seen Jes?"

"They fled ahead of the invasion," one of the kids said boldly. Michaelis pointed at them.

"Amani," he said. They beamed at having been recognized. "Good to see you again. Which direction did they go?"

A couple of hands pointed up.

"Yes, I…assumed that," he said.

"Boss said they were going out on the lake," Noah said. "They asked if you'd stick around for another ten minutes until everyone had to go."

"Ah. Conscription. Carry on, then. Will anyone need a ride home?"

"No, we're gonna walk down into town, people will get rides from there."

Michaelis nodded, duty mostly discharged, and took up a strategic position in the corner, far enough away that he wouldn't be obtrusive. He reviewed the following day's calendar and paged through a script Jes had sent him for editing until the children began trickling out. Noah, last to leave, waved at Michaelis and said, "Dismissed, ensign," and Michaelis nodded.

Upstairs, he changed into a swimsuit and ambled down to the dock, walking to the end. Jes was in the boat, well out in the middle of the lake, with what looked like a cooler. He stepped out of his shoes and dove in, enjoying the brief, brisk swim out to the boat. By the time he reached them, they were sitting up, arms on their knees, a skeptical look on their face.

"If you capsize me, I'll end you," they said.

"How long do you think I've been doing this?" he asked, hefting himself into the boat without even rocking it that much. It did require an undignified tumble onto his back, but from there he could dangle one leg out of the boat and look up at them upside-down, which he knew charmed them.

"All the kids gone? The noise was starting to get to me and I figured they couldn't get into too much trouble," they said.

"Yep. Nice to see Noah with so many friends." He sat up and shook water out of his hair, sliding around so that he fell into their lap backwards, head on their chest, arms resting on their knees. "Bliss."

"Closest I've found," Jes agreed. "Beer and snacks in the cooler if you want something."

"No, I'm fine. Are you comfortable?" he asked.

"Yep." One of their hands rested over his heart, and he felt a kiss dropped into his hair. "Can I run something past you?"

"Of course."

They propped their phone on his chest, open to an image of a person in a tuxedo that flowed into a dramatic, elegant ball gown in the lower half.

"Couldn't pull that off, not with my hips," he said.

"Don't sell yourself short. This is option one. Option two," they said, and flicked to the next image, which showed a vivid orange sheath dress, rather traditional for their usual tastes, shot through with gold. "And option three..."

The third outfit was a midnight-blue men's suit with velvet lapels. The model wore a shimmering blouse under the suit jacket, with a banded collar and a cutout below it, deep to show decolletage. He whistled low.

"These are for the coronation anniversary ball?" he asked.

"Considering my options. I'd like to stun, but subtly."

"You'd look fine in any of them, but you could have something made. Or buy a couple, pick out what you want on the day. Won't be the last formal you have to attend, probably. I'll be in the uniform, so it's easy to coordinate with anything you wear."

"I'm thinking option three," Jes said contemplatively.

"I like it, but you don't normally do cleavage."

"True. I don't know, it seemed like somewhere I'd like to go a little femme. Would you mind?"

"Not in the least, you know that." He turned his head to look up at them, nose bumping their collarbone. "We aren't being presented to court. Eddie has to follow the rules, for once in his life. You never have to, Caez."

"Too late for Caez. I'm relegated to Consort of the King Emeritus."

"Caez of my heart," he said. They scruffed his hair gently.

"All right, I'll make a decision tonight," they said. "I was going to stay out here another hour or so."

"Perfect. Mind if I sleep?"

"Keeps you out of mischief," Jes said. Michaelis settled in, eyes closing, and didn't even startle when he felt their arm drape over his shoulder and their palm drift down his abdomen, fingertips tracing gently across the skin.

"I love that," he said drowsily, and felt Jes smile against the crown of his head.

"What, belly rubs?" they asked, amused. He shifted a little, eyes slitting open.

"I love the touch," he said, pleased with how easy the words came. Sometimes they didn't, but he was working on it. "And I love that it's you doing it."

"I'm glad," they said. "I love you too."

"Hm." He closed his eyes again. "Wake me when you get bored."

"Sleep a while. We have plenty of time," Jes assured him.

He heard, distantly, a beep, and then the soft chatter of voices. He fell asleep to Jes's breathing and the low murmur of their headphones as they caught up on the day's listening.

THE REVERB PODCAST NETWORK
ASKAZER-SHIVADLAKIA OFFICE

JES DEIMOS:
Executive Producer, CEO
Host, *The Echo*
Host, *All On Mike*

LACHLAN HINES:
Executive Producer, COO
Producer, *The Echo*
Producer, *The Echo Junior*
Host and Producer, *How To Make Some Noise*
Producer, *All On Mike*

NOAH DEIMOS:
Junior Producer, Staff
Host, *The Echo Junior*
Host, *How To Make Some Noise*
Host and Producer, *Being On Boats*

MICHAELIS BEN JASON:
Partner Producer
Host, *All On Mike*
Host, *How To Make Some Noise*
Host and Producer, *The Royal Reads*

THE LADY AND THE TIGER

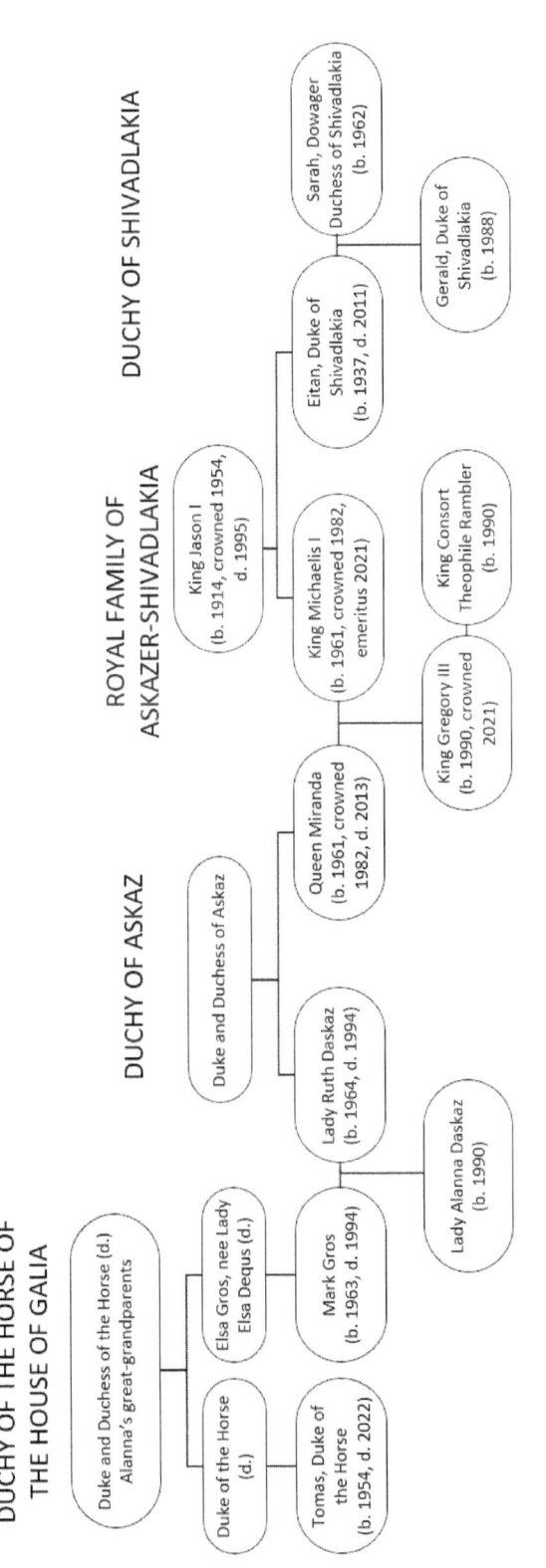

DUCHY OF THE HORSE OF
THE HOUSE OF GALIA

DUCHY OF ASKAZ

ROYAL FAMILY OF
ASKAZER-SHIVADLAKIA

DUCHY OF SHIVADLAKIA

Duke and Duchess of the Horse (d.)
Alanna's great-grandparents

Duke of the Horse
(d.)

Elsa Gros, nee Lady
Elsa Dequs (d.)

Tomas, Duke of
the Horse
(b. 1954, d. 2022)

Mark Gros
(b. 1963, d. 1994)

Lady Ruth Daskaz
(b. 1964, d. 1994)

Duke and Duchess of Askaz

Lady Alanna Daskaz
(b. 1990)

Queen Miranda
(b. 1961, crowned
1982, d. 2013)

King Jason I
(b. 1914, crowned 1954,
d. 1995)

King Michaelis I
(b. 1961, crowned 1982,
emeritus 2021)

King Gregory III
(b. 1990, crowned
2021)

King Consort
Theophile Rambler
(b. 1990)

Eitan, Duke of
Shivadlakia
(b. 1937, d. 2011)

Sarah, Dowager
Duchess of Shivadlakia
(b. 1962)

Gerald, Duke of
Shivadlakia
(b. 1988)

CHAPTER ONE

LADY ALANNA DASKAZ – Al to her friends and colleagues, the Lady Alanna on the rare occasions she made it into the press – often thought that palace breakfast was the highlight of her day. She loved her work, of course, serving as right hand and head of Royal Operations for the king; sometimes she even worked during breakfast. But just the act of being in the royal dining room was a pleasure.

When she was a child, her mother brought her to palace breakfast several times a week, mainly because Lady Ruth loved to visit with her sister Miranda, the queen of Askazer-Shivadlakia. Alanna had made friends with her cousin Gregory, now the king, while sitting under the dining table and earnestly discussing dinosaurs.

She and Gregory were sometimes mistakenly labeled in foreign press as siblings, even as adults. They both favored their mothers, the Askaz side of the family, slightly built with olive skin and dark hair, though Gregory's was curlier, more like his father's, and Alanna's hair lightened to a pale brown as she grew older.

After her parents passed, her grandmother still brought her at least once a week, often leaving her there for the day for Aunt Miranda and King Michaelis to look after. Once she was old enough she'd traipse down to the palace on her own, to make mischief with Gregory and his cousin Gerald. Most often, they eavesdropped on Michaelis's meetings with important ministers of Parliament. In hindsight, he had probably known and allowed it, as much to train them early in palace business as because he was indulgent of his only son, his wife's niece, and his brother's rambunctious boy.

As an adult, working in the palace after Gregory's election to king, Alanna found breakfast a useful time to bring things to Gregory's attention, get the occasional opinion from Michaelis, and tweak Jerry, who had never left the mischief-making phase. Saturday brunch at the palace was less useful, since business was largely banned from the table, but it was by far the best breakfast of the week.

It was particularly boisterous that Saturday morning. Michaelis's partner Jes and Jes's teenage son Noah had come to breakfast, and Noah's curiosity about pretty much everything in the world meant that his primary source of entertainment, Gregory's fiancé Eddie, was excitedly explaining something to him. Jes, who never met an opinion they weren't prepared to express in strong terms, was bickering with Gregory about taxes. Jerry, who used to show up to Saturday brunch hungover and occasionally still drunk, looked like he'd had a full night of sleep, hazel eyes sharp as he contentedly grazed on fruit and cracked jokes. And there was Michaelis, presiding over the table as patriarch, offering commentary on every conversation regardless of his previous participation in it.

Nobody else paid any mind when her phone beeped softly, but Alanna looked down at it immediately. She got enough notifications throughout the day that she'd taken to setting the Do Not Disturb function to run all weekend long. Notifications that got through her complex Do Not Disturb filter were few and far between – it usually meant either her grandparents or someone important on the palace staff was trying to get in touch.

This time, it was the palace communications team; the on-call public relations officer had messaged her. She opened the text curiously.

Sorry to interrupt your Saturday, but I thought you'd want to see this sooner rather than later, the message read, attached to a news service link. When she saw the headline, she said, "Gregory?" with enough alarm in her voice that even Eddie fell silent.

"Something wrong, Al?" Gregory asked, following her gaze to her phone screen.

"The Duke of the Horse of the House of Galia is dead," she said. "News is just getting out now. Looks like he passed late last night from a stroke."

"Good fucking riddance," Michaelis said, and every head immediately turned from Alanna to him. "Pardon my language," he added, a little sheepishly.

"I don't know who the Duke of the House Horse is but it sounds like you have something to share," Eddie said to Michaelis.

"Isn't that the fellow…?" Gregory asked, and Michaelis nodded. "Well. Good riddance indeed. Can I see?" he asked Alanna, who passed her phone to him.

"Who is he?" Noah asked, looking amongst the adults in the room.

"He's the king of Galia, functionally," Jes said. "They haven't had an actual king in what, a couple of centuries?" they asked Michaelis.

"Something like that. The royal line died out, so whoever was Duke of the Horse at that point took over. Probably because he had command of the biggest portion of their military – the 'horse' in the title refers to the cavalry forces the dukes led, back when they kept a standing army. Throne's been in the ducal family line since. The current duke had no children, either, which means the throne may go vacant. If I were you, Gregory, I'd invade," Michaelis said with a grin.

"Mm, don't know what I'd do with Galia," Gregory said absently, scrolling through the story. "But of course we will extend our deepest condolences and offer any aid we can provide in this time of uncertainty."

"I'll get people started on the draft letter to their government and a press release," Alanna said, taking her phone back from Gregory and adding it to her previously blank to-do list for the day.

"Don't let it interrupt your meal, at least," Gregory said.

"Indeed, Alanna. I doubt anyone else is mourning him very deeply," Michaelis added.

"Relatively young, though," Gregory continued thoughtfully. "He was only a few years older than you, Dad."

"He's not family, is he?" Jerry asked, brow furrowing. "Don't we traditionally just...not deal with Galia?"

"Not family, no," Michaelis said. "Well, I should say, not on the royal side. Possibly distantly through your mother, Gerald. Have to look that up, but most of the old nobility around here are related somehow."

"Who is this dude anyway, beyond the whole House Horse thing?" Eddie asked.

"I am loving that you're just calling him the House Horse guy," Jerry said.

"The Duke of the Horse of the House of Galia," Michaelis said, with a sharp look at them both, "is, or rather was, named Tomas, and if you don't want to speak ill of the dead there's really nothing to be said about him at all."

"Babe, you're a historian. You love speaking ill of the dead. It's literally your second career," Jes said.

"They've got you there, Dad," Gregory said. "Besides, it's not like you spoke well of him while he was alive. We've technically been in a cold war with Galia since Dad punched him in the face before I was born," he told Eddie.

"You did *what*," Eddie said gleefully.

"You have a cold war?" Noah asked, face lighting up. "Do you have spies?"

"It's not a cold war, and there are no spies," Michaelis declared. "We have had what the newspapers refer to as 'frosty diplomatic relations' since my last state visit to Galia, which was before most of you were born. It's not public knowledge that I assaulted a fellow head of state, Noah, so that is not to go beyond this room. If I'd known Gregory was going to announce it at brunch, I wouldn't even have briefed him on it."

"Yes, I announced it to my father who did it, his partner, their child, two of my closest advisors, and my future husband. Clearly I'm a menace to national security," Gregory replied tartly.

"Okay, but can I at least know why?" Noah persisted. Gregory just looked at Michaelis, who scowled and made a gesture of surrender.

"First, I didn't like how he spoke to my wife, and neither did she," Michaelis said. "On the rare occasions we visited, we had to arrange to bring only male staff, and make sure one of them always escorted Miranda if I couldn't be there. That was irritating, but not enough to warrant a diplomatic incident." He paused, considering, and then added, "I'm also going to preface this by saying that I was very young – younger than you are now, Gregory – and while it is an extenuating circumstance, it's no excuse for either one of us."

"Just tell the story. I promise not to use you as precedent," Gregory replied.

"I think the Duke of the Horse had some misguided image of me and he was trying to befriend that image rather than actually interact with me. We were having drinks in a very small party, and he was playing what in retrospect was a peculiar game of masculine one-upmanship," Michaelis said. "Started with talk of sport and hunting, which I didn't mind at all, but then he steered it towards women in a way I did not like. When I didn't play along, he thought I would perhaps appreciate his low opinion on Shivadh attitudes towards sexuality, and Shivadh culture more generally."

"Oh," Noah said, and then echoed Michaelis and Gregory. "Good riddance."

"Indeed. In any case, between what he'd already said and his mounting criticism of my country, I unfortunately escalated to violence at a certain point, and the next morning we were politely escorted to the border by his personal guard."

"Officers of the House Horse," Eddie said sagely.

"Guard of the Horse," Michaelis corrected.

"Is it really," Eddie replied, amused.

"Duke Tomas didn't want to admit he'd been sucker-punched by a fellow royal, and I certainly didn't want my poor behavior getting out, so nobody said anything about it at the time, or thereafter. And that's the last we spoke. About thirty-two, thirty-three years ago now," Michaelis said. "Except for the occasional back-door diplomacy lower down in the administration, but even then."

"There were a few Galian diplomats at the coronation," Gregory said. "Officially-unofficial. Nobody from the administration directly."

"It hasn't generally mattered," Michaelis continued. "Galia hasn't really got anything we want other than money, which we have enough of, and they don't want to spend their money on what we have to offer, other than the prodigious amount of seafood that Galian restaurants buy from the fishing fleet. So it hasn't been a huge loss on either side. I wonder who takes over if the seat is fully vacant," he added. "They might even decide to try democracy."

Gregory's phone interrupted with a ring, and both he and Alanna looked at it. Much like her notifications, his phone had a lot of filters to get through. He checked the caller ID, raised his eyebrows, and answered.

"Gregory ben Michaelis," he said, and then smiled. "Milo, hi. I saw your name come up but I didn't know if it was actually going to be you. I understand condolences are in order. Ah…yes, I can see how that would be the case. My father certainly has strong emotions he wishes to convey," he added. Michaelis looked extremely curious. "No, it's no bother, I'm just at brunch." There was a longer pause, and then he said, "I see. Give me one moment, would you?"

He took his phone from his ear and muted the microphone. "Galia wants to send a diplomatic team to the palace. Today. They'd be here by evening."

"They're going to make you king of Galia!" Jerry said. "Askazer-Shivadh-Galia, here we come!"

"No problem," Alanna said, giving Jerry a quelling look. "Get the number of people coming and ETA and I'll make sure the palace is ready. I can probably get some of our law team back in the office for tomorrow if need be."

Gregory nodded at her and unmuted the phone; she began to take notes as he repeated details to her. "Thanks, Milo, just had to check with my staff. When would they be arriving? Early evening, okay. How many? Including staff. Five, got it. Oh, it'll be nice to see you."

Alanna raised her eyebrows, intrigued.

"You might as well stay through Monday if you can. Yes, of course," Gregory continued. "Listen, between you and me and the satellites, do you have any idea what this is about? I mean, reopening diplomatic relations, political upheaval...succession. Say no more. If you need anything, the same number will get you through. Okay. Ciao."

He ended the call and set the phone down.

"You seem on very good terms with whoever that was in Galia," Michaelis observed.

"Yes – fortunate, but entirely by coincidence. He was at school with us. Did you know Milo Ansevali is the Secretary of the Duchy of Galia now?" he asked Alanna.

Alanna tried to place the name and came up with only a vague sense of familiarity. "I'm not sure I know who he is," she said.

"You remember Milo. He was a year below us, but in our classes half the time," Gregory said.

"The little guy, right?" Jerry asked. "Wasn't in any of my classes, but he was on the rifle team, I remember him."

"I have zero memory of this," Alanna said.

"I suppose you might not have noticed him. He was quiet, and you were in the girls' dorm. Anyway, he's done all right for himself. He's going to be here this evening to discuss succession. Which does in fact sound like they might ask me to take the throne," Gregory said, looking worried by this. "I do not love the idea of ruling Galia."

"Can't recommend it," Michaelis agreed. "A leader ought to be elected, even if he is king. Basis of our whole system of government."

"I'm going to go ahead and scratch that formal letter of condolence off my list and add about fifteen items pertaining to figuring out how to gracefully refuse a throne," Alanna said, making a list of people she needed to send carefully non-panicked texts to.

"If he doesn't want it, I'll take it," Jerry said.

"You'd be better than the old duke was," Michaelis said. "Alanna, you may wish to include that as a genuine option in your various contingency plans."

"Putting Jerry at the head of a country?" Gregory asked thoughtfully.

"I've lived my whole life preparing to become a puppet governor," Jerry announced.

Jes put their arm around Noah's shoulders. "I need you to understand," they told him, "that you're seeing history being made in this room right now, and 99% of all history is exactly as absurd-sounding in real time as this conversation is."

"I know I said this shouldn't interrupt brunch, Al, but I think it's now going to have to interrupt brunch," Gregory told her, and Alanna nodded. "What do you need from me?"

"Carte blanche on the entertainment budget and permission to forge your signature?" Alanna said.

"Granted."

"Overtime on staff? Five people means guest suites need to be aired out and prepped, and I'm going to have to bribe Simon not to take his usual day off tomorrow."

"Yes – and get some personal staff on standby in case anyone's fancy enough to need a valet," Gregory said.

"Got it. I should get to my office. I'll let you know when things are in motion," Alanna said, standing. "Anything else?"

"Yes," Gregory said. "This is a formal apology for your ruined Saturday and a promise to make it up to you."

Alanna smiled at him. "I'll slip a few trinkets for myself into the entertainment budget. You'll never know."

"You are my favorite embezzler," he told her. "Okay. Go on."

"I'm going to have a word with Simon about the food," Eddie said, rising to follow her out. "Everyone else, listen sharp. I want all other gossip involving His Grace punching people."

"You punch one duke, one time," Michaelis grumbled as they left. Eddie caught up to Alanna in the hallway and bumped her with his shoulder affectionately.

"Hey, leave the kitchen stuff to me. Staff, food, begging Simon to come in on his day off, I got that part covered," he said.

"You don't have to, Eddie. It's not in your job description."

"Not in the palace communications sense, but in the King Consort sense – this is stuff the spouse of the king would handle, right?"

"I suppose. In a weird, archaic, gendered way," Alanna said.

"And it'd help you, and I know what I'm doing, so let me handle it. Gotta learn this trade sometime. Also, if this Duke Tomas is any indication and Galia is full of homophobes, then when they show up to a reception catered by the king's boyfriend, it'll be just..." He made a chef's kiss.

"Eddie, I'm not only saying this because Gregory loves you," Alanna said, stopping in front of the kitchen doorway. "You should be proud of yourself, because you've just demonstrated a truly Shivadh fucked-up sense of humor."

"I take it as a great compliment," Eddie said. "Okay, this is my stop. Message me if you think of anything I should cover. Simon!" he called, walking into the kitchen. "I'm gonna give you five minutes of all the swearing your heart can handle and then we have places to be. Get ready for some really stupid news!"

Alanna laughed as she headed for her office, a small and cozy room across the hall from Gregory's. Her phone beeped again, a message from Jerry; it was captioned *Milo's the one in the headlock* and featured a grainy pixelated photograph, clearly taken by an early digital camera, probably pulled off someone's social media.

The boys were all in the uniform of Institut Alpin, the boarding school she, Gregory, and Jerry had attended; most of them looked to be thirteen or fourteen. She could pick out Gregory in the middle, and two boys she recognized vaguely on his right. On his left, Jerry – already a head taller than everyone else in the picture, with the same broad shoulders and sharp angular features as his father, Michaelis's brother Eitan – was beaming at the camera. Jerry had a small sandy-haired boy in a loose, affectionate headlock; the younger boy looked thrilled to be there, a huge grin on his face, green eyes alight with laughter.

Looking at the photo, she thought she remembered him in the back of a math or a history class, but she'd never really paid much attention to most of the boys at Institut Alpin until her last few years at school. And then she'd really only paid attention to the tall ones (well, hormones were shallow). By the time Milo was old enough to interest her she'd probably been working through her crush on Jerry, actually.

Am I a bad person that I still don't remember him? she texted back.

Society will judge you, I cannot, Jerry replied. *Want me to bring you lunch when you inevitably forget to eat?*

Snack around two would be great, she replied.

I attend! Jerry said. *I'll see if I can remember any tall tales from school days in the meantime.*

It was probably to Gregory's credit that calling the staff back in on a Saturday went pretty smoothly. Most of them understood that emergencies sometimes happened and seemed fine with a few hours of overtime, especially paid and catered overtime. By late afternoon, all of the rooms were prepared, Simon had stopped swearing, and the weekend PR officer had a series of templates ready for whatever Galia might get up to while visiting Askazer-Shivadlakia semi-officially for the first time in decades. Michaelis had made himself tactfully scarce but told Alanna he'd keep his phone nearby. Helpfully, Milo had sent them a guest list, so they weren't wholly unprepared.

Milo Ansevali, secretary of the duchy, was not a member of the peerage but must have been well-connected to have been educated at Institut Alpin; he was now in charge of general staff operations under the Duke of the Horse, a high office for a relatively young man. But then, Alanna supposed, he was more or less her counterpart, doing a job that was demanding but not particularly overwhelming, and he seemed well-qualified.

His older sister, Ofelia Ansevali, was also in the delegation. She was a lawyer somewhere in the diplomatic office, and she was bringing two assistants, one a paralegal. Alanna wasn't sure how much legal business they were going to be doing, but Galia was certainly coming prepared. The notes Gregory sent along said she'd been educated in Galia, so at least Alanna wouldn't be expected to remember her as well. The image palace comms had found of her showed the same striking green eyes and sandy blonde hair as Milo's, but with a solemnity Milo's photos didn't have.

The last member of the party was the royal historian, Bruno

Sheff, and Alanna knew enough history to recognize Sheff as a Galian corruption of Shivadh – probably the descendant of someone who'd moved across the highlands back in the day and taken up residence in Galia. He'd only been in the job two years, and the shine hadn't yet worn off his doctorate, which he'd earned from a prestigious university in Italy. His faculty photo from his teaching days showed a square-jawed man with an unkempt shock of black hair and eyes almost as dark.

By evening, they were as ready as they were going to be, and Gregory had gone out to wait in the reception yard of the Shivadh palace, where the kings traditionally met incoming guests. Alanna and Jerry had settled into an upper window overlooking the yard, which they'd used for spying since they were children, so they had a fantastic view when the Galians arrived.

"Mm, handshakes all round and Italian cheek-kisses for Gregory from both Ansevalis. If they are homophobes they're doing a good job of hiding it," Jerry said, watching Gregory greet Milo with a smile.

"I don't think it's out of the question that an entirely new generation might be a little more liberal in their thinking than the duke was thirty years ago," Alanna said. "Also, I thought you said Ansevali was a little guy. He's as tall as Eddie."

"Haven't seen the man since school, Alanna. You didn't remember him at all," Jerry reminded her.

"Gonna remember him now. Very cute," Alanna pronounced.

"I am offended and delighted that you are rating the hotness of the guy who's probably about to offer Gregory a kingdom," Jerry said.

"Whenever I delight you I know I've done something worrying," she told him, watching the Ansevalis, Bruno Sheff, and the support staff follow Gregory inside. She caught Gregory glancing up at them briefly, well aware they were spying. So did Milo, who followed Gregory's look and met her eyes for a split second. His eyebrows raised; she didn't even have time to duck back before he looked away and stepped inside.

"Oooh, spotted by the cutie," Jerry said. Alanna crossed the hallway to the staircase, where she'd be able to hear them from above as they passed through.

"...dinner ready soon if you're hungry, or we can hold dinner if you'd like to settle into your rooms first," Gregory was saying, voice echoing upwards.

"A quick refresh, perhaps," someone replied, with a light Italian accent. A woman's voice, so probably Ofelia Ansevali. "Half an hour or so should suffice."

"Staff will show you to your rooms. I'll have them check in to bring you to the dining room when you're ready," Gregory said.

"Thank you. Will your family be joining us for dinner?"

"My father has an unfortunate prior engagement," Gregory lied. Alanna supposed Michaelis probably did consider "toasting the duke's death over a cookout dinner at the fishing lodge" a prior engagement. "The Lady Alanna Daskaz and Gerald, Duke of Shivadlakia, will be joining us – Milo, you remember them from school?"

"Certainly. A pleasure to see them again."

"And my fiancé, of course, Eddie Rambler," Gregory added.

"Ah, I'm glad to hear it!" said another voice.

"Bruno's a fan," Milo said. "I'm sure we'll be delighted."

"I'll see you for dinner, in that case. This is where I leave you; if you need anything, staff will be nearby."

Gregory came bounding up the stairs as if he had someplace to be, quietly skidding to a stop at the top in front of Jerry and Alanna. All three listened for the fading footsteps of the envoy below.

"Milo saw us spying," Jerry said. "Also, Alanna thinks he's hot."

"I said cute, not hot," Alanna replied.

"I'm going to allow us to consider him hot," Gregory said.

"Sister's very attractive too, speaking as the only one who'd appreciate that here," Jerry added.

"Much as I'd love to continue this conversation, it's not the most relevant, and I'm on a schedule," Gregory said. "Eddie's dressing for dinner. We'll be in the dining room pretty much from now until whenever they show up. Do you want to be there early before our guests show up, or fashionably late?"

"Early," Alanna said, at the same time Jerry said, "Late."

"Perfect," Gregory said with a grin. "Do either of you need outfit approval?"

"I'm good," Jerry said. "I promise nothing too loud."

"I'll be in the usual Lady Daskaz getup," Alanna sighed. "Conservative jewel-tone sheath dress number eighty, here I come."

"Love you in pearls," Gregory told her, kissing her cheek. He kissed Jerry's too and then headed off towards his apartments, presumably to fetch Eddie.

"Feels like old times," Jerry said, as they strolled in the other direction, towards the little suite they sometimes used as a dressing room before state events. "Getting up to trouble with you and Greg. If this is going to be our life all the time, now that he's king, I can't say I mind."

"Do you honestly think they're going to offer him Galia?" Alanna asked.

"I don't know if I'd bet on it, but you heard Gregory say it, they're here to talk succession. If they aren't here for him, then they clearly need some kind of advice or guidance. They might be here to ask him to help them install a democratic monarchy, like old Gregory II did for Askazer-Shivadlakia."

"Best possible outcome, I suppose, but kind of a big ask to make us do all the work," Alanna said.

"If you were asked to organize an election, would you?" Jerry asked.

"Not while I'm also about to start planning Gregory and

Eddie's wedding, not to mention someone's got to keep you in line," Alanna replied. "Why?"

"Dunno, I think it would be kind of fun. Putting everything in order, setting up voting districts, polling places, all that," Jerry said. "Lots of moving parts, though."

Alanna ruffled his hair. "I'm sure you could do it, but you should probably be grateful nobody's ever going to ask. Seems stressful."

"Story of my life," he told her with a sunny grin. "Failing to live up to potential is a career, not a hobby."

There was definitely something unusual going on at dinner, Gregory decided, but he was having trouble determining what it was.

Milo seemed composed, but there was something slightly off in his manner. Bruno, the historian, was clearly there to follow the Ansevalis' lead, but seemed perplexed by something as well. The support staff, Ofelia told Gregory, preferred to dine in their rooms to allow the royal dinner to be a little more intimate; that wasn't unusual, and wasn't what was raising Gregory's red flags, but something was. Ofelia herself was difficult to read, but perhaps that was normal for her.

Eddie was his usual charming, enthusiastic self, and Jerry was matching Eddie's energy. Alanna had her Lady Daskaz face on, welcoming Milo as if she hadn't forgotten his existence and making small talk with Ofelia over dinner while Bruno peppered Eddie with questions about cooking and Gregory with questions about local politics. Nobody brought up the multiple elephants in the room: Galia's poor relationship with Askazer-Shivadlakia, the death of the duke, or the reason they were there. At least, not until coffee was served.

"I was wondering," Milo said, after the waitstaff had poured the coffee and left, "if you've considered what the death of Duke Tomas will mean politically for the country."

"I think it's safe to assume that I've been considering it all day," Gregory said. "Who's currently holding the reins?"

"The senior advisory council, on an ad-hoc basis," Ofelia said. "But the consiglieres aren't empowered to do much without the approval of the ducal office."

"Which is why we need to move swiftly," Milo added.

"I'm not going to lie," Gregory said, "I'm interested in who you mean by 'we,' and what swift movements you have in mind."

"Well – to install the new head of state," Milo said, eyebrows rising as if he was surprised by this. "That's why we're here. We've brought the formal paperwork, of course, although that can all be dealt with later – "

"You're not thinking of me on the throne of Galia, are you?" Gregory asked.

Milo and Ofelia exchanged a look.

"Ah. Were you...not aware?" Bruno asked.

"Aware of what?"

"His Grace died without issue, and has no siblings, but his cousin married into the Shivadh nobility," Bruno said. "His nearest heir is one of your people. We assumed you knew..."

"Oh, no," Alanna said, putting her cup down sharply enough that coffee splashed into the saucer.

"Alanna?" Gregory asked.

"I didn't even think of it," she said. "Oh, no, this is – they're not here for you, Greg."

Gregory stared at her. "What?"

Jerry was doing something mentally, one hand hovering in the air, moving up and down as if in an imaginary family tree.

"Father's...sister's...son," he said absently, then looked at Bruno. "Right? The duke's paternal aunt moved across the highlands and her son married into the duchy of Askaz. He'd be Alanna's dad. But he died years ago, so..."

"The Lady Daskaz is the next in line to the duchy of Galia," Ofelia said. "Technically, even now, you are the Duchess of the Horse of the House of Galia, whether you knew it or not," she said to Alanna.

Gregory could see Jerry and Eddie's eyes lock; he knew they were both thinking it. *Duchess of the House Horse*, he thought, panickedly trying not to laugh as all three of them struggled, for Alanna's sake, not to say it out loud.

"We had come prepared to discuss what needed to be done to invest Her Grace on the throne of Galia, but I can see we miscalculated," Ofelia said. Alanna still hadn't spoken.

"This must be a shock," Milo added gently.

"Alanna, you're going to be a queen," Eddie stage-whispered to her. "Are we freaking out good or freaking out bad?"

"Uh…" Alanna looked from Gregory to Milo to Jerry, which seemed to galvanize him.

"I think you're right," Jerry said, standing up. "This is a little shocking. To Gregory, too. I think he was expecting to have to graciously decline," he said, and Gregory saw his look – *sorry to humiliate you, please play along.*

"I have to admit that was part of it," he said. "And the political ramifications of having a meeting with Galia after such a long estrangement were also top of mind, rather than the genealogy of it."

"Obviously Alanna's going to have to confirm this with her people, and speak to our legal team," Jerry continued. Gregory resolved to forgive Jerry all past and future transgressions if he got Alanna out of this somehow. "I think we had probably better stop there until we're on more even footing."

"Agreed," Ofelia said, smiling at Jerry. "And we wouldn't mind an early evening-in after traveling, would we, Milo? Bruno?"

Both men took their cue, rising when Ofelia did; Gregory saw them to the door, where staff would escort them back to their rooms.

Once they were gone he turned around to find Alanna standing up as well, leaning into a bewildered-looking Eddie for a hug. He was hugging back, but clearly didn't know why. It was true that in any given group of people, Eddie was probably the best person to get a hug from.

"Are they gone?" Alanna asked.

"At least for tonight," Gregory said.

"Shit, shit, shit," she said, leaning away from Eddie and dropping back into her chair.

"She seems less than thrilled," Eddie said to Gregory.

"I'd definitely be in shock," Jerry said.

"Both of you, please be quiet for a minute," Gregory told them, before crouching in front of Alanna, taking her hands in his. "Hey, Al. This is going to be really complicated and weird, but I promise I am not going to throw you to the wolves. There is nothing this fixes that can't be left broken. You understand?"

She gave him a weak smile.

"What does this fix, exactly? Why is her becoming queen attached to you betraying her?" Eddie asked. "Gregory, please, I'm a clueless American."

"There is nothing that would be better for Askazer-Shivadlakia, in terms of our relationship with Galia, than a Shivadh noble on their throne," Gregory said. "A Shivadh noble who isn't the king but has a strong relationship with him, training for governance, and no spouse. It's basically bloodless conquest. I secure familial ties to the Duchess of the Horse – "

"The House Horse," Jerry blurted, clearly unable to keep it in any longer.

Alanna's face crumpled for a half second and then she burst out laughing, which was such a relief that Gregory started to laugh too.

"I saw you think it," she said, her voice high and thin. "When Ofelia said 'Duchess of the Horse' I saw you BOTH think it and then I saw *Gregory* see you think it."

"House Horse," Gregory repeated helplessly, still crouching, leaning his forehead on Alanna's knee.

"Okay, I'm sorry," Jerry said, still laughing. "Gregory, please, Eddie is a clueless American."

"If Alanna takes the throne, her children would still be considered Shivadh by our standards, but if she marries a Galian, then the child is acceptable to Galia as future heir. Even without kids, we become favored trading partners and close family combined, very suddenly. If she has a child, we have *influence*," Gregory finished. "That's what Alanna could achieve for us. However," he added, giving Alanna a stern look, "it also means Alanna has to quit her job, accept the throne, move to Galia, marry whatever Galian noble is least offensive, and have a baby. I'm not going to make her do any of that when Galia hasn't really got anything we want and she doesn't even want to be Duchess Askaz here in her home country."

"So there are all these shiny, great things that could happen, but only if the rest of Alanna's life sucks," Eddie said.

"Yes and no," Gregory said. "Yes, in theory, but no, because I'm not going to let that happen. All three of us are going to back whatever Alanna decides, unconditionally, regardless of the politics of it. And nothing needs to get decided tonight. Jerry?" he asked.

"I stand and wait," Jerry said, squaring his shoulders.

"Whatever else happens between now and tomorrow morning, I want you in the dining room at eight to meet with the Ansevalis. Your job is to make sure they're kept entertained."

"This is why he made me Grand Vizier," Jerry said to Eddie, taking his phone out. "Setting my alarm. I'll put some contingencies in place. Al, you want me to take you home?"

"No, I uh...I'll stay at the palace tonight," she said. Gregory stood up, offering her a hand to help her out of the chair.

"Okay, then I'm heading out." Jerry kissed her cheek. "Call if you need anything. I mean it."

"Thanks," she said. "Greg, can you walk me to my room?"

Gregory gave Eddie an apologetic look, but Eddie waved it off. He probably knew Alanna needed a moment to decompress.

"I'll see you upstairs," Eddie said. "Al – "

"If I need anything, I know," she said with a small smile. Eddie gave her finger-guns as he left.

"It's a little like having three big brothers with you guys sometimes," she said.

"We all mean well. Come on," Gregory replied, leading her out into the hallway, heading for the old nursery, which had been turned into a room for Alanna to sleep over in as a child. The bed was narrow and the bedroom itself still had a decidedly "little girl's princess room" cast to it, but Alanna had never seemed to want to change it.

"Someone's going to have to tell Nonna and Grandfather," Alanna said. "And Michaelis should probably know."

"Only if you want to. Our grandparents have no stake in it, and if Galia was going to be public about asking you to take the throne they would already have made a press release. If you really want to tell the grandparents now, I can do it."

"No...they'll be asleep, and you're right, it's not their problem, at least not yet," she said.

"It's not anyone's problem until we decide it is. You don't even have to tell Dad – he's retired and he knows it. He'll be annoyed, but he'll live if he isn't told for a few days."

He stopped in the doorway as she walked into the room; it had been made clear to him at a young age that this was Alanna's room, and he needed permission to go in. He hadn't really had to ask in years, but the habit still held strong.

"We'll get this figured out," he said.

"It's just really...I didn't even think of it," she answered.

"Nobody did. And I think..." Gregory wondered if he should even bring it up. Alanna waited. "Clearly someone in Galia did. They knew who the heir was and they got people here fast."

"What does that gain anyone?"

"I'm going to think about that. Above and beyond the fact that this is awful for you, Alanna, this is also political. It's not necessarily strange to know who the heir is, but not to tell them they are? Who gains from that? You should have been made aware, by Galia, long before now. Something to consider," he said thoughtfully.

Alanna nodded. "If I think of anything – "

"Put it in a note in your phone and try to sleep," he suggested. "We both need to be rested for tomorrow."

"Gotcha. Thanks for backing Jerry when he was kicking the Galians out, by the way."

"He made a good call. Can't say his career as a vizier hasn't been a useful one so far," Gregory said. "Goodnight, Alanna."

"Night, Gregory," she said, and he closed the door, heading upstairs, where Eddie was waiting to pounce with a hundred questions.

Alanna tried not to stay over at the palace too often, just to keep some kind of work-life balance, but she always kept some clothes in her old room. Pajamas, for sure, and a couple of comfortable outfits in case of emergency, which this clearly was. She struggled out of her formal clothes, sighing with relief, then pulled on some spare jeans and a shirt she suspected she'd stolen from Gregory at some point.

Are you awake? she texted Michaelis.

For another hour or two. How's it going? Are they still mad at me? he replied.

Mind if I come down to the lodge? Easier to talk in person, she said, hoping she didn't sound weird or desperate.

I'll be here, he answered, imperturbable as usual. She found a pair of sandals in the closet, pulled them on, and slipped out of the palace, heading for the lake.

The lakeside trail from the palace to the fishing lodge wasn't lit, but she knew it by heart, and there was enough moonlight to follow it easily. Michaelis was on the front porch when she arrived, leaning on the railing, clearly waiting for her. Retirement agreed with him, she thought; here at his home he was comfortable, barefoot, in a pair of loose trousers and a worn rugby shirt. The hard set of his shoulders that he'd had in the last few years of his reign had eased. He looked like a man on vacation, not a king.

"It's either gone excessively well or excessively poorly if Gregory's sending you here to break the news," he said, when he saw her coming.

She nodded, climbing the stairs to join him on the porch. "Kind of both, but he didn't send me."

"Did they offer Gregory the throne?"

"Not exactly." She tried to figure out what she wanted to say – had been trying the whole walk over – and she could see Michaelis waiting patiently. "Did you like being king?" she asked at last.

"I wouldn't have done it for forty years if I didn't," he said.

"But you also knew you were the best person for the job, right?"

"Well, I was unusually arrogant at twenty," he said with a smile.

"What I mean is…if you knew you were the best person for the job but really didn't want to do it, would you have done it?"

Michaelis considered her. Finally, he said, "This feels like a trick question, Alanna."

"My father was the duke's cousin," she said. "I'm the Duchess of the Horse of the House of Galia."

Michaelis nodded slowly. "There's wine inside. And harder stuff, if you want."

"Wine, please," she said. He held the door for her, following her in.

"When you texted, Jes suggested we might want some privacy. We won't be interrupted," he said, taking down wine glasses and pouring for them both, filling hers generously. She sat at the little breakfast table, trying not to gulp her wine, while he leaned on the counter and regarded her.

"I'm so sorry, Alanna," he said at last. "I didn't even think of it. I knew your father's mother had immigrated from Galia, but that was before he or I were born, and I didn't know her well. I just always thought of Mark and his mother both as Shivadh."

"Nobody else thought of it either. Gregory's suspicious that I wasn't told earlier," she said.

"He's right to be, but that's neither here nor there." Michaelis sipped his wine thoughtfully. "To answer your earlier question, no. If I hadn't wanted the job, even if I knew I was the best person for it, I would not have taken it. It's not that I lack patriotism, but there's simply no way to do the job well if you hate it. For evidence, I present to you the entire British royal family, many of the Tsars, and at least a few American presidents."

"Gregory said he'd back me if I refused the throne."

"Good. I can think of problems your being ruler of Galia solves, but – "

" – none of them actually need solving?" she asked. He nodded. "That's what Gregory said."

"He is my son. You're likely to get much the same answers from me as from him." He tilted his head. "Not that I'm not always pleased to see you, but it is a little strange you're coming to me, instead of going to him."

She nodded. "It just got a little…Eddie and Jerry were hovering, and Greg was really worried that I'd think he wanted me to take the duchy. It was all a lot. I love the boys, but you're, um." She took a second to phrase it correctly. "You've been good about letting us be adults. Gregory's always going to treat me like a sister. It's not bad, it's just not helpful right now. You know how to be more impartial."

"Yes, I suppose I see that."

"And I know if I asked Gregory this question, he'd say it was my choice and he couldn't tell me what to do, but you might actually give me an answer," she continued. Michaelis smiled. "If you were me, what would you do?"

He gave it all due consideration, puzzling out the angles thoughtfully. Finally he said, "Hm. It's nonsense, isn't it?"

"What is?" she asked.

"You can't possibly be the only heir. You might be the first in line, but if they're going up two generations of the family tree and coming back down in Askazer-Shivadlakia, they ought to be willing to go one branch further out to find a native Galian, or at least a Shivadh who wants the job," Michaelis said. "They have to make you an offer, but you can decline. And you should even be able to do it pretty diplomatically if you can offer them someone else instead."

She could feel herself slump with relief. Of course; that was an easy solution, and any of them should have seen it. Trust Michaelis, who never saw a problem he didn't want to immediately solve, to be the one to spot it.

"The real issue isn't whether to take the job, it's how to find someone else to take it," he continued. "Difficult to do that if the only information you have is coming from Galians in Askazer-Shivadlakia who clearly want you to be the one. You need more data."

His face took on a sudden, distant expression that she'd seen before – it meant he had an idea, didn't like the idea, and didn't want her to know he'd had it. She considered what Michaelis's mind might have suggested that would be so distasteful.

"But I could go to Galia," she said, sitting up straight again. "And then I'd be in Galia, and I could get the information for myself. And, being duchess, any other information we might want."

"I didn't say that."

"You didn't have to," she replied.

"I am not saying accept the duchy. But it would be possible for you to consider accepting the duchy, inspect it thoroughly in person, investigate the royal genealogy, and then renounce in favor of whoever you find," he admitted. "After that, you can come back here to tell your dear cousin the king all about your visit. I know, Alanna, that you like to be useful. That would be useful."

"Gregory would be so mad to hear you say that," she said.

"Wouldn't be the first time he's been irritated by my good advice," Michaelis said with a smile. "I also know you well enough to know that Gregory is being redundant when he reminds you that you don't have to bow to royal pressure. You'll do as you please, you always have. Very like your father that way, actually. While it's been frustrating, on occasion, you've rarely been wrong. This is up to you, Gregory is correct about that, and it's his job to tell you so. I don't have that same responsibility, not anymore. Frankly, I think two weeks in Galia, poking your nose in where it doesn't belong, would be a lovely holiday for you and very helpful to him. I'd go with you myself if that wouldn't cause an incident."

"Not very kind to the Galians, deceiving them like that," Alanna said, studying the last of her wine.

"In many ways it's kinder than the alternative – either flatly denying them and leaving them to flail, or taking up the throne and bending it to Shivadh interests," Michaelis pointed out. "Though I will say, having read the lives of your ancestors, the truly noble Askazer thing to do would be to accept the throne of Galia, raise an army and invade Askazer-Shivadlakia, take the throne from Gregory by force, and then rule both countries through benevolent yet ruthless absolute fiat. Now that is an epic in the making," he finished with relish.

"You seem very into invasion," Alanna said.

"I never got to do any invading myself. One likes to see one's protégés achieve more," he said, affecting a false modest tone.

"I'd probably have to have you beheaded," Alanna pointed out.

"Oh, I'd flee to Paris and live in genteel poverty," he said. "Gregory's the sort to fall in battle so I shouldn't worry about him either." He studied her. "Are you going to tell your grandparents?"

"I thought about it. I suppose I'll have to tell them something," she said. "It's just such a mess. They're not very happy with me anyway. They still think I should quit the job and go find a husband, start producing heirs."

"I can't throw stones there. I made that mistake myself with Gregory, trying to push him into marriage. But I thought you were getting on all right with them at Gregory's engagement ball."

"That's just how the old guard is," she said, and saw his mouth curve with amusement at not being considered part of the old guard. "You know what I mean! They were there for Gregory and so was I. We weren't going to make things awkward for him. But they're not big on family for family's sake. Family for the sake of the duchy only."

"Yes, I do know. Your grandmother was thrilled her daughter was marrying the crown prince, and simultaneously did not care much for me as a person," Michaelis said. "I think Miranda was happy to get away from her, to be honest. I'm sure your mother Ruth was, too. It's why we always insisted you spend so much time at the palace after the accident. We wanted to make sure you had someone who wasn't your grandparents helping to raise you."

She didn't blame him, but Alanna did always find it darkly amusing that Michaelis never referred to her parents' deaths directly. His wife Miranda, her mother's sister, hadn't either when she'd been alive. They always called it *the accident*. As if her parents just vanished one day, swept away by fate, instead of dying in a car crash that would definitely have killed her also if she'd been with them.

"I could just tell my grandparents I'm going on vacation,"

she said.

"I think probably there will be Galian press releases about your visit," he pointed out. "But you don't have to have a confrontation of any kind. Leave them a note, that'd be a very royal thing to do. Dear Nonna, gone to Galia to investigate the throne. For any questions, please see my social secretary." He sipped his wine. "Send them a postcard from Galia. Your grandfather will appreciate the brevity."

"Maybe. Maybe I just won't say anything and won't answer the phone when they call."

"Also an option. In this, not to echo Gregory, but I will support your choices. I've had forty years of handling your grandparents, there's not much they can do to me."

"Thanks." She finished the last of her wine and he took the glass from her, setting it next to the sink. "I should go back. Nobody knows I came to see you."

"I won't mention it. Although if Gregory thinks you came up with this spy job all on your own, that may color his opinion of you. He already knew I was like this," Michaelis added.

She gave him a quick hug, and let him kiss her forehead. "I appreciate the counsel."

"Remember: invasion is an option," he said, walking her to the door. "And if you decide you want to throw the Galians out of the palace, I'm happy to come help."

CHAPTER TWO

GREGORY WOKE IN the morning to a text-message alert; he rolled onto his side and picked up his phone, squinting at the screen.

Gregory, message when you're up, Alanna had texted, although she'd sent it to the group chat that included Eddie and Jerry. Eddie had stolen Gregory's phone at some point and named the group The Royal Pal-us.

I'm awake, he sent. *What is it?*

Almost before he sent it, the next text appeared. *I have an idea to present for your almost certain disapproval.*

He rubbed his face. *If you're pitching bad ideas you have to be the one to put real clothes on and come up here. I'm not wandering the palace in my pajamas.*

If I have to wear clothes, so does Eddie, Alanna said.

"I don't know where she gets these ideas about me," Eddie said from behind him, apparently following the chat on his own phone. He sat up and threw the blankets off, photographing his own lower half, clad in pajamas printed all over with flamingos. A few seconds later it showed up in the group chat.

On my way, Alanna said.

By the time she arrived, knocking as she entered to announce her presence, Eddie was brewing coffee and Gregory had pulled on a robe over his pajamas, settling into the sofa. He waved her into the nearby chair.

"You look like you actually got some sleep," Gregory said. "I'm a little impressed."

"I got the idea last night," she said. "I put it in my phone, per your command," she waved her phone, "and when I woke up it still seemed like a good idea that you will absolutely hate."

"You know," Eddie said, bringing her a cup of coffee and handing Gregory one before sitting down next to him, "it might be a terrible plan, but you may as well pitch it. The last time you screwed up, Gregory got a husband out of it."

Alanna choked on her coffee and glared at Gregory. "You *told* him I hired him accidentally?"

"I wasn't going to build an entire marriage on a lie, even one of omission," Gregory said. "He thought it was funny."

"I did," Eddie chimed in loyally. "If I could return the favor I would. I don't know what your type is."

"Patient, handsome, and emotionally self-sufficient," Alanna replied.

"Good, cheap, and fast – you can only have two," Eddie replied.

"Good and fast," Gregory said, and then laughed when Alanna said the same thing at the same time. "We both have expensive tastes."

"I'll have you know I'm extremely cheap," Eddie said.

"It's charming you think that," Gregory told him, then turned back to Alanna. "Come on, Al, tell me what it is."

"Well, there has to be some other heir, right? There have to be alternatives. Besides, you want to know why they're so hot to get me onboard," Alanna said. "So I was thinking, I could pretend I was considering accepting the throne, demand to inspect Galia in person, dig around in the archives, maybe do a little light desk-rummaging… then renounce in favor of another heir and report back to you."

Gregory narrowed his eyes. "I'm going to strangle my father."

"How do you do that?" she demanded. "How did you know he came up with it?"

"Because any other rational human being would tell you that

it's your choice while gently nudging you towards the safe and sane option, which is to say no and then stop answering their calls," Gregory said. "We had no relationship with Galia before yesterday. It's not like we could make the situation worse. Except by sending you to a *whole entire other country* to spy on them!"

"What are they going to do, arrest me?" Alanna asked.

"Yes, actually! If you're brought before The Hague for international espionage there's not a lot I can do for you."

"I can do plenty," Eddie volunteered. "Fuck the cops, I'll break you loose."

Gregory knew what Eddie was doing, and normally loved him for it – Eddie, perhaps because he was the oldest of five siblings, knew exactly when to insert himself into a conversation to relieve tension, to stop fights. It was already invaluable at parties. But it was also highly annoying when he did it to Gregory.

"I'm not saying this is a cold war on a level with, you know, the Cold War," Gregory said. "But it isn't a game, Alanna. If you are caught accessing or removing state secrets you can be prosecuted and imprisoned. Being the cousin of the king and heir to two duchies isn't going to change that."

"Okay, fine, but I can still go and look," Alanna pointed out. "I can see a lot, legitimately, as the heir to the throne, and I can get into the genealogy books to find a suitable replacement."

"And there's also a question of whether, once you say no, they'll let you come back," Gregory said darkly.

"This isn't the 17th century," Alanna said. "They won't lock me in a tower. They don't have a tower to lock me in. Send some security with me if you're worried."

He was opening his mouth to reply, because he understood he'd been suckered into turning this from a request for permission into a negotiation for support, when there was a rap at the door.

"It's Jerry," Jerry called.

"Come in," Gregory called back. Jerry put his head in.

"Thought I saw you were here, in the texts," Jerry said.

"You're up early," Eddie told him.

"Wanted to make sure I was on time for my breakfast with the Ansevalis. And I'm bored, so I'm glad you're all awake and apparently up to something," Jerry replied.

"We're discussing our options. Come sit, Jerry, you can give your opinion," Alanna said.

"Actually, I have an option I thought of to present to you," Jerry said, sidling through the door and letting it close behind him. "Okay, think on this," he said, pacing and gesturing as he spoke. "We support Alanna, of course, but we obviously don't want her to accept the duchy because we know it'll make her unhappy. I was thinking about that on the drive home last night. We'd be mad if she said yes, right? Supportive, but mad! And what would be the advantage if she said yes? Why would she do that? And then I thought, what does she get if she says yes...but then doesn't follow through?"

Gregory looked at Alanna, who was watching with an almost anthropological fascination.

"She gets an invitation to visit Galia, and she gets to go anywhere she wants in Galia," Jerry said, spreading his hands to demonstrate how exciting this would be. "Not only can she do a little light spying, she can figure out why Milo is – he's acting weird, right, Gregory? I didn't make that up in my head?"

"He is acting a little weird," Gregory agreed. "I can't figure out how."

"Me either. Pin in that. Anyway, if Alanna goes to Galia under the pretense of maybe accepting the throne, she can also find someone else to shove in front of them when she says no, so they won't even *suspect* she was lying," Jerry finished. "Now, before you tell me this is a terrible idea, I know. It's extremely unsafe. I agree. So I think she'll need an escort. I mean, definitely at least one lawyer, and if she's taking one she might as well say she's taking two and bring security along. I recommend Georgie.

But also, here's the brilliance of my plan: me."

"You...are the brilliance of your plan," Alanna said.

"I come with you. I am known universally as a politically unimpressive gadfly, but I am the Duke of Shivadlakia and I have land on the border. Even if they wanted to fuck with the Lady Alanna Daskaz, they are not going to fuck with *two* royally connected Shivadh, one of whom is the grandson of a king. Also, I can accomplish quite a lot while looking extremely harmless. So what do you think?"

"Did he just..." Eddie said quietly, pointing back and forth between Alanna and Jerry.

"Yes," Gregory sighed.

"Did I just what?" Jerry asked.

"I think it's a fine plan, Jerry," Alanna said, and Jerry beamed at her. "The kind of thing Michaelis would come up with. Great strategy. I especially like the part where you come with me to keep me safe. And Gregory," she added pointedly, "did promise that all three of you would support whatever decision I made. Even if you're mad about it."

Gregory could tell he was about to lose this strategy session very badly. He had dealt with professionally trained political operatives who were easier to debate than his own family. He rubbed his forehead with his fingertips.

"All right," he said. "But let's be smart about this, because neither Milo nor Ofelia are oblivious and you're going to need to be on the historian's good side."

"Good morning," Alanna said later that morning, as she swept into the dining room. Pretty much everyone was already assembled; Milo and Bruno were standing at the sideboard with coffees, conversing with Eddie, while Gregory sat nearby with Ofelia.

"Good morning – should I call you Your Grace?" Milo asked.

"I'd rather you didn't – Alanna's just fine," she replied, taking a pastry from the tray and pouring herself a coffee. "Listen, I need to apologize for last night. It just caught me so off-guard. None of us here had thought about – oh, obviously we thought about the succession, but not in terms of our own family trees. We thought Jerry might actually be distantly related."

"Well, you are cousins, aren't you?" Milo said.

"Not by blood, surprisingly," Alanna said. "His uncle married my aunt. The real problem is we forgot my father was Galian – he was born here, and he married into a prominent Shivadh noble house."

"I know how strong the national identity is," Milo said with an easy smile. "I'm sure any Galian immigrants are thought of as Shivadh very quickly."

"Exactly. Actually, that's what's been on my mind since," she said, leading Milo and Bruno to the table. "I was thinking about – this sounds terrible, but I was thinking about the Empress Alexandra."

"The wife of Tsar Nicholas?" Bruno asked, picking at his pastry. "Brutally murdered in a revolution?"

"That went straight for the most unforgiving path," Ofelia said, amused.

"I was thinking of her because I remember in school, learning about how she became empress – she had to marry Nicholas very suddenly. She wasn't trained for it yet and she barely even spoke the language. She was never happy at court. I find myself feeling sympathetic. Galia's not Russia, obviously, but we haven't had good diplomatic relations in my lifetime. I have no idea how to behave in a Galian court, I don't know any of the law. I speak Italian, but that's roughly what I have going for me. You have to admit, it's not ideal."

"Well, no. But we can provide training. And you'll have no lack of advisors," Ofelia said.

"I'm sure, but...I don't know either way, do I? My first

reaction was reluctance, but that's not fair to me or to Galia. I'm trying to be sensible about it, but to do that I think I need data," Alanna said, making the opening with care.

Because really, as Gregory had pointed out, they wanted her in Galia. Away from the Shivadh palace, somewhere they could convince her to take the throne. Even if they had the best of intentions, Alanna going to Galia was good for them.

"I'd like to do a sort of inspection tour," she said, and Bruno was already nodding. Milo looked pleased. "I can't accept – or decide any other way – until I've had some time to learn about the country. A few weeks in Galia would help me out, and I'm sure it would…"

"Calm concerns from the populace," Ofelia said. She glanced at Gregory, who had a cautious expression on his face, equal parts hopeful and apprehensive. It was a hell of an acting job. All she had to do was convince the Galians that Gregory had persuaded her, and she just needed a little extra nudge…

"I believe this is a good solution," Ofelia continued. "It provides you with information to make your decision, and provides Galia with time to recover."

"To mourn," Milo said, his voice so dry that Alanna fought a smile. "And to make plans."

"I'm going to need an entourage," Alanna said. "Not large, I don't want to inconvenience you. I'll be bringing a Shivadh lawyer, possibly two, just to ensure any legal dealings can be handled smoothly."

"And I'd like to come as chaperone," Jerry said. Milo glanced at him, then back at Alanna. "She should have some kind of escort from the royal family. Gregory can't go, and I think we can all agree the King Emeritus probably shouldn't."

"I asked Jerry if he'd attend and provide advice," Gregory said. "He is my vizier, after all."

It looked – at least, Alanna hoped it looked – like two big ruling-class boys were strong-arming the Lady Alanna into the modern-day equivalent of a political marriage.

"We can make appropriate preparations for anyone you'd care to bring," Milo said. "Were you thinking of returning with us, or...?"

"I need to put a few things in order here," Alanna said. "If we leave tomorrow afternoon – "

"You'd arrive late, but not so late as to be uncomfortable," Ofelia said. Bruno, the historian, was watching everything curiously.

"Let's plan on that, in that case. Which happily means there's not much paperwork for any of us to review today," Alanna said. "I can attend to my work, and you and your staff can have the day off."

"Jerry's volunteered to show you around Fons-Askaz if you want, or you're welcome to make use of the palace and the grounds," Gregory said. "I won't be available for lunch, and I suspect Alanna's going to be packing, but I thought I might arrange a small going-away party – a cruise on the harbor this evening."

The Galians exchanged looks, but they seemed pleased with the outcome. Ofelia spoke first, turning to Jerry.

"I'd love to see Fons-Askaz," she said. "I'm afraid Milo probably has work – his job is not limited to office hours – but I'd be glad of an excursion. Bruno?"

"I'd actually like a few hours in your library, if it's accessible," Bruno said. "I've had questions for years about some finer points of international relations that I think documents in the library could answer."

"I could call the royal librarian – he knew he might be needed," Alanna said to Gregory. "Excuse me, I'll just let him know."

She stepped outside and sent a quick text to the royal librarian *–Confirmed request for access, please come asap* and got an almost immediate response in the form of a book emoji. She flipped over to the phone app and dialed.

"Good morning! How is your planning coming?" Michaelis answered. It sounded like he was outside.

"Gregory absolutely knew it was your suggestion, so you're in trouble," she said.

"I can take him," Michaelis said easily. A seagull screamed in the background.

"I'd pay to see that fight," Alanna replied. "Where are you?"

"Down at the beach. Jes took us out for breakfast."

"Nice work if you can get it."

"Fortunately, I can. I suppose I owe Gregory some form of apology, or at least I owe him ten minutes of berating me for it. What did he think?"

"It took some persuading, but he bought it, and we've just sold it to Galia. I leave for Galia tomorrow. Jerry's coming too."

"You're taking Gerald?" he said, sounding surprised.

"He actually had some really good points about why he should come along. Tell you later."

"It's true he's good in a pinch. Not the most reliable soul, but he never got you into any trouble he didn't also get you out of. And he's very sociable, good at making himself agreeable."

"I think one of the Galians thinks he's cute."

"All the better," Michaelis said, which irritated her for reasons she couldn't define.

"I should go, they think I'm calling the librarian."

"This cloak and dagger business is fun, isn't it?" he asked. "Be safe. Text me."

"Of course. Bye," she said, and hung up just as Milo emerged from the dining room. "Librarian's on his way for Bruno. Do you need a workspace? We have empty offices."

"No need, you provided me with a very nice suite. We don't get sea views in Galia," he said with a smile. "I'm on my way back to the suite now. I'm so glad you chose to consider the throne. You'd be a breath of fresh air."

"From what you've said so far, I think you think anyone would be," she said.

"We should speak more on that later," he said. "But yes. I think you will find at least some of Galia extremely welcoming to any fresh blood after the old duke."

"Alanna," Jerry called, and they both looked back into the dining room. "Do you know where Uncle Mike keeps the Jag?"

"Yes, at the fishing lodge, because he's using it," she replied. "If you want to drive into town, take one of the government cars."

"I'll find something better than that," she heard Jerry say to Ofelia.

"I'd say we'll try to restrain Jerry but we've been trying for years with limited success," she told Milo.

"Ofelia can handle him. She likes a challenge," Milo said. "Until this evening, I think, Alanna."

"Looking forward to it," she replied.

Alanna went to her office first, because her mind was already filling with lists of things she needed to see to, particularly things she needed to tell her assistant, Darien, who would have to step up to help Gregory while she was gone. She had to bow out of meetings for the next few weeks, set an out-of-office, and send a memo to the team outlining how to handle the media. She'd need to talk to someone – probably Milo, maybe Ofelia – about how Galia would handle her visit.

She spent an hour trying to work out what to tell her grandparents, and in the end took Michaelis at his word about handling them.

I've been offered the Duchy of the Horse of the House of Galia, including the throne of Galia. I'm considering my options and will be in Galia for a few weeks to gather more information. Michaelis can explain it better than I can, and you can ask him if you have questions. I'll write from Galia when I'm able. Call anytime.

Her grandmother, who hated text messages and emails, would appreciate the physical note. Her grandfather, who didn't like long conversations, would enjoy how short and informative it was. It also neatly cut off any suggestion that her grandparents should offer her any advice. She did love them and knew they loved her, but their advice was usually terrible, because it was always about putting the estate first. Or at least, some idealized version of the estate that existed only in their minds.

"The thing I hate when it comes to media about the nobility," she'd said to Gregory and Jerry once, incensed by the very idea of enjoying *Downton Abbey*, "isn't that they get things wrong, or that they romanticize the nobility. It's that every plot, eventually, comes down to the same thing."

"Noble marriage?" Jerry had asked.

"No. Every plot eventually involves sacrificing personal happiness and freedom in the name of the title. The title, the estate, the continuity. If someone who is rich and powerful has to do something unpleasant, the writers have to find a reason for it, which is difficult when you're so insanely privileged. The reason they always give for the nobility having to do something they don't want to do is that they're doing it for the sake of their children, their legacy."

"Well, stability is important," Jerry had said. "It's why even when we elect a king it's a life term, eh? You can't do anything to make life better without a solid foundation."

"Sure, but when does the make-life-better part come into these stories? Everyone's always giving something up to nobly support the nobility for no good reason. It's why I hate the stupid ending of stupid *Roman Holiday*. If every generation is miserable for the sake of the next, what's the point of any of it? Why be unhappy just to pass on something to your children that will make them unhappy, too?"

Gregory had considered it, dark eyes thoughtful. "Put like that, it does sound pretty awful. Makes me glad I had to be elected."

"Wish I had to be elected, I'd refuse to run," Alanna had said. "Good riddance to the whole legacy. I'd have taken Gregory Peck over a kingdom any day."

"Who among us wouldn't be tempted?" Gregory had asked.

"Lord, imagine if I'd had to be elected," Jerry had said, and they'd laughed. "Mind you, I do love a show. I could have put on a hell of a campaign tour."

Now, trying to tie up loose ends before a weeks-long tour of a foreign country she was nominally already the head of, the irony of the situation hit home. She gave herself five minutes to feel upset without trying to rationalize it, then set the letter aside to be couriered over after she departed the following day. She locked her laptop and her desk, checked to make sure she wasn't missing anything vital, and went home to figure out what to pack for a royal inspection tour.

Jewel-toned sheath dress number eighty-one, she supposed. Pearls, heels, carefully expensive brand-neutral casual wear, tasteful athleisure. All of it on the blander end of her wardrobe, some of it downright uncomfortable.

What are you packing? she texted Jerry, procrastinating.

Loaded question, he texted back, and she smiled.

Seriously, though, I'm going very Young Conservative, do you think I should bring anything flashier? she asked.

I'll bring some suits and a tuxedo, casualwear. Wear what you want, I say. If Eddie could land Gregory wearing cargo shorts, you can snag at least an earl with capris and ballet flats, Jerry pointed out.

Very Mary Tyler Moore, good call, she said.

Instead of replying, he called; she put it on speakerphone as she looked through her closet.

"Words of wisdom in person, or just not willing to commit to writing it down?" she asked. He laughed down the line.

"Easier to talk this way," he said. "I'm still squiring the diplomat around Fons-Askaz. She's handbag shopping at the moment, which I'm enjoying pretending is a spy ruse of some kind. On that note, why pack a single high heel unless you want to?"

"I have to dress appropriately. You know how this game is played, Jerry, even if neither of us love playing it."

"Sure, but this isn't their game, is it?"

"How do you mean?" she asked.

"They know you're Shivadh. We've got a gay king and a notoriously relaxed attitude. You're also coming from a place of power – you don't have to impress them. If they want you to take the duchy, they have to impress you," he said.

"It's a real asshole stance to take," she said.

"Sometimes life forces us into the position of being assholes," he replied. "Furthermore, you know you're not taking the duchy so you don't even have to worry about first impressions. If they don't like you, so what? Oh, she didn't wear heels, pooh pooh," he groaned theatrically. "The fashion bloggers don't like what you wore to visit a country you don't want to rule and will probably never go back to? Big deal."

She considered the pile of dresses on her bed. "I can't go to Galia in Chuck Taylors and cargo shorts."

"Not with that attitude," he said. "But you're also not backpacking across the continent. You can bring two suitcases. I'll have at least two."

"One for suits, one for…?"

"Sex toys."

"Jerry!"

"Fine," he groaned. "It's for shoes. And also to bring back souvenirs. Hang on, looks like Ofelia's done. See you tonight. Oh, wear something in a cool tone – blue or purple."

She was about to ask why, but he hung up before she could.

It was early enough in the season that they hadn't had too

much trouble getting hold of a boat for the dinner cruise, although Gregory generally didn't have trouble in any case. It was a trim, elegant little yacht that Simon had taken possession of earlier in the day, loading it up with fresh food from the markets in Fons-Askaz. From the look of it, Eddie hadn't been far behind Simon in boarding. As she came onboard, he was just emerging from a changing cubby at the back, adjusting his formalwear for the evening.

Gregory had once told Alanna that Eddie reminded him simultaneously of a Viking and a tree, and she had to admit seeing him in a suit was always a little startling. Sometimes it was because he looked oddly out of place in them. Sometimes it was the suit itself.

"I see that eyeball, Madam Alanna," Eddie told her, as he adjusted the cuffs of the cream linen suit, heavily embroidered in blue with vivid flowers and songbirds.

"You look like an entire museum textiles gallery," she said. "I'm not complaining, just momentarily overwhelmed."

"Well, it was this or the chef's whites I've been sweating in all afternoon. Simon punished me for making him come in today by making me do all the hard prep. You look very nice, though," he said, gesturing at her deep blue dress.

"Jerry told me to wear cool colors, I'm not sure why," she said.

"Ah! I know. Stay there," he told her, and ducked into the kitchen. He emerged again with a little paper carton with a posy in it – a bundle of small, tasteful blossoms arranged in a blue-and-gold starburst. "Florist dropped it off earlier, Jerry set it up."

"Nothing for you?" she asked. He beamed, bringing his other hand out from behind his back. It held a trio of blue orchids, arranged as an overly large boutonniere.

"Go big or go home," he said.

"Oh, Eddie," she said, laughing, and kissed his cheek. "You are the best queen Askazer-Shivadlakia has ever had."

401

"I'm certainly trying for it," he agreed. "Would you – "

"Ah, yes," she agreed, undoing the little pin fixed to the orchids and passing it through his buttonhole, securing the bundle in place. She opened the carton with the posy and let him pin it to her dress at the hip, Askazer-style.

"Al, if you steal him, I will have you executed," Gregory said, joining them in the corridor. "And then I'll have to find a new boyfriend *and* someone to run my life."

"Alanna wouldn't have me," Eddie said, kissing him in greeting. "Though bagging a king and a duchess in the space of a year would definitely look great in my Wikipedia entry."

"Hm." Gregory adjusted the cuffs of his uniform, the sober black touched with gold that he always wore for formal occasions. "I can't approve of you being so interesting."

"Come on, squire me through," Alanna said, taking Gregory's arm and heading down the hallway, past the kitchen and into the opulent main cabin. There was a dining table at one end and a cluster of comfortable-looking benches and chairs at the other, all facing the wide glass wall that looked out on the bow of the ship. Beyond the glass, the harbor of Fons-Askaz was serene in the early sunset. They could hear Eddie call a greeting to Jerry and Ofelia from the hall.

Gregory went to the glass wall and began opening the panels, letting the warm salt air in. He leaned against one of the posts and admired the view, hands in his pockets.

"Something something the wine-dark sea?" Alanna suggested as she joined him.

"It really is beautiful," he answered. "I spend so much time looking at – the math, I suppose? All the ways we quantify the country. Spreadsheets of dairy production and olive yields and tourist spending, train timetables and bills passing through Parliament. Even when I look out the window I'm usually looking at Fons-Askaz. I can see why Dad always made so much time for the outdoors when he was king."

"You're in a very philosophical mood tonight," she said.

"Trying not to think about you and Jerry leaving tomorrow."

"We'll be fine."

"Well, I am worried about that," Gregory admitted. "But I'm also feeling sorry for myself a little. I'm going to miss you. I need my advisor and my vizier."

She patted his arm. "We're only going over the highlands. Back before you know it. And Jerry's surgically attached to his phone. If you can't get him by text, just post up a message on Photogram ordering him to call you."

"Who's calling me?" Jerry asked, strolling into the room, Ofelia following behind him. He'd changed into a fashionably nautical suit – navy blue with dark trousers, which looked a little silly but she couldn't deny was on brand. "Ah, you got the flowers," he said, gesturing at Alanna's waist.

"Yes, they're beautiful, thank you," she replied. Jerry went to Gregory, fixing an orange-petaled boutonniere, much subtler than Eddie's, on his uniform jacket. His own was already jauntily installed in his lapel, a small spray of blue-on-blue.

"And for the lovely Ofelia," he added, producing a different posy, this one of delicate purple flowers, the Galian national color. "May I?" he asked, gesturing between her dress and Alanna's. She nodded and held still while he pinned it in place.

"Bruno and Milo will be along shortly," she said, admiring the flowers. "I must say, Shivadh hospitality leaves nothing to be desired."

"I think we'd all like to mend fences," Gregory said. "Planting flowers isn't a bad way to start."

"True. Perhaps you and Bruno should speak about that," she said. "As a historian, he's aware of the fraught nature of the past few decades. He has some suggestions for reconciliation. Of course, if the duchy is to Alanna's liking..." She smiled at Alanna, warm and friendly enough that Alanna felt bad all over again. Ofelia seemed nice, and probably didn't deserve their duplicity.

On the other hand, Michaelis was right – better to find someone who could serve Galia properly.

"I don't think it needs to be passed through back channels that we'd like a better relationship with Galia," Gregory said. "To that end – aperitif before dinner?"

Milo and Bruno arrived as drinks were being poured, boutonnieres already in place, apparently handed to them by Simon as they passed through. Eddie mixed himself an Old Fashioned and then one for Alanna at her request, light on the bourbon; Jerry just dropped the ship's steward at the bar a wink and got something he'd apparently requested beforehand, gold and full of fruit.

"This is a new recipe," Gregory said, offering Ofelia a tumbler of light ruby liquid, small bubbles clinging to the inside of the glass. He had another one for himself. "After Davzda had its moment in the sun last year, Eddie did a survey of Davzda cocktails."

"Mostly just dressed-up margaritas," Eddie grumbled. "Nobody has any imagination when it comes to salt in mixed drinks."

"Where was I?" Jerry asked. "You didn't invite me to your tastings?"

"It wasn't an *event*," Eddie said. "Besides, most of them were terrible. I didn't actually taste that many. You can smell the bad cocktail coming off the page on 'em."

"Pomegranate?" Ofelia asked, studying it.

"Pomegranate, soda water, Davzda," Eddie said. "I call it the Royal D."

"It's certainly fragrant," she said, sipping the drink.

"I should warn you, he doesn't care about politeness," Gregory said, as she swallowed thoughtfully. "If it's awful, he'd rather know."

"A good quality in a royal spouse, I expect," she said. "It's actually quite good, thank you. Oh," she added, as the mushroom after-flavor hit the back of her throat. "And…layered."

Eddie grinned. "I won't be hurt if you want something a little more mainstream."

"I'll suffer through," she said, patting his arm. "Milo, Bruno, what will you have?"

"I'd better not," Bruno said. "I get motion sickness. Boat should be fine – boat and alcohol maybe not."

"I'll try one of these," Milo said, and coughed a little as he took his first sip of spiked pomegranate. "Well. That's adventurous."

"Ah, and it looks like the meal is nearly ready," Gregory said, as a waiter brought out a tray of nibbles – Simon's usual well-crafted food, but nothing Alanna hadn't had at dozens of parties before. "Please. Enjoy. How did you like Fons-Askaz?" he added to Ofelia, as Bruno pulled out her chair for her. Jerry jockeyed with Milo for a second, then let the Galian pull out Alanna's chair while he sat next to her, Milo on her other side. Eddie watched the little dance, amused, and then pulled Gregory's out for him, a gallantry he normally didn't bother with. Gregory gave him a look.

"It's delightful. So quaint, just like in all the Photograms," Ofelia said.

"Oh hey, what's your handle?" Eddie asked. "Did you post at all?"

"Yes, some very pretty vistas, here…" Ofelia held out her phone for Eddie to examine.

"That reminds me," Jerry said, leaning over to speak quietly to Alanna. "Brought you something."

"You already got all the flowers," she said.

"Those are palace business. Actually, that may have been me getting carried away, but the palace is paying, regardless. Anyway, I didn't buy this," he added, handing her a small velvet envelope, a little worn-looking. "Stole it from Mom. She doesn't really wear it much but she thinks it's lucky, and stolen things are double-lucky."

"Not sure that's how it works," she said, shaking the contents out into her hand. "Oh, wow."

In her palm lay a City of Gold, a ring cut in the shape of a city skyline. Usually they showed Jerusalem – she had a Jerusalem City of Gold tiara from her bat mitzvah – but this one was clearly Fons-Askaz. The Grand Synagogue was visible on one side, the palace on the other. The line of buildings along the harbor ran from the synagogue to the palace, and from the palace back to the synagogue were rolling hills broken by a small, distant, but unmistakable outline of Jerry's ancestral home, the seat of the Dukes of Shivadlakia.

"You don't have to wear it or anything, just thought it might be a nice lucky charm," he said as she examined it. It was loose on her fingers when she tried it, but fit snugly over her thumb. "Hey, that looks good. Very post-fashion."

"Sarah won't miss it?"

"If she does, she'll know who took it," he said, grinning. "She's got rings for years, she'll be fine without it. It's not an antique or anything, I think Dad had it made for her as a birthday present one year. We have to take a little Shivadh with us, right?"

"I'm glad you're coming with me," she said, making sure she was still speaking too quietly for the Galians to hear.

"Me too. It'll be fun. And if you decide you want the throne after all, you've got me to help you pick out an appropriate husband."

"Can you imagine," she laughed.

"Imagine what?" Gregory asked, glancing over at them.

"Jerry says, if I decide to stay in Galia he'll help me find a good Galian husband," Alanna said.

"You know, I distinctly remember your horrified reaction when I asked you to find me one," Gregory said. "What was it you said? I couldn't meetings-minutes myself a partner?"

"Very traditional royal thing to do," Bruno said. "Arranged marriage for the king. You'd hardly be the first."

"That's what I told her! But I can't imagine I'd have managed to go through with it. That was a stressful time for everyone," Gregory said, and Eddie reached over to run his fingers through the hair at the base of his neck, a quick affectionate touch.

Every so often – not frequently, but once in a while – she would see Eddie do something like that, or Gregory reach for Eddie, in a way that made her heart hurt a little. Gregory was a brother, Eddie a good friend, and she was happy they'd found each other, but it made her envious. She had her hands full with life, her own and Gregory's, and what romance came her way was fine, but the Shivadh kings seemed... especially fortunate, these days, when it came to love.

She twirled the City of Gold on her finger and listened to Eddie tell the story of their first meeting, when Gregory had been so unbelievably awkward that Alanna had to high-five Eddie as his stand-in.

"I think it's quite fortunate, you falling next in line for the throne," Milo said, as Bruno and Ofelia engaged with the king about some point of obscure historical protocol and how it might apply to the high-five. "I know it's perhaps not the most politic thing to say, especially when you still don't seem thrilled by the idea."

"It's just a lot at once," she said.

"But you are extremely well-trained for this, pragmatic, with useful skills," he said.

"Duke Tomas must have at least had some kind of handle on things, to keep power as long as he did," she said.

"He wasn't elected. Who was going to remove him? And under what process? Short of mass revolt, anyway."

"And there's no parliament. Just him and his advisory council," Alanna said, considering this.

"Well...now you and your advisory council," Milo pointed out.

"Maybe," she said, not enjoying the lie at all. "But you

worked for him, and Milo...I know we didn't know each other that well at school, but you don't seem like someone who bows to power for power's sake."

"It's a strange compliment, but I will take it," he said. "Galians aren't like Shivadh, you know – we don't like excitement and pageantry. We're stoics. But more to the point, Ofelia and I both watched Duke Tomas rule, practically since birth. We saw the only way to change things was from the inside. So, that's where we went."

"A conspiracy of two, eh? And you managed to get sent to fetch me?" she asked, thinking of Michaelis and his remarks about cloak-and-dagger.

"We do what's best for Galia. I hope that's not at the expense of Askazer-Shivadlakia, but if it is, it is," he said. "Your king would probably agree," he added, raising his voice a little to get Gregory's attention. "Political expediency occasionally demands sacrifice for the sake of the state, especially from those who are in a position to see it clearly."

"Alanna doesn't necessarily agree with you there," Gregory said. "And we try to keep it to a minimum. The state is made up of people, after all. Harming the people can't be good for the country."

"Milo and I argue about that sometimes too," Ofelia said. "Your father has a saying I like," she added, and Alanna felt the tension in the room jump up a notch. "A king isn't a person, he's a king – but only during working hours."

"More or less," Gregory replied, tilting his head. "Where did you hear him say that?"

"I listen to his podcast," she replied. "He has many useful things to say about governance."

"I think we were all given to understand he's *persona non grata* in Galia," Eddie said slowly.

"In some circles," she replied. "But radio doesn't stop at the border, fortunately for us. Regardless, I assume you aren't in working hours now. Or are we considered a late evening for you?"

Gregory smiled, but Alanna could see the politician in it. "This is a farewell party for two much-loved cousins. Couldn't be more off the clock if I tried."

Eddie changed the subject with his usual skill, leaning forward to observe that a chef was rarely off the clock, and he was interested in any Galian variations on Shivadh dishes. Alanna ate lightly from the courses that were served and mostly listened. She saw Simon hovering in the doorway at one point, clearly checking to see if the food was approved-of, and gave him a smile. He'd done a lot of her and Jerry's favorite dishes.

She knew she'd picked up enough politics in the palace as a child, and was generally adept enough at them, to play Gregory's sort of political games if she wanted. But that was why she worked for Gregory rather than serving as an MP, or anything more overtly political: she didn't care to. She didn't find politics interesting in the way Gregory did, or entertaining in the way Eddie had come to. Ofelia, on the other hand, seemed to be from Gregory's school of thought, appreciating the intricate challenge of it, so it was more fun for Alanna to watch her and Gregory play the game than to participate. She was still trying to make up her mind about Milo's attitude towards such things when they brought in the sorbet for dessert.

After dinner, most of the party drifted outside onto the deck. This far out on the water, the air could be chilly but the stars were bright and stunning. Alanna leaned on the railing and listened to Eddie and Jerry, who were competing to see who could make the most puns about boats.

"I keep trying to think of a way to strike up a conversation that doesn't make it sound like I'm flattering you," Ofelia said, joining her at the railing. "Unfortunately, I was trained to open diplomatic talks with a compliment. And those two are very distracting when I want to strategize."

She nodded at Eddie and Jerry, and Alanna grinned.

"You learn to listen around it, after a while," she said. "But I'm open to being complimented. Sounds like it's a royal privilege at the duke's court."

"You certainly won't lack for it once you arrive," Ofelia said. "Everyone's going to want to curry favor. Stay on staff, on the council."

"Including you and Milo. He's already made a sidelong pitch for being my trusted advisor."

"Pushy as usual," Ofelia said, sighing. "You'll need to see for yourself, I think. But when you do, I imagine your choice of who to trust will be correct. In the meantime, a little advice?"

Alanna gestured for her to continue.

"When you get to Galia, let them – let us – call you Your Grace. At the moment it is your title, and it will get you the respect you're going to need."

"Spoken as a Galian?"

Ofelia tilted her head. "Spoken as someone who knows what it's like to be the only woman in a room very full of men."

Alanna glanced past Jerry and Eddie to where Gregory was talking with Bruno and Milo.

"I take your point," she said.

"In any case, I understand you'll need tomorrow morning to tie up loose ends, but it would be better for Milo and myself to return sooner, and there's no requirement to travel together. We may leave tomorrow morning, if you don't have any objection."

"No, none here."

"Then we'll leave a driver with you, to ensure a safe arrival," Ofelia said. "I think we're looking forward to seeing how you fare in Galia."

"Me too," Alanna said thoughtfully.

CHAPTER THREE

JERRY AND EDDIE didn't often text each other anymore. It was rare that they wanted to share something with each other that they didn't also want to inflict on Gregory and Alanna, because both of them were big talkers who liked attention. Even so, Jerry knew that Eddie would be the most amused by what he'd found, so when a friend sent him a link to a Photogram post that morning, he passed it on to Eddie privately.

Someone, probably a late-shift worker at the harbor, had seen the farewell party disembarking from the yacht the previous night. Most of them were in dark clothes, but Eddie's embroidered cream suit stood out like a beacon. Eddie had his arm around Gregory's shoulders, saying something into his ear, and Gregory was turned into him, laughing, clearly enjoying himself. In the background, Alanna had Jerry's elbow, although they weren't very visible except for the little gold sprig of flowers at her waist.

Whoever took the photo clearly agreed that they looked nice; they'd captioned it "The hottest royals in the hemisphere."

I will never be over my dorky cousin's social media glow up, Jerry texted, still lying warm and comfortable in bed.

Honestly, me neither, Eddie replied, and Jerry laughed. Another message came through. *Hey, travel safe today. Can't be there to wave you off but I packed you guys some food.*

Not one for big goodbyes anyway, but thanks, I love snacks, Jerry replied, and sent a couple of food emojis for the hell of it.

He rolled onto his back, letting his phone tip gently out of his hand so that it came to rest on his forehead, closing his eyes for a last few minutes of peace. He didn't really want to think, yet, about the trip to Galia and all that entailed. He was going willingly – more than – but that was for Alanna's sake, not because he had any special desire to see Galia. Someday he was going to have to shake off his bad habit of following where she led, but it wasn't going to be today.

His "you do actually have to get out of bed now" alarm went off while his phone was still sitting on his head, vibrating his teeth together. He silenced it and struggled his way upright, then reached back into the blankets for the phone.

His luggage had been packed and was waiting by the front door for one of the family servants to load into the car; all he really had to do was bathe, dress, and ride down to the palace in time for their noon departure. These days it made him a little itchy, waking up early and then having nothing to do, but a regular sleep schedule was more and more appealing, past thirty.

He set some music to play on his phone, bumped the audio up, and took it into the bathroom with him while he washed and shaved. That done, he dressed in a suit laid out by his valet, decent for traveling as a visiting dignitary to Galia, and set out to acquire breakfast.

His mother and the dogs had already eaten and she was no doubt in her office, seeing to her correspondence (voluminous, never quite organized, and all done in longhand). Her days rarely varied and, while he knew she was always pleased to see him, it didn't often feel as if they even lived in the same country anymore, let alone the same house.

The dogs, meanwhile, were out being exercised, yelping joyfully in one of the gardens. He wasn't quite sure why they still bothered keeping dogs after his dad, the real dog lover of the family, had passed. Still, a dozen Shivadh Hunthunds – big, noisy, curly-coated retriever types with uncanny intelligence and no fear in their hearts – did at least fill a lot of empty space in the vast old ducal seat. The long gallery from his bedroom to the reception room, full of portraits of past dukes and duchesses, echoed with his footsteps.

The reception room itself held his favorite portrait – it showed a garden party, in the style of Matisse, featuring the last few generations of Shivadh nobility. In it, his grandfather Jason sat centrally, resplendent in an old-fashioned suit of deep blue and a spectacular, neatly-kept grey beard. His sons were seated on either side of him, Jerry's father Eitan on the right, Michaelis on the left. Eitan, already middle-aged, had his arm around Jerry's mother Sarah, significantly younger than he was; both were in Shivadh blue as well. Jerry was a kid, crouched nearby to poke at something in the grass with a stick, wearing a little navy suit but with bare feet.

Michaelis, on the other side, was only a little older in the painting than Gregory was now, but he'd already been king for several years. He was in the royal uniform of black and gold, seated, holding hands with his wife Miranda, in the vivid orange of the house of Askaz. Her sister Ruth was next to her in an almost identical outfit, holding Alanna, a cherub in a fluffy pastel ruffled dress, in her lap. Ruth's husband Mark, the cousin of the infamous Duke Tomas, was sitting in the grass at Ruth's feet, in a nondescript brown suit. He was bent over a book, studying it with Gregory, a grave-faced little boy in the royal black. He'd never actually worn the black uniform as a child, but the symbolism was meaningful; everyone was already well aware by then that serious, bookish little Gregory was the heir apparent to the throne. Michaelis had protested for years that Gregory should choose his own destiny, but Gregory's mind had been made up by the age of five.

Jerry wasn't sure why the painting was in the home of the Duke of Shivadlakia, rather than in the palace. Art did tend to get shuffled from place to place, but he suspected the royal family might have found it difficult to look at, after Alanna's parents had died. Michaelis might have palmed it off on Jerry's mother. Lord knew there were enough portraits of various dead royals in the palace as it was.

In any case, Jerry had always liked it, especially seeing himself off in the corner making mischief. As they'd all begun to grow up, he'd found it entertaining to remember Michaelis and Miranda so young, to see the hints of the adults Alanna and Gregory (and himself) would become in the children in the portrait. He liked to see his own brow and nose in the severe features of King Jason, who he barely remembered.

He passed the painting by and turned down another hall to the kitchen. Their kitchen staff weren't nearly as friendly or as entertaining as Simon or Eddie, but if Jerry wasn't at breakfast they knew to leave out something he could take on his way through. This morning there was a whole carton of food – granola bars, dried figs, little sweet oranges, and a tea-towel full of pastries. Travel treats. He took the hint, tucked the box under one arm, and went back out to the reception room. He set the box on the suitcases, looked at his luggage, looked at his watch, and said "Well, hell with it."

Ten minutes later, car loaded with his bags, music blaring through the speakers, and an onion knish between his teeth, he was driving down the winding road through the western edge of the family seat, heading for the palace. He'd be early, but it wasn't like that was going to be *bad* for his reputation, and he could get underfoot and entertain himself in the palace as easily as anywhere else.

When Darien finally tapped Alanna on the wrist in the middle of their handoff meeting and said, "I can take it from here. You need to go, the car's waiting," she felt a little twist of internal anxiety.

"Jerry's probably running late," she said, but she began shutting things down and packing up her purse and laptop case.

"Jerry's been here since breakfast," Darien said with a smile. "It's fine, Alanna. I'll handle the king in your absence, and I promise not to be so competent he replaces you. Go, enjoy your visit."

She might have stalled a little longer, but at that point most of her entourage arrived. Will, one of the palace legal team and chosen to go along because he was fluent in Italian legalese, was a small tidy man with sharp, intelligent eyes, as attached to his tablet as Alanna often was to hers. With him was Georgiana, taller than him and somewhat severe, with short ruffled hair and in a suit cut a little loose. She too had a law degree, but she was also a highly-trained bodyguard, one of the very few the Shivadh royalty bothered to employ.

"Ready to enter the lion's den?" Alanna asked them, as she left the office and they turned to follow her to the car.

"It's just Galia," Will said with a sniff. "It's not like we're going behind some iron curtain. My dad goes there every year for vacation."

"What is there to do on vacation in Galia?" Alanna asked.

"Gamble, mostly," Will replied. "He likes the horses, but the casino's pretty fun too."

"Fortunately, this time we'll be in the royal quarters, not the local casino," Alanna replied. "You've both had briefings?"

Georgie gave her a curt nod as they stepped out into the afternoon sunshine. Jerry, leaning on one of the palace cars they'd requested, looked up from his phone and waved. He looked like a model in a photoshoot, lounging in a casually rumpled but clearly expensive suit, the sun picking out gold highlights in his auburn hair. Alanna was secretly glad it was Jerry going with her. Gregory and Michaelis were both astute men, but they were also very serious sometimes, and Jerry could at least take her out of herself once in a while. She twiddled the City of Gold on her thumb idly.

"Adventure awaits, Your Grace," Jerry said, pulling open the door. "Georgie, are you riding with us?"

"In front," Georgie said, then lowered her voice. "Keeping an eye on the Galian driver. Not sure I trust him with one of our cars."

"Perhaps not, but I trust you with my life," Jerry told her earnestly, as Alanna got into the car. He closed the door after her and circled to clamber into the other side, while Georgie and Will loaded their luggage into the second car, which would follow them with Will driving. Inside, the barrier between passenger seats and driver was already raised, giving them some privacy.

"Away we go," Alanna said, as the cars pulled out of the drive, heading east towards the highlands and the passage through to Galia.

Jerry was on his phone almost immediately, scrolling through social media or perhaps reading the fashion blogs; he had little patience for long car trips. Alanna watched the scenery roll past for a while, enjoying the grassy fields and groves of fig and olive trees until they began the climb into the highlands. Most of the land around them either belonged to Jerry's family or had at one time, and it was pretty country.

She turned away from the window after a while, realizing her phone hadn't had any text or email notifications in ages, panicking briefly before remembering everything was being rerouted to Darien. Jerry, who had put his own phone away, cocked an eyebrow at her questioningly but let it go when she didn't offer an explanation for her sudden rushed consultation of her screen. He returned to the laptop he'd taken out – it was a newer model that could be folded to use as an extra-large tablet, and he was working over it with a stylus, moving abstract shapes on an irregular grid.

"What are you up to?" she asked, leaning on his shoulder to watch the shapes flick around the screen.

"Just a new puzzle," he said, giving her a quick smile. "Got tired of Sudoku."

"What's the goal?"

"Still working that out, actually," Jerry said. "It's one of those games where you're not sure what you want to achieve for a while."

She nodded and looked back down at her phone, scrolling through various apps, still leaning on his shoulder. After a minute, he shifted his arm back and around her, pulling her in more comfortably against his right side, still working away with his left hand.

"What do you want to do when we get to Galia?" he asked, eyes on his screen. "I assume there'll be some sort of formal welcome, but outside of all the usual stuff."

"I thought tomorrow I'd introduce myself to the royal genealogist, so I can start looking for a replacement," Alanna said. "Then I should talk with Milo about operations. I need to know who actually cuts checks and issues permits, that kind of thing, because I need access to the paperwork, the…bureaucracy. Although that's actually lower priority. In theory the national budget is public but it's actually very difficult to access, so I'm going to work on getting that, that'll be the most helpful. I'm going to need to speak to some of the advisors too – "

"Lord, I regret asking," Jerry murmured, amused. "All in the same day, Al?"

"It's not much more than about an hour's work in terms of networking – it's just asking other people for things with delays in-between," Alanna said. "Why, what's your plan?"

"Well, since we're there for two weeks, I thought I'd play it cool and not tip our hand wholesale," he said with a grin.

"I like to get things done," she replied, mock-prim.

"I know, which makes you amazing, because there's nothing I hate more than getting things done," Jerry replied, then shook his head. "I mean, I like getting them done, but the work to get there is irksome."

"You think it's a little much to try for all at once?" she asked.

"They know you need information, but they think you're trying to make up your mind. They don't know you already have and you're just looking for proof," Jerry said. "Let stuff flow. Get lost in the offices after seeing the genealogy records and ask who you should go to for palace operations. Find out from them where the budget data lives. Or send me, your faithful hound, to charm a clerk in the house of budgets."

"Seems like a lot of work," she said.

"The cost of sneaking around," he replied. "Or the joy, depending."

"On what?"

"On whether you're me, a man who makes trouble for the sake of it," he said, jostling her affectionately.

"You don't, really, though. You get into a lot of it, but you don't make it for no reason."

"Only with the best of intentions, you think?" he asked.

"Well, you are the vizier. You wouldn't be you without a little hint of mischief," she said.

"Spice of life," he replied. He did something to his game and it lit up with various colored patterns; perhaps it was one of those coloring-book apps. "We're about to lose signal until we're down from the highlands."

"Good to know," she said, texting the group chat. *Going silent in the last internet-free place on Earth. See you in a few.*

She had books on her phone she could read, or some podcasts downloaded – there was Michaelis and Jes's latest, about Shivadh-Spanish cooking, and a few of Noah's new one with his classmates, all about boats. Boats were not, Alanna felt, inherently fascinating; she didn't share Michaelis and Gregory's love of the outdoors. But the kids were funny, and some of the history was interesting.

"Why do you suppose it is that Askazer-Shivadlakia has

olives and Galia doesn't?" Jerry asked, as she tried to decide what to listen to.

"Wrong side of the mountain, maybe," Alanna said. "Gregory might know. Or someone in the agricultural cabinet, *great for growing tomatoes*," she said, as Jerry chimed in on the joke Eddie wouldn't stop making. *The agricultural cabinet? Oh yeah, had one of those for my tomatoes.*

"I'll have to ask when we get there. Good excuse to get out and have a look around, maybe," Jerry said. "Oh, perhaps the terroir for growing them is wrong."

"What do you know about terroir?" she asked, curiously.

"This and that," he replied. "Are you listening to music?"

"Just deciding what I want to listen to," she said.

"Gimme an earbud, you can DJ for me," he said.

"Gross, I'm not giving you an earbud. I can just put the phone on speaker," she replied.

"Is sharing headphones gross?" he asked. "A philosophical debate."

"Do you want the podcast I was going to listen to or do you want to be my own personal podcast?" she asked.

"You know me, I can improvise an hour's worth of content, but I prefer to save myself for a more appreciative audience," he said. "As the lady prefers."

She consulted her podcast player again and then decided on music; something with a nice thump of bass and generic lyrics she wouldn't have to pay too much attention to. Jerry hummed idly along with the music, and she scrolled through one of the books on her phone until they were back in cell range and notifications began to pop up from the Ansevalis.

"Ofelia says Galia knows we're coming," she told Jerry. He reached over to tap her music silent.

"Ofelia says Galia, like the whole country?" he asked.

"I assume so. She says to look out for crowds, but we probably shouldn't stop. Not a security thing, we've just got somewhere to be."

"They aren't playing around, are they?" he asked. "I've got snacks if we don't want to stop for dinner." He kicked his heel against something under his seat. "The estate chefs and Eddie both packed us stuff. Pretty sure Eddie made fried chicken, because he loves us."

"Maybe in a bit," she said. "Formal evening reception, 8pm, Milo will brief us when we get there. Milo says he's sorry it's unavoidable."

"It's not like we're not used to unavoidable social obligations," he said. "The lot of a Shivadh noble is a hard one."

"Yes, very difficult," she replied, gesturing around them at the car, the driver, the bodyguard in the front passenger seat. "Especially for you. You blow off social obligations whenever you like."

"You made the genuine error of allowing people to know you're reliable," Jerry said. "Now they're trying to give you a country to run. The only reward for hard work is more work."

Eventually the road down out of the mountains widened, and the occasional building started appearing again. It was only a few isolated farm houses at first, but then residential neighborhoods began scrolling past and, off to one side for a while, a golf course. The signs, when visible, were in Italian.

They passed through one small Galian town, sleepy and quiet, and then another larger one; this one had the purple of the Galian flag strung up as bunting, and a hastily hand-painted sign in the small plaza of a city center, facing the road, reading *Welcome Duchess of the Horse* in Italian.

Duchessa del Cavallo. Alanna didn't care for it. It sounded... uncomfortably operatic.

The capital city of Levaldi lay on a river that passed around it from northeast to southwest; at the bridge in the southwestern corner, a crowd had gathered. The cars were technically unmarked, without even the royal seals on the doors that some of the Shivadh palace cars had, but they did have Shivadh parking stickers on the corners of the windshields. And, well, they were big flashy cars that looked very royal.

"Time to smile and wave," Jerry said, lowering his window and putting an arm out to wave as they passed by. Alanna did the same on the other side, smile fixed on her face. People shouted in Italian, mostly friendly, and one ambitious young Galian man threw a bouquet with astonishing accuracy, right into the window. When she picked it up, the ribbon holding it together had a phone number written on it.

"Marriages are built on worse," Jerry told her, laughing.

There weren't any more huge crowds, but there were certainly people lining the streets to watch them pass; Levaldi, like Fons-Askaz, was a labyrinth of small streets cut through with big thoroughfares, full of open-air cafes and wide pavements where people congregated. There were small river-fed canals that cut through the city like efficient blades, paying no heed to what streets they interrupted, making for dozens of decorative little bridges. And everything seemed to radiate outwards from the Palazzo Cavallo, the center of the duke's power, a large domed building in the center of the city, set slightly higher than most of the buildings surrounding it. The vista was spoiled only by the giant, ugly modern casino situated directly next to it.

They took a service road up to the back of the Palazzo, pulling into a little turnaround clearly meant for deliveries to the kitchen. Milo, notified by the security gate that they were near, was waiting for them with several men and women in Palazzo livery.

"Your Graces, welcome to Galia," Milo said, offering his hand to help her out of the car.

"Glad to be here," Jerry said, stretching his legs and rotating his shoulders as a valet opened his door for him. "And we beat the deadline."

"Barely. Hello again, Milo," Alanna said, accepting polite

cheek-kisses. "Thank you for coming to meet us."

"Yes, Ofelia tells me you got her message about the reception. I'm so sorry, the council strong-armed us into it. They clearly want you tired and off-balance for your first meeting."

"What's the advantage there?" Alanna asked, and then realized she was already treating him like one of Gregory's aides or her own researchers, there to answer questions and gather intel for her. She reminded herself that Milo was not necessarily a reliable source – and he had his own job to do in any case.

"Establishing power early, I suppose," Milo said, seeming pleased by her question. "Or one of them wants to convince you to accept the duchy and thinks he can do it tonight while your guard's down. This way," he added, leading them up a handful of steps and into a back hallway. "There's a changing room we've set aside for you – your bags will be taken to your actual rooms – "

"No – let me take that one," Alanna said, pointing at one of them. "I need a dress from it."

The man handling the bag looked perplexedly at Milo. Alanna remembered herself, repeating the request in Italian. His face broke into a grin.

"Yes, of course, Your Grace," he replied in Italian, apparently delighted she spoke the language.

"This one for me," Jerry said in less perfect Italian, pulling one of his bags after him, pre-empting a liveried attendant. "It's fine, I can do it," he told the man. Then, after a second of consideration, he reached into his pocket and found a crisp Galian cash bill. Alanna heard him murmur, "If our bags reach our rooms without being searched, there's another for you."

"Half will need to go to the officer," the man said. Jerry sighed and gave him another bill. "You're a generous man, Your Grace."

"Why not let them search the bags if they want? Nothing incriminating in them," Alanna said in an undertone, following Milo inside.

"Speak for yourself, I might have controlled substances in mine," Jerry told her with a grin. She swatted his arm. "Why should they get to search us? They've got no business poking through our stuff."

"How did you even know they would?"

"I didn't, but I don't like it when my luggage is out of my sight, and now I've confirmed someone was going to," he replied with a shrug.

"You know, sometimes I think you have a lot more of your grandfather Jason in you than you let on," she said.

"I've just spent years stealing Uncle Mike's trashy spy thriller novels," Jerry replied.

"In here," Milo said, holding a door for them. Inside was a small office with a sitting area, a bathroom off to one side. "You can change, wash – have you eaten?"

"We had food on the trip," Jerry said, looking around him. "I assume there'll be nibbles at the reception, too. Can't drink on empty stomachs."

"It would certainly be an interesting first impression if you did," Milo said. "Anything you require that we can provide within the next ten minutes or so?"

"We'll be fine," Alanna reassured him. "Just let us get changed and maybe…if there's anyone who can stay close to us at the reception, someone to offer context…"

"I unfortunately can't escort you, but Ofelia will be escorting His Grace if you've no objections. As duchess, you're expected to attend unescorted if you're not married."

"Well, that's helpful," Alanna sighed. "Can Jerry and Ofelia stay close, at least?"

"I recommend it," Milo agreed. "I'll let her know."

He gave a little bow and left, and Alanna went to her bag, opening it and shedding her traveling clothes while Jerry changed into something less rumpled, backs to each other out of politeness.

"Thank goodness it's not black tie," he said, coming over to zip up the back of her cocktail dress. "My tuxedo is a wreck."

"We can unpack tomorrow morning and get things laid out," she said. Jerry wrapped his arms around her shoulders, hugging her from behind, and she leaned into the comfort of it for a moment. He smelled better than anyone had a right to, having spent that much time in a car. Probably something his valet did to his clothes before packing them.

"Let's go dazzle 'em," he said, and let her go, heading for the door.

When Jerry walked into the reception that evening, it was like every party his father had ever thrown, without the benefit of Shivadh liberality.

It was almost entirely men; Alanna and Ofelia were two of about a dozen women, not counting the servers. There were perhaps three times that many men, and most of them looked to be over fifty.

"It's the duke's advisory council," Ofelia said, her arm in Jerry's but her head inclined a little towards Alanna, on her other side. "Plus wives, and well-connected political hopefuls."

"Yikes," Alanna said.

"Tits and teeth," Jerry replied.

"Charming," Ofelia told him.

"Wasn't my idea," Jerry shot back, and just then there was the thump of a staff on the ground.

"His Grace, Gerald, Duke of Shivadlakia, and Ms. Ofelia Ansevali," a pair of voices announced, first in Italian and then in English, and Jerry left Alanna behind for a heart-dropping moment as they entered the room properly. All heads lifted, all eyes fixing on them. Jerry tried to radiate authority and nobility, but he suspected they'd figure out his real deal soon enough.

"Her Grace and Majesty, Duchess of the Horse of the House of Galia, the Lady Alanna Daskaz," came the same dual-language voices.

"We can drop the English if you want, by the way," Jerry said to Ofelia. "We both speak Italian. Or anyway, I get by. Alanna's fluent."

"Very helpful, and considerate. But you, perhaps, don't let on yet," she replied. "Always an advantage when they think you don't understand what they're saying."

"I like you more all the time," he said. She showed her teeth gently.

The reception wasn't all that different from various events he'd had to attend as Gregory's cousin – an introduction line, the presentation of dignitaries' wives, extremely brief small talk until everyone had at least had a chance to shake hands. Then a subtle jockeying to see who would get the ear of the duchess first. The Shivadh kings preferred dancing before conversation, but Jerry estimated roughly half of the men in the room might collapse if they tried anything more vigorous than a slow waltz. He snagged a handful of snacks that were being passed around, then lifted a glass of champagne for Ofelia from another tray, passed it to her, and looked around for the bar.

Once he'd found it, he said "Stick with Alanna," in Ofelia's ear and abandoned her. He headed for the corner, where a handful of men, on the younger end of the fifty-to-five-hundred range, were gathered around two harried looking bartenders.

"Ah, do you know how to make a Gunner?" he asked the nearest one in a low voice. She gave him an uncomprehending look, then held up a finger and tugged on the sleeve of the man working next to her.

"Repeat, please?" he said. "My English is better."

"Oh, thanks, sorry," Jerry replied. "A Gunner? Type of drink?"

"That is...ah, yes," the man agreed, cutting himself off with a nod. "I believe I know."

Jerry leaned back on the bar, snacking on the appetizers while the bartender measured and mixed, and it took about three seconds for one of the other men at the bar to approach. No-fail. Jerry grinned.

"Your Grace," the man said. "Not a champagne drinker?"

"Not allowed anymore, I'm afraid, after an incident with a fountain," Jerry replied. "It's Consigliere Riva, isn't it?"

"A good memory, given how many names you've just heard," Riva said with a sharp smile. "How are you enjoying Galia?"

"Haven't seen much of it yet," Jerry replied, accepting his drink from the bartender and dropping a tip in the glass behind the bar. "These nibbles are very good though."

"We were pleased to be able to promptly offer such hospitality. Obviously very important to make the duchess feel welcomed," Riva said. "She'll have a long night ahead of her, I expect," he added, watching Alanna and Ofelia speak with one of his colleagues.

"Ah, fortunately Alanna's used to it."

"And she speaks Italian! An added benefit, although you'll find most of us on the council know enough English," Riva continued. "Anyone who says they don't is pulling your leg."

"I'll bear that in mind," Jerry said soberly. "You aren't going to go circle with the others?" he added, watching the subtle way people tried to find strong positions from which to approach Alanna.

"No. I have no pressing concerns, and there will be time enough in council meetings to become better acquainted."

Jerry knew this score. Some of the men wanted direct access, but Riva was smarter than that. He wanted a connection, like the one he could get through the duchess's chaperone. Well, there was nothing inherently wrong with that, Jerry supposed.

He made small-talk on autopilot, and suspected Riva was doing the same, both of them with half their mind elsewhere. Jerry had his eye on Milo, who was helping to manage the crowd, moving between knots of people, shaking hands here and there. It was beginning to be much clearer to Jerry why Milo kept pinging him as off, somehow.

Milo, he decided, wasn't concealing anything specifically from the Shivadh nobility. He was concealing something from everyone, and they only noticed because they'd known him at school. Jerry even thought he could put a finger on what, generally, was wrong: Milo Ansevali was furious about something, the kind of low-banked, long-burn anger that was constant and therefore hard to see. He could only see it now because this was clearly touching on whatever enraged him. Jerry watched one of Milo's hands flex open, curve back into a fist, and then force open again as he spoke, smiling, with one of the older men casually waiting his turn to speak with Alanna.

Jerry supposed he had plenty to be angry about. He clearly hadn't liked Duke Tomas, and having brought the new duchess here, he now couldn't do much to defend her. Milo couldn't know how little Alanna needed defending, and might even be annoyed with Jerry as well for abandoning her. Certainly Milo was keeping an eye on both of them, glancing over every so often between being obviously condescended to by members of the council.

Why take the job if he hated it so much? Or at least if he hated the people surrounding him. Something to investigate while they were here, perhaps.

He turned his full attention back to the small-talk with Riva, mainly because someone new had entered the conversation – Bruno, of all people, the quiet nerd who got motion sickness.

"So good to see you again, Your Grace," Bruno was saying.

"Pleasure's mine," he replied. "I never got to ask how your research in the Shivadh archives turned out."

"Very well indeed," Bruno replied. "Consigliere Riva, did you know His Grace here is actually, hereditarily, a prince?"

427

"Only by certain rules," Jerry cautioned. "You'd need to be very careful making that claim in Askazer-Shivadlakia."

"You're only a prince in some places?" Riva asked, eyebrows rising.

"Well, we're democratic, as you know," Jerry said, and Riva nodded. Jerry checked on Alanna, estimating he had about five minutes before he should go back to Ofelia. "The king is declared by vote only. Can't be a king without a popular vote. But the king's children should always be referred to as royalty. It reminds people of what they had to put up with, more or less, as children of the ruler."

"But your father was a prince, properly titled, son of the king directly," Bruno said.

"Mm, yes," Jerry sipped his drink. "But that was honorary. It wouldn't pass down to me unless he became king. My uncle was king before he retired," he said to Riva, just to see what kind of reaction that got. Mostly a poker face, which was interesting. "So my cousin Gregory was prince, and then elected king. His children will be princes and princesses, or princeps, I suppose – that's the suggestion we've had for the gender-neutral, you know, going forward."

"How...progressive," Riva observed, lip wrinkling a little.

"Must move with the times. In any case, it was less confusing to refer to my father as a duke than a prince, since he was never going to run for the kingship even if my uncle left office. No interest in that kind of bureaucracy. Can't blame him."

"And now you are the Duke of Shivadlakia," Riva said carefully. "With land bordering on Galia, in the highlands."

Jerry bit down on the urge to make the old joke, *Just the one highland, really*. Instead, he smiled. "Yes! It's one reason I was so pleased to accompany Alanna. Great to see more of the place. That reminds me, Bruno, I'd love to know if you could show me where the original ducal holdings might have ended. I believe Shivadlakia sold a lot of land to Galia and I'd be interested in seeing the areas that might have been kept by my ancestors."

"Of course," Bruno said, but he looked confused by the request. It was mostly nonsense, but it was a good reason to tromp around the country a bit, while Alanna had to put up with all of these…delightful consiglieres. "I'll see about locating some maps for you."

"Great. Consigliere Riva, it's been splendid, but I'm neglecting my date. If you'll excuse me," he said, and headed back towards Ofelia. She gracefully made space between herself and Alanna.

"Just how awful is it?" he asked.

"Not any worse than what I've seen Gregory put up with," Alanna replied. "You can have about a minute and a half before someone is going to get impatient."

"Nothing to report here that can't wait. I – " he stopped, because someone had just entered the room, a late arrival who looked like he still felt he was too early. He wore a suit that was both expensive and several years out of style, though it looked new, and the light caught the shine off his mostly-bald head, where he didn't have any short, bristling white hair. He looked faintly like an overdressed turtle.

"Is that Brasolin?" Jerry asked, indicating the old man with a slight jerk of the head. "Holy shit, what an old bat."

Alanna followed his gaze. "It must be him. I wish we'd had time to get some kind of brief on the council."

"That's Consigliere Brasolin," Ofelia confirmed, following their gaze. "Alanna, this may not be pleasant, but…"

"No, I agree," Alanna said, and Ofelia patted Jerry on the shoulder and left, crossing the floor to where Brasolin seemed to be imperiously waiting for her.

"He can't be very fond of you," Jerry said. "Or me, for that matter. If I'd thought about it I'd have brought a pie."

That got a sharp noise out of Alanna, who bit her lip briefly.

"Don't make me laugh, he's about to come talk to us," she said.

"I'm going to find the video," Jerry said, reaching for his phone.

"No! Jerry, don't you dare," Alanna told him. "Seriously. You know how important he is in Galia."

"I know how funny it is watching him get hit in the face with a pie," Jerry said.

"Not right now. Behave yourself."

"Yes ma'am," Jerry replied, as Brasolin reached them.

Alanna offered her hands. "Consigliere Brasolin, how nice to meet you," she said in Italian.

Alexandros Brasolin, the overdressed turtle, took her hands and bowed over them, but when he straightened, his eyes were narrowed. Forty years earlier, Brasolin had been one of the candidates running against Michaelis for the kingship of Askazer-Shivadlakia, claiming citizenship through a Shivadh grandmother and blatantly, at least to the history books, looking for power. He'd never had a strong chance of winning against the charismatic younger son of the sitting king, but it was the pie that had sealed the deal.

Jerry wondered if Brasolin could see on their faces that all they could think of was the film footage, shown in Shivadh history classes, of a political activist who favored Michaelis, hitting Brasolin in the face with a pie during a campaign debate. One of Michaelis's first acts as king had been to quietly pardon the man who'd done it.

"A pleasure to meet you, Your Grace," Brasolin said to Alanna, also in Italian. Jerry had to give him this, he seemed sincere. "Kind of you to arrive with such speed."

"It seemed like it needed immediate attention," Alanna replied. "His Grace was young to have passed so suddenly."

"Indeed. Quite the loss. Still, there seem to be some benefits," he said. "Your presence. Perhaps a reconciliation between nations."

"Perhaps so. I'd be interested to hear your thoughts on it," Alanna said, which was something she absolutely had learned from Eddie, Jerry thought. It was a key phrase of his for when he wanted someone to feel like he was listening despite having already made a decision about what to do. "I believe Milo is setting my agenda – I'll make sure to find some time on it to speak with you further."

He gave her a nod, seemingly satisfied with this for the night, and retreated strategically.

"I'm texting Michaelis," Jerry said.

"If you really have to. Tell him from me that Brasolin has not aged gracefully."

"He has a face meant for pies," Jerry said, taking his phone out again. He shot a quick message to Michaelis, then managed to find a set of animated images of Brasolin getting the pie in the face, and sent those sequentially to the group chat. Alanna's expression didn't change as her notifications began beeping while she was being buttonholed about urgent paperwork by one of the other consiglieres.

Gregory, uncharacteristically, sent a string of laughter – *ahhahahahahah hahahaha* – and then a second message, *Sorry this is Eddie, Greg just explained it, I was holding the wrong phone.*

"Jerry, would you send a message," Alanna said, handing him her unlocked phone. "Tell them that the Duchess of the Horse simply cannot surround herself with a trio of buffoons any longer, and I have fired all three of you."

Ofelia looked amused. "Chaperone and social secretary?" she asked Jerry.

"Not as of ten seconds ago, I've been fired," Jerry said, hitting send and handing Alanna back her phone. "It's something Gregory does sometimes," he told Ofelia, more seriously. "He can't really be seen to be on his phone at official functions, so he asks one of us to send a message if he needs to. Used to be Alanna or me, now it's usually Eddie. Everyone expects Eddie to be on his phone."

"A strategy I hadn't considered," Ofelia said thoughtfully. "Duke Tomas didn't use his phone for communication."

"What did he use it for?" Alanna asked.

"Videos, mostly," Ofelia said, with a vagueness that told Jerry very little but apparently spoke volumes to Alanna, who wrinkled her nose.

"Brasolin's very powerful here, though – you aren't wrong," Jerry said, considering the room, the way people were moving and the change in dynamic since he'd arrived.

"Something we would all do well to remember," Ofelia agreed.

"Ofelia, if I want to circulate more, do you need to come with me?" Jerry asked. "I don't want to be seen to abandon my date."

"It's all right, I can handle things at this point, most of the introductions have been made," Alanna said. "Go entertain yourself, Jerry. Ofelia, do what you need to."

Ofelia looked like she was pleased, in a way, that Alanna was giving the orders. Jerry offered her his elbow.

"I think you should know," he said, as they left Alanna to some new would-be advisor, "one of my favorite things to do is meddle. It's mostly for my own amusement, but if it can serve the crown I always like it that much more. I feel there is fertile soil for that here, with you."

"What kind of meddling did you have in mind?" Ofelia asked, sounding more than mildly interested.

"I'm not picky," he said, but he narrowed his eyes, sweeping them around the room. "Wouldn't mind thinning the herd a little. Some of these fellows are just annoying Alanna, and I can't allow that."

"You'd like a target?" she asked.

"I'd like to know who the bad eggs on the council are. Not the competent ones who are just unpleasant. I want the boat anchors," Jerry said, making a little slashing motion with his free hand. "Cut 'em loose."

"I can offer intelligence, if nothing else," she said. "Introduce you to a couple of the heaviest of boat anchors."

Jerry beamed at her. "Let's have some fun, then."

It really was an endurance race, these formal occasions; Alanna knew they wore Gregory out, much as he enjoyed them. Now, after a long car ride and an evening full of introductions, re-introductions and discussions, it was starting to take its toll. But then, that was what Milo had meant – they wanted her off-balance. At least some of the council members had left early, and the longer conversations were easier, with less shifting between people and remembering who was who.

Then there was a break, someone leaving before someone else arrived, and Milo and Jerry both stepped in at the same time to block out anyone else.

"Just the man I wanted to see," Jerry said, and Milo pivoted, clearly a little startled. "I suspect you know how to get the bartenders to issue last call. Al's fading and I'm bored."

"I was about to ask," Milo said. "Technically, you can leave at any time, of course, but now would be good timing. Ofelia and I can circulate, help the exodus along."

Alanna nodded gratefully.

"If you leave through there, someone will take you up to your suites," Ofelia added, indicating the door they'd entered through at the start of the night. "You should leave first," she added to Alanna. "His Grace can go once you have."

"I'll be three minutes behind you," Jerry promised Alanna, giving her a formal Shivadh bow and a grin. Alanna, gratefully, retreated back through the door, watching as Ofelia deftly blocked someone who clearly still wanted another word with her. In the corridor behind the door, she leaned on a handy table and took her shoes off, groaning. A man in the ducal livery jumped up from a chair.

"Your Grace," he said. "Would you care to retire? I can show you to your suite."

"Please," she said. "And please say it's not far."

"Not at all, just up these stairs."

"Lord, stairs," she mumbled to herself, but he heard her; a smile flitted across his face.

"His Grace never allowed guests to stay on the ground floor," he said. "He believed the rooms were not sufficiently secure or private," he continued, as they slowly climbed the stairs.

"So what does he...did he do with the ground floor?" she asked.

"Storage. Offices. Some of it was converted for a menagerie, and the animals' kitchen and veterinary office take up a good deal of space," the man said. They reached the top of the stairs, thankfully, and he crossed the hallway to indicate a door. "Here you are."

"Thank you. Oh – my guest, Gerald, Duke of Shivadlakia – "

"Next to you on the left. Your entourage is across the hall. If you require anything, there's a buzzer on the bedside table."

Inside, there was a little sitting room with a very nice view of some manicured, parklike grounds, including what looked like a decorative iron gazebo. There was a long, wide arch leading into the bedroom – not much privacy, with no door on it – and beyond that she could see a bathroom. Across from the bedroom was a small alcove with a very basic little kitchen arrangement. She flopped on the sofa in the sitting area, wondering if she had the energy to write up notes from the night – something Gregory usually did, dictating them into his phone and putting his thoughts in order later with her.

She could probably talk them out like Gregory did, at least. She was just getting her phone recorder app open when she heard clattering from the other side of the wall, then a knock on her door. "Al, it's Jerry."

"Come in," she called. He walked in, and she smiled at the sight – shoes off, tie and jacket already gone, probably dumped somewhere on the floor in his suite. He'd popped his cufflinks, so his sleeves swung a little loose, and he had something in one hand, like a bocce ball.

"Is that a pomegranate?" she asked, blinking at it.

"It is, in fact, a mysterious pomegranate," he replied, holding it up for her to examine. "I found it sitting on my luggage in my bedroom. I don't imagine you arranged for cryptic fruit to be provided."

"No, but I love pomegranates. Very cultural, too," she said, as he put it into her palm and wandered away, exploring. "National Shivadh fruit. Someone was being thoughtful."

"You've got one too," he called from the arched doorway into her bedroom.

"Do you suppose they'd try to poison us?" she asked, laughing as he came back to the sofa with a second pomegranate. He sat down on the ottoman across from her and took his own back, considering both together.

"Well, I've been back and forth to the bar all night and you've had snacks and champagne, it seems fruitless to try and kill us with something as difficult as a pom," he said, and then laughed. "Fruitless!"

She recognized the loopiness of exhaustion in his voice. "You should get some sleep."

"So should we both."

"Agreed, but I still have to dictate my notes," she said, holding up her phone. "And I've had just enough champagne that I should have some water, too."

"Fair enough. You dutiful types," he said, putting one pomegranate aside and taking a little folding knife out of his pocket. "Couldn't be me. Anyway, go on. Your bags are in the bedroom. Talk your notes out while you're getting your pajamas on. I'll fix us a snack."

"Don't hurt yourself," she said, as he started to work the knife into the top of the pomegranate, carefully pivoting the blade around his thumb to slice the rind open.

"Not to fret, done this a million times," he replied. "Go. Sooner you get your notes in, sooner you can sleep. Ofelia said we had nothing tomorrow until ten," he added, rising and going to the little kitchen as she headed for the bedroom.

He worked quietly while she talked to her phone, her voice low enough that he probably couldn't hear more than the rise and fall of her tone. She tried to get down as much as she could from memory as she changed into a pair of sleep pants and a t-shirt, taking the phone with her into the bathroom, washing her makeup off and running a wet comb through her hair. By the time that was finished, she'd covered as much as she could think of. If it was possible to be *more* tired than she had been, she was.

Jerry brought over a plate full of pomegranate sections from the kitchen as she came back into the room; he'd rolled up his sleeves to the elbows and sectioned the fruit so neatly that there was hardly a seed out of place.

She felt a warm swell of affection for him that she didn't often allow herself. Jerry was a good friend, and she'd known as a teenager that she could have all the crush on him she wanted as long as she never did anything about it. Alanna knew how to spot a heartbreak in the making and avoid it. Still, it was nice sometimes to let herself enjoy looking. The affection was banked down low enough it wouldn't harm anyone, including her.

Jerry, oblivious to her private thoughts, set the plate down and went back to the kitchen, returning with a tray that had a carafe of water, two glasses, and a clean but crumpled handkerchief containing some slightly-dented appetizers from the reception, clearly stolen off a tray and stuffed into his pocket. He gave her a cocky grin.

"Take half an hour, come down from all the excitement a

little," he said, offering her a section of pomegranate. "Want to hear all the cool stuff I learned from Ofelia?"

She did, but she also knew this was an excuse to let her be silent; Jerry could fill a room with noise for hours, effortlessly, and mean nothing by any of it. He wouldn't expect her to retain any of it, either, well aware it was nonsense. So she sat on the sofa, sipping water, eating pomegranate seeds and weird little finger sandwiches while he laid out his own evening, which sounded like a lot more fun than hers had been.

"Anyway, my Italian was never great but it is very rusty now, so just as well I pretended I haven't got any," he said, as her eyelids began to seriously droop. "I think I get the gist of most of what's being said, but I couldn't hold an intelligent conversation in Italian. Barely manage that in English," he added.

"Ah, don't say that," she said, and he cocked his head at her.

"Yeah, you're right. I usually keep up with you and Gregory, anyway, so I must do okay," he said, as if he'd genuinely considered it and revised his opinion. "And you look bushed. Go to bed."

"You too? No more mischief?" she asked, standing and accepting a hug and a cheek-kiss.

"Not tonight. I'll be up a little while yet, might unpack. Want me anywhere specific tomorrow?" he asked, gathering the remains of their late-night snack back onto the tray and carrying it to the kitchen.

"No. Well, breakfast. What time is it now?"

"Nearly one," he said, and then, clearly seeing her struggle tiredly with the math, he said, "I can set an alarm for nine."

"Not early enough."

"I won't go earlier than six."

"That's…" she frowned.

"Five hours," he said gently. "How about I come get you at seven-thirty if you aren't up. I can't imagine breakfast will be ready before then anyway."

She nodded, heading for the bedroom. "Night, Jerry."

"Night, Duchessa," he said, and laughed when she threw an obscene gesture over her shoulder at him. She could hear her suite door open and close, and then his own; she thought possibly he slammed it for her benefit, to let her know he was in for the night.

CHAPTER FOUR

ALANNA DID SLEEP that night, if not particularly well. Her bed was softer than she was used to, and the room was so quiet. Her snug little apartment in Fons-Askaz was close enough to the harbor that she was used to coastal noises in the night – waves and the odd creak of boats, the cries of seagulls.

She figured that there was probably somewhere they were meant to go to get breakfast, or that it could be brought to her room, but instead she was up early enough, and Jerry was prompt enough, that they went in search of it. It caused a flurry of excitement in the kitchen when they arrived, but Jerry charmed the head chef with broken Italian and Alanna found herself sitting at a little table at the back of the kitchen, eating brioche and drinking extremely good coffee with Jerry, a companionable little meal for two.

"It's all about twenty degrees off normal, isn't it?" he asked, watching the kitchen staff work as he ruminated. "It's like home but not quite home. Brioche instead of scones, jam from the wrong side of the mountain…" He tapped the side of the little pot of jam with the handle of his knife, where it bore the ducal Galian seal instead of the Shivadh royal arms. "Coffee's all right, though."

"It's just more Italian. The English never made it over the highlands after they took Askazer-Shivadlakia," Alanna said, opening her phone to check her Photogram feed. The palace didn't seem to have burned down without them. Eddie had posted a few more photos from the farewell cruise, including a very sweet selfie he'd taken with her, captioned "Already missing #ladydaskaz," which had lots of well-wishes for her visit to Galia. She suspected either Eddie or the staff had gone through and excised a bunch of negative comments about Galia, its relationship to Askazer-Shivadlakia, and whether or not it was stealing *their* duchess out of spite.

"Do you suppose they could make a brioche scone?" Jerry asked, as she continued to scroll. "Like a cronut, only unbearably European. A scioche. Brione?"

"Isn't that just a currant bun?" she asked absently, trying to get past all the recommended-for-you posts – then stopping and scrolling back up as something caught her eye.

"I suppose it would be. Wouldn't mind that, either. I'll make some requests, I think. I like a good pastry, but I'd like an egg even better. Anything you'd like requested for breakfast tomorrow?" he asked, but Alanna barely heard him. "Al?" he prompted.

"Sorry, I'm – have you looked at Photogram this morning?" she asked.

"Only to post, I had extremely photogenic bedhead. I try not to read my feed before nine anymore. Too much input too early in the morning," he said.

"Very mature of you."

"One does one's best. Why? Gregory post something inflammatory?"

"No, it's the algorithm," she replied. "Now that we're in Galia it's throwing recommendations for Galian Photograms into my feed and they're…strange."

"How so?"

"Well, they reference us, sometimes. More, obviously, right now, but if you scroll back…" she flipped through the accounts, curious. "There's an expression they use. *How Shivadh.*"

"Really," Jerry said, leaning over interestedly to inspect her phone, then getting up and moving his chair around to sit next to her. "How are they using it?"

"Seems to be...I'm not sure, actually. This is like when Gregory was trying to figure out what 'yeet' meant because he thought it was a dance move," Alanna said. Jerry chuckled. "It's not a hashtag, more like a saying that's just been imported to social media. Seems like it's a response to...it's like a specific kind of aesthetic, maybe?"

"Good or bad?" Jerry asked. "Are we the Beautiful People or are we the embarrassing next-door neighbors?"

"Could be value-neutral, or contextual. It seems like it refers to modern things. Maybe like avant-garde," she said. "Like they're saying, if something is progressive, or even just new and shiny, it's Shivadh, but that isn't always a good thing. I've never seen it before. Comms should have briefed me on it if they're aware of it."

"Maybe because we ignore Galia as a rule?" Jerry said, leaning his head on her shoulder, still watching her scroll through Galian Photograms. "What I want to know is how Eddie doesn't know about it."

"Almost all Galian Photograms are in Italian, and he doesn't speak Italian."

"Ah yes. I believe the excuse he gave was *California Public Schools*," Jerry said, amused.

"He's monitoring half the social media in Askazer-Shivadlakia anyway, unfair to make him do Galia as well. Definitely unfair to make him learn Italian when he's already learning Hebrew."

"Is he?" Jerry asked. "He hasn't mentioned that."

"Gregory said he didn't have to convert, but I think he's secretly very pleased he's trying to."

"Those two are going to raise some real weird kids," Jerry said.

"Strange to think about, isn't it?" Alanna asked.

"I suppose. Wonder if the ducal line will end with me like it did for old Tomas," Jerry said.

"Why? You're not a particularly objectionable man like he was, and Shivadh men often have children late in life, especially in the nobility. You're only thirty."

"Yeah, Dad was over fifty when I was born. Still, not being particularly objectionable and actually being marriage material are very different," Jerry said. "I could get married tomorrow if I wanted, but whoever it would be, she'd only want me for my title. Hard to find someone who'd take me on non-titled terms. Anyway, I have hang-ups."

Alanna leaned back and looked at him. "Like weird kinks or something?"

"No – oh, maybe. I don't know what lies in my subconscious, and I refuse to excavate. No, I get hung up on people, and usually for really terrible reasons."

"Huh. How Shivadh," Alanna said to him, and Jerry grinned. "Anyway, this whole Photogram thing is exactly the kind of information we thought we could find and make use of. I'll send a brief to comms and ask them to take a look."

"Ah, and I suspect the Ansevalis are looking for us," Jerry said, leaning back and lifting an arm. Alanna followed his gaze and saw Bruno Sheff in the kitchen doorway, clearly looking for something, probably them. "Bruno! Sheff! Over here!"

"There you are," Bruno said, dodging deftly past hurrying staff members to reach them. "Milo just went to fetch you both for breakfast and found you missing. I said I'd help the search. But I see you shifted for yourselves," he added in amusement, taking in the remains of breakfast strewn across the table.

"The Shivadh palace keeps an informal house," Alanna told him. "But if there's somewhere we ought to be…"

"Well, not ought, exactly, but Milo would like to brief you on the day's agenda, that kind of thing," Bruno said. "Come with me?"

"Do you usually breakfast in the Palazzo Cavallo?" Alanna asked, as he led them out of the kitchen and down a hallway.

"I live here," Bruno said. "Perk of the job – the Palazzo has housing for about half the staff who work in it. There's a dining room we eat in, that's where I'm taking you now – although in future we can have meals brought to your room if you prefer. Duke Tomas ate in his rooms, or in the menagerie patio."

"Someone mentioned that last night – he kept a little zoo?" Alanna said.

"Yes – we put you in a suite that looks out on it. It's very pretty, if…" Bruno considered how to word it. "Old-fashioned," he decided.

"I don't mind eating with the staff," Jerry said. "Seems more useful."

"It would be seen as very democratic of you," Bruno told Alanna. "Whether that's the impression you'd like to give is up to you."

"Seen by whom?" Alanna asked, and Bruno gave her a surprised look.

"Shrewd question. Depends on who you'd like to see you there. If you were to, say, post an image of yourself with the staff to Photogram, the people of Galia would no doubt appreciate your, ah, common touch? In a good way. The consiglieres might feel markedly different – like you weren't respecting the office. That said, very few of them have that sort of nuanced understanding of the younger generation. Or know what Photogram is."

"We'll eat with staff until further notice, but I'd appreciate no Photograms for now," Alanna said.

"I'll make sure it's understood. Most wouldn't anyway; the Palazzo has some stringent rules about photography on-grounds."

"Lord, have I already broken a rule?" Jerry asked.

Bruno's mouth quirked. "I think bedhead selfies are exempt," he said. It occurred to Alanna that it was a little strange an archivist should be aware of what Jerry had posted that morning, but she set that aside for now. Milo had said Bruno was a fan of Eddie's; perhaps that extended to Jerry as well.

The staff dining room wasn't at all the institutional canteen she expected; it was an airy, high-ceilinged affair with tall windows, fitted with decorative grilles on the outside. Inside were a series of round wooden tables and comfortable-looking brocade chairs.

"Ah, you found them," Milo said, rising from his seat. "Thank you, Bruno. Would you let Ofelia know?"

"Already done," Bruno said, waggling his phone. "I'm afraid I can't stay, but it was good to see you again, Duchess Alanna. Duke Gerald, I'm working on those maps," he said to Jerry, and withdrew.

Milo led them to one of the round tables, past a few other staff members who gave them covert curious looks. Alanna noticed Will and Georgie dining at a table near the window and gave them a wave.

"Sorry we slipped our harness," Jerry said, settling in, lightly making their excuses. "We weren't sure where to go. Bruno told us we can eat breakfast here most mornings?"

"Yes, by and large – you can almost always get a meal here, any time of day. There may be one or two breakfasts that local concerns would like you to attend, but we can go over all that," Milo said, turning to Alanna. "Have you eaten? I can wait to review your schedule for the day."

"We ate in the kitchen. By the way," she added, "someone left pomegranates in our rooms last night, do you know anything about that?"

"Oh! Yes, sorry, I arranged that. Didn't remember to tell you."

"As gifts go, a little cryptic," Alanna said, but she gave him a reassuring smile.

"Was it? I know they're a particular Shivadh symbol. I thought it would be a nice touch of home, and maybe a decent snack after the reception."

"He's got us there," Jerry said to Alanna.

"We did appreciate them," she agreed. Milo looked pleased as he opened his folio case and handed them each a printed schedule.

"Ordinarily the council meets from ten to one every day," he said. "Luncheon, then individual meetings and paperwork and such in the afternoon."

"Three more hours with the council this morning sounds excruciating after last night," Alanna said, consulting the agenda. "But it does say here that I'm due for only half an hour today."

"Yes – I agreed with your assessment," Milo said. "The council can carry on without ducal approval for a few weeks, at least, before things start to catch on fire, so you won't be obliged to attend every meeting for the full time. The duke rarely did, after all. This morning is just to familiarize you with the proceedings. We've scheduled a tour of the Palazzo for the morning, and then a driving tour of Levaldi in the afternoon. Some of the younger nobles have asked you to dinner tonight, which should be a lot lower-impact than last night's reception, but you can decline and rebook if you think it's a bit much."

"No, the dinner sounds fine," Alanna said, "but I'm not sure I want two tours today – and I actually…" she took out her phone, consulting it. "I have a list of things I'd like to do and see as well, beginning…"

She trailed off, because Milo had laughed –quietly, clearly trying not to, but all the same. When she glanced at him, he shook his head.

"Apologies, it's only – I think your job for His Majesty in the palace was very similar to my job for His Grace here in the Palazzo," he said. "It's just pleasant and a little funny to find you appreciate the, ah, operations of it all."

She smiled back, pleased he'd recognized that she might be a duchess by birth but was an administrator by trade.

"Now, what's on the agenda you made?" Milo continued.

"Introductions at ten to the council is fine," she said, looking through her notes. "I'd like to meet with the royal genealogist after, if I can – I'll bring Jerry for that, and maybe get some printouts for our legal team, just to confirm that everything's in order."

"Certainly. Bruno can help, he shares an office in the archives."

"And I think we talked about a review of the national budget?"

"That's a little sticky, but I'm working on it," Milo said. "Won't have it ready for you today. The lower you go in a bureaucracy, the tighter people tend to hold on to their paperwork."

"Then let's push the tour of the Palazzo to this afternoon, after lunch. Where is this dinner – here?"

"No, they've booked one of the nicer restaurants in town."

"Oh, perfect, then I can see at least a little bit of Levaldi, and I'll do the official tour some other day."

"Certainly. Anything else?"

"Those were the big priorities. I'd love to see some kind of information on the major industries in Galia, there's not much available online," she said. "Maybe tour some factories or farms or similar."

Milo considered this. "Off the top of my head, it's almost entirely hospitality. Casino, restaurants, hotels, golf courses. We're heavily – perhaps overly, but that's just my opinion – invested in tourism. There's some agriculture, but it's on the outskirts. Not much manufacturing, but I can arrange for you to see what there is."

"What do you think we should be invested in?" Alanna asked. She saw Jerry mouth 'we' to himself as he fiddled with his phone.

"I'd like to see something along the lines of the Shivadh model. More food production in-country for the country, more luxury exports. We couldn't work quite the same way, but there are steps we could take to be less wholly dependent on gambling for our major revenue stream. The money coming into Galia is mainly from casino tourism, and most of it goes right back out again because we have to buy food and goods from outside our borders."

"You've put some thought into this," Alanna said.

"Couldn't avoid it, in my job. And Duke Tomas didn't want to hear it, so I've had a lot of time to refine the pitch," Milo replied.

"There goes that bid for trusted advisor again," she told him, and he shrugged, guilty as charged.

"I'll arrange your new schedule for today and begin setting up a few future meetings based on what you've said," he told her. "Jerry – " He caught himself, shook his head, and smiled. "I mean, Your Grace."

"Ah, Milo," Jerry waved it off. "Unless Brasolin or that other guy – "

"Riva," Milo said knowingly.

"That's the one. Unless they're in the room, Jerry's fine. You've seen me in my underwear at school, I think we can stick with first names."

"Regardless, would you like to be duplicated on Her Grace's schedule, or have one of your own?" Milo asked.

"If you can give me her schedule, a driver who speaks English, and a key to the front door, I'll entertain myself most days," Jerry said. "Although – is there anywhere off-limits around here? I'm a notorious wanderer and I get lost easily."

"Most of the council have offices on the fourth floor," Milo said in measured tones. "They tend to be a little touchy about their privacy, and legally of course could have you arrested for being in an office uninvited – that's a matter of national security."

"Good to know," Jerry said thoughtfully.

"The casino also has very strict security, but they make a

point of having friendly staff, and I'm sure I could arrange a backstage tour, if you'd like one. But if you really want to stay out of trouble I'd simply stay out of the way of the consiglieres. Power in Galia is compressed down into the hands of a very few, but that makes the balance very precarious."

"Ah, yes. Ofelia and I had some discussions about that last night. I appreciate the warning," Jerry said.

"And – importantly, this is for both of you – if you encounter a locked exterior door?" Milo pointed at a door, or what had once been a door, leading out into the courtyard. It had been sealed off with a couple of decorative horizontal bars across it. "Don't try to open it or get around it. If they're locked, they open into the menagerie."

"Well, I think I can handle a few birds, or some roe deer or whatever you keep around here," Jerry said.

Milo studied them both. "Perhaps you should come with me."

He stood, gathering up his paperwork, and led them towards the far end of the dining room.

In one corner, facing outward, was a door that wasn't locked or barred; Milo pushed it open easily, then swung another, slightly heavier door open in the little foyer on the other side. It led into a peculiar sort of outdoor corridor – a long walkway through the grass of the courtyard, hemmed in by thick wrought iron bars that arched over top of them, forming a tunnel. A few birds were perching on the bars, chattering to each other. Most of them took off in flight when Milo passed nearby, or fluttered over to an ornamental birdbath nearby.

"Oh, this is the gazebo you can see from my windows," Alanna said, following him. "I didn't realize there was a walkway to it. It's beautiful ironwork – is it historic?"

"Relatively new, but done in a period style," Milo replied, sounding a little grim. "The menagerie was put in when the duke came to power. He's been augmenting it over the years. There are some roe deer, actually, in the northeastern enclosure," he added to Jerry. "The birds come and go, but there's food and clean water, so they mostly stay. There was a capuchin monkey but he, ah, passed a while ago. Some wild rabbits got in, bred ferociously, and never left, but they're not an enormous concern."

"Why all the bars, then?" Jerry asked, as they reached the gazebo. Milo opened his mouth to reply, but Alanna's soft, sharp intake of breath interrupted them.

Because she had seen the obvious, evident reason for the bars, both on the windows of the ground floor and surrounding them now. A pair of amber eyes gleamed at her from a thatch of tall, waving grass that blocked some of the nearby windows from view.

"Ah. Yes. That would be why," Milo said, following her gaze.

"That's a tiger," Alanna said, hating how high and tense her voice sounded. Jerry tucked the knuckles of his left hand under his nose, cradling his elbow with his right, clearly a stress reaction. "That's a tiger on, like. On a lawn."

"That's Athena," Milo said. "She's very mellow most of the time, and she doesn't like to attack the bars. You're in no danger, as long as you're in here."

"She's massive," Jerry said. "Is it just that we're closer than we'd be in a zoo, or is she unusually enormous?"

"She's Siberian – they're a big breed. Duke Tomas acquired her about fifteen years ago as a cub. Hand-raised her, until he got bored of doing it and hired someone else to. He was very fond of her, though," Milo said. There was something hard and unpleasant in his voice.

"How big is her enclosure?" Jerry asked, processing this with a lot more speed than Alanna. She was still caught in that amber stare. She could see for herself how harmless the tiger was currently – lying on her belly, paws tucked in front of her like a housecat, simply watching them from the shade of the grass. But she could also see those paws were about twice the size of her hands, tipped with wicked claws.

"Not nearly big enough," Milo replied. "But she is the reason you should not go through any locked doors into the courtyard. It's her territory. Here, or on the private patio, she can come to you and that's fine, I suppose, if you want to get up close. Anywhere else in the courtyard, she'd possibly consider you prey. She got over the fence into the roe deer enclosure a few years ago and went straight for the humans feeding them, not the deer. Close call."

"This can't be good for her," Alanna managed.

"It's not great for us, either, I feel," Jerry said.

"No. But the duke was fond of her, or claimed to be, and it's shockingly difficult to rehome a tiger raised by humans," Milo said. They both looked at him. "I wanted to propose sending her to a preserve or at least a better zoo. He wasn't going to listen unless I had a solid plan, and I couldn't ever get that far along. The only people willing to take her were private wildlife parks that weren't any better, and now even a lot of those are closed."

"Poor trapped thing," Alanna murmured.

"She'll try and eat you if you annoy her, so keep your sympathy measured," Milo said. "But yes. It's not ideal."

Athena chose that moment to chuff loudly, a noise between a growl and an indignant huff. Her eyes closed in a long slow blink as she rolled over onto her side, claws raking the air.

"Duke Tomas must have been an extremely unlikable man," Alanna said. She looked at Milo. "He's eternally on my shit list at this point, so don't mince words if you don't want to. I certainly won't be, at least with you and Ofelia."

"I think he was morally bankrupt, not very bright, corrupted by power, and driven by his hungers," Milo said. "I was close enough to his inner circle to have heard the story about the last Shivadh state visit – do you know what happened?"

Alanna nodded.

"The thought of anyone punching the duke in the face is the

kind of thing that keeps you warm at night," Milo said. "You'll find I'm not alone in wanting to shake your uncle's hand. I disliked working for His Grace intensely. But he was never going to leave power, and someone had to be his brakes."

"And that was you?" Jerry asked.

"Me, Ofelia, a few others. Believe it or not, he could have been worse, these last few years. Still no idea why he hired us, given he had to have seen we were working in our best interests, not his, but for whatever reason..." Milo gestured haplessly.

"What about his council?"

"Mostly men like him, if not quite on his level when it comes to being an appalling person. They do not want you here for your liberality of spirit or your progressive ideals," Milo told her.

"Yeah, that's been made clear," she replied.

"And they have a level of power that means you can't just wholesale clear them out and bring new people in. But there are more...aggressive things that could be done, with a strong hand on the wheel. Which is why Galia needs you. Your Grace," he added, as if he'd overstepped his bounds.

Alanna felt a little thrill of sensation run through her – not excitement or pleasure, but not precisely fear. Her objection to being the Duchess of Askaz had always been that it was so pointless – her grandparents paid someone to manage the land, and otherwise did very little for either good or ill. Being the Duchess of the Horse...she didn't care for power, but she did care about fixing things, and there were things here to fix.

"Well," she said briskly, turning away from the tiger and beginning to walk back towards the dining room. "As long as I'm here, I should make a start, whether or not I mean to continue. I'll look into getting her removed from here myself."

"Very good, Your Grace," Milo said. "I'll send you my notes, so you won't duplicate my work."

Jerry's phone beeped, and when he consulted it he frowned.

"Ah, left something in my room," he said. "Listen, I'm going to run up and get that and handle a few things – meet you for the big genealogical summit? Milo, where should I go?"

"I'll send someone for you," Milo said, making a note. "Just be in your suite around ten thirty. About the rest of the menagerie…"

"The water and food for the birds can stay," Alanna said. "I'm fond of birds. We'll deal with the rest of the animals once Athena's been handled."

She wondered, as Jerry ran off and Milo took notes, if this was what Gregory felt like most of the time. There was a certain charm to it.

It would be especially funny, she thought distantly, if she came all this way, only pretending she was considering the throne, and then took it after all.

Bruno was in the office of the royal archives when they arrived; to Jerry's delight, he was leaning back in an office chair, twirling slowly, firing rubber bands at a hook mounted in the ceiling which already held several. When Milo cleared his throat from the doorway, Bruno nearly fell out of the chair.

"Ah!" he managed, righting himself. "Good morning, Your Graces! Happy to see you again so soon."

"Keeping busy, I see," Milo said.

"Composing my mind. A very important part of the research process," Bruno replied.

"Be kind, Milo, the poor man's stuck in here all day," Jerry said, peering around. Unlike the bright, comfortable royal library of Askazer-Shivadlakia, the archives of the Palazzo were in a squat, long, narrow room that buzzed faintly with fluorescent lights. Smelled nice, though, like archives often did, all dust and, what was the stuff? Lignin, the stuff in paper that made old books smell the way they did. A cluster of desks near the entrance spoke to a communal workspace, though Bruno was the only one there. The stacks behind the desks vanished into darkness, but they looked clean and well-organized at least.

"It's hardly a chore," Bruno said with a smile. "Although a brisk walk in the sunshine is occasionally recommended. Milo said you'd like to look over the genealogy," he added to Alanna.

"Just to make sure everything's in order. And I don't know much about my father's people – the duke's people, I suppose – so I wouldn't mind a little tour of his side of the family," she replied.

"Of course. Well, you have a couple of options," Bruno said, "starting with the fact that the royal genealogist is a volunteer position and he decided not to come in today."

Milo rubbed his face. Jerry grinned sidelong at him.

"That said, as long as you don't actually need any specialized research done immediately, I can get you access to the files," Bruno continued. "There are several ornate family trees on paper, there's a book, or we've been working on digitizing the complete tree. We're waiting to connect with a couple of other countries to link our people to theirs, but that shouldn't be a concern for you. I assume if you need to go into your family tree on the Askaz side, you know who to call."

"More or less," Alanna agreed. "If you could give me access to the digital version, I should be fine."

"Let me show you how it works," Bruno said, guiding her to a chair at one of the other desks and pulling his over. "Your Grace, can I help you first, before Her Grace and I dive in?"

"Ah, I'll just wander, if that's okay," Jerry said, gesturing at the stacks. "I mean, not if you think I'll break or nick something, but I promise to keep my hands in my pockets."

Bruno matched his gesture with a smile. "The fragile stuff has been archived; you can't do much damage unless you steal something. If you can find something left worth stealing, you deserve to get away with it."

"Very permissive. Love that in a librarian," Jerry said, and wandered off into the stacks, listening with one ear while Bruno showed Alanna how to move around the digital family tree.

"Do you suppose I've got any hidden cousins or aunts or things?" she asked, and he heard Bruno laugh.

"It's possible, but if so they're not on the tree. Further out than first-cousin? Probably, and those we could find."

"Like who? How would I find that?" she asked.

"There's a macro, actually. The program itself will go up the tree and come back down with your closest relatives, then those further out, and further out."

"Is that how you found me?"

"I didn't find you," Bruno said, still sounding amused. "But you weren't hard to locate – not like we needed the macro. Especially since I've been staring at this thing for months, inputting new names."

"Why new names?"

"Filling in blanks. We're always finding new information. That's why this is here," Bruno said, and Jerry leaned around a shelf, trying to see what he was pointing at. He couldn't see much, and Milo seemed to be watching him, so he ducked back into the shadows.

"See, if you click on Duke Tomas, you get this ghost that shows up," Bruno said. "Well, we call them ghosts. It's a hidden family member you don't see unless you click."

"But that's a child," Alanna said. "I thought the duke didn't have any children."

"He doesn't, that we know of. But the Guard of the Horse was in his office after he died, and they found a letter that mentioned an heir. No name, no gender, no mention of who the heir's mother was. For all we know it was some kind of code or joke, but it hardly matters. We put in a space for an heir, should one pop up, and that lets us put this in…" he clicked something, "which is a list of known female associates of the duke who might have had a child with him."

"He...certainly got around," Alanna said in a measured voice. "My goodness, there's a second page."

"There's a fifth page," Bruno sighed.

"Huh. And nobody's found any other mentions?"

"Not so far, but the duke's got about fifty years of paperwork to go through," Milo said.

"Surely this interferes with my succession, though," Alanna added. There was a silence long enough that Jerry looked out again. Alanna was looking back and forth from Milo to Bruno.

"Even if there is a child, it's out of wedlock, so their claim would compete with yours but not preempt it," Milo said at last. "And we can't delay on the off-chance we come across them someday. You're still the legitimate heir. And you've got the support of the council."

Jerry held his tongue, but only just; it was such a good opening, but Alanna had to be the one to say it —

"Be that as it may, I don't like this," she said. "I don't like even the whisper of an idea that there might be competing heirs. Can something be done about finding them, or disproving their existence?"

Jerry punched the air, just a little, making sure he couldn't be seen doing it. Of course she'd said the right thing; Alanna never failed.

"As of right now, you are the duchess, and your request is reasonable," Bruno said. "If you'd like to make this a priority, we certainly can. As long as I have permission to say it's ducal business."

"Of course. Use what resources you need. In any case, it does seem like everyone's very excited for the idea of me taking over," Alanna said, quieter now.

"And why not?" Jerry asked, emerging again from the shelves. "They saw you ruling Gregory with an iron fist and thought, *we'll have a bit of that.*"

"Jerry, don't make it sound dirty," Alanna said.

"Can't help it; I was born for innuendo. Speaking of, Milo, you really shouldn't have to babysit us. Bruno can keep us entertained. Or I can entertain Bruno," Jerry added. "Al, you're good, aren't you?"

"I'd just like an hour with the genealogy," she said. "Then I'd love to see some of the archives, if you're willing to show me around."

"I'm at your service, Your Graces," Bruno said, nodding at Milo.

"I'll come retrieve you for lunch – if you need me, you know how to reach me," Milo said. Jerry sat in the chair at the desk opposite Bruno's and stretched, preparing to do what he did best: talk absolute nonsense in the most distracting way possible and for extended periods of time, while elsewhere other people got up to the important business.

They didn't really get the chance to confer in private that afternoon; lunch, it turned out, involved Alanna hosting a gathering of the consiglieres' wives, including looking at a suspiciously large number of photos of unmarried sons (and one daughter, which she thought was rather brave of the mother). Jerry cooed over grandchildren, looked at a few unmarried daughters himself, and distracted people whenever she gave him a particularly desperate look.

The tour of the Palazzo Cavallo – complete with a much closer look at the menagerie grounds, which didn't improve with exposure – took up most of the afternoon. They only had about an hour to get ready for the dinner, most of which Alanna spent trying to wash off the crazy of the day. There'd be time for her to discuss the paperwork with Jerry later; she'd already photographed printouts of the family tree and sent them to the group chat, copying Will, the palace lawyer. She emerged from the shower to find Eddie and Gregory had filled her text notifications, texting each other while sitting in the same room. At least it was about the problem at hand, but still.

She hadn't mentioned the mysterious possible child, wanting to see if Bruno would find more about them first.

There were a few likely candidates to take Alanna's place, at least, but they were all Shivadh – when the nobility of Galia had a fall from grace or lost all their money, they tended to jaunt over the highlands, settle in Askazer-Shivadlakia, and become normal, everyday people in the way a noble just couldn't do in Galia. Her father's mother had done exactly that. So had a lot of other Galians loosely related to her father. Those names were fine, possibly useful, and Will was vetting them to make sure none of them were obvious criminals. But none were the bullseye she was hoping to offer.

Then Gregory looped Michaelis into the group text, and the genetic nerdery of the royal family took over. Michaelis was sure he could find someone on the Galian side if he could talk to a genealogist of his acquaintance in Milan.

How do you know a genealogist in Milan? Jerry asked, which must mean he was nearly ready to go.

Mind your business, Michaelis replied. *Shouldn't you be escorting Alanna somewhere?*

She grinned and typed, *He should indeed. I'm ready to go when you are, Jerry.* She turned off her notifications and was on her way to the door when Jerry knocked. "Come in!"

Jerry put his head in. "Ready to be dazzled?"

"Am I ever," she sighed.

He stepped into the room, spreading his arms grandly. He was wearing a deep purple crushed-velvet dinner jacket, over a purple shirt and patterned purple tie. The trousers, at least, were black.

"I call it my 'When in Rome malicious compliance' suit,"

Jerry said. "I'm leaning so hard into Galia that I lean right back out again."

"That's a heavy philosophical statement to put on a crushed velvet dinner jacket," she said, but she took his arm and collected up her purse. Out of habit, she opened it and let him drop his phone in. Half a dozen lost phones in the last decade meant if he was going out with her, his phone went in her purse. He'd tried carrying his own bag for it, but when he did that he just lost the bag as well.

There was a car waiting, with a Galian driver at the wheel. Georgie was leaning against the car, talking to the driver.

"Good evening, Georgiana mine," Jerry called, beaming at her. She smiled back. "Are you coming along?"

"Only if you like," Georgie said. "I cleared the attendees, and the restaurant's fine," she added in an undertone to Alanna.

"I'm sure it's safe," Alanna said. "Take the night."

"Phone's on, though. If you need me, call."

"We'll be home by midnight, Mom," Jerry told her.

"Grounded if you aren't," Georgie replied, and waved them off.

It wasn't a long drive, though the route to the restaurant did take them past the casino. Jerry tilted and twisted his head, trying to take it in as much as possible, while Alanna watched the other side of the street, where a busy public park was full of people out for an evening stroll.

She knew exactly one person in the room when they walked in – Carlo, the son of a count on the council, who'd been at the reception the night before with his father. At least it was a very small crowd, only about eight people, and Carlo introduced them around as they seated themselves at the long, dimly lit dinner table.

At that point it got…slightly surreal. Very surreal, later, but when she considered it, she felt that was probably when it started.

She knew, of course, that Eddie's Davzda cocktail recipes had been put on Photogram, and she knew that he was famous;

she'd been a fan before she'd hired him for Gregory's coronation. But long exposure had converted him from "famous person Eddie Rambler making cocktails for Photogram" to "my best friend's weird boyfriend who occasionally makes terrible drinks." When the servers brought an entire round of Davzda cocktails, clearly based on one of Eddie's early experiments, she shot a confused look at Jerry on her left. He was busy trying not to bump elbows with the woman sitting next to him, who looked like she honestly wouldn't mind bumping more than that.

"Shivadh fashions are en vogue right now," Carlo said, seeing her expression. "Did you not know?"

"We all want to drink what they drink, wear what they wear," one of his friends said, and it was true that she was in the latest style Alanna had seen in all the stores in Fons-Askaz. "Nobody wants to be a stodgy Galian stoic anymore."

"I can't say I've seen much of Galia that I didn't see from a car window, but you have a beautiful city," Alanna replied. "Surely Galia has a lot to offer."

"Maybe," a man who looked like he was probably a less interesting version of Jerry said. "Maybe more, if you become duchess."

"Aren't you going to?" someone asked, and Alanna wasn't sure how to respond to that. She was saved by Jerry, who leaned in and shook his finger at them.

"No peer pressure, friends," he said. "Al's just here to make sure she's the woman for the job. Now, if you really want to know what's fashionable in Askazer-Shivadlakia, I can show you a new drink that's making the rounds, a pomegranate soda…"

"He's very protective of you," Carlo said to her, while Jerry talked at the rest of the table. He'd spent most of the day talking; Alanna hoped he was hydrating.

"Jerry just can't stand not being the center of attention," she told him with a grin. "Very trying, me being up for the duchy."

"He holds court well enough," Carlo said, as food began to

emerge from the kitchen. "All right, everyone," he added to the table at large, "Time to show Her Grace a good meal and then a good time. Dozhine," he said, lifting his glass, and they all toasted and drank.

"This is what they mean when they say *How Shivadh,* I think," Jerry said, leaning in. "I think we are the cool kids, Al."

"Well, what do I do with that information?" Alanna asked.

"Milk it for all it's worth. I plan to," Jerry said, and turned away again to ask his seatmate something.

It was, actually, a nice dinner. Alanna didn't get out to many meals with people her own age that she didn't actively work with. She had friends in Fons-Askaz, but – like her – most of them had pretty intense jobs, and it was rare they could all get together at once. The Galians were a little eager to please but they were also lively people who had a lot of opinions and suggestions, and they seemed to like both her and Jerry not just for what they were but who they were, at least by the time the meal was winding down.

Several of them had taken their drinks out onto the restaurant's terrace after the meal, and a handful were at the bar, which at that point left just her, Jerry, and Carlo, their nominal host and emcee. Jerry announced he was going for a drink, but Carlo said, "I wonder if you'd stay, just a moment."

"Ah, sure," Jerry said, settling back down.

"As much talk as there has been tonight of Shivadh culture, I have to admit, I'm a Galian through and through," Carlo said. "I don't like to waste time and I haven't much sentiment in me, when all's said and done."

"You're a rare bird in the nobility, then," Alanna said with a smile.

"Perhaps. The point is, many people in Galia do want you to take the duchy, and if you did, you'd need connections – a guide, someone who can arrange nights like this," Carlo said. "To make sure you meet the people you ought, and that you're in good company."

"I appreciate that, but Milo – "

"Is a good man to have at your side in a finance meeting or a treaty negotiation," Carlo said. "I'm talking about something deeper."

Alanna steepled her fingers, because she could not believe that she knew what was coming, and also could not believe it was coming. "You'd better be a plain Galian, in that case," she said.

Carlo grinned. "I like that, a plain Galian. Very well. It may come across as hasty, even importunate, but if you do take the duchy, I'd like to be the first to make you an offer of marriage. Obviously a political contract, but I think in time I might be able to charm you sufficiently for more," he added, with the shit-eatingest grin she'd ever seen.

"Can I ask why I'm here?" Jerry said, into the silence that followed.

"I wouldn't dream of proposing a marriage like this without the presence of her chaperone," Carlo said. "You represent all of Askazer-Shivadlakia standing behind her. If you disapproved, the thing would be a non-starter. I know that."

"Ah," Jerry said. "Al, do you have some input on this?"

Alanna tried to decide if she was offended, and came to the conclusion that she wasn't – this big dumb son of a count didn't mean any harm, he just had a practical view of the world and thought she might, as well.

"Carlo, this is honestly one of the nicer things anyone in Galia has done for me since I got here," she said, and Carlo looked pleased. "You put together this whole little soiree just to welcome me and pitch yourself as the guy who can help me out. I appreciate that. But I'm afraid I can't even promise you I'm going to accept the duchy, and if I do, I have to give everyone a fair chance."

Jerry's face, trying to suppress laughter behind solemnity, was priceless.

"Of course I'll keep you in mind. You're a very strong contender. But this will be a long audition process, you know," she continued.

"Very wise of you," Carlo agreed. "You understand my expediency, however."

"Completely. Does you credit. And dinner has been lovely. But as I'm sure you can understand, today's been long and I'd like to consider things a little more. Would it be absolutely a mood killer if we went home?"

"Of course not." He took one of her hands and kissed it. "Especially if it helps keep me in your thoughts. And if you have any desire for another dinner, or a tour of the finest nightlife…"

"You'll be the first person I call," she promised. "Jerry?"

"Yeah, I'll get the car," he said, voice suspiciously strained. "Back in a flash."

He was uncharacteristically silent until the pair of them were in the car, doors closed, on the way back to the Palazzo Cavallo, and then he turned to her and cracked up laughing.

"That was," he said, "the best proposal I've ever been a part of. That was *mental*. Positively medieval in the strictest sense, proposing a business marriage in front of your chaperone. I wanted to ask him for his prospectus. I bet he has one. I bet it's a headshot on the cover and a bunch of impressive financial statements inside."

"Hey Alanna, how did your first day in Galia go?" Alanna asked, in a passable imitation of Greg, which set Jerry howling. "Oh, not bad. We met a tiger. Count Carlo proposed to me."

"Oh, no, when his dad kicks it he'll be Count Carlo." Jerry gasped with laughter. "Make way for Alanna, Duchess of the House Horse, and her consort, Count Carlo. It's a cartoon."

"You should have tried to accept," she said.

"What, accept him on your behalf?"

"No, you should have – "

"Pretended he was proposing to me!" Jerry clutched his chest. "I can't believe I didn't think of that! Next time. Bound to be a next time. I'll start a pool."

"What if Carlo's the one, though?" Alanna asked. "What if he's my soulmate?"

"Stop, I can't breathe," Jerry wheezed. He thumped his chest and then shook himself to calm down. "Hoo, wow. I hope every night in Galia is this fun."

"I don't think I could take this much fun on a regular basis," Alanna replied, and Jerry regarded her from where he had propped himself up in the corner of the seat. "But I do have a job for you as vizier. From now on – I'm serious, no joke – your job is to run off anyone you see trying to propose to me."

"Nothing easier," he said, folding his hands over his chest and relaxing. "Unless you give me some kind of secret signal. If you tug on your earlobe it means *I like the look of this one, let me take him for a spin first.*"

"Yeah, that's fair," she agreed. "Just in case."

"Not to be an elitist monster, but also your grandmother would have kittens if you married a mere count."

"Someday I'm probably going to marry a commoner. I can only hope that doesn't kill her," Alanna said.

"Very respectable in Askazer-Shivadlakia, the nobility marrying commoners," Jerry said. "She'd probably be fine with you marrying a fishmonger or a schoolteacher or something. But it's got to be one or the other. High rank – higher than a count, anyway – or no rank at all."

"Lord, is that what you're getting from your mother?"

"It's what I hear her saying. Not to me directly. I don't think she often considers my love life, which is probably for the best."

"Well, you're a boy. Different standards."

"Yeah, that blows for you, for sure," he said. "But you always say you haven't got time for a husband anyway, so I suppose the poor tailor you could have married will have to marry the baker instead. Would you consider a noble, or is that an automatic disqualifier?"

"I don't automatically disqualify anyone, until they give me reason," she said. "But – you know how it is. We're different."

"Are we?"

"You and me. I work for a living, I'm not part of the party set."

"I am," he said, puzzled.

"Maybe you're in it, but you're not part of it, not the way Count Carlo is. You're the vizier to the king," she said. "I know we all say it's a joke, but Gregory really does value your advice and your presence. There are other peers in Askazer-Shivadlakia, some very highly trained, and he doesn't make any of them come to the official royal events."

"That's just because Eddie likes me."

"Eddie does like you, but Gregory needs you. And me," she said, a little satisfied. Nice to be needed, after all. "So we're special. Well, maybe not special – maybe different. I couldn't marry most of the Shivadh nobility. I'm related to half of them and three-quarters of them are boring. I mean, have *you* ever had a steady girlfriend? One you'd consider settling down with?"

"Haven't been looking for one," he replied. "But I see your point. Do you think," he began, and then pressed his thumb to his lips, as if preventing himself from saying something. "Ah. Do you think Eddie's got a sister who'd have me?"

She laughed. "I do wonder. He has several siblings, one's bound to work for one of us."

"I look forward to meeting them someday. A whole family of Eddie Ramblers would be very entertaining," Jerry said. "Hey, can I get my phone back? I need to send a few texts."

She passed it over and unlocked her own while he tapped away. The group chat about the family tree had been lively while they'd been at dinner. It looked like Jes and the royal librarian had become involved. And, she noted, Michaelis's phone was still autocorrecting "Theophile" – Eddie's real first name, which Michaelis insisted on using – to "trophies". She was pretty sure Eddie had somehow done that to his phone on purpose as a prank.

"Are you texting the chat?" she asked. Jerry had been texting for a while.

"Ah, no, just a pal of mine," he said, looking up briefly. He tipped his head back, arching a little to crack his spine. "Going to sleep well tonight, at least, I hope. Milo send you tomorrow's schedule?"

"Yes, but it starts at ten a.m. again, so I'm not looking at it until breakfast," she said resolutely.

"I do like Galian hours," Jerry yawned. "Nothing nicer than beginning the day halfway through the morning."

It wasn't even that late, but Jerry was definitely crashing by the time they got to their suites; he mumbled a sleepy goodnight at the door and disappeared into his rooms. She sat up for a little while, texting with the group, but the chat status window said he'd turned off notifications.

Jer's in bed early, Eddie said. *For him, at least.*

Tell you about it next time I call. He had a long day of playing decoy for me followed by the best laugh we've had in a while, Alanna replied.

Miss you both, love you both, Gregory sent.

Go to bed, children, Michaelis added, so Alanna did.

CHAPTER FIVE

THE NEXT FEW days did become a little less crowded, or perhaps she became more accustomed to what was expected of her. Milo was still trying to wrestle a budget out of the finance office, and Bruno reported that his people were researching, and sometimes speaking to, the duke's old *amores*, but no children had turned up so far.

Otherwise, Alanna felt that things were going as well as she could expect. In the mornings, she attended the council meetings, though she was asked to leave the room when they were discussing sensitive matters she wouldn't have access to unless she actually took the throne. In the afternoons, she went into town, shopping and exploring, or touring factories and offices. She did get the backstage tour of the casino, where Jerry almost got arrested five separate times for going places he shouldn't and generally enjoyed himself hugely.

And it was pleasant to be out in Galia, because the people *loved* her. Jerry, too. They were starved for a royal they could feel happy about, and the Galian passion for Shivadh culture wasn't confined to Galia's upper classes. Shivadh fashion, Shivadh food – no wonder Galia bought so much of their seafood, with trendy little Shivadh seafood joints on every block. You could go into a gift boutique in Galia and buy posters of Gregory, most of them slightly pixelated prints bootlegged from high-resolution photographs, or vintage posters of Michaelis from the early days of his rule. She couldn't imagine what Duke Tomas must have thought of that, if he knew about it. She knew what Michaelis thought of it, because Jerry wouldn't stop texting him photographs of the old posters and getting endless grumbling in reply.

There were no other dinner offers from eager suitors, but she did meet a lot of the unmarried sons of the council. Ofelia suggested, as a joke, that she should keep a shortlist of contenders. Milo, the kind of brother who leaned into his sibling's madness, started one. As promised, Count Carlo held top position.

On Thursday, with an afternoon that was mercifully empty, she curled up on the sofa of her suite with her laptop and tried to make progress on Project: Rehome Athena.

Milo hadn't been kidding. Alanna had Will working on the legal paperwork they'd need to ship Athena anywhere in the world, but there weren't a lot of places she could go. According to her patchy records, she was not only captive-bred but inbred, as many captive tigers were. They were kept as exotic pets with enough frequency that zoos didn't need to look very far to get one, and didn't want Athena anyway.

It felt weirdly personal. She could see the metaphor, that she and the tiger were both snared by this stupid situation, that Galia and even the Duchy of Askaz were enclosures too small for her, that she wanted meaning they couldn't provide. Well, she couldn't know if Athena craved a deeper, personal satisfaction she couldn't get from being a pet in a courtyard, but if you were going to project emotions onto a tiger, you might as well commit.

Now that she knew to listen for it, at night she sometimes heard Athena chuffing in the grass. It was oddly comforting. And it was still satisfying to work on getting her out of there, even if she wasn't making much headway. It felt like a little slice of her real job, waiting for her back in Askazer-Shivadlakia.

She was just reflecting on this and wondering if she wanted to eat something before dinner when there was a knock at the door, and Jerry's voice – "I have tea!"

"Come in," she called, and Jerry entered with a tray of food and a small teapot set on it.

"Dinner's not until nine tonight, I guess because whoever we're eating with isn't sure his balls are big enough and just had to make us wait an extra two hours for a meal," Jerry said.

"Not like Milo to allow that kind of nonsense," she said, shuffling paperwork and half the contents of her purse to one side on the coffee table.

"Ofelia's going to be there, so I suspect he's more important than first blush," Jerry said. He offered her a plate of crackers with various toppings. "You certainly do settle into a place, don't you?" he asked, sifting through the paperwork idly.

"Casting aspersions on my organizational skills?" Alanna asked.

"Not at all. Complimenting your ability to make yourself at home in strange worlds," he replied. "You've moved in. I still feel like I'm here on tolerance. Any progress from Bruno on the hunt for the missing heir?"

"He's ruled out a lot of names," she said. "He feels there must be a more efficient way to do it."

"Have we tried one of those DNA test things?" Jerry asked. "Upload spit to a database and see what it pushes out?"

"I think they're holding that as a last resort. You need a lot of DNA for it, I guess, and it's very public. Can you imagine what would happen if we uploaded his DNA and a dozen matches popped up?" she asked. "Chaos."

"Still, it'd be efficient. And extremely fun," Jerry added with a grin at her. He sat in the wing-chair at one end of the coffee table and leaned forward to pour the tea. "Anyway. Tomorrow's Friday; I was wondering if you'd given any thought to dinner, or attending shul while we're here."

"I hadn't," Alanna said regretfully. "Do you think we ought?"

"I'm of two minds. On one hand, I like a nice Shabbos dinner, and I'm sure the kitchen would do something passable, but I know your family doesn't really observe," Jerry said. "And shul could be…how to put this."

"Gregory's had to deal with some ugliness as king," Alanna said. "From outside the country, I mean."

"I suppose that's part of it, but also…it doesn't quite feel right, does it?"

"It's not our shul, and we haven't given them any warning," Alanna said. "Galia isn't Askazer-Shivadlakia, either; I'm sure we'd be welcome, but it would draw a lot of attention to the community here. Better not, this week. Maybe next. I would like a quiet dinner, though. Especially because Saturday night – "

"Ugh," Jerry groaned, leaning back, tea cradled in his lap. "That's right, the Eligible Bachelors' Ball."

Technically it was simply a formal reception to invite prominent Galians who weren't on the council; not just the nobility or the politically connected but business owners, wealthy citizens, prominent local figures. As Ofelia had put it over breakfast one morning, it was actually to introduce Alanna to every acceptable marriage prospect between the ages of twenty and fifty.

"I tried very hard to discourage the council," Ofelia had said. "But they're extremely focused on finding someone to tie you off to. Pin you down here, ensure the child's half-Galian, all of that. I imagine this has occurred to you, too."

"What would the council say if I told them I didn't want children?" Alanna had asked. "Not saying I would say that – I wouldn't mind kids, someday – but just to tweak them."

"Have you ever tried to tell a male relative you're not living to give birth?" Ofelia had asked. "Did you get the you'll-change-your-mind head pat?"

She had, from her grandfather. Ofelia had smiled at her expression and spread her hands.

"Better get a nap in on Saturday afternoon," Jerry said, bringing Alanna back to the present. "If I'm going to spend all evening shoving your would-be husbands off you."

"Well, it'll be public and pretty formal. I don't think anyone will get aggressive. Why don't you call up Carlo? I'm sure he'd help," Alanna said. Jerry laughed.

"He probably would. Actually, he'll probably be there. Ah, and Milo's just sent tomorrow's schedule," he said, consulting his phone. "Want the rundown?"

"Please."

"Bruno wants to see us at nine. Apparently he's finally got that map for me. You've got a morning jaunt to the boutique with Ofelia to do final fitting for your dress for the ball on Saturday, and then you're requested to attend the council but only from noon to one – ah, probably because you've got lunch with some of them afterwards."

"Which ones?"

Jerry made a face. "Riva and Brasolin."

"What the fuck," Alanna said, although without particular surprise. Riva was fine – stodgy, conservative, boring, but fine – and Brasolin was obnoxious but intelligent; neither of them seemed to like her much, but both of them did seem to want her on the throne. It was obvious they also didn't like each other, even though they had common interests. She thought both were angling to be her vizier, or whatever the Galian equivalent was, and wouldn't let the other see her alone.

"After lunch, you're booked in with Milo for something called Finance Review, which might be that budget you've been wanting to see," Jerry said. "Ah, and nothing planned for dinner. I think I will ask the kitchen for something a little special, if you're fine with it."

"Yes – a taste of home would be welcome, I think."

"Mm, I'll talk to the chef," Jerry said. He leaned back in the chair, studying her. "How are you holding up? Busy days for you."

She considered the question. "Well, I'm sleeping like the dead now that I've gotten accustomed to the mattress," she said at last. "They are busy days, that's true, but I like the work. I could do without the consiglieres, but if I actually took the job I could bring in fresh blood."

"I wonder. There's a power dynamic I don't think we fully understand. If you punted Brasolin to the curb, what could he do to you? What does he know, and who does he influence?"

"I haven't a clue," Alanna said.

"Me neither, but if he could ruin you it'd be good to know before baiting him. And presumably if you took the job you could find out – have someone prepare dossiers, like the palace research office."

"It does…" She thought about how to say it. "It offers a better understanding of why Gregory keeps the staff he does, I guess. I know why he has me, but I always wondered if he actually absorbed all the research and data and reports that I arrange for him to have. I think he must, though. I certainly am," she added, nodding at the paperwork.

"Better you than me. Sounds exhausting."

"I don't know," she said. "I feel like I'm good at it in the same way Gregory is. It feels satisfying, like putting a jigsaw puzzle together. Being honest, I think I'd be really good at ruling Galia," she said to him. "It'd be slow going the first few years, because the place really hasn't been well governed in ages, but I think I could create change here. And it's easier when you don't have to convince a full-on parliament, like Gregory does. If my word were law? The things I could do."

Jerry laughed. "Don't get corrupted by power."

"That's why I'd have you, to keep me humble," she said.

"Court jester! Gosh, even better than being a vizier," he said, but the amusement in his eyes dimmed.

"Don't want to be my jester?" she asked with a knowing look.

"No, that'd be fun," he said. "I'd ditch Greg for you in a heartbeat. But Galia isn't my home, is more what I was thinking. I'd need either very generous vacation or to be allowed to telecommute. That'd be funny, though. Get a tablet, put it on a little motor scooter, I'll just roll about the halls from my bed in Askazer-Shivadlakia."

"That would certainly take me out of myself," she said with a smile. "All right. It's not going to happen, anyway; we have plenty of names to suggest when I renounce. So right now, I'm going to enjoy these very nice snacks you've brought me, thank you, and keep working on finding a new home for a tiger."

"Want me to go?"

"No, finish your tea at least, and I'd rather you stay. If you haven't got anything to entertain yourself with, I can give you work."

He held up his phone. "All the world in my pocket, I'll be fine. In fact, I'm going to be Alanna to your Gregory and send some important emails," he added.

"Like what?" she asked suspiciously.

"You just do your work," he told her, nose in the air. "Your vizier has machinations to put into motion."

"Emailing the chef to request no pork ribs for Shabbos?"

"Something like that," he agreed with a grin.

Admittedly, she might have told Jerry that she was fine, and that was mostly true, but Friday did put it to something of a trial.

Alanna was accustomed to having to buy dresses for various galas, although Gregory tried to give her as many breaks from the formal events as he could. She did like wearing nice things, it was just... tiresome to always be *made* to. The dress fitting she went to with Ofelia, for her formal gown for the ball, would have been more fun if she didn't know she was going to be auditioning potential spouses all night.

"At least they're the ones in the meat case, not you," Ofelia said philosophically.

"Are you sure about that? I do feel very put on display."

"Yes, but you have the whip hand."

"Kinky," Alanna said before she thought about it, and Ofelia laughed. "Sorry, that was probably inappropriate."

"I like that you feel you can say such things. Milo might be pleased you're a strong political pick – trained, noble born, intelligent, all the rest – but I like that you're a pleasant person," Ofelia said.

"I think that's a compliment?"

"I just mean I think you and I could be friends, and we could both use one."

"Very much the truth," Alanna agreed, as the dressmaker circled around behind her. "Wish you could come to lunch with me today."

"Ah, Brasolin doesn't like me, and you'll have your hands full with Brasolin and Riva disliking each other already."

"What's his reasoning? For not liking you."

Ofelia looked away politely as the dressmaker zipped Alanna out of the dress, and she went to change out of the edifice of engineering that was the bra the dress needed.

"On one level it's as simple as being a woman in politics," Ofelia said, disdain in her voice. "He thinks it isn't their place."

"He likes me, though. As a candidate, if not personally."

"Yes, he does, thankfully," Ofelia agreed. "I think it's also that…he's not fond of me and Milo. You know they call us the Jumped-Up Ansevalis. We have ideas above our natural station."

"I thought you must have some kind of link to the upper class. Milo went to Institut Alpin. You have to be connected to get in there, let alone pay for it."

"Askazer-Shivadlakia has a scholarship program, though, yes?" Ofelia asked. "High-achieving Shivadh students can apply for the king's aid in admission? Milo got in through something similar here."

"Oh, I suppose I hadn't thought of that. I didn't know Milo was there on scholarship."

"Not through the school, no. The state paid for him to attend."

"But not for you?" Alanna asked.

"It's the girl-in-politics problem, but I'm not particularly upset about that. I never wanted to board. Didn't want to leave Galia, and our mother thought it best if I was educated here in any case. I had a scholarship to a very good school as well, just...locally."

Alanna pulled her shirt on. "All right, I'm presentable. Doesn't seem to have hurt your prospects, anyway. Whoever takes the throne, you'll be right there, won't you?"

"I hope so. Without ego, I think Galia needs people like me and Milo."

"I don't disagree," Alanna said. "And we ought to get back so I can go have my unpleasant hour with the council and then my even more unpleasant lunch."

People snapped pictures of them as they left the dressmaker's arm-in-arm; Alanna appreciated the fact that Ofelia tried to shield her, at least a little, with medium success.

"If this keeps up you'll be a fashion idol like I am," she told Ofelia. "Stick with me and you'll go places, baby."

"That's the idea. I'm only in it for the fame," Ofelia replied, amused. "Driver – back to the Palazzo Cavallo, if you would."

Alanna reflected later that Gregory – and Ofelia – would have enjoyed the lunch with Brasolin and Riva. She could see the undercurrents of the conversation, could tell when they were jabbing at each other and at her, and she could ignore the latter. But she didn't like that kind of business, all sly innuendo and nothing productive. She did her best to block it, which she could see frustrated and surprised both of them. She suspected they were as relieved as she was when Bruno came to get her for the finance review.

"A word of advice, if I may," Brasolin said, catching her elbow firmly as she bid them goodbye. Alanna looked down at her arm pointedly, flexing a muscle, and Brasolin let her go. He didn't look apologetic, let alone apologize. "You must understand whatever you see of the budget is not the full story. Galia's economy is an intricate one, and it takes time and depth of knowledge to understand how it functions. Do not be misled by simple columns of numbers."

She resisted the urge to pat his head just to piss him off. "I'll bear that in mind. Admittedly my MBA comes from a French school, not a Galian one, but I do feel Université Paris Dauphine is equally good at imparting a nuanced understanding of columns of numbers."

"Just so we understand each other," Brasolin said. Riva, who was being helped into a jacket by a valet, looked murderous that Brasolin was getting a private moment with her.

"I think we do, thank you," she said. "I really must be going, however. Do have a lovely afternoon, both of you."

Once they were outside in the hallway, on their way to the archives, Bruno shook his head.

"People who have to deal with Brasolin should be issued tasers," he told her. "If he grabs you again, I'd yell *ouch* and jerk away. Or give Duke Gerald permission to object on your behalf. He seems the type who'd challenge someone to a duel over you."

"Much as I'd love to, it's not diplomatic," she told him. "And the more he talks, even if he's giving me a creepy touch, the more I learn."

"He hasn't tried anything ugly with you, has he?"

"No – I think he's the sort to treat a person as a trophy, not as a toy. Fine distinction, but a fortunate one for me."

"Let's see if we can't show you a few interesting columns of numbers," he told her, holding open the door of the archives.

"I'm looking forward to it. You and Milo both wear many hats around here these days," she added, as Milo looked up from pushing two desks together to make a sort of improvised conference table.

"How so?" Milo asked, pulling out a chair for her.

"Well, Bruno here is a historian, seems to do most of the genealogist work, and is helping you present the national budget, such as it is," she said. "And you're social secretary, political advocate, and paperwork wrangler all in one, plus now financial advisor. I also think Ofelia's somewhat overqualified to take me to get a dress fitted, fun as it was. One might accuse you of a conspiracy," she added with a grin.

Milo looked perturbed by the idea, but he looked to Bruno and not to her; Bruno ignored the look and also the implication, which she hadn't meant seriously but which Milo seemed to take as such.

"Like Askazer-Shivadlakia, Galia is small," Bruno said. "I'm sure the Shivadh palace has people like us. Young strivers, or in my case simply people with extensive interests in very boring subjects."

"Like finance?"

"It's similar to history, in some respects. Cross-references, citations, research," Bruno replied.

"In that case, you'd better show me what you found," she said.

It didn't take long to see, first, why staff hadn't wanted to part with the data. Second, she could now see why Brasolin had warned her not to trust in it. The longer Milo and Bruno talked her through it, the worse it looked.

Galia was running at a deficit and had been for years, despite the presence of a massive casino and an uptick in tourism, which Milo thought was overflow from Askazer-Shivadlakia. There was an issue with inflation, not easily solved, and an issue with the hoarding of wealth by the upper class – the consiglieres and their families. Duke Tomas hadn't seemed to give much of a damn, but even if he'd wanted to fix things he'd have been hamstrung by the economic power of the other nobles. He would have needed a fast, large, and discreet infusion of cash to keep Galia going another two or three years without defaulting on loans or stopping payment on civil services. The data wasn't complete, but she didn't see how more information would make it less dire.

"This is what nobody wanted me to see," Alanna said.

"Some of it is speculation," Milo admitted. "We don't know for sure that there isn't a secret Swiss bank account somewhere we could fund Galia on for a decade. And His Grace never seemed troubled by concerns about money."

"An indictment in itself, perhaps," she remarked.

"If you'd like my opinion as a historian," Bruno began. Alanna waved him on. "Some of the senior advisors – probably led by Brasolin – have been setting him up for years. If he hadn't died he would have had to go to the consiglieres for a very large loan. Then they'd control Galia – and the succession. They could still do the same to you. They're aware you could go to the Shivadh government for money, but only if you understand the finance side enough to know you should."

"Just how stupid do they think I am?" she asked.

"Very," Bruno said. "Unfortunately. It's no reflection on you. Most of them just assume you're an inexperienced young woman. Not to flatter you, but they're not accustomed to a noble who is also both intelligent and well-educated."

"The question is what you want to do about it," Milo said. "Seeing all this – it's bad for Galia. On the one hand I wouldn't blame you for turning around and going right back to Askazer-Shivadlakia."

"And on the other?" she asked.

"You could be the woman who saves our country," he said. "For what that's worth. You have the power to right a listing ship with about a million people on it. Not to lay a guilt trip on you."

She rested her forehead on one hand, elbow propped on the desk. "Appealing to my work ethic is a real dick move, Milo."

"Unfortunately I can't appeal to your greed or vanity, like I did with Duke Tomas," Milo said with a small smile.

"I need to think about this," she said. "Not about what it changes, although that too, but about the budget itself. Can you send me the documents, Bruno?"

"Of course. Review at your leisure, you understand the work," he said. "Now that we have certain keywords and codes from these documents, I can start ferreting out others, too, but there's no point unless it's going to be helpful. If you find something you want more information about, do let me know."

"Thank you. Thank you both for your work on this. It must be... frightening, to have uncovered it."

Milo and Bruno exchanged a look.

"It's not great," Bruno said. "But worst case...if we leaked it..."

"Please don't, not yet. Maybe we will have to but – it wouldn't help right now, and people might panic."

"Could Askazer-Shivadlakia help?" Milo asked.

"To an extent. It's a risk I'm not sure Gregory would take, to fully fund what Galia would need. But we could do some kind of structured loan for part of it, or a guarantee of purchase if Galia issued bonds," Alanna said. "Gregory knows other heads of state he could speak to about funding. Whatever happens, we can't let the country founder. I will find a solution for this. Don't let it keep you up at night."

"You should take your own advice," Milo said, rising when she did. "Can I get you anything else?"

"I think I'm just going to take a walk," she said. "Still learning the palace layout. Who knows, maybe I'll find a secret treasure room."

"If you do, call me. I'll show up with a wheelbarrow," Bruno said.

Alanna left them in the archives and took a roundabout way down to the courtyard, following a complicated route to a back set of stairs that had windows looking out on the city – it was stuffy, but the windows appeared to be rusted open, and every time she passed one of the narrow openings she got a whiff of fresh air. And the stairwell, she knew, opened into a hallway that would take her through a mostly unused wing of the building, out to the menagerie garden.

This was clearly where the duke had gone to see Athena. Her enclosure, though small, was grassy and had a pond in it; at one end was a high metal grille in the same style as the gazebo, which blocked Athena off from a patio attached to the building. There was a gate in the grille, with cavorting tigers on it, and a key in the gate; Duke Tomas used to let Athena into the patio to keep him company. Athena saw her at the gate and came over to inspect her. Alanna didn't get too close.

"Another couple of years and he'd have had to sell you off, I imagine," she told Athena, who regarded her with deep amber eyes that gave away very little. "Bet you're an expensive beast to feed. And it's awful to be owned by someone like him, isn't it? Doesn't love you. Definitely hasn't given you the home you should have."

Athena chuffed softly.

"I'm working on it. Try not to maul anyone before I can find you a nice big preserve," she said. Athena, apparently resigned to not getting to come into the patio, flopped down and rolled onto her side. Alanna tapped one of the little tigers in the gate with a hand, like she could comfort Athena through it, and went away again.

As she was heading back towards her own suite, a text message buzzed her phone – Jerry, asking if she was still stuck in finance with Milo and Bruno.

No, just got out, she said. *It's bad news.*

Care to tell me? Come to mine. Or don't, if you want to digest. Dinner in an hour, you can always tell me then.

Be there in a few, she said, and added a tiger emoji on a whim. He messaged back with a roast beef emoji, which was so tasteless that she laughed as she knocked on his door.

"Come in!" he called, though he wasn't visible as she let herself inside. "Just got out of the shower, avert your eyes."

"Were you texting me in the shower?" she asked. "How do you keep the phone dry?"

"I was bored. I do it all the time. Put it on a ledge outside the shower and voice-to-text," Jerry replied. "The places I've texted you from would curl your hair."

The suite was a mirror of hers, with the same wide, no-privacy archway between the sitting room and bedroom. She could see him moving around, towel slung on his narrow hips. She went to the little kitchen to get a drink and give him the privacy to dress.

"I think I'll go casual for dinner tonight, since it's just us. If that's all right with you," he continued.

"That's fine," she agreed, filling a glass at the tap.

"So, your peek at the budget with Milo – is it just scary, or is it Necronomicon-level bad?"

"There are some gaps, but Milo wanted me to see what there was, at least, and I'm glad he did. What I could see was food for thought. It's not good. We might have to bail them out."

"You think Gregory would go for that?"

"Depends on how. It'd be a good thing to do, but none of us are stupid, and Galia's in real trouble. Gregory won't bankrupt us to save them, and he shouldn't have to. Milo and Bruno think Duke Tomas was being set up for a bailout by the consiglieres, who could control him with large loans. Probably high-interest ones."

"What absolute dickheads. The council, I mean, Milo and Bruno are fine," Jerry replied. "How'd lunch go with the chief dickheads, by the way? I'm mostly decent, you can peek."

"It was fine, I guess. Actually sort of validating," she said, turning around to lean on the counter. "Handled myself very well against them, I thought. I don't know that they expected that."

A flash of color caught her eye as she turned; next to the sink, sitting in an empty drinking glass, was a slim cardboard carton – orange, with a white sleeve. She paused, saw him pass the bed with a shirt in his hands, and turned back to the little carton in the glass.

"Of course you did fine with them. Bet you're glad we're done with business for the day, though. I know I am. I am very tired of neckties," Jerry continued, monologuing in muffled tones as he pulled the shirt over his head. "I should have packed sweaters, nothing says casual-formal like a nice sweater, but I thought they'd be too warm…"

She listened without paying attention, reaching out for the carton. Printed in large blue letters on the sleeve were the words *Adderall* and below that, (*Amphetamine*). She opened one end, without even thinking about it. Inside was a half-empty blister pack of pills.

"…don't know if it would be considered gauche to go clothes shopping again, because…" Jerry's voice came back into her ears, closer, as he emerged from the bedroom. He trailed off, and when she looked up from the carton, she saw him watching her.

"Ah," he said, guilt etched on his face.

"Jerry," she said, taking the blister pack out, showing him the empty pockets. He opened his mouth, but didn't speak.

"You brought this across the border?" she asked. He blinked at her. "Party drugs right now, really? Amphetamines? Thought you'd do some intense clubbing?"

"There's," he managed, almost rallying his usual light tone, "…nothing wrong with clubbing. You learn a lot rubbing elbows with the locals. And other parts."

"I know you like to have fun, but this is really dangerous stuff," she said. Her heart was in her throat – this was more than a small problem, if he had to bring this kind of thing with him. "Jerry, this is – are you drinking when you take them? Or is this what you're doing instead of drinking now? Where did you even get – "

She stopped, because she'd looked down at the carton again,

and it had a label stuck on the sleeve on the other side – legal disclaimers, dosage instructions, and the name of the patient prescribed. Gerald ben Eitan Dux Shivadlakia, his legal name.

Mr. Shivadlakia, he'd said, a long time ago, joking about it. *Didn't even have to compete for the title.*

"Who prescribed this for you?" she asked, anger mounting.

Jerry closed his eyes and rubbed his forehead. Alanna waited.

"My therapist," he said.

"Like some kind of pill mill, or – "

"Alanna, my psychiatrist prescribed it," he said, voice terrifyingly loud for a second, an echo of the basso-boom she'd heard from his father Eitan when he was angry. "He prescribed it." He lowered his voice. "For my rampant, previously undiagnosed neurodivergence."

It was the way he said the word that convinced her – the way he half-laughed on *neurodivergence*, stumbling over it as if he wasn't used to saying it out loud. He probably wasn't, she realized. She stared at him, at a loss for words.

"It's not fake," he added, looking down at his hands, flexing in front of him. "And not an excuse to get drugs. Honestly, if I couldn't get illegal drugs without a doctor, what kind of life have I lived – "

"Like – it's really for...?" she managed.

"Yeah," he said, looking back up at her. "Go figure. Fucked up, right?"

"Jerry – I'm so sorry, I just – "

"You and everyone else. It's a natural assumption," he said lightly, like he was talking about the weather and not something heartless she'd just done, assuming he was high when he was *medicated*. "I mean, I'm me. Like you say, the drinking, the partying. Having fun."

"How long...?" she asked.

"Since last year. Right around Gregory's coronation."

"That recently? How? You went to one of the best schools

in the world – "

"Where they are invested in assuring the parents that we're all very normal, and tolerant of misbehaving children," he said, gesturing with one hand. "I went to a school so good they didn't need to diagnose me. They just gave me average grades and graduated me. How can I possibly need medicating? I speak four languages and play polo."

He dropped into a wide wing chair, bending forward to lace his hands over the back of his neck. She came to sit on the edge of the sofa cushion, knees almost touching his.

"How'd you find out?" she asked quietly.

He laughed a little and leaned back, meeting her eye for the first time. "You're not allowed to be mad at me when I tell you. You were the one snooping in my meds."

"The box was on the kitchen counter."

"Forgot to put them away this morning. Ironic, si?" he asked.

"Jerry."

"Fine. How I found out. I was dating a woman, nothing serious. I don't have a pill problem, Alanna, but she did, which no, I didn't know when we started seeing each other. Although it's not like that's to my credit, wouldn't be the first time I've made dumb choices when it comes to women. But I was having a shitty week and not hiding it well. She gave me a pill, said it'd take me out of my head for a little while."

The idea of Jerry having a bad week felt foreign – like he floated through life ignoring all the crap other people had to deal with. Which was probably something he'd cultivated. Alanna realized she was still holding the box, and set it down on the end table.

"It wasn't even this," he said, gesturing at it. "She had Ritalin. I thought hell, why not, maybe it'd help."

"Help with what?"

He shrugged. "Whatever it was that the drinking wasn't helping with anymore? Or the not-drinking, at that point. I'd gone dry that week because I was starting to be concerned, which is a big reason it was such a bad week. But I didn't feel high when I took the pill. I felt weirdly functional. Like I could see clearly for an hour. And I'm not stupid, I knew that was potentially a big problem – I'm given to understand that's also how *cocaine* makes you feel – and it could be dangerous."

He picked up the box and studied it, then got to his feet. "Stay there. I'm not done, I promise, but if I don't put this away while it's literally in my hands, I'm going to forget again."

She nodded, and he kept talking as he walked into the bedroom, stowing it wherever it was normally kept.

"So I did some research," he said, voice raised so she could hear him. "Turns out, the way I felt taking a party drug is the way most people just feel all the time. It's fortunate that I wasn't drinking, actually. It made it more effective, enough for me to notice. That's not how these meds work for some people. Lucky me, I guess."

He returned, dropping back into the chair, legs stretched out.

"I talked to a guy and got some tests done and it turns out that impulsive behavior, alcohol misuse, and poor academic performance are all symptoms of being a useless royal cousin *and* ADHD," he said, folding his hands over his stomach. She could see how forced his relaxed pose was, but now wasn't the time to call him on it. "My therapist says given what I've told him, my mother should get tested, but try talking to her about stuff like that."

"And you didn't tell anyone?" she asked.

"No real reason to," he said. "I'm not active in the government, so it's not impacting policy or endangering Gregory's administration. Haven't got a partner to tell, and it'd only cause problems with my mother. It doesn't affect you guys at all, except I'm more likely to be on time for things and remember birthdays now."

"So Gregory doesn't know."

"No. It felt weird to imagine, you know? Walking into a room and announcing it. And I'd rather everyone think I was unreliable and now I'm improving, than treat me like I'm sick or stupid or something. I'm used to being unreliable."

Alanna got up and went to the chair, poking him to make him scoot over. She slipped into the gap he left and put an arm over his shoulders, leaning her head against his.

"I have never once thought you were stupid," she said. "Silly, maybe, but not stupid. And I don't think you are now. I'm thrilled that you got help you needed and I'm upset you had to do it alone. And, honestly, a little angry at Institut Alpin right now. Mostly mad at myself for yelling at you. I'm sorry."

"I'd have made the same leap to conclusions you did, knowing me. And another school would just have drop-kicked me and I'd have ended up at Eton or something," he said, with a dramatic shudder. She laughed, more because she knew he wanted her to than because it was funny. He was quiet for a while, then turned into her a little, nose brushing hers. "I gotta ask, Al. Are you going to tell Gregory?"

"Of course not. Not my news to tell. But he's not just your cousin, he's your friend, and he cares about you," she said. "If you want me to tell him, so it won't be weird for you, I could. No big deal between you guys that way."

"Yeah, maybe, but that's not your job. No urgency to it, anyway. He and Michaelis both think I'm just trying to turn over a new leaf, and that's mostly the truth. I get so much *done* in a week now," he added, turning away again, body relaxing a little. "Next year the duchy's going to turn a profit on olive oil because I hyper-focused on olives this year."

"Oh, no," she said, realizing what he was saying. "Michaelis has always griped at you about doing better with the estate and staying out of trouble, that must have been – "

"Alanna," he said, gently. "Michaelis sometimes shows he cares by noticing my fuckups, yes, but it's not a big deal. Now I know there's a reason for at least some of them, life finally makes sense. He's even been kind of impressed by me, lately. Fun to take people by surprise. Anyway, I'm *less* angry and sad than I used to be, and I didn't even used to be angry or sad all that often. Please do not be angry and sad on my behalf now. Or if you are, dump it somewhere else, okay?"

She considered this, nodding. "Okay. Fair. But you can tell me when you feel that way, you know. And I'm glad about the stopping..."

"Drinking?" he asked. She nodded. "Yeah. That took a little time to sort out. Not super proud of not handling my champagne better at Gregory's engagement, but I misjudged my tolerance, that's all. Funny story to tell. Did I ever thank you for saving me from drowning?"

"You fell face up in an ornamental fountain," she said.

"Still. Thanks."

She kissed his temple. "Tell me how I can help, when you need it. Otherwise I promise not to let it be weird between us, okay?"

He leaned into her, nodding. "Solid deal. Right now, though, I'm supposed to be helping you," he added, leaning back again. "And more importantly, taking you to dinner."

She knew what it was – a change of subject meant to move them away from something delicate and painful, a sign that he'd had enough and needed to back away. She climbed out of the chair carefully.

"We could have dinner here, if you want," she said, gesturing at the table by the window where she'd eaten a few hasty meals in the past week. "Little more private than being served in the dining room."

He considered this, then shook his head. "Unless you want that, I'd rather go to the dining room."

"No, I don't mind," she said. It was understandable; sometimes you needed a reason to pull yourself together.

"You know, after the finance review I went down to see Athena this afternoon," she added, as he got his shoes on. "I told her she was a very expensive and annoying child. She didn't seem impressed."

"Poor kitty. Nobody loves a spoiled tiger," he replied. "I say we throw the gates open and let her loose. Hell with Cavallo, it's Palazzo Tigre now!"

"As amusing as it might be, it probably wouldn't be very good for Athena in the long run," she said.

"I suppose you're right. Still, it'd keep the annoying consiglieres to a minimum." He held the door for her, following her out. "Let's talk about something happier. I did get out to see the old land today. Very pretty. Galia isn't doing enough with what natural beauty it has left."

She took his elbow, which seemed to please him, and smiled and half-listened to his idle chatter until they reached the dining room.

CHAPTER SIX

ALANNA DIDN'T BACKTRACK to the topic of medication at dinner, for which Jerry was grateful; she didn't seem inclined to ask him anything more about it afterward, either, which was probably kind but possibly also because it sounded like she'd had the longest day ever *before* finding his meds. They were quieter than usual, both of them.

It had been incautious of him to leave the meds on the counter for several reasons, not least that any Galian who didn't like his presence could probably use them against him. At least it had only been Alanna who'd seen them. The way their conversation had gone didn't exactly make him want to tell anyone else, but it did feel good to have someone in his corner that the national health service wasn't paying to be there.

After dinner was over he left Alanna at her suite, probably to go over the budget numbers again. In his own suite he changed into his pajamas and settled on the bed with his phone in his hands. He had plenty of options if he wanted to reach out – he could message the group chat, call his psych, or go next door and tell Alanna he'd like to keep her company after all. She'd let him; Alanna was good like that.

Instead he opened his contacts list, tapped Eddie's name, and hit dial.

"Hey, bud," Eddie answered on the second ring. "How's foreign affairs? You're on speakerphone, by the way."

"Hi, Jerry," he heard Gregory's voice, fainter.

"Hey," he said. "Good to hear you both. Thought I might

get through on your phone easier than on Greg's."

"Good call," Gregory said, closer now. "Business or pleasure?"

"Oh, the pleasure of hearing you boys' dulcet tones, mostly," Jerry said, wondering what to say now that he had them on the phone. "Al's probably going to be up half the night with some spreadsheets. I didn't want to pester her."

"You know, if we have to lose her to another job," Eddie said, "at least it takes a whole country to replace Gregory as her boss."

"It's not even a very good boss," Jerry replied.

"Ah! You don't like Galia?" Gregory asked. "I thought Alanna was enjoying it, at least in part."

"Galia's fine. Galia's government is a hot mess," Jerry said. "Might be something in the water, I feel like a mess myself."

"Oh?" Eddie asked. "Rough day?"

"Not as rough as Al's. More a rough week. I did go to boarding school for years, I know how to be away from home," Jerry said. "But a week here, all I want is to run back over the mountains."

"That sounds about right, actually," Gregory said.

"How do you mean?"

"You were always homesick that first week back at school," Gregory said. "You didn't eat, you moped around."

"Did I?" Jerry asked, trying to recall.

"Don't you remember? Pretty much every year," Gregory said.

"Maybe I didn't know I was doing it."

"Wouldn't surprise me. I used to come sit in your room and share my snack box treats with you, and you just acted like you were humoring a weird little brother."

He did remember that. "Sure. A well-loved weird little brother, but that's definitely how you came across. I thought you wanted to hang out with me because I was cool."

"I did, and you were," Gregory admitted. "But mostly it was that Al and I knew if you weren't eating my snacks you pretty much weren't eating, that first week every year. It was fine, I had fun and you always got past it eventually."

"Blasphemy," Eddie said. "Wish I'd been there. Trash Tower all day every day."

"I do love the Trash Tower," Jerry said wistfully.

"I'll stock up on chicken wings for when you get back."

"Thanks, I'll enjoy it and Al will enjoy being grossed out by it. Anyway, how's the palace? Things ticking over all right?"

"As much as they ever do," Greg agreed.

"Michaelis and Hugo are locked in mortal combat," Eddie added.

"They're having a spat over wine for the wedding," Gregory said.

"The wedding nobody is yet planning and Eddie's probably going to have to cater himself?" Jerry asked, eyebrows drawing together.

"Hugo, in his official capacity as palace sommelier, thinks we should have a Syrah for the reception," Gregory sighed.

"Hugo is out of his mind," Jerry said, beginning to enjoy himself. "Uncle Mike's never going to go for a red. He doesn't like tannins and also liquids that stain clothing. Although there is room here to pick a fight with him over why he's dictating the wine at your wedding when you are a full-on adult. He was barely an adult at his *own* wedding."

"Look, Hugo is a workaholic who only gets to shine when we're throwing big parties, and Dad's retired," Gregory said, but he did sound amused. "If it keeps them busy I'm not going to wade in."

"I am," Eddie said. "I'm a wader. Not that hot on Syrah either."

"Wish I could be there, I'd help," Jerry said.

"I'm going to try to distract them by asking Michaelis to host

Greg's birthday party at the lodge this year," Eddie said. "Then they can argue about new, different inconsequential things."

"What else is life for?" Jerry asked. "Glad we'll be home soon, I miss the chaos."

"Just another week," Gregory agreed. "And you both know to call if you need anything. Personal or royal."

"Yeah, will do. I'll keep you posted. Night, boys. Don't do anything I wouldn't do."

"Too late for that," Eddie said, and Jerry laughed as he hung up.

It was a good reminder that one more week and they'd be home, and everything would go back to a new normal that he'd just been starting to enjoy in the past year. He could figure out the rest of life when he wasn't sharing a wall with a tiger and fending off petty nobility trying to weasel their way into Alanna's good graces.

The petty nobility did keep on coming, and Saturday night got a little out of hand. Not unmanageable, especially compared to most of his twenties, but definitely wilder than he'd anticipated.

He could have planned for it better if he'd thought of it ahead of time, but Jerry knew himself to be the sort of person for whom inspiration strikes at the last possible minute. In this case, it was half a dozen dances into the ball on Saturday, watching Alanna smile politely and suffer through whatever pitches the eligible bachelors were making as they waltzed with her.

It was a nice party, generally. Good food, open bar, decent music for dancing, and company that knew how to make itself pleasant. Alanna looked amazing; Ofelia had picked out a gown in purple and gold, just on the tasteful side of vivid, sleeveless to show off her shoulders and the elegant rise of her throat. The dress accentuated her figure, fitting to the curve of her hips, with the skirt of the gown flaring off to cascade to the floor. She looked, in the best possible way, like an exotic bird meant to be strutting through a jungle somewhere. Jerry was considering paying Ofelia to pick out all of Alanna's dresses from now on.

But it was also difficult, watching people he couldn't even consider competition try to make nice with Alanna. It wasn't like he'd ever been brave enough to suggest himself as an appropriate consort for the Someday Duchess of Askaz, despite her being one of the more significant hang-ups he'd had in recent years, so he was well aware he couldn't think of her as his, even though he wanted to. Watching everyone else suggest themselves as consorts for the Duchess of the Horse was somewhere between absurd and excruciating. She even seemed to enjoy dancing with a few of them.

So he was trying to focus on something else, anything else really, when he ran into Carlo while he was picking up a second mocktail from the bar, the bartender giving him a smile and a wink.

"Your Grace," Carlo said, nodding at him pleasantly. "How are you enjoying the festivities?"

Technically, of course, Carlo being only the son of a count, Jerry was still Your Grace to him; it struck him as funny that a noble elite with a good deal of money like Carlo had to call him by the same title a palace staffer would. Or even funnier – Milo sometimes slipped and called him Jerry even in front of strangers, because they'd known each other at school, but Carlo would have to be given permission for that.

Which also made him wonder if perhaps Carlo was the answer to a question they hadn't been asking.

"Oh, Jerry's fine, you know. I don't stand on ceremony," he said. "It's really Alanna's party. I'm just window dressing in any case."

"Aren't we all? Her world, we're just dancing in it," Carlo said. "But you must at least find it amusing, all this fuss over a friend."

"Honestly, it's always been her world that I'm just dancing in," Jerry said with a grin. "And she's supposed to be flirting with all the men tonight, so I can't even chaperone her properly."

"Tedious for you," Carlo remarked, considering it.

"Yeah, but isn't it all? Much rather have a night on the town, but duty calls."

"Well," Carlo said consideringly, and Jerry glanced at him. "I'm sure in Askazer-Shivadlakia you must have the concept of an after-party."

"In Askazer-Shivadlakia, I *embody* the concept of an after-party," Jerry assured him. "Why, are you planning one?"

"There are enough of the younger set here that I could," Carlo said. "Say we leave in an hour or two, after most of us have had a chance to woo the duchess. You and I and some others could find somewhere a little louder and more interesting to be."

"In that case I'll be here at the bar, getting warmed up," Jerry said. "Come find me when it's time to go."

"I'll just have a few words with a few friends," Carlo agreed. As soon as he was gone, Jerry leaned over to the bartender.

"Whatever I order in front of anyone else, you keep giving me these," he said, pointing at the drink in his hand. "Everyone who serves me tonight gets a bonus if you manage it."

"His Grace is generous," the man observed.

"His Grace needs to leave here sober," Jerry replied.

"Be careful of that one, then," the man told him, nodding at Carlo. "Go out with him and the drinks get a heavy pour."

"I'll bear that in mind and order my own," Jerry replied.

He slipped away from the bar briefly, near the end of a song, and cut in between dances with the universal "I only need a minute" gesture at Alanna's next partner. He leaned in close and put a hand on her waist, as if paying her a compliment.

"I'm about to make trouble," he said.

"Jerry, not here – "

"No, I promise," he told her. "But I've got a line on something and I need to be a little bit visible to do it. Whatever you see here or on Photogram tonight, I promise you two things."

"Okay," she said slowly, leaning back a little to look at him.

"One, I know what I'm doing, and two, I am not drinking," he said.

"Lord," she sighed. "What are you doing?"

"Impressing Count Carlo, ironically," he told her. "That dress looks amazing, by the way. Your boobs are out of this world."

"You're an ass," she said. "But thank you, I thought they looked great."

"Dance your butt off, and don't worry about me," he told her, and then stepped back, gesturing for her next suitor to come up while he went back to monopolizing the bar.

He actually managed to leave the ball pretty quietly when the time came. He'd planned, if necessary, on picking a minor fight with someone and getting thrown out, but Carlo just said, "Hey, time to go," grabbed him, and began towing him calmly towards the door, both of them staggering a little.

"We're leaving in shifts," Carlo said, once they were in the corridor beyond the ballroom, which was significantly cooler and didn't smell like people sweating in formalwear. "We've got time for a cigarette and to have the car brought around before everyone else joins us."

"Hope you've got a ride, I'm not fit to drive," Jerry said, as they walked out onto the front steps. There were several cars, with various drivers and attendants lounging around on them – a few were playing cards on the hood of a BMW, and Jerry kind of wanted to join in, but he made himself accept a cigarette from Carlo and inhale just enough to get it lit, puffing the smoke in his mouth so he wouldn't cough.

"We're not savages," Carlo laughed. A woman in a ball gown joined them, and Jerry offered her his smoke. "Of course we have drivers."

"Should I change?" Jerry asked, indicating his tuxedo. "Should any of us?"

"No. We go out like this, people will know we were at the Palazzo. Very good tables, very strong drinks," Carlo told him.

"Can't hate that," Jerry agreed. "What's the plan?"

"Early yet," Carlo said thoughtfully. "I think karaoke, at least until midnight. Then better dancing than this," he added, nodding in the direction of the ballroom. "Not that I am not still charmed by Her Grace, and I hope my name still tops the list – "

"I've seen the list, it does," Jerry grinned.

"Splendid. But I don't think she loves this any more than we do. Ah! Would she come meet us, once her duties are discharged?"

"I doubt it – she's going to be exhausted. Maybe some other night," Jerry said.

"Perhaps we should make you Duke of the Horse instead," the woman smoking his cigarette suggested. "More stamina than Her Grace."

"I'm just less useful, so I don't spend all my energy doing the work," Jerry told her.

"Leaves plenty for us," she said with a wicked grin.

By the time a pair of limousines pulled up, Carlo had amassed a dozen people for the party, some familiar from the dinner, none without a title of some kind to their or their parents' names. Carlo packed them into the cars with the care of a DJ setting up a night's set. He knew where he was going, too, which Jerry appreciated in a party manager.

The karaoke bar they ended up in was loud, not just with music but with voices raised to be heard above it, and the English of the lyrics and the Italian of everyone else started to grate on his nerves almost immediately. He liked a nightclub; he liked the wall of sound that could shake you out of your body, get you out of your head. He used to need that a lot more than he did now, though, and even then he'd never liked karaoke. It felt too much like a form of ritual humiliation.

Still, this was where Carlo and his friends had dragged him, and they did manage to find a corner booth that was at least mostly shielded from all the…sound.

They'd also all been drinking at the ball, and more in the car, and after an hour in the karaoke bar most of them were hammered. Jerry had learned very recently how uninteresting it was to be sober in a room full of drunk people, but it was also terribly useful.

He stirred his soda water – "Davzda soda, hold the D," he'd said to the bartender, laughed at his own joke, and then tipped extra because they had to put up with him – while he waited for the right moment. Didn't take long; most of them wanted to talk about Alanna anyway. In Italian, which made it a little difficult, but he found if they spoke Italian and he spoke English back, mostly the message got across.

"She's so glamorous," one of the women sighed. "It's internal beauty, you know. Not that she's not pretty! But she obviously doesn't care what anyone thinks of her. Such confidence."

"She's the coolest," another woman agreed. "But His Grace is cool too," she added, leaning against his arm. Her hand kneaded his thigh under the table, and he smiled down at her.

"You never know – if Al stays, I might have to stay too," he said. "At least for a little while, to make sure everything's stable. There's a lot to worry about, big job like this."

"That's the great thing, though," Carlo said. "She worked for the king! She knows what to do."

"Mostly. She can't control everything," Jerry said pensively. Carlo really never could resist rising to a lure, he decided.

"What does she need?" Carlo asked, and then turned away to hiccup discreetly. "What kind of help could be provided?"

"Oh, this and that. Milo's doing a great job – " Jerry broke off, distracted by a snort from Carlo. "What's wrong with Milo?"

"Nothing," Carlo said. "Sister's all right, too. But neither of them, you know, *are* anyone."

"Hard workers, though," Jerry said, determined not to pick a fight with Carlo over Milo and Ofelia when he had more important information to wriggle out of him. "And he's helping Alanna with the big problem."

"Dirty," one of the women put in.

Jerry faked a laugh. "Not a problem like that, and don't go spreading lies," he told her. "No, it's this issue of the duke's other heir."

"Other heir?" Carlo asked, eyebrows rising.

"Sure. Apparently there's some kind of rumor that His Grace had a kid. No evidence of it, nobody's come forward, but it makes us all nervous, you know? What if she does stay in Galia and a year from now some kid pops up? Who gets to keep the throne?"

"That old story," one of the other men waved a hand dismissively. "It's like the. The whatssnames."

Jerry waited patiently, volunteering nothing. Irritating drunk people was the most fun you could have if you weren't drinking yourself.

"The princesses," the man finally managed. "The Russian ones."

"Anastasia!" another said, snapping his fingers. "Yes, it's like that."

Someone new got up on stage to sing and the music changed beat. Jerry resisted the urge to rub his temples.

"It's a dumb old rumor," the man continued. "Just persistent, because people like the idea. Oh yes, old Duke Tomas has an heir somewhere. Very romantic. Even if he did, so what? It's not like they'd be acceptable."

"Why not?" Jerry asked.

"Have to be low born, wouldn't they?" Carlo said. "I mean, your people go in for that, all this lord-marrying-the-milkmaid and such. Can't be having it in Galia. I wouldn't care personally but the council wouldn't allow it."

"Why would they have to be low born?" Jerry asked. "Explain to a poor Shivadh, whose grandfather was an immigrant."

"Your grandfather was a king," a woman said.

"His mother was a foreigner. Greek, married a Shivadh. Anyway, we aren't talking about my parentage – my other grandfather's grandfather owned the land this bar is built on, probably. Why would a duke's by-blow have to be a commoner?"

"You don't get a noble lady pregnant, or if you do she takes care of the problem," Carlo explained. "But the old goat chased the help, and anyone else he could chase. No, if he's got a bastard out there, it's the son of a cook or a chambermaid. At best, some professional woman in Levaldi he set up with an apartment somewhere."

"He kept mistresses that way?" Jerry asked. The woman sitting next to him slid her hand up the inside of his thigh, apparently enjoying all this talk of mistresses, and he gently rested his hand on hers, shifting it to the top of his leg.

"Not many, but when he did, no expense spared, so they say," Carlo told him.

Jerry made a thoughtful noise. Most of the women on Bruno's list had been nobility. He wondered how one would even go about making a list of non-nobles. Start with the staff, he supposed.

Carlo raised a hand, signaling a server. Without even ordering, he received a tray of shots. Jerry tipped a finger over the top of his, and when everyone else leaned back to swallow theirs, he let it pour out over his finger onto the floor, then wiped his hand across his face.

"Did the old man have any particular favorites, do you suppose?" he asked, once everyone had recovered from the shot. "It's wild he managed all that while ruling the country."

"If he did, they can't have been the jealous type. He always had two or three on a string," someone remarked. "Some of the staff at Palazzo Cavallo were there for thirty, forty years, so if they minded they can't have minded too much."

Jerry had his own thoughts about that, but he set them aside and let the conversation happen around him. Nothing much else of use got said, but it did help paint a fuller picture of the duke's proclivities. By the time midnight hit, he was yearning for either a vodka neat, just to numb the senses a little, or an aspirin for the headache.

"Hey," he said, catching Carlo as they made their slow way out of the bar, heading for the first of a likely string of clubs. "I think I'm going to peel off. There's a waitress in there who doesn't know she's about to be swept off her feet by the Duke of Shivadlakia."

Carlo grinned at him. "Well, you gave us an excuse to come out tonight, I won't blame you. Got a way to get home?" he asked, which was actually very thoughtful.

"Oh sure, I'll call my driver. Give everyone my regards."

"Have fun," Carlo said, patted his cheek, and fortunately left.

Jerry about-faced and headed for the back of the bar; he pushed through and into the brightly-lit kitchen, dodged down the length of it, and emerged into the alley behind, which was quiet except for the bass thump from inside. One of the bartenders was standing in the alley, smoking and chatting with someone, and looked alarmed as Jerry leaned against the wall, taking in a few deep breaths of nice, cool fresh air.

"Are you all right, Your Grace?" he asked in English. Jerry blinked at him.

"How do you know who I am?" he asked.

The man gave him a sardonic look. "You're the cousin of the Shivadh king – the fun one. Everyone knows who you are."

"Oh. Thank you, that's very nice of you," Jerry said.

"Are you ill? You don't look well."

"Just stepping out for some air, had a little too much a little too fast," Jerry told him. He took out his phone and texted Georgie, which he probably should have done earlier. *Sorry in advance. Are you awake? I need a pickup.*

"I can bring you water, if you like," the bartender said. "Or something to eat."

"Thank you, but I'm fine," Jerry told him, smiling. Galians, he decided, were mostly decent people once you got past the weird inner layer of nobility the palace surrounded itself with.

"Would you mind a selfie?" the man asked, and Jerry laughed.

"No, of course not," he said, and the man stepped in close, holding up his phone and snapping a picture of them both that did look pretty flattering. "Uh, if you post that anywhere, please say I was the life of the party and not sadly standing in an alley waiting for my ride."

The man nodded agreeably, and Jerry's phone pinged.

Not a problem. Where are you? Bless Georgie.

He sent her a map with a pin-drop in it and went to the mouth of the alley to wait for her. Within ten minutes the car was pulling up; Georgie was at the wheel, Will in the passenger's seat.

"Georgiana, whatever we pay you, it isn't enough," he said, climbing into the back. "I'd kiss you but I absolutely reek."

"Who says I want a kiss from you?" she asked, amused. "Wouldn't say no to a raise, though."

"I'll talk to Gregory. Will, did she drag you along for a reason?"

"Off-chance you were under arrest for something," Will said, turning around to grin at him. "Besides, going in pairs is safer, in case it was a trap. Georgie has a twisty mind."

"Someday one of you is going to be kidnapped, and then you'll be glad I'm so paranoid," she said. "You royals drive me nuts. No security detail, no alarms anywhere in the palace, the King Emeritus just wanders into town whenever he pleases…"

"Not at midnight, Georgie, I'm begging you," Jerry pleaded. "I'm sorry I didn't warn you sooner I'd probably need a ride, but

I didn't know and then I didn't think. Hope I didn't get you out of bed."

"No – your friend Milo saw you leaving. He let us know you might need a ride at some point, so we waited up."

"Very useful, our Ansevalis," Jerry mused. "Back to the Palazzo, if you would."

Georgie nodded and pulled into traffic; she and Will spoke quietly together and left him alone. He closed his eyes and breathed.

"I should tell you," Georgie said, as they pulled through a security gate and back up to the palace, to the kitchen entrance, "the ball's over. Staff said they saw Alanna heading for your room."

"Nasty gossip?" Jerry asked, sitting up sharp.

"Oddly enough, I don't think so. They seem to think you're the older brother," Will said.

"The third wheel," Jerry replied, rolling his eyes, and they both laughed. "Thanks, I'll make sure she sleeps in her own bed tonight."

"I think we'll all be happy to be home soon," Georgie said.

"You don't know the half of it," Jerry agreed. "You can both go to bed. And sleep in tomorrow, for sure. We will."

"Goodnight, Your Grace."

He passed through the kitchen on the way to his suite, lifting a plate of savory pastries left over from the ball and taking them along.

Alanna was asleep on his sofa when he came in. He considered her – cheek on one of the throw pillows, hair in disarray, makeup still on, his robe wrapped around her over the ball gown – and went to wash, so he wouldn't upset her with the smell of him, and also a little so he wouldn't try to hold that picture in his mind for later. She woke as he was damply pulling on some pajamas in the other room.

"Hey, I'm back," he called. "You'll get the worst kind of

cramp sleeping there."

"Sorry, I thought I'd wait up for you," she yawned.

"Sorry I'm so late," he replied, settling next to her. "Do I still smell like desperation, cigarettes, and cheap booze?"

She sniffed him. "No. Why? I thought you said you weren't drinking."

"I wasn't, but I smelled like I was. I had to get Carlo and his entourage loaded. Fortunately they were already on the way, and he paid."

"What exactly were you doing?" she asked. He leaned back, spreading his arms over the back of the sofa.

"I had the idea that – much as we like Ofelia and Milo, much as they know – they work in this life, they weren't born in it," he said. "They don't run with the young nobles, the Bright Young Things. Bruno neither, he's an academic."

"I think that's to their credit."

"So do I, but it means there are things they don't know. Things you or I would know, for example, that say – Jes's kid Noah wouldn't, or Eddie. Not their fault, it's just a class divide that it's hard to get over."

"Oh, fair enough."

"So I thought I'd see if Carlo knew anything about this supposed heir. Maybe there are rumors. Maybe there's someone in their set who claims to be of higher birth than their rank suggests. There's always one asshole in a group like that who tells you a secret, then tells you not to tell anyone, and everyone knows and nobody believes it," Jerry said.

"Find out anything juicy?"

"One thing," Jerry said. "Nobody knows if he has a kid or who it would be, but Carlo insists it has to be the child of someone outside the peerage. Staff in the Palazzo or someone who works in Levaldi. He'd be more cautious with someone in the nobility, and so would they. And I see what he means, as elitist as it is, but I think there's another angle Carlo isn't thinking of."

"I should hope you'd see angles he wouldn't. He didn't strike me as very bright."

"I don't know, he might have depths. I don't strike a lot of people as very bright either," Jerry pointed out. "I think what Carlo's missing is that a woman of the nobility doesn't need a royal heir to maintain her status. But if you are, say, a chambermaid, and you have the duke's child…well, he'd set you up, wouldn't he? He might send you away, but he'd make sure you didn't want to tell anyone. Especially if they were around our age – born in the era of the paternity test."

"Doesn't make our lives easier," Alanna said. "Just widens the pool."

"Yes, but there's somewhere to start. Bruno can look at payroll, see what women on staff might have had an affair with him. I can ask him, if you want," he said, taking his phone out to add it to his notes.

"Thanks," she said. "How'd it go, partying with Carlo's crowd?"

"How do you mean?" he asked.

"You sound exhausted," she said gently. "And you look sad, Jerry."

He studied her. "I am tired," he said. "It was the kind of loud I don't love. Hard to pull my usual tricks when I'm translating Italian in my head half the time." He rubbed the back of his neck. "I'm not sad. I just have a headache, and I'll be glad when we get to go home."

"If you need to go back, you know you can," she said. "I can handle Galia on my own."

"Don't you miss home?" he asked.

"Of course, but we text with Gregory and Eddie all day, and I know we'll be going home soon. And I've got you here," she said.

"And I've got you," he replied. "Anyway, I can handle it, it's only another week. I just miss the palace. I wanted brunch from

Simon this morning. The food here's good but it's not his cooking. Also, Galians will put bacon in literally anything they can fit it into."

"I'm sure you'll be forgiven if you accidentally get a bite of pork," she said.

"It's not that – all right, it's that a little – but mostly it's that bacon is gross," he replied. "It tastes like being downwind of a bonfire. Mleh," he added, showing his tongue.

She laughed. "Fair enough. Anyway, you should get some sleep and I should take this makeup off. This was good work. Much more useful than me dancing with a bunch of men who are only horny for the throne I'm supposed to sit on."

"Oh, did you get to dance with that one lesbian who wants your throne?"

"I did! She's delightful, actually. No aspirations to royalty, just came to make her mother happy," Alanna said. "We're going to have drinks next week. You can come if you promise to behave. For now, go to bed."

"Yes, yes, I'm going," he sighed, pushing himself up off the sofa. "You too. Sleep in tomorrow, if you can. I'll talk to Bruno."

"Leave the poor man alone, it's the weekend," she said.

"Mysterious heirs wait for no weekend," he told her, walking her to the door. "I'm going to have awful karaoke dreams all night. Go get your beauty sleep."

She gave him a hug in the doorway and then walked back to her own suite; he managed to make it to the bed and flop down on it, face-first, but he didn't quite get a pillow under his head before he was asleep.

CHAPTER SEVEN

THE JOKE ABOUT karaoke dreams proved prescient; after the first crash, Jerry woke up around two am and from there onward didn't get a full solid hour, but also didn't feel awake enough to get up and do anything about it. He just roamed around in the bed, with various snatches of pop music stuck in his head, until he startled awake one last time around eight and gave up, fumbling for the bedside buzzer he hadn't used since they'd arrived.

"Yes, Your Grace?" came a tinny voice.

"Please save my life, bring me coffee," he mumbled.

"Of course, Your Grace," was the reply, and a few minutes later, while he was sitting up on the edge of the bed and trying to determine how well he could stand, there was a knock at the door.

"Come in," he called, and one of the staff entered with a tray – a carafe of coffee, cream and sugar, plus a plate under a domed cover.

"In bed, Your Grace, or in the sitting room?" she called.

"Ah. Sitting room," he said, staggering upright. She set the tray on the table by the window and began unloading it, pouring the coffee, adding cream and a spoonful of muscovado sugar, just how he liked it.

"You are a delight," he told her, and she smiled.

"Our pleasure, Your Grace. I took the liberty of bringing up breakfast, as well," she said, unveiling the plate. Underneath were eggs, toast, and fried potatoes, unusual for Galia; next to it, he noticed, was a little bowl of ice chips with a smaller bowl of fruit salad in it. The general Galian breakfast was pastries-and-fend-for-yourself.

"What did I do to deserve all this?" he asked, beaming at her.

"Chef likes you," she replied. "And we're all very pleased you've taken so well to Galia. We hope maybe when Her Grace is invested as duchess, you'll consider visiting often."

"And how do you know I love Galia so much?" he asked, plucking up the fruit salad and stuffing his mouth with apples.

"You should look yourself up on Photogram this morning," she replied. "Will that be all, Your Grace?"

"Yes, thank you, and please send my thanks to the chef," he said. "I'll leave the tray outside when I'm done."

She gave him a bow and left, and Jerry pulled out his phone.

His hashtag was pretty busy even at the quietest of times; not Hollywood Celebrity busy, but he got out and about, even once he'd left off the more frequent partying, and people were always taking pictures. Eddie posted up a lot of pictures of him too, though he always checked in first. This morning, however, it was party city.

Jerry's exciting night at karaoke was laid out in all its glory from evening well into the wee hours, with exclamations of *partying like a Galian!* and plenty of admiring comments, mostly in Italian. Like once he'd gone out drinking, they could claim him. And yes, there was the photo taken in the alley with the bartender. He hoped his bartender friend got some real street cred out of that.

Someone had also snapped the moment he'd put his hand on the excitable young woman's, under the table, and moved it from crotch to leg – but they'd caught it before he'd moved it, so it did look like he was having an excessively good time at karaoke. He sent that one to the group chat with *I swear I was just removing her hand* and dug into his eggs.

I'm telling Michaelis, Eddie replied.

What are you, a cop? Jerry asked.

You all realize I'm still receiving these messages, Michaelis texted. Jerry double checked and, sure enough, he'd messaged the genealogy chat by mistake.

I would very much like to be removed but I don't know how, Michaelis continued. Jerry had a suspicion that Michaelis knew how to do a lot more on his phone than he pretended, but he'd never been able to prove it. Before he could reply, Jes chimed in.

Kind of like Jerry and the young lady's hand.

Jerry pressed the edge of the phone to his forehead and closed his eyes. It buzzed, rattling his teeth.

Be nice, he did me a favor last night, Alanna said.

He was still typing out *Thank you, at least someone vindicates me* when she texted a second time.

And I see the evening had a happy ending.

Jerry set his phone face-down on the table and ignored the cackling series of texts that followed.

Once he'd finished breakfast and was feeling fully awake, he spent the morning working his way down his to-do list. Over the past few days he'd thrown notes in there at random, which he now had to puzzle out and deal with, along with the recurring action items like answering his email. The email itself ate up a significant portion of the morning, but at least the urgent stuff got taken care of. He had a handwritten letter from his mother, too, which he replied to using some stationery he found in a search of various drawers. At least he could just put that out with the breakfast tray and a note reading *Please stamp and mail*. He wasn't sure he was up to trying to find a post office.

Alanna had lunch with Milo listed on her calendar for eleven-thirty, and he technically wasn't on the invite, but he didn't figure they'd mind if he sat in. With the five-minute warning going off on the calendar, he slipped out of his suite and knocked on Alanna's door, pushing it open when she called for him to enter.

"Oh! Hey, sorry, I was expecting Milo," she said, looking up from where she was settled in a wing chair with her computer. "How'd you sleep?"

"Poorly, but I also got roasted by everyone I know on group chat this morning, so life's going great," he said, smiling to take the sting out. "Hope at least one of us slept well."

"I've still got dents in me from that ball gown, but otherwise I'm doing all right," she said. "You know, I'm glad you didn't, but you could have gone home with that girl, if you wanted."

"I can't explain to you how much I didn't want to," he said. "Besides, going home with her would have meant two, probably three hours of going out with her, first."

"Anyway, Galia adores you, and if you want a nightcap tonight you could probably have your pick," she said. Jerry was trying to decide how best to reply to that when there was a knock on the still-open door to the suite, and Milo arrived.

Jerry had seen him, so far, only in formal clothing for state affairs or in the slightly rumpled suits of a royal functionary; he'd apparently broken out something special for lunch, charcoal dress slacks and a soft knit sweater-vest over a dress shirt, all of which made Jerry narrow his eyes. He knew that outfit. He'd worn that outfit on first dates.

"Your Graces," Milo said with a small smile, but he looked as perplexed to see Jerry as Jerry was, very suddenly, annoyed to see him. "You've had a pleasant morning, I hope. You're a big hit with the karaoke crowd," he added to Jerry. "Though nobody seems to have video of you singing."

"Couldn't find my signature song," Jerry replied.

"I'm sure if you make a request, every bar in Galia will leap to obey," Milo replied, and turned to Alanna. "Ready for lunch, or do you need a few minutes?"

"Mostly, but I suspect we're not staying in the Palazzo," she said, gesturing at his outfit. Jerry realized Alanna looked very nice too, in a simple, pretty sundress that showed off her shoulders, and began to wonder if he *actually was* the third wheel Georgie had joked about.

"I thought you might like some fresh air after last night," he told her. "There's a park that cuts through the city, the grand promenade, and a stroll around it would be nice. Very good restaurant at the northern end – authentic Galian fare, lots of fresh fruit and good bread."

"Huh," Jerry said, hearing himself and a little bit hating himself, but doing it anyway, because he saw where this was going. "Sounds delicious. When do we leave?"

Alanna and Milo were both watching Jerry with something between suspicion and annoyance.

"Ah," Milo said, glancing between them. Jerry just kept smiling. "As much as I'd love to show you both the grand promenade – this is awkward – I had intended it as a date."

Alanna's expression at Milo flat-out saying it would have been funny if Jerry wasn't standing slightly outside of his body, watching himself do something terrible.

"That is awkward," Jerry agreed. "I know that, Milo. I was trying to be subtle as well."

"About what?" Milo asked.

"Preventing it. Look, I like you, and I'm sure Alanna does too," Jerry said. "But you can't think you'd be an appropriate marriage if she does stay in Galia."

Milo seemed dumbstruck by this. Alanna, however, had rarely been dumbstruck in her life.

"*Excuse* me?" she said.

"Well, we are being political, aren't we? And this is why you brought me, you know," Jerry said, talking faster so she'd have less space in which to interrupt. "I can't advise it, Alanna. You know they call him and Ofelia the Jumped-Up Ansevalis. It's an awful name!" he said, holding up a hand to stop Milo from talking. The funny thing was, it worked; Gregory used to joke that the Dukes of Shivadlakia bred for charisma, but there was something to the idea of eleven generations of imperious, grasping egotists producing Gerald ben Eitan, who struggled with basic math but could shut up a room simply by holding up a hand.

"It's an awful name," he repeated. "But I'm telling you this, which is nothing you didn't know, because it's a sign of what would happen. If Alanna stays here, she's got to marry someone with real status and power and Milo, that's simply not you."

"You," Alanna said, her tone icy, "are advising me on policy, Jerry, not on my love life."

"Unhappily, this is both," Jerry said, shoving his hands in his pockets. "The Duchess of the Horse cannot marry a palace administrator. Back home? Perhaps. Our king's marrying a cook."

He overplayed it there, and saw it. Alanna's whole expression changed to one of confusion.

"In any case, here, she's going to need at least a count, and hopefully someone a little brighter than Count Carlo," he finished. "She can't waste time pretending she could be with you in anything other than an adulterous situation."

Milo's mouth was open, eyes darting back and forth between them.

Alanna stood and shot Jerry a glare, going to Milo and taking his hands in hers.

"Milo, I'm sorry. Jerry is being insufferable and he does not speak for me," she said, and Jerry finally located his ability to shut the hell up. "I said yes when you asked because I'd like to go out with you. I'd love to go to the promenade. But right now it's clear that Jerry and I need to discuss some of the finer points of protocol he just violated, and that may be a long discussion. We're all tired after the ball last night, too. So I'd like you," she said, bouncing their hands together a little for emphasis, "to give me some time. We'll talk about this at breakfast tomorrow, and I'll take a promise of a future trip to the promenade this coming week, if you would do me the honor."

Milo bowed lightly over their hands. "As the duchess likes," he said, without a tremble in his voice, and Jerry had to respect him for that one, because if someone had done to him what he'd just done to Milo, he'd be *livid*. "Your Grace," he added to Jerry, and if there wasn't a tremble, there was a lot of venom.

They were silent until the door clicked shut after him, and then Alanna said, "Went too far with that crack about Eddie."

"Oh, is that where I went too far?" Jerry asked lightly, wondering if he could still get out of this.

"You towering asshole," Alanna said, so probably not.

When Jerry opened his mouth about Milo, she'd wanted to punch him. When she heard what he was saying, she'd wanted to murder him for a hot, angry second. Until he called Eddie a cook, and then she knew something else, something darker and weirder, was at play here.

Because yes, Eddie was technically a cook, but he was actually called a chef, a title he'd earned, and both of them knew it. Jerry had been in the room at least twice when Gregory had gotten mad at gossip blogs for calling Eddie a cook. Jerry knew better and respected Eddie too much to insult him so offhandedly. And Jerry, who had grown up in the nobility and gone to an elite boarding school and spent a decade with the party crowd, absolutely knew how to find the tender places and jab a blade into them.

Jerry wasn't a bully, but he knew how to act like one, and he would bully anyone threatening her – but he had zero reason to do that to Milo.

"You towering asshole," she said, turning to fully face him. He was pale, arms at his sides, not nearly as casual as he was pretending. "Why the hell did you do that? He asked me out!"

"Yeah, exactly," he replied. "You're not staying here, Alanna, and if you did you couldn't – "

"That's beside the point and you know it. So what if I'm not staying here? That doesn't mean I can't date someone from Galia!"

"You think he'd leave Galia and come running across the highlands to be with you?" Jerry asked scornfully.

"I'd like half a minute to find out. He wanted a first date, Jerry, he wasn't asking for the throne."

"Good, because he's not getting either."

"Go fuck yourself," Alanna said. "You don't decide that. Even if it's a matter of *policy*, you don't choose who I go out with, and you don't get to make assumptions about Milo's pretensions to rule."

"Oh, for the love of – I didn't run him off because I think he wants the throne, of course he doesn't want the throne, have you met him?" Jerry said. "What he wants, apparently, is you."

"Even better," she snapped. He looked like he'd been slapped. "Do you know how many people want me for me, Jerry? You're in the same messed-up boat and you know what we deal with! You've said it yourself, nobody's taking you on non-titled terms. You're being – you're being so stupid about this I feel like it has to be intentional."

"Intentional that I don't want someone else asking you out? Of course it's intentional!" he threw his arms in the air, frustrated.

She opened her mouth and then caught herself. Something about what he'd said –

"Someone else?" she asked.

"What?" Jerry yelled.

"Don't yell at me, that doesn't scare me," she retorted. He at least looked a little abashed at that. "You said, 'someone else.' You don't want *someone else* asking me out," she repeated.

"Yes?" His voice was quieter now, but he still seemed confused.

"Wait, just…" she rubbed her forehead. "If Milo isn't a fortune-hunter, if he's just a guy who likes me and wanted to take me to a nice lunch, and you couldn't let that happen…why not,

Jerry?"

A muscle jumped in his jaw. Gregory did the same thing when he was preparing to lie – usually to himself. Michaelis did it too, although he had better control over it. It was a very subtle tell, one most people didn't notice. Jes did, but Alanna'd had to explain it to Eddie.

"Okay," Jerry said finally. "You know what, you're right, that was – that was shitty of me," he added, clearly working hard to get the words out. To his credit, he sounded sincere. "That was a real asshole thing I did just now. Milo didn't deserve it just because he clearly sees how great you are, and it was way over a line with you. I'm not the duke of your social life. I'm sorry."

It was a little startling, and it almost put her off the line of thought she'd been following. None of the royal family liked to admit when they were wrong, and for him to do that without trying to misdirect or put off taking blame meant something else was going on.

"But why did you do it?" she asked. "If it was such an asshole thing to do, Jerry…"

He ran a hand up into his hair, letting it rest on top of his head. He closed his eyes. "Because I didn't want him going out with you, but it's not up to me," he said. "Fuck, this isn't how I wanted to do this."

"Do what?" she asked.

"Nothing," he said, muscle jumping in his jaw again. "It's fine."

"Jerry – "

"Sorry," he repeated, lowering his hand. "I'll talk to Milo, I'll apologize and tell him I was out of line. I will fix it."

"I think what's happening right here and now is way more important to fix," she said slowly. "But I don't actually understand what's happening."

"I'm being a dickhead," he said, voice careless. "Still happens sometimes, unfortunately."

"Impulsivity problems?" she asked, trying to match his light tone.

"I'm trying to take responsibility for my actions, so yes, but also no." He gave her a tired grin. "Look, here's what's happening. I overstepped and you called me on it, which you are extremely good at doing. You were right to do it, and I'm sorry. So as long as you accept my apology, or at least let me work towards making it up to you, we're fine."

"Okay." She took a breath in, exhaled. "I do accept your apology as long as you give Milo one as well. So we can hug now, right?"

He laughed. "Is that what you want?"

"Yeah," she said, going to him, and he folded her into himself the way he always did, warm and familiar. She leaned back just a little so she could rest her forehead against his.

"Now stop lying," she said quietly. His entire body tensed.

"For fuck's sake, Al," he finally said, voice as quiet as hers. "For someone who's so relentless, you are absolutely oblivious about what you're even chasing. You're making this worse than it has to be."

"Why?"

"Because I'm in love with you," he said. It was a shock hearing him say it, even if she'd been hearing him carefully not say it for the last five minutes. "You are the person I'm hung up on. And that makes it so much worse. I don't own you, I don't have any claim on you at all, and I ran Milo off because I was jealous and worried you'd like him more than you like me. *What* an asshole."

It was difficult to catch her breath, and her throat had tightened too much to speak. He began to disengage slowly – leaned his head back, loosened his arms around her shoulders.

She swayed forward and kissed him, a little off-kilter but hard enough he jerked forward into it instead of slipping away. He caught her head in his hands and leaned in for a few intense seconds before he pushed gently, and she let him escape for the moment.

"Al," he said softly, eyes on her face, like he was looking for something specific. "Do not do this to make anyone but yourself happy. I'm dealing with this, you don't have to – you don't owe me anything."

"You know, Michaelis says," she started, and then had to swallow. "He says you and Gregory do this."

"Do what?" he asked, genuine confusion on his face.

"You treat me like I don't always do exactly as I please regardless of your opinion," she said. "Have you ever seen me kiss anyone I didn't want to kiss?"

"Well, I haven't been there for all of them," he managed. She hooked two fingers in the collar of his shirt, knuckles pressed up against his neck. She could feel his pulse thud against her skin.

"Do you think I would hurt you?" she asked. "Lie to you just to make you happy this briefly?"

"No," he admitted, and let her kiss him again. "No, I – I'm just..." He waited until she was done kissing him, "...not used to getting what I want this easily. Not when it's important like this. And especially not when I've just been a towering asshole."

"This has absolutely not been easy in any way," she told him. She kissed him again and started using her fingers at his collar to work the button free.

"Ah, I don't..." he started, and then she could almost hear it happen – somewhere in his mind, a loose gear clicked into place. His whole body relaxed against hers, one hand sliding around to cup the back of her neck, the other dropping to her waist to hold her against him. "I could be easy," he said.

"Could be cheesy," she retorted. He laughed.

"Sure, that too. Um, say the word and I can stop," he added, "but otherwise I would love to make the last ten minutes up to you and then prove a couple of points in my favor."

"Yeah, kinda counting on that," she agreed, and let him pull her slowly towards the bedroom of the suite.

It was a roar that woke her, late that afternoon. The sun was moving towards the horizon, and sometimes in the early sunset hours Athena would feel compelled to roar, for whatever reason – maybe calling out to see if she could hear another tiger, maybe at the lengthening shadows, or maybe just because she was waking up after sleeping most of the day.

Alanna stretched a little, slowly, conscious that there was another body in the bed; she didn't want to risk waking him yet. He was lying on his stomach, face mostly concealed by the pillow it was pressed into. His left arm was flung over her waist, hand curved into the blanket.

The signet ring of the duchy of Shivadlakia, the only jewelry he wore, was heavy and loose on his index finger, and had slipped around so the seal hung inward. It wasn't like the City of Gold he'd loaned her, a pretty ring with a bad fit – he'd had the ring sized to his index finger when he inherited it after his father died, and he wore it constantly enough that it should sit properly. He must have lost weight, and he didn't have a lot to spare.

She turned carefully onto her side, facing his hand and the ring. He shifted, turning as well, arm curling inward to pull her close from behind. The soft breaths behind her told her he'd done it unconsciously.

If he'd found out around the time of Gregory's coronation, then he'd been dealing with this for a year. He looked all right, even out of his clothes, not especially starved or frail. He looked great out of his clothes, actually, but she saved that for later consideration. All taken together, maybe he was healthier now. He'd stopped drinking, he said. He'd certainly started showing up to palace breakfast looking less rough, but she wasn't sure when.

He'd had some drinks since, at least –

Although, honestly, it would explain the drink he'd had on the yacht at their going-away party. It had been something pre-mixed, with fruit in it – but that didn't mean there was alcohol, too. It might have been orange juice for all she knew. And at the anniversary ball, he'd had what looked like a cocktail when they were only serving wine. Until the proposal, when the champagne was poured.

Thinking on it, she could pick out a dozen times she'd seen him with a drink she had assumed was alcoholic. Always mixed drinks, never wine or beer. Even in Galia, she didn't know what was in his glasses.

She twined her fingers in his, fiddling the ring into its proper place, and lifted his hand to kiss his fingertips. This time he did wake, but with a kind of slow calm that said he knew he was somewhere safe.

"Wha'sat for?" he asked, throat raspy from sleep.

"Gold star for overachieving," she said.

"First time for everything," he mumbled into the nape of her neck. Then, a little more alertly, "Of course, never leave the lady wanting."

"That too. But I was thinking about your little game with the cocktails," she said, rolling over to face him. His eyes opened a fraction wider than they had been, curious. "You've been drinking juice for months."

"Yeah, more or less," he agreed, hand coming to rest on the nape of her neck, his arm curved around her shoulder blade. "Told you I was handling the drinking better, shouldn't be a shock."

"Bribing bartenders?"

"Tipping bartenders. They don't care what they make me. At this point, at least in the Shivadh palace, they bring me the soft stuff automatically. The bartenders here all know my drink now too, but I still get the odd glass of wine handed to me."

"What's your poison?"

"It's called a Gunner. Lemonade and ginger ale, mostly. Easier to make than a lot of cocktails, tastes fine, looks nice."

"Seems like a lot of work for you, though, always trying to get a mocktail on the sly. You could just say you're off alcohol. You know none of us would hassle you about it."

He laughed quietly. "I suppose, but that's hardly *fun*. I like pulling a fast one for the sake of it. I like cocktails, even the mock ones. The lack of alcohol doesn't impact the aesthetic. I like fruit juice, too."

"That's a point. You must be getting lots of vitamins."

"Every party's a smoothie," he agreed, yawning.

"Your ring is loose, though," she said, turning it on his finger, one way and then the other. "You're okay, right? Healthwise?"

"Yep. Fewer drunken 3am kebabs and more horrible morning runs with Greg, that's all," he said. "Nothing to worry about, promise."

"So how long has it been?" she asked.

"Since what, I started running with Greg? Feels like a damn eternity, I assure you."

"Since you got sober," she said, smiling to soften the harshness of the question.

"I'm not," he said. "I mean, not the way you're thinking. I didn't join a group or decide on abstinence or anything. I still have a drink now and again. But not very often, and not very much. When you're no longer frantically self-medicating, it gets easier. At least, for me."

"That makes sense, I suppose," she said.

"Thank you. But to answer what I think you're actually asking, I got on meds about ten months ago. That's when the self-destructing stopped. Hard month between stopping drinking so the drugs could work and getting the dosage right, but I got through it."

"And none of us noticed."

"Yeah, but that was on purpose," Jerry said. "I made myself scarce. It was right around the time Jes and Noah moved into the lodge, so Uncle Mike was…"

"Distracted," Alanna suggested.

"Yeah. You and Gregory were still figuring out how to run the palace in practice. Eddie was very new. Easy to disappear for a while, especially since we could text, so it didn't even feel like I wasn't around. Actually pretty great timing, though I say it myself."

"This will be the last time I say this, I promise," Alanna said, "but I wish you'd told me."

"I know, dear heart," Jerry said, nosing into her shoulder, kissing it before pulling back again. His voice had a certain tone to it, like the pet name was a little daring of him, like he wasn't sure even now that he was allowed. "Maybe I should have. But sometimes you gotta grow up on your own. I knew that if I came to you and asked for help, I'd get it. It wasn't about not trusting you. It was about whether or not I could stand on my own for a little while. And all of this is awesome pillow talk," he sighed.

"I like that name," she said, uncertain how to respond to the rest of it, wanting to reward him for the endearment in any case.

"What name? Dear heart?" he asked.

"Yeah."

"You would always have been dear to me. Even if we never…" He gestured between them. "Like, love has many floors to it, and I've been on this landing between the two of them, with you. But the foundation doesn't disappear just because you climb the stairs. On the other hand, if you never go upstairs, it's still there. Just…empty, for now."

"Very poetic."

"Comes naturally to Shivadh men," he said with a grin. She smiled back. "I didn't do any of this specifically for you, but the last couple of months I've felt like I could deserve you, and that's been pretty…uh, cool," he said. "For lack of a better way to put it. You were always going to be someone I loved, but you weren't always someone I would have been good for. I was at least that self-aware. I was just, you know, picking my moment."

"Took your time," she said gently.

"What's the saying? It was a calculated risk, but man am I bad at math?" he said. "There was just a lot going on, and then the damn Duke of the Horse goes and kicks it and we end up in a whole separate country where suddenly everyone sees you like I've always seen you. Or if they don't, they're still angling to get close to you. And honestly…" He tilted his head against the pillow, studying her. "I didn't know how you felt. Realistically I still don't. I hate to ask this after the fact but do you even know? How you feel about me?"

"If you think I didn't care about you and still – "

"No! It's only that I have been deliberately working to figure this out and that's not actually something a lot of people do, or need to do. So I don't know if you think this is love, or that's too fast, or this could be love but I'm coming on kind of strong, or it's definitely something really deep…I don't know. Inscrutable sphinx," he added, and kissed the palm of her hand, so he couldn't be too worried, she decided.

"I think," she said slowly, "that this was probably a very rash decision that is going to pay off big time for you."

He laughed. "It's a good place to start from."

"Also," she added, "if you asked me to marry you here and now, I would lose my shit, say it's too fast, and run away, and that'd be smart."

"Wow, Al, I'm not – "

"And then tomorrow I'd come back and say yes," she said, rubbing his cheek with her thumb. He looked stunned. "A week ago I would have said I knew you better than anyone else does, except Gregory. Now there's – a whole new part of you that you've been building with your own hands, and I'm the only one who's really seen any of it, and I'd like to see more. A year ago if you'd asked me out I'd have said yes. Would have been a mistake, but I would have done it anyway. I had a huge crush on you in school, and I got past that, but it's not like I don't know I love you. I am more than willing to spend some time figuring this out, whether that's a functional love, but – I don't think this is actually all that sudden for either of us."

"Well," he said thoughtfully, and then, "Fuck me, that's pretty great, Al. Oh, hey – hold on," he said, and rolled out of the bed. Alanna watched him hop into his underwear and pull his shirt around his shoulders, then dart towards the little vanity where she'd laid out her makeup and jewelry. He picked something up and returned, hands behind his back as he sat cross-legged on the bed next to her. He brought his hands around to show her two level fists, a traditional Shivadh marriage proposal. They'd watched Gregory pull this on Eddie, not long ago.

She looked at his eyes, not his hands, and there was humor in his face but also a weird, desperate earnestness.

"The Dukes of Shivadlakia have long engagements," he said. "We can take years, if we want. You and I don't have to ever marry. We can take our time and then decide we just want to be together, or even that we're not meant for each other and break up. But I would love to make our incredibly rash decision official. Even if it's only for us."

She sat up, kissed his cheek, and rested her fingers on his left hand. When he turned his hand over, she looked down and took the City of Gold ring out of his palm.

"First try, good job," he said.

"You're left-handed, it wasn't rocket science," she replied.

"That is the beauty of me – I will never be rocket science," he told her.

"Are you going to work on self-esteem with your therapist at any point?" she asked, sliding the ring on, and his mouth dropped open.

"Catty!" he managed. "You are cruel to your affianced! Cruel to poor Gerald! Also yes," he added. "I have been. And he's going to be super happy about this, you have no idea. I've been having a slow-motion nervous breakdown since we left Askazer-Shivadlakia and I owe him a win."

"Good," she said. "Should I – would it have been better if someone else came with me instead of you? So that you wouldn't be dealing with all this, I mean."

"No," he said firmly. "I wanted to come. I wouldn't have let you leave me behind. And look," he said, lifting her hand to kiss the ring on her thumb. "Big win."

"We're such...such nobility," she said. She'd have to talk to Jerry's mother Sarah, get the ring sized or maybe have a new one made. Eventually. No hurry. "Thirty seconds of courtship and we're engaged."

"Don't look now, but that's title number three for you. You officially have a collection," he said. "You are three whole duchesses. Galia through your father, Askaz when your grandmother dies, and Shivadlakia because you seduced that poor, witless Duke Gerald. You can't have every duchy in Europe, Al."

"I could if I wanted," she replied. She turned the ring so that the engraving of the palace was facing up, the Grand Synagogue on the other side tucked snugly against her palm.

"Yeah," he agreed, and she saw an entire future for both of them in the look he gave her. "You probably could. I'd help. Given the damn ring's not going to fit on the right finger, do you want to play it cool or tell the world?"

"We can't, not yet," she said. "Not until Galia's been dealt with."

And that was a sobering thought; she could tell he felt the same in the way his face darkened.

"We are behind enemy lines," he agreed. "Okay. Good call. I should mend fences with Milo regardless, and the sooner the better. *He's* not the enemy."

"No. But at least now you can explain, if you want. Why you

were such an asshole to him."

He let his head fall back, staring at the ceiling. "Making amends blows. But yeah, I'll go say I'm sorry."

"Shower first," she told him, and he smiled and kissed her ring one more time, then got off the bed to go wash.

When Jerry emerged from the shower, Alanna was on the phone with Gregory, hopefully not immediately telling him they were engaged, although he supposed it was a good sign for the future if she was. He held up a finger, tipped to one side, and raised his eyebrows, a question mark of sorts. She shook her head and mouthed, *paperwork*.

He dressed enough to be presentable, then found his phone in the sitting room and opened a text window to Milo.

I owe you a million apologies and probably something expensive, he wrote. *Alanna isn't making me do this, I know I was a huge asshole and you didn't deserve it. I will come to wherever you are to make good, unless you'd rather it be in public at breakfast tomorrow.*

He could see in the status bar that Milo was reading it, and then tapping a reply; when it arrived it was better than he deserved. *I'm still in the Palazzo. In the archives. Please do not bring anything expensive.*

Jerry waved for Alanna, who said, "Hang on," and held the phone away from her face. "What's up?"

"Going to see Milo. Wish me luck," he said. She gestured for him to come over to the bed, then kissed him when he got close enough.

"Be a grownup about it," she said, and he smiled and nodded and called "Hi Greg!" loud enough for him to hear, then left while Alanna was laughing with Gregory about Jerry's irreverence.

The archives were cool and mostly dark; when he arrived, Milo was sitting at Bruno's desk, feet up on the edge of it, working on a laptop propped on his thighs. He closed it and set it aside, fixing Jerry with a level look.

"First," Jerry said, "I am going to say that while I did not mean a lot of what I said, I still meant to say it, and that was really stupid and wrong. I don't think you're a jumped-up file clerk, I think you're one of the best people working in this cursed place, and I said all that because I knew it would piss you off."

"Well, you aren't wrong," Milo allowed.

"Whatever anyone says, I think you'd probably make a great Duke of the Horse, and either way it's not my job to tell Alanna who she can or should date. Having met some of her dates, you definitely are a cut above the crowd."

"Still haven't heard an *I'm sorry*," Milo pointed out.

"I am," Jerry said, coming to lean against the edge of the desk. "I'm really sorry I hurt you, Milo. I shouldn't have done that."

"Thank you. I'm glad you realized it. I assume with a hand from Alanna."

"Even as I was doing it I knew I was being an asshole, so lord knows why I kept on," Jerry said. Milo tilted his head, his glare going more studious. "I think…you understand how special she is."

"You care about her."

"Well, yes. Not sure if this is evident, and it's no excuse, but I'm in love with her," Jerry said.

"Suspected that much when you started in on me," Milo agreed. "It did not make it more pleasant, Jerry, I have to say."

"I can imagine." Jerry studied the ceiling, sighing. "But I like you, as does Alanna, and both of us need you. I did you dirty for no good reason. So I need to know how to make amends, as much as I can."

Milo made a thoughtful noise, and Jerry glanced at him. There was a lot of emotion on his face.

"I think you and I are working at cross-purposes but for the same goal," Milo said. "So perhaps it's time to put some cards on the table. I can't tell you that I was acting out of romance when I asked Alanna out. Do I want to be duke? No. Do I want some other idiot to be duke? Even less. I don't want us to have a Duke of the Horse. I want us to have a real government, with open elections. That's what Bruno was doing in your archives when we came to the palace, you know."

"What, having an election?" Jerry asked, and then snickered.

"I have known you were stuck at twelve years old since we met when you were thirteen," Milo said.

"Then you were an astute judge of character for an eleven-year-old. Everyone else expects me to be an adult, which is frankly a lot of responsibility."

"Bruno was – still is – studying Gregory II, the man who democratized a kingdom," Milo said. "He's working on a long-range plan to do the same for Galia. I know Alanna doesn't want to be here. I think she's trying to figure out a way to get out of being duchess. While I want to help her, I also think perhaps she ought to know that even if she becomes duchess, we don't intend to let her stay on the throne."

"I hope this is less beheading and more impeachment," Jerry said.

"Or they might try to elect her once we get that far, who knows? The point is, until we can put the elections in place, someone's got to take charge and if it's one of the old guard, we're just...fucked, Jerry. Really, really fucked."

"Mm. So you and Bruno – and I assume Ofelia?" he asked, and Milo nodded. "Are trying to make sure power keeps moving away from the council and towards you."

"Well, that makes us sound a little craven, but essentially. If it helps, we don't want it or intend to keep it. But if not us, then who?"

"So – when I told Alanna in the massive fight we just had that I thought you liked her for her, and didn't want the throne,

I… misjudged."

"I do like Alanna greatly. I'd do a decent job as a husband," Milo said. "But I'm already seeing someone and also not attracted to her, so yeah, we were both being assholes, just in different ways."

"Now I'm intrigued," Jerry said. "Who catches the eye of the covert revolutionary Milo Ansevali?"

Milo gestured at the desk he was sitting at. Jerry blinked.

"You and Bruno?" he asked. Milo gave him a small, curt nod. "That explains a few things."

"Does it?"

"Sort of. Both of you raised some red flags for us. Nothing bad, just…unusual. Greg and I thought you were acting weird, and Alanna was kind of wondering what Bruno's deal was," Jerry said. Milo looked away, seemingly in thought. "But if you two are together and awkward about hiding it, or even just awkward about hiding all the plotting, maybe that's why. Is it okay, you outing him to me?"

"He won't mind. He's not in the closet, it'd just be…difficult for my career if I was out," Milo said. "But I don't think you're the kind to use that against us, all recent evidence to the contrary."

"No, I wouldn't do that. And I can see why you wouldn't want it gossiped about in Galia. You've already got a bunch of people taking aim at you. I thought you'd have higher sights than an archives nerd, but I have to admit Bruno's very nice. And he presumably was cool with you making a play for Alanna," Jerry added with a grin.

"I don't feel great about that, but we're working to save a country," Milo said, and then inhaled. "Uh, in *full* disclosure, he's not a historian. I mean. He is. But that's not why he's here."

Jerry leaned forward. "Then why's he here? Unless it's one of those *I could tell you, but then I'd have to kill you* deals." At Milo's expression, he sat back again. "Uh. Is it?"

"Bruno's a member of the Guard of the Horse," Milo said.

"He's a spy. Sort of. No, that's not a good word…" He shook his head. "The Guard of the Horse is supposed to be the elite guard for the duke. There's a large faction that hated the duke, though, including Bruno's brother, who's pretty high up in the Guard. He brought Bruno in, undercover. The Guard's been working – with us, that's how Bruno and I even met – to make sure whoever succeeds the duke is…different. He's spent two years in the palace, trying to find ways to fix this *mess*. And then the duke dropped dead and Alanna fell into our laps. We thought if she had reason to stay, stronger than just knowing how much trouble we're in, she might accept long enough for us to organize free elections. But we could see her pulling back, so I was supposed to be an attempt at bait to keep her here."

Jerry rubbed his lips with his thumb. "Wow. Milo. That sounds stressful."

"Little bit," Milo agreed. "But desperate times."

"Alanna won't thank you for it."

"I didn't expect she would," Milo said with a sigh. "And in the cold light of you kicking my ass just now, it looks more and more like a bad, dumb, panicky idea."

"Was Bruno even trying to find a direct heir, like she asked?" Jerry said.

"He was, actually, still is – a Galian heir would solve some problems. And then Alanna could go home and report back to her king," Milo said, with a sharp grin.

He'd guessed, then, that they had ulterior motives for being here. Well, no point in obfuscating now. "Politics," Jerry said, shrugging.

"That's an excuse, but we've both had a rough weekend, so I'll give it to you," Milo said. "Besides, if I thought Gregory had ill intentions, we'd have kept Alanna out of the sensitive information."

"I'd like to see you try," Jerry said. "But no. You know Gregory. He's a diplomat, not an empire-builder. He wasn't lying when he said he'd like to have better relations with Galia."

"Good. We want that too."

"Then I also happen to have some new leads for Bruno to chase down, if you'd like to carry them along," Jerry said. "I talked to Carlo – the party count?"

"Ah, Carlo. He's dim but harmless. Useful in his way."

"Glad my assessment is confirmed. He says there are rumors the duke had a direct heir, but he doesn't think the mother was nobility. The Bright Young Things all think if he had kids it was with the help – Palazzo staff, or a professional in town. The kind of person who might use a child to maintain their position, or even just the kind of person he wouldn't be as careful with as he would someone in the peerage."

"That makes…actually a lot of sense," Milo said. "He definitely seduced the staff. Some willingly, but I'm sure there were some who just wanted to keep their jobs. What a creep he was. I almost wish he'd lived to see himself get dropped into the shit by Brasolin and his ilk."

"Anyone come to the top of your mind?"

"A few. I'll talk with Bruno and get back to you," Milo said.

"As apologies go, this was super productive," Jerry said, as Milo stood to walk him to the door.

"How's Alanna? Still furious with you? I should probably talk to her, say I'm sorry. But if she's still breathing fire, maybe it can wait."

Jerry clapped him on the shoulder. "She's quick to heal. I'll be fine, I'm going to go talk to her now. I'll clue her in on all this, if that's okay. That way when you do say sorry, at least you won't have to go through this twice."

"Yes. She should know. Thank you," Milo said.

"As you may remember from school, I have a lot of experience being dumb and panicky," Jerry told him kindly. Milo gave him a rueful grin. "You go have a nice evening with Bruno, don't work too hard, and tell him he doesn't have to worry about losing you to the duchess."

"He'll be thrilled," Milo said drily.

When he got back to the suite, Alanna was dressed again, slouched on the sofa, staring at the ceiling.

"I am exhausted," she announced. "You speak to Milo?"

"Boy did I," he replied. "Not to annoy you and then insult you but apparently his motives were not pure."

She threw an arm over her eyes. "Can anyone in Galia just say what they mean?"

"Apparently not. He's dating someone else. He was trying to lock you down so he could marry you, become duke, overthrow himself and you, and institute a democracy. It's extremely exciting and, yes, also very tiring, and explaining why he owes you an apology even bigger than the one I owed him might take a while," he agreed, sitting next to her, wrapping an arm around her shoulders and kissing her hair. Then, realizing he could, he pulled her arm down and kissed her properly.

"Just what I need, more excitement," she said. "At least now I don't have to worry about letting him down easy."

"No, indeed not," Jerry agreed.

"Gregory sends his love, by the way," she added. "He just needed to know where some files were and Darien's off because it's Sunday. Took us some time to get to them."

"He'd be lost without you. As would I."

"Nice to be needed," she said. "I didn't tell him about us."

"Seems like a face-to-face kind of conversation," he agreed. "Maybe after we've been dating for more than an hour."

"That's what I thought. So now what do we do with ourselves?"

"I sent Milo home to his *amore*. We could stay in and I will do my best to entertain you. Or we could go get dinner in the dining room, it's coming up on mealtime. I think we should go out, though. Be seen around Galia. I'll take you to a steakhouse, load you up with protein, and make you laugh," he promised. "I can tell you what Milo told me in the archives, it's a lot of good gossip. I also have extensive questions about your very offhand remark that you think I didn't notice, about having a crush on me at school."

"If I let you take me out, will you promise not to ask me about that until we're both at least fifty?" she asked.

"No, but I promise not to ask you about it tonight," he said, kissing her again. "Let's give the people a thrill and go be glamorous and seen."

"I'm not wearing heels."

"Say the word and I will," he replied, grinning at her.

"No, you're tall enough already."

"Woke up this way," he told her. "I promise a good dinner and an early night in. I'll even go back to my own rooms and sleep alone in the big cold bed if you decree it."

She rested a hand on his chest, head on his shoulder, and he managed to keep quiet and let her think.

"I'd like to go out," she said at last. "Not just to dinner. There's one of those outdoor shopping plazas past the casino – looked fake and dumb but also kind of pretty. We can buy some presents to take home. I just want a nice evening like we could have in Fons-Askaz. Dinner somewhere fashionable. Then back here, and you can stay a while, but you can't sleep the night in my rooms. The staff would know."

He hadn't considered that, and it felt a little bittersweet, but he nodded. "All right. Let me change and see about a car. You find wherever you'd like to eat."

He had seen Alanna smile countless times, at friends and boyfriends and people she didn't even like that much, but when he stood up and kissed her before heading back to his own room, it felt like she offered a completely new smile just for him.

CHAPTER EIGHT

IT WAS PROBABLY just as well they'd had an early night; on Monday morning, things took a sharp turn.

Alanna was at breakfast; she'd woken early, and decided to fortify herself in case Milo still wanted to have a conversation. Instead, before she could text Milo to ask him about their meeting, a woman sat down across from Alanna in the dining room and offered her a slip of paper over her half-eaten pastry.

Alanna saw Will, at the back of the room, start to get up; she gave him a small shake of her head, and he settled back down but narrowed his eyes. She picked up the paper and studied it, glancing back and forth between it and the woman sitting across from her. Handwritten on the paper was a digital path – a route through one of the Palazzo Cavallo's administrative shared drives, presumably to the location of a file.

"I only just have known Milo asked for a full budget," the woman said quietly, in heavily accented English.

"I was beginning to think one didn't exist," Alanna replied in Italian, setting the paper down, and the woman looked relieved.

"It does. We have to have one copy, so the departmental budgets reconcile," she replied. "It's part of my job to keep the master book."

"Why you?" Alanna asked. "I'm sorry, I don't know who you are."

"Because I'm the lowest rung on the ladder, and it's very boring work," she answered, ignoring the implicit question of who she was. "That's an archive," she added, nodding at the paper.

"It's accessible to anyone with a login, it's just nobody ever looks for it. I knew someone should see it, but I didn't know who before now. Hard to know, in the Palazzo, who to trust. But everyone trusts the Ansevalis, and we like you. If Milo needed it, I knew you'd have a use for it."

"Thank you," Alanna said. "For the trust and for the information. This will be helpful."

"Just don't get me fired," the woman said with a smile, and left the dining room at a casual stroll. Alanna tucked the paper in her pocket, took a last sip of coffee, and tried to be as casual going back to her rooms.

Laptop open at the table by the window overlooking Athena's enclosure, Alanna followed the path on the slip of paper through five nested folders, some of which were only identified by a series of numbers. Eventually she came to a folder that was full, row upon row, of spreadsheets. Each of these was simply marked with a number.

She opened one – 2020.xlsx – and found that it was the year for the information stored inside. At first blush it did look like a budget, but then she frowned and studied some of the codes. This wasn't a projection, a guess at what would be spent where, or even a statement about what could be spent where.

It was a ledger. It was what *had been* spent. What had been deposited and moved around, too. It was an avalanche of information, compared to the little trickle Milo had been able to source.

It could also be a trap. If one of the council wanted to imply to them that there was nothing wrong with Galia's finances, a fake archive would be the way to do it. She copied the files over to her laptop's hard drive while she considered what to do.

Well, she knew a few things about Galia, enough to do a random audit and see if things that should be in the files were there. If she had at least that much confirmation, she could call Milo and Bruno about it.

The files were dense with information, but the current year's budget was easily sorted; once she worked out some of the codes, she could even find entries paying for her own stay – extra food, musicians, alcohol for the receptions. There was her ball gown, too.

"Yikes," she mumbled, when she saw the price of the gown.

She also knew, in a general sense, when Michaelis had been in Galia last; she opened the year she thought it might have been, as well as the two around it, and combed through the much less detailed numbers in those files. This data would all have been entered from paper records, or imported over from earlier spreadsheet programs if the duke had been particularly progressive about digital archives, which he probably hadn't. The poor clerk who had given this to her might have been the one to build them from paper. In any case, there wasn't much in the way of text, just codes and numbers. There were clearly several receptions in those years, marked by expenditures on food and drink, music and staff, but they weren't broken down by who had visited, and some didn't have exact dates attached.

She considered this, closing the older files. Even if they weren't big fans of computerized bookkeeping, they'd probably begun keeping digital records at least twenty years ago. She counted backwards, to one year after her first year at Institut Alpin, and opened the file. What she was looking for didn't show up under any designation she thought of at first – the name of the school, anything to do with education or scholarship funds. Finally, she just searched "Ansevali", and that turned it up immediately: "Ansevali M" in a notes column.

There were a handful of expense entries tagged with Milo and Ofelia's names. They came from the duke's discretionary fund, not an educational fund, but there were entries in late summer, several years running, that were about the amounts one would pay for a year's tuition at Institut Alpin, or at an elite school in Galia.

Perhaps the duke's personal staff had administered some kind of named scholarship fund, so that it wouldn't come out of the allocations for local education.

It probably shouldn't be so exciting, finding one or two particular numbers in column upon column of them, but she'd always enjoyed this kind of detail work. It was why she'd loved being Gregory's right hand at the palace.

Still loved it, she reminded herself. This was temporary. He was waiting for her to come home. Hopefully she could, in another few days.

She took her phone out and sent off a text to Bruno and the Ansevalis, asking if any of them were in the Palazzo and could come to the suite. She was just texting Jerry the same when there was a knock on the door and Jerry's voice on the other side calling in Italian.

"Good morning, Duchessa! Don't behead me for oversleeping."

"Come in," she called in English, and he put his head in the door, grinning at her. "Your breakfast manners are as appalling as your Italian, but your timing's good regardless," she said. Her phone beeped and she consulted the lock screen. "The Ansevalis are on their way."

"Why, what's going on?" he asked, coming inside. He leaned over her and tipped her chin up to kiss her, albeit briefly. "Also, shouldn't you be getting ready for council? They want you at ten today, don't they? Half past nine now."

"Damn – I'm going to have to cancel," she said, gritting her teeth.

"Send me instead," he suggested, settling next to her on the sofa. "You and I both go to meetings for Gregory, it's not unheard of. And it'll put them in their place, you sending the idiot to deal with them."

"Self-esteem," Alanna sing-songed.

"I was speaking from their point of view, that's others-esteem," he protested.

"Just watch yourself, I'm going to call you on that from now on. Anyway, I'm not sure if they'd let you in – might be a bigger deal than just me canceling. We can ask Milo when he gets here."

"Why do you need to cancel, anyway? Find something juicy?" he asked.

"I think so," she said, gesturing at the laptop screen. He turned from studying her face to look at the screen instead, and then leaned forward to see it better.

"Whoa. Is this..." He touched the trackpad on the laptop, scrolling up and down. "Looks like the ledger they use on the estate back home, only about a million times more complicated."

"You read your estate's ledgers?"

"I do now, have for the last three quarters. Have your grandparents not shown you the documents for your estate?"

"No, they have – they wouldn't give me the birds and the bees but they went through the operating budget with me very thoroughly when I was fourteen. I check in every so often, but mostly Grandfather manages it. It just didn't strike me as something you'd be interested in," she said, derailed from explaining how she got the ledgers by the idea of Jerry, their Jerry, poring over spreadsheets and doing pivot tables.

"Oh, I'm not interested in them, they're mind-numbingly boring," he said, eyes still on the sheet. "It's the worst part of the gig. But one has to make sure the steward's not embezzling and such, and if my mother's not going to do it – and she's not – I might as well. Fortunately our household manager is as honest as he is uninteresting. Ideal man for the – "

He broke off abruptly, head tilting, and was opening his mouth to speak again when there was another knock at the door.

"Come in," she called, and Milo entered, followed by Bruno and Ofelia. "Close the door. Milo, you may need to make an excuse for me to the council this morning."

"I told her she can send me if she wants," Jerry said,

highlighting a line in the spreadsheet and continuing to scroll. "Not sure how the council would take that."

"Probably find it welcome; they'd rather deal with a man," Milo replied. "Tell me why, first, if you can?"

"Someone from the finance office just sent me these," Alanna said, removing the laptop from Jerry's grasp and turning it around to show them. Milo sank down into a chair, taking the laptop from her. Ofelia sat in the other chair, and Bruno looked around before dragging one over from the table near the window.

"It's full ledgers going back decades," Alanna said. "Apparently they made it this one poor clerk's job to keep them all – "

"Of course they did," Milo murmured.

"We should have expected that. For years the duke's personal security codes were kept on a flash drive in someone's pocket," Ofelia groaned. Milo was blinking at the sheet, hands moving quickly on the trackpad and keyboard.

"This is everything," he said, astonished. "Payroll, deposits in, expenditures – if someone embezzled, it's probably in here. If someone transferred money to a bank in the Bahamas it might even outright be called 'Bank in the Bahamas' in this notes column. This is madness. It's our own national Panama Papers," he said, looking up at her. "Half the council is implicated here. Maybe more. Is this real?"

"As far as I can tell," Alanna said. "There's real entries, across several years. It looks like I'd expect it to look overall. But I haven't been able to systemically audit it."

"Who gave it to you?" Bruno asked.

"I don't know her name. She just told me where to find it all and left."

"Smart woman."

"I don't think Milo spoke to her when he was trying to get this kind of data – she said she didn't know until just now what you were looking for. I get the sense she's been dying to know who to give it to," Alanna said.

"Bruno," Milo said, and Bruno got up immediately, crouching next to his chair, one arm slung over his shoulders as he studied the screen with him.

"Yes, I see. I don't know if I understand, though," Bruno agreed, when Milo pointed at something. He looked over at Alanna. "I – no offense, I know you're trained in this kind of work, but I'd like to take this to…my people."

Ofelia raised her eyebrows at him, then looked pointedly at Alanna.

"I told Jerry yesterday, about Bruno being in the Guard," Milo said. "Sorry, Ofelia. Didn't have time to brief you."

"Important information to have," Ofelia said sharply.

"It was a very long day," Alanna put in gently.

"There's data here that could ruin any councilmember that's been maintaining power through financial control of the duke," Bruno said. "The Guard of the Horse has access to discreet, thorough forensic accounting. With these files, we might be able to bring down the council. No wonder they wouldn't give them to you, Milo. And some…some clerk just had them all?"

"She told me, everyone trusts the Ansevalis," Alanna said. Bruno's mouth curved upwards and he glanced affectionately at Milo, who didn't appear to notice, still studying the sheet.

"With this, and with Alanna on the throne, Galia could be holding elections in two years. Maybe less," Milo said, looking at Ofelia.

"Does it have to be me?" Alanna asked. "If we have this, can we force them to accept a different heir?"

"Very possibly. But is there anyone you'd trust to serve in your place? You know the potential heirs you've found. Do you know any of them personally?"

"Not well enough that I'd tell them what we in this room know," Alanna admitted.

"I have a question," Jerry said softly. "Two, actually. Promise they're relevant."

"Go ahead," Alanna said.

"Does the Guard of the Horse also have access to a reliable DNA testing lab?" Jerry asked. "One that can do a rush job discreetly."

Bruno looked perplexed. "Probably," he said. "I can ask. Why?"

"It's relative to the second question. Milo, scroll up – there's a line item highlighted. Can you tell me what it means?"

"Yes, I see – " Milo began, and then his eyes narrowed, mouth thinning.

"That's a relative of yours, isn't it?" Jerry asked. "Not M for Milo or O for Ofelia."

"Milo?" Ofelia asked.

"When I came in, Alanna had a filter on the sheet," Jerry said. "She'd been searching your surname."

"I was trying to confirm the sheet was real. I thought, you both went to school on scholarship from the state…" Alanna gestured at the laptop. "I found the lines for your tuition."

"This one isn't school tuition, though," Milo said. "This is six figures paid out."

"To a relative of ours?" Ofelia asked, perplexed.

"To Mama," Milo said, looking up at her.

"*What?*" Ofelia asked.

"Ansevali C. is Catrina, our mother," Milo said to Jerry. "But this can't be right," he continued, turning his attention back to the laptop. "It's got to be a mistake. She was employed by the Palazzo, it's probably misplaced from the payroll sheet, and it's about what she'd earn if you took a zero away – "

"Your mother was staff here?" Alanna asked, the details beginning to fit together.

"She was one of the duke's personal secretaries. It's how we know so much about palace operations," Ofelia said. "We grew up in the Palazzo, practically. That's how she got the scholarship money, too, she knew who to ask – "

"She asked the duke," Alanna said.

"Yes, probably," Ofelia said dismissively.

"No. Personally," Milo said. "She asked His Grace. The school money's from his discretionary fund."

He opened a different file, studied it, opened another one.

"There's…I think there's no scholarship program," he said. "I'm not seeing anyone else under these codes. I've never spoken to any other Galian who went to Institut Alpin, but I thought it was just because there's such a stigma against taking charity in Galia – nobody wanted to admit…"

"The duke sent you both to school on his dime," Jerry said. "And he gave your mother some kind of payment."

"Yearly," Milo murmured. "There's at least three – no – at least five yearly payments here."

Ofelia had her hand over her mouth.

"We used to joke that Mama stole a house," Milo said, voice tight. "When we were little she bought a house near the Palazzo – mostly it's apartments around here, but there are a few houses. They aren't cheap. There was no way our mother bought a house, that house, with a nice yard and a good view of the promenade, not for what she made in the Palazzo, with no husband in the picture. When we were young, she joked she stole it. When we got older she used to say she got a lucky break. That's why they call us jumped-up, you know," he continued, bitterness in his voice. "Not just because we went to Institut Alpin and the Galia School for Youth Leadership or because we're good at our jobs. It was because we were a secretary's kids but we always dressed like a duke's kids. Looked nice, good manners, fine house, new car…"

"You're calling our mother – " Ofelia began, and then swallowed. "Milo, Mama didn't take money for sex with the duke."

"That's not what he's saying," Jerry said. "She was taking the money for you two, to give you a good life." Ofelia looked at him. "Ofelia. Do the math. You're the oldest. You're the heir."

She looked away, and Alanna realized that she'd known since Milo mentioned the duke's discretionary fund. She just didn't want to admit it. Alanna wouldn't either, in her position.

"Jerry," Alanna said.

"Yes'm."

"Go to the council. Take Will if you want. Tell them I'm unwell and you're there to stand in for me. You'll need to sell it a little."

"No shortage of selling it," Jerry said.

"Milo, Bruno, you should leave my suite before someone sees you here," she continued. "Call your friends in the Guard, only people you trust. I want a single sheet of paper, two days from now, that I can use to ruin the council. Is that doable?"

"Might be two pages, the way these files look," Bruno said, seemingly torn between amusement and disgust.

"Even better. Can you figure out a way to get a paternity test done?" Alanna asked.

"Sure. I'll see what's available."

"Ofelia," Alanna said, and Ofelia, who had bowed her head, looked up at her. Alanna gestured to the sofa cushion next to her. "You and I are going to stay here and figure something out."

Ofelia chewed her lip, then nodded and got up, coming to the sofa to sit. Alanna put an arm around her shoulders.

"This is a good – " Milo began, and Alanna shot him a look. "But politically – "

"Milo, she's your sister, give her five damn minutes," Jerry said, standing up.

"If he does that he's going to realize she's not the only child of the duke in this room," Bruno said, and Milo went pale. "Milo. Come on. Let's do this somewhere else."

Jerry walked them to the door, Milo cradling Alanna's laptop. She didn't really want to let someone else take her laptop, but she did trust Milo, and anyway she suspected he was in enough shock it would be hard to get it back right now. In any case, they probably wouldn't go exploring on her hard drive, and it wouldn't be a disaster if they did. She didn't have anything dangerous unlocked and there wasn't anything incriminating, though there was a collection of Star Wars fanfic she didn't care to be judged for. Jerry saw Milo and Bruno into the hallway and then leaned back in.

"I don't care if I'm arm-wrestling Brasolin for the fate of Galia, if you need me, you text," he said. "I'll come running."

She nodded. "Text Gregory and Michaelis for me? I'm going to need a call with both of them later."

"Sure. I've got calendar access, I'll book you in," he said, and closed the door behind him. Ofelia, her forehead resting on Alanna's shoulder, shuddered.

"It is good, Milo's right," she said.

"It's not good," Alanna said. "It's helpful. Not the same thing. If you are the duke's child, you can take Galia in hand. If Bruno can come through with evidence to ruin the council, you can do everything you and Milo set out to do. And not to be poetic about it, but there's…something very mythical in the idea of two children of the sitting ruler, without knowing it, growing up to be such staunch defenders of the country he almost ruined. But we don't have to think it's good, Ofelia. I didn't even know the duke and I don't like him. I can't imagine knowing him personally and finding out you're his child."

"We probably should have known," Ofelia murmured, leaning away from her. Alanna kept her arm over her shoulders, but very lightly, ready to let go if need be. "It's not like the pieces weren't there."

"Why would you assume, though? Everyone knows the duke didn't have children. Everyone told you that you were middle class."

"Heh," Ofelia said, rubbing her knuckles against her nose. "Middle class would have been a promotion."

"Well," Alanna said reflectively, "the next time someone calls you a Jumped-Up Ansevali, you can have them imprisoned."

That got a laugh, at least, and Ofelia dug in her pocket for a handkerchief, blotting her eyes, wiping her nose.

"We still don't know, anyway," she said to Alanna. "Jerry's right. We'll need to do a test and it'll need to be unimpeachable."

"Not necessarily. Not at first, anyway," Alanna said. "We can have one done today, if we can get some of the duke's DNA. Think that's possible?"

"His rooms are on the third floor. They've been sealed since he died," Ofelia said. "Bruno can get access. There must be a hairbrush or something similar."

"We'll confirm what we think is going on, here," Alanna said. "Maybe confirm with the Guard of the Horse and then use an independent lab for proof. We have a little time. Even if you aren't, the financial data alone is going to give me what I need to start fixing this. But I think we both know you are."

"Do you suppose the council would accept me? I'm not nobility – it's not like they were married. I have political capital, but not nearly as much as you do just by virtue of being close to the Shivadh king."

"No…but Milo is friends with the king. Old school chums. And you…are close with me," Alanna said. Ofelia looked skeptical. "You could be. I'd like us to be friends, too, you know. Either way, it's in our interests to support you. If you go into the council with the backing of Askazer-Shivadlakia and enough evidence to ruin them…well. I've never project-managed a coup before, but this could be fun," she said. Ofelia smiled at her. "Want to help me plan it, Your Grace?"

"Lord." Ofelia put the handkerchief away. "Yes, I suppose I'd better."

Outside, under the window, Athena chuffed in the long grass as they hatched their plan.

A lot had to happen, very quickly and very discreetly, that day. Jerry, realizing this on his walk to the council chambers, squared up and took a hit for the team, making himself so obnoxious for the entire duration of the council session that they were too busy being annoyed he wasn't Alanna to wonder why she wasn't there.

By the time he got out he felt he'd crammed an entire week of bad behavior into three hours. He carb-loaded with pasta at lunch in the dining room, flirting with the staff who came and went as he texted the Shivadh palace.

Gregory, of course, generally had full Mondays, and Michaelis was technically retired but functionally a busy man. It wasn't that they didn't want to talk to Alanna, but they had to push things around to make it work, including both of them hating the conference call feature and thus wanting to be in the same place at the same time when they called her. He kept an eye on their conversation, but he'd had at least a firm commitment from them to both be present in some form or other at two o'clock, and the rest was just them wrangling with each other.

Bruno, just after Jerry walked into the council, had texted a group chat that included Milo, Ofelia, Alanna, and himself, plus a number he didn't recognize. He scrolled through it at lunch, but it seemed to be mostly logistics surrounding a rapid DNA test, so Jerry sent a series of gif images showing various talk show hosts announcing "You ARE the father" and otherwise left them alone. Alanna sent a private message thanking him because he'd made Ofelia laugh.

It's what I do, Jerry said. *I'll take that jester job if it's still open, I do better at that than vizier.*

You are helping to mastermind the downfall of a royal government. You've never been more vizier-like, she replied.

Jerry chuckled. *Should have packed my medallion of office.*

You mean the video game character costume medallion you bought at the street market? Alanna asked.

It looks very dramatic, Jerry replied. *Want me to bring you up some lunch?*

We've eaten. Bring me up yourself, though. You should be on the call with Greg and Michaelis.

He sent a thumbs-up and stood; he was almost to the doorway of the dining room when Brasolin entered, and the way he moved made it clear he was there either to see Jerry or prevent him from leaving.

"Consigliere," Jerry said. "Nice to see you again so soon."

"Your Grace," Brasolin replied, and then just stood there.

"Anything I can help you with? I wouldn't try the chicken today, the sauce is a little spicy for my tastes," Jerry said.

"I wanted to inquire after Her Grace. I hope she's not too ill."

"Just a headache. I think she'll be fine."

"I noticed also that Ms. Ansevali has called in sick – perhaps there's something going around," Brasolin said.

"Really? I saw Milo this morning, I hope he's not a carrier," Jerry replied. "You know how these big, badly-ventilated old buildings are – one person gets sick and comes into work, everyone gets sick. I don't think it's a flu, though, not in Alanna's case anyway. She had a rough Sunday," he said, which was completely true.

Brasolin gave him what Jerry could only identify as the stinkiest stink eye of his experience. He supposed the man had been working on it for about fifty years, and it showed. Jerry didn't believe in the Evil Eye but his mother had given him a hamsa ring to protect against such things as a child and in that moment he wished he'd brought it along. He rubbed the signet ring on his finger with his thumb.

"Please convey my wishes for a swift recovery," Brasolin said at last. "We would hate for her to be absent again tomorrow."

Message received, you unpleasant gargoyle, Jerry thought. Out loud, he said, "I'll convey your sentiments to Her Grace."

Upstairs, in Alanna's suite, he announced, "Brasolin knows Ofelia called in sick and he's being very weird about it. We may have to sneak her out later. I volunteer to serve as a diversion while you dress her like an old woman and wheel her downstairs in a chair."

"If I can't sneak out of the Palazzo, I don't deserve to be here," Ofelia replied. She seemed to have rallied, at least, from the shock of the morning.

"That's the spirit. Hey, I was thinking, Count Carlo's marriage bid was for the duchess, not for Alanna; he just wants to be duke," Jerry said. "You should give it some thought. He'd put in the work, and when you overthrow yourself he'd probably fall on a sword for you."

Ofelia sniffed. "I can do better than Carlo."

"Yes, but can you have more fun?" he asked.

"Welcome to your future, where every man wants to marry you off, usually to himself," Alanna said, coming out of the bedroom. "Jerry won't tell you this but he'd be an okay husband if you asked."

"I'm taken," Jerry said with a grin.

"Yes, I saw the photograph from your karaoke adventure," Ofelia replied. Jerry covered his face with one hand.

"Milo's working up an exciting new agenda for the week," Alanna continued. "How'd council go today?"

"Fine," Jerry said, "but I hope his agenda includes you being in council tomorrow, because Brasolin will get even edgier if you aren't."

"Damn, we'll have to go shopping in the afternoon," Alanna said to Ofelia.

"Don't have anything to wear to seize power?" Jerry guessed.

"PR campaign. Ofelia and I are going to be seen out on the town. The more visible she is with me, the better. And technically we are distant cousins, not that anyone knows that, but she's some portion Shivadh, if only by marriage," Alanna said.

Jerry did the family tree in his head, something he actually wasn't that bad at; he lifted his hand to map it out.

"You are Ofelia's paternal great-aunt's granddaughter," he said at last. "Oh, make it daughter of the paternal cousin, that simplifies it. Sort of. Second cousins."

"Handy skill," Ofelia observed.

"Only in very niche situations, but yes," he agreed. "Love any other reason to be useful, though, if you two have any. Milo and Bruno took the boring jobs, at least."

"Bruno's probably standing over a scientist as we speak, watching the DNA test develop. Milo's working on the blackmail."

"Isn't blackmail if you aren't asking for money," Jerry replied. "Technically, it's coercion."

Both women looked at him.

"Blackmail is when you want money, coercion is when you want *results*," Jerry said.

"Legally speaking, he's correct," Ofelia said, a little perplexedly.

"And how do you know this?" Alanna asked.

"I've known some unfortunate people in my time," Jerry replied. "Never had either done to me personally, but it's on the bucket list. So what's the plan?"

"Working that out now," Alanna said. "Although I will say, if the Galians didn't want drama, they shouldn't have called a Shivadh."

"I can't wait," Jerry said.

All three of their phones went at once; when he looked down he saw a message from Bruno. *Confirmation. Ofelia is daughter. Milo full sibling. Be there in a few with documentation but they agree it wouldn't hold up in court – lab's not impartial.*

"Another puzzle piece falls into place," Jerry said. His alarm went off to mark five minutes to the call with the palace; he'd barely registered it when Alanna's phone rang. She put it on speaker.

"You're early," she said, but she sounded pleased.

"Only me, I'm afraid. Gregory will be here soon. Didn't see the point in waiting," Michaelis replied. "Am I coming through clear?"

"You are, Uncle Mike," Jerry said. "Hear us okay?"

"Yes, Gerald. I should have known you'd be where trouble was."

"I had a question, actually, if we have a few minutes before Gregory gets here," Jerry said. "Do you have the recipe for the pie that hit Brasolin in the face forty years ago?"

Michaelis's laugh was deep, booming down the line. "I believe it was just a pie tin full of whipped cream, actually. Would have been a waste of good fruit if they'd used a real pie."

"No argument here. Also, we need to introduce someone to you," Jerry said.

"Wait, hold on, Gregory's here – " There was a rustle and the sound of voices talking distantly.

"I am indeed here," Gregory said finally. "Sorry for the delay."

"Good timing, actually," Alanna said. "We have some news, and we need some help."

"Of course. What can we do?" Gregory said.

"It turns out the duke had a child," Alanna said. "Two, actually."

"Oddly unsurprising," Michaelis said. "Have you found them?"

"They found us," Alanna continued. "It's Ofelia and Milo."

"The Ansevalis?" Gregory asked, stunned. "Did they know?"

"We didn't," Ofelia said. "We wouldn't be in quite the same mess if we had. Mind you, we'd be in a different, more complicated mess, so there's that, at least."

"Good point," Jerry murmured. "Uncle Mike, that's Ofelia Ansevali. Her Grace, I should say."

"Not to state the obvious, but this is good news, isn't it?" Michaelis asked. "It gets you out of being duchess, Alanna, and brings you home fairly quickly, I'd imagine. From what I've heard of you, Ms. Ansevali, either you or your brother would make a fine ruler."

"Little more complicated than that," Alanna said, while Ofelia looked pleased by the compliment. "Which is why we're calling. Gregory, I don't think we need you to do anything, but we might need documents attesting to our ability to throw some money behind Ofelia."

"I hate to be crass, but I am king and I need to ask, how much money?" Gregory said.

"Nothing that would break us. We might not even need to commit to sending it, just to…"

"Threaten to," Ofelia said. "Perhaps not even that."

"This is sounding more fun all the time. I'm sorry I'm missing it," Michaelis said.

"That's the other part of the plan," Alanna told him. "I have a front row seat for you, if you're willing to run an errand for us."

"You have my full attention," Michaelis said.

It was difficult to maintain a sense of normality, that Monday and the two days following. They'd fixed the day they would go to the council as Thursday: it gave them time to make arrangements, but left Friday for what they hoped would be the work of cleaning up, of putting the word out and sweeping away the dust left behind.

But in the meantime, Alanna still had to attend council on Tuesday, all three hours, and for an hour on Wednesday. There was a luncheon to attend, and a tea, and she had to be seen out with Ofelia. Jerry had to call up Carlo and arrange for another night out, mentioning that he'd be bringing both Alanna and Ofelia along, which meant Carlo had to compose a very careful guest list.

"He's a little bit of an ass, but he does seem to like being helpful," Jerry said, hanging up on a skeptical Carlo. "You might replace his dad with him on the council. He'd at least be better than Senior."

"Not sure he'll want it, once we remove his father," Ofelia said.

"Don't prosecute and you'll be okay. Carlo knows where the payday is," Alanna said. "And it'll keep the old man from retaliating."

"I'm more worried about Riva," Milo said, studying the dossiers that Bruno had brought them. "There's nothing in the ledgers that incriminates him. He might not actually have done anything wrong. But he's still very powerful, and he is going to hate Ofelia taking the throne."

"If he's honest, then he's probably capable of seeing reason. Or at least of knowing when he's beat," Jerry observed.

"Let's hope," Ofelia said.

"Anyway, if we're going out Wednesday evening and committing treason on Thursday morning, I want a curfew," Jerry said. "I need a reason to be back here and in bed no later than two in the morning. Midnight would be better."

"Emergency call from home?" Milo suggested. "Gets both of you out of there at once."

"It does leave Ofelia to the tender mercies of the Bright Young Things," Jerry said.

"I've handled them before. And I'll have to anyway, when you leave," Ofelia pointed out. "Chivalrous of you, Jerry, but not necessary."

"Well, if you change your mind, let me know and I'll start a fight with Carlo. Alanna can hustle you away in the melee," Jerry said.

For all of Jerry's fretting, Alanna found their night out with Carlo and the Bright Young Things sort of fun. None of them were willing to be rude to Ofelia's face, at least with Alanna there, and everyone wanted to be near Alanna. It required Jerry and Carlo to bookend her, and it was fun to be charmed by Carlo while Jerry leaned into her and smelled good and smoldered subtly. And when the call came in from Georgie at midnight, purporting to be from the Shivadh palace, he handled it so completely that she mostly listened to him sell it to Carlo and then let herself be pulled out of the bar.

"Sorry to leave you like this," he yelled over the music. "Little thing but it just can't wait. Carlo, can you look after Ofelia for us? Huge favor to me," he added with a wink. Carlo blinked at him and then nodded, a knowing grin spreading across his face.

Georgie was down the block, and when she saw them come out of the bar, she flashed her lights. Jerry slung an arm over Alanna's shoulders companionably, as if a little tipsy, and then held the door for her, posture straightening as he climbed inside after.

"Someday," he said in her ear, as they zipped back to the Palazzo Cavallo, "when we are not engaging in high adventure in foreign lands, I'll actually get to take you out and kiss you in public and everything."

"Looking forward to it," she replied, twining her right hand in his left. He clicked his signet ring against the City of Gold, scrolling through Photogram.

"PR campaign is working. Ofelia's got her own hashtag," he said. "Also, it's hard to look good in photos taken in dim karaoke bars but you and she are both managing it, duchessa mine."

"Glad we've got our priorities settled," Alanna sighed.

CHAPTER NINE

THURSDAY MORNING, ALANNA arrived at the council chamber with an entourage: not only Milo, who often sat in on council meetings as secretary, but Jerry, who had been there only once, and Ofelia, who hadn't ever been there. She also brought in a handful of sergeants-at-arms: Palazzo security officers who, in this case, had been hand-picked by Bruno as friendly to the cause. The security already in the council chambers looked perplexed at the last minute shift-change, but left easily enough for an unexpected paid day off.

And it meant that Alanna and Ofelia were already there, chatting amiably with each other and surrounded by trusted people, when the council members began arriving. It was almost ten when Riva approached and coughed discreetly.

"Your Grace," he said to Alanna. "We should begin soon. We'll need to clear the chamber."

"I'm afraid there's been a slight change of agenda," Alanna replied. "We'll start on time, but I need to address the council on the question of my succession to the throne."

"Ah, you've made a decision!" Riva looked pleased. "And your...colleagues?" he asked, eyes flicking from Jerry to Ofelia.

"I have some legal needs that Ofelia will be helping with," Alanna said. "Jerry's just here because he's a hanger-on."

Jerry gave Riva a crooked grin. He'd pulled up a chair next to Ofelia's, so that he and Alanna sat on either side of her, although Alanna was at the head of the table, with Ofelia off to the side. "Can't get enough of all these politics," he said.

"Well, we wait on Her Grace's pleasure," Riva said, giving

Jerry a dark look, and took his seat down the table. Brasolin, across from him, was reading some brief or other; most of the other consiglieres were chatting or waiting to begin. Alanna confirmed that everyone who was going to arrive had arrived, and then knocked sharply on the table to draw their attention.

"Gentlemen," she said, when they were all looking at her. "I'm afraid I need to interrupt our regular business. I have some happy news for Galia regarding the succession of the duchy."

"I'm sure we're all pleased you've come to a decision, Your Grace," Brasolin said.

"I hope you'll be downright delighted," she replied. Brasolin's eyes narrowed. "In determining whether I should take the throne of Galia, I wanted to make sure there were absolutely no other pretenders who might interfere. I decided that if I was going to make the sacrifice of moving here and ruling, there should be no question of my legitimate claim to the throne. Such diligence is sometimes rewarded – fortunately or unfortunately – and in my case, I discovered someone else had a better claim to the duchy and the throne of Galia than mine."

The men began to murmur among themselves.

"Steady on, Brasolin," Jerry said quietly, much too quiet for him to actually hear. Brasolin wasn't talking or fidgeting like the others, Alanna saw. He was looking at Ofelia.

He knows, she thought. And then, *Wonder just how much he knows, and when he learned it.*

"There have been rumors since I arrived that the duke had a direct heir, a child who could claim the title," she continued, "I've since been able to confirm it. Just this week a DNA test – "

"Your Grace, I'm sorry, could you repeat that?" Riva said.

"She said, *the duke has a child*," Jerry said in Italian, raising his voice. Riva looked like he wanted to murder him. Jerry seemed to be enjoying himself.

"A DNA test was performed this week," she said. "Confirming the duke has two biological children, born and raised here in Galia."

"Two," Riva said skeptically.

"Nonsense," Brasolin added.

"I'm afraid it's true. However, I'm pleased to say that the duke's eldest child is not only qualified to take power in Galia, but I think ideal for the job," Alanna said. "Ofelia Ansevali, therefore, will be invested as Duchess of the Horse this morn – "

The council burst into uproar, a dozen voices shouting at once in Italian. Alanna could see, under the table, that Ofelia's hands were shaking, but her only visible reaction to the yelling was a small smile.

"Absolutely not, this is a coup by the Ansevalis – "

" – can't possibly be true, I won't accept less than an independent lab's test – "

" – the hell is Ofelia Ansevali? Should I know her?"

"You did this, Milo, you ambitious little prick – "

"Gentlemen," Alanna said, and then louder, "Gentlemen!" When that got her nothing, she turned to Jerry. "Would you?"

"Love to," he said, and tucked his tongue behind his teeth. The shrill whistle he blew was loud enough to make her molars hurt, but it did silence them.

Into the silence, there was the sound of a door opening.

"Anticipating turmoil, I had a few extra measures put in place," Alanna said, as an aide entered. He went to Brasolin first, something all of the council aides had a habit of doing, and which Alanna decided it was time to put a stop to.

"I think the person you want to speak to is me," she said loudly. The aide glanced at Brasolin. "He doesn't control who enters this room. Currently, I do. I also control who is employed by the Palazzo. So if you want to have a job in five minutes, you tell me," she added more gently. That got his attention.

"Your Grace, there's an…individual from Askazer-Shivadlakia who says he is here to see the council," he said apologetically. "He's demanding entrance."

"I know. Let him in."

There were quiet murmurs at this, until the aide went to the main entry doors and, with a regretful look, opened them fully.

Alanna had watched a lot of political theater, over the years; the Shivadh palace had a policy that the children in it had free access to almost all proceedings. She and Gregory, and sometimes Jerry, had seen dramas play out on the floor of Parliament, in the grand reception hall, at balls and small parties. So she knew that the vast majority of the time, Michaelis was remarkably unassuming. Gregory referred to the Shivadh royalty as "functionally bureaucrats" and he wasn't far off the mark.

But Michaelis had also spent twenty years learning rule at his father's side and a further forty in politics, and there was a certain switch he could flip – he'd taught Gregory, as well – that changed that.

Even out of the royal blacks, which would have been inappropriate to the situation, Michaelis had a gravitas that could silence a room. He hadn't had much occasion for suits, lately, but he was in one now, neutral brown with an antique gold shirt under a high-collared waistcoat. He walked into the council chamber with his shoulders back, head high, eyes sharp, and mouth set – there was a mixture of solemnity and displeasure on his face that Alanna could recognize as an act, but she doubted anyone else could. He stopped at the foot of the table, hands clasped lightly behind his back.

Next to her, Jerry let out a low whistle.

"Lady Daskaz," Michaelis said. "Thank you for your invitation to attend. Gentlemen," he added, nodding around the table, and then to Ofelia, "Duchessa."

There was another eruption of murmuring at that, but at least it wasn't shouting. Michaelis cleared his throat. Silence fell.

"Welcome to Galia, Your Majesty," Alanna replied. She knew that he preferred *Your Grace*, now that he was retired, but there were enough Graces in this room without adding one more.

"We appreciate your presence."

"The pleasure is mine. I understand there's a dispute I may be able to resolve."

Brasolin scowled. "We have no need of washed-up former monarchs – "

"Brasolin, from now on you will speak when spoken to," Alanna said sharply. He opened his mouth. One of the sergeants-at-arms, at a gesture from her, put a hand on his shoulder, and he closed it again.

"We may have words later about that remark, Brasolin," Michaelis added in a gentle tone, like a parent scolding a toddler.

"Your Grace," one of the senior consiglieres said, and the way his eyes drifted it was impossible to tell if he was addressing Alanna or Ofelia. "While I don't necessarily agree with Consigliere Brasolin's assessment of the situation, traditionally we have not, ah, resorted to diplomats of other nations to resolve our own internal disputes."

"I understand your reserve," Ofelia said, and Alanna shot her a smile. "However, Galia was ill-equipped to provide what was needed in this case. His Majesty isn't here to offer diplomatic or political aid, merely data." She turned back to Michaelis, who nodded. "You've brought us some documentation, I believe."

Michaelis unbuttoned his suit jacket, taking an envelope from an inside pocket.

"This is a DNA test," he said. "Performed in Genoa by a lab unaffiliated with Galia or Askazer-Shivadlakia, using anonymous codes for those involved. Would you care...?" he offered it to Ofelia, but she gestured for him to continue. He opened the envelope and took out a few folded sheets of paper. "It concerns, primarily, two individuals, female contributor 8857 and male contributor 8858. On testing, the laboratory confirmed that male contributor 8858 – "

"This is a farce," Riva said. "The lab could be forged, the submissions falsified – "

"I wasn't finished," Michaelis said mildly. The men on either side of Riva subtly leaned away. "Male contributor 8858, whose DNA was collected by the Guard of the Horse from the bathroom in the suite of the Duke of the Horse Tomas of the House of Galia, is confirmed to be the father of female contributor 8857, collected by the Guard of the Horse from Ofelia Ansevali directly. This one," he added, turning to the second page, "identifies male contributor 8859 as the son of male contributor 8858 and full sibling of female contributor 8857. 8859 was collected by the Guard of the Horse from Milo Ansevali directly."

"Now," Alanna said, and every head in the room turned back to her. "You can question whether the results are valid, Consigliere Riva. Have your own performed, if you like. And when they come back valid as well, see how popular you are with the Duchess of the Horse."

Riva was pale, anger in his eyes. "You cannot simply assert a duchy and have done," he said.

"Why not? You did to me," she said. A few of the men blinked. "You looked at a family tree and assumed I was blood of the duchy and wanted the title. I was ideal, after all – a young, foreign woman with no partner, with close ties to someone you need right now – "

"We do not need Askazer-Shivadlakia," Brasolin blurted.

"Our national budget very much says otherwise," Ofelia replied. "Mostly thanks to you, Brasolin."

"I beg your pardon – "

"Gentlemen, I'm circulating a memo to the council," Ofelia announced, and Milo took a sheaf of papers out of his folio, passing them around the room. As Bruno had predicted, the memo took up two full pages per copy, and a lot of consiglieres turned as white as the paper it was printed on when they saw what it said. "You may review it at your leisure. In the next week or so, we'll discuss which parts may be made public. And which parts may become evidence in criminal court."

"This is blackmail," another man said.

"Coercion, actually," Jerry corrected. The man shot him a poisonous look. "Don't hate the player, you volunteered for this game," Jerry told him. It earned him a quiet chuckle from Michaelis.

"In any case, you can't have it both ways," Alanna said. "You can't believe we are sneaking Shivadh liars when we tell you who Ofelia is, but also ask us to rule your country. Either I'm a double-agent or a duchess. If I'm a double-agent, you can't possibly want me on the throne. If you want me on the throne, then I must be unimpeachable. And if I am, then when I say that I renounce the duchy in favor of the duke's natural heir, you're going to have to eat it."

"Sort of how this works," Jerry added. "Absolute power, invested in a single biological heir. Seems like it backfires sometimes."

"Can't say I support it," Michaelis said.

"You were a king," Riva retorted. "Your son is king even now."

"We were both elected," Michaelis replied. "You should try it. Brilliant for the ego. At least, when you're not getting a pie to the face."

Even Alanna inhaled at the audacity of that, but it had the desired effect. Brasolin stood so quickly his chair was shoved into the sergeant-at-arms still behind him; the man staggered backwards, and only a quick headshake from Ofelia kept him from diving in to tackle Brasolin, whose fists were clenched. Michaelis tilted his head at him as if he were an interesting painting.

"If this man is not removed from the council chamber as a spy and an insurrectionist, you can have my resignation," Brasolin spat. "These insults – "

"Okay," Alanna said. Brasolin stopped mid-rant, turning to

stare at her.

"Your resignation, if you please," Ofelia added. She set her copy of the memo on the table, smoothing it out. The first paragraph concerned Brasolin.

His mouth worked silently for a moment. Then, without another word, he turned and left – through a side-door, so he wouldn't have to pass Michaelis, who watched him go.

"Any other resignations immediately pending?" Ofelia asked. Alanna, with a small smile, stood and stepped aside from the chair at the head of the table. Ofelia, nodding at her, rose and took it. Alanna stayed standing, resting an arm on the back of Ofelia's chair.

"I'm not a vengeful person, on the whole," Ofelia said. "I like to think I serve the interests of the duchy. And I do see your point, Consigliere Riva, about unsealed lab results and DNA tests done in private. We will have a proper, detailed, and public test performed at our leisure, which you may supervise yourself if you like. However, that will take place after I am invested as Duchess of the Horse. It's past time someone took the reins of the country properly. In the meantime, Your Majesty, we appreciate you...running this errand for us."

"Always pleased to oblige," Michaelis replied. A few of the men in the room exchanged glances. Alanna could tell what they were thinking: that Ofelia Ansevali had the power to make a former king her errand-boy – to summon a man who hadn't been in Galia for thirty years to bring her a piece of paper. And from there Alanna could see the realization rippling outward.

Ofelia Ansevali was trained just as much as Alanna was to rule, and still connected through some unknown bond to the Shivadh nobility. She could give them everything Alanna could, and more – she was a native Galian, known to the people, but touched with glamor through her association with Alanna and Jerry. She was willing to threaten the council with the memo instead of simply ruining them. She could be expected to play their game, at least to an extent.

And all they had to give up to get her was the illusion of control, which Alanna wouldn't have let them keep in any case.

Ofelia Ansevali had also just driven Alexandros Brasolin out of the council. There was not only a power vacuum where he'd left, but an unspoken threat: *If I can remove Brasolin, I can remove anyone.*

"I'm sure we can arrange for a more transparent test at a later date, as you say," Riva said at last. "However, this does radically alter the political situation of the entire country in ways that I think none of us were prepared to consider. Perhaps a few days to…meditate on this would be advisable."

"I entirely agree," Ofelia said. "The country will need to come to grips with this new situation. Therefore, we will allow for a grace period before the enthroning ceremony. Must find a good caterer, in any case," she added with a smile, and stood. Almost instinctively, so did the men. Ofelia shot Alanna a dry look. Michaelis was not bothering to hide his amusement.

"However, I will not wait for my title," Ofelia continued. "The business of running the country must be taken in hand. I intend to go into the reception chamber and, with legal witnesses, sign the documents that will invest me as duchess. I assume anyone who wishes to remain on my council may attend as witness and sign a brief affirmation of their loyalty to the Duchess of the Horse. Anyone who does not wish to remain on the council is, of course, free to leave. You will not be allowed to take copies of the memo with you; leaving the council removes you from the benefit of its confidential information."

"Your Grace, not to offer advice where it's not asked for," Michaelis said, "but as someone experienced in this sort of thing…"

"Suggestions welcome," Ofelia said.

"Perhaps a pension, for those who wish to resign. In recognition of their service."

Clever old fox, Alanna thought. This hadn't been planned; Michaelis was improvising, but doing an extremely good job of it. *Leave now with a payout, or get cleared out later with nothing if you step out of line.* Most of the consiglieres were already wealthy men, but their wealth was tied up with the state's, and some of them were just grasping old codgers whose pride would be balmed by a bribe.

Ofelia nodded. "We'll put something in place. Alanna, Milo, Gerald?"

She stepped out from behind the council table and walked, without hurry, towards the entry doors; Milo, tucking his folio under his arm, stepped in front to lead the way. Alanna took Jerry's arm, falling in behind, and caught Jerry laughing a little when Michaelis offered Ofelia his elbow as she passed.

"Wonder how many of the consiglieres are going to follow," Jerry murmured to her.

"Don't look back," she replied.

"No fear. Do you suppose if he wanted, Uncle Mike could have invaded and taken the throne?"

"I can hear you," Michaelis said from in front of them. "And yes, looking at those sad bastards? I absolutely could have."

"Be kind," Ofelia said. "A number of them are about to lose their jobs."

"Couldn't happen to a more deserving dozen," Michaelis replied. "Pleasure to meet you in person, by the way, Your Grace."

"Charmed, Your Majesty," Ofelia replied. "I'm a great follower of your podcast. As I've told Alanna, I think you offer a number of useful lessons about rule. Allow me to invite you to lunch after I ruthlessly seize power."

"Gladly. It was a long drive from Genoa."

Alanna leaned into Jerry, who shifted his arm, lowering his hand and pulling out of her grasp so that he could twine their fingers together instead.

"Is it wrong that watching you and Ofelia devastate a room full of appalling old men really got me going?" he whispered in her ear.

"It absolutely is. Also, thank you," she whispered back.

"Are we going home after this?"

"Apparently we're going to lunch. If you're nice you can sit next to me."

"When do we go home?" he asked, and she could hear in his voice a plaintive echo of her own yearning.

"Soon," she said, patting his arm with her free hand. "Maybe as soon as tomorrow. This afternoon I have a job for you."

Late that afternoon, while Alanna and Ofelia were enjoying drinks and pretending to work in Ofelia's office, Jerry arrived with a file box. He set it down with the look of a man bringing home a trophy of war.

"You found something," Alanna observed. "What did you bring us?"

"Varied delights," Jerry said. "You were right. Brasolin pitched the biggest fit imaginable when he found that he was locked out of his office. The Horse...Guard...guy that I talked to said they had to remove him from the building. They say they should have arrested him but you gave orders not to."

"There's no need to be vicious as well as political," Alanna said.

"I would have had him arrested," Ofelia replied.

"Her reign of terror begins," Jerry said. He popped the lid off the box. "The Guard has his computer now, anyway, but as instructed I had a rummage around in his office."

"Jerry's great at finding things people want to hide," Alanna said.

"Comes of my devious mind," Jerry replied. "Behold, highlights of an eighty-year-old career politician's home away from home. This," he said, pulling out a heap of files, "is information he shouldn't have had, according to Bruno."

"Good to know, but I must say, most of us have some of that around here," Ofelia said.

"Yeah, I asked Uncle Mike, he said it's pretty normal for people to end up with stuff that wasn't meant for them, especially after a couple of decades. I haven't read it in detail – you're the lawyer – but it seems harmless enough. That said, if you wanted to arrest him for treason…" he waggled the files.

"It's a point. What else?"

"Very boring pornography," Jerry said, flashing a magazine with a topless woman on the front. "For a man in his position, he had what I'd consider extremely plain tastes. Runs to boobs and blondes."

"Were you looking for the rougher stuff?" Alanna asked. Jerry grinned at her.

"I wasn't looking for porn at work at all, but I guess it's something people do. And lastly, I have a present," he said, taking an envelope out of the bottom of the box. "Which explains why he was absolutely enraged he couldn't get in. This is a duplicate birth certificate for Ofelia Ansevali which lists Tomas, Duke of the House Horse, as her father, with a countersignature by the duke himself. I'm guessing any certificate you've seen leaves that part out," he said to her.

"Our father's name was always blank. Mine and Milo's both," Ofelia said, holding out a hand. Jerry put the envelope in it.

"I've got one for Milo, too," he said sympathetically.

"So Brasolin knew," she mused, opening the envelope and studying the certificate. "But he didn't want me on the throne."

"You would have been too powerful," Alanna said. "A direct descendant, with a younger brother for social capital – you with legal training, and the knowledge you have of the inner workings of the Palazzo? I was the much better candidate to have my strings pulled by all of them."

"So they thought," Jerry said.

"I wonder how he got it," Ofelia said. "I wonder if the old

duke gave it to him, or if he stole it somehow."

"Possibly that's how he got to be so powerful," Jerry said, nodding at the birth certificate. "I'm sure the duke's affairs weren't secret by any means, but there's a difference between chasing the staff and having two children with one. Begging your pardon," he added to Ofelia.

"Perhaps it was ill-gotten dirt, but I imagine not. I think he was keeping them safe for my...father," Ofelia said, as if trying the word out.

"Is there a chance Tomas didn't know about the two of you?" Jerry asked. "Someone else arranged for the payments, maybe?"

"No," Ofelia said. "Money didn't leave his discretionary fund without him knowing. And there was no reason for anyone but him to send Milo to a school for kings or me into a diplomatic career. I think he was grooming us for rule. I think he wanted to put Milo on the throne. The male heir, you know. I wonder when he was planning on telling us," she added, looking down at the birth certificate again.

"Got more than he bargained for," Jerry said. Ofelia frowned at him. "Well, from what I've heard of him, I'd bet he wanted what they all want. That puppet they thought Alanna could be. He set you two up to be his proteges. Doesn't appear to have taken. Ungrateful, I call it," he added in an imitation of Riva at his most pompous. Ofelia snorted.

"Yes, well, I will repay all of this with some brisk housecleaning," she said. "What's the English? Sunlight is the best soap?"

"Something like that," Alanna agreed.

"A year or two to get the books in order and prosecute those who need prosecuting. A propaganda campaign perhaps, and some public opinion polls. As soon as possible, a constitution and a general election," she said. "Parliament and a prime minister. No more dukes for Galia. We don't love our dukes as you love your king."

"Fair," Jerry pronounced. "Don't be surprised when you get elected, though. Galia's got a lot in common with Askazer-Shivadlakia, deep down."

"I'll remember that." Ofelia set the birth certificate on the desk, gently. "If you don't mind, I need to make a few calls, and speak to Milo."

"His birth certificate is under the rest of the porn," Jerry said, pointing into the box.

"He will no doubt appreciate that," Ofelia drawled. Jerry held the door for Alanna, following her out.

"Rough on the poor kids," Jerry said, once they were out of earshot.

"She's your age, you know."

"Yes, but I've lived a debauched life. In noble years I'm nearly fifty," he told her, and she laughed. "Very appropriate age to wed, fifty, especially to a young delight such as yourself."

"You are the grossest," she told him.

"I do my best. We have all afternoon ahead of us, and I got a favor out of Uncle Mike," he said, taking a set of keys out of his pocket – the keys to Michaelis's prized Jaguar.

"A favor, or did you steal them?" she asked.

"He's tied up with Bruno in the archives; he won't miss the Jag if we take it out. I'm only a new version of me, you know, not a completely different person," he said, when he saw her expression. "A quick drive. You should see the vineyard terraces on this side of the mountain."

"Terroir nerd," she told him.

"A man could get used to being called names by you," he replied.

Jerry was well pleased with himself by dinner that evening. He'd gotten to drive the Jag with Alanna on the bench seat next to him, tucked under his arm, and she'd been impressed by both his driving and the vineyards, which gave him a weird sense of gratification. The pretty terraces full of vines weren't even his, but the land had once been his family's, so he allowed himself a little pride in them. The winery nearby poured tastings for Alanna and sold them a few bottles of what she liked, and they made it home in time for a nice dinner that evening.

It was probably wise not to be seen out too much, and Alanna seemed just as happy to stay in, so they had a simple meal – just Alanna at the window, Jerry next to her, and Michaelis across from them, smug at having spent the day irritating every Galian politician he could find and exploring the royal archives with Bruno as his guide.

And then, just as they were finishing up the meal, the best thing in the world happened.

"That's a very pretty ring, Alanna. I don't think I've seen you wear that before," Michaelis said, nodding at her thumb as she finished her glass of wine. "Reminds me of one Eitan gave to Sarah, years ago."

"That's the one," Jerry said. Michaelis looked at him, surprised. Alanna was hiding a smile so hard he could almost hear it. "I got it from Mom before we left for Galia. Looks good on her, doesn't it?"

Michaelis' surprised look turned into a baffled stare, and it was so rare that Jerry got to troll his uncle that he couldn't resist. He gave Michaelis the most innocent face he could, for a beat longer than was comfortable, and then turned to Alanna. "You'll need to get it sized, though. Can't wear it on your thumb forever, it's not proper."

Alanna played into it so beautifully he could have kissed her (would, later). "I thought about that, but it's so intricate – we might need to just have a new one made. That way I could have it done in the traditional silver, and you could get a matched one with the Askaz estate on it, if you liked."

Michaelis gestured between them with his fork, then looked at the fork like it annoyed him and set it down. "If you two are playing some kind of joke on me…"

"No joke," Jerry said casually. "Planning on a long engagement, though. Can't steal Gregory's thunder, after all."

Michaelis was so silent and still that for a second Jerry began to worry he really was having some kind of attack.

"Well," Michaelis managed, then cleared his throat. "Well, I imagine Sarah will be pleased. You know how fond of you she is, Alanna. I can't fathom what your grandmother will say, but I hope I'm there to see her reaction."

"There's that royal will of iron," Jerry said to Alanna. "He wants to give you a hug so badly. It's destroying him that he has to pretend he's not absolutely losing his mind that you're going to marry me."

"You're making that a lot easier," Michaelis told him.

Alanna got up from the table and came around to hug Michaelis from behind while he was still seated, her chin hooked over his shoulder, arms looped across his chest. Jerry watched, pleased, as he squeezed her wrist and then turned to press his forehead to her temple affectionately.

"Not that anyone asked *me*," he added, with a sidelong look at Jerry, "But you have my blessing should you need it."

"We haven't told anyone yet," Alanna said, releasing him and going back to her seat. "It's still very new. We wanted to make sure Galia was stabilized first."

"Wise of you. But we are going home tomorrow. Will you tell Gregory?" he asked. Which Jerry knew was his way of saying *Can I tell Jes?*

"Jes can keep a secret," Alanna said, clearly also reading the question correctly.

"Thank you," Michaelis said, without apology, and took his phone out. About thirty seconds after he sent the text the phone began beeping. He looked down at it. "Jes is very pleased for you, and says congratulations. Noah's going to dust off his horrible wedding Powerpoint."

"I love that thing. Tell him I want it updated with this season's worst," Jerry said.

"You are my nephew, Gerald, and I could not be more pleased with either of you just now, but I cannot bring myself to encourage you," Michaelis said. Jerry noted his smile and basked in the approval regardless. "Besides, Noah's a self-starting young man, he doesn't need to be told."

"That reminds me," Jerry said, getting up to go to his jacket, where it lay across the back of the sofa. "There's still some business to wrap up in Galia, and here's me doing my part."

"What is this?" Alanna asked, studying the bundle of paper he handed her.

"Those are Athena's travel papers," Jerry said. "Last week when you started making calls, I thought I'd do a few too. For two people who live less than twenty minutes apart and work in the same building, we have *wildly* different spheres of influence," he added. "But I used to date the sister of a big Hollywood guy who comes to Italy to make cheap slasher films. Put in a call to him because he knows every movie star who thinks they're an eco-activist for paying carbon credits on their private jets. Several of them could use the PR boost of rescuing an exotic animal."

"Ah. Like Cher and that elephant," Michaelis said. Alanna, distracted, looked at him questioningly. "It was in the news. I do follow current events, even when they're ridiculous. She helped rescue an elephant and got it sent to a park somewhere. You can't read an article about the elephant without her getting dropped in there."

"Big fan of elephants, are you?" Jerry asked.

"Everyone likes elephants," Michaelis said dismissively.

"My point," Jerry said, leaning into Alanna, "Is that a very famous movie star with a slight image problem is going to pay for Athena to be shipped to a tiger rescue in Texas. They weren't accepting new beasties, but they are accepting large sums of money in exchange for taking in one more tiger."

"Unfortunate but true that hard work often fails where good connections succeed," Michaelis said.

"It was hard work too," Jerry protested.

"It looks like it," Alanna said, giving him a reassuring smile. "You're sure this place in Texas is all right?"

"Yep. They're a closed preserve. No tours, no breeding. She'll get to hang out with all the other old lady tigers and dish dirt on the duke," he said.

"So," Alanna said. "Happy endings all around."

Jerry waited, resigned, for her to finish the joke, but before she could, Michaelis did.

"Especially for Jerry," Michaelis murmured, and Alanna erupted into laughter.

CHAPTER TEN

THEY LEFT THE following afternoon for Askazer-Shivadlakia with a mostly quiet send-off, if a little later than planned.

"I had the situation in hand," Michaelis insisted, as staff loaded Jerry and Alanna's luggage into the car Will would be driving back. Georgie was in the other one; Michaelis's Jag, parked nearby, was waiting for him.

"You left the Palazzo on foot, with no security or staff," Milo said. "What did you expect to happen?"

"Absolutely nothing, which is what happens when I do it two, three times a week in Fons-Askaz," Michaelis replied.

"I told him not to!" Georgie yelled from the car.

"I wasn't expecting anyone to recognize me, especially out of uniform, let alone want to talk to me," Michaelis protested.

To say he had been mobbed was probably overstating things, Alanna reflected, but she'd seen images on Photogram of him surrounded by young Galians, looking baffled by all the attention but smiling and chatting with them regardless. They'd had to send Georgie with a car to rescue him. Jes probably hadn't stopped laughing yet.

"Why on earth did you leave the Palazzo alone?" Jerry asked, not looking up from his phone.

"I wanted to see the city. Thought I might find a nice cafe for lunch. Possibly even pick up some postcards. It's what normal people do," Michaelis told him.

"The fact that you think you're normal is endlessly funny to me," Jerry said. "Gregory does that too, I think it's some kind of delusion."

"I beg your pardon, *twelfth Duke of Shivadlakia*," Michaelis replied.

"Exactly. I'm not in denial that my life is super weird," Jerry replied. "We're burning daylight and I want to go home. Al?"

"Waiting on you, far as I'm aware," Alanna said, and Jerry raised an eyebrow and pointedly climbed into the car. "Are you going back to the lodge, or stopping at the palace first?" she asked Michaelis.

"Best report in to Gregory first, I think," Michaelis said, accepting his keys from a staff valet. "Yourself?"

"I want to see Gregory and Eddie, and I think Jerry's dreading going back to the estate. He's homesick for the people, not the place. We might stay the night in the palace."

"Come to the lodge if you like," he said. "There's room to stay over, and we have plenty of food. Might ask Gregory if he and Theophile want to join us, actually. Celebrate your engagement, if you're planning to announce."

"I think so, at least among friends. But are you sure you don't want Jes and Noah to yourself for a while?"

"I saw them yesterday before I left. You've been gone weeks," he said, and kissed her forehead. "We'll sort it out when we get home."

He jogged off towards the Jag, clearly ready to be on the road, but Alanna didn't get into the car yet; she turned back towards the Palazzo, and saw Ofelia standing on the steps. When she approached, Ofelia smiled.

"Hate to dump a country on you and run, but I think you'll do better with us out of your hair," Alanna said. "How's your first day going?"

"About two-thirds of the council didn't show up this morning. Couple of them sent their sons, including Carlo. Couple of daughters too, which was nice. The wind is blowing change," Ofelia said. "Milo's pleased by it all. You have no idea how much paperwork something like this generates, but he was born for that."

"The next few months probably won't be easy on either of you."

"Well, they'll hardly be more difficult than working for the Duke. Although I'm hoping I can count on the group chat when I need to vent," Ofelia added, holding up her phone.

"Such times we live in," Alanna said. "I'll ask Jerry to do something humorous every few weeks, he enjoys entertaining people."

"I wish you would. And you know you're both always welcome here...as long as it's not in the next six months or so," Ofelia said.

"I can't promise Michaelis won't be back sooner. He really hit it off with Bruno."

"His Grace is always welcome. I imagine if he showed his face in Galia again, a few of the old council might decide to permanently move to Italy." Ofelia closed the gap between them and kissed her on the cheeks. "Travel safe. Thank you. It hasn't been easy on anyone, but at least it's been usefully difficult."

"That's the Shivadh spirit in a nutshell, usefully difficult," Alanna said with a grin. "Call anytime."

When she climbed into the car Jerry scooted over, buckling up the middle seatbelt and crowding her comfortably into a corner, arm over her shoulders. He had his laptop, turned to tablet mode, and that program open again.

"What is this, really?" she asked, poking at it as the car pulled out of the drive. "I've seen you messing with it since we left home. It looks like a logic puzzle, but it's not a video game at all, is it?"

"It's definitely a puzzle," he said, using the stylus to draw a diagonal slash across the screen, zooming it out. "It's a diagram I had our steward build. Digital map of the ducal seat. I am lord of all you survey," he added, rotating it slightly until it made sense — there was the palace, down in the southwestern corner outside the boundaries of his estate. There was the main building, and beyond it the landscape on her ring – hills and terraces, pastures, orchards, and ponds.

"What are you doing with it?" she asked, studying the map.

"Laying out a new land management program. Crop rotation, orchard plantings, stewardship of old orchards we left to run wild. Turns out if you don't prune an olive tree it goes feral, so I've got prunings planned for the really old groves. Might double crop yields on what we have, and we're putting in new crops as well," he said. "Converting a lot of the lawns into growing terrain. But you have to kind of fit everything together – make sure the right plants are in the right zones, check the soil acid levels, that kind of thing. It's not as interesting as an actual video game, admittedly. I won't drone on about it."

"You could," she said. "I mean, I'm not interested in this stuff the way you and Gregory are – "

She broke off, because he'd made a thoughtful noise.

"Never considered it that way," he said. "Gregory and I both being interested in the agriculture. I guess it's true. But that doesn't mean you want to hear it."

"What I was going to say," she said, grasping his left wrist with her right hand, rubbing the City of Gold against his skin, "was that I'm not interested in this the way you are, but I wouldn't mind hearing. You've been hearing me talk about governing Galia for days on end. You talk, I'll rest. I might not hold onto much of what you say but I like the sound of your voice, and you like talking."

He smiled and kissed her. "I do like talking. Do you really like my voice?"

"Of course. Very soothing."

"Then I won't be hurt if you fall asleep, my dear heart," he said. "Would you like the olive groves first, or the apiary? I have plans for new pomegranate trees, and I can show you the fields we're going to open up for next winter's lowland dairy herd grazing. I've also found hardwoods over by the river – there's a lot of prospect there for sustainable exotic woods, although that's very long term. Kind of thing the next generation or two might see better returns on. And I have to watch the runoff, can't disturb Uncle Mike's fishing down at the lake. Best start with the olives," he decided, and she watched him move the diagram around, idly listening, until she drifted off.

Gregory must have seen them coming, or possibly he heard the Jaguar's engine; in any case, when they pulled into the little yard at the kitchen entrance, he was coming out of the kitchen to meet them.

"I'm so glad you're back," he said, enfolding Alanna in a hug. He let go with one arm to grab Jerry by the shoulder, then released her so he could hug Jerry as well.

"Thank you for going with," he said in Jerry's ear.

"It was fun. Let's never do that again," Jerry replied.

"Certainly not," Gregory agreed, leaning back. "Father, I hope you brought me a souvenir."

"Bringing these two back isn't enough of a present for you?" Michaelis asked, gesturing at Jerry and Alanna, but he also tossed Gregory a small box. Gregory caught it, gave Jerry a startled look, and then popped the flap up, opening it. Inside was a small cheap tchotchke – a figurine of a man on a horse, a replica of a statue of a previous Duke of the Horse from one of the local parks.

"It's the Duke of the House Horse," Jerry told Gregory, who laughed.

"I love it. I'll keep it on my desk. Now, come inside and you can tell me all about it," he said, leading them through the kitchen. Simon gave Alanna and Jerry a wave as they passed.

"Missed your cooking, Simon," Jerry called.

"Of course you did!" Simon replied. "Galians will put bacon in anything, the monsters!"

"Eddie's picking up food, he'll meet us at the lodge," Gregory said, leading them into the family dining room. "I'd love to get a full report, but I think the details can wait given I'm already seeing Galian press releases, and I'm sure you're all tired. Perhaps just the basics."

"We do have news to share," Michaelis said, pulling out a chair and settling in. "Gerald, Alanna, would you like to go first?"

Gregory looked at them curiously. Jerry turned to Alanna, only to find she had turned to him. Nobody was going to make this news more interesting than he could, so he squared his shoulders and said, "Your Majesty, I've asked for the hand in marriage of the Lady Alanna Daskaz, prospective Duchess of Askaz, lately of Galia, and she has consented. We are here to request your permission – "

At that point Gregory's jaw dropped and Alanna broke down laughing.

"You two," Gregory said. "You – did you propose?" he asked Jerry. "Did you propose to Alanna? Like...not as a joke?"

"Stop, stop," Alanna squeaked.

"When were you even dating? Because you I love," Gregory said, pointing at Jerry, "but you, I know you're not *insane*," he finished, pointing at Alanna.

"I'm marrying him for his money," Alanna said, voice about an octave above normal.

"And I think she'll be a good and obedient wife," Jerry said. "Tractable. Knows her place."

"Is that the face I made?" Michaelis asked Alanna, indicating Gregory. She nodded. "Lord."

"Father, is this real?" Gregory asked.

"Yes. They told me in Galia. I have no explanations, I'm afraid, but they seem sincere."

"Being away from home offers a lot of clarity," Jerry said,

and caught Alanna's hand in his, lifting it so he could kiss her thumb, where the ring sat. "And also I had to pin her down before some trashy Galian count made a play."

"That's – congratulations to both of you," Gregory said. "That certainly blows my plans for asking all about Galia's government and finances out of the water."

"We do actually have a brief for you," Alanna said, seating herself. "And Jerry tells me the dukes have very long engagements so there's plenty of time for that later."

"Well, you know better than I do what I need to know," Gregory said, as Jerry sat next to her. "Tell me everything relevant. I didn't actually expect you two to destabilize the country and then install a new duchess friendly to my administration. I feel like I should give you some kind of bonus."

Alanna did most of the talking, after that. Jerry was aware she'd make a better narrative of it than he would, and she'd be more concise than Michaelis, who like Gregory had a perhaps over-powerful inclination for detail. Gregory listened intently, drinking it all in.

"I think I'll have to appoint an ambassador," he said when they were done. "Certainly send some of our people to offer support to the new duchess. Not you two," he added, because Alanna did look like she was about to yell *not it*. "I'll give Milo a call on Monday and discuss options. I'd like to set up a regular chat with Ofelia."

"I think she'd appreciate that," Michaelis said. "She's a bright young woman and eager to learn the craft."

"He just likes her because she's a fan of the podcast," Jerry said.

"Shows impeccable taste, to my mind," Michaelis replied.

It was a relief when they reached the fishing lodge that

evening. Travel was done for the day; they'd given Gregory their report, and Alanna was tired enough not to feel guilty that she wouldn't need to speak with her grandparents until at least tomorrow. Jerry had already had a cordial homecoming phone call with his mother, and didn't sound eager to go back to the ducal seat full of empty rooms and loud dogs. Alanna was now in charge of nothing, for the first time in weeks – for the first time since Gregory had hired her, if she was being honest. It felt wonderful.

All they had to do was settle their bags in one of the upstairs suites (it would be a little warm, but Jerry opened the windows and got a breeze blowing through) and then come downstairs. There, they could peacefully sit at the kitchen bar and watch Eddie take over the old lodge kitchen, press-ganging Noah into service as sous chef. Although he did first spend roughly two minutes yelling loudly and hugging them when Alanna told him they were engaged.

Jes poured the wine while Eddie prepared appetizers; they gave Jerry a raised eyebrow when he gestured for them to skip him, but didn't say anything. A minute or so later, he got up and circled around to slip into the kitchen, deftly avoiding Eddie and Noah at the stove.

"Don't touch the cheese," Eddie ordered, as Jerry opened the refrigerator door.

"I try not to touch anything in here, this fridge is older than the lodge. It was probably here first," Jerry said, taking out a bottle of orange juice. "Mind if I pilfer some?"

"Go ahead," Michaelis said.

"Learn some new cocktail recipes in Galia?" Jes asked.

"Oddly enough, no," Jerry said, coming to the bar, facing Alanna, who passed him his wine glass. "They're all crazy for Eddie's Davzda cocktails. Taught them your new pomegranate soda one, in fact."

"Nice to be a legend in my own time," Eddie said, tending to the sauce that was bubbling on the stove. Jerry filled his glass halfway with juice, sliding it back across the bar. Alanna took it and put it at his place.

"I'm mostly off alcohol these days, you know," Jerry said casually, putting the orange juice away. "Never was a fan of wine."

Alanna beamed at him, but he was hiding his face in the fridge; when he finally did emerge, he caught her eye and nodded before dodging around Eddie to get back to his seat.

"Wine or not," Gregory said, holding up his glass, "a toast to Jerry and Alanna, who managed to overthrow a government and get engaged in under two weeks. I can't fault your efficiency."

"And on that note, prepare for your first course of challah bruschetta alla Theophile," Eddie said, taking a pan of toasted bread slices out of the oven and beginning to plate the food. Jerry slid an arm around Alanna's waist and she pressed her hand over his, twisting his signet ring around his finger.

That night, lying in the slightly undersized guest bed in the breeze-cooled suite, listening to the soft clatter of Michaelis and Jes doing the last of the tidying-away downstairs, Jerry pulled her up against his side, kissed her hair, and said, "I'm going to do my very best not to kick you away in the night, but I'm sometimes a restless sleeper."

"I promise not to take it personally," Alanna said. "You realize this is the first full night we get to spend together? In a guest suite at the fishing lodge, on a bed that I'm going to have replaced as soon as I'm back in the office."

"Better than my place," he said. "A dozen Shivadh Hunthunds yelping around outside and all my ancestors glaring down at us."

"And my apartment would have been desolate, after the last two weeks," she said. "Better to have family around, just for tonight. Very proud of you, by the way."

"For what?" he asked, amused.

"Orange juice at dinner."

"You took it well enough, thought I'd press my luck," he said.

"Gregory didn't blink," she told him. "Nobody did, really. Bet you this time next week Eddie's cooked up a dozen mocktails from what he knows of your tastes."

"I won't say no," he said. He ran his free hand over his face, then up into his hair. "Speaking of."

"Speaking of," she repeated, when he was silent.

"I genuinely don't want to make this your job," he said. "But…if you want to. If you'd like to tell Greg. About the ADHD stuff. Maybe Uncle Mike too? And that it's okay for them to tell people if they want. I don't mind, I just…don't really need to have that conversation." He turned his head to rest his chin against her forehead. "If that's okay. It doesn't have to be. You don't have to, I mean."

She nodded, tapping her fingers against his chest. "Yeah. It's fine. I'll let them know. I won't make a big deal out of it."

"Gregory probably will anyway," he sighed.

"Well, he is Shivadh."

It wasn't Gregory in the end, though. It was Michaelis who, a few days later, caught Jerry as he was leaving breakfast at the palace.

"Do you have time for a walk?" he asked, and Jerry frowned at him, perplexed. "Now or later. I'll be around today."

"I can do now," Jerry said. "Why are we walking?"

Michaelis just tipped his head in the direction of the side entrance, the one that let out near the lake. Jerry followed, neither of them walking particularly quickly, Michaelis ambling and seeming to gather his thoughts.

"I had a word with Alanna," he said, after a while. "Once things calmed down after we returned from Galia. About how things went while you were there."

"Is this the shovel talk?" Jerry asked, and Michaelis frowned.

"The what?"

"It's slang. Is this where you threaten me if I hurt her?"

"Ah. No, Alanna's capable of managing you if anyone is," Michaelis said. "Besides, if I thought you were going to hurt her, I'd strike first."

"That's..." Jerry searched for a word. "Proactive of you."

"I do what I can. No, this is somewhat the opposite, in a way."

"How so?"

Michaelis put his hands in his pockets, frown deepening. "I think, Gerald, I owe you an apology."

"An apology? For what?"

"When you were younger, when your father was still alive – Eitan and I weren't especially close. He was so much older than I was, and we had rather different upbringings, which affected how we raised our own children. I knew you weren't getting the same kind of parenting as Gregory was. But we also knew you had two competent parents, and you were clearly bright and well cared-for. Between the country, and Gregory, and Alanna after the accident – Miranda and I didn't pay as much attention as we should have."

"I didn't expect any extra attention," Jerry said.

"No, why would you? You were a child, you didn't know to expect it. Doesn't mean you shouldn't have had it," Michaelis said. Jerry considered this, and it struck him that this was a different conversation than the one he'd expected. He stopped walking, struck by it.

"This is about the ADHD," he said.

"Alanna – perhaps rightly – observed that if I had paid more attention, you wouldn't have had to figure it out yourself, alone, at the age of thirty," Michaelis said, stopping as well and turning to face him.

"I asked her to tell you, not give you a damn moral lecture – "

"She feels protective of you. There's nothing bad in that, Gerald. Extremely good quality in a partner, in moderation."

Jerry kicked a rock off the path. "She said she wouldn't make a big deal out of it."

"Then nobody should have told me, an infamous lover of drama," Michaelis said with a smile. "She isn't wrong. If I'd known then what I know now, I would have done things differently. I certainly would have taken more of an interest in your grades at school. Rather than only taking an interest in your mistakes afterward."

"I knew it was because you cared, though. I never thought you...you know, didn't like me or whatever," Jerry said, gesturing large enough that he knew, really, he was flailing.

"Hm." Michaelis regarded him. "That's good. Considering what I do know now, I think you should hear this anyway: I'm sorry we didn't do better for you. And I'm very proud you've done so well regardless."

Jerry felt his face heat, looking away to try and hide it. "Well. Thanks, I guess."

Michaelis, mercifully, let him have the moment; he walked on, turning on a gentle arc back towards the palace, and didn't speak again until Jerry caught up.

"In any case, she mentioned your new interest in agriculture," Michaelis said when Jerry joined him, as if they were picking up where they'd left off on some other conversation. "I thought I should remind you that what resources I have are at your disposal. Politically and as your uncle. I'd like to hear about your work, if you have the time. It sounds like you're experimenting with techniques that Gregory should bring to the agricultural cabinet – "

"*Great for tomatoes,*" Jerry chimed in, and Michaelis chuckled.

"I enjoy the fact that Theophile thinks we don't know that's actually a joke about growing marijuana," he said.

"Uncle Mike!"

"Don't tell him. I'm seeing how long I can stretch the joke before he works it out," Michaelis said. He regarded Jerry sidelong as they walked. "Have you and Alanna thought about how a marriage would impact the estates? Unless one of you gives up a title, you're going to unite them unavoidably. Not necessarily a bad thing, but it could grow complicated, legally speaking. Especially if you have children."

"Was that a hint?" Jerry asked, grinning.

"While I would love nothing more, I'm focusing my efforts on Gregory and Theophile right now," Michaelis replied. "Enjoy the margin Gregory has bought you."

"I usually do. As for the estates, I've been looking at some options for mine. Nothing I've talked to Alanna about yet, but I will eventually, before I do anything. I have to get the new plans in place first. Have to pitch it to my mother, too. But I'm thinking of collectivizing. Incorporating the estate as a holding company and splitting stakes among the staff."

"That would destroy the duchy as we know it," Michaelis said.

"Who cares? The land would still be there, and more useful than it is now. I'd still have my title. Some of the staff have been working there for generations, since before the duchy was even established. The longer I look at it, the more I think it's not mine to own."

"You'd give it all up?" Michaelis asked. "Twelve generations of your people on that land?"

"Yep," Jerry said simply. Michaelis was quiet as they walked.

"You'll have to make sure the workers are protected," he said finally. "Limits on stakeholding. Nobody can own a majority stake or form a bloc majority. But done properly, it would be a great step for the country. And as you say, there's no reason you couldn't keep the title. Or get yourself a new one. Gregory minted one for Theophile."

"I could be Duke of the Horseshit," Jerry said, and Michaelis let out a bark of laughter.

EPILOGUE

THE KINGS OF Askazer-Shivadlakia did not, by preference, work on the weekends. Even Gregory, who liked his work and had a young politician's drive to overachieve, tried to arrange life so that his time was free for his family.

Still, sometimes it was unavoidable. If they were going to push through the bond deal, with Askazer-Shivadlakia and its neighbors helping Galia get back on its feet, he was going to have to make a few sacrifices. Ofelia, at least, tried to be as efficient as possible.

"I know it's a handshake deal," Gregory said that Saturday morning, leaning back in his chair and studying the ceiling, phone on the desk next to him. "Earliest I can get any kind of complete documentation to you will be Wednesday. But if you're ready to push the bond sale on Monday, the cash from the Shivadh government to cover sixty percent of the investment will be there. We're representing four separate smaller nations with that amount, I do expect France to try and pick up some leftovers, and Italy's documented they'll cover whatever we don't. So if I screw this up I'm on the hook with them, too, because they'll be overinvesting. I'm very motivated not to screw it up."

"I think a handshake deal with Askazer-Shivadlakia is sound," Ofelia said over speakerphone. "We appreciate your help too much to waste your time, Gregory. We can open the sale on Monday as planned."

"In that case, congratulations, Your Grace – on Monday afternoon we will be united by something even stronger than marriage or children."

"Cash," Ofelia said, with exaggerated relish. "And I won't

keep you – I know how Alanna values your weekend brunches."

Gregory checked the clock. "Ah – thank you. Say hi to Milo and Bruno for me. They should try to get here for a visit before summer ends; we'll take them to the best beaches."

"I'm sure they'll enjoy that. Ciao."

"Ciao, Duchessa," he replied, and hung up the phone, shoving it into his pocket as he hurried down the hall.

He could hear the royal family at brunch long before he reached the dining room. Generally Alanna was one of the more well-behaved brunchers, but Eddie did have a knack for setting her off, and he could hear her lecturing him about some food or other.

"I am not responsible for the fact that every language in this part of the world steals from all the other languages and none of them have more than five words for breakfast pastry," she was saying.

"Croissant, brioche, danish," Jerry began listing. "Cornetto – ooh, baguette – "

"Not a pastry," Michaelis said, voice a low rumble even under Jerry's.

"But you eat it at breakfast," Jerry said.

"We're not talking about bread for breakfast, she specifically said pastry."

"Wait, what's the difference?" Noah asked.

"Between a bread and a pastry?" Eddie said, as Gregory reached the doorway. He leaned against the door jamb, unnoticed for the moment, watching the debate rage.

"This is going to get into the area of 'what is a sandwich' very quickly," Jes said.

Eddie began ticking things off on his fingers, clearly searching his memory for some culinary class in his past. "Fat ratios, amount of gluten, amount of water – texture, but that's really based on the other three – oh, pastries sometimes have fillings."

Odd how the heart could beat a little faster, Gregory thought, just watching someone you loved be pedantic about something.

"So do some breads," Alanna said. She was leaning against Jerry, his arm slung over her shoulders. One of her hands rested on his, twisting his signet ring around on his finger. "Anyway, this is missing the point, I cannot be blamed for the fact that brioche means a different kind of food in every town in Italy."

"They probably do it just to annoy the French," Michaelis said. "Given what we do to annoy the French, I can't fault Italians for that."

"What do we do to annoy the French? All I've ever done is buy their chocolate," Jerry said.

"Institutionally. We're flagrant anglophones right on their border," Michaelis said. "And they're very mad Gregory's cut them out of the formal bond deal with Galia."

"I did it just to annoy them," Gregory said. The reaction was both swift and gratifying; his father looked over and smiled a welcome at him, eyes lighting up, and Alanna and Jerry both waved him into the dining room. Eddie scooted to make room next to himself, and Jes gave him a nod while Noah hovered, wanting to sit on his other side. He helped himself to a scone and a cup of coffee and settled in next to Eddie, bumping him with an elbow affectionately.

"Bonds all stitched up?" Jerry asked, picking at the last of a croissant (possibly a brioche).

"Yes – the wire transfer's set for Monday morning, paperwork to follow, as soon as the bonds are legal," Gregory said. "That reminds me," he added, taking an envelope from his pocket and handing it to Noah. "Thanks for doing the podcast about the Galian infrastructure bonds. It really did help get people on board."

"Whoa," Noah said, unfolding the onionskin sheet inside the envelope. It entitled the bearer to one hundred Galian liry at two percent interest, payable after ten years minimum. "Is this what they actually look like?"

"Technically it has no face value. It's just a souvenir," Gregory said, accepting a brief sideways hug from the boy. "But the digital bond'll be in your name tomorrow, and Ofelia understands the power of an elaborate document."

"Look, there she is," Jerry said, leaning over to point out her portrait in the intricate series of engravings around the border. "There's Milo, nice to see him getting credit for setting it all up. And Gregory, because he brokered it. Ugh, Riva. Suppose they had to put him on there to shut the old man up."

"At least he seems to have accepted Ofelia as his fate," Alanna said.

"Ah, look, there's Athena," Jerry added, indicating the little prowling tiger in one corner. Noah swept crumbs off the table and spread the bond out so he could go over it in detail; Jerry sat back so Michaelis could lean in and explain the terms printed above the engraving to Noah, who was still in a beginner's Italian class. Eddie tugged Gregory gently away so he could wrap his arm around his waist, and Gregory let his whole weight rest on him, relaxing.

"Not bad work for a Saturday," he said to Eddie, watching the others. "And a good reward to come back to."

"Yeah? Not mad I divided the room with questions about brioche?"

"They look like they've recovered," Gregory said. He rested his head against Eddie's, pleased with his little family – happy, safe, mostly sane, all together in one place. "Glad you're here with me."

"Yeah, me too," Eddie agreed. "Second luckiest bastard on the planet, me."

"Oh yeah? Who's the luckiest?"

"You," Eddie said, grinning at him.

"Sure," Gregory agreed, the last of the morning's stress bleeding away. "No argument here."

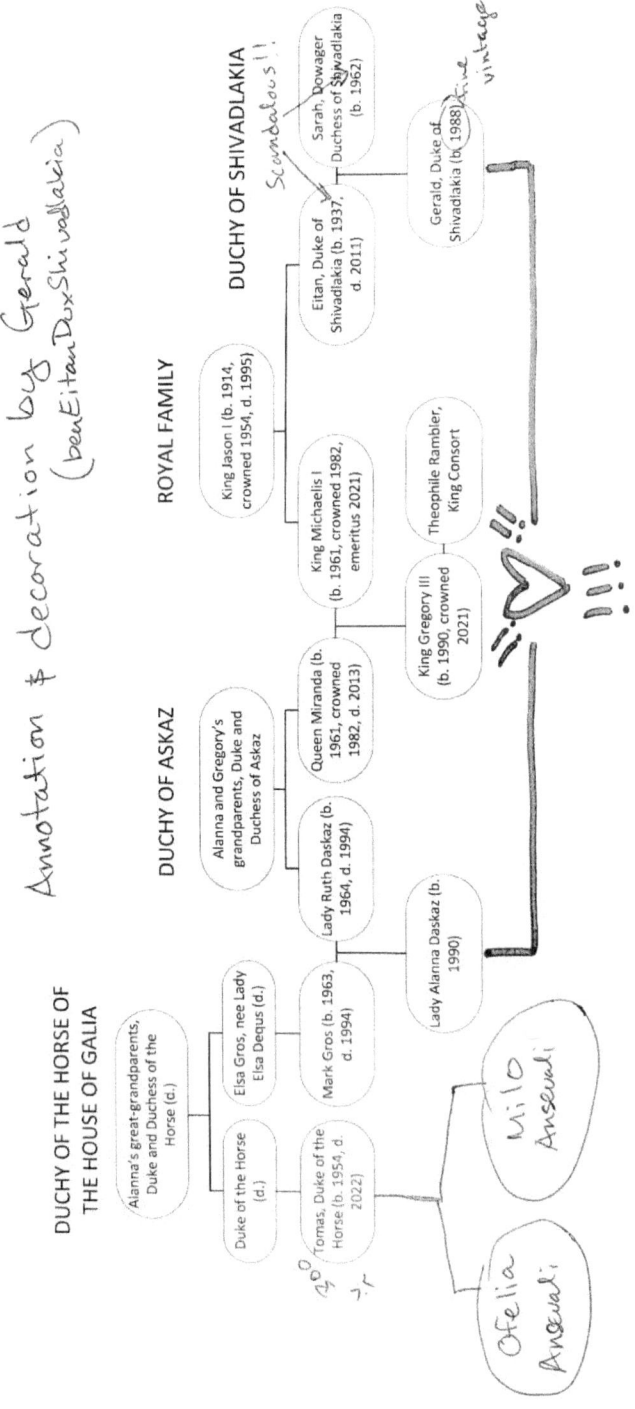

INFINITE JES: CONTENT WARNINGS:

- Brief mentions of spousal death and grieving (throughout book). Michaelis is still grieving his wife, who passed several years before, and processing the grief throughout the story.
- Brief discussion of family-related trauma (Chapter 4). Noah speaks with Michaelis about Jes's relationship with their parents; this does not involve transphobia regarding Jes's gender, just their parents being run of the mill assholes.
- Extensive discussion of alcohol and drinking (Chapter 5; some discussion of hangovers etc. in Chapter 6). Jes and Michaelis play a drinking game where Michaelis becomes progressively more intoxicated. No trauma or negative consequences result.
- Mention of injuries and description of wounds and blood (Chapter 9). Nothing graphic; Michaelis receives scrapes and cuts that bleed somewhat before being treated.
- Child briefly endangered (Chapter 9). Noah ends up trapped underground by an accident and must be rescued; no permanent harm or trauma.

THE LADY AND THE TIGER: CONTENT WARNINGS:

- Brief mentions of parental death (Chapter One); Alanna's parents passed when she was young and the specifics are occasionally referenced.
- Discussion of potential drug misuse (Chapter Five); Alanna discovers Jerry is taking Adderall and confronts him, assuming he's taking it as a party drug. Jerry reveals that it is prescribed medication for previously-undiagnosed ADHD, but he discovered his ADHD while using Ritalin as a party drug.
- Discussion of alcohol misuse (Chapter Five and onwards);

Jerry mentions some issues he had with alcohol prior to his diagnosis, his process for easing off use, and whether or not he is considered "sober". Throughout, he entertains himself by pretending his mocktails are actually cocktails to everyone else.

- Discussion of neurodiversity (Chapter Five and onwards); Jerry has chosen to keep his ADHD diagnosis from his family and expresses some attitudes, his and others, surrounding it that aren't entirely healthy. Chapter Six includes a description of what could be considered a sensory overload episode; Chapter Ten has a brief but emotional discussion of parenting issues surrounding neurodiversity, mainly positive in outcome.

- Brief discussion of food issues (Chapter Six); Gregory mentions Jerry used to stop eating when he was homesick at school for brief periods.

- Bullying scene (Chapter Seven); Jerry is angry at Milo and lashes out inappropriately in a way Alanna explicitly describes as bullying towards Milo. He later makes a full apology and it's clear that Milo, while not enjoying it, also knew it wasn't really about him, so there is no lasting trauma.

- Surprise paternity reveal (Chapter Eight); the reveal of a parent's identity leads to uncomfortable feelings for various parties.

www.ingramcontent.com/pod-product-compliance
Lightning Source LLC
Chambersburg PA
CBHW051054030726
47504CB00006B/1623